S0-BBI-739

ACCLAIM FOR SHELLEY SHEPARD GRAY

"Shelley Shepard Gray has written a riveting tale that captures all the heartache, guilt and shame left by the Civil War. The historical details, memorable characters and sacrificial love combine to make *Love Held Captive* a compelling and enjoyable read."

—MARGARET BROWNLEY, *NEW YORK TIMES* BESTSELLING AUTHOR OF *LEFT AT THE ALTAR* AND *A MATCH MADE IN TEXAS*

"Be still my heart! Shelley Shepherd Gray has masterfully married the romance of the Old West with rich post—Civil War history to create a truly unique tale unlike any you have ever read. Without question, *An Uncommon Protector* is an uncommon love story that will steal both your heart and your sleep."

—JULIE LESSMAN, AWARD-WINNING AUTHOR OF *THE DAUGHTERS OF BOSTON*, *WINDS OF CHANGE*, AND *THE HEART OF SAN FRANCISCO* SERIES

"Gray is a master at integrating rich details and historical accuracies to create an engaging tale that will take the reader back in time. Strong secondary characters are well integrated. It is a shame to see this series end."

—*RT BOOK REVIEWS* 4-STAR REVIEW OF *WHISPERS IN THE READING ROOM*

"Shelley Gray writes a well-paced story full of historical detail that will invite you into the romance, the glamour . . . and the mystery surrounding the Chicago World's Fair."

—COLLEEN COBLE, *USA TODAY* BESTSELLING AUTHOR OF *ROSEMARY COTTAGE* AND THE HOPE BEACH SERIES ON *SECRETS OF SLOANE HOUSE*

"*Downton Abbey* comes to Chicago in Shelley Gray's delightful romantic suspense, *Secrets of Sloane House*. Gray's novel is rich in description and historical detail while asking thought-provoking questions about faith and one's place in society."

—ELIZABETH MUSSER, NOVELIST, *THE SWAN HOUSE*, *THE SWEETEST THING*, SECRETS OF THE CROSS TRILOGY

"Full of vivid descriptions and beautiful prose, Gray has a way of making readers feel like they are actually in Chicago during the World's Fair ... The mystery surrounding the 'Slasher' keeps the reader engaged throughout."

—*RT* BOOK REVIEWS, 4-STAR REVIEW OF *DECEPTION ON SABLE HILL*

A Lone Star Hero

3-IN-1

LOVE STORY COLLECTION

OTHER BOOKS BY SHELLEY SHEPARD GRAY

CHICAGO WORLD'S FAIR MYSTERY SERIES

Secrets of Sloane House
Deception on Sable Hill
Whispers in the Reading Room

A Lone Star Star Hero

3-IN-1
LOVE STORY COLLECTION

THE LOYAL HEART
AN UNCOMMON PROTECTOR
LOVE HELD CAPTIVE

SHELLEY SHEPARD GRAY

ZONDERVAN

The Loyal Heart © 2016 by Shelley Shepard Gray
An Uncommon Protector © 2017 by Shelley Shepard Gray
Love Held Captive © 2017 by Shelley Shepard Gray

This title is also available as a Zondervan e-book. Visit www.zondervan.com.

Requests for information should be addressed to:
Zondervan, *Grand Rapids, Michigan* 49546

CIP data is available upon request.

Scripture quotations are taken from the Holy Bible, New Living Translation. © 1996, 2004, 2007, 2013 by Tyndale House Foundation. Used by permission of Tyndale House Publishers, Inc., Carol Stream, Illinois 60188. All rights reserved.

Any Internet addresses (websites, blogs, etc.) and telephone numbers in this book are offered as a resource. They are not intended in any way to be or imply an endorsement by Zondervan, nor does Zondervan vouch for the content of these sites and numbers for the life of this book.

All rights reserved. No part of this publication may be reproduced, stored in a retrieval system, or transmitted in any form or by any means—electronic, mechanical, photocopy, recording, or any other—except for brief quotations in printed reviews, without the prior permission of the publisher.

Publisher's Note: These novels are works of fiction. Names, characters, places, and incidents are either products of the author's imagination or used fictitiously. All characters are fictional, and any similarity to people living or dead is purely coincidental.

Printed in the United States of America

17 18 19 20 21 / LSC / 5 4 3 2 1

CONTENTS

THE
Loyal Heart

To my husband Tom

Create in me a clean heart, O God.
Renew a loyal spirit within me.

—PSALM 51:10

Let us go home and cultivate our virtues.

—ROBERT E. LEE, ADDRESSING HIS SOLDIERS AT APPOMATTOX

PROLOGUE

Johnson's Island, Ohio
Confederate States of America Officers' POW Camp
January 1865

THEY WERE DIGGING ANOTHER GRAVE. THE THIRD THAT week, which Devin Arthur Monroe, captain in the C.S.A., reckoned was hard enough without knowing it was for Rory Macdonald. Rory had been all of nineteen, the youngest member of his unit by far. Because he had been a private, he shouldn't have even been imprisoned with them in the first place. He wouldn't have been, except for some clerk's error.

The clerk's mistake had been Rory's good fortune, however. Conditions had been better for him here than they would have been in the enlisted prisoner-of-war camp in Columbus. Devin had been grateful for that. Rory had been a good man. He'd been a good soldier too. If they hadn't been captured down in Tennessee, he would have made sergeant before too long. The Confederacy had needed more young men like him.

Devin had been certain Rory was going to walk out of their prison in the middle of Lake Erie, go home to his family's loving arms, find a pretty girl to marry, and accomplish something great.

In short, Devin had been sure Rory Macdonald was going to do them all proud.

Instead, the best of them was going to spend an eternity in an unmarked grave surrounded by Yankee soil.

Just thinking about it stung.

"I still can't believe he won't be heading back to Texas. Ever," Lt. Robert Truax said as he tossed another patch of dirt over his shoulder. "Why did God have to go and decide the kid should die of pneumonia?"

Devin said nothing. Merely looked toward the dead zone—a line of fencing surrounded by a three-foot gap and another higher wooden fence. Their worthless Yankee guards were instructed to kill on sight any man who went beyond their restricted boundary.

Devin had seen them do it.

Lord knew, none of the structures that confined them were all that well put together. But that was the charm of their prison—at least for the Yankees. Even if a Rebel was able to escape the barricades without being shot and killed, the broad expanse of Lake Erie surrounded them. If the swim in the frigid waters didn't kill them, the frozen Canadian wilderness on the other side surely would. They were good and trapped. And for the most part, bored out of their minds.

"It should've been me," Robert muttered as he propped a boot on the edge of his shovel, using his weight to help him dig into the frozen ground.

Robert had taken the boy's death especially hard. Devin figured that was to be expected. For all his rough-and-tumble ways, his second lieutenant had a soft heart. But the man's tone was dark enough to pull Devin out of his reverie.

Turning to him, he glared, his expression vivid in the

moonlight. "Nothing we can do about the dead. Rory is in a better place. I thought you would have come to terms with that by now."

Impatience flashed in Robert's eyes. "The kid was only nineteen. Too young to die."

"You know the answer to that," Devin chided. "A great many men have died in this war who were too young. What you need to remember is that Private Macdonald definitely did not consider himself too young. And he'd likely try to box your ears if he could hear you saying that."

"He would box your ears for even thinking it," Sgt. Thomas Baker pointed out as he thrust his shovel into the hole they were digging. "Mac had no patience for anyone discussing his age."

"Well, now he's dead," Robert said. "He should have had his whole life ahead of him."

"I reckon the good Lord didn't see it that way. A great many men should have been looking forward to a bright and sunny future." Thinking of Gettysburg, Devin felt his throat clog. He cleared it, at the same time pushing away the gruesome memories that never completely went away. "But they're gone too."

"It doesn't make any sense."

"War doesn't."

"Neither does a healthy nineteen-year-old boy dying from pneumonia."

"It was a real bad case of pneumonia, though," Thomas muttered. "The kid was having so much trouble breathing, he was blue for days."

Robert tossed his shovel to the ground. "Show our private some respect."

Thomas sneered. "Or what?"

"Settle down, Lieutenant," Phillip Markham hissed under his breath as he knelt to smooth away a chunk of earth. For some reason, he was still recovering from a bullet's graze. While some days it seemed like it pained him something awful, for once he didn't seem to be suffering too much. "If you don't lower your voice, you're going to get our fine Yankee hosts to put us in lockdown." Phillip's light blue eyes glared as he continued, as always their voice of reason. "That would be a real shame, 'cause we've got a body to bury." Looking up at Devin, he said, "I think the grave is deep enough, Captain."

Devin nodded. "Let's do this, then."

Devin, Thomas, and Robert carefully picked up Rory's body and lowered it into the ground. After Rory was settled, they surrounded the grave in somber silence.

When Devin was able to push through the lump that had formed in his throat, he led them in prayer.

After another moment of silence, Thomas and Robert picked up shovels and began the painful work of covering Rory's body.

Devin and his major, Ethan Kelly, stood to one side and watched. Devin figured he'd now stood in respectful silence dozens of times since the war began. It never got easier.

When the grave was finally filled, they started walking back to their two-story barracks. Now that the dreaded chore was done, their mood seemed better.

"I'll write Rory's mother tomorrow," Devin said as they went inside. "Let's hope and pray this will be the last note of its kind that I'm going to have to write anytime soon."

"I'll do my best to stay alive," Ethan quipped.

"Me too," Phillip said with a ghost of a smile. "Don't forget, I've got Miranda."

Pure relief filled Devin. That comment had been exactly what they needed to get back on track. Phillip's devotion to his pretty brown-haired wife was legendary—and the source of much ribbing.

"Oh, we know you have Miranda, Phillip," Ethan teased. "You never let any of us forget you've got a beautiful woman waiting for you at home. You lucky dog."

"I received not one but two letters from her today. So yes, indeed, I am lucky." He stretched his arms. "Actually, I'm blessed beyond measure." As always, Phillip never pretended he felt anything but enamored by his wife.

Devin had always thought it was rather an endearing trait in their best sharpshooter.

But Robert was still staring at Phillip in confusion. "You never complain, Lieutenant. You never say anything except you're biding your time until you see her again. I don't see how one woman can make all the difference."

This time, Thomas grinned, showing a full set of exceptionally fine white teeth. His smile was undoubtedly his best feature and he used it to his advantage every chance he got. "If you don't know how one woman can ease a man's burdens, then you've got problems, Truax! Shoot, I'd say you've got more problems than being locked in a POW encampment in the middle of Lake Erie."

Ethan smiled. "I don't mind admitting that I'm looking forward to my fiancée, Faye, easing my burdens the moment I see her again."

Devin tucked his chin so Robert wouldn't see his grin. He'd never had a sweetheart, but he reckoned Ethan and Thomas had a point.

Unfortunately, Robert didn't care to see it. "I'm just saying, a man needs more than the comfort of a good woman. No offense, Markham."

Phillip grunted but didn't say a word.

Devin didn't really blame him. He'd seen a tintype of Phillip's wife. She was lovely, everything a man would want to fight for.

But, Devin supposed, he could see Robert's point. If a man didn't have a good woman waiting for him or a home to return to, there was a strong possibility of feeling out of sorts with their mission. Especially now that it seemed the war was almost over and all points were turning toward the inevitable loss for their side.

Perhaps they did need something more. Something more than dreams and elusive promises. Something dear to hold on to and grab hold of. Something to live for. "How about we make a pact, then?"

Ethan looked at him curiously. "What you got in mind, Captain?"

"Just something to make sure we remember."

Thomas raised a dark eyebrow. "Remember what, Cap?"

"To remember when one of us is sitting in the dark and wondering why he should live to see another morning."

"Bring it on, then," Ethan said. "I could use some of your words of wisdom."

"How about we make a promise right here, right now, to live for each other?"

"I'm already doing that." Thomas grinned. Looking at his major, he said, "I'm already keeping you warm at night, aren't I?"

"Don't remind me," Ethan said with a scowl. "You snore like a banshee." They all slept two by two. It was too cold otherwise.

Devin stood up, warming to his topic. "Come on, men. I'm serious. I suggest that from now on we do everything we can to help each other survive."

"We are in prison barracks, sir. Unless we get pneumonia, we'll live to see the end of the war."

"No, I'm not talking just about now. I'm talking about in the future too. Even after we get out of here."

"Sorry, Cap, but I don't follow," Thomas said. "After we get released from here and the war's over, I'm not gonna have one thing to do with a uniform."

Thomas was truly like his name. He needed a literal, tangible reason to believe in something. Otherwise he couldn't see it.

"Back in Gettysburg, we were once a band of eight. Then we lost Tucker and Simon. This morning, we were six. Now we are five. I propose, gentlemen, that when this war is over, we keep a promise to ourselves. Let's promise to always look out for each other."

"Always?" Robert asked.

"Yep. Even five years from now. Even ten. I think we're going to need to know that no matter what, we have each other."

Ethan nodded. "You might have something there, Cap. I like it."

"I don't," Robert said as he picked up a stick and tossed it into the dwindling fire in their old stove. "When the war is over, we're not going to need to be looked after. Everything's going to be fine again."

"Will it?" Thomas muttered.

"All I'm saying," Robert said, "is that most of us will have lives to go back to. We'll be free. We won't be worrying about dying or someone attacking us in our sleep. It's going to be better."

"I hope it is," Devin said. "But if it's not, let's promise we'll still have each other."

"I'm in," said Thomas. "This promise is as good as any, I reckon."

"Me too," Ethan said.

Phillip nodded. "I'm in too. But, uh, can I ask . . . if something happens to me, would one of you look after Miranda?"

"You'll get back to her," Ethan said.

Phillip nodded, but still looked alarmed. "Just in case I don't?" Phillip pressed.

"If you don't survive," Devin said, "I promise one of us will make sure Miranda is all right. Gentlemen, do you promise?"

Ethan pulled his shoulders back and looked at Phillip straight in the eye. "Upon my honor as a gentleman and a Southerner, I will make sure your wife is taken care of, Lieutenant."

At last Phillip breathed a sigh of relief.

Feeling satisfied, Devin finally looked at Robert. "Are you in?"

After a pause, Robert nodded. "I'm in, Captain. No matter what happens, I will honor this pact."

"Good."

Each lost in his thoughts, no one uttered a word until the last of the fire died out.

But as he thought about what would happen when the war ended, Devin knew they'd all be going back to a world different from when they first put on their Confederate uniforms. It was likely that their troubles would begin anew.

Some of them wouldn't even have their farms and houses, thanks to the Yankees' penchant for burning down everything in their path.

Yes, Devin Monroe feared that, after the war, when the world was at peace but so terribly upside-down, they were going to need each other even more.

1

Galveston, Texas
January 1867

AT TIMES, THE PAIN WAS SO INTENSE, SHE WANTED TO DIE.

With a new sense of resolve, Miranda Markham skimmed a finger along the second-floor windowpane just outside her bedroom door. As she did, frigid drops of condensation slid across her fingers, moistening them, transmitting tiny bursts of pain along her skin. The glass wasn't thick, surely no more than a quarter inch. It seemed, to her eyes at least, that the frame was rather rickety as well.

It would be so easy to break.

Miranda wondered what it would feel like to perch on the edge of the windowsill like one of the gulls that rested on the weathered wood from time to time. She wondered what it would feel like to open her arms. To finally let herself go, to lean forward into nothingness.

To be free.

Perhaps she would feel nothing beyond a cold numbness, accompanied by an exhilarating rush of fear . . . followed by the blessed relief from pain.

Did pain even matter anymore?

The iron latch was icy cold as she worked it open. Condensation sprayed her cheeks as the pane slowly edged upward. Tendrils of hair whipped against her neck as the winter wind seemed to beckon.

She breathed deep.

If she could just garner what was left of her courage, why, it could all be over. Within minutes, in seconds, even, she'd no longer be awake. No longer be reminded. No longer be sad.

She'd no longer be afraid to rise each morning.

And wasn't the absence of fear, that intangible notion of confidence that children enjoyed and the elderly remembered, worth everything?

Reaching out, she clasped the metal lining of the frame. Felt the iron bite into her palm as she edged closer. At last, it was time.

"Mrs. Markham? Mrs. Markham, ma'am? Where should I put the new boarder until you are ready to talk with him?" Winifred called up from the base of the stairs.

Slowly . . . too slowly perhaps . . . one corner of Miranda's dark cloak of depression lifted. She realized she was still standing on the landing at the top of the stairs, the window open.

Winifred's voice turned shrill. "Mrs. Markham, do ye hear me?"

Miranda dropped her hands. Turned. "Yes. Yes, of course." Peering through the maze of mahogany spindles, she looked down. Blinked as her home's long-time housekeeper came into focus. "A new boarder, did you say?"

Winifred stared back. "Yes, ma'am. 'E's here a wee bit early. A Mr. Truax, his name is. Mr. Robert Truax."

Though the name sounded familiar, Miranda couldn't place it. Why couldn't she?

"Madam," Winifred began again, her voice holding the slightest tinge of impatience now. She was a reluctant transplant from England and seemed to always stare at her surroundings with varying degrees of shock and dismay. "Madam, don't you remember?" Winifred added, raising her voice just a little bit higher, as if she were talking to a child. "We got the telegram yesterday that said he was arriving today."

She didn't remember much after receiving another threatening letter in yesterday's post. "Yes, of course."

"I been working on his room all morning, I have." Looking pleased, Winifred added, "It sparkles and shines, it does."

"I'm glad," she said absently.

Until and unless Phillip's family found a legal way to run her off—or made her miserable enough to leave on her own—she was in charge of the Iron Rail. It was her house, and with that came the responsibility of at least pretending she cared about the running of it. With a vague sense of resignation, she turned back to the window. Set about cranking it shut before locking it securely.

"Mrs. Markham, he's cooling his heels in Lt. Markham's study. What shall I do with him?" The housekeeper's voice now held a healthy thread of impatience. "Do you want to do your usual interview for new guests, or would you rather I take 'im straight to his room?"

Miranda truly didn't care where the man went. Any room would do—the farther away from her, the better. But she had a responsibility to the staff to at least meet the man she would be allowing to lodge in the house for a time.

Phillip would have expected her to do that. Summoning her courage, she said, "Please escort him to the parlor. I'll be down momentarily." Stepping forward, she smoothed the thick wool of her charcoal gray skirt.

She avoided glancing at her reflection as she passed a mirror.

Though she was out of mourning and no longer wore black, no color appealed. Hence, gray. Though they'd never said so to her face, she'd overheard her four employees talk about her appearance more than once. The general consensus was that the hue didn't suit her any better than unrelieved black. Actually, Cook had remarked more than once that she resembled a skinny sparrow.

Continuing her descent, she said, "Please serve Mr. Truax tea. I believe we have one or two muffins left from breakfast as well?"

"We do. Since you didn't eat."

Miranda almost smiled. "Today it is most fortunate I did not."

Grumbling, the housekeeper turned away.

When she was alone again, Miranda took a fortifying breath. Realized that a fresh scent wafting from the open window had permeated the air. Salt and sea and, well, something tangy and bright.

It jarred her senses, gave her a small sense of hope.

Perhaps today was not the day to die after all.

By the time Miranda went downstairs, she'd made the poor man wait for almost fifteen minutes.

Yet instead of looking irritated, he stood and smiled when she entered the room, bowed slightly, as if she were wearing cerulean instead of gray. Just as if the war hadn't come and gone.

As she studied him, all traces of oxygen seemed to leave her. Robert Truax was terribly handsome. And for some reason, she thought perhaps she should recognize this man whose name had also seemed familiar. Tall, finely muscled, and—dare she admit—exuberant? So different from most of the men living on Galveston

Island. Most of the men looked hard, either from their years fighting the Yankees or from a lifetime sailing the open seas. Rarely did any of them smile at her. She was not only Phillip Markham's widow, but she now had the dubious reputation of housing strange men under his family's roof. Neither attribute endeared her to the general public.

As she crossed the room, Mr. Truax stood quietly. As if he had all the time in the world to stand at attention.

His good manners embarrassed her. She shouldn't have been so negligent. "Mr. Truax, I am terribly sorry to have kept you waiting." Since she had no excuse, she offered none.

"I didn't mind. I've been looking at your books. And your housekeeper brought me some tea." He flashed a smile. "With cream."

Cream was a rare treat for most people. These days, with so many having so little, she'd almost forgotten their blessing. "Yes. We, um, have a cow."

His grin widened. "Seems she did a real fine job of it today."

The artless comment was unsettling. His accent was also unfamiliar. It lacked the usual soft r's and smooth cadence of south Texas. "You are not from around here."

"You are correct, ma'am. I am not. And this is my first time in Galveston. However, I don't hail from too far away. I was raised in Ft. Worth." He paused. "Then, of course, serving during the war took me all over the country. I spent a portion of it in the North. I think my accent might have altered after being around all those Yankees for so long."

She winced. Remembering how much Phillip had hated to talk to her about the war, she quickly said, "Please forgive me . . . I shouldn't have pried."

"You didn't pry, ma'am. You may ask me anything you'd like. I'm not a man of secrets."

He was disconcerting, that was what he was. Attempting to regain control of their conversation, she gestured to the crimson-colored velvet settee. "Please, do sit down."

He waited until she sat on the brocaded chair before he took his own seat at the end of the settee closest to her. But instead of leaning back against the cushion, he turned to face her. Leaned slightly forward. So close, she noticed he smelled of mint and leather. So close that their knees almost touched. It was unseemly and rather too forward.

However, she couldn't think of a polite way to withdraw.

"Mrs. Markham, where did you imagine I was from?"

She noticed his gaze had turned a bit more piercing. She also noticed she was finding it increasingly hard to look away. "It doesn't matter."

"But still, I'm intrigued."

She couldn't tell the truth. She would never tell a man that he sounded like a Northerner. To say something like that would be close to unforgiveable.

Almost as unforgiveable as what people said her husband did.

She cleared her throat. What she needed to do was complete their interview, put him in Winifred's capable hands, and retreat to her bedroom. "Mr. Truax, I like to know a little bit about the people staying in my home. Could you tell me about yourself?"

"Not much to tell, ma'am. I grew up in Ft. Worth, spent a good four years in the army. Now I am in Galveston to see to some business."

His answers seemed purposely vague. "Perhaps you could share the nature of your business?"

"It is of a personal nature."

"And for that you will need to stay here . . ." She tried to recall his telegram. "For one whole month?"

"I believe so. It might be longer. We'll see."

"How did you hear of my boardinghouse?"

His dark gray eyes somehow became even more unfathomable. "People talk, Mrs. Markham. What I heard brought me here." He paused. "That isn't a problem, is it? I mean, you do have a room open, don't you?"

His piercing gaze was more disconcerting than her in-laws' frequent unannounced visits. "Of course we do. It is simply that there are other, better establishments on Galveston Island that I feel would be far better suited for your kind." She smiled. He stilled.

"Did you say 'kind'?"

Her cheeks heated. "Most men of worth stay at the Tremont, for example. You look as if you have money to spend. Most of my boarders don't."

He crossed one leg over the opposite knee. Infiltrating more precious space. "Actually, a friend told me about your board-inghouse. He said it was clean and reasonably priced. The perfect place for a weary soul to find solace." He brazenly met her gaze, then let it drop. "I could use some solace, I think," he added, his voice sounding troubled.

His tone caused goose bumps to form on her arms. What could he mean? More important, why did she care? She averted her eyes, not liking her body's response. How could she be this aware of a man who wasn't Phillip?

"This house has a good reputation, ma'am."

"I see," she said. Because she felt some response was necessary. However, his words were disconcerting. They'd all recently survived a war. Barely. No one's personal reasons for anything meant much these days.

Furthermore, she doubted her house would have garnered

any type of good reputation. Most people felt that her husband's sins stained her own reputation. And, of course, the old, drafty house she'd lived in since her marriage to Phillip.

Before she could comment, he shifted and spoke again. "I really do need a room. And I would like to get settled, if you would have me."

If you would have me.

His words reverberated in her mind, causing her hands to shake. Phillip had said those exact words when he'd asked her to marry him.

I'd like to be yours, Miranda . . . if you would have me.

She clasped her fingers together.

"Tea?" he murmured.

"What? I mean . . . beg pardon?"

He gestured to the china pot and pair of cups. His almost empty. Hers hadn't yet been filled. "May I pour you a cup of tea, Mrs. Markham?" A dimple appeared. "It's cold as Hades in here, if you don't mind me saying."

Before she thought better of it, she wrinkled her nose. "I've never heard that expression before."

"Oh?"

"Yes. I mean, I thought it was hot in Hades." Feeling awkward, she bit her lip. Why had she even uttered such a thing?

Instead of replying, he lifted the teapot. The fragile china, marked with a profusion of poorly painted pale pink roses, looked absurd in his masculine hand.

"I'll pour, Mr. Truax."

"It's already in my grip, though. So may I pour you some tea now? I don't dare drink another drop without you."

Oh, those words. That direct, heated look. It was nerve-racking. Whoever spoke so freely? So openly?

"Mrs. Markham?" He set the fragile teapot back down on the small table in front of them.

It was all Miranda could do not to grimace. She needed to focus. To be the lady he assumed she was. "Yes. I mean, sir, I'll pour. That's a lady's job." She blinked in frustration. "That is, I'm sorry you are chilled." She didn't dare offer further apology. The reason for the cool rooms was obvious. All of them had so little now. And living as they did in Galveston?

Timber for fireplaces wasn't an easy commodity.

Miranda picked up the teapot. But from the moment she held it aloft, it was obvious her tremors hadn't abated.

He noticed.

"Let me help," he murmured. Gently, he curved his fingers around her own and supported the bottom of the pot with his opposite hand. Easily, he guided her, pouring hot tea into one cup, then the other.

His hands were comforting. His rough, calloused palms reminded her that he was so very different from her. Those hands were wide enough to completely cover her own. And warm enough to tease her insides—like heated caramel syrup. For a moment, she was tempted to close her eyes, to imagine a man's arms holding her once again. Warming her. It had been so long.

She trembled.

After setting the pot back on the table, he leaned closer. "Ma'am? Are you all right?"

"I'm sorry." She forced a weak smile. "I guess a ghost crossed my path."

Instead of grinning, he merely stared at her, his manner filled with concern. "Are you feeling better now?"

She nodded. "Yes." Oh, but she felt so strange!

She watched as he poured a liberal dose of cream into his cup and sipped appreciatively. "I do love hot tea. It's been ages since I've had any."

"Why is that? I thought you folks in Ft. Worth had most everything you needed."

"Not everything, ma'am."

His presence still confused her. "Mr. Truax, when, exactly, did you arrive in Galveston? Did you arrive on the ferry from Houston this morning?" She couldn't recall if the boats ran this early.

The secret amusement that had played around his eyes faded as his expression clouded. "Yes."

"And what business have you had before coming here?"

"Work that has taken me all over the state."

Work? He sounded as if he'd been on a mission.

What kind could that be? Was he a soldier still? Yet he wore no uniform. He said he needed rest, but he didn't look weary.

"I hate to point out the obvious, but you haven't yet actually told me my fate."

"I beg your pardon?"

"Did I pass the test? May I stay here with you, Mrs. Markham?"

She blinked. Perhaps it was her imagination, but she kept getting the feeling that he was talking in riddles. Almost as if he knew something she didn't.

The idea was disturbing. She should probably ask more questions. It wasn't safe for a woman to be living with people she didn't know. Especially not a strange man who smiled too much and evaded questions like they were intricate steps in a quadrille.

However, it didn't really matter, did it? Her reputation was in shreds and it wasn't like she didn't have rooms to spare. She had far too many empty rooms.

But most of all, overriding everything was the fact that she was too tired and too numb inside to really care. Numbness, she had learned, was the key to survival. And if she were going to decide to live, she needed to survive in this house as long as she could.

Eager to end their conversation, she at last answered. "Yes, Mr. Truax. You may stay."

A dimple appeared. "I'm so glad. Thank you."

They stood up. "Winifred, my housekeeper, will give you a key and show you to your room when you finish your tea."

"I have already finished," he said lightly, illustrating that she'd very likely been staring at him, lost in thought for longer than she realized.

She really should be doing better with him. After taking a fortifying breath, she got to her feet. "Mr. Truax, I just realized I haven't yet given you a tour of the house. Or told you about mealtimes. Or explained our fees."

"I'm sure we'll take care of everything in time, ma'am," he replied, his voice gentle. "And don't you worry none. Fact is, I don't need very much at all. Why, I'd bet a three-cent piece you'll hardly know I'm here."

When he left the room to find her housekeeper on his own, she sat back down.

As she sipped the rapidly cooling tea, Miranda knew one thing for certain. It was extremely unlikely that she would forget Robert Truax was there.

2

ROBERT WAS NEVER COMFORTABLE IN A TAILORED SUIT. Growing up the way he had on the streets of Ft. Worth, he'd been lucky to have a shirt on his back, never mind anything that actually fit him. After he entered the service, his uniform had been cut for the active life of a soldier. The fabric had been thick and hardy, turning soft after many washings. The cut had been generous through his chest and shoulders too. A man needed room to point and shoot.

A lot had happened in the last seven years, however. When the war broke out, he'd been one of the first to enlist. Given the circumstances of his youth, he was tough. He was good at street fighting and had little to no fear for his person or his life.

Those qualities, while not serving him all that well in the businesses of Ft. Worth, were highly valued in the military. He worked hard to gain acceptance and be valued. It became apparent that, whereas he had no reason to return home, he had every reason to excel in his unit.

It seemed his soul had been aching for a life filled with purpose.

Perhaps because he was so eager—or maybe it was because he was so obviously lacking—he'd gotten a good education from both his fellow enlisted men and his officers. Bored men greatly improved his literacy and taught him to write. Lazy supply officers taught him rudimentary math skills.

Eventually he'd garnered the attention of Captain Devin Monroe and the officers in his unit. Over time, they more or less adopted him, teaching him manners and correct grammar.

After Gettysburg, he fought hard enough and displayed sufficient skills to become an officer. A second lieutenant. Later, when they were captured and moved up North, Robert concentrated on making the best of the experience.

Consequently, he was probably the only man to feel he came out of the prisoner-of-war camp in better shape than when he entered. Those men had not only continued his education in history, science, and literature, but they'd managed to teach him how to waltz one very long stretch of days when the temperatures loomed around zero and the snow and ice covered the ground in thick blankets.

He'd also made some close connections. Soon after their release, he'd gone to work for a locomotive company. The owner had been looking for someone with Texas ties to help encourage new business.

Just as he had in the military, he'd quickly risen through the ranks and reaped the financial rewards. And though most men might not consider him wealthy, he now was blessed with far more in his pockets than he'd ever dreamed of—and he looked the part as well.

When his former captain had asked a favor, it had never occurred to Robert to refuse. He owed that man and his former unit both his life and his peace of mind, so he left the locomotive company's employ and came here.

Most days he didn't think much about how his clothes fit.

That moment, however, as he followed the curmudgeonly housekeeper up a flight of stairs into a surprisingly well-kept and spacious room at the far end of a long hall, he was sure the collar of his close-fitting shirt was in danger of choking him.

That was what he deserved, he suspected, for lying through his teeth to a beautiful widow who looked so fragile that a strong wind would likely toss her off her feet. When he quickly realized Miranda Markham had no idea who he was—perhaps Phillip had never mentioned him in his letters?—he followed through with his intent to keep his connection to her husband to himself. His plan might be more successful that way. Mrs. Markham seemed like she was barely hanging on.

However, though he had the best of intentions at the moment, he felt lower than he could ever recall. Well, not since he'd followed his captain out of the prison he'd shared with his four best friends in the world, leaving Phillip and so many others in unmarked graves in the small cemetery just outside their barracks.

The housekeeper fingered the coverlet on the bed. "I trust everything is to your satisfaction, sir?"

He didn't bother to look around. In truth, his surroundings didn't interest him as much as the woman downstairs did. It was true, as well, that rooms and amenities meant little to him now. If he was warm and dry, he would be a far sight better than he'd been on Johnson's Island. "It is. Thank you."

Her expression flattened. "I'll be seeing you, then. Let me know if you'll be needin' anything." She took a breath. "That ain't to say that I can find it, but I can try," she said as she started toward the door.

"Times still hard here?"

She drew to a stop. "War ain't been over that long."

"I meant in this house." Of course, the moment he said the

words he wished he could take them back. The woman had had to open her house to strangers. Things were obviously not good at all.

She turned, umbrage in her posture. "Mrs. Markham runs a respectable establishment, sir. I don't expect you'll be finding anything remiss."

"Of course not. I suspected nothing less."

She nodded. "Good. I'll expect you ta remember that."

"Shame she lost her husband," he interjected quickly. He needed information and so far she was his best and easiest option to get it. "I mean, I assume she is a widow."

"She is." After eyeing him for a long moment, she said, "Lt. Markham died near the end of the war." Her voice lowered. "He perished less than a month before Lee surrendered at Appomattox."

"Shame, that," he said lightly.

"It was worse than a shame, sir. It was a tragedy."

"Indeed."

He considered his ability to even say two words to be something of an accomplishment.

Because the fact was, he remembered Phillip's death well. Too well. Phillip had lingered, fighting the inevitable with each breath. Robert had painfully watched him fight that losing battle, helpless to do anything but watch him waste away for days. On his last day, Robert had held his hand for hours, attempting to give him some degree of warmth in a very cold existence. Then, after he'd left his side and Devin Monroe had gone to take a turn, Phillip had passed on.

"He died in a Yankees' prison barracks, he did," the housekeeper blurted. "He would write Mrs. Markham letters from there, trying to sound positive, but we all knew he weren't doing well."

Robert had watched Phillip write those letters. They all had.

But because he didn't want anyone in Galveston to know that yet, he kept his expression impassive. "Oh?"

"Oh, yes. He died up in Ohio, he did." She grimaced. "Poor man, forced to live and die on an island in the middle of Lake Erie. Don't seem natural, if you ask me."

He agreed. "I would imagine any prison would be a hard place to live. Or die."

After eyeing him carefully, she said, "I should probably let you know that if you stay on Galveston Island for any length of time, you're going to hear a lot of talk about Lt. Markham and even more talk about Mrs. Markham herself. Some of it is ugly." She closed her eyes. "Actually, the majority of it is ugly."

He knew she was warning him for his own good. He was more than willing to heed it. "I've never given much credence to idle chatter."

"If you are living here, that would be good to bear in mind," she advised. "Sometimes life interferes with all our best intentions."

Robert felt as if the walls surrounding him were closing in. Remembering the drafty barracks, how cold it had been in the winter, how endless the days had lasted, he felt a thin line of perspiration form along the middle of his back. "Some might believe there's more glory from dying on the battlefield, but I imagine there's just as much honor dying in prison."

She lifted a graying eyebrow. "You really think that, don't you?"

"I do." It took everything he had not to embellish his statement. He wasn't ready to discuss his own imprisonment. Still less ready to remember his comrades' pain, suffering, and eventual death. The memories were too crystal clear—the damp smell of their cells, the faraway look in his commander's eyes, the long hours spent in boredom.

Those memories, it seemed, were reserved only for the middle of the night.

With a new awareness in her eyes, Winifred looked him over. She seemed to hesitate, then blurted, "Since you're going to be hearing things anyway, you might as well know that folks not only say he died a coward's death in that Northern prison, but he also died while being interrogated and gave secrets to the enemy."

Only by digging his fingers into the palms of his hands was he able to remain impassive. "I don't understand."

"I know. It don't make no sense at all. If he died while being questioned, it would mean he kept his secrets, don'tcha think?" Before Robert could comment on that, she continued on in her loquacious way. "Sir, anyone who knew the lieutenant knew he would no more share precious secrets with the enemy than he would have harmed a hair on Mrs. Markham's head. He was a good man."

Phillip had been better than that. He'd loved his wife, yes. But he'd also loved the men he'd served with. He'd been loyal to the cause. Even more than that, he'd been loyal to the men he served with and led into battle.

As far as he was concerned, Phillip Markham had been the best the South had to offer. Anyone who said different was surely a liar and a scoundrel.

"So you don't believe he did share military secrets?"

She shook her head. "No, sir, I do not, and neither does Mrs. Markham. Even if one didn't call into account the fact that he'd been injured, captured, then hauled up to the middle of Lake Erie, therefore not able to share anything of use, he weren't that kind of man," she murmured, her English accent sounding more pronounced. "That said, if he did say anything he shouldn't, I'm of the mind that he should be forgiven, don'tcha think?" She stared at him, her pale gray eyes practically daring him to refute her.

Or, perhaps, she was looking for hope instead?

Robert stayed silent.

He wasn't sure who should be forgiven. They'd all committed atrocities in battle. They'd all done things in captivity they'd never imagined they would do before they'd donned a uniform.

Visibly uncomfortable with his silence, the housekeeper spoke a little faster. "I mean, six months before General Lee signed that treaty, well, things were already a foregone conclusion. No Yankee cared about what a Confederate lieutenant had to say. And especially not one locked up on an island." She looked at him worriedly. Practically begging him to reassure her. "Don'tcha think?"

She was wrong, of course. Their enemy had cared about everything they knew. Then there were guards who cared about nothing other than recriminations.

Though they were treated with a light hand compared to the atrocities of Andersonville or even in some of the other Union prisons, their guards hadn't been especially kind to them. Why, once word got out about the horrors of the treatment in the Confederate prisons, their rations had been cut in half. Hunger and cold had been constant companions.

Robert now knew any confinement was debilitating. "I couldn't begin to guess."

She waved an impatient hand. "Whatever the reason, it would help Mrs. Markham if you kept the gossip you hear to yourself. I promise, nothing you could say will sway the gossipmongers, and it ain't anything she hasn't heard before."

"Understood."

Her face cleared then, seeming to come to a decision. "We're pleased you're here, whatever the reason, Mr. Truax. We serve supper at six and breakfast at seven. Don't be late."

"No, ma'am."

"Charmer," Robert heard her say under her breath as she walked out of the room.

The moment the door closed behind her, he strode to the desk, found a letterhead, envelope, ink, and quill, and sat down to collect his thoughts. Though he would have preferred to simply telegraph his progress, he couldn't risk anyone discovering his real mission. His job was to get to know Phillip Markham's widow, ascertain how she was truly doing after her husband's death, and make whatever changes he could to ease her life. Then he was to leave and go on about his life—unless Monroe summoned him for another assignment.

This duty had seemed so easy when he learned its details from their former captain. His mission had felt cut-and-dried. He'd been certain he would have been able to remain carefully distant, even if she had known from the beginning that he served with Phillip. He'd imagined he would feel nothing more than pity for her. After all, she was merely one of hundreds—if not thousands—of women struggling to reconfigure their lives without husbands by their sides.

But from the moment she'd entered the room and he'd caught sight of her beauty and heard her slow drawl, he'd been mesmerized. Then he'd noticed that her eyes were a curious shade of blue—almost lavender in color. And that they were framed by dark circles, illustrating her lack of sleep and an abundance of worry and stress. His heart had been lost.

Miranda Markham was a woman in need of a savior. And though he was no heavenly angel, he was determined to do what he could to make her life easier. The first step in making that happen was to gain her trust. A tall order when he was beginning with a lie.

With bold strokes, Robert wrote that he had arrived, made contact, and would be in touch with an update soon.

For the first time since he'd come to terms with the outcome of the war, Robert had a new goal, a reason to step out into society, and, for once, to look forward to another day.

"He's a right one, he is," Winnie declared when she stepped inside the kitchen. "At least six feet of muscle and brawn, all wrapped up in a handsome package."

Belle Harden glanced up from the pot of chowder she was stirring. "Who is?"

"Our new boarder," Winnie said as she trotted into the room, looking much like a pigeon. She was round and gray haired. By turns sharp and nurturing. Belle had loved her from the minute Winnie had invited her in to have a bowl of soup at the end of the war.

Within an hour of Belle's stepping into the kitchen, Winnie had procured her a job in the expansive mansion, known to everyone near and far as the Iron Rail. At first she worked for room and board, but once Mrs. Markham opened for business as a boardinghouse and business was good enough, Belle received a small salary. It was enough to save and fuel her dreams of one day working in a dress shop. To do that she was going to need money to pay for her own room. Until that time came Belle planned to stay in the confines of the Iron Rail and help out as much as she could.

After all, Mrs. Markham needed them.

Brought back to the present by Winnie's bright expression and even brighter tone of voice, Belle put down her wooden spoon. "How did Mrs. Markham receive him?"

"About the way you'd expect. She looked like she could hardly do anything but summon the energy to walk down the stairs to greet him in person." Winnie's warm expression fled just as quickly as it had come. "She's in a bad way today, Belle. If she doesn't improve soon, why, I don't know what we're going to do."

"There's not much we can do. There's only four of us—you, me, Cook, and Emerson." She didn't add that Cook and Emerson were recently married, and while they did a fine job with their duties—Cook in the kitchen and Emerson filling every job from handyman to coachman when needed—they spent any moments to themselves wrapped up in each other.

Winnie said, "We can start by trying to convince everyone who has been so unkind to her to let the past lie buried in Ohio like it should."

"That would be a hard thing to do given the fact that Mrs. Markham owns this here house and any number of people want it out from under her," Cook said.

"Not everyone," Emerson pointed out. "Only Mr. Markham's mother and sister."

"And every third ship captain who sails through and sees the dock," Cook added. "Why, a man could sail here from any part of the world and walk right into the house without anyone knowing the difference."

"I wonder why she doesn't simply give in," Belle said. "It would make things a bit easier."

"Maybe, maybe not. She likes this house and everything it reminds her of," Winnie said. "If she left here, it would be like she left Mr. Markham too."

Emerson grunted. "You women are far too sentimental. It's not just the memories keeping her here. We all know she needs the money. Plus, running a boardinghouse keeps her occupied."

Cook guffawed. "I can think of any number of things to keep a woman occupied besides opening up her home to strangers."

Pulling out a fresh rag, Emerson continued to polish silver. After carefully holding up a tray and looking for signs of tarnish, he placed it in one of the many cabinets underneath the counter. "Winnie, have you seen any more of those letters lately?"

"I found one she received yesterday in the trash this morning."

"I don't understand how Sheriff Kern can't do anything to stop them," Belle mused. "They are terrible."

"It ain't like they're signed, Belle," Cook said. "All we know is that they are local."

"Well, that eliminates no one. Whoever started those tales about Mr. Markham did a good job. Nobody hardly speaks to her anymore."

Winnie poured herself a fresh cup of hot tea. "You should say something to someone."

"Me? I don't think so."

"Why? Everyone seems to like you."

Belle knew the men who liked her were secretly hoping she was a sporting girl. The good men, the churchgoing men, didn't give her the time of day.

The women who were of Mrs. Markham's class didn't even see her. To them, she was yet another young woman of questionable means cleaning rooms and peeling potatoes.

"I don't know who you think I'm friendly with, but I surely don't carry that kind of weight in this town," Belle replied. "And beg pardon, but you three don't either."

"Maybe not," Winnie agreed. "But Sheriff Kern might listen to you. I think he's sweet on ya."

Belle shook her head. "I don't think so." Sheriff Kern had moved to Galveston in the summer of '65 and quickly been appointed sheriff. At first everyone thought it was because he was friends with the Northerners put in charge of their island. In no time, he'd corrected that misunderstanding. He told everyone that he had been loyal to the South and that it was simply his experience in the war that had enabled him to be appointed so quickly and easily.

Most people took him at his word, but Belle had never been positive he was telling the truth. After all, he never talked about the war or where he'd served.

Blowing out a deep breath, Cook blurted, "All I do know is that Mrs. Markham needs a champion, she does. Someone somewhere needs to step up and help her before she loses hope."

Belle completely agreed. But she also knew it couldn't be her. She needed this job. The last thing she wanted to happen was to be let go for being impertinent, and denied a little recommendation to boot. "Someone will, I bet."

"I hope that someone does soon." Winnie's lips pressed together tightly. "I swear, every time I think about the way her supposed best friend Mercy Jackson turned her back on her, I want to spit nails."

"When I spied her pointedly ignoring Mrs. Markham on her last visit to the bank, I considered whacking that woman on the head with a saucepan, I did," Cook stated. Glaring at Winnie, she said, "Don't know what possessed you to mention that vixen's name in my kitchen. You're liable to make all the milk curdle, you are."

"I'm simply saying Mercy should be acting a little bit kinder to poor Mrs. Markham, seeing as her man came back from the war with hardly a scrape. She should be acting more like her name, you know."

"If I know anything, it's that pain comes in all sorts of names and appearances," Cook said. "All of us know that. Especially Mrs. Markham."

And, Belle realized, especially herself too. She also had suffered during the long, bloody War of Northern Aggression. All she could hope for was that no one would ever discover the things she'd had to do to survive.

If anyone here found out, well, even these women in the kitchen would no longer give her the time of day. She'd be out of a job and out of a home.

And once again, she'd have nothing. Nothing at all.

3

It was a journey she hated, but it had to be done. Every Friday Miranda made her way to the downtown business district, most of which was located on the Strand. It was a pretty area, and flourishing even after the war. So much so, many folks called it the Wall Street of the Southwest.

Miranda only thought of the walk as something she had to get through as best she could. She walked quietly, striving to attract no attention to herself as she passed the row of Victorian office buildings, most of which had survived the war intact, thanks to their brick structure and cast-iron fronts.

She would cross the small grassy expanse that filled the center of it, bypassing any number of horse-drawn carriages, groups of freedmen, exhausted from long hours working in the cotton warehouses, and noisy dockworkers eager to collect their pay. Then, at last, she would enter the bank. Once inside, she would stand in line and pretend she didn't feel everyone's eyes on her. As she was both ignored and observed, she would stand as straight and tall as her five foot six inches would allow. And act as if she didn't hear the whispered comments about Phillip and the woman they all thought she'd become.

The line would feel endless, even if there was only one person in front of her. Her nerves would grow taut, and she would coax herself to pretend nothing was amiss, that her skin hadn't turned cold or her breathing hadn't turned shallow.

Then and only then would it finally be her turn with Mr. Kyle Winter, the teller. He'd look down his nose at her while he collected her week's deposit. He'd double- and triple-check the amount, making her wonder if he'd believed her husband had been both a thief and a traitor.

Just when her nerves would be stretched so tight that she feared she would either collapse in dismay or give in to weakness and allow her tears to form, Mr. Winter would nod. Smile crookedly.

"Your business is concluded, Mrs. Markham," he'd say. Then he would look beyond her to the next person in line, triumph lighting his eyes.

She hated every minute of it.

All four of her employees had offered to do the errand in her place. Miranda knew it would probably do everyone, including Kyle Winter, a service if she accepted that help. But she also knew no good would come from avoiding the chore. If Phillip could go off to fight, get injured, and eventually die in his captors' prison, she could survive one grueling half hour a week doing her banking business.

At least, she hoped so.

With a sense of doom, she put her carefully counted money in her wallet and placed it in her reticule. "You can do this, Miranda," she muttered to herself. "It's only a trip to the bank. Not a battle."

Feeling a bit better after her talking-to, she reached for her favorite black wool cloak lined with a dark mauve satin. At least the beautiful cloak would give her some comfort. She was just about to slip it over her shoulders when she heard her new boarder's footsteps on the stairs.

"Going out, Mrs. Markham?" Robert asked.

"Yes."

"Allow me," he said as he took the cloak from her hands, gently covered her shoulders with the wool, then circled around her to fasten the closure at her neck. "Will this be warm enough? The wind is particularly powerful this afternoon."

"It is January," she stated. Which, of course, didn't answer his question.

He smiled pleasantly. "Where are you off to this afternoon?"

"The bank."

"Is that nearby?"

"It's on the Strand. Only a fifteen-minute walk."

He looked around the foyer. "I don't see a maid," he said, sounding concerned. "Are you going by yourself?"

"Yes. Of course."

"Surely not."

"No one puts on airs like that here in Galveston." She tried to smile.

But instead of looking reassured, he only looked worried. "May I accompany you?"

"Accompany me?"

"I'd like to. If I may."

Obviously he was worried about her safety. "There is no need."

"Perhaps. But may I?"

"Why do you want to?" she asked suspiciously.

"I'd enjoy getting the opportunity to walk by a lady's side for a spell," he answered easily. "Plus, I'm trying to get the way of the land. Per se."

"While I can understand that, I don't need any help." She also was in no hurry to see his expression when he realized just how vilified she was. Once he understood that, there was a very good chance he would remove himself from her home, and then she wouldn't even have a deposit to make.

He continued to look at her directly, his gaze steady and sure. Somber. "Even if you don't need any help, it would still be my honor to accompany you. May I? I promise, I'll be a perfect gentleman."

There was something startling about the way he was staring at her so solemnly. Almost as if he cared about her. Almost as if he already knew how difficult her weekly banking journey was for her to take.

How could he have any idea? And even if he did, why would he care? They were strangers. There was little chance they'd even become acquaintances. After all, when his business was concluded, he would leave. It was likely she'd never see him again.

But as she looked at him, noticed how sincere he looked, she found herself thinking it would be nice not to have to make this weekly journey by herself. "Mr. Truax, if you would care to accompany me, I would be obliged."

His lips curved upward. "Thank you, ma'am. You honor me."

With effort, she bit back a smile. His words were so gallant, so different from the way most people spoke to her, she'd almost felt giddy. "You, sir, are quite the gentleman."

"Hardly," he said as they exited the old house. "I'm afraid my skills in that area are rather rusty."

"That's all right, seeing as how my skills are virtually nonexistent."

"Tell me about the square. What is its name again?"

"It is called Recognition Square."

He looked rather unimpressed as he eyed the small expanse of land lying just off to the side of the main thoroughfare. "It seems to me that it's a rather big name for such a humble area."

"Yes. Um, well, I suppose it is." For a split second, she was tempted to apologize for its state. Why, she had no earthly idea. She'd neither named the square nor spent time there. Feeling uncomfortable, she pointed to the stately Victorian on their left. "That house over there is owned by the McKenzie family. They hail from Scotland."

Mr. Truax didn't even look. "What is it recognizing?"

"Recognizing?" she repeated.

"Yes. The square."

With a start, she realized she'd been staring at his expression—and maybe his dark gray eyes—for far too long. "Oh, the, um, dead." She pointed to the monument that had been recently erected on the far side of the square. "Both the name and the monument are to honor the heroes fallen in the war. It was just completed and dedicated two months ago."

"I'm surprised the Yankees let you erect such a thing."

"I was, too, as a matter of fact. However, to be fair, we, um, don't get a lot of reconstruction supervision around these parts. And a few of the wealthier shipping merchants paid for it." Allowing a bit of humor to touch her, she added, "The Yankees seem to prefer to oversee the city dwellers."

"I see."

She doubted he did. She didn't, not that it mattered. Their town had been filled with Union soldiers by the end of the war. When the fighting had stopped and the treaty had been signed, Galveston had reinvented itself, becoming a rather booming port city with a decidedly ribald atmosphere. Anything could happen in Galveston, and often did.

Now, except for the monument, all that reminded one of the war was a sense of injustice, a loss, and the vacant stares of a great many widows like herself.

His expression turned sympathetic as he offered her his arm. "Come, show the monument to me."

"I'd rather not."

"It won't take up too much time." Gesturing toward the stone, he said, "I see a great many names carved here. At least fifty, or thereabouts."

"There are seventy-five," she blurted before thinking the better of it.

"Seventy-five fallen. A shame. Where is your husband's name? I understand from your housekeeper that he was one of our cause's heroes."

Such a simple question. It was a shame she didn't have the correct answer. "I am afraid I can't show his name to you."

"Why not?" As if he'd just realized he'd been holding up his arm for a full moment, he let it fall to his side. "Are you worried we'll cause a scene? If so, I promise I will be on my best behavior."

"No. I, um . . ." Why was she being so hesitant? Phillip's name's absence on the monument wasn't a secret. Why, any person in the town would most likely be thrilled to share the awful truth. "Phillip is not listed," she said at last.

His expression seemed to harden, but that was likely her imagination. "But he was a Confederate soldier. An officer, yes?"

"Yes. He was a lieutenant."

"And he died during the war."

"Yes. In captivity. He was a prisoner of war on Johnson's Island."

"Therefore, his name should be listed here. Honored." His tone held a new edge to it.

It took her off guard. "Yes," she said hesitantly. "But, well, there are some, I fear, who feel that he died betraying the South. The townspeople elected not to include him."

His expression turned murderous. "That is most unfortunate, ma'am."

She didn't quite understand why he even cared. "Yes. Yes, it is." Just then she noticed several people staring at them curiously. "We best go. We're causing a scene."

But he didn't budge. "How would we do that? We are merely standing here. Reading the names of the fallen heroes."

She didn't miss the sarcasm in his voice. Or the fact that his tone had risen enough to carry.

"Please, Mr. Truax. I am still unsure as to why you decided to accompany me. But since you did, I must ask you to abide by my wishes. I rarely leave the house and of late I never am accompanied. Your appearance and anger are going to cause further talk about me. And though it pains me to admit this, I have been a target for gossips and conjecture. I'd rather not give them any more ammunition."

He backed down at once. "Of course not. Please forgive me." Looking a bit abashed, he said, "Like I said, my manners have become quite lackluster. Any refinement I've ever had has taken leave."

"There is nothing to forgive. I simply need you to see how things are."

"I hope your circumstances change soon."

She did, too, but she doubted they would change. Well, at least not for the better.

The rest of the way to the bank, Miranda tried not to be aware that his hands now remained clasped behind his back. That he was keeping a respectful distance from her side. That he remained stoically silent.

The first thing Robert noticed when they entered the ornate building was that it was in far better shape than most likely any other bank building in the state. The woodwork gleamed. The brass fittings on the drawers and cabinets sparkled. The marble floor looked shiny enough to eat off of.

In short, it could hold its own against any grandiose building in Philadelphia or even New York City. Which, of course, was impressive, given the fact that they were in the post-war South and living in the throes of Yankee Reconstruction.

However, even the building's imposing beauty paled compared to the second thing Robert took note of. And that was the way the teller eyed Miranda with a combination of disrespect and lewd appreciation. It was blatant. Bordering on how many men had eyed the sporting girls when they'd come to their camps during the war.

Robert was shocked, seeing as how Miranda was everything the camp's fallen angels were not. But what was more surprising was how everyone in the building allowed the man's behavior to go on. Did no one see or hear how a bank employee was speaking to her? Or was it simply that no one cared?

Before his eyes, Miranda retreated into herself. She quietly stood in the short line and waited far too long to be served. A few ladies held glove-covered hands to their mouths and smirked.

Robert's jaw clenched as he understood that the teller's behavior was an intentional oversight. He was playing a game at Miranda's expense. Only when the man noticed Robert watching him coldly did he call Miranda forward.

"Mrs. Markham, if you're ready?" His voice was laced with sarcasm.

She started. And, Robert was dismayed to see, a hot flush rose up on her neck. "Yes, sir." Before she stepped forward, she looked back at him in some sort of apology. "I'll be right back, Mr. Truax."

It took everything he had not to step in front of her and guard her from everyone else's interested eyes.

But that was neither what she needed nor why he was there. "Take your time, ma'am," he said gently. "I've got all day."

However, when she moved toward the teller, and Robert noticed that the smarmy man boldly scanned her body as she approached, he realized it was going to be impossible to remain off to one side.

Instead, he followed, stopping just short of her. Close enough to hear every word spoken but far enough to provide the illusion of privacy. When a man behind him started to speak, obviously confused as to why Robert wasn't waiting his turn, he looked over his shoulder and glared. Now every person in the building was aware that Miranda Markham was no longer alone.

A new, uneasy silence permeated the room.

She glanced his way nervously, then timidly opened her reticule and her wallet and laid a small stack of money on the counter. "I have a deposit, Mr. Winter."

Instead of taking the bills and collecting it in an expedient fashion, the teller sighed. And started counting the bills out loud.

Stopping.

And then beginning again.

He looked up once to peer at Robert.

"I guess some people don't care where they stay. They'll even consider the Iron Rail." He paused, glancing at her with a wicked gleam in his eye. "Kind of makes me wonder what services you offer there." He smirked again and glanced up at her face.

Obviously, Mr. Winter was double-checking to see if his words had made a direct hit.

Robert clenched his fist as Miranda said nothing.

Looking pleased with himself, the teller jabbed again. "Do you ever tell your guests about your husband? About what he was really like?" he continued, his voice oily. Slick. "Do you ever admit to those folks what he did? Or do they simply prefer you to keep silent?"

Robert tensed as he prepared himself for Miranda to berate the man for his poor manners. After she had her turn, he was looking forward to speaking a few choice words himself.

However, she only inhaled before speaking. Her voice trembled but was thick with emotion. "I simply wish to conclude my business, Mr. Winter."

"Do you? What is your hurry? Do you have new boarders to entertain?" He leered at her.

Robert had had more than enough. Gently, he took her arm and moved her away from the teller's window. "Mrs. Markham, perhaps you'd like to sit down while I take care of this for you?"

"Mr. Truax—"

"It would be my honor, ma'am." He kept his voice hard. Firm.

When at last she nodded and moved to do as he bid, the teller sputtered. "I can't allow that."

Once he was satisfied that Miranda was out of earshot, Robert pressed both hands on the counter in front of him and leaned close. "I know you can allow me to see to her business. And once more, you will allow it," he said. "Furthermore, I suggest you conclude Mrs. Markham's business in a more expedient fashion."

"Who are you?"

"No one you would have ever heard of. Simply a friend."

Winter's expression was filled with derision. "I see. You're one of her men."

"No. You do not see." Lowering his voice, he said, "It has come to the notice of several people that Miranda Markham has been in need of some protection. I have come to offer that. You would be wise to change your attitude toward her."

"Because?"

"Because I am not helpless. I am not demure. I am not used to men in ill-fitting, cheap suits telling me what to do," he continued, his voice rising. "Most of all, I am most certainly not used to explaining myself."

The teller inhaled sharply. "Are you threatening me?"

"Sir."

"Pardon?"

"You forgot to add 'sir.'" When the teller gaped, Robert added, "If you are going to ask me a question like that, be sure to address me properly." After the briefest of pauses, he murmured, "Now give it another try, Mr. Winter."

For the first time, Mr. Winter looked shaken. "Are you threatening me, sir?"

"I don't make threats. I make promises." He lowered his voice. "As of today, Mrs. Markham's circumstances have changed. You would do well to take note of that."

Mr. Winter's eyebrows rose. "Yes, sir."

"I'm glad we see eye to eye. Now, if you would, finish the lady's banking needs in a more expedient fashion."

Immediately, Mr. Winter looked down to his hands, which were now clutching the crumpled bills. After smoothing them out, he began counting them, all in lightning-quick motions. After writing the amount in a ledger, he tore off a receipt. "Here you are. Sir."

"I'm glad we understand each other now." Robert took it, then turned back to Miranda, who was perched on the edge of one of the dark wooden chairs. "Mrs. Markham, are you ready to leave now?"

"Yes, I am." She rose gracefully, then took his elbow. She looked wary, but her eyes were shining.

Robert wondered if that new gleam was from happiness, unshed tears, or amusement. He hoped it was the latter. He would like to think she had enjoyed seeing that little worm of a teller finally get his comeuppance.

As he guided her out of the ornate building, Robert didn't look at the teller again. He didn't make eye contact with any of the men and women who had been eavesdropping curiously.

But most important, he made sure not to look at Miranda. There was only so much a man could handle at any one moment. He wanted to enfold her in his arms and promise that she would never be treated so shabbily again.

Furthermore, he knew if he saw that it wasn't amusement shining in her eyes but new pain, he would be very tempted to go back into that building and punch that teller for his insolence.

But that was not what she needed. She needed a protector, not a bully. And for her to accept his protection, she needed to first trust him. That meant he couldn't do anything to make her fear him.

He couldn't afford to do that. She couldn't afford that.

When they stepped outside, the cold air slapped their cheeks, making his eyes water and, as he saw when he finally looked down at her, her skin flush.

He wished he had a soft scarf to wrap around her.

She paused on the steps and breathed in deeply.

"Are you all right, Mrs. Markham?"

As she turned to him, he noticed her eyes were no longer shining but were a clear blue. "I believe I am. Thank you for what you did in there. Mr. Winter has always been rude, but he has never said such things to me before."

"You never need to thank me for defending your honor."

"He looked browbeaten."

He wished he could have simply beaten the man. "Mr. Winter was insolent and disrespectful. He needed to be reminded of his manners."

"I believe you did that."

He couldn't resist smiling. "I think so too." He gestured toward the street. "Shall we?"

She nodded, leaning into him when he rearranged his hands so one was resting on her back while the other was gripping her elbow.

He liked how she was depending on him to help her.

He probably liked it too much.

But at times like this, he missed the easy retribution that he'd learned on the streets of Ft. Worth. There, violence wasn't a last resort; it was the norm. Men didn't hold their tongues; they spoke their minds and made sure each word was sharp.

Reputation was everything, and a healthy dose of intimidation was often employed.

He had known that life and had been good at it. Robert also realized right then and there that if there came a time to unleash his baser qualities, he would look forward to it.

Perhaps far too much.

4

FROM THE TIME HE'D RETURNED MIRANDA TO HER HOME, Robert fumed about his visit to the bank with her. At first, he'd been so angry about Winter's treatment of her that he'd been tempted to return to the bank and show the man what happened when someone was rude to a woman Robert cared about.

Just imagining how good it would feel to knock some sense into the clerk had made Robert smile. But of course, no doubt Miranda would not appreciate the use of such violence on her behalf.

He made do with going for a long walk before supper, stopping and chatting with assorted passersby on the Strand and around the port. He'd learned a great many things about the island, its part in the war—and the rumors swirling about Phillip Markham and his widowed bride.

After supper, when Miranda had actually apologized for making him witness her abuse, he'd gotten angry all over again. He'd paced back and forth in his room, silently fuming. Over and over Robert reminded himself that he was no longer a daredevil soldier in the wilds of Arkansas. Instead, he was a gentleman whom Miranda needed to trust. That helped a bit, though punching a hole in the wall or ripping something into shreds was tempting.

Now, in the dim, winter morning light, Robert realized what

the correct course of action needed to be. He needed to write that letter to Captain Monroe.

With a new intent, he sat down at the small corner desk, dipped his quill into ink, and began. After writing a few lines about his travels and the state of Miranda's boardinghouse, he got to his point.

The situation here is beyond disturbing, sir. In fact, it borders on disbelief. The woman is treated like a pariah. She is avoided by practically every man and woman in the city, both because of rumors that Phillip was a traitor and because they think her boardinghouse is not a respectable establishment, though it most certainly is. It is as if everyone feels the need to make sure she is held in contempt, which makes no sense. Phillip told me she was from a good family and that their courtship, while impetuous, was not out of the ordinary.

He paused, letting his quill drip ink onto the corner of his paper. Only a quick dab of blotting paper prevented it from bleeding onto the rest of the page.

After reviewing what he'd written and being satisfied that he was neither exaggerating nor presenting Miranda Markham's situation too lightly, he continued.

Furthermore, from what I understand, no one has any true knowledge of what Phillip Markham actually did other than "giving the enemy secrets." It's all innuendo and veiled accusations. However, those allegations have already done terrible damage to our friend's reputation.

He gripped the quill, holding it so tightly he feared he was in danger of snapping the instrument in two.

He forced himself to inhale. Exhale. Repeat the process. Gathering his wits, he added:

I will attempt to further investigate this matter and discern how these rumors started. I will also do my best to try to alleviate some of Mrs. Markham's worst fears.

I'll write again in a few days.

He reviewed his words one more time, then signed his name. Next, after blotting the page, he carefully folded the paper and stuffed it into the awaiting envelope.

It was time to post it and move forward.

If he thought too much about his words, he would be tempted to tear the missive and rewrite it. But that would prove to be unnecessary and foolhardy. There was really nothing else to say and not much else to report. If he added too many of his thoughts or emotions, the captain would suspect that he had already begun to become too involved in the woman's life.

And that was not why he was there. No, it was far better to let the letter speak for itself and concentrate the rest of his energies on calming down and appearing detached.

Yes, that was how he needed to be. Detached.

At last satisfied that he had regained his composure, Robert carefully splashed water on his face, rolled down his shirtsleeves, slipped on his coat, and headed downstairs.

As he walked across the foyer, he passed a maid. She was small in stature, slim and petite. She was also on her hands and knees, scrubbing diligently at a scuff mark on the floor. Unable to help himself, he paused to watch her, enjoying how her black dress and crisp white apron coordinated with the black-and-white floor.

As if she noticed his regard, she stopped and stared up at him. "May I help you, sir?"

"No. Thank you." He turned on his heel and walked out the door before he did something foolish and started asking about her employer's mood that morning.

Now just past noon, the sun lay nestled in a mass of low-hanging clouds. Rain was in the forecast, he supposed. Perhaps it would be welcome. Though the temperatures were hovering around the forties, the air was thick with a strong, clawing humidity. His shirt stuck to his back and his lungs felt parched.

The humidity brought back memories of marching for hours in the Georgia heat, the red dust staining his uniform and black boots. Instinctively, he reached for his collar, his fingers fumbling with the starched seams, reaching for the button before remembering that he was no longer in a snug uniform. He was also no longer in a Yankee prison camp. He no longer had to fear running out of breath.

Would he, too, be forever marked by his months in captivity? Inwardly scarred from the traumas that had befallen him, that had befallen all of them?

Shaking off the doldrums, he crossed the road and headed toward the mercantile. He assumed he could post a letter from inside. Then perhaps he could find a place for some lunch and a drink.

A striking young woman with golden hair and wearing a well-tailored shirtwaist greeted him as he approached.

"Sir. How may I help you?"

Her voice was lilting. Melodic and surprising to find in the city. Since he'd arrived, a haze of depression had seemed to encompass almost everyone he met. Though it was no different from the atmosphere throughout much of the South, he'd naively expected something different in Galveston.

After all, it had survived the war better than most places. Its port was bustling, and it was the ranking port when it came to exporting cotton. The crowded warehouse district was full of it, and he'd heard that the business provided many men, both white and freedmen, with work.

So different from the parched plains of northern Georgia when he'd marched and fought there that one awful summer. There, pain and suffering and deprivation were daily occurrences.

In spite of the direction his thoughts were heading, he found himself smiling at her. "I need to post this letter, miss. Would you be able to assist me?"

A dimple appeared in her cheek, giving that final touch of ingénue and beauty that he hadn't even believed she lacked. "Of course." After taking the letter from him, her blue eyes examined him curiously. "You don't sound like you're from here."

"That's because I am not."

The dimple disappeared as a new suspicion appeared in her eyes. "You from the North, sir?" Her voice now sounded brittle, as if her composure could easily break.

"No."

"Forgive me. It's just that you sound different."

He knew his captivity on Johnson's Island had altered his accent. Maybe it had altered many things about him. "I'm from all over," he said simply.

Then, because he knew his answer told her nothing, he smiled again. Though this time, his smile was forced, brought forth for him to get his way. As much as he was eager to be done with the girl's company, he wondered if she might be the person he needed to discover just how Miranda Markham was doing among the people with whom she surely did business.

"I see," she said, her eyes lighting with interest, just as if he'd uttered something of value. "I've never met anyone who was from all over before."

Her gentle flattering inspired his vanity. He'd never been a man especially in need of female appreciation, but he couldn't deny that it did his soul good to realize he was not without certain charms.

Or perhaps it wasn't his charms. She was likely very skilled in conversation.

The thought amused him.

Remembering his goal, he lowered his voice. "More of us are from nowhere than one might assume," he murmured. He knew, of course, that this answer, too, told her nothing. Therefore she had nothing to remark upon. "How much?"

"Two bits." She smiled, revealing her one flaw, a set of crooked teeth. "Are you here for very long?"

"A month. Maybe longer."

"Oh? Where are you staying? At the Tremont?"

"No. At Mrs. Markham's house, the Iron Rail."

She blinked. Then visibly straightened. "Forgive me for being so blunt, but you really shouldn't be there."

"Why is that?"

She looked ready to blurt something, then glanced away. "It's just that the Tremont is far nicer. You should consider relocating."

"Relocating sounds like a lot of trouble. I'm sure Mrs. Markham's boardinghouse will suit me fine."

Her expression darkened. "You won't find many here of the same mind. Trust me, sir. You should take heed to what I say."

"You sound sure of yourself."

"I am. And you should listen. It's for your benefit, you see."

Seeing as he had no one standing behind him, Robert took the bait. "Why would you say such a thing? Is it because of the rumors surrounding her husband?"

"You've heard of them?"

"It's hard to be in Galveston five minutes and not hear them."

"There is a reason for that. He was a traitor." She lifted her chin. "As far as most good people are concerned, Miranda Markham should have done the decent thing and left Galveston Island. She could have sold her house and left the rest of us in peace. Not set up a boardinghouse."

"You'd ask her to leave her home? That sounds exceedingly harsh."

The girl looked as if she considered arguing that point, but instead simply stared steadily at him. "Sir, you have not paid me yet. Do you intend to?"

He dug in his pocket and pulled out the coins, slapping them on the counter with, perhaps, a bit more force than was actually needed.

She palmed them with alacrity. "Good day, sir."

He tipped his hat before turning, realizing several men and women were now behind him.

Had his skills deteriorated so much that he hadn't even been aware he was surrounded? The thought was disconcerting. If the captain had been around to see that, the man would have boxed his ears good. The childish punishment would have been no less than he deserved too.

With effort, Robert hid his chagrin and nodded at the four or five pairs of eyes watching him suspiciously.

It was time to exit the building, take a stroll back to Recognition Square—or whatever the Sam Hill that place was called—and make himself focus. He needed to get his head back on straight and become more alert. He needed to concentrate on the reason for being here. The multiple reasons for being here. Then, once he was firmly reminded of that, he needed to make a plan.

"Excuse me, sir?"

Robert looked to see a dapperly dressed man, perhaps five years younger than him, staring at him intently. He was standing a good two yards away, almost as if he didn't trust Robert enough to venture closer. His denims were new, his chambray shirt worn. On his feet was a fine pair of brown leather boots, the likes of which Robert hadn't seen in ages. Not since he'd witnessed a trio of cavalrymen taken to their barracks back on Johnson's Island. A Yankee soldier had claimed one of the men's boots in exchange for a freshly washed blanket. While Robert had burned at the indignity of it, the cavalry officer had merely shrugged, saying there wasn't a great need for good riding boots at the moment.

Hating that the memories he'd held at bay for so long seemed to be creeping back into his head like forgotten relatives who refused to stay away, Robert cleared his throat. "Yes?" he finally muttered.

Looking pleased that Robert had acknowledged him at last, the man stepped forward. "My name is Jess Kern, Mr. Truax."

The name meant nothing to him. But then, as the man's intent dark eyes remained steady, a sudden memory returned. "You were there," he said. "You were at Johnson's Island too."

Looking pleased to be remembered, Kern nodded. "I was. Though not too long. Only a few months." He added, "I was captured in January of '65."

Robert remembered his long captivity in terms of how cold he'd been. "Just in time for the lake to freeze."

"We marched on the ice from Sandusky to the barracks."

Robert felt chill bumps form on his skin just from the memory of it all. "January was a difficult month on the island."

Kern shivered dramatically. "If I close my eyes, I can remember the chill that permeated my skin. Some nights the men in my unit huddled together. We told ourselves it was for company, but it was certainly for warmth."

They'd done that, too, though he and his comrades had been there long enough to not need reasons to share cots. They simply were glad there was someone near enough to take the edge off the constant ache.

Those memories were so clear, so piercingly real, that he had to close his eyes to forget them.

"There were a lot of men there. Over two thousand at the end of the war. I'm surprised you recognized me."

"Everyone knew who you were."

Robert lifted his chin. "Why is that?"

"You were with Captain Monroe." Looking a little sheepish, Kern said, "He was a formidable figure, even though he was only a captain."

"He was a formidable figure." Looking at Kern intently, he added, "He still is." No man would ever get far if he dared to say anything bad about his commanding officer.

Kern's eyes widened. "Hey, now. No need to get riled up. I meant that as a compliment. After all, there were generals in camp with us."

"There were." They'd been impressive. Some had been West Point graduates. Yet even those men had treated their captain with a combination of awe and respect.

Eager to find a few minutes of solitude, he stared at his interloper coldly. "You have the advantage of me. While we might have both had the misfortune to be detained in the middle of Lake Erie, I do not know you. Furthermore, I am afraid I don't take pleasure in remembering my time in captivity."

Something uneasy flickered in Kern's eyes. "No, I don't reckon you would."

That told Robert nothing. Losing patience with the man's lack of information, he bit out, "Any particular reason you wanted to say hello?"

"There is." After another brief moment, the corners of the man's lips turned up. "Though I told you my name, I should also let you know I'm the sheriff here." He paused, presumably waiting for Robert to give him his due.

However, Robert could find no reason to respond to the lawman. He'd done nothing wrong and was far beyond feeling impressed by men wielding authority, especially men in power with such a lazy drawl.

Therefore, he merely stared.

A flash of awareness filled Sheriff Kern's features before he attempted to smile again. "Don't want to trouble you, but I'd like a few minutes of your time. If I may."

All of Robert's defenses went on alert. The lawman knew his name and had sought him out away from Mrs. Markham's boardinghouse. Both things gave him pause. "Is there a specific reason you've sought my company, Sheriff?"

"Yes."

Impatience gnawed at him as he realized the sheriff had no intention of providing any information without Robert investing a considerable amount of time and energy. "I am at a loss for what we could possibly have to say to each other."

"I aim to rectify that if you would kindly spare me a few moments of your time."

Robert knew he had no choice. He was going to have to listen to this man no matter what. But still he muttered, "I don't believe I've done anything here in Galveston you might find fault with."

"Neither do I—especially since you have been here barely more than twenty-four hours." After another weak attempt of a smile, Sheriff Kern said, "I promise, this won't take up much of your time."

Robert searched the man's features. Noticed the freshly shaven cheeks, the earnest look in his eyes. His solid stance. Then, upon further examination, Robert saw a hard glint in his eyes, a faint scar marring one of his dark eyebrows.

And an air about him that warned most everyone to give him respect. This man might not have fought in the war for years like the rest of them, but he was no tenderfoot. There was a will of iron lurking behind his easy, relaxed expression and slow Texas drawl.

And in that hint of iron, Robert found a measure of respect for him. The sheriff grew in his estimation. "Where would you like to talk?"

"Not here. It's too public."

"No offense, but I'd prefer not to meet in your offices." A lawman's offices were always barely one step away from his holding cells, and Robert had no desire to ever be that close to a set of iron bars again.

"None taken." Sheriff Kern looked amused. "Perhaps you would join me on a walk? I could show you the sights. Galveston is a progressive city with a lot to be proud of."

Satisfied that Kern didn't seem to be harboring any ulterior motives, Robert gestured to his right. "I was about to revisit your square."

The lawman frowned. "Ah. Well, if you don't mind, I'd rather not go there right now."

"Anywhere else in mind?"

Looking as if he'd just discovered oil, his expression brightened. "I know. There's a place at the end of one of the docks that I find particularly pleasing. How about there?"

Robert was officially intrigued. "I can't think of a better spot I'd like to see."

Kern turned on his heel and started down a nearby alleyway that Robert hadn't even noticed. After a moment's hesitation, Robert followed, wondering all the while if he was about to be set up to be ambushed.

Though it was midday, the alley was dark and narrow and smelled like forgotten trash and desolation. It was also damp and held a peculiar chilliness, in direct contrast to the relative warmth on the public square. Here and there sat poor lost souls—some men, some women holding a child or two. Their disinterest in both the sheriff's approach as well as the unfamiliar stranger's appearance spoke volumes. They'd been through much and didn't hold out hope for anything to change.

Just as Robert slowed to stare in wonder at one of the women who looked like little more than skin and bones, he heard the rustling and squeal of a rat racing across his path. He released a low cry of alarm before he could stop himself.

Kern glanced over his shoulder with a chuckle. "There are more rats here in Galveston than people. You'll get used to 'em."

Robert sincerely hoped he did not. "You need some cats."

"Not for those rats. They're big as coons and mean as snakes. I wouldn't put any creature I liked in their paths. But don't worry, Billy'll catch him sooner or later. He always does."

"Billy? He your rat catcher or something?"

The sheriff let loose a bark of laughter, its sound reverberating around the brick walls of their enclosure. "Heck no. This ain't England. He's just an old codger man with a way with rodents. He says they're good eating."

"You haven't tried?"

Sheriff Kern visibly shuddered. "To my good fortune, I have

not. Even when times were tough around here, they were never that tough." As they exited the alleyway, Kern gestured to the harbor looming ahead. "'Course, I'd rather eat a fish any day of the week. What about you, Lt. Truax?"

Robert was momentarily taken aback by the title. It seemed that the sheriff, for all his good-ole-boy persona, was actually far sharper than he let on. He wondered how he'd discovered his rank in twenty-four hours. Or had he known on Johnson's Island? "I've had rat," he said at last. "But only once. It wasn't a meal worth repeating."

"Don't imagine it was. Fan of fish?"

"From time to time."

"I'll see if my sister, Diana, can cook up some while you're here visiting. She has a way with catfish and frog legs."

"I'll pass on the frogs, if you don't mind."

Kern grinned. "You're kinda particular for a man who has spent time in prison."

He was particular because he'd spent time in prison. Instead of sharing that point, Robert kept his silence as they walked toward the harbor. The few men loitering around watched them with silent, steady expressions. Sheriff Kern ignored them, his lanky, relaxed way of walking giving the impression that they were strolling along a boulevard in Savannah.

Not along the rundown docks of the former Confederate port.

His guard relaxed when they at last approached a pier. The air smelled both of the sea and the fetid remains. A cross between fish and decay and coal and debris. The scent was acrid and strong. And though far different from the smells he remembered coming off Lake Erie around his prison, not completely dissimilar.

The memory, like all the others, threw him for a tailspin. He inhaled the cloying air, attempting to locate something fresh weaving in the middle of it. Anything to clear his head yet again and bring him back to the present.

As his vertigo dissipated, he breathed deeply and cautioned his body to remember that he was no longer at another's mercy. No more bars separated him from freedom.

He wasn't cold. He wasn't shooting his mouth off about things he had no knowledge of. Phillip Markham wasn't dying next to him.

Once he got his bearings again, he realized the dapper young sheriff was staring at him with concern. "Mr. Truax, you've grown pale. Is something distressing you?"

It seemed he could either pretend he had no past or admit what was really the matter.

His instincts told him telling the complete truth at this point in his mission would be exceedingly foolhardy, not even to a lawman. "My body seems determined to take its time getting acclimated."

Instead of letting his comment pass, the other man looked at him curiously. "To what do you need to become acclimated? The ocean? Or the South?"

Despite his vow to remain distant, Robert felt his eyes flash in annoyance. "As you well know, I was an officer in the Confederate army, sir. I have no need to become acclimated to the South."

When Kern took a page out of his book and merely stared steadily at him, silently daring him to reveal his dark secrets, Robert gave in and admitted the rest. "As much as I don't care to think about our time in captivity, sometimes the memories still inundate me."

Kern winced. "I dream about all that water that surrounded our encampment. In my dreams I relive the feel of the ice under my worn boots and my fears about being forced to march on it during the spring thaw. I think those pieces of ice floating in it scared me more than anything."

Robert couldn't believe they were currently making small talk about his months in captivity. Discussing the weather like it mattered. But as he involuntarily shivered, his body recalling the chill against his skin that he could never seem to completely forget, he nodded. "I was always cold. And damp." And though the sheriff hadn't prompted any more confidences, he found himself continuing to talk.

"Every once in awhile, something triggers my body, and for a brief amount of time I imagine I'm back. A loud crash, or the smell of burning fibers. Cold, damp air."

"It seems no matter how one might wish otherwise, the past always treads on our present."

Kern's tone wasn't light. Instead, it gave Robert a reason to believe he wasn't the only man present suffering from the war. "Do you, also, have demons that you find difficult to escape?"

"I do."

"I must admit I'm surprised. You don't look old enough to have fought, let alone been sent to Johnson's Island."

"Toward the end of the war they didn't just send officers. Anyone would do."

The younger man's simple statement shamed him. "Forgive me. I didn't mean to negate your experiences."

"There ain't a thing to forgive. We've all experienced loss, sir. Only some of the things, I think, are harder to imagine than others."

Robert blinked. It seemed this young pup had more to him than he had anticipated. The other man's acceptance of Robert's weaknesses felt like he was being exposed. Opening a wound, leaving himself bare for further viewing. For pain.

And though one might argue that uncovering such a wound might eventually give a man the hope of healing, Robert wasn't exactly ready for that. No, it would be far easier to live with the dull ache that filtered through his heart and soul.

At least he was used to that.

Obviously seeing that Robert was done sharing his experiences, Kern cleared his throat again. "Well, we are here. How about we take a seat at the end of the dock?"

The dock looked rickety. "You sure it can hold both our weight?"

"Only one way to find out, Lieutenant," Kern called out as he walked to the end of the pier and sat down with little fuss or fanfare.

Wondering how his errand of posting a letter had come to a sojourn down memory lane with a youngish sheriff with a penchant for good humor, Robert followed the sheriff's lead and made his way down the pier.

When he reached the edge, he sat down. The wood felt warm underneath him. And with his legs dangling over the water, he felt both younger than he had in years and curiously ancient. He couldn't remember the wood ever feeling so unforgiving when he had been younger.

"What did you want to speak to me about?"

"Miranda Markham."

Robert held his temper with effort. "Don't tell me that you, too, seek to warn me about her?"

"Definitely not. On the contrary, I was hoping you could tell me more about your relationship with her."

"We have no relationship. I am a guest at her boardinghouse."

"Is that right?" Kern's lips pressed together. "That's all?"

"Do you expect more? I only met her yesterday morning."

To Robert's amazement, Kern relaxed. "I see."

Again, he was feeling like he'd stepped into the middle of a maze for which there was no way out. Tired of such foolishness, he hardened his voice. "What, precisely, do you see?"

The muscles in Kern's throat worked a bit. "Nothing."

"Except?"

"Except that Mrs. Markham attracted my notice from my first day here over two years ago. I suppose I feel a bit protective toward her."

"If you do, I would venture that you'd be the only one. The few townspeople I've met seem to treat her as a pariah."

Kern stiffened. "I know. I don't understand it myself."

"It's my understanding that many believe her husband is responsible for betraying the Confederacy."

"I've heard that too. But beg pardon, I don't know how that rumor started, though it was about a year ago. It coincided with her opening the Iron Rail as a boardinghouse. And furthermore, even if her husband did betray the South while in prison, he was only a lieutenant. And he was only imprisoned at the end of the war. What could he have possibly said that would have made much of a difference?"

"Any idea who is responsible for the rumors?"

"I can only surmise that it is the same person who sent her a threatening letter."

Everything in Robert froze. "What letter? I haven't heard anything about that."

"Mrs. Markham brought it to me the day she received it, just after she opened the Iron Rail for boarders. It was an ugly piece of work," he said with a grimace. "The author threatened to reveal missives supposedly in Phillip's handwriting, ones that supposedly proved he had been a traitor."

"That means nothing. Anyone could say the missives were in his hand."

"I agree. I told her to ignore it as best she could. There was no way to trace where it came from and therefore it would be better to simply dispose of the letter and forget it ever came."

Robert was incredulous. Sheriff Kern seemed to be telling him that Miranda's concerns meant nothing. "Is that how you handle most problems that come your way? You simply tell the victim to forget about it?"

"Of course not. However, I didn't see any other course of action. There was nothing I could do and she was terribly agitated. I decided to err on the side of caution. After all, Mrs. Markham had already been upset by her husband's imprisonment and death. She was barely out of mourning. No reason to make her suffer more."

Though Robert wasn't sure he would have given her the same advice, he wasn't exactly sure he would have said anything much different either.

"If you weren't worried about her, then why are you so concerned about her now?"

"She hasn't seemed well. Actually, it looks to me like she's fallen into melancholia. She looks like she's lost weight and she hardly leaves her house now."

"I am not sure why you sought me out."

"I heard about your walk with her yesterday. I heard that you stood up for her with that weasel Winter." Kern turned his head and stared at Robert directly. "Beg your pardon, but those actions are not things a man who just happened to be in Galveston would do."

"They might be."

"No, I don't think so. Mr. Truax, I'm going to be honest with you. Mrs. Markham knows I served in the war; everyone in town knows that."

"But?" Robert pressed.

"But I've never told anyone I was on Johnson's Island when Phillip Markham was, not even his wife."

"It seems to me that news might have eased her in some way."

"I don't think so." He shifted, his expression pensive. "Fact is, I didn't want to add to her pain when I didn't really know anything about what happened to the lieutenant. I don't have any proof to refute the rumors about him." Before Robert could comment on that, Kern turned his head to stare at him directly. "Say what you want, but I don't think it's by chance that you're here. I think you knew her husband because you both served under Devin Monroe."

"I did know Phillip Markham. Furthermore, I sat by his side in his last hours."

Kern relaxed. "Was he actually the kind of man Mrs. Markham believes him to be?"

"Yes. We talked a lot, you see." Actually, there hadn't been much else to do. But every time they'd complained about their lack of activity, of their inability to help their comrades still battling across frozen fields, Captain Monroe had chastised them. All they needed to concentrate on was living. Survival—that was the key to life in a prison camp. Nothing else mattered.

They'd known it, and the soldiers guarding them had known it too. As the battles became even more one sided and rumors flew about Lee's eventual surrender, even the guards had lost their interest in keeping a vigilant guard. All of them were missing their sweethearts and families.

Why, they'd even all shared stories about their homes one long snowy evening, all of them huddled around their meager stove, burning scraps of wood and one soiled blanket.

Of them all, Phillip had spoken the most lovingly of his wife. He'd talked about her beauty. About how strong she was, how she'd never even led him on a merry chase when they'd been courting. She'd simply gazed at him with her blue eyes and asked if she could trust him.

They'd all gazed at him with mixed emotions. For Robert, jealousy combined with a healthy amount of incredulousness had filled him. He had never heard of a woman so well regarded. Actually, he'd been more of a fool than that. He, in all his inept naiveté, had doubted their lieutenant's word. He'd also been resentful of a man who had been so blessed, not only with good looks but property and an adoring wife.

It had seemed like too much. Too much when he'd had so little.

Two days after they'd all sat around the fire and listened to Captain proclaim they needed to look out for each other after the war, Phillip's wound took a sudden turn for the worse. His arm began to swell.

Twenty-four hours after that, he'd spiked a fever and his injury became visibly infected. Then, unfortunately for all of them, he lingered. For weeks. Gangrene settled in. And with that came pain for Phillip and the helpless knowledge for the rest of them that they could do nothing of worth for him.

His death had upset them all. Even the guards stood in silence while Robert and the rest of Phillip's comrades buried him. Their pickaxes and shovels had clanged against the frozen ground. Jarring their muscles and helping to take the sting off tears.

They'd all been hurting about the injustice of it all, and none more than he. Because he had been so full of himself. Instead of agreeing that Phillip had been blessed, Robert had thrown it in his face.

And Phillip had no doubt died thinking Robert hadn't believed in him.

"When I heard you were being so kind to Mrs. Markham, I wanted to touch base with you," Kern explained. "If you hear that she's had another threat or if she confides that anything else worrisome has happened to her, will you tell me?"

Robert wasn't following. It was a lawman's job to help, not stand back in the shadows and wait. "Why haven't you asked her yourself?"

"Because I let her down before," he explained. "She doesn't trust me."

"Why not?"

"I told you. I denied her request for help. I didn't investigate the letter."

"She may not trust you, but she doesn't know me."

"Then get to know her." Kern's cheeks flushed. "After all, she's a beautiful woman. A beautiful woman in need of a man to care for her. A woman like that shouldn't be living alone. It ain't right."

"And you'd like to be the man to offer her companionship?" Robert made sure he infused his words with a healthy amount of sarcasm.

The sheriff drew himself up to his impressive height. "Suppose I did. Do you have a problem with that?"

Robert knew he shouldn't. From what he'd learned so far, Kern was truly concerned about Miranda. He cared enough about her to approach Robert and make his concerns clear.

And hadn't that been what Devin had asked him to do? Yes, he was supposed to discover why Phillip's widow was having such a difficult time. But he was also supposed to try to help her, to perhaps be her friend. She was lonely. A good, caring man who would happily face the gossips and the naysayers was a blessing. Someone worth holding on to.

But though all those reasons made sense, Robert couldn't do it. At least, not yet. "I know nothing about you."

Kern's eyes narrowed. "I didn't realize my background or interest was any of your business."

"I've made it my business."

"I don't know why. I was under the impression that you didn't know Mrs. Markham before you came here."

Robert's earlier doubts about Kern were becoming stronger. The man spoke in circles. "I'm starting to think I might know Miranda Markham better than most," he stated with a new edge in his voice.

"Is that right? Even though you've only just arrived on Galveston Island?"

"I have learned she is a gently bred lady who has already had her fair share of pain . . . and that she is in dire need of a protector."

"That occurred to me as well, Lieutenant. That is exactly why I asked you to talk with me," he continued, his expression hard. "Therefore, sir, if you know something about her to help me in my goal, I respectfully ask you to share. I don't cotton with cowardly fools who prey on the weakness and fears of women."

"On that, we are in agreement."

Kern nodded. "Good to know. Now that we have that settled, if you learn of even a hint of who was behind the letter she received and who started the rumors about Phillip Markham, I hope you'll share that information with me as well."

"Nothing would make me happier than to give you that name."

"I'd be obliged." Slowly, he added, "Finally, like I was saying, I have an interest in Mrs. Markham that is aboveboard and completely respectful. I hope you do not intend to stand in my way."

"I don't intend to, but like I said earlier, I don't know you yet. I don't plan to make any promises."

"Take your time," the sheriff said easily. "Unlike yourself, I have all the time in the world to win her trust."

Robert nodded, then turned away and started back to the Iron Rail. But as he walked, he realized that much had already changed in his heart.

5

IT MADE NO SENSE. IN JUST FOUR DAYS, ROBERT TRUAX HAD managed to become a prominent fixture in her life.

Miranda figured the reason for this was that she simply did not have enough to occupy her mind. Most days, she mended linens, planned menus, welcomed her few guests, and kept up with correspondence. Conversations with her staff were pleasant but impersonal.

None of those tasks took much time or thought. Until Mr. Truax's arrival, it had been a struggle to merely get through each day without succumbing to depression, especially since she had been forced to open the boardinghouse to survive and the rumors about Phillip had started. Moreover, she had felt empty inside. Devoid of any joy or goals.

And she had received the last letter.

Now, however, wherever she was, Robert found her. He engaged her often, sometimes talking of nothing more than the weather or some interesting tidbit he'd discovered about one of the buildings or Galveston Bay. He asked her questions. Made jokes and asked her opinion. In short, he gave her no choice but to interact with him.

After the first couple of times, she'd dared to respond. Every time she did, Robert would look pleased.

She'd likely smiled and even laughed more in the past week than she had since Phillip died. So much so that she found herself forgetting to mourn for him, and she was even able to put her worries aside for hours at a time.

Miranda knew she'd be a liar if she said this transformation in herself didn't feel strange. On the contrary, she worried about what was going to happen when Robert left and the support she was gradually getting used to accepting vanished.

Would she delve back into her dark depression? Would the blackness consume her, finally pressing in deep enough to give her the courage to open that windowpane again?

The idea was frightening.

"Knock, knock."

Looking up from her desk—and her musings—she saw Robert standing in the parlor's doorway. He wore dark denims and black boots this morning. He had on a dark brown shirt and a thick vest as well. He looked almost like one of the cowboys who came onto the island from time to time, intent on sampling the wares of fallen women in the warehouse district.

His dark hair was curved behind his ears and he was freshly shaved. And he was watching her closely. Once again there was no judgment in his dark eyes. Instead, only a lazy appreciation that she would have to be dead not to appreciate.

"Good morning, Mr. Truax. I trust you slept well?"

A half-smile formed on his lips. "I did, thank you. And you?"

"Me? Yes, I did sleep well, thank you." To her surprise, she realized she wasn't lying. She had fallen asleep soon after she'd slipped into her bed and had enjoyed a lengthy, peaceful slumber. She'd slept better during the last two nights than she had in the previous two months.

Realizing he was still standing in front of her waiting, she smoothed the fabric of her pale lavender gown. No gray today. "May I help you, sir? Or did you simply stop by to say hello?"

His smile grew as if the question amused him. "I came for a reason, of course."

She got to her feet. "Yes?"

"I had a hankering to take another walk on the Strand today."

Though she still wasn't sure what that had to do with her, she responded. "Oh! Well, I hope you have an enjoyable time. As you have already seen, we are fortunate to have a great variety of shops, restaurants, and businesses to sample. Many claim it is Galveston Island's crowning achievement."

She didn't think it was quite that, but it was a lovely area. Many of the fronts were ornate and built in the Victorian style. Furthermore, each was showcased in its own right. "My husband told me many of the buildings are made of cast iron and brick because the architects hoped the expensive building materials would help withstand the storms and hurricanes that wash ashore from time to time."

"I didn't merely come to inform you of my plans, ma'am," he said with a meaningful look. "I had another goal in mind."

"Oh?"

"You see, I am standing here in the hopes that you would consider accompanying me."

She stilled. Not since before the war had she gone for a simple stroll by a man's side. When Phillip got leave one summer, they had walked down on the Strand, stopping for ice cream. Once, they'd dined out, just like some of the ship captains who arrived from all over the world or the cattle barons who vacationed in the Tremont.

And though Robert had walked with her to the bank, this offer was different. She was sure the whole experience would be different, and she wasn't exactly sure how she felt about that.

No, to be fair, she wasn't sure how she would be able to do such a thing without having it affect her. Or, for that matter, what would everyone say? Of course, did it even make a difference?

Even thinking about the distaste she would encounter from passersby, she tamped down her wishes. "As you know, the Strand is nearby, sir. I doubt you'll have difficulty locating whatever shop you are hoping to find."

He chuckled. "I'm not worried about getting lost, Miranda. I am asking because I would enjoy your company."

"My company?"

"Yes." He looked at her curiously. "Surely you can understand that I would want to spend an afternoon with a beautiful woman?"

He thought she was beautiful. It had been a long time since she'd thought of herself as attractive, as anything other than a shell of the person she once was.

And though she knew she should ignore his flowery words, her insides warmed and that same cautious burst of nervousness mixed with butterflies settled in her stomach. "Thank you for the compliment and the invitation, but I am afraid I cannot do that."

"Why is that?"

Yes, why was that? Scrambling for a real reason, she ventured, "Well, first of all, it wouldn't be seemly."

"Why not?"

Oh, his questions! Some days she was sure he had a never-ending supply locked in his head. "It wouldn't be seemly because we are both unmarried. That is obvious."

But instead of looking as if he understood her point, he looked amused yet again. "Perhaps that might have mattered if we were eighteen, but we are of age, ma'am." He paused. "I am thirty and survived a war. And you, well, you are a widow," he added. "I consider both of us past the age of needing to justify our actions to anyone."

He was right. He was thirty and she was twenty-six. Both of them had a number of experiences that could neither be ignored nor simplified.

But it was because of those events that she was reluctant to make a stir. Because she'd rather be blunt than simply refuse him and inadvertently hurt his feelings, she said, "Mr. Truax, the truth is that while I would enjoy accompanying you, I don't know if I could survive the talk that would ensue."

"Do you truly think two people walking out together would cause so much notice?"

"If it was you and someone else, no. However, I am afraid everything I do now causes notice." Hating how terribly pitiful she sounded, she added, "Other than Mr. Winter, you might not have noticed anything out of the ordinary when we went to the bank, but—"

All traces of amusement vanished as he stared hard at her. "I noticed," he interrupted.

She wasn't sure if she was glad he understood or if she was now more embarrassed than ever. "I've begun to hate leaving the house."

"We need to put a stop to that."

"There is nothing one can do."

"I disagree." He stepped forward. "Ma'am, I think it's time you ignored the looks and the criticism and enjoyed your days. We need to get you out more. Go on the offensive, per se."

"Spoken like a true military man."

He shrugged. "I am used to finding solutions to problems, ma'am. It is second nature."

He was so sure. So confident. Miranda was tempted to simply agree, to let him make decisions about what was best for her.

If he was going to stay, she might even give in enough to let him.

But eventually he would be gone and she'd be back to being

alone. When that happened, she would have to bear all the consequences, and no doubt they would be dire indeed.

Not wanting to let on just how much his kindness meant to her, she kept her voice light. "Sir, I must admit to being tempted. But again, I must decline. The talk would be even worse than normal after last week's visit to the bank."

"Because?"

"Well, Mr. Winter has undoubtedly already turned your defense of me in the bank into something ugly."

His expression turned ice cold. "He wouldn't dare."

"Oh, I am afraid he would. I know we've already talked about this, but there are rumors circulating about Phillip. His reputation isn't ensuring my protection, and for some reason, Mr. Winter in particular has an interest in me."

She paused, mentally preparing herself for Robert to take back his offer to go on the Strand.

But instead of retreating from this latest bit of news, Robert stepped closer. And with that increased proximity came an increased awareness of his scent. Sandalwood and soap. The combination shouldn't have been appealing. She found it masculine and irresistible.

Her attraction to it—and the man it belonged to—also worried her. She'd promised to love Phillip forever. Until Mr. Truax appeared in her parlor that first day, she'd had no doubt that she would never love again. Would ever even look at another man.

But now she was discovering that was not going to be the case.

"Miranda," he drawled, "how about if I promise you that when I leave, no one will dare to disparage your character ever again?"

"I doubt such a promise can be made."

"Let me prove you wrong."

"Sir, trust me when I say it is better that I keep to myself."

"You can't imagine your life being much different because you have given up." His voice hardened. "It's time to try harder."

He was baiting her. Goading her.

It wasn't fair and she knew better than to let him.

But sometimes even she wasn't capable of continually saying no.

And sometimes she didn't even want to.

Robert hadn't been lying when he told Miranda he'd been his unit's problem solver during the war. Whether it was a by-product of living a childhood devoid of assistance or he simply had been blessed with a devious mind, Robert Truax had always been able to obtain anything he or his friends needed. He could pick locks. He could lift produce without notice. He could charm old women and crusty men and bitter scoundrels.

Monroe had called him a master manipulator. Phillip Markham had said he was far too conniving. Other men had called him names that weren't half as kind.

Robert had never cared. He'd liked being useful and he liked being able to depend on his brain to survive. He had secretly felt it was a far more gentlemanly way to go through life than the way Sgt. Thomas Baker had, which was to use his bulk and his fists to convince others to follow his lead.

However, though he'd been on many missions and had stolen, lied, and grinned his way toward food, shelter, ammunition, and even medical help, Robert wasn't sure if he'd ever had to be as patient and persistent as he had to be with Miranda.

Her stubbornness would give a mule a run for its money! He'd never been so glad he was as stubborn as she was.

It had all been worth it, though. Now he was reaping the

rewards. He was walking along Market Street with Miranda on his arm. She was wearing an attractive wide-brim hat and a navy day dress that favored her blue eyes. She'd also forgone layers of petticoats and had opted for one of fashion's newer looks, the bustle. She looked very fine.

He soon found out she hadn't been exaggerating. His escorting her to the bank and the mercantile had not been so bad, but today one would have thought they were notorious bank robbers or visiting royalty, the amount of attention they were receiving. At first he'd glared at anyone who dared to stare at them too long.

But he soon discovered Miranda also had a certain number of skills. She was a master of walking along and mixing in with crowds. She could talk to him without making eye contact with anyone surrounding them.

And she could look at ease and serene even when it was obvious that people were whispering about her.

He instinctively knew she hadn't been born with such skills or had even practiced such behavior in her childhood. When she let down her guard, Miranda seemed bright and vibrant. That was who Phillip had spoken about with such care. Robert believed her husband would have been truly dismayed to see the way she was forced to behave now.

After she led him into a sweetshop where he bought some hard candies, he walked with her down the street until they were looking only at the ocean beyond them.

The air was ripe with the scent of salt and ocean and decay and mildew. The combination was unusual, but it wasn't unpleasant. It was also decidedly distinct. Right then and there, Robert knew if he ever smelled it again, he would instantly think of this moment with her.

He was about to comment on a flock of seagulls circling a

shrimp boat when he noticed Miranda had her chin slightly lifted. She looked bright and alive and vibrant. Beautiful.

"You like it here in Galveston, don't you?"

She laughed. "I suppose I do. Even though I've had so many difficult days here, there is something wonderful about standing here at the pier. I enjoy the water."

"You don't mind the fishy smell?"

She laughed again. "Not so much. I've grown used to it, I think. The air is odorous, but it is pungent and fresh too. And if I stand still, I can feel faint droplets of water from the ocean. And taste the salt. I don't think I'll ever forget the combination of it all, even if I move far away from here and live for thirty more years."

Her comment made him curious. "Where did you grow up?"

"In a small town west of Houston. We had a ranch and my father ran his uncle's mercantile." She sobered. "Everyone is gone now, of course."

"And you met Phillip there?"

"Oh, goodness, no. Phillip would have ridden right by my dusty town without a second look," she said without a trace of embarrassment. "Actually, my cousin Carson joined the army around the same time Phillip did. Somehow they bonded during basic training and Carson's letters were always filled with stories about Phillip."

"So you started writing to him?"

"Not at all. Phillip and I met when I went with some other cousins to a dance in Houston."

"It must have been quite a dance," he teased gently.

"Oh, it was. Phillip had recently graduated from West Point and was in his uniform. He looked resplendent."

Her words were sweet, her voice softly lilting.

No woman—no person, really—had ever spoken to him or about him that way.

Robert carefully bit back the sharp taste of jealousy that coursed through him. "I imagine he was quite a sight to see."

Still looking moony, she sighed. "He was. But everyone was dressed to the nines." Giggling softly, she said, "My mother and aunt had outdone themselves, outfitting my cousin Beatrice and me." She giggled. "We arrived at that dance in beautiful dresses."

"What did yours look like?" he asked, hoping to keep that soft smile playing on her lips.

Her voice took on a dreamy quality. "Mine was white with pink bows along the bodice and the capped sleeves. I also had the most beautiful long white gloves. And a bonnet with silk roses! It was gorgeous and so, so heavy!"

Though it wasn't that long ago, she was referencing a time that most every Southern man tried to forget. The memories were too sweet. "I'd almost forgotten about hats like that."

"Bea and I had our fancy bonnets and our princess dresses. We were sure we were the most fetching young ladies in attendance. Why, we were sure we were sporting the biggest hoop skirts this side of the Mississippi."

He laughed. "I most definitely do not miss those skirts."

"Because they got in the way of everything?"

"Because a man could never get close enough to the woman he was flirting with," he teased.

When she laughed again, he smiled at her. He liked seeing her like this, so carefree and happy. He liked it almost as much as the idea of her being all dressed up in a white dress and gloves and dancing with Phillip for the first time.

"I bet you took his breath away, Mrs. Markham."

"Maybe I did," she mused. She bit her bottom lip. "I'm sure I couldn't say."

"Surely your husband paid you many compliments."

"He did. But he was the person who looked so dashing." Her voice went soft as she rested her elbows on the wooden railing. "He was handsome and tall and so very kind."

"He sounds like a true gentleman."

She sighed. "He was. Even with everything that's happened since, with all the rumors and innuendos and pain, I've never regretted falling in love with him."

"I would wager that he would have been happy to know that, ma'am." The moment he said the words, he tensed. No doubt they sounded too familiar for a man who was a stranger to say.

But instead of looking confused, she simply shrugged. "Maybe."

She looked away from him then and stared back out at the gulf. Below them, water lapped at the wooden pilings under their feet. The faint echoes of fishermen coming off boats floated toward them, their sharp orders and barks of laughter and raucous conversation mixing in with the shrill cry of the seagulls overhead.

"No . . . I mean, I know so," she said after several minutes. "We were a love match. He would be pleased to know that my love for him has never wavered."

He made no reply. Instead, he leaned his forearms on the weathered railing and simply let the moment wash over him. After years of barely surviving, it seemed especially sweet.

Far too soon, Miranda stepped away. "I think we had better get back, Robert. I'm no longer a child or a young bride. I have things to do."

"Yes, it is probably time we returned." He had been too entranced by her for his own good.

As they started walking, she said, "I'm sorry, I chattered on about myself this whole time."

"I enjoyed your chatter."

She smiled. "No, I meant, I bet you probably have your own stories to tell about those dances. Do share."

He laughed. "I most definitely do not have any stories about officer dances."

"No? Why not? I was under the impression that all officers were expected to attend those assemblies."

"They were, but I did not enter the army as an officer, Mrs. Markham. I could never have afforded that." For the first time that afternoon, he felt a small burst of pride. He could never compare to a gentleman like Phillip Markham, but he wasn't without any redeeming qualities.

"Robert, you earned your rank?"

"I did."

Her eyes widened. "I've heard that is hard to do."

"It would have been near impossible . . . if we hadn't been at war." He shrugged. "My captain needed men unafraid to take chances. I was fearless."

Thankfully, she didn't ask him to divulge stories about the battlefields. "So you mean to tell me you never had a sweetheart? I'm sure you eventually attended a dance. They were all the rage here."

He debated about how much to tell her, then realized it was of no consequence what she thought. It wasn't as if he ever had to worry about truly impressing her. No matter who he was or what he'd done, he was never going to be good enough for a lady like her.

Especially not after she'd had a husband like Phillip Markham.

"Miranda, when I first entered the army, I had no manners to speak of. I was as unruly as a bobcat in the wild."

She looked skeptical. "I am positive you weren't quite that bad."

"I was. My only redeeming qualities were my size and my lack of fear. My officers taught me discipline and deportment while my captain and men like your husband taught me everything else."

Thinking of how awkward and frustrating those lessons had been for all involved, he shook his head. He thought he would never conquer proper table manners.

"It is actually because of them that I'm even fit company for a woman like you," he added.

She tilted her head to one side. "Robert, why was that? Did your parents not teach you those things?"

"I had no parents to speak of."

Her eyes widened. "Who raised you?"

"Experience, I guess." He didn't want to sound too ram-shackle, but he didn't want to sugarcoat his past either. Miranda had been too brave, too vulnerable about her faults and hurts for him to attempt to hide his past. "My mother died in childbirth and my father . . . well, he took off as soon as he could. Though some of his neighbors helped me out from time to time, for the most part I grew up on the streets in Ft. Worth."

She looked shocked. "I . . . I'm sorry."

He was too. For most of his life, he'd always felt rather bitter about the things he didn't have and the care that had never been given. He'd wondered how the Lord could have overlooked the basic needs of a young child. Surely he couldn't have been that much of a brat?

But now he realized all of that had brought him to this place and this moment. He was walking sedately next to a true lady. She was holding his arm and he was not only protecting her but making her happy.

"Don't be sorry, Miranda," he said lightly. "I am not."

When she blinked, then cautiously smiled, he smiled too.

And realized he'd told her the truth.

Captain Monroe would have been pleased.

6

TWO DAYS AFTER THEIR WALK ON THE STRAND, MIRANDA
was still reliving the outing. She found herself dwelling on the
feel of Robert's arm under her hand. Of how safe she felt by his
side—as if no one would dare to slight her out of fear of incurring
Mr. Truax's displeasure. For a few hours, she'd allowed herself to
forget all about her problems. She'd forgotten her pain, pushed
aside her worries, even managed to stop thinking about what
would happen when Robert left and she was alone again.

Instead, she had let herself remember the feel of the ocean
breeze on her skin, the scent of the wharf, the antics of the peli-
cans and seagulls. She'd smiled more than she had in months.

For a little while, she'd simply been a woman on the arm of a
handsome and attentive gentleman.

Last night she'd fallen asleep remembering their conversation
about their childhoods. Somehow, remembering how idyllic hers
had been while Robert's had been so painful had helped her heal
even further. It seemed she'd needed to remember that no one ever
had an easy life. Instead, there were gaps and curves and dips and
valleys. Men and women of strong grit survived instead of giving up.

She certainly liked the idea of being a survivor.

Indeed, that small outing had changed her in ways she hadn't
expected. As had the man himself.

Today the house had felt abnormally silent without Mr. Truax. Cook had informed Miranda that he'd left shortly after breakfast, saying he would likely not return until close to nightfall.

But even though she'd known not to expect him, throughout the day Miranda still found herself looking for a sign of her new boarder. In spite of her best efforts to remind herself that one lovely walk didn't mean they would go out on another outing anytime in the near future.

But as she walked down the empty hallways, it was apparent that Mr. Truax was not only still not about but he hadn't been for some time. He was an unusually messy boarder. He left his papers and his handkerchiefs and his books all over the place. She and Belle and Winifred had even started placing everything they found in a little basket in the dining room. That way he could deposit his articles back in his room easily.

And since he was paying extra to have his room cleaned, Miranda had also learned he was just as messy in his room. Clothes were left on the floor, his bed was a constant rumpled tangle of sheets and blankets, and blotting papers were strewn about his desk and on the floor underneath.

More than once Miranda had wondered how an officer in the military could have such untidy habits. Now, though, his basket was empty and the table and chair where he ate his meals were absent of his usual disarray.

Picking up the empty basket, Miranda realized she missed the clutter. Missed all signs that made Robert unique. How could one man make such an impression on her, and so quickly too? She'd hosted many guests in the mansion over the last year. For one man to mean so much, well, it hardly seemed fair.

"Oh! Hello, Mrs. Markham," Winifred exclaimed as she entered the dining room. Right away her gaze zeroed in on the basket in her hands. "Is everything all right?"

"Yes, of course. I, um . . . well, I was just thinking I should put this someplace out of the way."

"No real reason you should, if you don't mind me saying so. We both know we're gonna be filling it up with Mr. Truax's items soon enough."

Hastily, she set the basket down again. "Yes. I imagine so."

But as if her housekeeper was used to her making no sense, or maybe because she didn't know Miranda had ever acted differently, she smiled brightly. "It's right quiet without him here, don'tcha think?" Winifred asked as she pulled out a rag from one of her pockets and started wiping down the shelves on the top of the server.

She was too embarrassed to lie. "Yes. He not only is rather messy, he's loud."

"I don't mind a man making a noise every now and then myself. Makes me think of my pa. When he got to talking, well, no one else could ever get a word in edgewise."

"My father was quieter, but I know what you mean. Thank goodness for Emerson or we'd be a quartet of women."

"This is true." With a wink, she said, "I won't tell him that, though. It'll cause him to get a big head, it will."

"We can't have that."

Winifred giggled. "Anyways, Cook told you Mr. Truax left just after breakfast, saying he had several people to meet and might not be back until nightfall, didn't she?"

"Yes, she did. I wonder whom he needed to meet," Miranda mused before she stopped herself. All sorts of activities and projects came to mind, all of them nefarious.

"I expect he'll tell us when he returns," Winifred said, her voice suspiciously bright. "He's a friendly sort, he is."

"He is, indeed." Needing to get her mind off the man before she was reduced to watching for him out the window like a love-sick girl, Miranda picked up the stack of letters Winifred had left neatly folded for her on a small table by the door. "I'll be in the parlor sorting the mail, then."

Winifred paused in the doorway before taking her leave. "How does some tea sound to ya? Belle can bring you a cuppa."

"Yes, thank you." A cup of piping-hot tea was exactly what she needed to get through the rest of the day. It would settle her nerves and hopefully rejuvenate her enough to sort the day's mail in lightning speed.

Moments later, Belle arrived in the parlor with a cup and teapot, along with a freshly baked scone. "Hot tea and a currant scone, ma'am."

Miranda smiled at her. Today Belle was wearing a light gray dress. It should have made her look washed out and tired but, as everything did on her pretty maid, it only seemed to emphasize her beauty. "Thank you, Belle."

"Oh, you're welcome." Smiling at the plate she'd just set on the corner of Miranda's desk, she added, "You're in for a treat, Mrs. Markham. The scones are especially good today."

"I think we say that every time Cook bakes."

"I guess we do." She shrugged. "But it's better than thinking they could always be better."

Miranda chuckled. "Indeed. Thank you for bringing me this treat." Belle set about straightening the room, and after taking a fortifying bite of the scone and a bracing sip of tea, Miranda pulled out her letter opener and began slicing open the envelopes.

The first five were reservations, two others were bills. One was a letter of appreciation for a restful visit.

And the last was another threat.

Hating the sight of it, her hands shook as she pulled out the letter. The handwriting was familiar. The letters were ill formed and slightly block-like. Though she wanted to do nothing more than crumble the offending paper away, she forced herself to read it.

I know what he did. I know he betrayed the South. I know how you have been dishonoring his memory. And I can prove it all. Soon, everyone will have the proof if you don't leave Galveston and never come back. I've been warning you for a year, and my patience is gone. Your time has run out.

Her hands were trembling so much that the paper fell through her fingers. Panicked, she grasped for it but knocked the tea over instead. Hot liquid splattered over the desk and on the rest of the correspondence.

Miranda jumped to her feet to escape being burned. That action caused the rest of the letters to drift to the floor.

Tears pricked her eyes as every worry she'd pushed aside came back, tenfold. The return of her fear was almost as frightening as the letter itself. She had thought the letters couldn't be any more threatening, but it seemed she was wrong. She'd thought she was done being afraid of everyone in Galveston, but that fear was still there. Alive and well. Stronger than ever.

But what if the rumors were true? Even if they weren't—and she was desperately clinging to that belief—what if this monster had falsified documents that made it look like Phillip was a traitor? It had to be someone who hated her enough to torture her and blackmail her into leaving her home. Did she dare to contemplate who that might be?

Belle rushed to her side. "Oh, Mrs. Markham! Are you all right? Did you get burned?"

Miranda worked her mouth but, try as she might, no sound came out.

"Here, come sit down, ma'am. I'll get this cleaned up in no time."

Miranda said nothing as Belle wrapped an arm around her shoulders and guided her to the chaise lounge in the corner. "Here, ma'am. You just rest for a moment."

"I . . . I am fine, Belle. Yes, as you said, it's merely tea. I don't know how I managed to spill it. I'm not usually so clumsy."

"We know you ain't clumsy at all, Mrs. Markham. It was just an accident. That's all. Everyone has them."

Relieved that Belle wasn't making a fuss over her anymore, Miranda attempted to smile. "Yes, they do. I guess it's my day."

"Wish my day didn't come up quite so often," Belle said as she wiped up the tea with the tea towel. "I'm forever knocking into things."

As Belle continued to prattle on, Miranda closed her eyes and tried to breathe deeply.

"Now that it's all spick and span again, may I bring you some more tea, Mrs.—" She abruptly cut off her words with a gasp. "Oh no. You got another one of them."

Miranda popped open her eyes. When she realized Belle was staring at the letter on the floor like it was about to gain legs and jump out at her, a terrible realization settled inside of her. "What did you say?"

Belle stood up slowly. "Beg your pardon, ma'am," she whispered, her cheeks turning bright red. "I didn't mean to look at your letter."

"My letter?" She cleared her throat.

Wringing her hands, Belle whispered, "I am sorry I said a word. I promise, it won't happen again."

It was a sweet apology. However, it most certainly wasn't a retraction. "You, um . . . you have been aware that I've been receiving letters like this? Threatening letters?"

Belle swallowed. "Yes, ma'am."

Shock, mixed in with a bit of paranoia, set in. For a split second, Miranda considered the possibility that someone on her staff might very well be behind them. It would be so easy for them to make sure she received them on a regular basis.

But then, as she remembered how hard they all worked, how much they put up with her, with their mistress's mood swings and self-doubts and, yes, self-loathing, Miranda knew no one who acted like they did could be so duplicitous.

"Belle, when did you first discover them?"

Her maid's eyes darted around the room. Settling on anything but herself. "Well, ma'am, I don't rightly know. I couldn't say for sure."

"Please, do try to remember. It is important to me."

"Yes, ma'am." Looking truly miserable, Belle swallowed hard.

Miranda knew she needed to get control of her patience. "I promise, I won't get mad," she said as gently as she could. "I simply want to know. And it must be said that I feel I deserve an answer."

"Yes, Mrs. Markham. Yes, you do." But instead of blurting out the information Miranda had asked for, her maid was chewing on her bottom lip.

With a sigh, Miranda got to her feet. "Belle, I am doing my best not to lose my temper, but I have a feeling that I'm about to lose that battle. Answer my question, if you please."

At last, Belle visibly steeled her spine and took a fortifying breath. "To be real honest, I don't recall that single moment when I discovered you were getting those awful letters. It was more like I simply became aware that you were receiving them."

"Simply aware? That makes no sense."

"Well, um, it kind of does. Because, you see, we all know about them."

Miranda didn't know if she was more shocked, embarrassed, or bemused. She never would have thought that something she had tried so hard to keep hidden would be common knowledge . . . and that her servants were attempting to keep their own secrets too.

However, she could almost hear her well-bred mother's voice in her ear, reminding her that servants know everything that happens in a house and a good mistress made sure that nothing untoward happened. "We? All?"

Belle shifted uncomfortably, looked down at the soiled towel in her hand, and deposited it on the tea-filled plate. "Well, me, Winnie, Cook, and Emerson know about the letters."

"All of you do." She raised her brows. "And not a single one of you decided to speak to me about it?"

"As a matter of fact, a couple of times one of us made that very suggestion, but then the others knocked that idea down. You see, we all kinda figured it would be best if you thought these letters were your secret."

"Because?"

"Because we all saw how upset they made you," Belle said. Looking decidedly more uncomfortable, she added, "We thought if you believed no one knew, then you might not worry about them so much."

All this time she'd been living in fear of Belle or Winifred discovering the letters, fearing that once they saw she was being targeted by a stranger they would finally decide to quit. Every time a letter arrived she would break out into a cold sweat, force herself to read it again and again, and then become so desolate and afraid she'd hide in her room until she could act in a calm and genteel manner.

But it seemed all that hiding had been for nothing. She never expected they would look through the things she threw away.

"I see." Once again Miranda felt as if she'd stepped into a play about another person's life. Here she'd spent months doing her best to pretend she was okay. That life was normal. That she had no cares beyond the Iron Rail and missing her husband.

But it had all been a lie, and once more it had been a useless one. She could have saved all that energy.

She wasn't exactly sure how she felt about her big secret being not so secret after all.

She didn't feel embarrassed. Instead, she felt a curious sense of relief. As if she could maybe—just maybe—not be quite so alone anymore. That would be so nice.

"I am glad this is out in the open now," she said at last. "Thank you for telling me the truth."

Belle looked extremely distressed. "I really am sorry, ma'am. Both about the letters and about knowing your secrets and never saying a word. I never thought you'd be so understanding."

How did one respond to that? "Perhaps we should simply drop this subject."

"Yes'm." Belle nodded. Then blurted, "You see, I don't think any of us wanted to make you more upset than you already were."

"Pardon me?" Just how pathetic had she been?

Belle winced. "I know you don't like to speak about your personal life. I mean, I know we aren't supposed to talk about you. On account that you employ us and all—"

"You are right. Most employers value their privacy."

"But, ma'am, well, I just want to say that I've felt real sorry for you," Belle continued in a rush. "I mean, those letters are cruel, that's what they are."

"They have been difficult to read." Raising a brow. "I am

guessing you felt the same way?" She didn't mean to be sarcastic and unkind, but this conversation was becoming increasingly uncomfortable.

Belle's eyes widened. "Oh, I haven't read them!"

"No? I thought you could read."

"Oh, I can!"

"Then?"

"It's just that . . . I mean, I've only read one," she sputtered. "Emerson, Cook, and Winnie told me what the others said."

"So all of you have taken to reading my disposed correspondence without my knowledge and then discussing it in secret?"

Miranda truly had no idea how to handle this. She fervently wished her mother were sitting next to her. Then she could have educated Miranda about the best way to handle this sticky situation.

Whatever she would advise had to be better than what Miranda was contemplating, which was to call all four of them to the parlor, chastise them soundly, and then promptly fire them all. Servants who disrespected their employers' privacy were worse than useless.

But of course, they had been some of her only defenders in the city. If she let them go, who would even consent to work for her?

She sagged as tension filled her neck and shoulders. What she wouldn't give to go back in time to just an hour ago, when she was still reveling in yesterday's walk in the Strand!

"Mrs. Markham, please don't be upset. It's just that, well, Winnie found one on the floor about a year ago. She'd been in the hallway when you'd opened it. You'd cried out and ran upstairs to your room. It was obvious you were upset."

"Yes." Unfortunately, she remembered that day well. It had been the second time she'd received a letter. She'd been forced to accept that whoever was behind the threats wasn't going to go away. And she never realized she hadn't thrown the letter away.

One of Belle's hands was twisting the edge of her white apron now. "Mrs. Markham, I'm sure Winnie only meant to pick up your letter. I'm sure she didn't actually mean to read it, but . . ."

"But she did." With a sigh, Miranda sat down at her desk chair. "I suppose I don't blame her for that. It was human nature."

"Yes." Belle nodded. "It was that. Exactly."

"I suppose she couldn't resist telling the rest of you about it, either." Miranda supposed she would have been tempted to do the same.

Belle winced. "It wasn't like that. We don't gossip about you. And I promise, no one has said anything to anyone outside the house." She bit her lip then.

"But?" Miranda asked, wanting to get the rest of this awful story out in the open.

"But, well, it's just that we're all real worried about you. Like I said, those letters are cruel, especially with you being a widow and all. And with Lt. Markham's mother and sister nagging you something awful."

Ruth and Viola did nag her something awful. The description was so fitting, she almost smiled. Why, if she didn't know how much they had cared for Phillip, she would suspect them of spreading rumors about him and sending threatening letters to get her out of this house rather than depending on their lawyer to find a way.

Yes, Phillip had known his mother and sister loved him, but he was reluctant to spend much time with them because of their dispositions. He was just as happy when they decided to move to Houston rather than live in the mansion with them.

Wearily, she ran a hand along the muscles supporting the

back of her neck. They were bunched and knotted. In need of a small massage.

It was moments like this when she missed having a husband. Someone to share her burdens and take charge. Someone to help her figure out how to speak to servants about letters she wished she hadn't received. Someone to help her talk about things no one was supposed to know about in the first place.

Yet, on the other hand, she no doubt wouldn't have received such letters if Phillip had still been alive.

Because she was alone, she was at a stranger's mercy. He could freely play with her emotions, threaten to harm her reputation, practically do whatever he wanted because he knew he could.

She wasn't from Galveston. She had no family or long-standing support system here to help her through trying times. And Phillip's mother and sister still resented her keeping the house and not giving it back to the Markham family.

All she had was a large house that she'd inherited on a prime piece of real estate. She had that, which many valued highly, and the name of her husband.

Which, until recently, had kept her feeling secure. Now that so many people had besmirched his name, Phillip's reputation didn't keep her safe anymore.

"I don't know what to do," she finally admitted. "I've tried to be strong, but someone desperately wants me gone. But if I leave, I have nowhere to go and no way of surviving or making a living." She couldn't emphasize enough how much that idea scared her. "I did tell Sheriff Kern about the first letter, but he brushed off my worries as a feminine drama."

For the first time since their conversation began, Belle looked certain. "That was wrong of him."

"I thought so too. But he made me so worried, I was afraid to go back to him."

"Beg your pardon, ma'am, but I don't reckon admitting you are afraid or need help is a sign of weakness. I think it simply means you're like the rest of us."

"Thank you for that, Belle. I have to tell you that though this conversation is difficult, I'm thankful to be able to discuss the letters with someone."

She sighed in relief. "I'm thankful things are out in the open now, too, ma'am."

"So, um, if I was your sister, what would you advise me to do?"

"You need to get help," she replied instantly. "And though all of us here would be happy to help you do whatever needs to be done, I think you need to go back to ask Sheriff Kern for assistance."

"But what if he doesn't listen to me?"

"Then go talk to him again."

"Yes, I suppose you're right." She bit her lip. "Now I wish I would have saved the letters. Then I could prove to him how vicious they have become."

"You don't need to worry about that. Winnie saved them."

"Of course she did."

"I think you really should talk to Sheriff Kern, ma'am. The sooner the better."

Before she lost her nerve, Miranda nodded. "I think you're right. Belle, please go to the sheriff's office right now. When you get there, ask Sheriff Kern to pay me a visit at his convenience."

"Are you going to write this down? I could hand him a note."

Miranda shook her head. "No. I'd rather not have anything more in writing. Simply tell him it's about the letters and that you and I've talked." Aware that Belle wasn't exactly comfortable with the errand, Miranda added, "While I realize visiting the sheriff's office is not the easiest errand to run, I can assure you that Sheriff Kern is polite and gentlemanly. I'm sure this visit won't take up much of your time."

"It ain't that, ma'am."

"Are you concerned about what to say? Simply tell him I've received more letters and I would like to speak to him without the whole city knowing I am in his office. He'll understand that."

"Yes, ma'am."

"Thank you, Belle. I appreciate it."

Looking a bit more confident, Belle smiled. "I'll go speak with Sheriff Kern straightaway."

"Thank you. When you return, I'll probably still be here in the parlor. If not, please look for me. I'll want to know what he says as soon as possible."

"I'll do that." Just before she turned to leave, Belle smiled. "This is nice, isn't it?"

In her opinion, the conversation they'd just shared had been one of the most difficult in recent memory. "I'm afraid I don't understand. What is it that is nice?"

After visibly weighing her words, Belle said, "I think it's going to be a real good thing when we all know you are no longer at this coward's mercy. And that it's going to be nice to know all of us can now speak freely about your letters. It's nice when secrets are unveiled, I think."

Though she had no idea what was in store for her future, Miranda had to agree. No matter what happened, anything was better than being at a stranger's mercy.

Anything had to be better than that.

7

THE MOMENT AFTER SHE CLOSED THE DOOR IN THE STUDY to allow Mrs. Markham some privacy, Belle scampered down the hall, hurried down the stairs, ran out to the walkway, threw open the door, and at last burst into the kitchen.

When she saw Winnie, Cook, and Emerson all look up in alarm, she grinned. "Oh, good. You all are here."

Instead of smiling in return, Cook frowned. "We're here, but you aren't acting like you belong here, attending to your duties. What has gotten ahold of you?"

"Mrs. Markham."

Cook dropped the heavy knife she'd been holding. It clattered onto her work surface with a noisy clang.

Emerson glared. "Belle, some complete sentences would be real welcome right about now."

"Yes. Of course." Forcing herself to calm down and try to make a lick of sense, Belle took a fortifying breath. "When I served tea to Mrs. Markham, she was opening her mail."

Cook shrugged. "And?"

"And inside one of the envelopes was yet another one of those letters!"

"Oh my word."

"She gasped when she saw it and spilled her tea."

Cook wasn't even pretending to cut vegetables now. "Did she burn herself?"

"No, but to be honest with ya, she was so upset I think even if she was burned she wouldn't have noticed."

Emerson stood up from the chair he was sitting in and began to pace. "I'd like to wring up that coward by his neck, I would."

"I would help you too," Cook said.

Winnie stared at Belle impatiently. "Well, don't keep us in suspense. What did you do?"

Kind of enjoying the fact that she had their undivided attention, Belle drew out her answer. "Well, I would have ignored the letter, her manner, her tears, everything. You know, like we always do."

"But?" Winnie asked sharply.

Belle knew that tone. It meant Winnie wanted some answers and she wanted them fast. Feeling a bit uneasy again, Belle sputtered, "But . . . well, I made a mistake. Before I knew what I was saying, I told Mrs. Markham I was sorry she received another one."

Cook's eyes widened. "Please say you did not do that."

"I'm sorry, but I really did. I couldn't help myself." When three disbelieving pairs of eyes stared back at her, Belle backtracked. "Well, I mean, I know I should have been able to, but I couldn't hold my tongue. Before I knew it, I was telling her I was sorry. Then, next thing I knew, Mrs. Markham was asking me all about what I knew about the letters she'd been receiving."

"And then?" Winnie asked.

"And then I went and told her I've known about them for some time. And, that, well, you all knew about them too."

Emerson moaned, Winnie was visibly gritting her teeth, and Cook . . . well, Cook pressed a hand to her chest and glared. "You just had to go and bring the rest of us into it, did ya?"

"I didn't mean to," Belle replied, knowing deep in her belly that her explanation could use some work. "But Mrs. Markham wanted some answers. I couldn't ignore her questions. And I'm not good at lying. I am sorry."

"I suppose we should all be glad you aren't a liar," Winnie stated. Looking at the other occupants in the room, she shrugged. "No use crying over spilled milk. What's done is done."

Emerson whistled softly. "It's done all right. We're all going to get fired. We might as well sit down with a cup of tea and prepare ourselves."

Cook left her cutting board and stood next to Emerson. "My daughter lives in New Orleans. We could go there, I suppose."

Winnie frowned. "I got nowhere else to go."

Belle cleared her throat. "I don't think we're about to get fired."

Emerson folded his hands across his chest. "Because?"

"Because Mrs. Markham just asked me to go to Sheriff Kern's office. She wants me to ask him to come here, to pay her a call." Daring to smile, she added, "I think she's finally going to tell him everything."

"Do you think so, truly, girl?" Emerson asked.

Belle nodded. "Mrs. Markham even said she was glad her secret was out in the open. She said she'd been afraid we would all leave if we found out about these letters."

Winnie shook her head. "Our lady is a lamb. Doesn't she realize she's not the one who has done something wrong? It ain't her fault some mean coward is sending her ugly letters."

"She seemed a lot better when I left her just now," Belle said.

Cook clasped her hands together. "Praise God! Maybe things are finally going to get better for Mrs. Markham. I was beginning to think he wasn't listening to my prayers."

Winnie made a shooing motion with her hands. "Well, off with you now before she up and changes her mind."

Belle decided right then and there that she didn't need to be told twice. She'd already disobeyed Mrs. Markham by tarrying in the kitchen. After running to her room to put on a real dress and not her faded work one, she refashioned her hair. Finally, she put on her best bonnet. It was felt and navy and had dark purple ribbons around the brim.

After slipping on her cloak and pulling on gloves, she decided she now looked suitable enough to visit the sheriff's office. She told herself she had gone to so much trouble because she wanted to do her employer proud. Not because she was about to have a conversation with the most attractive sheriff in the great state of Texas.

Fifteen minutes later, Belle was sitting on a hard wooden chair inside the sheriff's small waiting room and doing her best to avoid the dark stares of not only Sheriff Kern's deputy, but also two men who appeared especially weather beaten and rough.

All three of the men had raised their brows when she'd asked to speak with the sheriff and looked at one another in disbelief when she'd refused to explain why she needed to see him.

When she resolutely refused to answer any questions, Deputy Banks told her to sit down and then went about his business.

The other two men, however, merely turned so they faced her and looked at her with increasingly lewd expressions. She felt exposed and at a disadvantage. And, frankly, wished she was sitting anywhere else but where she was.

Her only consolation was that she was the one sitting in the waiting area and not her employer. Imagining gentle, shy Mrs. Markham being subjected to such disrespect was difficult to contemplate. Belle might be small but she knew she was far tougher. She'd also had plenty of experience with men who had next to no manners and little respect for a woman like her.

But as the minutes passed, some of her confidence faded. The men's too-forward stares were making her uncomfortable. She could practically feel their bold, assessing eyes drift over her body. Their disrespect made her feel like she used to when she stood by her mother's side back in Louisiana.

After her mother died, Belle had promised herself she'd do everything in her power never to be at such a disadvantage again. If she hadn't promised Mrs. Markham that she'd contact the sheriff, Belle would have stood up and walked away.

But Belle had promised, and she was willing to do whatever it took for her employer to feel safe. Therefore, she had no recourse but to sit with her hands pressed in a tight knot on her lap and pray for Sheriff Kern to arrive sooner than later.

But as the clock's minute hand continued to move at a glacial speed, the tension in the room rose. Belle could have sworn the very air she was breathing had become thicker.

Though she was trying hard not to look at them, she could still feel the men's appraising leers.

After another five minutes passed, one of the men kicked a boot out. The sudden motion forced Belle to turn her head their way.

"Where do you work?" one asked, his voice sharp and staccato, betraying that he was a Yankee.

The wariness she'd begun to feel was replaced by fear. "That is none of your business," she replied when it became apparent she had no choice but to answer him.

He lumbered to his feet. "Ain't no shame if yer a sporting girl," he said. Almost kindly. "All I is aimin' to know is what house you're a part of." He leaned closer, bringing with him the faint scent of fish and onions and stale clothing. "That way I'll know whether to bring a quarter or a dollar."

She was both appalled and saddened by his comment. Pity for the soiled doves who frequented the port and warehouse district overwhelmed her. It made her ill to think that a man like him could have his way with a woman for less than the cost of a meal.

Against her will, memories of the men who frequented her mother's room hit her hard, causing her mouth to go dry. "I am not a . . . a prostitute."

"But you could be, if you had a mind to it," he said, as if he warmed up to the idea. "Shoot, a pretty thing like you? Chances are good you could earn a decent living on yer back. Heck, you could even buy a better hat."

She folded her hands tightly in her lap and remained silent. Where was Sheriff Kern? And why couldn't Mrs. Markham have simply written a note that needed to be dropped off?

He grunted. "What's wrong with you?" He scowled. "Can't you talk?"

She didn't want to talk to him. Feeling more anxious, Belle glanced at Deputy Banks. Waited for him to intervene. Unfortunately, he was leaning back in his chair eyeing the interplay with a bored look.

The swarthy man's voice turned rougher. "Or do you consider yerself better than the likes of me?"

Worried that he was going to approach her if she didn't respond, she spoke at last. "I am waiting for the sheriff. That is all."

He coughed. "Where I come from, women know their place. They don't ignore a man when he's speaking to them. They know actions like that have consequences."

His threat did not fall on deaf ears. She believed he would

happily retaliate for her rudeness if he felt he could. The fact that not for Winnie and Mrs. Markham taking her in Belle could be at the mercy of a man like him made her tongue sharper than was wise.

A sudden memory returned of her mother pretending that the men who called on her actually cared, and Belle's anxiety transformed to fear.

But she wasn't weak. Not yet. Forcing herself to look far braver than she felt, she raised her chin. "Where I come from, women do not speak to strangers."

The man's friend chuckled. "She's a fiery one, she is, Jeb." Standing up, he stepped in her direction. "Don't be acting like you're a real *lady*, now, 'cause we all know you ain't that." His assessing look turned into something else. "Now, why don't you answer me? Who are you?"

She looked at Deputy Banks yet again. Surely he was going to help her now? If not for her, for her mistress?

After the span of a heartbeat, he colored. "Sit down, Henry. Belle here is right. You ain't got no call to be speaking to women like that."

"Or what?" the Yankee asked, just as the outer door swung open at last. "What are you gonna do, Banks? Tell me I gotta start bowing and scraping to all the girls that walk through yer door?"

She and the three men inhaled sharply as Sheriff Kern entered the room with none other than Mr. Truax on his heels. It was obvious to all that they'd heard the Yankee's words—and Deputy Banks's allowing of it.

Deputy Banks jumped to his feet.

Both of the other men took their seats, looking cowed and bedraggled all of a sudden.

Belle breathed a sigh of relief. Maybe she was going to be all right after all.

"Miss Harden, good afternoon," Sheriff Kern said politely. "May I help you?"

"Good afternoon, Sheriff. I, um, was hoping I might speak with you for a few minutes. If you wouldn't mind."

"Of course I don't." Glaring at the two Yankees and his deputy, too, he gestured toward his office. "Why don't you go into my office? I'll be there directly. I must attend to a piece of business first."

"Hold on," Mr. Truax said. "Belle, is everything okay at the Iron Rail?"

She shook her head. "I don't believe so, sir."

Sheriff Kern raised his brows. "Is this an emergency?" He turned to Banks. "Why didn't you assist her?"

"She said she would speak only to you."

"You knew I was having lunch. You should have gone to get me."

"I couldn't leave her alone in here. Sir." Reddening slightly, he said, "Besides, you know what everyone says about Mrs. Markham. It ain't like Belle here is working for a real lady."

One of the Yankees grinned. "So that's why the girl didn't tell us who employed her. There's only one person around Galveston Island who is even less welcomed than a couple of Yankee dockworkers! No wonder you didn't want us to know about you."

Sheriff Kern looked from Belle to Mr. Truax to his deputy. Then he scowled. "Robert, why don't you join Miss Harden and me?"

"I think that would be a good idea." Without sparing the deputy or the two men another glance, Mr. Truax strode toward Sheriff Kern's office door, gallantly opened it, and waved on through. "Let's go inside, Miss Harden."

"Yes, sir." She stepped inside Sheriff Kern's office, glad to be out of that awful front room and away from the terrible men.

But now that the time had come to speak to the sheriff, she realized he was simply not going to let her share Mrs. Markham's message and leave. No, he was going to want her to share everything she knew. And when she did that, Belle was going to have a whole new set of worries on her shoulders.

She was going to need to find the right way to tell the sheriff and Mr. Truax everything she knew . . . all without betraying Mrs. Markham's privacy.

Was that even possible? And how did Sheriff Kern and Mr. Truax know each other anyway? They seemed too comfortable with each other to have just met.

As she gingerly sat down on the padded leather chair Mr. Truax held out for her, Belle exhaled.

Then, as they waited for Sheriff Kern to join them, she at last did what she should have done in the first place. She prayed that she'd find the right words to do the most good.

8

AT THIS POINT IN HIS LIFE, ROBERT TRUAX KNEW SOME things to be true. One, C.S.A. bills were worth less than the paper they were printed on. Another was that regrets were a waste of time, as was foolishly hoping that something good would last forever. Nothing was always good and nothing ever stayed the same.

Robert knew better men than he had died far too young. He also knew men who were not as honest as he was would live far longer than he would.

And finally, he knew Belle Harden was currently scared out of her mind.

Once they were alone in the sheriff's office with the door shut firmly against prying ears, he said, "Tell me, are you frightened because of the news you are about to share or because of something those men did?" Already thinking the worst, he added, "Do you need me to deal with them?"

She shook her head. "No, Mr. Truax. I am fine."

Each word sounded so brittle that he was surprised she didn't break down right there in front of them. "We both know that is not the case."

"I am tougher than I look, sir."

"You are all blond hair and blue eyes. You look like an angel. You do not look tough at all."

"That may be true. But still, I wasn't scared." When he merely stared at her, silently willing her to stop lying, she bowed her head. "Well, I will admit to feeling a bit frightened before you and Sheriff Kern came in."

Few things made him more upset than men ganging up on helpless women and children. He'd seen men prey on the weak all his life and had been their unwilling victim more times than he cared to remember. When he was seven, he'd promised himself that one day, when he was old enough to protect those weaker than him, he would.

For the most part, he'd done just that.

Now, knowing that this young woman had been afraid while waiting for the sheriff in the waiting area outside his office—one of the few places in Galveston where a woman should feel safe—well, it irritated him to no end.

"What did they do?" he asked as calmly as he was able. She didn't need him to make things worse or more frightening than they already were.

Belle folded her arms protectively across her chest. "Nothing you need to worry about, sir."

"Miss Harden, although we don't know each other much, I hope you will trust my reputation as a former Confederate officer to know that I only mean to help you."

"I trust that, sir. However, I promise that my problems should not be your concern."

When the door opened and Sheriff Kern strode in, looking vaguely put-upon, Robert unleashed his frustrations on him. "What kind of deputy did you hire, Jess?"

Giving him a sardonic look, Kern paused. "A rather weak one, it seems," he said lightly. "He can't seem to understand that he's in the office to help people, not make friends."

Crossing the room, he reached for Belle's hand. "Belle, Chet said those men did nothing more than ask you rude questions. Is that the truth?"

"Isn't that enough?" Robert interjected. "A woman should be able to come into this office without being afraid she is in danger of being accosted."

"I completely agree." Kern's expression turned hard. "He made a mistake and I told him so. That said, he's also in a difficult position. His older brother works with the shipping companies and brings in a lot of business to the island. Because of that, it's in Chet's family's best interests to get along with our city's visitors."

"If that is the case, then he shouldn't be deputized," Robert said bluntly.

Wearily, Sheriff Kern nodded. "You aren't saying anything I haven't thought more than once myself."

"Please, may we not talk about this any longer?" Miss Harden asked. "There was no harm done, and it was nothing that I haven't encountered before."

"Which is a problem," Robert said.

"We both know I'm not a lady. I'm made of stern stuff." She drew a breath. "Plus, I would have been willing to put up with all sorts of things to help Mrs. Markham." Looking from one to the other, she continued. "Mrs. Markham is why I am here."

"What happened?" Robert asked, already mentally planning the quickest route back to the Iron Rail. "Is she hurt?"

"Not exactly."

Robert stood up. "What does that mean? Does she need medical attention?"

Belle shook her head. "No, sir. It's nothing like that."

Sheriff Kern walked to the front of his desk and perched on the edge of it. Staring at her intently, he said, "What, exactly, is it like?"

But instead of relaying the problem, she continued to hedge. "Mrs. Markham asked if I would come here and ask if you could pay her a call soon. At your convenience, she said to tell you."

Too agitated to sit down, Robert leaned against the wall and studied the maid closely. "What has happened? She seemed well enough yesterday."

Kern ignored him. Instead, he was staring at Belle intently. "Do I need to walk over there this minute?"

"It's not an emergency. At least, I don't think so. The fact is, Mrs. Markham has been receiving a lot of terrible letters. Threatening ones."

"I was aware that she received a letter. She showed it to me."

"Oh, no, sir. It wasn't just one."

"Really? How many has she received?"

"Lots."

Robert felt as if ice were flowing through his veins. "Define 'lots.'"

"At least one a week."

Robert pushed off from the wall. "Kern, you made it sound like the letter was a one-time occurrence. Have you been ignoring her?"

"I have not, Truax," he bit out. After taking a breath, he stared at Belle. "Did she receive a letter today?"

Belle nodded. "I think you should visit her soon. Very soon."

"Have you seen any of these letters?"

She nodded again. "They are bad. Real mean. Some are so threatening it's a wonder she doesn't faint."

"What do they say?" Robert asked.

"They say bad things about Mr. Markham, like the rumors that have been going around for so long. Most also promise that something bad is going to happen if she doesn't give up the Iron Rail."

Robert was so agitated, it felt as if his spine were about to snap. "When did today's letter arrive?"

"This morning. I brought her some tea, and then she was opening her mail." Looking increasingly distressed, Belle said, "I don't know what it said, exactly, but it was bad enough for her to spill her tea. Sheriff Kern, what are we going to do?"

"*We* are not going to do anything."

Looking alarmed, Belle gripped the armrest of her chair. "No, we must—"

"*I*, on the other hand, will. Now, please, Miss Harden, don't trouble yourself any further."

Sheriff Kern's expression softened as he stared at Belle, making Robert realize that while the sheriff might think he had a soft spot for Miranda Markham, he had true feelings for this petite woman sitting across from him. Kern was gazing at her the way Phillip had gazed at the tintype of his wife.

"I'll pay a call on Mrs. Markham today and see if she'll let me see the letters. Then we'll see if we can get to the bottom of this." After a pause, he murmured, "I promise, Belle. I will not let you down."

Robert knew this to be true. After he had finally decided over lunch to take Jess into his confidence about his mission, he knew him to be a man he could rely on.

"It doesn't matter if you let me down, sir. I can handle it. But I really hope you won't let Mrs. Markham down. If you do, I simply don't know if she'll survive." She stood up, and with a flick of her wrist shook out her skirts and petticoats. "Thank you for seeing me, sir."

Robert walked to her side. "Allow me to walk you back."

"That's not necessary."

"Yes, but it would be my honor."

She smiled softly at him. When she glanced the sheriff's way, her gentle smile turned into a cautious look. She abruptly turned and walked out the door.

Looking over his shoulder, Robert caught the reason for Belle's awkward expression.

Sheriff Jess Kern was glaring at him. "Watch yourself, Truax."

"Always," Robert replied as he walked to Belle's side.

As they walked through the front room, he was pleased to see that only a chagrined deputy remained.

When they stepped onto the street, he couldn't resist grinning. Then, because it felt so good, he gave in to temptation and laughed. Loudly and without compunction.

"What is that for?" Belle asked.

"Nothing important. I was only thinking that some things never cease to surprise and amaze me. And that I'm so glad about that."

Robert changed his mind about that less than an hour later when he spied Miranda standing at the landing window, her hand pressed against the cold condensation. She looked extremely beautiful. She also looked desperate and afraid.

"Anything special going on out there?" he asked lightly. He hoped he would make her smile. Encourage her to tease him back.

Instead, he'd managed to startle her. "Mr. Truax. Hello. I didn't know you had returned."

"I got here a bit ago. I came in the servants' entrance."

"Why on earth would you do that?"

He debated telling her the truth, then decided there was no help for it. She was likely to find out. "I ran into Belle while I was out. I volunteered to escort her back."

"I see." Her mouth worked, betraying her curiosity. "Did she, um, happen to tell you where she'd been?"

"She didn't need to. I saw her at the sheriff's office."

"Oh?" Her mouth worked again. "Yes. Well, I asked her to run an errand for me."

"I know. Kern said he would be by here before too long."

Her hand dropped from the pane. He wondered if that was because it got cold or that she suddenly realized she'd been standing with it pressed against the window. "I should go freshen up for his visit."

Her words caught him off guard. Did she have feelings for the sheriff?

Jealousy at the thought of her primping for Kern flowed through him. Knowing his thoughts were inappropriate and unwanted, he ruthlessly tamped them down.

He wasn't there to have a liaison or to develop any romantic attachments. No, he was there to help her and fulfill a promise he'd made not only to his captain but to her husband. He'd vowed that he would look after Miranda for Phillip.

That was what mattered. That was all that was important.

With that in mind, he stepped away. "I'll let you get to it, then."

Looking adorably awkward, she went into her room.

When she was out of sight, he crept up the stairs and placed his hand on the pane where she'd had hers.

Looked out.

And wondered what she saw. Had she been looking forward to the sheriff's visit . . . or had she been remembering how her life used to be?

"Well, you were gone a long time, Belle," Cook said. "I trust you were able to speak with Sheriff Kern?"

"I'm sorry it took me so long. When I arrived, Sheriff Kern wasn't in the office. I was forced to wait."

"And when he did arrive? What did he say?"

"He happened to be with Mr. Truax. Both of them talked to me. After Sheriff Kern promised he'd stop by, Mr. Truax walked me back."

Winnie stopped scrubbing a silver tray and looked over at Emerson and Cook. "There's something going on with that Mr. Truax, mark my words."

"Like what?"

"He's not here just to visit and conduct business in Galveston. He's here for a reason, and I think it has something to do with Mrs. Markham."

"Do you think he's someone from her past? Do you think they knew each other?"

"No. But either he knows something he's not sharing or he knows something about her past. I aim to discover what that is."

Emerson grunted. "That's all we be needing, another batch of questions and a mystery to solve."

Belle was about to offer her guess when they heard the light footsteps of their employer.

All four of them turned to her when she entered the kitchen.

"Good afternoon, Mrs. Markham," Winnie said as she dropped a quick, impulsive curtsy. "Is there something ya need? What may I help you with?"

Their employer looked from one to the other to the other in confusion. "I . . . well, I was wondering where all of you were. The house seemed especially quiet."

"It's my fault, ma'am," Belle said. "I, um, was telling them about my visit into town."

"Oh?" She paled. "What were you telling them?"

This was why it was a bad idea to lie. Instinctively, she knew it was also a bad idea to mention the sheriff or Mr. Truax. Mrs. Markham would misunderstand why she was sharing. No doubt she would think Belle was gossiping about her instead of being concerned.

Therefore, she let the lies continue. "Um, two new ships arrived at the port today," she blurted.

Mrs. Markham blinked. And who could blame her? Now that the war was over, since when did any of them care what ship pulled into port? "Oh?"

"Yes." When all of them were looking at her expectantly, she babbled on. "One . . . um, one looks to be from England. Or France!"

Mrs. Markham tilted her head to one side. "You don't know?"

"No. You see, I couldn't see the flag."

"Then how did you know it was from another country?"

This was terrible. But in for a penny, in for a pound. "The . . . um . . ."

"She was just telling us about the sailors' uniforms, ma'am," Emerson said quickly. Just as if he noticed sailors' uniforms all the time. "They were white."

"I see. Well, as interesting as sailors' uniforms are, I need your assistance, if you please."

Emerson strode forward. "How may we help, ma'am?"

"We have a new guest waiting in my husband's study to be escorted to his room. The sheriff has just arrived as well."

Immediately, the four of them set into motion.

"I'll go out to see to the guest," Winnie said importantly. "Belle, you accompany Mrs. Markham and see what refreshments the sheriff would like."

"Yes, ma'am," Belle said, leading the way out of the kitchen, outside to the short gap that separated the kitchen from the main house, then into the hall leading to the parlor.

Beside her, Mrs. Markham's movements were wooden.

Though it might have been a bit cheeky, Belle asked, "Are you ready to speak to the sheriff now, ma'am?"

"No, but I guess it's time. So I had better be ready." Looking Belle in the eye, she said, "Try as I might, I haven't been able to forget the past. I guess it's time to deal with the present."

Belle thought truer words had never been said.

9

Johnson's Island, Ohio
Confederate States of America Officers' POW Camp
February 1865

PHILLIP MARKHAM'S STATE OF HEALTH WAS WORSE.

The gangrene that had settled in his arm had spread to his shoulder. Angry red welts radiated from his wound, ran down to his fingertips and up along the lines of muscle and veins that marked his upper arm.

Fever had set in, along with delirium. The man's only source of relief was the cool compresses they placed on his skin and the water he drank. Robert would have given a mint for a healthy dose of laudanum or a bottle of whiskey. Anything to give Phillip a few moments of relief from his misery.

Yet, true to form, even though Phillip was undoubtedly in extreme pain, he never complained. His stoic determination to even die like a gentleman humbled them all. Especially Robert, who had never claimed to be anything close to a gentleman.

Even their idiot Yankee guards had seemed to pity Phillip. One stopped by daily to see how he was doing. Another guard had even given Thomas a jug of fresh water for Phillip to drink. He'd gone so far as to assure them they only needed to let one of them know when it needed to be filled again.

That, perhaps, was the true testimony to the man Phillip was. Even their enemy knew they had someone special in their midst.

Because they'd known Phillip's time was near, four of them had been taking turns sitting with him. It was degrading enough for one of the finest men they knew to have to die as a prisoner of war. No one wanted him to have to die alone in their barracks.

Robert had been sitting with him for three hours. He'd bathed Phillip as best he could but hadn't been able to coax him to drink any water. Instead, his friend had simply been lying listlessly on a pallet on the floor.

Robert had placed his hand on Phillip's pulse more than once just to make sure the man was still alive.

Now his shift was over. "I'm going to let someone else take a turn with you now, Lieutenant," he said. "You're in for a treat too. Next up is none other than our esteemed captain."

Though he was fairly sure Phillip wasn't even aware he was there, Robert continued. Maybe he was speaking more for himself than for Phillip. "If you can, be sure to give Captain Monroe some grief. He's been altogether too confident and merry of late."

Robert chuckled, his forced laughter sounding hollow even to his own ears. "You know how Cap gets—always thinking daisies are gonna start blooming and tomorrow is gonna be brighter."

When Phillip didn't so much as flinch, Robert knelt down and clasped his thin, lifeless hand. "Don't give up, Lieutenant. I'll be back tomorrow, and you better plan to open at least one of those eyes for me."

Still reluctant to leave his side, Robert pressed his other hand to Phillip's, curving his palm around Phillip's limp one, attempting to impart some of his strength to him.

But still, Phillip's hand only hung limp between his own.

Feeling more depressed than usual, Robert turned away and walked out of the dank and dark room. The moment he stood outside, he inhaled deeply. It was a relief to feel fresh air on his skin and to be away from the cloying scent of Phillip's disease.

Of course, he immediately felt guilty for even thinking such a thing.

After taking a number of fortifying breaths, Robert spied Captain Monroe. His back was facing Robert, his front leaning against a fence. His arms and elbows were resting on the top rung. For once their captain didn't look like he was plotting or worrying about anyone. Instead, he seemed captivated by the expanse of water that could now be seen, thanks to some recent chinks in their outer fence.

When they'd first arrived at their camp, Robert had been shocked at just how big Lake Erie was. Though he'd learned about the Great Lakes in a geography text, he'd never imagined anything quite so large.

Now he was used to their surroundings enough to feel something of an authority on them. At the moment, white caps dotted the waves.

Robert predicted they were in for another rough night. He'd been there long enough to take notice of the changes in the water's patterns. He hoped a storm wasn't on the horizon. A storm would bring a fresh blanket of snow and hours of pounding ice on their buildings.

It would also make their barracks blindingly cold.

For a moment Robert considered sharing his weather report, then decided against it. No doubt their captain had already surmised the same thing.

He'd just opted to leave and find someone else to sit with Phillip when Monroe turned to face him. "How's he look?" he asked.

Robert exhaled. "Like a man facing death." There was no other way to describe it.

Devin flinched. "Don't expect it will be long now," he said after a pause. "He'll be in heaven before we know it. Too soon."

"Maybe a day or two at the most." Robert was torn between hoping he was wrong and praying he was right.

Cap nodded. "Figured as much." Still looking out at the waves, he said, "Heck of a way to die, though."

Robert had learned from an early age that death was always unpleasant. His experiences on the battlefield reinforced that idea, along with the knowledge that, while death was unpleasant, there were worse ways to die than others.

But yes, Robert understood his commander's statement. Phillip was a good man. A true Southern gentleman. Loyal and true. It was going to be hard to come to terms with the fact that this good man could meet such a painful and dark death.

Just as Robert was about to say something about pain and suffering and how he wished the Lord would decide to go easier on Phillip, Devin spoke.

"Truax?"

"Sir?" Robert realized he had unconsciously stood at attention. "When you sat with Markham . . . did he say anything?"

All of Robert's senses went on alert. There was a new thread in the man's tone that signified his question was important.

After reflecting on the last three hours, he said, "Yes, sir, he did speak. Well, he spoke for a bit the first hour I sat with him, though I couldn't be sure if he was speaking to me or merely talking in his sleep."

The captain tensed. "What did he say? Tell me exactly."

"I don't recall his exact words, sir. They were a mumbled mash."

"Try, Lieutenant."

"He, uh, was talking about Miranda." Though he was a grown man and had grown up on the streets, he felt himself blush. "Something about her skin, sir." He truly hoped Captain Monroe wouldn't ask for more details than that.

Captain relaxed. "Is that it? He only talked about his wife?"

Robert stared at him curiously. "Yes, sir. Isn't that enough? Ever since we've known him, she's been his favorite topic of conversation. He used to talk about that woman most every waking minute."

"I hope that continues to be the case."

His words were cryptic. And though it wasn't usually his place to question his commanding officer, he asked, "What is on your mind, Captain? Does Markham know something you're worried about getting out?"

After looking around their vicinity, Captain Monroe lowered his voice. "Phillip was a skilled horseman. Skilled fighter. "

"Yes, he was." For the most part, they all were. Well, except he'd been one of the few men in his unit who had never ridden a horse before the war. It had caused an endless amount of ribbing.

Monroe shook his head. "No, he was a better soldier than you know. He was a better fighter, better at strategizing, braver than most people would ever imagine. He was educated too. He knew several languages." Devin paused, stared at him. "Did you know that?"

"I knew he went to West Point. But about the languages? No, sir, I did not."

"Fluent in French and Spanish. It came in handy."

"I didn't know about that." Their job had been to kill Yankees, not speak to them.

"That's good. He was charged to keep it a secret."

Robert wondered if his captain was reminding him of Phillip's qualities to illustrate that the wrong man was dying. If so, it was an unnecessary step. Robert already knew he could never compare to the man Phillip Markham was.

"He was an exemplary officer. The Confederacy will miss him." Robert knew most men who knew him would have blinked twice to hear such words flow off his tongue. Robert was a loyal man but never one to speak in such a flowery way.

"No, Robert. You aren't understanding what I'm trying to say. Phillip often went behind enemy lines. He was a spy."

"What?"

"Markham could lose that Texas drawl and charm-school demeanor faster than you could say 'buttercup.' He's received all kinds of commendations for his missions. One of the generals here pulled me aside yesterday and said that some of the information Phillip shared saved hundreds of lives."

To say he was stunned was an understatement. "I . . . I had no idea, sir."

"That is good. Lee himself swore him to silence. He would have been shot for insubordination if he ever talked about his missions."

"He certainly never betrayed himself to me, sir."

Monroe turned to him at last. "To be honest, by the time he came to report to me, he was done with all that. The powers that be were worried he'd be recognized. Because of that, he was placed into the regular cavalry and asked to serve under me."

"He often told me it was his lucky day when he received orders to come to your unit."

His captain waved off that remark. "I didn't know much of what he'd done. All I'd ever been told was that Markham was valued, with a capital *V*. I took that to mean I should try not to get him killed." He flashed a smile, then sobered. "But then one night I learned a lot more about him."

"When was that?"

"It was back when we were in north Georgia. I was visiting a couple of men at a hospital tent, paying respects and so forth, when a major general stopped me. After I sat down next to him, he pointedly asked how Phillip Markham was doing."

Robert stared. "What did you say?"

Monroe smiled slightly. "About what you'd expect me to. The man's question seemed pointed and out of character. After all, it wasn't like we all went about and checked on our men like they were children." Monroe met Robert's gaze, then turned back to stare at the water. "I kind of shrugged and said he was doing all right. I think I said something about him being good with horses or some such nonsense. That's when the blasted general told me about Phillip Markham's true contributions to the war."

"I must admit I'm shocked."

"I was shocked too. For a while there I even found myself strangely tentative around the man. Phillip had been important enough to the effort to earn the rank of a general. He would have far outranked me . . . if he hadn't agreed to keep all his missions a secret."

"I wish he wasn't dying like this. Seems a poor end to such a great man."

Impatiently, Monroe shook his head. "That isn't why I told you this, Robert."

"What, then, was the reason?"

"I've decided to ask this of you, not Ethan or Thomas. I . . . I think you will be able to handle it the best. From now on, you or I need to stay with Phillip until he passes on. *Only you or me.* No one else. He cannot start telling tales about his past escapades."

"He probably won't. He seems—"

Monroe shook his head again. "He very well might. He's going to start forgetting about where he is. You and I have both seen men do that. It won't be his fault. But the fact is, no one can know about what he's done. No matter what you hear him say, you need to keep it to yourself, or if you truly feel you need to share it, speak to me. That is it." His voice turned hard. "And if you aren't able to quiet him, you will need to silence him yourself. Understood?"

Robert felt as if all the blood were rushing from his face. "Yes, sir."

Monroe continued to stare at him intently. "Do you promise?"

"Yes, Captain." Above all, he was loyal to this man and to the cause.

Captain Monroe exhaled. "Thank you, Robert. And don't forget . . . no matter what, we need to continue to stress that Phillip Markham was nothing more than one of my lieutenants who happened to have a good seat on a horse."

"Yes, sir. And, uh, let us not forget he was a gentleman who really loved his wife."

Captain Monroe smiled. "That will probably be the truest thing we've ever said during our time here. Phillip seems to be fairly sure that the sun rises and falls on his Miranda. The man is still smitten after several years of marriage."

Glad to be talking about something that wasn't so uncomfortable, Robert said, "Do you think any woman can be that wonderful?"

Monroe looked at him sadly. "I would like to think there is at least one woman who is. If Miranda Markham loves Phillip even half as much as he loves her, I shudder to think how she is going to receive the news of his death."

Much to his shame, Robert hoped she was desolate. It was going to be difficult to bear if the woman who was everything to Phillip hadn't actually felt the same way about him.

10

SHERIFF KERN WAS STANDING AGAINST THE FIREPLACE mantel, Phillip's tintype in his hand, when Miranda entered the parlor.

When he saw her, his expression softened. "Mrs. Markham, you're back."

As she watched him clumsily attempt to replace Phillip's tintype, she couldn't help but smile to herself. His awkward way of moving and conducting himself was rather endearing. It set her at ease, unlike Phillip's perfect manners. His perfect comportment often made her doubt herself.

Briefly, she wished her situation were different. She wished she trusted Sheriff Kern more. She wished they were friends, or at least friendly.

She would give a lot to be able to look forward to enjoying his company after Robert left. It would be nice to have a good friend.

However, it was likely that such a moment would never come. Or at least not anytime soon.

"Sheriff Kern, thank you again for coming so quickly. I do hope I haven't inconvenienced your day?"

"Not in the slightest."

"I am fairly sure you are lying, but I'll pretend I believe you."

Instead of correcting her, he bowed slightly. "May I say that you look quite fetching today?"

"You may." She curtsied slightly, realizing as she did so that she was blushing. The clumsy compliment eased her like little did anymore. Funny how some things that were drilled into a person's head by force and cajoling could ease the greatest tensions years later. "Won't you please sit down?"

When his gaze darted toward Belle, who was standing silently beside her, Miranda felt her blush deepen. "Please forgive my manners. Sheriff Kern, Belle came in to see what kind of refreshments we might serve you. Would you care for tea or coffee?"

"Coffee would be much appreciated, Belle. Thank you."

"Of course, Sheriff," Belle said before turning to Miranda. "Coffee for two, ma'am?"

"Yes. And if Cook has any blueberry bread, that would be good as well."

After another nod, Belle departed.

After gazing at Belle's retreating form a moment longer, Sheriff Kern took a seat across from Miranda and stared at her expectantly.

Miranda knew she needed to get to the point and fast. No matter how kind the sheriff was, he was not going to have time to sit and stare at her while she behaved like a ninny.

"As I said, I appreciate you meeting me here, Sheriff Kern," she began before sputtering to a stop. Perching on the edge of the settee, she tried to control her onslaught of nerves. It was obvious that she was doing a sorry job of it, however. Her hands were clenched in tight fists and she no doubt looked anything but relaxed.

Sheriff Kern, on the other hand, leaned back in the chair

across from her, one of his elbows resting on the arm as though he was simply taking an hour's respite from work. "Do you think we could move to a first-name basis, ma'am?" he said with a small smile. "We've known each other for some time now."

"About a year, I believe."

He raised one eyebrow. "Since that is the case, perhaps you would be so kind as to call me a friend?"

"Yes, of course." Had he just read her mind?

"Therefore, may we be on a first-name basis?" He raised a brow. Goading her on.

There really was no other choice. Though she felt as awkward as a wallflower at her first ball, she smiled softly. "Please, allow me to introduce myself. I'm Miranda."

"Miranda, I am Jess."

She felt herself blushing again. Her reaction was troublesome, indeed. She had never believed a man—any man—would cause butterflies to flutter in her stomach again. But now it seemed she truly was not immune to masculine appreciation. First she experienced this with Robert, and now Jess Kern.

Or perhaps it was simply that she wasn't dead.

If anything, he looked even more relaxed. "I'm glad we got that out of the way."

"I, as well."

He smiled at her again, and then, before her eyes, his whole manner changed. "Miranda, I don't believe you brought me here simply for coffee."

She gulped. It was time. "I'm afraid I wanted to discuss something of a serious nature with you." She paused, mentally trying out several different ways to discuss her problem. She wanted to share her concerns in a quiet, easy way. She wasn't sure if that was possible, however.

But instead of making her wait, Jess said, "You want to discuss the letter you received today."

She exhaled a breath she hadn't even realized she'd been holding. "Yes. Belle must have told you."

He uncrossed his legs and leaned forward. "May I see it?" His voice had become all business.

"Yes, of course. Though, um, I'm afraid I must tell you I've been receiving letters like this with startling regularity."

All traces of ease vanished from his expression. After he read the letter, he asked, "How often have you been getting these letters, Miranda?"

His use of her Christian name jarred her composure. It was going to be next to impossible to tell him anything but the stark truth. "Almost every week." Either Belle had not told him that, too, or he was pretending not to know, protecting her maid from her employer's possible anger for discussing her private affairs. But she didn't care anymore. She wanted it all out in the open now.

"You've been receiving a letter every week. For the past year?"

"Yes. Since, um, around the time I opened the Iron Rail for business."

"So you've received at least fifty letters."

"Yes."

His expression was incredulous. "Miranda, I know I did not take the first letter seriously enough, and I'm very sorry about that. But why didn't you come to me when the letters continued?" His voice was harsh. It was obvious that he was trying hard not to scare her, but he was upset.

"I don't know why I didn't come to you," she blurted, then forced herself to be honest. "No, that isn't true. At first I started thinking that maybe those letters were nothing less than I deserved."

He inhaled sharply. "Why on earth would you think you deserved to be the recipient of such abuse?"

"Because I'm alive, I suppose, and Phillip is not." Her heart started beating faster. She hadn't allowed herself to verbalize these thoughts before. It was amazing how ridiculous her reasoning sounded. Her husband would have given her a good talking-to for turning those letters into something so convoluted.

Jess's expression flickered from anger to confusion to pity. He got to his feet, turned from her, and paced. Then after a pause, he walked toward her again and sat down. "Phillip was a good man, Miranda. Though I didn't know him, many officers I met in the army knew of him and thought very highly of him. He was well respected."

"He was," she said quickly. "He was a wonderful man. He treated me well. He was better than I deserved." Lowering her voice, she said, "We married in haste, were hardly more than strangers, really. I was so young, and here he entrusted me with so much. No doubt he would wish I was stronger and wiser."

"Stronger?" He cocked a brow. "Wiser?"

Even to her ears, her words sounded convoluted. "Oh, I don't know . . . better?"

Jess shook his head. "No, Miranda. Phillip Markham was exactly who you deserved. You deserved a good man. You are worthy of that love."

Just as she was about to murmur something inconsequential, he continued. "However, even though Phillip was good, I am sure he was not perfect. He had flaws just like all of us. He was no better and no less. And more than that, I'm told he loved you dearly. Nothing would make him more upset than to realize that someone was taking advantage of your widowed state and preying on you. And . . . that you felt guilty about living."

"Perhaps you are right."

"No, I know I am right. Promise me from this day forward you will cease to assume that you deserve anything but happiness."

"I will try, sir."

"That isn't good enough. I promise you, dear, you being miserable will not make either Phillip's reputation or memory better. It will simply make you worried and upset." Looking at her intently, he said, "Will you promise me?"

She nodded. She didn't know if it was a fool's promise, but she saw Jess's point.

His eyes flickered beyond her again. "Ah."

She turned to see that Belle had returned with a coffee cart. And that Mr. Truax was entering the room just behind her.

Uneasiness jangled her nerves as she noticed he seemed as confident as ever.

Confident and full of his own secrets. She suddenly realized the letters had taken a stronger, ugly turn after his arrival. Did that mean something?

Could he have had something to do with them?

"Belle told me you both were in here. I thought I'd join you," he said with a charming smile.

When Jess merely stared at him, not looking pleased by his appearance in the slightest, Miranda drew herself up. "I'm sorry, Mr. Truax, but you will have to excuse us. This is a private conversation."

"I'd like to think I can help you."

"I don't believe you can. It's of, um, a somewhat confidential nature," she replied. Beside her, Jess continued to stare at her boarder.

It was beginning to make her worried.

But instead of abiding by her wishes, Robert simply sat down next to her. Uninvited. Immediately she was surrounded by his masculine scent. Against her will, she was aware of everything about him.

"You see, the fact is, I have knowledge of your problem, Mrs. Markham. I was at the sheriff's office when Belle arrived and I know about your letter."

Sheriff Kern propped one leg on his other and glared. "Truax, I'll take care of this. Watch yourself."

"That is what I'm doing, Jess."

As Miranda stared at the two men, she realized they were speaking to each other with a measure of comfort, as if they had already met. Perhaps even with a compatibility? And why was Robert at Jess's office when Belle was there?

While Jess looked ready to spit nails, Robert lazily leaned back and propped one foot on an opposite knee and smiled at Belle. "Bring me a cup of coffee when you can, would you, please, Belle?"

"Of course, sir," she said easily. Just as if she were used to taking orders from him!

Feeling both confused and frustrated, Miranda watched Belle set china cups in front of her and the sheriff, then pour piping-hot coffee from a pot. Finally, she set out a small plate of Cook's berry bread.

Jess took a sip, while Mr. Truax reached over, rudely picked up a piece of bread, and took a large bite. A faint sprinkling of crumbs littered his vest. He brushed them away.

"Perhaps you would care to explain yourself?" she asked, somewhat caustically.

"I'll be happy to. As soon as Belle returns with my coffee. In the meantime, I think it would be wise for me to see the letter that came today."

Instead of arguing with him, she sipped her coffee as Jess handed him the letter. When Belle returned, she served Mr. Truax, then finally left them.

Through it all, her suspicions grew. Jess Kern and Robert Truax were no strangers.

"You two know each other?"

For the first time since his entrance, Robert looked uncomfortable.

The two men exchanged glances and seemed to come to the same conclusion.

After setting down his fork, the sheriff said, "We actually met for the first time the other day, but Robert and I also have much in common because of the war."

"You mean . . . you two served together?"

"Kind of. We were both in . . . the same place once."

She barely refrained from rolling her eyes. That answer told her absolutely nothing. "Why did I not know this before?"

"It never came up in conversation. You know I only recently arrived here," Robert answered.

She clenched her hands in a last-ditch effort to calm her temper. "Don't prevaricate, sir. You knew the fact that you served together would have been meaningful to me. Yet, for some reason you chose to keep it a secret." Looking from one to the other, she said, "Both of you did. I suspect you actually knew each other before Robert came to town. You've been lying to me about this."

Robert bristled. "I didn't do anything of the kind."

"You did. I was led to believe that you knew no one here. That you were a stranger." Remembering her chatter about the park, remembering how inane, how foolish she must have sounded, she said, "You've probably been here before. You should have told me."

"I didn't lie about that, Miranda. I've never been to Galveston before."

Suddenly hating that she'd been so familiar with him, hating how comfortable she'd felt walking by his side on the pier, she flinched. "You may call me Mrs. Markham."

Looking contrite, Robert nodded. "As you wish. The truth is, I have not revealed everything about my visit."

"Give him a chance, Miranda," Sheriff Kern said.

Glaring at him coldly, she said, "I think it is best if we go back to a more distant relationship, sir."

Hurt flashed in the sheriff's eyes before he nodded. "If that is what you wish, Mrs. Markham."

When she noticed the men exchange yet another cautious glance with each other, her pulse started racing. "Explain yourselves, gentlemen," she bit out, hardly able to keep her anger and dismay at bay.

"I served the Confederacy in the war, ma'am," Sheriff Kern said. "Just as Robert did. And Phillip."

"A great many men served the Confederacy."

"That is true. A great many men also died."

"I am aware of that."

Mr. Truax's jaw tightened, then he said, "Several thousand men were also imprisoned in a camp in the middle of Lake Erie, off the coast of Ohio. It was called Johnson's Island. Most of the captives there were officers but there were also a smattering of privates and grunts like me."

She felt as if the wind was getting knocked out of her. "Johnson's Island is where Phillip was imprisoned."

"Yes, it was. Johnson's Island is also where I was imprisoned, Mrs. Markham," Sheriff Kern said quietly. "Robert was too."

"You . . . you two knew each other there, then?"

"No. We never met there, although Jess told me the other day that he remembers me, and I remember seeing him," Robert said. "All three of us were taken to be prisoners of war in early 1865. There was a large group of us. Some were great men. Even generals. We were bored. And some of us bonded."

"Did you know Phillip, Mr. Truax?"

"Yes, I did."

"You served with my husband."

"Yes. And may I say that he was everything you knew him to be. A true gentleman. Heroic and brave."

Robert had known her husband. He'd known Phillip. He'd seen him before he died.

"How did he die?" she whispered.

"He died in his cot surrounded by friends," Robert said. "He was injured. He had gangrene. It spread. He died just weeks before we were released."

She knew that. She'd received the telegram. "Were you with him when he died?"

"I was," Mr. Truax said, his eyes looking strangely vacant. "Well, I was there shortly after. Another officer was taking a turn by his side when he passed."

Though their words were far beyond anything she'd ever imagined, she forced herself to focus on one thing. "So he didn't die while being interrogated and giving secrets."

"None of us was interrogated," Robert said. "Not really. It was at the end of the war. There was no point."

She gasped. Tried to hold her tears at bay. "But . . ." Her voice drifted off as she tried to wrap her mind around what she'd just learned. "I mean, everyone's been saying he betrayed us all."

"They are wrong," Mr. Truax said without a moment's hesitation. "That rumor is wrong. Phillip betrayed no one. If you only believe one thing I say, ma'am, please know that Phillip Markham died a hero. He was honorable and stoic. He also loved you more than mere words could ever describe."

Tears pricked her eyes. Tears that she'd thought she'd long since stopped crying. The feeling of despair that had clung to her like a heavy, prickly cloak dissipated. It was replaced by something new—a hot, vigilant anger.

She got to her feet. "Why haven't you said anything, Mr. Truax? Why did you not tell me who you were to Phillip when you came? I remember now. Phillip wrote about you, just as he wrote about his other friends. You know how I've been treated here in Galveston. You know how Phillip's memory has been vilified with these lies. How could you have let that continue? How could you have kept your silence?"

"I had no choice."

"Of course you did."

"Ma'am, I did not. I could not betray a confidence."

"What confidence?" she scoffed. "Phillip is dead."

"You don't understand, Miranda. There are things I can't tell you."

"Obviously," she said bitterly.

"There was more at stake than your husband's memory," Robert whispered. "We couldn't betray the cause."

"The cause? As you said, the war is over and we lost. We lost!" she cried out, not even caring that she sounded out of control and shrill. "We lost and so did Phillip."

Sheriff Kern clumsily got to his feet. "Mrs. Markham, please take a chair. You must calm yourself."

She ignored him, still staring in wonder at Robert. "Why? Why did you keep your silence?" She was shaking now. "What confidence are you talking about? The war is over. Nothing that used to matter does anymore."

"That is where you are wrong, ma'am. Everything that happened matters. And everything we shared in that god-forsaken camp matters now. It is not forgotten."

Tears now fell unashamedly down her cheeks. "What happened there means more to you than I do? Than what I've been going through? I've been so upset by the rumor everyone's believed . . . I've been hopeless."

"Yes. Well . . ." Sheriff Kern leaned forward, as if he was intending to clasp her hand.

She was very glad he did not. And though it was so difficult, so painful, she forced herself to continue. "I have not wanted to live anymore."

Though both men flushed, neither spoke.

Which was why a sudden, terrible thought entered her mind, took hold, and fairly took her breath away. "Sheriff, are you the one who has been writing me those letters? Are you the one who has been torturing me all this time?"

"Of course not."

But when Kern and Mr. Truax exchanged glances, she felt her insides practically fall apart.

They were still keeping secrets.

And that made her realize her situation wasn't just bad.

It was actually far worse than she'd believed it to be. Maybe far worse than she'd ever imagined.

11

ROBERT WAS AFRAID IF HE TOUCHED HER, MIRANDA WOULD lose the last bit of control she had over her emotions.

She looked that fragile.

She was staring blankly into space. Tears ran unabashedly down her face, unchecked. Robert figured she either didn't notice or didn't care that the tiny drops were cascading down her cheeks. Each one landed on the bodice of her gown and made a small stain.

As he stared at the water marks, the self-loathing he felt deepened.

Across from Robert, Kern stared at her in much the same way Robert was assuming he looked. The sheriff's expression reflected a hundred emotions, each one guiltier than the next.

They needed to do something. Fix this. Fix her pain.

But was there a way to tell Miranda—and Jess—enough about Phillip's undercover work without ignoring Captain Monroe's orders or betraying the very men Phillip had risked so much to protect? Though the war was over, both sides hadn't completely put the battles, injuries, or losses behind them. No soldiers wanted everything they'd done in the name of war to come to light.

As soldiers and officers, they were trained to put their mission and their cause above personal needs. Above any one person's feelings. But their cause had died, along with so many of the men they'd sworn to protect and serve.

And here was a widow who had dealt with the consequences of their actions. In many ways she'd suffered as much as they had.

Was there a way to ease her suffering and make things right . . . without betraying his vow to Captain Monroe? He wasn't exactly sure. All he did know was that he had to at least make an attempt.

"Miranda," he began haltingly. "I know how you must be feeling."

Her eyes flashed. "Forgive me, but you have no idea." Somewhere inside her, she seemed to find the strength to raise her voice. "Ever since I learned Phillip was gone, I've been alone." More tears filled her eyes.

Kern shifted uncomfortably. "I'm sorry for your loss, but of course you are not the only Confederate widow."

"I am not. But I am the only widow in Galveston, Texas, who was burdened with her husband's sins." Looking at Robert with a barely concealed contempt, she added succinctly, "Sins I never believed he had."

"He was a good man, Miranda. What I knew of him, he was brave," Kern said.

She glared at him. "Forgive me, Sheriff Kern, but I don't have any desire to hear you talk about my husband ever again."

Kern flinched. "I never meant to hurt you."

"Yet neither did you help."

"Don't forget, madam, that you kept much of your pain to yourself. I had no idea you had received so many letters."

"I won't forget. How could I ever forget what it felt like to be vilified by my friends? I came here as a young bride, moved into Phillip's house just days before he left for battle, and with his death turned from his bride to his reminder. At first, he was considered a hero like all the other men who fought. But then the lies started, and everyone turned their backs on me."

She drew in a breath, then added, "All because someone made up rumors about him that I now know for certain are not true."

"I will discover who did that," Robert said.

She stilled. "How?"

"I'll find a way."

"Thank you, sir. That explains so much."

Robert knew there was no way he could fully explain either his motives or his reasons. "Let us not dwell on the past, Mrs. Markham. There is nothing we can do or say to make it easier to bear."

"I agree. However, the past is all I have."

He leaned forward. "Not anymore, ma'am. I am here to make sure your future will be far better. Please, trust me to make things right."

But instead of looking relieved, she merely stared at him in loathing. "I don't intend to ever trust you again. You lied to me about who you were as well as your past."

"I did not lie about my past. I told you I served."

"You did not tell me the whole truth about your connection to Phillip. When you arrived, you should have simply told me you served with my husband. I would have been glad to meet you."

"I couldn't. I was bound by my promise to our captain."

"What promise could you have possibly given him that affected me?"

"I was asked to visit you, to make sure you were all right. If you were, I was going to leave and not disrupt your routine."

"My routine. And never tell me who you were?"

He exhaled. "It all sounds convoluted now. All I can say is that my intentions were true. And I will help you now. I promise, I will not leave here until your burdens are lighter."

"Even if I did let you help me, I don't see how you will ever be able to make my life easier. I don't know how either of you will be able to discover who wrote these letters, who started these rumors."

"We will, Mrs. Markham," Sheriff Kern said. "Whether or not you believe me, I can promise you I intend to keep my word."

"I will earn your trust, minute by minute, hour by hour," Robert vowed. "And while I am working toward that goal, I will do everything in my power to seek out this blackmailer."

"Everything in your power?" she echoed, her voice thick with doubt and sarcasm. "What power could you possibly have?"

At that moment, Robert would have liked nothing better than to share his whole past with her.

Instead, he ached to describe to her in more detail what his childhood was like, to describe just how dirty and hungry he'd been. How lonely. How bitter. How it had felt to join the army and to be so grateful for his meals in basic training that it had caused the other men to ridicule him.

How it felt to fight next to men who believed they were so much better than he was because they were blessed enough to be born to parents who cared.

He yearned to describe the battlefields of the war to Miranda. To tell her the things he'd done.

He ached to share with her the conditions in their prison camp. The despair they'd all fought. The melancholy, hope, and guilt that filled them, knowing they were merely biding time while their comrades were putting their lives on the line.

Maybe if he shared those things, she wouldn't think he was merely some polished dandy filled with nothing more than empty promises. Maybe then she'd look at him in the eye again. Look at him like he was worth something.

Look at him like he was worthy of her.

But of course, he did none of those things. Instead, he said stiffly, "I would like to think I have some power. But the man your husband and I served under has even more influence than I. I'll send a dispatch to Devin Monroe immediately."

She blinked. "Captain Monroe?"

"Have you heard of him?" Kern asked.

"Yes, of course. Phillip wrote of him. Often." Some of the bitterness that had enveloped her evaporated. "I wasn't aware he had survived the war."

"It is my honor, then, to inform you that he not only survived, but he's made it his calling to ensure that we all survive the war's aftermath. He's the reason I came here to check on you. Once he discovers how terrible your situation actually is, I have no doubt that he will come here to join us."

"But why? Phillip is gone."

"Phillip has passed on to heaven, that is true. But what you might not understand is the depth of his love for you."

"How would you know?"

"He spoke of you often." Feeling a bit bashful, he corrected himself. "Actually, he spoke of you all the time, ma'am. And he made us all aware of you and your goodness." He also told them about her beauty, but he kept that to himself.

Her blue eyes widened. "I . . . I had no idea."

"Before he died, he asked us all to look out for you," Robert continued as he got to his feet. "To my shame, I haven't done much of a good job of that. But eventually I will do him proud."

"We all will, Miranda," Kern said as he stood up. "Somehow, some way, you will be avenged and Phillip's true heroism will be celebrated once again. That is my vow."

Still sitting, she stared up at both of them in obvious wonder. Gazed at them as if she'd never seen them before in her life.

And then, at last, she smiled.

Her smile was beautiful. It was a gift.

Once more, Robert knew it was everything he'd ever desired and never believed he could have. The appreciation of a beautiful woman.

One day, he vowed, he would deserve it.

Bowing slightly, he said, "Again, I am sorry for my deception. I'm going to move out of here, find somewhere else to stay. Perhaps you have a spare room at the sheriff's office, Jess?"

"You don't wish to be around me anymore?" What was she asking?

"Given the circumstances, I think it would be best for both of us if we had some space between us."

"No. Please, don't go." Her tone was desperate.

She'd managed to shock him. "I won't ask for a refund of money," he said slowly.

"It's not the money. It's . . ." She closed her eyes, then stammered, "I simply don't think I can bear to feel like I'm by myself again."

Her honesty was humbling. "Are you sure?"

She nodded. "I have much to come to terms with, but I'd rather have you here than not."

Robert inclined his head. "Thank you, ma'am. I will stay until you tell me otherwise."

"I had best take my leave." Turning to Miranda, Kern bowed stiffly. "Mrs. Markham, I am sorry for my deception. I hope in time you will be able to forgive me."

"I hope so too, sir," she said before he took his leave.

When they were alone, Robert stared at her. Noticed how pale and exhausted she looked.

Wished there was something more to say. But because he felt

as if he was out of words, he simply turned and walked with leaden steps to his room.

He needed to go to his desk and write another, more urgent note to his captain. But at the moment, all he wanted to do was sit and stare out the window and think about all he had almost lost.

Belle approached him just as he reached his room. She looked as hesitant and worried as she had when he'd found her at the sheriff's office. "Belle, what is wrong?"

Her hands were clenching the sides of her white apron. "Mr. Truax, you're not going to leave, are you?" Had she listened to their conversation?

"No, though I probably should. It's improper for me to continue to stay."

"Of course it isn't. Though your reasons for being here might be different, your circumstances haven't changed."

"They have." No, everything had changed. Miranda now thought of him as a liar.

The maid looked skeptical, but still she pressed. "But you're still going to stay."

"I'm going to stay," he promised.

"Good," she said before turning down the hall.

Leaving him with his thoughts.

And he? Well, he now realized Miranda had gotten under his skin. He didn't look into her blue eyes thinking about her husband or his quest to make things right. Instead, he only thought about how he could make a living out of simply gazing into her eyes. Or making them shine.

He no longer sought only to redeem her husband's memory.

Instead, when he thought about her, he thought about how gentle she was. How much he cared about her.

He thought about how he wished she was his.

He found himself plotting in the middle of the night ways in which he could try to win her over. Win her heart.

As if he were worthy of such a woman's love.

It was selfish too. Yet again, he was betraying his humble roots. Or maybe it was his selfish, rough nature. He was used to fighting for things he believed in and clawing and grasping at everything he wanted. Somehow in his goal to clear the black mark around Phillip's name he'd interjected his own wants.

This wasn't right in any shape or form. In fact, it was nothing like what he should be doing and everything that was detrimental to both his honor and the honor of his brothers-in-arms.

If Devin Monroe ever discovered just how much he was in danger of losing his heart, he would no doubt demand an apology and expect Robert to bow out of any future missions. Deservedly so.

But until that happened, something had to be done.

He needed to distance himself from her. But more important, she needed distance from him, because if he stayed this close, he was going to find multiple opportunities to seek her out. If he was able to accomplish that goal, he knew he'd use every wile and trick he'd learned on the streets to cajole her to trust him. Eventually, she would grow to trust him. He would take that trust and hold it close.

But he knew himself well. He recognized what he was good at and what he would always be a dismal failure at. Because of that, he knew it was very likely that, sooner or later, he would make an even greater mistake than the ones he was contemplating. He was going to hurt her. Or ruin her reputation.

Or, even worse, she might be so desperate for a kind word, for protection, that she'd grow to depend on him. Maybe even develop feelings.

With him!

If that happened, just like in the thick of battle, he wouldn't hesitate. He'd ask her to marry him. With haste. Because she was, without a doubt, the most enchanting woman he'd ever met.

And if she said yes and they did marry . . . it would be such a mistake. Oh, he'd try his best to be everything she wanted him to be. He'd show her how much he cared for her. He'd profess his love as well.

It would only be later, when the pleasure of waking by his side faded, that she'd at last look at him with clear eyes. See him for exactly what and who he was and everything he wasn't.

He was a former Confederate officer whose best friends in the world were men he'd met during a long and difficult war.

A man who had learned social niceties from a variety of people, none who would ever be fit company for a lady like her.

She'd see he was a man who was quick to temper and slow to feel remorse. She'd see him for who he was.

And when that happened, he'd see some of the glory fade from her expression. She'd realize that she'd become tainted. And when it was too late, after she'd given him her heart and trust, she was going to wake up one morning and dare to compare him with Phillip Markham.

And the moment she did that, she would realize just what a sorry comparison that was.

He doubted she would ever utter such a thing aloud. Instead, Miranda Markham Truax would most likely keep her regrets and dismay and worries to herself. She'd simply continue to care for him with her head high and her spine straight.

But they both would know.

And then she'd live the rest of their days together pretending she hadn't made a terrible mistake, and he'd spend every moment of it watching her swim in an ocean of regret. It would be tortuous and painful. As painful as getting captured by the enemy and being forced into a Yankee prison camp.

As painful as spending countless days passing time, watching his fellow prisoners write and receive letters home . . . and realizing that he had no one to write to.

It would no doubt be just as painful as watching Phillip slowly die.

That was unbearable.

Therefore, as Robert slowly walked up the stairs, his hand on the gleaming wood banister leading to his room, he came to a decision. He would do everything in his power to uncover the blackmailer, improve Miranda's reputation, and then get out of Galveston.

As soon as possible.

12

HOW WAS IT THAT SHE COULD EXPERIENCE BOTH DEVASTATing heartbreak and exhilarating euphoria in the span of one hour?

Miranda reviewed everything she'd just learned as she paced across the width of her room, paused for the briefest of moments, then turned and paced again.

Never would she have imagined to hear that Robert had actually known Phillip and that he came to see her out of some misplaced vow on her husband's deathbed.

Never would she have imagined that Sheriff Kern, who had practically brushed off her worries a year before, was now offering to be her friend and practically turn the city upside down to find the author of the letters. Both revelations had been such a shock, she felt like crying and laughing at the same time.

However, all that would do was cause her staff to worry about her even more. What she actually needed to do was compose herself and think.

With that in mind, she stopped her relentless pacing and breathed deep. Trying to find comfort in the cool shades of chocolate brown, mint green, and eggshell white that she'd painstakingly decorated with when she and Phillip had first married.

In her naiveté about marriage, she'd attempted to create an

oasis of sorts for her husband. She'd had visions of him entering their bedroom, seeing how comforting and beautiful she'd made the room, and somehow feeling refreshed.

In those first days of war, when everyone had reassured each other that their men would be coming home in a matter of days, that there was truly nothing the Yankees could do that their men couldn't do better, she'd sat by the window and waited for Phillip to return.

But as the days turned into weeks and eventually months, she'd known their circumstances were never going to be as easy as she'd hoped and believed.

Later, when Phillip had gotten leave, the man she'd brought to their bedroom was far different from the one she'd first said good-bye to. This Phillip was harder, moody. More sullen and physical. There was a new struggle behind his smooth words and quiet stares that had never been there before, and she hadn't known how to react to it. Small things set him off, sudden movements did too. And when she'd teasingly wrapped her arms around him from behind, he'd turned to her with a curse and almost hit her.

She'd cried out. The look that had appeared on his face was one she'd never forget. Complete devastation and remorse. That hadn't been hard to accept. Though he'd refused to talk about his life in the cavalry, she'd had a very good idea that war was a terrible, bloody experience. After all, everyone read about the accounts in the papers, heard stories from other men who were far more forth-coming, and, most heart-wrenchingly of all, saw the names of the injured and dead on the lists that appeared in the papers.

So she'd been understanding of his need to keep his secrets. She'd come to realize that he wasn't going to be the same. That war had changed him.

But what had been much harder to come to terms with was

the way he'd turned away from her. His smiles had vanished. He'd become silent. And he insisted on sleeping in a separate room, stating that his restless sleeping habits would keep her awake.

No protests from her had made a difference. Neither had her smiles, her understanding, or even her one failed night of seduction. He'd been distant.

The only time she'd found an inkling of the man she'd fallen in love with had been their last moments together. He'd held her almost painfully close, run his hands over her face, over her hair, over her body as if he needed to remember her by touch alone.

She'd been so grateful for his attention she'd clung to him and allowed him to grip her just a little too hard. Allowed him to mess up her hair, wrinkle her dress. She hadn't cared about anything other than she'd gotten him back for a few precious seconds.

It seemed that she, too, had needed to keep hold of their memories. She'd needed to remember what he felt like against her body. She'd needed to remember everything about him.

And then, of course, all too soon, he was gone.

His loss had been devastating. What had followed had been even harder to live with. Though she'd always been a solitary person, she'd learned that living as a shunned one had been almost unbearable.

And now she learned that, despite his distance, Phillip had loved her very much, so much that he told others about her until his dying days. That was worthy of the euphoria she had felt.

But worse, the cause of the devastation she felt was discovering how many lies she had been told. And the one man in Galveston whom she'd trusted had known they were lies. And now claimed he had to keep more.

She pressed her cheek against the cold windowpane, remembered how cold the windowpane on the landing had felt the morning of Robert Truax's arrival. Back then, the frosty pane had served to wake her up.

Now, however, it merely served as a reminder of just how much she'd lost and how, for some unknown reason, she was still alone.

"Jesus, why?" she whispered. "I thought you suffered so much so I wouldn't have to. Why do I have to keep being reminded of how hard life is and how fleeting the feeling of security is?"

Closing her eyes, she thought of the verses she'd read time and again. Of how all Jesus' disciples had moved away from him when he was whipped and nailed to the cross. Though she'd never compare her relationships to Sheriff Kern and Robert Truax to Jesus' to his disciples, she couldn't help but feel she had been receiving a hint of what her Savior had been going through. Trusted friends had betrayed him. Trusted friends had chosen other causes instead of Jesus' teachings.

Jesus, of course, had forgiven them.

But now, as she came to terms with the fact that everything she'd believed to be true was once again turned on its side, Miranda realized the unavoidable, ugly truth.

She was not Jesus.

Moreover, it seemed that her suffering was not about to end, either.

Moving from the window, she unfastened her kid boots, pulled down her window shade so darkness penetrated her world, and lay down on the bed. If she couldn't summon up the nerve to end her life, she was simply going to have to escape it for a while.

At least the Lord was still letting her sleep. She took refuge in that and fell into an exhausted slumber.

After Mr. Truax went into his room and Mrs. Markham's room fell silent, Belle wandered about on the upstairs hallway as she contemplated what to do next.

Should she report what she'd heard to the rest of the staff? Surely Winnie and Emerson and Cook would know what to do. However, if she did that, she would be betraying Mrs. Markham's privacy and trust. And though the lady of the house was the primary topic of conversation, it still seemed a betrayal to share something that was most definitely the woman's private business.

But what if she didn't share her news?

Mrs. Markham had looked decidedly depressed and hopeless. Winnie had whispered to her that they all had to be on the lookout for times when their employer got a case of the blues. Because she actually didn't just fight a case of the blues, but battled serious depression.

Winnie had even confessed that once she had seen Mrs. Markham open an upstairs window and lean so far out that she was sure she'd been contemplating a fall.

Was the devastated expression Belle had seen a sign of something horrible about to come?

And what if it was? Miranda Markham's mental state was not any of Belle's business. A grown woman should be able to do harm to herself if she wanted to.

Shouldn't she?

Belle bit her lip. She simply wasn't sure.

As she stared at Mrs. Markham's closed door yet again, she felt her stomach roll into tight knots. How could she live with herself if she didn't do anything?

But . . . what if Mrs. Markham was just fine? The lady would no doubt not thank her for disturbing her rest! And if she had an inkling about what Belle was suspecting of her, there was a very good chance she would get fired. Winnie, Cook, and Emerson wouldn't come to her defense, either. No, they'd let her accept the consequences of her foolish thoughts completely on her own.

But what was the right thing?

She knew. She knew what Jesus would do. She knew what she should do. After all, the Lord never promised an easy life, only that he wouldn't forsake her.

Resolve straightened her shoulders. She was going to have to do this. She was going to have to knock on Mrs. Markham's door and check on her. And if the lady needed her, she was going to have to counsel her. Somehow or some way, Belle was going to need to be the person she'd always hoped to be.

Her mind made up, she turned on her heel and started toward Mrs. Markham's door.

Just as her fist raised, the door behind her opened.

"Belle, what has you in such a dither?" Mr. Truax called out.

"Did I disturb you? I'm sorry, sir," she sputtered.

He ran a hand along his brow, smoothing back a chunk of hair from his face. Revealing his startling dark gray eyes. "You didn't disturb me, but I did hear you mumbling to yourself. It sounded like you were having quite the conversation too."

This was just getting worse. "I'm very sorry."

He paused in mid-nod, then looked at her more closely. "Care to tell me why you are so distraught?"

"Not especially."

"Now I'm afraid you actually are going to have to tell me. I'm intrigued."

"I was just, um, trying to decide whether or not I should knock on Mrs. Markham's door."

"Why would you worry about that?"

"Because . . . I am afraid she is resting?" She couldn't help but pose her statement as a question. Because it was a ridiculous statement, after all. If Belle thought she was resting, then she should leave her in peace.

"You know you are making no sense, right?" He walked toward her. All traces of humor gone from his eyes.

"Yes." She opened her mouth, then shut it just as quickly. Mr. Truax was simply a boarder. She knew she shouldn't bother him with her worries.

But he also seemed to have formed a bond with Mrs. Markham. Did that mean she should trust him?

Folding his arms over his chest, he stared at her intently. "Perhaps you should tell me what you are concerned about."

She bit her lip. Belle knew confiding her worries to a guest was even more of a bad idea than telling Winnie or Cook. However, she also knew Mr. Truax was part of the reason Mrs. Markham was in the state she was in.

A muscle in his jaw jumped. "Let's make this easy, miss. You will tell me what has you concerned. Immediately. And the truth, if you please."

His words might have been cloaked in niceties, but he'd just given her an order. One she didn't dare refuse. "I am worried about Mrs. Markham's emotional state, sir."

He paled. "Say again?"

"I saw her expression when she walked up the stairs," she whispered. "She . . . well, she wasn't in a good way. Sir."

"You mean she was upset."

In for a penny, in for a pound. "I mean she looked hopeless." She licked her lips. "As if she didn't want to live anymore." There. She said it. "We—I mean Winnie, Cook, Emerson, and I—have seen this look before, you see."

Mr. Truax's stunned expression turned hard. "I see. And you . . . ?"

"I was debating whether I should check on her."

His expression became an impassive mask. "Thank you for confiding in me. I'll take care of this now."

"Sir?"

"Go on downstairs, Belle. And please send word to the others that we are not to be disturbed."

Feeling as if she'd just not only lost her job but part of herself, she clumsily curtsied. "Yes, sir."

The moment she started walking down the stairs, she heard Mr. Truax open Mrs. Markham's door. Without knocking.

And then, to her shock, he walked in and shut it behind him.

She would now be left to only guess what he would find on the other side.

13

SOME MEMORIES OF THE WAR WERE SO PAINFUL THAT Robert would gladly trade the loss of one limb if the Lord would remove the images from his mind.

However, since he was pretty sure God didn't necessarily appreciate a man bargaining with him, Robert had long since resigned himself to cope with his flashbacks as best he could. Some methods worked better than others.

After spending too many hours nearly paralyzed by his thoughts, Robert had begun to try to ease those dark thoughts in a variety of ways. So far, the best way he'd found to find relief had been to consciously attempt to never think about the war.

Ever.

After a bit of practice, that method worked rather nicely. Every time his mind would drift toward a particularly horrific event that had played out on the battlefield, Robert would stop himself and concentrate on something at hand. Like music, for example. Or the way a woman smiled at a shopkeeper. Puppies and kittens and babies he saw. Anything that was the complete opposite of the grim realities of war.

But now, as he walked into Miranda Markham's darkened bedroom, his mind drifted back to one of his most painful nights on Johnson's Island . . . the night after they'd buried Phillip Markham. The burial ceremony itself had been a rather grand affair, given their circumstances. Over a hundred men had gathered together to pray before Robert, Captain Monroe, Thomas, and Major Kelly laid him to rest in the Confederate cemetery.

Captain Monroe, a man always to be counted on for eloquence, spoke about Phillip's love for Galveston Island, honor and chivalry, and of course, his beloved Miranda.

Robert had committed much of Monroe's speech to memory, it had been so beautiful. Their captain had spoken of living life to the fullest, even if it was a shortened one. He'd talked of finding joy in most every blessed event—even those events that didn't seem blessed at all.

And for a while, Captain Monroe's words had given them all a measure of hope and solace. His speech had offered a small amount of understanding in a time when so very little of what had happened to them was understandable.

But then the night had come.

And with that night came silence and men's cries. For Robert, it had also brought with it the realization that never again would he hear Phillip's slow drawl. Never again would Phillip chat incessantly about love and marriage and his beloved Miranda.

Late in the evening, long after midnight, Robert had felt a desolation so strong that it had hurt to breathe. He'd remembered all the men he'd known who had already died. He'd even forced himself to remember the day Rory had passed away.

And then his state of mind had gotten even worse.

For one long, interminable hour, he'd gazed at his sheet and contemplated making it into a rope.

All that had stopped him was the thought of the other men having to bury his body. Digging graves was a grueling and daylong affair. It left one sore and dirty and feeling hopeless. Then, of course, was the pain that he would put his captain through. He'd have to stand up once again and fashion words to comfort the other men.

He'd gone to sleep that night taking some comfort that he was sparing his fellow prisoners that, at least.

Now, as Robert opened Miranda's door, he was instantly inundated with the faint scent of roses that always clung to her skin and hair. Though his instant reaction was to breathe deeply, he pushed that thought away and forced himself to remember that long, painful night when he'd convinced himself to stay alive.

At that moment, even though they were so very different, he realized he felt as one with Miranda. After all, he knew what it felt like to give up hope.

But more important, he also knew the sharp relief that came from making the decision to not give in to despair.

"Lord," he whispered, "please help me out here. Please help me be of use to this woman . . . and not scare her half to death when she realizes I've entered her bedroom unannounced and uninvited."

After waiting a second for the Lord to process his request, Robert cleared his throat. Paused.

His muscles were so tense, he was pretty sure he would be able to hear his heart beating.

When he heard nothing, he cleared his throat. And into the silence, he called out, "Miranda?"

He heard a gasp, then a rustle of taffeta.

Then he could almost feel the tension reverberating from her. "Miranda, it's me. I mean, it's Robert. Truax." He winced. Why was he sounding so tentative now? After all, he came into her boudoir without knocking.

"Robert?"

Her voice sounded confused, not frightened. And not angry. That was something, he supposed. "Yes, it is I."

Through the faint shadows, he saw her scramble from where she'd been resting on top of the bed covering.

And that was when it hit him. She'd been resting, not attempting to kill herself. She'd been asleep and he'd woken her up.

A mere hour after she'd told him he could stay instead of leave. What had he been thinking?

Robert stumbled backward until his shoulder blades were touching the door. In all of his thirty years, he doubted he'd ever been more embarrassed.

"Why are you here?"

There was only one answer he could give, and that was the truth. "I was afraid for you, ma'am."

She stepped into the light cast by the sheer fabric covering the narrow window next to him. Her dress was rumpled, her hair in disarray. It wasn't loose, but it looked as if a faint breeze could loosen it from its confines.

Her eyes were sleepy looking, her eyelids lower than usual. And her face . . .

He inhaled sharply. There was a sheet mark on her cheek, giving evidence that she'd been sleeping hard.

He had never seen a lady in such a state. Not languid, freshly awoken. Smelling of roses and slumber and still throwing off the faint vestiges of sleep.

His embarrassment faded into longing.

The polite thing to do would be to excuse himself. To turn away. To give her some privacy, or at the very least, the semblance of such. But he found he could no more do that than he could have kept his distance from her if he'd thought she was hurting.

She was everything he'd ever dreamed a fine woman could be. Beautiful and feminine. Gentle. She encouraged every protective instinct he'd ever had and quite a few feelings of longing that he hadn't known he possessed.

Actually, Miranda was everything her husband, Phillip, had ever claimed her to be when he'd waxed poetic tales about her over the campfires. She was everything he'd said she was and far more than Robert had ever imagined.

And, he realized, she'd taken his breath away.

"Robert, why are you afraid?"

He hated what he was about to say, but he couldn't afford not to be blunt. Looking at her directly, he said, "One of your servants feared for your mental state, ma'am. I decided to make sure you were all right. Perhaps sit with you if you were doing, uh, poorly."

She curved a palm around the top of the wing chair that sat between them. "I don't understand."

He knew she did. Though the light was faint, the rays that did enter the room rested on her face. Illuminating the guilt that shone in her eyes.

"I heard Belle outside your room, ma'am. When I asked her why she was doing that, she confessed she was worried about you. She didn't want to bother you . . . but felt you needed to be checked on."

She shook her head as if she was having trouble organizing her thoughts. "Mr. Truax, I am so sorry. It seems my servant has overstepped herself. Terribly. I'll speak with her."

"You'll do no such thing."

"Pardon me?"

"You heard me," he said. "She was near tears, she was so worried about you."

"Yes, but—"

"She cares about you, Miranda," he said frankly. "And what's more, she told me only out of kindness to you. You cannot think of punishing a servant for that."

"It was a kindness for my maid to tell one of my guests that she was concerned about her employer's mental state?" Her voice was filled with derision. "Perhaps you were used to such insubordination in the service, but I am not."

Her chin was lifted, her eyes were full of fire. The last of her languidness was now only a memory. She looked indignant and like everything a well-brought-up woman of worth should look like.

But he could tell it was only an act. Her voice was brittle and her posture was so stiff that he feared there was a very good chance she would break.

"Sit down, Miranda," he said harshly.

"It is not your place to tell me what to do. You need to leave."

Ignoring her, he stepped closer. "Madam, I have been through too much in my lifetime to pretend with you."

"Don't you mean 'anymore'? As in pretend anymore? You lied to me. You knew Phillip. You came here to check on me. Yet, you let me believe you were merely a guest."

"If we're going to say so much to each other, then let us be completely honest," he said, stepping to his left and taking a seat on the small eggplant-colored velvet sofa. "Your husband was a good man. A wonderful man. Furthermore, he was an outstanding officer. He saved all of our lives in one way or another, and observing his death was one of the worst times in my life. But more than anything else anyone will ever know about him, he worshipped you, Miranda."

Her lips parted.

Robert leaned closer, close enough to see the band of dark blue that surrounded her irises. "He. Loved. You," he said slowly, taking care to enunciate each word. "He loved you more than he loved anything else in this world."

"I loved him."

"I know you did. And that is why when it came to our attention that you were not doing well, we decided to pay you a visit."

She sat down. "Who is we?"

"Captain Monroe and me, Miranda. Someone is blackmailing you, threatening you with so-called proof Phillip betrayed the Confederacy if you do not sell this house and leave Galveston."

After a pause, he said quietly, "And I now know that you are at the end of your ability to handle it. Miranda, please allow me to assist you. Please allow me to be someone you can trust. Please allow me to take care of the person who is making you so miserable and ruining one very fine man's reputation."

"Robert, you don't understand. This person is skilled at deceit. If he follows through on his latest threat—even using documents somehow falsified—everyone will believe him, no matter what you say. I will have no choice but to sell this house, and I won't know if I am selling it to the blackmailer or not." Her words were uttered in a halting, clumsy manner.

When he said nothing, only waited for her to continue, she said, "I will lose everything but the money from the sale, which won't be much, given I am branded a traitor's wife. I have little money . . . your help is too late."

"It is not," he replied quickly. Wishing she could trust him, could understand the depth of his regard for her, he added, "I can help you."

"I don't want your money."

"I am speaking about your problems, ma'am. When we discover who has been doing these things, I will ensure that he pays and everyone will know about his lies."

"How could you?"

"That is not something you need be concerned with." The fact of the matter was simply that he knew a great number of ways to bend men to his will. He'd learned many skills when he served, the least of which was strong-arming men to do what he wanted. "Miranda, you need to trust me."

She looked at him with longing in her eyes . . . but it was mixed with doubt. It was obvious that she yearned to trust him but was too afraid. "I trusted the sheriff," she said at last.

"You still can. You can trust Jess Kern."

She shook her head. "You are wrong about that. He lied about being imprisoned with Phillip. It would have meant so much to me to have known that they shared a history, but he didn't care enough about my feelings to inform me of that fact."

"I don't think that was exactly how it went, Miranda."

She continued as if he'd never spoken. "Furthermore, Sheriff Kern never stopped by to tell me who you were when he recognized you."

"Just because he didn't feel he could divulge another man's secrets doesn't mean he won't hold your needs close to his heart."

"Are you on my side or his?" She paused, then asked quietly, "Or are you still more worried about dispelling military secrets than being completely honest with me?"

In spite of himself, he flinched. "We are all on the same side, Miranda. I promise you this." Leaning forward, he rested his elbows on his knees. "If you believe anything I say, please know that you can trust Jess Kern, Miranda."

She bit her lip. "All this sounds too good to be true."

Perhaps it was. No doubt something would go wrong in their plan to follow up on their suspicions, and there would be snags.

When she moved to stand and dismiss him, he held up a hand.

"I know you would like me to leave, but we still need to talk about the original reason I came in here."

"I cannot discuss that with you."

"I feel differently. Your staff is concerned about you. They are very worried about you."

"I . . ." She swallowed. "My personal problems are not their concern."

It would be so easy to accept her statement. To promise that he would alleviate her worries and then be on his way.

But he had begun to see that he cared about her too much now. She'd become not a mission but a reason to get through each day. In short, she had bewitched him.

Perhaps it was time to see if she, too, was under such a spell. Looking at her closely, he took care to be blunt. Jarring. "I have heard you have been depressed. Beyond depressed." He lowered his voice. "Some might even say suicidal. You said yourself that you have not wanted to live. Do you want to die?"

She gasped, but said nothing.

Robert took her silence as an invitation to push even more. "Miranda, do you, in fact, want to die?"

"I cannot believe you asked me that."

"Yet you didn't answer." Staring at her coolly, he said, "And that, Miranda, is why I am here."

She met his gaze. Stared hard at him. Then got to her feet and strode toward the window and pressed her hands on the cool glass.

If she thought he was going to leave now, then she was sadly mistaken. He was willing to sit on the lumpy settee and stare at her back for as long as it took to get some answers.

After all, as far as he was concerned, that was the real reason he was on Galveston Island. Beyond his loyalty to his unit, beyond his promise to her husband, Robert had agreed to this mission because he needed to know more about himself.

He needed to understand why he'd done the things he'd done and why he'd survived.

He needed to understand why he had been able to get a job and finally flourish while so many men were still suffering from wounds and mental anguish. He needed to understand what was in his soul and in his heart. Only then, at long last, would he be able to find any peace.

14

Do you want to die?

The question was blunt and bordering on blasphemy. It was one she felt no one should ever ask.

Yet Miranda had a feeling she might be the only person on earth who was afraid to answer it.

Which was the problem, Miranda realized. She'd been drifting in and out of her pain for so long, she'd begun to wear her depression like a mantle on her shoulders. After the mind-numbing grief she'd felt from Phillip's death had begun to fade, she'd been at a loss for what to do about her future. For too many years she'd felt confused and adrift.

But she'd had her home. Phillip's mother and sister were bitterly hurt that Phillip had made provisions to ensure she would always have the house as her home and not his family. But then she learned they were working with lawyers to try to contest Phillip's will, and she'd known she must do something.

When Winifred and Emerson, her longtime servants, had suggested that she turn the big mansion into a boardinghouse as a way to solve her financial problems, she'd first been aghast. Phillip would have never wanted her to live with strangers. He had often told her he liked taking care of her and seeing to her needs, much to his mother's dismay.

Miranda couldn't come to terms with the idea of converting his family's home into a place of work. But when their lawyer's letters had gotten forceful enough for Miranda to have to hire her own to fight them, the little money she had left began to run out.

Uncovering a force of will she hadn't even known had existed inside of her, she'd known it was time to take action. Therefore, she'd followed Winifred and Emerson's advice and opened the Iron Rail to boarders.

Oh, but those first few days after she'd placed that advertisement had been nerve-racking! Many of their friends had been scandalized, and acquaintances who had always looked down on her because she was not from Galveston blatantly turned their backs on her. Doubts had begun to set in.

She'd been sure she'd done something unforgiveable.

But then, one Tuesday, two things happened within three hours of each other. She'd received a telegram reserving a room for two weeks. Moments later, a gentleman had showed up and asked for a room for the evening. God had provided.

He'd paid when he arrived and had been both extremely respectful of her and appreciative of the mansion.

Winifred had cooked him a simple supper and Emerson had shined his boots. And in the morning he'd not only left a sizable tip, but promised he would return . . . and spread the word about her charming establishment.

And with his departure, she'd realized there was a chance that she was going to be okay after all. She'd started to think of herself as a survivor. She wasn't broken; she was mending. She was going to make Phillip proud.

However, she soon received her first threatening letter. The words had been ugly and cruel. That note had torn her apart and had reminded her of just how alone in the world she was.

But boarders and guests had continued to come and their company had soothed her soul. Until the letters came every week and the animosity she felt from everyone in her circle of friends had become more intense as rumors about both Phillip and her spread.

She hadn't understood it. Couldn't think of what she had possibly done to deserve such ire, such treatment. Why did everyone believe these lies? She even asked her best friend, Mercy, about it. Mercy had been by her side when she'd married Phillip, had held her hand when she'd first heard that Phillip had been captured.

She'd stayed with Miranda for days after they learned he'd died.

Miranda had turned to Mercy when Mr. Winter had first leered at her and the first time two women she'd known walked by her without acknowledging her. Almost as if she were a fallen woman.

But as she'd confided all her fears and worries to her best friend, a change had occurred. Instead of being supportive and optimistic, Mercy's expression had become shuttered. Instead of offering Miranda advice, Mercy had shuttled her out of her house.

And then had become as distant and aloof as everyone else.

That betrayal had been so difficult, almost as if she were experiencing another death. But this time, there seemed to be no one around her to lean on. Somehow, for some reason, she was all alone.

She'd begun a downward spiral after that, and it had culminated with the morning she'd not only contemplated jumping from the window, but gone so far as to open the pane.

But yet . . . she hadn't jumped.

Did that mean something? Did that mean she cared enough about her life to keep it? Or was she merely too afraid about failing in her suicide attempt?

Only to herself had she been able to admit that she hadn't been sure.

But now, with Robert staring at her, practically willing her to confront the truth, even when it was so shameful that she knew she'd barely been able to admit it to herself, she yearned to say that she did not want to die.

She blinked. Realizing that she felt more certain about that than ever before. She did not want to die. She wanted to breathe and walk and talk to other people and plan.

And even remember.

"I . . ." Perversely, the words felt stuck on the tip of her tongue. It was as if her brain was telling her one thing but her mouth was completely incapable of following its directions.

Still Robert watched her.

His attention, so intent, so unwavering, made her lungs tighten. It made her pulse skitter and race in a panic.

Abruptly, she looked at him, afraid he was going to stare at her impatiently. Show her that he was like everyone else in her life. Remind her that she wasn't worth his time, his conversation, or even his compassion.

But when their eyes met, she saw only acceptance. And patience. He wasn't waiting for her to be a different person. No, he was simply waiting for her to find herself.

That enabled her to find her bearings. She breathed deeply and forced herself to concentrate on this moment. Not the past, not an uncertain future.

Buoyed by that, she gathered herself and breathed in deeply. Finding success, she inhaled again. And felt hope.

It was as if God had finally spoken to her and blessed her. He'd taken so much, but he'd given her this man.

Oh, she didn't expect Robert to stick around. She didn't

expect him to even become her friend. But he was there for her at that moment, and the feeling of happiness that accompanied it was so sweet she almost felt giddy.

Suddenly, Miranda knew she had to tell Robert about her thoughts and her worries. About her hopes too. She had to convince him that she wasn't as bad off as everyone feared.

And, she realized, she had to convince herself that she was worth his time and attention. Somewhere inside of herself she was the same person she'd always been. The girl who had met handsome Phillip Markham at a soldiers' ball and enchanted him. The girl who had bravely hugged her husband with a bright smile before he went off to war, not wanting his last memory of her to be one of tears.

Suddenly, she was living, breathing, feeling.

She was alive.

"I do not want to die," she said at last. "I . . . I, well, for a time, I wasn't so sure about that, but now I realize I want to live this life that was given to me. Even if it's not perfect." She closed her eyes. Had there ever been a greater understatement? "I mean, even if it is painful, right now I realize I want to feel that pain."

Slowly, he got to his feet. Looked at her steadily. And finally nodded. "Good."

She thought he was going to turn around. She was certain he was ready to leave the room. Be rid of her now that he wasn't afraid she was going to jump or collapse or do whatever else he imagined she was on the verge of.

But he didn't do that at all.

"It's going to be all right, Miranda," he murmured as he approached her. "You are not alone any longer. I will not leave you to face everything by yourself," he said as he carefully wrapped his arms around her.

"I, too, have suffered, but I got stronger. You will get stronger too," he whispered as he brought her into his embrace and held her close.

His warmth, his very being, felt so comforting that she allowed herself to relax. With great deliberation, she placed one hand around his waist, then the other. Leaned her cheek against his clean, starched shirt.

And clung to him.

Robert Truax, former second lieutenant in the C.S.A. and comrade of Phillip's, had become important to her. Not just because he was a handsome man. Not just because he had almost become a friend.

But because he believed in her.

And because right then, right at that moment, she believed in herself too.

She wasn't perfect, but she was alive.

She wasn't strong, but she could be.

She wasn't happy, but she had hope.

Furthermore, she was standing. She was blessed. She was being held.

She had not fallen yet.

15

IT WAS NEVER EASY TO ASK FOR HELP. HOWEVER, ROBERT
had learned the hard way that it was far more difficult to face the
consequences of failing by himself.

Because of that, combined with last night's memory of holding Miranda Markham fairly burning in his chest, he'd pulled out
his quill and forced himself to compose the letter he hadn't wanted
to write. Jess was now an ally, but Robert needed more.

> I have learned, sir, that Mrs. Markham's difficulties are even
> worse than I had surmised. I have told you that her friends
> have abandoned her, even her best friend. Men who are so far
> beneath her that they should be doing nothing but begging
> for a kind smile are treating her as a pariah. Now I've learned
> that she has been receiving threatening letters for a year and is
> being blackmailed with the threat of some kind of false proof
> that Phillip was a traitor. All that on top of insinuations that
> she has dishonored her husband with other men.
>
> In addition, she is still recovering from the loss of her
> husband.
>
> In summation, she is a woman who has been through too
> much and has almost given up hope.

As Robert stared at his last sentence, his handwriting barely legible with poor penmanship and hopelessly cramped, he found himself smiling.

Because he'd been able to add one single word that changed everything.

That "almost" meant the difference between a chance of optimism and the knowledge that there was very little anyone was going to be able to do for Miranda Markham.

Last night, she'd realized she had much to live for.

When he'd thrown caution to the wind and enfolded her in his arms, she'd clung to him. That moment, that experience of holding her close, smelling her sweet scent, of knowing that she trusted him when she trusted so few . . . well, it had changed him.

Over the last two weeks, Robert's goals had changed. He'd come to Galveston to honor his friend, to fulfill a promise he'd made to a dying man whom he greatly admired. Then he'd gotten to know Miranda. Little by little, he'd begun to understand Phillip's fascination with his wife. Then, practically out of the blue, he'd felt a tenderness toward her that had nothing to do with dark promises and everything to do with the woman he couldn't seem to take his eyes off.

He'd become smitten. No, entranced. She was a wonder. No, wonderful. He now wanted to make her happy. Not because he could ease her problems but because he, Robert Truax, was a man she had come to admire too.

He wasn't necessarily proud of his feelings. Part of him felt like he was betraying a close friend's trust. However, the greater part of him, the part that had survived life on the streets and a long war, was far more pragmatic. Life was meant for surviving. And sometimes, if a person was blessed, he might experience love too.

Blinking, he pushed last night's memories from his mind and refocused on his report to Captain Monroe.

Because of the wealth of her problems, and because I did not at first tell Miranda my connection to Phillip and have for the time being lost some of her trust, I feel I must stay here even longer. The sheriff here is Jess Kern. Though I do not remember him, he tells me that he, too, was imprisoned at Johnson's Island the same time we were. He has fostered a tenuous friendship with Miranda. I believe he sincerely wants to uncover the author of the threatening letters, and I have taken him into our confidence. Not about everything, of course, but about our mission to help Miranda. I trust him.

Taking all the above into account, I am humbly asking for assistance, Captain. I fear if I continue to navigate her problems single-handedly in light of all you and I know, there is a chance of failure.

We both know that is not an option. Please advise at your earliest opportunity.

Yours respectfully,
Robert

After marking and sealing the letter, Robert addressed it neatly, blotted the ink, and walked downstairs.

To his surprise, he didn't come across Miranda, any of her servants, or even another guest. In fact, it was unusually quiet for eleven in the morning.

He wondered why. He knew enough about the workings of the house to have a pretty good idea of what everyone usually did at this time of day. Actually, this late-morning hour was one of the busiest. Winnie and Belle cleaned rooms and Emerson was either cleaning fireplaces, washing windows, or tending to the winter garden outside.

Miranda herself spent her time working in her parlor, answering correspondence or greeting new guests. Not that he had seen more than one other guest the entire time he had been there.

But there was no sign of anyone anywhere.

His curiosity was slowly being replaced by worry and a vague sense of trepidation. Stuffing the letter in his vest pocket, Robert headed toward the kitchen. Perhaps Cook had prepared some jam tarts or some other delicacy and they were sampling the items. Miranda had told him that happened from time to time.

Just outside the kitchen, he heard voices. He breathed a sigh of relief and congratulated himself on not jumping to conclusions and making things seem worse than they were.

Opening the door, he grinned. "Cook, what treat have you made today? And please tell me you saved me a sample," he called out.

Then he froze.

Miranda and her four servants were standing together and staring at a pair of thin women dressed in unrelieved black. One was older and looked to be in frail health. She was sitting on one of the hard kitchen chairs, grasping the armrests as if she was using them to keep herself upright.

The other woman had dark hair and hazel eyes. High cheekbones. She looked like the feminine version of Phillip Markham.

But that was where the similarities ended. Whereas Phillip always had a smile on his face and a rather easygoing patience about him, this woman was birdlike and sharp and agitated.

She was also staring at him in the way he'd always looked at two of their Yankee guards. Those men had been sloth-like and unkempt. Unfit and undisciplined. They were men who would have done poorly in Monroe's unit, and presumably weren't even fit for fighting in the Union army since they'd been able-bodied and designated to serving on an island in the middle of the Great Lakes.

Because he was as different from those men as night and day, Robert raised his chin and boldly stared right back at the woman. Phillip had never told him he had living relatives, and why had Miranda not mentioned these two?

"Who are you?" the younger one asked rudely.

Before he could answer, Miranda walked to his side. "This is Robert Truax, Viola," she said in a tremor-filled voice. "He served with Phillip."

Viola scanned him with disdain. "What is he doing here?"

"He is staying as a guest," Miranda said quickly. "I believe he has some business to tend to here in Galveston."

She was attempting to shield him, Robert realized with a bit of shock. Miranda was trying to shield him from these two spiteful women.

He would have been amused if he hadn't been so sincerely touched. He was six foot one, was well muscled, and had been blessed with a bright mind. He'd grown up unafraid to use his fists to get what he wanted.

In addition, he had been an officer in the Confederate militia. He was used to commanding scores of men. He was used to being the person doing the shielding and guarding.

On top of that, he'd made himself into a gentleman. He prided himself on his ability to shelter the weaker sex.

He accepted that and had enjoyed the feeling of worth that had given him.

He did not enjoy the sight of Miranda fretting about him.

"Yet another man ruining your reputation, I see," the old lady muttered.

When Miranda shook her head and visibly prepared herself to respond, Robert had had enough. "To whom am I speaking?" he asked curtly, in the same tone he'd used to snap at insolent corporals during training exercises.

When the lady did not answer, only inhaled sharply, Miranda once again rushed to the rescue. "Forgive my poor manners. Robert, may I present Viola and Ruth Markham, Phillip's sister and mother. Ladies, as I said, this is Robert Truax. He was one of Phillip's fellow officers in the C.S.A. and one of his best friends. He was also captured and imprisoned at Johnson's Island."

The elder Mrs. Markham sniffed. "But you lived."

It seemed her audacity knew no bounds. Lifting his chin, he stared at her directly. "Indeed, I did."

Noticing that Miranda was wringing her hands, he looked at the servants. All four of them were wearing pinched, uncertain expressions.

That made no sense. He knew enough about the management of a household to realize that a mistress's ill-behaved guest had little effect on the state of the servants. Even as close as their bond was with Miranda, there was no reason, as far as he could see, for why they were standing in the kitchen and looking so awkward and nervous.

"Why is everyone in the kitchen?"

"It is no concern of yours, boy," Viola said.

Before Miranda could run interference again, he spoke. "No one has dared to call me that since I was old enough to make sure they regretted it, Miss Markham. I have no intention to begin accepting it now."

Viola flinched, but otherwise had no response.

"Viola and Mrs. Markham arrived an hour ago, sir. They came to share with me that their lawyer has discovered a way to take the house away from me." After visibly gathering her composure, she added, "After this announcement they insisted on a tour of the home."

"A tour? If this was your son's, I am sure you know it well."

"Mrs. Markham wanted to meet the staff. Her new staff."

"We were interviewing them to see if they have any qualities that would necessitate them staying," Viola said with a note of satisfaction in her voice.

"Is that right?" he drawled.

Miranda's eyes flashed. "I put a stop to it." Her voice turned to ice. "As a matter of fact, I was just attempting to tell them that this was not settled when you came in."

"No, it does not seem settled at all," he agreed as he noticed that both Viola and her mother looked terribly uncomfortable. And Miranda? Well, Miranda looked madder than a wet hen.

Robert was so proud of her. This was the first time, at least in his presence, when she had believed in herself enough to stand up to the naysayers. It proved that she truly had had a transformation the evening before. But again, why hadn't she told him about these two presenting yet another threat to her well-being?

He hated that he couldn't smile at her and tell her how proud of her he was. Instead, he did something that was probably even better, and that was to succinctly inform these two biddies that they were mistaken about the house becoming theirs. Miranda and her staff needed them off the property as soon as possible.

"Miranda was Phillip's beloved wife," he said.

"She was his wife," Mrs. Markham said. "She was also his mistake."

Miranda shook her head. "No, that is not true."

When the old lady inhaled sharply, Robert hardened his voice. "You can say many things, ma'am, but you will never be able to deny your son's complete and utter devotion to Miranda. He adored her. He carried her picture around on his person and gazed at it constantly. He wrote to her daily. And when he wasn't doing those things, he was talking about her. She was his world."

Mrs. Markham looked like she'd just swallowed a particularly sour pickle. "She might have been those things, but she has since become his liability."

"Never that." He made sure to interject enough force in his words to cut off any further discussion, at least there in the kitchen. "Now, I suggest we leave this room and allow Miranda's staff to continue with their duties."

"You are overstepping your bounds, sir," Mrs. Markham said.

"I think not."

Just as the lady was about to speak, Miranda cut in. "Everyone, it is time for this discussion to end. Robert, thank you for joining us, but I feel we all have better uses of our time than continuing this debate. Viola and Ruth, if you would like to stay here for the night, please let Winifred know. She will take you up to your rooms. Otherwise, I fear you have outstayed your welcome. It is time for you both to take your leave."

Ruth got to her feet. When Robert attempted to offer her his hand, she batted it away.

"What about your staff?" Viola asked.

Turning to the four people who were still standing in a small row but now wearing far more relaxed expressions, Miranda said, "Do you need directions for your duties?"

"No, ma'am, we do not," Winnie said with a glare at the two interlopers.

"Very well then," Miranda replied. "Ladies, if you will follow me, please?"

Though Viola looked ready to argue, her mother walked toward the door. Robert stood to one side as Miranda led the ladies out of the kitchen, down the short gap between the kitchen and main house, and finally inside again.

When they heard the last door click shut, Robert turned to the servants. "How bad was it?"

"Not as bad as it could have been," Belle said.

"Do they come here often?"

"They used to come once a month," Emerson replied. "But it's been almost six months since they stopped by. I suppose they were due to make an appearance."

Winnie shook her head. "They're up to something. They must feel that they have something with that lawyer."

Belle shivered dramatically. "I am not going to be able to work for those biddies."

"You won't have to worry about them," Cook said. "They're gonna fire us right away. They're not going to want anyone who was loyal to Mrs. Markham. Mrs. Miranda Markham, I mean."

"I fear you are right," Robert agreed. "However, try not to let their visit worry you too much. Something about their confidence didn't sit well with me. I'll look into it."

"All I can say is that Mr. Phillip would be rolling over in his grave if he knew how his mother and sister were treating his wife. He treated her like gold, he did."

"I wasn't aware that you had worked here when Phillip lived here."

"I've been here for years. Mr. Phillip hired me when he first inherited the mansion. Emerson too. I was here when he brought home his bride, and thank goodness his mother and sister had already moved out."

"Besotted, he was," Emerson said.

Winnie shook her head. "They were in love. He doted on her.

And Miss Miranda? Well, she was a sweet little blushing thing. Remember, Audrey?"

Cook fanned her face. "Don't want to shock you, Mr. Truax, but Mr. and Mrs. Markham only had eyes—and hands—for each other. Practically spent their first week of married life in their room."

Robert laughed. "It's going to take more than the amorous affections of a newly married couple to shock me, Winnie!" Sobering, he said, "Your description doesn't sound much like the lady I've met."

"She was hard hit by him going off to war. He came back three times, but each time he returned, he looked more weary and thin. And, I am afraid, more distant. She worried about him fiercely. Then when word came about his imprisonment and then death . . . well, she changed."

"And his family didn't support her?"

"No. The older Mrs. Markham had a different woman in mind for Phillip. When he ignored her wishes, she wasn't happy. Then when he was on leave, he didn't want to give them any time at all and they resented it," Winnie said. "But they were still respectful to her."

"But when the lawyer read the will, everything changed."

"They became mean as snakes, they did," Winnie said. "To our Mrs. Markham and to us."

"I was afraid to be in the same room as them!" Belle said.

Robert didn't even try to hide his smile. "I can imagine why."

"Do you truly think you can help our mistress with them?" Winnie asked.

"Yes," he said after a pause. He almost said he would try his best. Then he realized that such a promise was not only going to mean little, it wasn't true. He'd come here to make Miranda Markham's life better and he was going to do that. If he couldn't handle these women and their lawyer by himself, he would contact as many of his fellow comrades as it took. They'd made each other a promise to see their lives through and he intended to do just that.

No one had ever claimed their journeys would be easy. On the contrary, no one had imagined it would be. Monroe had practically guaranteed that the road to recovering their lives after the war would be anything but simple or quick.

But after the things they'd been through, Robert felt he probably wouldn't even trust something simple or quick. Experience had shown that trial and pain and patience and hard work were what guaranteed success.

That was what he understood and had faith in.

"Now, I had best see how Mrs. Markham is doing with her relatives. Winnie, if you would accompany me, please? If the women are staying, we'll need you to see to that."

"Yes, sir," Winnie said as she bustled to his side. "Though, if I may be so bold, I have to tell ya that I don't think they'll be staying."

"You sound certain," he commented as he opened the back door to the kitchen and ushered the portly housekeeper through.

"I am." With a look of distaste, she added, "They come here to make her miserable, they do. If she's turned the tables on them, then their fun ain't going to be the same. They'll head back to their own home."

Opening the door to the main house, something occurred to Robert. Before they entered the doorway, he said, "Winnie, it just occurred to me that I don't know where they live. Are they on the island?"

She shook her head. "No, they live just on the other side of the bay. They'll have to take the ferry across. But if they can't take it today, they'll stay somewhere else."

"Such as?"

"One of the elder Mrs. Markham's friends. I believe she has at least one or two who haven't turned against her because of the rumors about her son."

Now that they were in the back hallway in the main house, he lowered his voice. "Do you know these friends of hers? Do you know anything about them?"

"I know staff at a couple of their houses, but we don't speak much to each other. Not anymore."

"Did they not have use for you after the rumors began or did you choose not to associate with them?"

"We chose not to associate with them, of course."

Robert shook his head. "I'm sorry. I was a soldier for years. I have no knowledge of what it is like to be a gossiping woman, or to have a staff to do that."

"It's like this, sir. Mr. Markham being thought of as a traitor is a terrible thing. But no one seems to know how such a rumor started. And Mrs. Markham's disintegrating reputation is difficult to hear but not so hard to believe. But her actions weren't what started the mean talk. And these threatening letters . . . well, they're filled with information that shows the writer knew a lot. A whole lot."

Now Robert wished he and Jess had asked to see all the letters.

Lifting her eyes to his meaningfully, she said, "All that got me to thinking about who has the most to gain from all this talk."

"I see," he said. "Any idea who it is?"

"Well, I've got my ideas, and they begin and end with the two women who were sitting in that kitchen like they have any business even to step foot in it."

"Do you think Mrs. Markham suspects them?"

"No, sir. I don't think any of us has imagined Lt. Markham's own family would want to hurt his reputation. But they do have resentments about this house."

"Thank you for your honesty, Winnie."

"No, sir. Thank you for caring."

Stunned at how much her words meant to him, he strode into the mansion's foyer. He'd intended to go up the stairs and knock on Miranda's door, but there was no need. She was standing by the front window, her focus completely fixed on the two women's retreating forms.

"Did they leave, Miranda? Or have they simply gone outside to tell their driver and collect their belongings?"

She turned his way. "They are gone," she said with a bit of wonder in her voice. Then, still gazing at him, she smiled.

Truly smiled. It was beautiful.

16

Though she couldn't exactly be sure, Miranda knew there had been a time when she had neither trusted nor loved Phillip Markham wholeheartedly. She was old enough and wise enough now to realize that love was not instantaneous.

It just was sometimes difficult to remember such a time.

She recalled their initial meeting as clearly as if it were yesterday. She'd gone in her family's carriage with her cousin Beatrice to Houston. After hours of primping and prepping, they walked into the assembly hall fairly bursting with exuberance.

An orchestra was playing, flowers were planted in vases, and there were so many men in resplendent gray and gold that Bea had actually gasped at the sight. And in the middle of it all was Phillip.

He had recently graduated from West Point. In addition, his family had purchased him commissions. Therefore, he was a striking, young second lieutenant who was a little in awe of his company when she and her cousin entered.

He and several men his age were talking to a pair of older-looking officers next to a table laden with lemonade and cookies. His hands were loosely clasped behind his back, and he was nodding at something one of the older men was saying.

Miranda thought he was the most handsome man there.

"Oh! There's James!" Beatrice had squealed.

Miranda giggled when Bea practically dragged her across the room toward the men. "Watch out, Beatrice," she'd cautioned. But in truth, she hadn't minded getting pulled along. The men they were approaching were handsome, debonair, and close to their ages.

They were also standing conveniently far from the long line of seated chaperones. The older women were gossiping and sipping tea. No doubt feeling they had fulfilled their duties by simply showing up.

Walking toward the young officers by her cousin's side, Miranda had felt so grown up and full of herself. At last she was in the big city. She was dressed like a lady and even had her hair styled into an elegant twist. She had on a tight corset that reduced her waist to nineteen inches and enough crinolines and petticoats under her skirt to feel as if she were floating instead of merely walking. She wasn't a particularly vain girl, but she knew she had never looked so fine.

And then Phillip lifted his head and looked her way. He had curly blond hair, light blue eyes, and dimples. She thought he looked like an angel. And then he smiled at her.

And she? Well, she lost her heart right then and there.

The rest of the night was a blur of emotion. He bowed gallantly when they were introduced. She stammered and pretended she wasn't affected. When he immediately asked for her dance card and filled in his name in three places, she stopped pretending and enjoyed the attention.

Dancing in his arms had surpassed every girlish dream. He held her properly and sure, his right hand curving protectively on her waist. In between dances, he stood on the side and watched her dance with his friends. She'd had no experience in courtship or relationships, but even she knew he'd marked her as his.

And instead of being dismayed or afraid, she'd been glad.

After their three dances and countless glasses of lemonade and one long stroll along the building's back balcony, it was time to go. And then he raised her gloved hand to his lips and pressed his lips to her knuckles. She was so entranced she wished she could feel his touch on her bare skin.

Miranda had no doubt she would have stayed with Phillip until dawn broke if not for Beatrice and her mother's insistence that it was time to leave.

But when she finally turned away from him, trying not to cry, Miranda knew that in that one evening she had forever changed. Phillip Markham might not have been perfect, but he'd been perfect for her. And by the time they settled back into their awaiting carriage Miranda knew she had fallen in love.

In fact, Miranda had known without a shadow of a doubt that if he had proposed to her that evening she would have said yes.

She did say yes not even one month later and they were married the very next day. Her love for Phillip had been wild and overwhelming and all-consuming.

And then, of course, he went to war, and the battles that no one expected to happen did. Phillip fought and marched and commanded men. He'd been imprisoned and finally gone to heaven.

And she learned that just as nothing ever began from nothing, nothing ever lasted forever.

Now, as she looked at Robert Truax standing in the foyer of her boardinghouse so seriously, Miranda didn't know if she was falling in love. Part of her hoped that certainly wasn't the case. If she was falling in love, why, it made no sense.

Robert was nothing like Phillip. He was hard and bull-nosed where Phillip had been caring and amiable. He was rough around the edges where Phillip had always been smooth elegance. He was also direct and blunt and loud and willful. She'd suspected Phillip was many of those things as well, but he'd always taken care to shield her from his baser emotions and actions.

Robert may have secrets, but he didn't hide anything he was.

For some reason, she found his honesty about himself strangely compelling. Attractive.

He was also going to move on one day soon. Even if he asked, Miranda wasn't sure if she'd leave with him. As hard as her life had been in Galveston, it was also her home.

All she currently understood was that she needed Robert right now. She was grateful for his presence, she liked being in his company, and she was tired of pretending that she didn't care about him.

Noticing that he was still standing still, his expression carefully void of any emotion, she walked to him.

Knowing he was still reeling from her in-laws' visit, she attempted to lighten the mood. "Before they left, my mother-in-law said I was a sinner and an embarrassment to the Markham name." She smiled slightly so he would know that she wasn't too terribly hurt by the hateful statement.

But instead of looking amused, a muscle in his jaw clenched. "And Viola? What did she say?"

"I believe it was something to the effect that she was glad her brother had died so he would not be able to witness the type of woman his wife has become." She did her best to remain looking amused, though Viola's words had been difficult to hear.

Robert sighed. "Miranda, I have heard a lot in my lifetime. But I have to tell you that I've never been forced to listen to any statements more appalling."

"It wasn't that bad. You've been on the battlefield, after all."

"I've also lived on the streets. But try as I might, I can't think of any person who would target a lady such as you with such purposely cruel words." His voice lowered. "I beg your pardon, but I don't believe I had ever had the misfortune to meet such ill-mannered women in my life before today."

Though the women's words did pinch her feelings, Miranda realized they hadn't devastated her. Furthermore, she couldn't help but agree with his assessment.

"They certainly did come here with cruel intentions. I think they would have fired my whole staff and put them on the streets if they had been able to." Thinking of how upset and dismayed they looked, she added, "I'm going to need to visit with them later and assure them that even if the worst happens I'll look after them as best I can."

Robert began pacing. "Have they always treated you as such?"

"No. They were nicer when Phillip was alive. But they were always rather judgmental, I'm afraid. As I told you, I didn't have a lot of city polish and Phillip was quite a catch. They never thought I was good enough."

"They were wrong. Phillip Markham was a man of many good qualities, and as far as I can tell, you are his equal in every way."

"I don't know if that is quite the case, but it is very kind of you to say. For what it's worth, Phillip was never particularly close to them. They didn't visit all that often."

Robert paused to stare at her. "I can't imagine that he would have wanted them here. What's more, I shudder at how he would have reacted if he'd witnessed such a scene. The man I was honored to know wouldn't have allowed any person to speak to you in such a manner."

"Well, they wouldn't have spoken to me that way if he was here."

Robert resumed his pacing. "I can't believe he comes from that same family! The women were cold hearted and vindictive. Even when we were in prison, I never heard Phillip speak unkindly to anyone." For the first time, humor entered his features. "Not even the guards." He waved a hand. "Why, even when he was bossing us around, he was a gentleman. It used to annoy me to no end."

"I imagine it would have. You don't seem like the kind of man to say please and thank you while being told to march."

He chuckled. "I'm afraid I wasn't that kind of man even on my best days. And that, of course, is why Phillip was about to be made captain and I was advised to shape up and quickly." At last, he stopped pacing and leaned against the banister leading upstairs.

"The problem, I believe, is that Mrs. Markham never wanted Phillip to marry me. She wanted him to marry one of the local girls."

"Instead, he chose you."

"He did. We had a whirlwind courtship. I think she might have come to accept me if Phillip had taken more of a concern for her feelings. I learned after Phillip brought me here that Ruth was hurt that he hadn't brought me to her for approval before he proposed."

"I wonder why he didn't do that."

"There wasn't time." Feeling her cheeks flush, she corrected herself. "Rather, we didn't make time. We fell in love almost on sight and corresponded with each other for barely one month before he proposed. Actually, the moment he was given permission to obtain a week's leave, Phillip came to my house, informed my parents that he couldn't go into battle without making me his wife, and literally whisked me away."

Robert fanned his face dramatically. "My goodness. Who knew Phillip had such impetuousness in him?"

"I suppose I did."

"Your romance sounds like a fairy tale. It's good your parents gave their permission." He paused. "I'm assuming they did give their permission?"

She nodded. "My father said he and my mother worried that I'd simply elope if they didn't give their blessing."

Robert raised both his eyebrows. "I guess you both were rather willful back then."

"Oh, yes. Seriously, I think they would have been shocked if it hadn't been Phillip. But it was." She shrugged. She had never been one to make the deceased into saints or paint them as perfect. But Phillip actually had been very close to perfect. "We got married that evening in Houston and he brought me here the next day. His mother and sister knew what he was going to do, and they left the premises immediately. My mother had all my things delivered here over the next few weeks, and we packed up theirs and sent them to their new home across the bay."

He stared at her for a long moment. "You are blessed to have known such love, Miranda."

"Yes, I am."

"Before all this hullabaloo, I came downstairs to post a letter. Would you care to accompany me?" His voice gentled. "We could take care of your weekly deposit at the bank as well."

"Yes, thank you. I would like to accompany you very much," she admitted. Perhaps it was time to reclaim a little bit of that impetuousness she once had.

Looking down at the gown she was wearing, she knew it wouldn't do. "Robert, would you be able to wait a few minutes? I need to change my gown. I promise I'll hurry."

For the first time since he walked into the foyer, something tender entered his expression. "Mrs. Markham, I may not be the gentleman Phillip Markham was, but even I know never to rush a woman." They had stepped from the foyer into the parlor, and now he walked over to one of the wing chairs situated in front of the for-once roaring fireplace. "I'll cool my heels here as long as you need. So take your time."

The absurdity of his words made her flirt a bit. "Your offer is very gallant, Mr. Truax. However, I'll do my best to make sure your heels don't have too long to cool in front of the flames."

He laughed. "Touché, madam."

His laughter rang in her ears the whole way upstairs.

Even though she'd told him she wouldn't take long, Miranda still tarried. For some reason, she decided her chignon wasn't pinned right. And then she had to try on two different hats.

Finally, she had to collect her latest monies to deposit. She had had even less business than normal, which meant that she had an even smaller amount than usual. If not for Robert's payment, her financial situation would have fallen into even further precarious territory.

Therefore, it was a full forty minutes later when she returned downstairs. "I do beg your pardon. Here I promised I would be quick and I took an even longer time than I usually do."

"I still didn't mind." Walking to the wardrobe, he pulled out her cloak. "Now, let's get you as warm as possible. I do believe there was frost on the ground this morning."

She doubted that, but she allowed him to assist her with her cloak. Moments later, they were walking together toward town. She wasn't clutching his arm, but she might as well have been.

The last time they'd walked together, she had been nervous and tense. Worried about not only everyone around them but also Robert himself. People like Kyle Winter and Mercy had tainted her trust. She'd been afraid of him and couldn't bear to believe anything he said.

Now, however, she felt as if he was her one true ally.

Whether from Robert's appearance or if her time of purgatory had finally ended, several men and women acknowledged her. Oh, they didn't actually greet her and stop to pass the time, but they didn't ignore her completely like they usually did.

The idea that she no longer was going to be despised made her feel like laughing. She settled for a bright smile.

Robert noticed. "What's that smile for? Did I do something to earn it?"

"Maybe." Looking up at him, she said, "Today is the first day in memory that no one on the streets has been treating me like an outcast. I am very happy about that. And I suspect it is because of you standing up for me."

"It's about time that nonsense ended, ma'am. You never were a pariah in the first place."

"Perhaps, but for some reason, people seem nicer. I am glad of that."

His lips curved up. "You, Mrs. Markham, are too easy to please."

"Don't get your hopes up," she teased. "I am only feeling that way this afternoon. Tonight, I feel certain everything and everyone will cause me to complain."

"I'll do my best to stay far away from you this evening then," he said as they stopped at a corner.

She was just about to tell him she wouldn't dare be mean to her social savior when her former best friend walked to her side.

Though it was tempting to say nothing—after all, that was what Mercy had done to her time and again—Miranda didn't want to create an awkward situation. "Hello, Mercy," she said at last. "I trust you are doing well?"

Mercy barely inclined her head. "Mrs. Markham."

When her gaze flickered over to Robert and stilled, he bowed ever so slightly.

"Ma'am."

"Sir, I'm afraid I have not had the pleasure of your acquaintance."

Though she had a feeling she was about to regret it, Miranda performed the introductions. "Mercy, may I present Mr. Robert Truax? He served with my husband in the war. Robert, this is Mrs. Jackson."

"Sir."

He bowed slightly. "Mrs. Jackson."

Mercy tilted her head to one side. "I haven't seen much of you of late, Miranda. Have you become even more a recluse?"

"I suppose I have."

"Perhaps we shall see more of you, now that you have decided to walk the streets with your boarders." She paused. "Or shall I say, too much of you?"

Before Miranda could give that the dignity of a reply, Robert took her elbow. "We should be on our way, Miranda. Let's go while there's a break in the traffic."

"Yes, of course." She allowed him to guide her forward, then started to look back to see if Mercy followed or what expression she was wearing.

"Don't look back."

"I'm only looking to see—"

"Don't. Forget about her."

"I cannot. You see—"

He cut her off again, his voice firm. "You can forget her, Miranda. It's possible. You owe her nothing."

She wondered what kind of man he was. Did he go through life firmly forgetting past friendships? Was that how a man survived without parents to guide him or protect him? "Robert, it isn't quite that easy. You see, she was my best friend for years. We were once quite close."

"If that is truly the case, then that is even more of a reason for you not to be kind to her now. She should have stayed loyal to you." He leaned down closer. "Miranda, she had a choice to make when your troubles started. She could have put you first or put you last. We both know what she did."

It was hard to hear about Mercy's actions in such stark terms. "I wish she had chosen my friendship over the gossip she heard."

"You do?" He looked down at her and smiled softly. Then, to her surprise, he ran two fingers along the slope of her jaw. Right there on the street! "Well, that makes two of us."

Before she could comment on that, he sighed dramatically. "Now that we've taken care of your former best friend, let us tackle the bank and the weasel otherwise known as Mr. Winter before we post my letter at the mercantile."

She dared to smile. Truly, he was being outrageous. "Goodness. He's a weasel now?"

"More or less. Other names are more fitting, but alas, they are not for your ears."

"I've noticed that you are not afraid to put everyone in their place today."

"Yes, it is true. Unlike you, it seems everyone has gotten on my nerves today. I have lost patience with Galveston Island's general population."

"I had better watch myself, then."

"No, my dear." Taking her elbow to carefully guide her up the steps, he said, "Be assured that you have nothing to worry about. There isn't a thing you could do to lower my estimation of you."

His words were so direct, so assured, that they made her a bit wary. He knew her, but he didn't know the things she'd done or contemplated. "Those are sweet words, but we both know they cannot be true. Everyone does something that another finds fault with."

"With you? No, I don't think so," he said without a trace of hesitancy.

Because she knew such words didn't always last and some feelings eventually faded, she didn't protest his effusive praise.

After all, even if he had no regrets, she knew another day things would go dark again.

If time had taught her anything, it was that nothing wonderful lasted.

17

Johnson's Island, Ohio
Confederate States of America Officers' POW Camp
March 1865

EVER SINCE PHILLIP HAD BEEN MOVED TO THE BOTTOM floor of their barracks, which was their makeshift infirmary, Thomas Baker had been Robert's new bunkmate. Baker, being only a sergeant, had been originally slated for the POW prison in Columbus, but through the wonders of red tape, and, no doubt, a certain captain's influence, he'd been shipped up to their island prison with the rest of them.

Robert had always liked Thomas well enough. They'd been sent on a few scouting missions together when they were stationed in Tennessee. After only a few hours in each other's company, it was evident they made a good team. Neither of them had much to lose. Because of that, they had little fear. They'd also had a lot of experience using force when necessary. Robert wasn't exactly proud of it, but he could use his fists with the best of them. Thomas was just as scrappy.

Thomas was street-smart, too, and the enlisted men had held

him in high esteem. Robert would fight by his side any day, and consider it an honor to do so.

All that said, Robert wasn't especially thrilled to have him as his bunkmate. The man was bigger than Phillip and, as far as Robert could tell, he'd never slept without shifting positions two dozen times. He was also a talker.

Robert was soon learning that the man required at least an hour's worth of conversation before he closed his eyes for the night. For two men stuck on an island with little to do but write letters to loved ones, pace, and whittle, Robert was amazed that the man had anything to say at all.

But each night Thomas came up with something, usually when Robert's eyes were drifting shut.

"Hey, Rob?"

Not bothering to move from his position on his side, he mumbled, "What?"

"Did you see the new men arrive this afternoon?"

Even though he'd almost been asleep, Robert found himself smiling. "Hard to miss them. They were walking across Lake Erie like their soles were going to slip through at any minute."

"I talked to one. They're from the Tennessee Army."

"Didn't know that. Do you know any of them?" Thomas, like Captain Monroe, had originally joined the Tennessee regiment before getting transferred.

"No. But they seem a well enough sort. Decent."

"Bet they're tired as all get-out." It was a long journey to be taken prisoner, shipped up to Ohio on a train, then eventually forced to march across Lake Erie's frozen bay to their camp.

"Yeah. Maybe." He paused. "One of the officers almost smiled when he saw our barracks. Said it looked like a college dormitory."

"I've heard that too." Phillip had once compared their lodging to his dorm at West Point. Thomas sounded more than a little wistful. Robert wondered where this conversation was going.

"You ever been to college, Lieutenant?"

Robert scoffed. "I never had any schooling."

"Not any?" Thomas sounded incredulous, and Robert couldn't blame him. Most people were lucky enough to have some kind of formal education, he reckoned. He just had never been one of those.

"Nope."

When a couple of men around them grunted, Thomas lowered his voice. "I thought you could read, though. Can't you?"

"I can read. But until I enlisted, only a couple of old men had taught me how to cipher, and a pair of sisters taught me to read a little." He frowned, thinking back to that summer when those girls had befriended him as their charity case. They'd let him use their barn's spigot, given him a cot to sleep on, and had even given him supper every evening.

But when one of them started acting like she liked him, he'd gotten smart and moved on. No amount of learning or stew was worth being some girl's kept boyfriend. Especially when her daddy would've likely shot him for getting close to her.

"What about you?" Robert asked, curious now. "I thought your childhood wasn't much different from mine."

"I was born north of Dallas, in Wichita Falls. I had a house and everything." His voice turned wistful. Almost sweet. "For my first eight years, I had a mom and dad and a big brother too."

Robert was shocked. Thomas was rougher around the edges than he was, and that said a lot. "Were they good people?"

"Yeah. They were real good. My ma liked to sing. She sang most every morning when she hung clothes out on the line. And my brother, Jeremy, was the best. You know how some older brothers act like their reason for living is to beat the tar out of their siblings?"

Of course he didn't; he had no siblings. But he answered anyway. "Yeah."

"Jeremy wasn't like that. He always let me follow him around. And when he was with his friends after church, he made everyone include me. He walked me to school every day too."

Putting off the inevitable question, which was what happened to them all, Robert said, "What about your dad?"

"He was stocky like me. He was a blacksmith. Funny, some blacksmiths are all about the iron, but my dad, he was all about the horses. He loved those horses."

"Now I see why you ride so well."

"Yep, he taught me how to ride. He rode like the wind. He taught me how to trust your horse too. Said a horse won't ever let you down. He was right." His voice drifted off, true sadness lacing every word.

Which prompted Robert to ask the inevitable. "What happened when you were eight?"

"Indian raid."

"What?"

"Shut up, Truax!" a major called out. "It's going on one in the morning!"

"Sorry," Robert mumbled. Flipping over on his back, he whispered, "What happened?"

"Some renegade Indians were out looking for food, I guess. Or maybe they were just sick of being forced from their homes and land and decided to make a point. Anyway, they killed 'em all but me."

"It's good you survived."

"I don't know," Thomas said in his halting way. "My ma made me hide, you see." He lowered his voice. "They all did. Jeremy said he'd beat me good if I showed my face, no matter what I heard. So I stayed hid, 'cause Jeremy didn't lie."

"I'm, uh, real sorry, Baker. That's a real shame about your family." It was more than that, of course. But what else could he say?

"Yeah. But what do you do? Everybody's got something. Now here you and I are, sitting in some Yankee barracks getting yelled at by guards who never saw action."

"This is true."

"And Phillip is downstairs dying inch by inch with that gangrene." Whispering now, he said, "Gangrene's a heck of a way to die."

It was.

The reminder of Phillip downstairs writhing in pain made him get up. "I better go relieve Cap."

"How come it's just you and Cap watching him now?"

"Don't know," he lied. "We might be in prison, but I still do what I'm told."

"Yeah," Thomas said, but it was apparent that he didn't believe Robert.

Not wanting to converse about it further, Robert slipped out of the cot, threw his boots back on, and walked downstairs, then through the middle aisle where most of the men there were sleeping.

No one asked him where he was going. Probably because they'd seen him walk through here dozens of other times.

When he got to Phillip's room, he saw Captain Monroe sitting next to him. Phillip's blanket was clenched in Cap's hands. The expression on their captain's face could only be described as devastated.

"Robert," he said.

"Captain, you okay?"

"Me? No. Phillip is dead."

The words, though expected, hit him with such force that Robert knew he was swaying on his feet.

Unable to completely grasp it, Robert walked to the side of Phillip's bed and sat on the edge of his cot. Phillip's eyes were closed, but his body didn't look like Robert would have expected it to. He looked tense, almost as if he'd been fighting something.

"What happened?"

"You know what happened, Lieutenant." He hesitated. "The man had gangrene and infection. This was inevitable."

"I know. It's just that when I was with him earlier, he seemed to be breathing easy. He even talked for a while."

Captain Monroe looked up. "Was he making any sense?"

"At first he was talking about Miranda and home, but then about squirrels and rabbits. And weasels, if you can believe that. He must have thought he was a kid out hunting with his pa or something."

Captain Monroe looked like he was about to nod, then, after looking over his shoulder, he shook his head. "He wasn't talking about hunting with his pa."

"You know what all that meant?"

Monroe nodded. "Yeah. I know."

"Was it . . . was it from one of his missions?" he whispered.

"It was."

"Did he say more while you were with him, sir?"

"Let's not talk anymore about this, Robert." After taking a fortifying breath, Captain Monroe stood. "If it's all the same to you, I think we might as well tell everyone about Phillip's passing in the morning. Let everyone who can sleep do so."

"Yes, sir."

He walked out then, head down. Robert was fairly sure he'd never seen Devin Monroe stand so dejectedly.

The door closed behind him. Leaving Robert alone with Phillip Markham's dead body.

Closing his eyes, he prayed for the man's soul. Prayed he'd find some comfort. And at last prayed for his beloved Miranda, whom he'd seemed to have loved more than anything else in the world.

Then, satisfied that he'd done his best for the man, he moved over to the chair their captain had just vacated and sat vigil by Phillip's side.

He told himself it was because Phillip Markham needed that kind of respect.

But what he really did was look at the door and think about the last time he'd sat with Phillip.

Phillip had been feverish and vocal. He'd cried. He'd talked about Miranda and Galveston Island. And he did talk about squirrels and rabbits and weasels. He hadn't lied about that.

But then he seemed to be talking to a phantom officer about the success of his latest foray behind enemy lines. Where he'd donned a Union uniform, adopted the East Coast accent he'd learned at West Point, and walked the halls at one of the hospitals.

Through it all, Robert had been stunned and terrified. Terrified to leave him to go get Monroe.

And more terrified to do what Monroe had insisted had to be done.

Soon, however, Phillip had stopped talking and fallen into a deep sleep. Robert dropped the jacket in his hands and sank back against the wall in relief. When Monroe arrived shortly after, Robert never said a word to him, too ashamed that he'd betrayed his captain's orders.

As he left Phillip's room, he noticed the two sick men in cots on the other side of the door staring hard at him. And the guard who was leaning against the wall seeming to stare at nothing.

Those three men had heard. But he walked out without a word.

What had he done?

Certainly not what his captain had been brave enough to do.

18

BELLE DIDN'T LIKE FISH. SHE ESPECIALLY DIDN'T LIKE going to the fishmonger early in the morning for Cook. Honestly, she wished Cook would send Emerson every once in a while. That man loved fish and he didn't even mind getting up an hour before dawn.

But of course it didn't really matter what she wanted. Sometimes a woman had to do the job that was asked of her, and this was hers.

After throwing on her cloak and a thick wool scarf to tie around her neck and face, she made the thirty-minute walk to the docks. In the middle of the day, it was a nice journey. Walking in the dim morning light on half-empty streets was another story. To make matters worse, a fog had come in with the tide and blanketed the outside market in cold mist. It was enough to make a girl wonder if she could ever get warm again.

As she got closer to the fishmonger, more people filled the streets. Roughnecks, sailors, and dockworkers were moving slowly through the haze, as were the unfortunate women who had worked the night before. In the middle of it all were domestics like her.

After sidestepping a pair of freedmen standing outside one of the cotton warehouses, she at last got to the pier where her favorite fishmonger set up shop.

"You're here early, Belle," Sam said with a smile.

"I am." She hated sounding so glum when she knew Sam had already been out in the gulf and had returned. "How was your catch this morning?"

"Good." He grinned. "Good enough to sell you a fish or two."

His good nature was infectious. "You always say that," she replied, stifling a giggle.

"You always laugh when I say it too. Makes me proud to get you to smile."

"You're my only reason to smile on this errand. You know I'm not one for getting out early."

He pressed his hand to his chest dramatically. "You wound me every single time you come, Belle." He started to say more, then shuttered his expression.

Surprised by his sudden change in attitude, she turned to see who he was staring at. It was Sheriff Kern. He was talking with some of the men coming off an expensive-looking freighter. She was surprised. The docks usually weren't where the local law enforcement presided. She'd learned they had their own set of rules and regulations. In the distance was another surprise—Mr. Winter. Though she hadn't had much reason to mix with the clerk, Belle certainly recognized him.

But his being down at the docks at sunrise was even more of a surprise than Sheriff Kern.

"You still friends with him, Belle?" Sam asked under his breath.

"Who?"

"Kern."

Belle finally stopped staring and turned back to her friend. "I wouldn't say we're friends, exactly. He's the sheriff." Remembering what she had overheard about Kern's service and imprisonment, she added, "He fought bravely during the war."

"We all fought, one way or another."

"He also has friends in high places."

"What does that even mean?" he scoffed.

"It means we don't run in the same social circles, Sam. He's a good four steps above me."

Sam grunted. "Hardly that. You're better than some of the folks I've seen him keep company with, I'll tell you that."

Wondering if he was referring to Mr. Truax, she asked, "Who have you seen him talking to? Anyone in particular?"

"You know Kyle Winter?"

"I know who he is. And I saw him standing nearby." Curious now, she asked, "Are you saying they spent time together this morning?"

Sam shrugged.

She was confused . . . unless the sheriff was doing some detective work. That had to be it. Surely the sheriff couldn't condone Mr. Winter's behavior toward Mrs. Markham. After all, she overheard that he and Mr. Truax were going to work together to solve Mrs. Markham's problems. After glancing around to make sure no one else might be listening, she said, "I doubt they're friends. After all, Mr. Winter treats Mrs. Markham badly and Sheriff Kern is her friend."

"I just assumed anyone who would be friends with Winter would not be a friend of yours."

"No, maybe not. Mrs. Markham doesn't deserve how Mr. Winter has treated her. But why do you think Sheriff Kern—?"

"Sheriff," Sam interrupted, suddenly straightening his shoulders. "Good morning."

Sheriff Kern nodded. "Morning, Sam." Turning to Belle, he smiled slightly. "I was hoping you might be out this morning."

She wouldn't have been more surprised if he'd told her he'd decided to move to New York City. "Oh? I wasn't aware you spent much time in this part of town."

"I do when I have business here. Then someone told me you often come here on this day of the week, so I thought perhaps if we could take a walk together."

"Kind of hard to be walking with your hands full," Sam mumbled.

Kern turned to Sam. "Do you have a problem this morning?"

Across from her, Sam stiffened. "No."

Though Belle wasn't sure what Sam had been getting at, as though Sheriff Kern was not being quite everything he said he was, warning bells were going off in her head. "Thank you, Sheriff, but I had best go right home."

Holding out her hands, she practically grabbed hold of the fish Sam had wrapped in paper and hugged it to her chest. "Fish don't keep for long, you know."

But to her surprise, Kern didn't shy away. "How about I walk you home, then?"

"Well, I, um . . ."

"I insist." He took her elbow and guided her away from Sam's stall and along the narrow passageways of the fish market. Though his hold was strong and unforgiving, she noticed it wasn't painful.

She also noticed that she couldn't help but be aware of his touch. Afraid to meet his gaze, Belle kept looking in front of her. When they got back to Market Street, she pulled her elbow away from his grasp. "There is no need to keep ahold of me, sir. I'm not going to run away."

"I wasn't trying to keep you," he said impatiently. "Only navigate through the crowded market." He waved a hand toward one of the many abandoned buildings on the edge of the warehouse district. "You know it's not safe here. Half the buildings are barely standing after the last storm. You could get hurt."

"By a collapsing building?"

"Vagrants and rats live around here too. I promise, neither are suitable company for you."

He was looking out for her. Trying to shield her. She stiffened as she realized she appreciated his efforts. It was so unexpected. He stopped and looked at her curiously. "Is anything wrong? You seem out of sorts."

"I am fine. I am simply not good company this early in the morning."

"I hope that is all it is." After they walked another half block, he said, "As I said, I was hoping to see you. I want to speak to you."

"About what?"

He glanced her way. "Well, how are things at the boarding-house?"

"About the same. We got two new boarders last night."

"Any other visitors?"

"No . . . well, no, unless you count the older Mrs. Ruth Markham and Miss Viola Markham."

Sheriff Kern's eyebrows rose. "They were there? Did they spend the night?"

"Oh no. They came in, talking about how they were going to be getting the house soon. We all thought we were going to get fired, for sure. But then Mr. Truax practically ran them off."

"I see."

Belle wasn't sure what he saw. "Has anything happened, sir?"

"I'm not sure," he said slowly. "I plan to ask Mr. Truax about his conversation with those women, though."

They were back in Mrs. Markham's neighborhood. The streets were wider, palm trees and mossy Spanish oaks lined yards, and far fewer people were out than when Belle preferred to be stirring.

Maybe because it felt as if they were the only two people

around, their conversation felt more intimate. "Is there a reason you are worried about that?"

To her surprise, Sheriff Kern now looked even more uncomfortable. "I simply want to make sure Mrs. Markham is in no danger."

That, for Belle, was the last and final straw. She was tired of him circling around their conversation, asking things yet not giving her a reason why he was so concerned. "Sir, are you sure it's Mrs. Markham you are worried about?"

He drew to a stop. "Please explain yourself."

"If you had really cared about her, you would have tried harder to figure out who sent her that very first letter. Instead, you made her feel like a fool. And then, when everyone started disparaging her character, you could have put a stop to it."

"And how would I have done that without causing her more undue gossip?"

"I don't know. But it seems to me that you could have tried. Mr. Markham gave his life for the cause. But you—and half the people in this town—act like that wasn't good enough."

"I did not start that talk."

"But you were in a position to finish it, sir. I know that. You could have done something, but you didn't." No longer caring that he was the one in the position of power and she was just a maid, Belle added, "You didn't want to offend the wrong people so you ignored her pain. Just like when someone started sending her awful, hateful letters you didn't want to get involved."

His brow wrinkled. "Belle, I promise, I had no idea who wrote those letters. I still don't know."

"But you didn't even act like you cared to find out. And by your reaction to the news that Mr. Markham's sister and mother came by, you must somehow know how they have been treating her. They act like Mrs. Markham is no better than a harlot. So does half this town. But you have let that talk continue. Only now that Mr. Truax is here do you seem to care."

He was pale now. "Perhaps you have a point."

"I know I do," she bit out as she turned to face him on the street in front of the Markham mansion. "Just as I know I am right about you not wanting to get involved, I know Robert Truax has done more to help her than you ever tried. And that is wrong."

"I am trying to make up for it now."

"I see." His tone was earnest, his expression haunted. She wanted to believe him. She wanted to believe he was talking to Kyle Winter to help Mrs. Markham, and she was tempted to ask him if that was the truth.

However, it was more important that she concentrate on Mrs. Markham herself. Actually, what she needed to do was stop trying to figure out if Sheriff Kern was her ally or one of the reasons her employer was so miserable.

"Do you have anything else to tell me?" he asked quietly.

"No. Just that I hope you will help Mrs. Markham solve her problems as soon as possible."

He stilled. "Is there a specific reason you are stating this?" Though she knew her employer deserved her loyalty, something told her the sheriff could indeed be an ally. Heaven knew Mrs. Markham needed more of those. She let her anger go.

At last, she said, "Because maybe I know we don't have much to lose. You see, before Mr. Truax arrived, we were worried that Mrs. Markham wasn't going to survive much longer. However, with Mr. Truax's arrival, I think she now has a reason to live and to be strong." Lifting her chin, she said, "Maybe I want a reason to live and be strong too."

His demeanor changed.

"Do you think I could ever be that reason, Belle?" His voice was plaintive, his gaze hopeful.

Her mouth went dry as she stared at him. He was handsome. He was powerful. When she'd first arrived in Galveston from Louisiana, she would have given anything for a man like him to even give her the time of day.

But now? Well, it seemed she was starting to want more out of life. She was starting to want people in her circle of friends whom she could depend on. People who cared about her even when things weren't going her way. She wanted a man who cared enough to take risks.

She simply wasn't sure if he was that man. She wasn't sure if she could trust him. Apparently, Sam did not.

"I don't know," she finally replied.

Instead of getting mad, he stared at her. "Will you give me a chance?"

Belle swallowed. Here she was, standing with Jess Kern as dawn was breaking overhead. He was asking for her to give him a chance to make amends. To prove that he was good enough for her.

All while she was holding a newspaper full of smelly fish.

It was unbelievable. It was also . . . well, it was also rather flattering.

"I will think about it, Sheriff Kern. If you really want a chance."

"I do." Looking over her, he suddenly smiled. "Will you call me Jess now?"

"Of course not. It isn't proper."

"Will you call me Jess in the early mornings . . . when you are holding fresh fish?"

She couldn't hide a slight smile. "Perhaps." She walked into the house then. Holding the fish to her like a newborn babe.

Maybe he was a man willing to take risks after all.

19

THE KNOCK CAME AT HALF PAST FOUR.

The moment Miranda opened the door to the man who should have been a complete stranger, she instead found herself smiling as though she'd suddenly met a long-lost friend.

Maybe it was the golden head of hair that looked to be ruthlessly kept short. Maybe it was the man's pale blue eyes that had too many wrinkles at their corners. Or his military bearing.

Or, perhaps, it was the way he looked—as if he was not only the most formidable man on earth but also possessed the kindest heart ever known.

None of that really mattered. It didn't matter how she knew him; she simply did.

As she stood there, fighting a smile, his own eyes scanned her face, seeming to memorize every detail.

And then he bowed from the waist. "Madam," he said, his voice halting and respectful. "You don't know me, but I am—"

"You're Captain Devin Monroe," she finished.

He blinked as if she'd taken him by surprise. Then, after a pause, he smiled. "I am, indeed. And you, I presume, are Mrs. Markham?"

"Yes, Captain, I am. I mean, I was Phillip's wife, Miranda."

His smile grew. "You are everything he said you were, ma'am."

"As are you. Phillip must have been better at describing people than I had ever realized. I feel like I would have known you anywhere."

"I am delighted to make your acquaintance at last."

"I am pleased as well."

After gazing at her face again, he folded his hands behind his back. "May I come in?"

"Oh! Oh, certainly." She stepped back. "I'm so sorry. I can't believe I kept you standing outside my door." She waved a hand. "Please, do come in."

After he'd followed her and she closed the door to shut out the wind, she held out her hands. "May I take your coat, Captain?"

He shrugged it off his shoulders. "Thank you. But please, simply call me Devin."

"I could not," she said as she hung his heavy wool coat in the wardrobe by the door. "You meant so much to my husband. To both of us."

"Then I guess it will have to be Mr. Monroe. I resigned my commissions, you see. I'm no longer in the military."

"I was not aware of that. Robert, I mean Mr. Truax, still refers to you as Captain."

He smiled again. "Old habits die hard with Robert, I'm afraid. He likes things to stay the same if at all possible. Change doesn't come easy. Perhaps you've noticed?"

"I can't say that I have," she said after a moment's reflection. "All I have noticed is that he is more than he seems at first glance."

Appreciation flickered in his eyes. "I dare say we all might fit that description."

She was embarrassed now. Had she just revealed too much of herself?

"Please, won't you come into the parlor and sit down?" she asked in a rush as she led the way. "Or may I serve you some coffee? Tea?" Another thought crossed her mind. "Or are you hungry? Perhaps you'd like a light repast?"

"I have no need of refreshment at the moment. Don't go to any trouble, Mrs. Markham."

His expression looked so serious all of a sudden that she sat down too. "All right."

He looked at her again, his eyes showing genuine happiness. Then, catching himself, he shook his head as if to clear it. "I'm sorry for staring. It's just that, well, you are almost all Phillip talked about. It's taken me a moment to put the lady in front of me with the words that so often rang in my ears."

"Phillip and I were a love match. I'm afraid we were both guilty of talking far too much about the other."

"I don't think that is anything to apologize for. Yours was a blessed union."

"Yes. Yes, it was." She folded her hands, then was suddenly embarrassed. "I'm sorry. I should have sent for Robert right away. He said he was asking for your help, and I'm sure he's been expecting you." Moving to get up, she said, "I think he is home. It won't take me but a moment to—"

"Mrs. Markham, I do want to see Robert. But if you can spare the time, I would like to talk to you first."

She felt more awkward than a schoolgirl attempting to please her teacher. "Oh. Yes, of course."

"You see, Robert came here to see how you were faring. I believe you know that."

She nodded.

"He's been mailing me updates about you and his visit. He also told me about the disturbing letters you've been receiving." He raised a brow. "And, I believe, you've also had some trouble with your in-laws?"

Everything he listed had happened. And while she supposed she was grateful to Robert for caring, she wasn't as pleased to hear about her problems on this man's lips. "I am not sure how I feel about Robert giving you updates on me."

"He didn't really have a choice, I'm afraid. You see, one night on Johnson's Island we made a vow to each other, a pact, if you will, to look out for each other. Phillip asked that you be looked after too."

Miranda didn't know whether to laugh or cry. Of course Phillip would have wanted her to be safe and secure. She could honestly see him, dressed in his worn uniform, standing with Robert and Captain Monroe and inserting her needs into their conversation.

It was sweet and so very thoughtful.

But she didn't think they honored that vow all that much. After all, Robert had only arrived to see her a few weeks ago. But she had been suffering for so long before his arrival.

"You don't seem all that impressed with our pact, ma'am."

"I'm sorry, but I am not. The war has been over for some time, and I confess I've been struggling on my own. I never thought your men would seek me out, so I don't want to sound ungrateful or bitter. It's just that, well . . . I hope you have been looking after the other parties in your pact a bit better."

He winced. "We scattered after we got out. I'd like to think the others are doing well now, but I have no idea. I, um, had some issues that I had to take care of directly after the war. I am only just now able to fulfill my promises."

"No, I am sorry. You owe me nothing."

He leaned forward, resting his elbows on his knees. "Mrs.

Markham, I disagree. Furthermore, I have heard that you have been experiencing some difficulties of late. Perhaps you could tell me a bit more about what has been happening with you."

She didn't wish to ask one more man for help with her laundry list of hurts. "I will be fine. Sheriff Kern is now helping me. The only problem I've been experiencing that you might find noteworthy is the rumor that has been circulating around Phillip."

It even hurt to say it. "About Phillip's role in the war. Someone is saying he was a traitor. That, I believe, is cause for your concern. I suppose that is why Robert sent for you."

Captain Monroe's whole bearing shifted. He looked angry and hard. At that moment, it was hard to locate the gentleman who had opened the door to her. "Phillip was not a traitor, Mrs. Markham."

"No, he was not," Robert said as he walked into the parlor.

Miranda rose to her feet. "Robert, your captain is here."

"Just arrived," Captain Monroe said as he stood up as well. "I came as soon as I read your last letter."

"So I see." He winked at her before walking directly to Captain Monroe and holding out his hand. "Devin, it is good to see you."

They shook hands, then to Miranda's surprise Devin pulled Robert to him and clasped him in a manly, rough hug. "We've been through too much to simply shake hands, Lieutenant."

"Yes, sir. I suppose we have." Turning to Miranda, he said, "I hope Devin here hasn't been filling your head with too many stories about our time together?"

She loved how he so easily used that euphemism. Instead of reminding them all that they'd fought side by side in the most terrible of situations.

"Mrs. Markham has just shared how she's been besieged by rumors about Phillip betraying the Confederacy."

"Which is where I came in," Robert said easily. Taking a seat next to Miranda on the sofa, he said, "I have to say that whatever Miranda might have told you about the pressure she's been under is probably at least ten times worse than she has led you to believe. I don't know too many men who could put up with so much, let alone a gently bred woman."

Captain Monroe's expression turned fierce. "I would like to spend a few days here if I may, ma'am."

"Yes, of course," she replied.

Then he eyed her gently. "I would like the opportunity to share some memories of Phillip with you. If that wouldn't upset you too much."

"I would love to hear your stories. Well, if you feel they are suitable for my hearing," she teased.

The captain grinned. "You're looking at a man who has spent the majority of his life in the company of ramshackle men. I doubt any of my tales are suitable for gently bred ladies. But if you think your ears can handle stories with a few rough edges, it would be an honor to share some memories about a man I held in high esteem."

"I might have been gently bred at one time, but now I'd like to think of myself as a survivor, sir. I promise, there is little you could tell me that I haven't heard before."

Robert chuckled. "Just probably not from Phillip."

Feeling her cheeks heat, she averted her eyes. "You are right about that. Phillip was always careful around me."

Monroe exchanged a meaningful glance with Robert.

"What is it?" she asked. "What did Phillip do? Robert, you told me Phillip was not a traitor. Were you telling me the truth?"

Captain Monroe stared hard at her again. Then, seeming to come to a decision, he sat back down.

"Phillip Markham was a smart and capable man, Miranda. He excelled at West Point."

"Yes."

"Did he, by chance, ever speak to you about his relationships there?"

"No. I am assuming they were the usual ones made between men at university?"

"I think one could safely say that is true. But what you might not have realized is that he was popular there. He had many friends. Many close friends from all walks of life."

"Yes?"

"When he attended, the war was not on anyone's mind. No one paid much mind to where men were from. Because of that, he became as close to men from the North as from the South."

"I thought that might be the case," she said slowly. "He never mentioned any man or state by name. But he did say from time to time that a man can't be judged only by the region where he lives or the dialect in his speech." She shrugged. "I think that was his way of reminding me that every soldier in the North wasn't a terrible person, just like every man in the South wasn't perfect either."

"That sounds like something Phillip would have said," Robert said easily. "He was always giving everyone a chance. Even a man like me."

Miranda smiled softly at Robert. "Even you."

Devin linked his fingers together. "Mrs. Markham, what I am about to tell you cannot be shared with anyone. This is for your ears only."

Miranda was sure she paled, but she leaned forward to catch every word.

"When we went to war, I was not with Phillip at first. Did you know that?"

"I did. He was under another captain. I can't recall his name now."

"I would be surprised if he ever told it to you. That captain had been assigned a job directly from Lee himself. He was to find men who could easily slip through enemy lines and gather information."

She felt her cheeks freeze. "What are you saying, sir?"

"That Phillip was one of the men recruited for that job."

She shook her head. "No."

"For two years Phillip Markham went behind enemy lines, donned a blue uniform, and mixed with Union officers."

She shook her head. "No, that is not possible. They would have known he was from the South."

"Some did. Some thought he was from Kentucky, and that state was pretty much split down the middle. But it didn't matter. He changed his name half the time. He changed his posture and his accent. To survive, he became another man."

"But—"

"To fulfill his missions, he never told anyone but his superiors about them. He kept his promises to the generals and such, who asked so much of him. He was loyal to the core."

Hardly able to believe what she was hearing, Miranda nodded.

Captain Monroe looked at her intently. "What I need you to understand, Mrs. Markham, is that there were many jobs and roles in our war. Not everyone who put his life at stake held a bayonet and charged across a field. Some, like Phillip, risked their lives for information. He was a hero, ma'am. He was a hero in every sense of the word."

Miranda knew it would be days before she would fully be able to let that sink in and come to terms with the fact that her husband had led a very different life from what he'd let on.

Perhaps it didn't matter. Maybe she didn't really need to know how much he sacrificed for the cause. But as she looked at both men and saw how unwaveringly proud they were of him, of how much they'd believed in him, she couldn't help but feel justified.

She'd wanted Phillip to be everything she'd believed him to be. And, it seemed, he was.

She was just about to thank Captain Monroe for making the long journey to meet her face-to-face and tell Phillip's whole story when she realized the question that had been hounding her had just become more complicated than ever. Perhaps the captain could help after all.

"Robert assured me Phillip was not a traitor, and now I know how false that rumor has been. But if no one knew about his undercover missions except for a very few select group of people . . ." She paused.

Captain Monroe nodded. "Yes, that is correct."

"Then there was no basis at all for the rumor. So who wants me out of this house so much that he would make up lies and threaten me with these letters?"

Captain Monroe exchanged glances with Robert. "That's a very good question, ma'am. Believe me when I say I aim to find the answer to it very soon."

"We'll discover what has been going on, Miranda," Robert said quietly. "I will not leave Galveston without knowing you are safe and secure once again."

Robert's words were reassuring. But they also filled her with a new sense of dread. Robert Truax wasn't planning to stay in Galveston. And what's more, he never had.

He'd come here for a mission. For Phillip. That was all.

20

Lieutenant Robert Truax's house, West Texas
Christmas Day 1866

THE CAPTAIN'S ARRIVAL WAS A WELCOME SURPRISE, BUT not a completely unexpected one. Once Robert's brain took a moment to register that he was actually seeing the captain and not some apparition from his many dreams and nightmares of the war, he drew himself up to an almost-forgotten military posture and inclined his head.

He had to remind himself that their army days were gone and therefore he shouldn't salute.

"Captain Monroe. Welcome," he said in a crisp, concise voice. "Happy Christmas."

Captain Monroe's clear blue eyes filled with an unfamiliar glint of amusement. "Happy Christmas to you, Lieutenant. Stand at ease now, man. We're not in the army any longer."

Somewhat embarrassed, Robert relaxed his stance. But he still felt awkward. Part of him wanted to hug his captain, the other part of him wanted to present the calm, relaxed stance he'd been so known for back when they directed their men at camp.

He settled for being direct. "What brings you here, sir?"

Devin rested his left hand on the doorjamb. "Well, I was first hoping that you might invite me into your rather grand home."

Feeling worse than foolish, Robert stepped back. "Forgive me. It's bitterly cold out. I shouldn't have kept you standing in the elements so long."

Captain Monroe stepped through the door. "I've stood in worse, soldier," he said as he passed. "I believe we both have."

"Yes, sir."

They'd shared three Christmases together. One in Tennessee, another in the wilds of Pennsylvania, the last in a flimsy wooden barracks in a prisoner-of-war camp.

That Christmas spent on Johnson's Island in the middle of Lake Erie had been bone chilling. Nothing could compare to that.

Robert closed the door with a firm clap and promptly turned the deadbolt. As he did so, he prayed to wrap his head around the fact that it was time to sound smarter than he was acting.

Luckily, his maid, Marisol, strode forward and held out her hands to Devin. "Take your coat?"

Captain Monroe blinked, then unfastened each button with care. After handing his wool coat to Marisol with a word of thanks, he looked at Robert. "You have servants now?"

Robert couldn't determine if his captain was impressed with his improved financial situation or taken aback that he'd hired people to do things he could easily do himself.

But perhaps the why of it didn't even matter.

"Sir, this is Marisol," he said. "She and her husband, Stan, live in a cabin on my property. They were looking for some work and, well, you know me . . . I need all the help I can get."

"Yes, I reckon you do, Robert." He directed a small smile at the maid, who was a good ten years older than either of them. "I hope you and Stan keep him in line, ma'am."

"We try, but it can be a challenge at times, sir," she admitted with a sparkle in her eyes. "Most days the hardest part of my day is reminding Mr. Robert that I am here to help him . . . and not the other way around."

"I'm not that bad, Marisol."

"Bad enough, Mr. Robert," she teased. "Now, may I serve you both some food?"

"Please do. Gracias."

"It's nothing," she said as she parted. "I'll bring it to you in the library, sirs. Stan's got a good fire going."

Captain Monroe had watched the interplay with thinly veiled surprise on his face. "It seems you are surviving fairly well these days."

"It does seem so. My work for the railway has proved profitable." Robert chuckled as he led the way down dark stained maple hardwood floors into a small room off to the side. His pride and joy, his library. For a man who'd grown up with next to nothing, the very fact that he had enough books to need a place to store them was amazing.

Sure enough, Stan had built a roaring fire in the stone hearth. That, with the pine branches Marisol had found and arranged on the mantel, gave the room a warm and Christmasy air.

Weeks ago, he had admitted to Marisol that he'd never actually celebrated a true Christmas. She'd taken his admittance to heart and had practically begun baking Christmas treats and decorating in the next breath.

"Have a seat, sir. Or, if you'd prefer, please warm yourself in front of the fire."

Captain Monroe walked right up to the fire and held out his

hands without a trace of artifice or self-consciousness. "Even after all this time, I still can't pass up the chance to get warm."

"I find myself doing that fairly often too." He shrugged, then said in a rare bit of honesty, "Old habits, I guess. Some blessings are too wonderful to ignore."

Captain blinked. "There you are."

"Pardon me?"

"Between your fine clothes and servants and fancy house, I was wondering if the man I fought beside at Gettysburg was still under there."

Robert barely refrained from tugging at his collar. "He's still there, sir. Just a little more polished and a whole lot more comfortable."

"That's a good thing, Robert. Don't be embarrassed about the gifts you have received."

"Thank you, sir."

Leaning back, Captain Monroe stretched his arms, then exhaled with a contented expression. After a second's pause, he focused on Robert. "Now, I suppose you are probably wondering to what you owe this honor of a visit."

"I figured you'd be ready to tell me in your own time. Even if you came all this way to simply wish me Happy Christmas, I wouldn't have been surprised." And that would have been the truth too. Robert held the captain in such high regard, he was fairly sure he could do just about anything.

"Though that thought might have crossed my mind, I did come for a reason."

There was a new, unfamiliar wariness in his captain's tone. Robert tensed. "Yes, sir?"

"I have something to ask you, but I'll wait until Marisol and Stan get us settled."

Robert turned with a start, realizing that his commanding officer had done it again. He was able to set him off without any difficulty at all.

"Shall we set everything on the card table, sir?" Stan asked when he entered the room.

"Yes. Yes, that will be fine. Stan, this is Captain Devin Monroe. He was my commanding officer in the war. We served together . . . and were imprisoned together as well."

"Sir," Stan said. "It's an honor."

"It's good to meet you too," Devin drawled.

"Will that be all then, Mr. Robert?" Stan asked.

"Yes, thank you. And, please, close the door when you leave."

Without another word the man did as he asked. Turning toward the table now heaping with food, Robert thought an explanation might be in order. "This is corn tortillas, refried beans, and steak with peppers. Marisol, being originally from Mexico, has a way with food like this."

"It looks good. A real fine Christmas meal."

"Yes, sir. Gives a man a lot to be thankful for." Robert didn't know if he would ever take a full plate for granted. He hoped not.

After he said a quick blessing, they ate. Once again, his captain looked like he enjoyed every morsel, taking in each bite as though it might be his last.

As Robert watched without trying to look like he was watching, a slow, sickening feeling settled into the pit of his stomach. Was his captain sick? Did he guess he was dying or something?

Afraid to know, his appetite left him. He picked at his food and started mentally reminding himself not to embarrass himself or the captain.

After a few moments, Captain Monroe set down his fork,

wiped his mouth with the bandanna on the table, and leaned back with a satisfied sigh. "Good food, Robert."

"Thank you. I'll let Marisol know."

"You've got a nice life now. Prosperous. Good fire. Help. Excellent meal." He eyed him carefully. "None of those things are to be taken for granted."

"No, sir, I do not. Since this is the first time I've ever had such things, I don't take them for granted at all."

"Are you happy?"

The blunt question took him off guard. "I am happy being warm and clean," he said. "I'm happy not being a prisoner and not being hungry." Most days, that was enough.

"Ha. So you've developed some simple needs."

Robert couldn't resist smiling. "I've always had rather simple needs. They've just never been met."

"Point taken." Captain Monroe shifted, looking slightly uncomfortable. Then he fastened his clear blue eyes on Robert and spoke again. "I'm here about Miranda Markham."

And just like that, all feeling of contentment vanished. "Yes, sir?"

"Robert, I want you to go check on her."

Even the thought of such a thing made him uncomfortable. "Why?" Remembering Phillip's constant concern for her, he grasped for a reason. "Is she unwell?"

"I fear so."

"What happened?" he asked, growing more concerned. "Did she get that influenza? Did she get hurt? Is she injured?"

"No, nothing like that. I have heard she is having a difficult time. Uh, emotionally."

"She is still mourning."

"Yes. But I fear there is more." He paused, then said quietly,

"From my contacts around Houston, I have learned that she has become something of a recluse. Some even fear that she will take her own life."

Robert rose to his feet. "That would have devastated Phillip. She was the reason he fought so hard to live." Maybe knowing there was a love like Phillip and Miranda's had given all of them a reason to live.

Even for Ethan Kelly, who'd received a letter just weeks before their release that his Faye had decided to marry someone else.

"I agree. Hearing that she is on the verge of giving up is difficult. It also doesn't make sense." Instead of standing up again, Monroe simply leaned back and stretched out his legs. Looked at him hard. "I worry that something else might be happening to her. After all, how can a woman who stayed strong throughout a long war suddenly give everything up?"

"I don't know."

Captain Monroe leaned forward. "Will you go see her? Will you go to Galveston Island, call on Miranda Markham, and stay with her for a few days? Maybe even a few weeks?"

"Stay?"

"She has turned her home into a boardinghouse. I hear the rooms are rarely filled," he said in his off-hand way. "I imagine you would make her very happy if you were to stay for a week or two."

This request was getting harder and harder to bear. "You want me to stay with her that long?"

"I'd like you to," he said easily, but Robert heard what was blatantly unsaid. It was more of an order than a simple request. "She could use a friend, I think."

"Do you think she'll welcome a friendship with one of her husband's comrades?"

Devin stared at the fire. "Perhaps you don't need to mention that you knew Phillip. It's been my experience that some friendships form best when there is little baggage attached. You might be able to ascertain she will be all right, then quietly leave. I don't think she needs any reminders about the war."

"You don't think she'll recognize my name?"

"She might . . . or she might not," he said slowly. Looking back at Robert, he said, "You have always thought quickly on your feet, Lieutenant. I'm sure you'll know how to present yourself when the time comes, just as I feel certain you will keep the exact nature of your service to the C.S.A. to yourself."

Before he realized what he was doing, Robert pulled back his shoulders. "I would never discuss my missions."

"Of course not," Devin said lightly. "Beg pardon. After all, it's not like you've decided if you are going to see Miranda."

"I will go," he said. He took care to keep his voice casual and contemplative, though there had never been any question of him visiting Miranda Markham. "I have been thinking about leaving my job with the railroad and finding something new."

"Thank you, Robert."

"But why me?"

Captain Monroe stilled. Stared at him directly. "We both know that answer, Robert."

Robert didn't do him the disservice of pretending he didn't understand what he meant. He'd been mesmerized by Phillip's love for his wife, and everyone at the camp had known it. He'd often gone to sleep wondering what kind of woman Miranda Markham was. Now, it seemed, he was going to find out.

They were still sitting in silence ten minutes later when Marisol stepped into the doorway. "Coffee, gentlemen?"

Devin got to his feet. "Thank you, but no. I should be going."

Robert stood up as well. "But it's Christmas. And it's getting late. It will be dark out soon."

"Indeed."

"I wish you would consider staying, sir. The area around here is not very forgiving at night. Especially not in the winter."

"I'll be fine. I have a feeling the only people who will be brave enough to be out on a night like this are me and any wayward wise men."

"But—"

"I came here for a reason, soldier. Now that is done, I think it's best I go on."

Without another word of warning, Robert led the way back down the hallway. Captain Monroe followed, Marisol on their heels.

All too soon, she produced the captain's coat. She and Robert stood quietly as they watched him fasten the buttons with the same care he had taken as he unfastened them.

When he was buttoned up and had his hat in his hand, he smiled at the woman. "Thank you for a wonderful meal, ma'am. Best I've had in some time."

"It . . . it was my pleasure."

He smiled at that, then turned to Robert. "Thank you for both the hospitality and your loyalty. Both mean a lot to me."

That was the thing. Robert knew his captain wasn't just giving him lip service. He was completely sincere. And that was why Robert knew that, as soon as the new year came, he would take a train down to Galveston Island and check on Miranda Markham as he was asked to do.

Even though the sight of her was likely going to rip him in two. He owed Phillip that much.

But he owed Captain Monroe even more.

"Merry Christmas, sir. Safe travels and Godspeed."

"To you, too, Robert. For all good things, you too."

And with that, he put on his hat and walked outside. Moments later, Robert saw him on his mount riding through the east pasture.

When he closed the door, Marisol was still standing in the foyer, looking at him with concern. "Do you think he'll be all right?"

"I hope and pray so." He shrugged. "I learned something about him years ago. With Captain Monroe, one doesn't argue or question. One simply does as he's bid."

He walked back to the library then. Found all traces of their meal and visit had been magically cleared away.

So he stood in front of the fireplace, raised his hands, and gave thanks for the warmth.

21

Not long after Captain Monroe and Robert made their promises to Miranda, she excused herself, citing a pressing need to answer some correspondence.

Though neither of them had actually believed her excuse, Robert let her go without comment. He knew Miranda likely needed some time to process everything they'd revealed about Phillip.

Soon afterward, Winnie directed Devin to one of the bedrooms down the hall from Robert. Thirty minutes after that, the two men went outside.

Devin was eager to see the Galveston Phillip had described in such detail to them all during their late-night talks. As for himself, well, Robert knew the time had finally come to admit to his captain what had happened the day Phillip died.

To have never told him about his inability to do his duty was pure cowardice.

They'd just stepped off the front porch when Devin looked back at the house curiously. "This house is rather close to the water."

"Yes."

"It would be so easy for one to slip down to the docks without notice."

Robert shrugged. "Perhaps. It has one of the finest locations in Galveston. It's close to the water yet off the main thoroughfare."

Still staring at the canal, Devin said, "Has Miranda told you if there has been much interest in her house because of its location?"

"All I know is that her mother-in-law intends to have the house. She and Phillip's sister resent Miranda's keeping it after Phillip left it to her, and especially for turning it into a boardinghouse."

"I bet they do," he mused. "It's Miranda's right to claim her home, though."

"It is. It's her house and her husband's legacy. But since I last wrote to you, I have learned firsthand that they are miserable women who gladly make Miranda miserable as well."

Still staring at the narrow body of water and dock behind the mansion, Devin said, "I don't know a lot about shipping and waterways, but I know a lot about military strategy. Water is desirable."

Robert felt a little slow, and he still wasn't following. "And?"

"And maybe someone decided they would like to have this mansion not for its beauty or sentimental nature, but because of its location. A man could bring all sorts of things into the country this way and no one would ever be wiser."

Remembering just how displeased Phillip's mother and sister had been when he'd told them he would make sure they never got the house, Robert said, "Let's go visit the older Mrs. Markham and her daughter, Viola, tomorrow. They might have some answers to some of our questions."

Captain Monroe's light blue eyes warmed. "If they are as truly unpleasant as you made them seem—"

"They are," he said quickly.

"And if they have truly been as disrespectful and impolite to Miranda—"

"They have."

"Then visiting them first thing tomorrow will be worth waking up for."

Robert smiled to himself. "In the meantime, would you care to see the Strand?"

Devin inclined his head. "I would indeed."

They walked up Market Street, then turned toward the busy city district. When they passed the infamous Recognition Square, Robert walked Devin over to it. "This is the memorial for the dead, sir."

Devin nodded, barely scanning the names. "Where is Phillip's name? Did they list his rank? I still wish I would have been able to get his promotion to go through before his death."

"It is absent, sir."

He turned to Robert. "What is? His ranking?"

"No, sir. His name."

"Why?" His words were fairly barked.

"I was told the memorial was for only the city's heroes. This is what the rumor has done, sir."

Devin jerked off his hat and stood at attention. It was obvious to Robert that he was forcing himself to read every man's name on the off chance he'd recall one of the honored fallen heroes. That, of course, was a vintage Captain Monroe gesture. He'd been exhausted for most of the war and paid attention to correct protocols only when absolutely necessary. Until something untoward happened to one of his men.

Then it was obvious that he would do anything and everything to uphold their honor.

Only when Devin had replaced his hat on his head and was staring at the statue in silence did Robert speak. "Did you recognize any of the names?"

"One. He was in the Texas Rangers with me."

"Good man?"

Devin thought for a moment. "Good enough. Too young to

die." At last turning away from the carefully carved list of names, he said, "Thank you for showing this to me, Robert."

"Of course."

Devin looked at him a moment longer, then instead of walking ahead, he took a seat on one of the vacant benches. "You look like you have a lot on your mind."

"I do. When I walked onto Galveston Island, I felt as if I was entering Pandora's box. It's been a challenge figuring out whom to trust. Fortunately, as I told you in my last letter, I have come to trust the sheriff, Jess Kern. But I am glad you are here, sir. Jess, of course, does not know of Phillip's true contributions to the war."

"I am pleased you wrote to me about the urgency of the situation," he said as they left the square. "However, I don't believe that is actually all that is on your mind, is it?"

"No."

"Is it Miranda Markham who has you so tied up in knots?"

That took him by surprise. "Sir, everything we are dealing with has to do with Miranda."

"Don't be dense, Lieutenant. I am not speaking of her problems, I am speaking about her."

"Sir?" Robert wasn't sure if he was offended or embarrassed.

"It has not escaped my notice that she's a beautiful woman. I also have not failed to observe that you've noticed her beauty."

"I would never force my attentions on a woman still grieving."

"Is she, though?"

"I know she misses Phillip. But that said, I don't know how much she misses the man versus what she'd hoped they would be together." Thinking about this further, he said slowly, "Wrapping one's mind around a new reality can be a challenge."

"This is true. However, it is the way of the world. Life and death can interrupt a great many plans."

"Indeed."

"That said, I think you should investigate Miranda's feelings."

Robert stopped and started several times, then at last uttered, "You don't think my . . . I mean, you don't think my admiration for her is wrong?"

"What? To look after her? To admit that you fancy her?" He paused, then grinned. "Or to admit that it is okay to fancy her?"

Robert decided to give up all sense of pride. "Yes to all of those things."

Captain Monroe laughed. "My forte is war, not love. But I will say that, as someone who has just stumbled upon the two of you? It's apparent there's something almost tangible between you. For both of your sakes, I think you should give it a try."

"I might." Staring down at Devin, Robert said formally, "Captain, I need to tell you something, but I'm afraid you're going to be so disappointed and upset, you'll think differently about me."

All traces of humor vanished from his expression. "It's that serious?"

"Yes."

Looking at him closely, his captain sighed. "I'm not going to make you any promises, Robert. I'd like to think I've learned something after all these years in the military."

"So, then . . ."

"So then, spit it out, soldier."

Inwardly, Robert gave a sigh of relief. At last he was going to be able to share his burden. He was ready to face the consequences, even if it meant that the man he admired the most was going to look at him as if he was a failure.

"You remember when Phillip was so sick. When he was slowly dying and started hallucinating."

The muscle in Devin's cheek jumped. "I remember."

"What you may not recall is that earlier that week I made a promise to you."

"No, I remember your promise." Devin stood.

Robert was standing almost at attention and couldn't even meet his captain's gaze. Belatedly, he realized he was staring just above the man's head. It was a classic soldier's pose. Men had done it to him all the time. Whenever they were ashamed or lying or afraid, they would stand tall and look slightly away.

It didn't fool anyone.

He had no doubt that he wasn't fooling Devin at the moment. Not even a little bit.

Feeling even worse because he was still acting like a coward, he continued. "Anyway, sir . . . I promised you I would do whatever was necessary to sustain the integrity of Phillip Markham." And, of course, the integrity of the South.

"Yes. You did."

"When I sat with him that day, he started talking. In an agitated way. At first I truly thought he was lost in a vision of home. Maybe back when he was a boy. He was talking about rabbits and weasels. Foxes and hounds, and you told me later, after he died, that he had been talking in code . . ." His voice drifted off, and at that moment the words Phillip had uttered were so clear in his head he could probably have recited them verbatim. "But I didn't tell you Phillip started talking about his undercover work. Not in code, but plainly."

His captain froze. "Yes."

Feeling as though it had all happened days ago instead of years, Robert felt as if his mouth were full of cotton. "I knew I should quiet him. I knew what my orders were. They were clear, sir."

"What did you do?"

Hating the memory, hating how it made him feel, he forced himself to say each word, even though admitting it all out loud made him feel even worse. "I took off my jacket, intending to . . . to stop him. But I couldn't."

"I see."

Robert glanced at Captain Monroe's expression. It was carefully blank. Feeling miserable, he said, "Sir, there's more. You see, when I left the room, a guard was standing nearby, and two prisoners were there in their cots. The sick men were staring at me with stunned expressions."

"So they heard." His voice was flat.

"They did. And I'm sure the guard heard too." Robert closed his eyes, hating this part of his story the most. Hating how weak it made him sound. How weak it made him feel. "I should have dealt with them there, sir."

"Should have? What did you do?"

"Nothing," he whispered. Then, forcing himself to remember that he was alive while Phillip was dead, he said clearly, "I did nothing, sir. I walked away." Robert swallowed. "And then I chose not to tell you either."

"Why didn't you tell me?"

"I couldn't bear to let you know that I wasn't man enough to kill Phillip. Or brave enough to deal with the three men who heard." Back then, every choice had seemed to have irrefutable consequences. If he'd killed the men, he would have very well been caught and put to death too. If he'd merely threatened them to keep their silence, the uncertainty would have been an insurmountable weight around his neck.

"I see." Devin stared at him for several seconds.

Robert forced himself to stand still. Unwavering. Whatever blame Devin heaped on him was what he deserved.

"Lieutenant?"

He braced himself. "Yes, sir?"

"When I went into Phillip's sick room to relieve you, just minutes after you left, he was dead." Looking hollow, Devin said, "He was already dead."

"What? But you seemed to . . . you never said."

"You're right, I didn't." He swallowed. "You see, I thought you ended Phillip's life."

"You thought I killed him. Yet you never said a word to me."

Monroe shrugged. "How could I? I thought you had done what a soldier—no, what an officer—needed to do. When I said, 'You know what happened,' I thought you knew I was acknowledging what you would not want to admit, not Phillip's inevitable death from gangrene. No words could have made you feel any better anyway."

He sighed. "Robert, I thought you had done what was best for our unit, best for the Confederacy, best for Phillip's memory." He laughed darkly. "After a while, I even said it was best for Phillip. He was in terrible pain. For weeks."

"When you said Phillip was dead, I assumed you did what I wasn't brave enough to do."

"I would have. I would have done it without much remorse. However, I did not end Phillip Markham's life."

"So it was one of the three men outside the door. Either one of the Confederate soldiers in the cots or the guard. As I think on what Phillip said, I'm not sure if it would have been clear that Phillip was a spy for us, and not the North."

"So it would seem. He did not look as though he died peacefully."

"All this time I've felt terrible about it. I wished I had been stronger," Robert said, feeling both confused and, for the first time, cautiously optimistic. "After all, I couldn't say how many times I fired bullets with my Remington. I killed dozens of men on the field."

"We all did."

"But I loved him."

"We all loved him too. He was a good man. The best."

"Captain, I think one of those three men must have either ended up back here or told someone here that Phillip was a traitor. That's the only way I can figure out how that rumor started. Someone either truly thinks Phillip betrayed the South or wants everyone to think that. Either way, he is bent on destroying Phillip's name and Miranda's life."

"I don't know if we'll ever find who killed Phillip. I'm not even sure if it matters. What's done is done." Looking grim, Devin said, "But whoever did kill him saved you and me from doing it. It might not be right, but I'm grateful for that. Ending Phillip's life would have been a heavy burden to bear."

"How is it that even after all this time, we're still uncovering the pain and secrets of war?"

"How can we not? We are men with hearts and souls, after all. We're scarred by our experiences. We also promised each other that we'd never forget."

As Robert stared at his former captain, he realized that was one promise that had been almost too easy to keep.

22

ANY IDEA WHAT YOU INTEND TO SAY OR ASK THESE LADIES?"
Captain Monroe said under his breath as they rode their rented
horses up a windy dirt road on the outskirts of Houston.

From the livery's directions, Robert deducted that the
Markham women lived in the modest ranch at the end of the lane.

"Not a one," Robert replied. From the time they'd left that
morning for their trip on the ferry to the quiet ride to Viola
and Ruth's home, he'd been playing over different scenarios.
Sometimes he imagined appealing to their love for Phillip.

Other times, he thought it was a better idea to go in strong
and assured, using Captain Monroe's rank to an advantage.
They'd seemed like women who valued Phillip's military career.
Therefore, it stood to reason that they'd value his captain's reputation as well.

Robert even imagined using a bit of force. Flatly refusing to
leave or doing his best to keep the women from their scheduled
activities until he got some answers.

But that didn't seem like the right method either.

"I've considered a lot of avenues," he replied at last. "Unfortunately,
none of my ideas feel like the right course of action."

Instead of looking aggravated, Captain Monroe grinned.
"Guess we'll figure it out when we get inside."

"If you have any bright ideas, feel free to take the lead. I'll be happy to follow your directives again. Sir," he added belatedly.

"Will do, but I don't imagine I'll know what to do any more than you will." He paused to move his horse around a parked buggy and a patch of debris on the ground. "To be honest, a part of me would like to simply yell at the women until they've told us what we need to know."

Robert was shocked. "I thought I was the only man who thought that way."

"I don't think you are," Monroe said as he dismounted and tied up the leads. Eyeing him in a bemused way, he continued. "Moreover, I spent far too much of my life on the battlefield. All men lose control at times, I believe."

"You think so?"

Monroe shrugged. "There's only so much one man can take before he gives in to emotions he usually tries to keep in better control." He paused. "That's when prayer comes in handy, I think."

After Robert tethered his mount, he steeled his shoulders and walked to the front door. Winifred had been extremely agitated when she discovered he and Devin planned to visit Mrs. Markham's in-laws that morning.

Though the housekeeper didn't say it, he had a sneaking suspicion that she feared those women would hurt his feelings. He didn't know whether he should be touched that she thought he possessed delicate feelings or simply be amused that she was hoping to protect him.

Now, though, it was time to get some answers and get back to her. He rapped his knuckles on the door twice.

"It will be fine, Truax," Captain said as they heard a quiet rustling on the other side of the door.

"I know. I just want to help her."

"You will. Once more, don't forget—no matter what happens, the future is already in God's hands. He knows what was meant to be."

Robert replayed that sentiment over and over again as Viola herself opened the door and stared at him and the captain as if they were thieving carpetbaggers intending to fleece them out of their life savings.

"You," she bit out. "What are you doing here?"

Ironically, her foul greeting made his mission easier. "Good morning to you, too, ma'am. I came to speak to you about Miranda."

"I have nothing to say to you."

"I beg to differ," Captain Monroe blurted as he walked right in, ignoring the small push on the door as he strode forward. "I have traveled a fair distance to speak to you and your mother. I intend to do just that."

Viola blanched. "Excuse me, but you may not barge into my home like you own it."

Her words rankled Robert to no end. "Tell me now what you said when Miranda told you that same thing."

"She never dared to say anything of the sort," Ruth Markham announced as she appeared from one of the back rooms. "She knew better than to speak to me with such disrespect."

Captain Monroe looked at her coolly. "Where may we sit?"

"We will not be leaving until we've gotten the answers we've come for," Robert advised. "How long we stay is up to you."

While her mother looked as if she was actually tempted to argue, Viola sighed. "Come into the drawing room. We'll conduct our business there." Then she turned and started down the short and narrow hallway.

After a brief second, her mother followed, her uneven gait looking painful even to Robert's untrained eye.

When they were alone in the entryway, Devin looked his way and smiled. "It seems the manner to deal with these women has been solved. We simply need to be direct, blunt, and if all else fails, rude."

"Agreed." He realized there had been a grain of hope that the women would be cordial enough to speak to him in an easy and open manner. It was obvious now that he hadn't been more wrong.

It made him sick to think that Miranda had been dealing with them all by herself for years now. They were thoroughly unpleasant.

Once all four of them took their seats in the small room that was filled with doilies, knickknacks, area rugs, heavy drapes, and an excessive amount of cat hair, Devin looked directly at the women.

"Even though you have not asked, I would like to introduce myself. I am Devin Monroe. I was Phillip's captain during his last two years of service in the army."

Ruth's expression softened. "He spoke of you often, Captain. He idolized you."

"I hope not. I was only his commanding officer," he said modestly. "However, I will tell you I thought very highly of your son. He was a good man, a good lieutenant, and above all, a true gentleman of the South. It was an honor to have known him."

"But he still died while in your care," Viola blurted.

"Phillip was not a child, ma'am," Robert replied. "Furthermore, he was suffering the effects of a gunshot wound. It festered while in captivity. There was nothing we could do."

"Perhaps."

"There was nothing anyone could have done. Like too many others to count, the Lord had decided it was his time to die."

Ruth's face pinched. "Sir—"

"We did not come all this way to discuss old injuries or Phillip's death," Devin smoothly intervened. "We want to know who is behind the letters to Miranda."

"What letters?" Ruth said.

"The threatening ones," Robert said. "The letters that disparage her marriage, her character, and her very self. The letters that come frequently. The letters that tell her to move."

Ruth frowned. "I have no knowledge of such things."

Captain Monroe eyed Viola carefully. "And you, ma'am? Do you have any knowledge of them?"

"I am not sure."

"I did not ask a difficult question," Robert said, leaning forward so his elbows rested on his knees.

Viola shook her head. "Perhaps, but still . . ."

"I saw the last one," Robert pushed. "It was not only vicious in content, but poorly written. Were you not able to have access to a good education, Miss Markham?"

Viola's face flushed. "I had a proper education. Just as Phillip did. I did not write letters such as the ones Miranda received."

Captain grinned. "So you actually do know about them, yes?"

Viola looked from her mother to Robert to Captain Monroe. Then, finally, she nodded. "I know about them," she whispered.

"You know more than that," Captain Monroe pressed. "If you did not write the letters, did you feed the information to the person who did?"

"I fail to see why any of this matters to you."

"A good woman has been tormented by them."

"You are painting a picture of Miranda that simply isn't true. She is far from being helpless, sir."

"Then let us make no mistake about this. I am not a helpless woman." He hardened his voice. "I expect you to answer me. Immediately."

"Mother, are you going to let him make such accusations against me?"

Ruth took a moment, then said, "I, too, would like to hear the truth about these letters, Viola. Speak."

A hand flew up to her chest. After several shaky breaths, Viola whispered, "I . . . I may have told him some things."

Robert leapt on that pronoun. "Him?"

Viola closed her eyes. From the position of her body, it was obvious that she was hoping the men would feel sorry for her circumstances and desist.

But Robert had no intention of backing down. "Who is he?"

"I shouldn't say."

Captain Monroe eyed her with a dark expression. "Oh, you should, ma'am."

Viola looked toward her mother. "Mother, say something."

Ruth, in contrast to her daughter, looked deflated. It was as if she was coming to terms with how their efforts to drive Miranda away sounded in the light of day and she wasn't proud of it. At all. "Viola, what have you done?"

"Nothing!" She leapt to her feet. "I only did what had to be done." She waved a hand. "Look at *where* we are living, Mother. At *how* we are living. We shouldn't be here. We should be in our home. In the home I was born in. In the house you raised me in!"

"I know that. But I didn't think you would have resorted to such tactics. It is most unbecoming."

"I need the name of the man," Devin said, his voice as hard and as unflinching as steel. "Now."

"Tell him, Viola," Ruth said. "You will not get any sympathy from me. Writing threatening letters is beneath us."

"Mamma—"

"Now, if you please," Captain Monroe said.

Viola glared at him, then exhaled, looking like her mother's twin. "Kyle Winter."

Robert surged to his feet. "So that worm of a bank clerk wrote these letters? The sheriff and I have suspected him. But why? Why do this?"

"Because his brother was killed at the Battle of the Wilderness."

Captain Monroe shrugged. "So were thousands of brave men. How was that Miranda Markham's fault?"

"Mr. Winter said Phillip told secrets about the South, maybe about the North too. Someone who was at Johnson's Island with Phillip told him so. He caused the fight to go so badly against the Confederacy."

Captain Monroe shook his head. "Winter was either misinformed or made that up. Phillip was . . . no traitor. He did not betray the C.S.A. You have my word on that."

Viola shook her head. "No, that isn't right. Kyle said the Union troops were too overwhelming in that battle. He was sure they knew too much about our soldiers' plans and strategies." Her voice rose. "He said there was no way they would have so soundly trounced our boys if not for Phillip's betrayal."

Robert shook his head. "Phillip did not betray us. We were out-funded, out-manned, and out-gunned. The Union army had almost twice as many men." He sighed, hating what he was about to say but unwilling to lie. "By the time that battle was fought, the South's loss was all but a certainty. The fact is that we were losing the war even then."

Mrs. Markham raised her voice. "The South had not fallen."

"No, ma'am, but many factors were against us. And even if

not, please believe me when I tell you that Phillip did not cause the rout."

Viola stared at him mulishly. "His brother still died."

"So did my brother!" Captain Monroe snapped. "So did half of America's brothers. It was war. It was terrible. It was bloody. But it was not Phillip Markham's fault."

Viola's eyes widened. She looked to be completely at a loss for words. "You sound so sure."

"I am sure," Monroe retorted. "But what I don't understand is your reasoning."

"Mine?"

"Yes, Miss Markham. What I want to know is why you didn't stand up for him."

She froze. "I tried."

"I don't think so." Staring at her intently, he asked, "Why didn't you stand up for your brother's memory? Even if you weren't close, he was your own flesh and blood."

Instead of answering, Viola colored and put her head down.

And it was Ruth who replied. "I believe I have the answer, gentlemen," she said, her voice flat. All trace of fire had disappeared.

"I did not know about the letters, nor that the hurtful rumors about my son"—she turned to stare at Viola—"came from Mr. Winter with Viola's knowledge. And while I do not care about that woman still living in the home my late husband built for me, I am dismayed that my own daughter betrayed Phillip's memory by helping Mr. Winter with these tactics."

Ruth straightened her shoulders before going on. "I am, however, certain I know the reason for her actions. Kyle Winter promised Viola if and when Miranda returned the house to us, she would be living there as his wife."

Incredulous, Robert turned to Viola.

"You agreed to Winter's plans in order to get married?"

"He said he loved me." She shook her head. "No, he does love me."

"He doesn't love you," Devin said. "Love isn't full of conditions or threaded with threats and pain. He was using you. I would be surprised if he even ever intended to marry you at all."

"You are wrong," Viola whispered. "You are all wrong."

"Believe that if you must," Captain Monroe said, his voice flat. "However, we both know if you believe that, you are lying to yourself."

"There's more," Ruth said. "I have also suspected that, rather than truly interested in marriage to Viola, Winter has desired the mansion itself. It's quite valuable, you know. And now that I know what he has done, I can see no better way for him to avenge his brother's supposed betrayal than to take over all Phillip's family has left. But I fear I have been turning a blind eye in my desire to return to my home and be rid of my son's wife."

Robert looked to his captain. "We have what we came for. I suggest we leave."

"I agree."

"Wait!" Ruth called out as she struggled to her feet. "What is going to happen to us now?"

"I have no earthly idea."

"Are you going to tell the sheriff?"

"Of course," Robert answered.

"But we are her family."

"I don't see how it matters," Devin replied. "You have already made your choices, you have been party to blackmail, and you will be answering for your actions for years to come and for eternity."

"You don't understand," Viola cried out. "We deserve . . . we need—"

"You need compassion and forgiveness and trust," Robert bit out as he slapped his hat back on his lap. "I suggest you begin searching for those things again. In the meantime, if you so much as glance in Miranda's direction, I will make sure you will be brought to Sheriff Kern."

Ruth had the audacity to roll her eyes. "Kern. He is no one. He has no power at all."

"That, Mrs. Markham, is about to change," Captain Monroe said before bowing slightly, leading the way out the door of the drawing room, and heading outside.

Robert followed, glad they had several hours before they were going to have the opportunity to face Kyle Winter. Robert knew without a doubt if the man walked in front of him at that moment . . . well, those would be the last pain-free steps he'd walk in months.

As far as he was concerned, it was past time for the man to get a taste of what it had been like to walk in Miranda Markham's shoes.

23

THE MEN HAD LEFT EARLY THAT MORNING. HOURS LATER, Miranda learned they'd asked her staff for directions to Viola and Ruth's home.

Miranda was mystified why the men hadn't asked her about the women or for directions. After all, she had been to their home several times, though only when Phillip had been home on leave. Had they worried about upsetting her? Were they planning to visit other locales besides that house? Or was it simply a matter of them not wanting Miranda to be present when they spoke to Viola and Ruth?

Especially because she had no idea what they thought the two women could tell them about her troubles, other than their own desire for her to leave this house, Miranda hoped Robert and Captain Monroe hadn't wanted her present when they talked to the ladies. Because, quite frankly, she had no desire to be around the women ever again. They were callous and selfish, and she'd had enough of their difficult dispositions for a lifetime.

Now that she had support and the dark depression that had hovered around her psyche for months had at last lifted, Miranda felt renewed. Instead of sitting and worrying, she was eager to do things again. To make plans for her future. To live. For the first time since she'd moved in, she was thinking about doing some redecorating. The idea of pulling down some of the old velvet drapes that hung over almost every window and sew some new, lighter curtains was appealing. Actually, the idea of working on any project for the house was as tempting to her as candy had to be to a small child.

With that in mind, Miranda slipped on an easy-fitting calico day dress and concentrated on work. A new guest had arrived just a few hours ago. She was an elderly lady, the mother of a ship's first mate or some such. She wanted to spend some time with her boy while he was in port.

The idea of the woman coming so far to spend a few precious hours with her son made Miranda smile. Perhaps that was the silver lining after spending so many years under war's thumb. No one took family or time spent with them for granted.

At that moment she remembered what she had told Robert after the two women's last visit. That she would let them know she would always look out for them. And she would, because that was what Phillip would have wanted.

After knocking on the guest's door and making sure she had everything she needed, she decided to sort through some of Phillip's favorite books. She had only begun when she heard a knock at the door.

Hoping it was Robert and Captain Monroe—perhaps they left their keys?—she rushed to the door. But instead of spying the two men she was coming to trust implicitly, she came face-to-face with a tall, extremely handsome man with a military bearing.

The moment he gazed at her, he smiled.

His smile was a beautiful thing. Straight, white teeth, framed by high cheekbones and a solid jaw. "You are Miranda."

She nodded. "I am Miranda Markham. However, I'm afraid you have me at a disadvantage. May I help you?"

He removed his hat. "My name is Ethan Kelly. I served with your husband, Phillip. I am actually looking for two gentlemen I believe are staying here. Robert Truax and Captain Monroe. Are they here, by any chance?"

There was something unique in the way he spoke. Maybe it was his cadence? He spoke in starts and stops. Maybe it was the way he was staring intently at her, as if a cannon could go off behind him and he wouldn't pay it any mind.

Suddenly, she knew who he was. Just as he did with Captain Monroe, Phillip had described him well. "You're Major Kelly, aren't you?"

"I was. However, I'm plain old Mr. Kelly now."

His smile was so warm, she felt as if she were greeting an old friend. "Please, do come in, Major Kelly." The moment she ushered him inside and closed the door, she held out her hand. "I'm honored to make your acquaintance. I feel like I am greeting another old friend. Phillip spoke so highly of all of you."

His brown eyes softened. "He was an excellent man. And he certainly thought the world of you."

"I'm beginning to realize that. Robert and Captain Monroe said much the same thing. He . . . well, he was a very good husband."

After taking his coat, she offered him a seat in the parlor. She was about to ask if she could call for tea or coffee or a light repast when Belle rushed forward.

"I'm sorry I wasn't here to get the door, ma'am," she said. "I went out to run some errands for Cook and lost track of time."

"You have nothing to worry about. I don't mind answering the door from time to time." Smiling in Major Kelly's direction, she said, "Especially to friends."

Belle's apologetic stance turned curious as she turned to look at Major Kelly.

He was already on his feet. "Miss," he said. "Good morning."

"Good morning. Sir." She opened her mouth. Closed it, then shook her head. "I'm sorry. I meant, thank you."

Miranda hid a smile. Her sweet maid looked entranced. Miranda didn't blame her one bit. Major Kelly was truly handsome. So handsome, he looked like he belonged on the stage.

But what Miranda also noted was that he seemed to be looking at Belle in appreciation.

Feeling a bit like a third wheel, Miranda cleared her throat. Instantly, both turned to face her. Belle's cheeks were lightly flushed.

"Major Kelly, this is Belle Harden. She works for me as kind of a maid of all work. Belle, this is Major Ethan Kelly. He served with Phillip."

Belle's eyes widened. "You're a major?"

"Yes. Well, I was."

"Goodness."

Major Kelly laughed. "I promise you, those days are in the past, thank goodness. And, well, I have to say that plenty of people were not terribly intrigued or impressed by my rank. My sergeant, for example, could have easily run our unit without my interference."

"I am sure I don't know about that," Belle breathed.

"Belle, I was just about to offer Major Kelly some refreshment. Would you prepare some coffee and a tray for us?"

"Of course. I'll get right on it." But to Miranda's amusement, her maid didn't move a muscle.

"Thank you. That will be all."

At last, the maid blinked. "Yes, ma'am." She turned away with a snap of her skirts and exited the room again. The minute they were alone Miranda couldn't help herself. She burst out laughing.

"I must admit that was a first for her and me, sir. She usually looks far less, well . . . far less spellbound by visitors."

"I'll take your word for it," he said with a hearty chuckle of his own. "At the risk of sounding too full of myself, her appreciation did my vanity good."

"I imagine it did, though at the risk of embarrassing you, sir, I would venture that her reaction is not as outlandish as you are making it out to be."

"In my current job, I promise you, I rarely get stared at like I'm someone of worth."

She noticed there was more than a trace of bitterness underlying his words. She wondered why. Was he thinking of the war or everything that had happened since? "You know, the first time Phillip left, when I knew he was going to be marching into battle, I barely slept. I was worried about him. Worried about him getting hurt, being without help, and dying. The stories that came back from the front . . . well, they were very bad."

"They were accurate. Our battles were difficult. Many, many men didn't survive."

"What I'm trying to say is that I didn't think I would ever have a longer evening than those nights. Long evenings spent with worry and doubts . . . but I discovered that life after is sometimes harder to handle."

"Yes. I would agree." He frowned. "And then one hates to complain because we're alive."

"Why are you here, sir? Are you on business with the men?"

"Devin Monroe contacted me. He relayed to me what Robert had relayed to him in a recent letter. I dropped everything and got on a train here from San Antonio."

She shook her head in wonder. "I find it amazing that you would come so far for me."

"You shouldn't find it surprising at all. We all wanted to be here for you. Thomas Baker would be here as well, if he could."

"Your loyalty seems to know no bounds."

"For the men I served with, it does not."

"I appreciate it more than I can say." Good manners might have expected her to say his visit wasn't needed, but she was too happy to not be alone to say that.

"Please don't mention it. Like I said, I am glad to be of use. It's good to have a worthy cause to fight for again."

"What do you do now? If I may ask?"

"I do several things in San Antonio. But by trade, I suppose you could say I'm mainly a gambler, ma'am."

A gambler! Staring at him, Miranda reflected that he certainly didn't look like any gambler she'd ever met. The gamblers she had crossed paths with in Galveston had come off the boats. Most were rather fidgety, pale, and thin men. This gentleman, on the other hand, looked tan and fit. Realizing she was staring, she said, "I must admit I haven't met many gamblers."

His lips twitched. "That is a very good thing, madam." He shrugged. "I am good at it, which some might say is not to my benefit. I, however, like to think it is a useful skill."

"Indeed." Smiling softly, she said, "I am not one to judge, sir. I have found that we'll all do what we must to survive."

"Indeed, Mrs. Markham. I have found that to be continually true."

It felt good to be back in the saddle. It felt even better to be riding alongside his captain. They'd spent countless hours on horseback together during the war, throughout most of Tennessee, Pennsylvania, and everywhere in between. Ironically, they'd never ridden together in their home state of Texas.

"These horses are in surprisingly good condition," Robert said as he patted his gelding's flank.

"I inspected several stables when I arrived in Houston two days ago. I wanted to have a good idea where the best horseflesh was in case we needed some mounts."

"What?" Robert had no idea that he'd been in Houston for any length of time before heading to Galveston.

Monroe shrugged. "It never hurts to be prepared."

"Obviously not." As Robert clenched his legs, prompting his mount into a canter, he said, "You never fail to surprise me, sir. I'm glad you're here."

"I am too. What's happened to Miranda isn't right."

Thinking of how Viola and Ruth betrayed both Miranda and Phillip, Robert thought that was something of an understatement. "At least we now know who has been behind the letters and the rumors."

Devin's expression hardened. "What do you know about this Kyle Winter?"

"Enough to know that it will be a pleasure to pay him a visit and escort him to Sheriff Kern. Jess will be glad his suspicions about Winter have been justified. He even followed the man early one morning to see what he was up to. He ended up down by the water, but when he engaged Winter in conversation, his excuse for being there didn't hold up. Now I wonder if Ruth is right about Winter's interest in the canal. You were right to suspect its worth had something to do with this."

"Too bad we can't dispense our own justice and string him up from a tree."

Thinking of how Winter had talked down to Miranda in front of the other customers of the bank and even in front of him the first time he accompanied Miranda, Robert didn't disagree. "I agree with you one hundred percent, Captain. This man deserves to be treated the way he treated Miranda. Harshly and without remorse."

"Where to next? The Iron Rail or the bank?"

"The bank," Robert said after a moment's reflection. "The next time I see Miranda, I want to be able to tell her that her troubles are over. At least with Kyle Winter."

24

MIRANDA HAD HOPED ROBERT MIGHT BE BACK IN TIME TO accompany her to her weekly visit to the bank. Unfortunately, he was nowhere to be found. After watching the clock tick past early afternoon and creep toward four o'clock, she knew she could wait no longer.

As she slipped the week's worth of receipts and notes into her reticule, Miranda resigned herself to the next hour's difficulty. Lord knew, she'd survived the encounter with Mr. Winter on her own plenty of times before. She would simply have to suffer through his rudeness again.

Unless . . .

Gazing up the stairs, she thought about Major Kelly. He was as close to Phillip as Robert and Captain Monroe were. He'd also already told her he took his vow to Phillip seriously. She hated to be so weak as to need him to accompany her on this errand, but in the scheme of things, it surely wasn't much to ask, was it?

And he did seem to be simply waiting for the men to return too. Running this errand with her would help make the time go faster.

Making a decision, she walked up the stairs and knocked on his door before she lost her nerve.

He answered immediately. "Yes, Mrs. Markham?"

He'd taken off his suit jacket, vest, and tie. He'd also rolled up his sleeves. He looked so much like how Phillip had after church on the few Sunday afternoons they'd had together. She soaked in his appearance, savoring the memory that she'd pushed away for far too long.

Then she recalled herself. "Major Kelly, I don't wish to inconvenience you, but I have a favor to ask."

He smiled, as if she'd truly made his day by needing him. "All you have to do is ask and I'll help in any way I can."

She smiled back before concentrating on her words. She wanted to beg his help in just the right way, so he would understand why she was asking. At the same time she wanted to be sure he knew this favor wasn't going to take up hours of his time. "You see, every Friday I must make a deposit to the bank. The teller there . . . well, he is rather rude. He . . . well, he says disparaging things to me."

He blinked slowly, as if he was trying to come to terms with what he was hearing. "He is rude to you. To Lieutenant Markham's widow."

"He . . . well, he is one of the people who has been saying Phillip was a traitor. And . . . well, he has suggested that my character has much to be desired."

"Your character?" he asked slowly.

"Yes. On account of the fact that I have turned Phillip's house into a boardinghouse."

"This is your house too, Mrs. Markham."

"Yes. And, well, I have had no choice but to take in boarders. The bills must be paid."

"Of course." His eyes narrowed. "Therefore, you would rather not go to the bank alone."

She swallowed. "Yes. Um, well, I did go by myself for several years. But since Robert has been here, he's accompanied me and the task has been much easier to bear. That is why I decided to ask you to come with me. If you wouldn't mind, that is."

"It would be my honor to go in Robert's place, ma'am. When would you like to depart?"

"As soon as it is possible. I am supposed to be there before five. I usually am there before four."

The muscle in his jaw jumped. "Let's not make him wait, then. I'll be downstairs presently."

Afraid she was making too much out of what was usually a routine errand, she said, "Please, take your time. I need to put on a bonnet."

"I'll await at your pleasure, ma'am."

"Thank you."

"There is no need for thanks. You have given me a way to help you. I am grateful for that."

Breathing a sigh of relief, Miranda walked to her room, only to find her door open and Belle dusting the furniture.

She started when she saw Miranda walk in. "I'm sorry, ma'am. I didn't realize you were coming back in here right now."

"No need to apologize. I came in to put on a bonnet and gloves. I've asked Major Kelly to accompany me to the bank."

"I'm glad of that. With you standing next to him, I have a feeling Mr. Winter will think long and hard about his manners today."

"I would be very happy if that was the case." She took a simple black bonnet out of the box, then sat down at her dressing table to fashion it on her head.

Belle came to stand behind her. "If I may, Mrs. Markham?"

"Of course."

Carefully, Belle took down her hair, brushed it, then pinned up her tresses again. As she looked in the mirror, Miranda saw that her hair was in essentially the same style as it always was. However, Belle had pulled her hair back less severely. The looser arrangement was more becoming. She looked more feminine, even younger.

Miranda was amazed. "I wasn't aware you knew how to fashion hair." And surprised Belle would want her to be more attractive in the presence of the man she had so recently admired. Actually, she suspected it was Sheriff Kern who had caught Belle's eye, but whoever Belle cared for, that was her business.

"I learned a long time ago." Blushing, she said, "Sometimes my mother would ask me to dress her hair." She picked up the hat, eyed two of the pale pink roses in the vase on her table, and threaded them into the brim. Then she pulled out one of Miranda's more ornate hat pins and secured it.

Looking in the mirror, Miranda tilted her head this way and that. The effect was very pretty. "I don't believe I've ever been so thankful to have received such pretty roses in the winter."

"They do you proud, ma'am."

"Major Kelly is waiting for me downstairs," she said as she pulled on her gloves. "Wish us luck."

"You won't need any luck. Mr. Markham's friends are at last making everything better."

"They are." She glanced at Belle and realized they were both most likely thinking the same thing. It was going to be so very hard when Phillip's comrades left.

When she appeared on the stairs, Major Kelly glanced up at her and smiled. "You look as pretty as a picture. All the men in Galveston Island will undoubtedly be green with envy."

After she double-checked her reticule for her deposit, she

closed the top of it with a firm snap. "The women we pass will no doubt feel the same way."

Major Kelly's laughter rang through the house. "I am beginning to understand why Phillip was so smitten, ma'am. Now, let's go take care of this odious errand."

Thinking that was the best descriptor yet, she allowed him to help her put on her cloak and then led the way outside.

Thirty minutes later, Miranda was trying her best not to clutch Major Kelly's arm as a lifeline. Because the atmosphere at the bank had not changed a bit. Not in the slightest. Not without Robert there.

Once again the various officers of the bank looked down their noses at her, the other customers barely acknowledged her, and Mr. Winter seemed to be as determined as he ever was to make sure she felt like a second-class citizen.

She could feel Major Kelly's ire rise as he took in every slight. From the hard expression that had appeared in his eyes, she was starting to even think that he was practically cataloguing each person so he could get retribution at a later date.

After Mr. Winter finished with the wife of one of the city's well-known cotton suppliers, he shuffled some papers on his counter, obviously taking his time to force Miranda to stand even longer for his bidding.

Major Kelly tensed up. She laid a hand on his arm. "I know it is hard, but please, don't make a fuss."

He leaned down. "Someone needs to make a fuss. This is inexcusable."

"I agree. But when you and Robert and the captain leave, I'll have to be here in Galveston by myself. And unless something changes, I'm going to have to continue to make my weekly deposit. This errand is hard enough. I don't want things to get worse."

"We will not leave you like this. Things will get better, I promise," he said before stepping forward to Mr. Winter. "Mrs. Markham has business to take care of," he said in a loud, authoritative voice. "She has waited long enough. You will see her now."

Mr. Winter lifted his chin. "I'll see her when I am ready."

Major Kelly's expression turned to ice. "I suggest that moment be now."

Unperturbed, the clerk wrinkled his brow. "I don't know who you are, and I don't care. As far as I'm concerned, you are simply another man warming the bed of a traitor's widow."

Major Kelly slammed his hand on the counter. "Bring me whoever is in charge here. Now."

"I don't answer to the likes of you."

Kelly glared at him, then turned and spoke to the room at large. "Who is in charge in this institution?"

The whole room—easily at least twenty-five people—went quiet. After a moment, Mr. Carrington stood up and approached. "I am. Is there a problem?"

"From the moment we arrived, Mrs. Markham has been both ignored and derided."

"Sir, I'm sure you have misunderstood the situation."

"Do not tell me what I witnessed. Furthermore, I don't care to learn why you have permitted such behavior in your establishment. But I will tell you that it will stop now."

Mr. Carrington blanched. "You should watch yourself, sir. If you are the latest guest in Mrs. Markham's boardinghouse, your concern is of no interest to me."

The cold, harsh stare Major Kelly sent to the bank president should have stopped him in his tracks. "I beg your pardon, but I am certain you should rethink your decision. As far as I'm concerned, there is everything for you to worry about."

"I beg your pardon," Mr. Winter said. Still standing behind the counter, he leaned his elbows on the top. "But you have obviously no idea to whom you are speaking. This is Mr. *Marcus Carrington*."

Miranda had had enough. "This gentleman is Mr. Ethan Kelly. He served as a major for the C.S.A. and was held prisoner on Johnson's Island. He is a decorated war hero. Do you truly dare to pawn off your prejudices of me onto him?"

The bank president paled. "You are Major Ethan Kelly? Of the Kelly family in Houston? Who rode with the Texas Rangers?"

"I am," Major Kelly replied, his voice like ice. "Are you going to tell me now that we have a problem?"

As low murmurings flew through the occupants of the room, the bank president paled further. "Of course not. I am sorry, Major Kelly." He snapped his fingers. "Winter, please see to Major Kelly and, uh, Mrs. Markham right now."

With a sigh, Miranda stepped forward, only to be pulled back by her escort. "I'm afraid, Mr. Carrington, that your apology is not sufficient."

After freezing for a second, the bank president stepped forward, his rotund appearance looking as if it was shrinking before their eyes. "Pardon me, sir? What else do you need?"

"I need you to apologize to Mrs. Markham. Immediately. Next, I will hear you order this . . . this clerk of yours to speak to her in a more respectful way."

Mr. Carrington looked at Major Kelly, then his clerk, then glanced around the room.

Miranda was surprised to find that most everyone present was glaring at the bank president. It seemed there were few people in Galveston who would disrespect such a war hero so publicly.

After swallowing hard, Mr. Carrington turned to her. "I do beg your pardon for my clerk's mistreatment of you, Mrs. Markham. I hope you will not hold it against us."

She was so surprised, she merely nodded.

"And?" Kelly prodded.

Sweat formed on the gentleman's brow. "And . . . and I will give you my word that you will be treated better in the future. I assure you."

Miranda wasn't sure if she believed such a pretty speech. She actually doubted the promise would last after Phillip's friends left. "Thank you."

"Very good," Major Kelly said with a nod of his head. "Now you will help Mrs. Markham with her deposit."

"What? No, that is Mr. Winter's job."

"Not today."

Mr. Carrington visibly debated whether to argue. Then, with a halfhearted shrug, he said, "Very well. Kyle, stand aside."

Mr. Winter paled. "But, sir—"

"Don't say another word," Mr. Carrington said.

But instead of listening, Mr. Winter puffed up, his whole body filled with indignation. "But you know who she is. You know who her husband was."

Major Kelly stepped forward, obviously intent on boxing the man's ears.

But before Kelly could do a thing, Mr. Carrington pointed to the back door. "Out, Winter. Now."

At last Mr. Winter stepped away. Looking increasingly upset with every step, he left the room and slapped the door shut behind him.

"Idiot," Kelly muttered under his breath.

Miranda stayed completely quiet.

By the time Mr. Carrington finished noting her deposit, which he did with shaking hands due to Major Kelly's fierce glare, Mr. Winter still had not returned.

Since several men and women were still waiting to be helped, the bank president himself beckoned the next person in line forward.

As Major Kelly took her arm, one of the women who had been standing in line eyed her in a confused way. "You certainly have some friends in high places, Mrs. Markham."

"No," Kelly interrupted. "I am the one who has that honor. Miranda is one of the finest women I've met. She was the wife of one of the best men I had the good fortune to serve with."

"Yes, well. There are some who say—"

"I would watch who you listen to from now on, ma'am. You may begin to regret your choice of causes."

Two men and one woman nodded. "It's about time someone put that clerk in his place," one of the men said. "It's been difficult to watch how they've been treating you in here, week after week."

Though Miranda ached to ask why he had never stood up for her, she merely nodded as they exited, her hand clinging to Major Kelly's arm like it was her lifeline.

The moment they walked down the stairs, Miranda blew out a breath of air she hadn't even realized she'd been holding. "Major Kelly, you are a force to be reckoned with."

"No, ma'am. I am simply old enough to be tired of having to put up with such foolishness."

"Thank you," she said. "Robert scared them, but you somehow made the threat stick."

Major Kelly looked pleased. "To tell you the truth, it felt really good to throw my weight around. I hadn't done that in a while."

"You don't do such antics in San Antonio?" she asked as they walked toward the edge of the Strand, next to the rows of cluttered warehouses, some damaged in storms or during the Galveston battle.

"No," he said quietly. "My—" Stopping abruptly, he reached for her elbow. "Get behind me, Miranda."

Startled, she did as he asked. But when she peeked around him, she saw what he was guarding her against. None other than Kyle Winter was facing them with a pistol. He was holding it in both of his shaking hands. Miranda wondered if he'd ever held a gun before. She hoped it was not loaded, but she had to assume it was.

"Come with me," he ordered her.

"Yes, yes, of course."

"You will not go anywhere with him," Major Kelly said. "I would have to be incapacitated for that to happen."

"That can be arranged," Mr. Winter said. Just before he shot Major Kelly in the thigh.

25

"HALLELUJAH!" DEVIN MONROE EXCLAIMED THE MOMENT they walked off the ferry and stepped foot onto Galveston Island. "I thought we were never going to get back on this island in one piece."

Robert chuckled. "I've been with you through battles and marches and prisoner-of-war camps. Through it all, you've never done more than press forward, hardly flinching. But today was a new experience."

Still looking a bit green, his captain attempted to draw himself up. "I don't usually get seasick. The sea was unusually rough."

"It was choppy, I'll give you that. But you were also unusually squeamish." He started laughing again. There was no hope of even trying to keep a straight face.

Devin looked away. "All I'm saying is that one would think our day's trip would have been easier. We were only going to Houston and back. Not Timbuktu."

"One would think," Robert quipped. Then as he remembered how callous the women were and how much they didn't seem to have a single moment's regret for their treatment of Miranda, he said, far more soberly, "Unfortunately, it was even worse than I remember."

"I swear, I think it was easier to direct two hundred men than those two women."

"Of course it was. The men listened. Those females did not."

"Neither did the ferryman." Devin rolled his eyes. "If he told me once, he told me a hundred times that he wasn't allowed to operate the ferry unless he was filled to capacity."

"He did stay true to his word."

"His sense of urgency has much to be desired," Devin said under his breath. "If there was ever a day that I wished I was still a captain and had some say in this world, today was it."

"Indeed, sir." Because he had experience with his captain's extremely rare loss of patience, Robert took care to look impassive. But inside, he was grinning like a loon. It had been quite a sight to see his captain, who held the respect of even generals, get beaten down by a pudgy ferryboat captain with a chip on his shoulder.

As they started down Water Street, Robert tipped his hat at an awaiting lady, then spoke. "Sir, it's late. I suggest we relax the rest of the evening. We can compare notes in the morning and visit with the bank clerk then."

"I like the way you're talking, soldier," Devin said with a grin. "I'm freezing cold and in need of a hot beverage, a bath, and a roaring fire." He paused. "Not necessarily in that order."

Robert was about to agree when he noticed Miranda's servant Emerson standing just beyond the ferry platform with a panicked expression on his face. "Something's happened," he said as he strode ahead.

The moment Emerson spied him he breathed a sigh of relief. "Oh, thank the good Lord. I didn't think you'd ever show up, sir."

That comment only made his heart beat faster. "What has happened?"

"Everything, it seems," he sputtered.

"Explain yourself," Devin ordered.

"Oh, yes, sir. You see, well, I have some news to tell you about Major Kelly. You see, he arrived earlier and . . ."

Emerson's words were almost too much to take in at once. Mind spinning, Robert turned to his captain to try to make sense of things. "Did you know Ethan was coming here?"

"I wasn't sure he would join us, but I hoped he would. After I received your letter, I wrote Kelly and told him what's been happening with Phillip's wife. I told him you've additionally been uncovering information right and left. I can only assume he took it upon himself to lend a hand."

"Well, he may be regretting that decision," Emerson said. "On account that he got shot, you see."

Time seemed to freeze. "Shot, you say?" Devin asked, his voice hoarse.

"Yessir." Emerson pointed down the street behind them. "Right outside the bank it was."

"Is he alive?"

Emerson brightened a bit. "Oh, yessir, he is. Matter of fact, he's with the surgeon now. He's a good one too."

"How good?" Devin asked.

"I promise, Captain, that he's a real particular doctor. Not a sawbones in the slightest. Keeps his offices spick and span, he does. Major Kelly is in good hands."

After mumbling something under his breath, the captain said, "Take me to him, Emerson. I need to see this for myself. I've yet to meet a surgeon I would trust not to make things worse."

"I'll go too," Robert said, wondering who would shoot Ethan and why. "If he needs anything, I can go fetch it. Emerson, please tell Mrs. Markham where we are, and that we'll talk to Sheriff Kern as soon as we can."

But Emerson shook his head. "No, sir. You see, that ain't

all. From what I understand, Major Kelly accompanied Mrs. Markham to the bank—"

"Miranda was with him?" Robert nearly shouted.

"Yessir. And he got mad when people there were being rude to her. Then he called out Mr. Carrington."

"Who is that?"

"The bank president himself!" Emerson declared proudly. "After Major Kelly told him who he was, and Mr. Carrington put two and two together and all, he apologized to Mrs. Markham."

Robert was interested in the story but was more interested in seeing to his old friend and making sure Miranda was safe and well. "Tell us about it later, Emerson. After you tell me how Mrs. Markham is. Did she accompany the major to the physician?"

The little man gulped. "No, sir."

"Pardon me?"

"You see, I ain't done."

"Finish up, if you please," Captain Monroe said.

"Well, Major Kelly wanted Mr. Carrington to help Mrs. Markham instead of Mr. Winter."

"That man is a worm," explained Robert. "If I could prevent him from even looking Miranda's way again, I would."

"Oh, yes, sir, he is," Emerson said. "See, you see . . . Mr. Carrington agreed, but Mr. Winter got mad."

"And then?" Monroe said impatiently. "Get to the point."

"And then Mr. Carrington told him to leave. And when Miss Miranda and Major Kelly left the building, Mr. Winter shot Major Kelly and took Mrs. Markham!"

He could sense Monroe's unease, but for Robert, time seemed to stand still. "Took her where?"

"I'm not sure, exactly. But by all accounts, everyone believes they darted into the warehouse district."

Robert's pulse started to race, not from fear but adrenaline. It was the same reaction his body had when they were mere minutes from going into battle. "Where is Mrs. Markham now, Emerson?"

"That's what I've been trying to tell ya," Emerson said with a pull on his collar. "Mrs. Markham is with Mr. Winter in the warehouses and no one has seen hide nor hair of her for hours." Looking both appalled and dejected, he said, "I'm sorry to tell you, sir, but she's been kidnapped."

Robert looked at the captain. His lips were pressed together in a thin line. "Did you say 'hours'?" After Emerson nodded, he barked, "When, exactly, did this happen?"

"At least three hours ago, I reckon. Maybe toward four?" Emerson scratched his chin. "You two have been gone a long time."

Though every muscle in his body ached to head directly to the warehouse district, Robert knew it would be far more prudent to ascertain as much information as possible before going off half-cocked. "Who has been searching for her?" he asked, hoping and praying the servant would give him a name and not a shrug.

Emerson's expression cleared. "Oh. Sheriff Kern is, Mr. Truax. The moment he heard about what happened, I heard he grabbed his pistol and went after them."

Some relief filled him, but not enough. With a start, he realized he didn't trust anyone to protect Miranda other than himself. "Who else?"

"I don't know." Emerson looked up at the sky as if he was attempting to pull the information out of thin air. "Maybe one of his deputies?" He frowned. "I have to tell ya, though, I'd almost rather Mrs. Markham be lost with Mr. Winter than 'rescued' by one of Kern's men. They're a sorry lot, to be sure."

Captain Monroe exchanged a glance with Robert. "What do you think? Do we have time to get our weapons?"

Though Robert was reluctant to spend one more minute simply standing and pondering, years of fighting made him cautious and able to see the benefits of thinking through the situation. "I don't think we have a choice, sir. If Winter shot Kelly, he's liable to shoot again."

"Good point. Lead us to the quickest way back to the house, Emerson," Captain Monroe ordered. "And be quick about it. We have no time to spare."

"Yes, sir," Emerson replied, then turned sharply to his right and picked up his pace, fairly running down a back alley, Robert and his captain on his heels.

As they ran, Robert left the rest of his thoughts unspoken. Mainly that if Winter shot Kelly, he might have also already injured Miranda. And that as soon as Winter met either him or Monroe face-to-face, he would be receiving his retribution. There was no way Ethan Kelly had survived Gettysburg and several months in a Yankee prisoner-of-war camp only to be bested by a disgruntled bank clerk with an ax to grind.

There was no way that was ever going to happen. Not if he could help it.

The moment they tore open the front door, Belle, Winnie, and Cook ran to meet them.

"Do you have her?" When the answer became obvious, Winnie sniffed. "Oh, where is she?"

"I don't know, but we're going to find her," Robert said. "We came in only for our weapons."

As he and Monroe rushed up the stairs, Belle followed. "Sirs, beg your pardon, but is it true about Major Kelly? Has he really been shot?"

Captain Monroe spared her only the briefest of glances. "That's what Emerson says. We haven't seen him."

"I know you both are going to find Mrs. Markham, and I'm real glad of that. But . . . would you mind terribly if I went and sat with the major?"

"I think that is a fine idea," Robert said as he reached into his knapsack, pulled out his Colt and a box of bullets, then began loading the revolver.

"Oh, I'm so glad. I would hate for him to be alone."

"I would too," he said as he raced back to the hall. Monroe was already trotting down the stairs. "Thank you, Belle."

"Of course. Please, please go find Mrs. Markham."

"I will find her tonight," Robert promised. He didn't dare add that he was hoping and praying he would find her alive.

"You need me to do anything besides look after your major?"

"Pray," Monroe called out as he swung open the door. "And, Belle?"

"Yes . . . yes, sir?"

"You tell that sawbones that Kelly keeps his leg," he said fiercely. "You hear me?"

"Oh, yes, sir!" she called. "I'll make sure that happens. You can count on me."

Robert hoped that really was the case, because it was now apparent that he was going to need to place his complete trust in her and Kern. And the Lord, of course.

He sincerely prayed that would be enough.

26

Galveston's warehouse district was a run-down hodgepodge of derelict buildings, thriving cotton warehouses, and empty storefronts. With every storm that had passed through the area, water and wind had caused a good bit of damage to some of it.

Never all.

For that reason, it was an area in constant change. It lay in between the port and the red-light district, and the businessmen who oversaw the area were generally thought to be unscrupulous. They were men just coming out of years of war with nothing to lose. Because of all that—as well as the well-known rat population— Miranda had stayed far away from this section of the city.

Until now.

She was currently sitting alone on the second floor of what surely was once a fishery. The building smelled abominable and creaked and groaned painfully with every burst of wind. Her hands were tied behind her back with rope, she was bruised, and she had a cut on her cheek that she feared would always leave a scar.

If she survived.

After shooting poor Major Kelly, Mr. Winter had jerked her forward, pulling her into the crowded alleys and passageways of the warehouse district. She'd screamed and cried, but no one they passed had given her any mind.

Any attempts of rescue wouldn't have been fruitful anyway. Mr. Winter had been dragging her along like a man possessed, calling her foul names and accusing her of awful things. She doubted he would have been any kinder to any poor soul who would have attempted to rescue her.

After he dragged her into the fishery, he forced her to climb the rickety stairs into an abandoned loft. Then he talked and talked, hardly taking a breath.

As much as Miranda could ascertain from the madman's ramblings, Mr. Carrington's bowing to Ethan Kelly's wishes had pushed Kyle Winter over the edge, and he'd finally had enough of waiting for his schemes to work. He told her how he blamed Phillip for his brother's death, and how he had been courting Viola to claim the house and its prime location as his ultimate means of revenge. Then how while Viola imagined they were going to live happily as husband and wife, he planned to sell the house to one of the many ship captains who often came in, to one of the Yankee profiteers, or to one of the men making fortunes in cotton as both the North and South struggled to pull themselves together.

He was going to destroy everything Phillip Markham had ever known, and, he said, the only real obstacle was her. She was made of far stronger stuff than he'd ever imagined.

Then he pushed her into a small space about the size of a storage room. The action had caused her to trip and fall. She'd landed clumsily. Because of that, she'd cut both her arm and cheek as well as bruised most of her limbs.

The moment she struggled to stand upright, Mr. Winter yanked her to her feet, then proceeded to pull her to the back of the musty space.

While she was still disoriented, he tied her hands, secured her to a rusty pipe, and left.

That had been at least two hours ago. Maybe three. She had no idea where he had gone or if and when he would return.

Now it was dark, though some shadows played along the walls, making the already-scary situation worse. She kept imagining someone was attempting to break into the room to join her. Whether it was a rat or a vagrant, she would have no way to fight back.

Miranda had known her situation would get even more horrific when darkness fell. She wouldn't be able to see anything and the temperature would drop even more. She'd been right.

Already bitterly cold, she rested her head against the wall of the room and closed her eyes. Tried to calm her nerves.

It was ironic that she'd fought her depression for months, contemplating suicide in much the same way a cook considered a new recipe. She'd spent hours in a fog, wondering whether it would be better to die by slicing her wrists or jumping through a window.

Only her respect and love for her staff had prevented her from doing either.

Or so she'd thought.

Now she wondered if she actually ever had wanted to die at all. Maybe it hadn't been fear that had stopped her but a deep-seated need to survive.

It was certainly how she felt now. She was willing to do anything to fight that dreadful Kyle Winter and his schemes to destroy her husband's memory, his very home. She did not want to spend her last hours on earth in an abandoned fishery. She certainly didn't want his to be the last face she ever saw.

There was no way she could ever simply lie down and give in

to a man like him. If she died in his captivity, it would make his life so much easier. It would be like he won. And she would be doing the exact opposite of what Phillip had done.

She couldn't let that happen. She was not going to make anything easy for Mr. Winter, and she was not going to die without putting up at least half as much of a fight as Robert and Devin had told her Phillip did.

She didn't know how she was going to survive, but she would. To perish this way was unthinkable.

It took Belle asking for directions several times before she located Dr. Kronke's offices. Of German descent, the doctor hadn't been in Galveston long, but it seemed he had already developed a formidable reputation.

Injured soldiers and ailing sailors alike seemed to praise his efforts. By the time Belle located the man's door and knocked twice, she had decided that Major Kelly was receiving the best treatment possible.

To her surprise, the doctor opened the door himself. Peering at her closely, he tilted his head. "Yes?"

"Hello. I'm, uh, Belle. I'm looking for Major Kelly. He received a gunshot wound to his leg, I believe?"

The doctor beamed. Beamed! "He did, indeed."

She thought his smile was strange, but it did give her a curious sense of hope. "Is he still here? May I see him?"

"Of course. Come in!" He stepped back.

She walked into a tiny receiving area, the whole space barely big enough for two rather uncomfortable wooden chairs and a small, very fine wooden table in between them.

The walls were covered in light blue wallpaper and framed prints of what she could only assume were scenes from Germany hung on his walls. It was a pretty, cozy little room, and a surprise when she'd expected to see a rather bare doctor's examining room.

He peeked at her a little more closely through his wire-rimmed glasses. "Are you the major's sweetheart?"

"Me? Oh, goodness, no. I'm, uh, well, I work for Mrs. Markham," she sputtered, feeling her neck flush. As he continued to stare at her with interest, Belle continued, attempting to make some kind of coherent sense. "She runs a boardinghouse. She's currently, um, hosting three men who served in the army with her husband."

He tilted his gray head. "So you are here for her?"

"No . . ." Why was she there, exactly? How could she explain her need to see Major Kelly? "Sir? I mean, Dr. Kronke, is he all right? We're all very worried."

"Yes, I imagine you are. As for your Major Kelly, he is doing well so far. I was able to remove the bullet without any consequence. He lost some blood, of course, but overall he doesn't seem too worse for wear." He shrugged. "We'll see what happens over the next twenty-four hours. Infection is any wound's worst enemy."

Belle was fairly proud of herself for not turning weak or light-headed at the mention of the officer's loss of blood. "May I sit with him?"

"He might not wake up for some time," he warned. "It might even be hours."

"That's okay. I don't want him to be alone."

Dr. Kronke grinned. "Of course you don't. Well, my dear, if you are willing to keep this major company, I'll even give you a job. When he wakes up, you may give him sips of water."

"Yes, I can do that."

After beaming at her again, he tottered to another door and quietly opened it. She followed right behind and was immediately struck by the scent of antiseptic, clean cotton, and lavender, of all things. When she fingered the bowl of dried herbs, the doctor chuckled.

"You have seen my weakness, I see. I have found that I grew weary of the smell of blood and sickness. The lavender soothes me."

"It soothes me too," she said, meeting his gaze with a half-smile. Then all thoughts of dried herbs were forgotten as she spied Major Kelly lying motionless in a small, neatly made cot.

The doctor bustled over to the lone utilitarian chair resting against the wall and carried it to the major's bedside. "Here you are, dear. I'll have someone bring in a pitcher of water and two glasses to you shortly."

"Two glasses?"

He bowed slightly. "Sitting bedside is hard work. You might need to take a sip every now and then too."

He turned and walked out the door before Belle could thank him for his kindness. When the door shut, and she was completely alone with Major Kelly, Belle allowed herself to look her fill of him.

He was still in his shirt, but his trousers had been removed. A white sheet covered him up to his waist, with only his left bandaged leg exposed. A small moss-colored blanket was neatly folded at the foot of the bed. Fearing he might be cold, she shook it out and placed it on his body and around his wound. He shifted and groaned from her administrations.

She started from the noise, then sat back and smiled. "Groan all you want, Mr. Kelly. All that means to me is that you're sleeping hard."

Minutes later, a serious-looking young man a few years younger than her entered with the promised pitcher and glasses on a small tray. He set them down without a word, ignoring her thanks.

Belle poured herself a half glass, sipped carefully, then kicked her legs out a bit.

Then, because she had never been completely comfortable in silence, she began to talk. In choppy, halting sentences, she told him about growing up in northern Louisiana and then finding her way to New Orleans and eventually ending up in Galveston.

It was the first time she'd ever dared to speak out loud about her whole past.

But even though no one's ears heard but her own, the confession felt cleansing.

27

So I hate to ask the obvious," Captain Monroe ventured as they made their way down two side streets that lined the warehouse district. "But do you have any idea where in this maze of alleys she might be?"

"Nope," Robert said.

"I see. Do you happen to have a plan that consists of something more than wandering around and peeking in doorways?"

"There's no reason to be sarcastic, Devin. We're not leading hundreds of troops into battle; we're searching for Miranda and a crazy bank clerk in a run-down warehouse district. Officer Candidate School didn't cover this scenario."

"Point taken. So . . . what do you suggest we do?"

"I thought we'd first patrol the area and interview anyone we see. Someone here had to have seen Winter and Miranda."

"And if no one did? What next?" Monroe didn't seem to be even trying to hide his skepticism.

Robert shrugged. "If no one did, then your guess is as good as mine. I guess we'll have to start searching through every structure until we find her."

After a pause, Devin smiled. "Sounds good."

Robert didn't respond. He could feel the same anticipation he was sure was running through his former captain. Though he was afraid for Miranda and hated that she was scared, possibly hurt and alone, he couldn't deny the satisfaction that ran through him.

Frankly, it felt good to be of use. Ever since they were captured and sent to Johnson's Island, he'd felt at a loss for what to do with the rest of his life. From the time he was a child he'd been used to frequent activity combined with the quiet sense of desperation that told him he needed to do everything possible to survive.

Their long period of captivity, though it had been filled with pain and more than a little suffering, had also been filled with guilt, knowing they were likely to survive while so many of their friends and allies would not.

After his release, when he'd spent two long years working seventy and eighty hours a week for the train lines, making money hand over fist, it hadn't brought him all that much satisfaction.

But this? Walking by his captain's side, revolver in hand, with a noble purpose in his heart? He hadn't experienced this feeling in years.

When they saw a pair of men and one woman loitering outside a warehouse, they stopped. The trio looked at them curiously.

"We're looking for a woman," Devin said. "Brown hair. Attractive blue eyes. She was taken into the area against her will earlier this afternoon."

The woman rolled her eyes. "If it didn't just happen, we ain't seen her. We've been working inside all day."

Robert had no doubt she spoke the truth. When he worked for the trains, he had the opportunity to step inside several warehouses and factories just like this. Workers were hardly given breaks, and they were supervised closely.

"I need to find her," he pleaded, not caring in the slightest that he sounded suspiciously like he was begging. "Who in the area might have seen her? It's imperative I find her as quickly as possible."

"I don't know, and I don't care."

Devin shot Robert a look that conveyed he'd told him so. "Let's go, Lieutenant. We'll ask someone over on the next block."

"No. Wait a sec," one of the men called out. "Who are you gents, anyway?"

Before Robert snapped that it didn't matter who they were, Devin spoke. "I'm Devin Monroe," he said easily, his voice as smooth and calm as if they were being introduced at an officer's ball. "This is Robert Truax. We're staying at Miranda Markham's house. She is the one we seek."

"Mrs. Markham has gone missing?" the woman asked.

"Yes. Kidnapped, in fact. Why, do you know her?" Robert asked.

The three exchanged glances. "Were you friends with her man?" the man asked suspiciously.

"We were. Her husband, Phillip Markham, served under me during the war." Devin paused and looked at him more closely. "Why? What do you know?"

"I know him," he replied. "I mean, I used to. We grew up near each other."

"You lived on Market Street?"

The man shook his head. "Nah. He was on Market. I was with my ma at one of the cottages nearby. But we still saw each other a lot."

"I'm sure you did," Devin said laconically, just as if they were discussing the latest weather report. "Did you stay in touch?"

The man looked surprised to be asked, then a bit embarrassed. "Nah. He went off to some fancy boarding school in Virginia and then on to a high and mighty military academy of some sort."

"He attended West Point. What did you do?"

"Me? I went to the shipyard. Good, honest work, it is. I worked there before the war. Then ended up here after." His chin lifted. "But I saw him later too."

"When?" Robert asked.

"After Gettysburg. I was getting sewn up from some shrapnel and he was walking through the hospital wards. When he saw me, he stopped and talked awhile." His expression softened. "He acted like we were friends. He acted like he was happy to see me."

"I'm sure he was glad to see you, as well as relieved you were surviving," Devin said. "Friends from home were always a bonus to us."

The man shrugged. "I don't know about that. All I do know is that we both served." Looking adamant, he blurted, "I don't care what no one says. He didn't betray nobody."

"No, he did not," Captain Monroe said.

The man stared at him in wonder. "You're sure, aren't you?"

"I wouldn't be here if I weren't."

The man seemed to weigh his words. He looked at his friends. Then, after an interminable amount of time, he pointed to a run-down, boarded-up warehouse. "Winter took Mrs. Markham over there."

Robert stepped forward, his expression intent. "You sure about that?"

The man didn't back down. "Sure as I can be without stepping foot in that place. It's an old fishery and smells to high heaven."

Monroe ignored the description and glared at the three of them. "How can you be sure it was them? We didn't tell you it was Winter who had her."

"Well, I know who Winter is and the woman was fighting him like her life depended on it."

"She was crying, sir," the woman whispered. "Then she stilled and looked our way."

"Yes?" Devin asked impatiently.

"That's when I saw her eyes. You see, I know who Mrs. Markham is too. She's got bright blue eyes, she does. Plus, she is a high-class lady. She stuck out like a sore thumb in these parts."

"She does have blue eyes," Robert said. "Beautiful eyes."

"Almost violet, they are," the woman said.

"Why didn't you go after them?" Devin asked.

For the first time, the man looked embarrassed. "Winter had a gun. And, well, you learn, living and working around here, to keep out of other people's business. Sticking your neck out don't count for much."

Robert felt as if he was about to expire on the spot. Looking at the building across the way, he gave a quick prayer of thanks. He'd needed the Lord to give him a hand, and it seemed that he had in the form of this loquacious fellow.

Devin put his hand out and steadied him. "Chin up, Lieutenant. She was alive then. That is something."

"Let's just hope she's still alive now. If she isn't, I don't know if I'll be able to bear it."

"Let's hope you don't have to find out."

"Do you need some help?" the vagrant asked. "If you want, I could go in and lend a hand."

Though Robert was more than ready to dismiss the man's offer, he knew how important it was for everyone to feel valued. "Thank you," he said finally. "If you and your friends could stand at the doorways and stop anyone who tries to escape, that would be a tremendous help."

The man seemed to stand a full six inches taller. "Thank you, sir. I can do that."

"Let's go," Devin said. "We can't wait another moment."

Robert couldn't have agreed more as he strode to his former captain's side and entered the building, his Colt cocked and ready.

Miranda heard the footsteps on the stairwell before her captor did.

Thirty minutes ago, Mr. Winter had returned and then had started pacing in the loft, stopping often to look out the dirty windows. For what, Miranda wasn't sure. She'd anticipated Mr. Winter yelling at her, or manhandling her, or doing much worse.

Instead, he seemed to be thoroughly confused about what to do with her next. Wherever he had gone before didn't seem to have helped him.

When Miranda heard the footsteps get closer and saw Winter turn toward them, she braced herself. She had no idea what was going to happen next, but she was prepared for it. She knew now that she was going to fight as much as she could. She was not going to give up. Not going to give in without a fight.

The footsteps were hard claps against the wooden floor. Only men in heavy boots made such a noise.

Trembling, Miranda kept her eyes focused on the door. Mentally preparing herself to call out for help. To scream. To do whatever it took to help herself and get free.

"Miranda!" A voice called out. "Miranda!"

"Don't say a word," Mr. Winter said.

Heart pounding, she drew in her breath. Ignored the cocking of his Colt.

And did the one thing she knew she had to do. No matter the consequences. "I'm here!" she called. "In here."

28

THE CLERK HAD A PISTOL TRAINED ON MIRANDA. HER EYES were wide with fright and glued on Robert.

Obviously waiting for him to do something. To save her.

That moment, all training, experience, and common sense flew out the window. "Don't do it, Winter!" Robert called as he raced into the room.

His exclamation seemed to be all anyone needed to push them forward. Devin cursed behind him, then cocked his own pistol and trained it on Winter.

Miranda shifted and pulled at her hands, which Robert now realized were tied to an old pipe.

And Winter pivoted and turned his gun on them. His hand was trembling. Right then and there, Robert figured there was only a fifty-percent chance that the clerk could hit either him or Devin.

That clerk's insecurity and nervousness was all Robert needed to calm down and focus. "Put the gun down, Kyle. You do not want to hurt anyone."

"We've all hurt people. This isn't any different than what happened to my brother in Virginia."

"It's everything different," Devin called out, his voice perfectly

composed and his dark eyes looking completely cool and unemo-
tional. "Your brother died in war. On the battlefield. You are
harming an innocent woman."

Winter shook his head, his gun waving with the motion. "I
wasn't allowed to fight," he declared with a pained expression.
"My brother, my parents, even the doctors said I was too unfit.
Too unhealthy." His voice cracked. "Can you even believe that?
The South needed everyone. Every able man. Boys volunteered!
Everyone but me. And then he died."

"Don't dishonor him by behaving in this manner, then," Devin
said. "If you want to serve the South, don't start shooting innocent
women and soldiers who already gave so much for our cause."

"I have no choice." Turning back to Miranda, he said, "Her
husband betrayed my brother. Her husband shared secrets and
spied." Lowering his voice, he said, "Somebody needs to pay. But
still, here she is, living in his grand house, smiling at the Yankees
who give her money to stay there. Flirting with men. She deserves
nothing. And since my brother is dead, I have to be the one to take
care of her."

"Killing her won't change the outcome of the war, son," Captain
Monroe said as he edged forward. "The hard truth is that our side
lost. All of us on both sides of the Mason-Dixon are grieving for
people we buried. There probably isn't a person in this country
who hadn't wished and prayed for more men to have survived the
war. However, that wasn't what the Lord intended to happen."

"What does God want? Do we even know?" As if his right
arm was paining him, Winter lowered it. The Colt now hung
limply in his hand. Still cocked and ready to go off at any second.

"He wants us to value what we still have," Robert answered,
realizing as he spoke that he was sure about his answer. "God
wants us to find solace in each other. To remember to give thanks

for what we have. To love the people we care about and show kindness to people we don't. He wants us to live and breathe and learn from our past." Taking a fortifying breath, he added, "He does not want us to find retribution. That is for him to do, not us."

Kyle's eyes filled with tears. For a brief second, Robert felt hope, hoped that he'd said something that would have struck a chord with him and defused the situation.

But then Kyle inhaled sharply and shook his head. "No!" he shouted as he raised his gun again.

And pointed it directly at Robert.

"No!" Miranda called out just as a shot rang out.

It came from Devin.

When Kyle Winter collapsed, Robert knew he'd died instantly.

Out of habit, Robert put the safety back on his revolver and slid it back into the waistband of his jeans, nestled in the small of his back. Then he ran to Miranda.

Thick tears were racing down her cheeks. "Oh, Robert. I was so scared. I was afraid he was going to kill you."

"Thanks to Devin, he did not." Kneeling by her side, Robert brushed some of her tears away, then gave in to temptation and kissed her cheek. "I was afraid for the same thing. I was afraid he was going to take you from me. I have never been more scared."

As her tears continued to flow, he reached for his knife. "Let's get you free."

Two sharp swipes with his knife freed her. The moment the rope fell to the ground, he inspected her wrists. Her tender skin had been rubbed raw and was bleeding. Her wrists were bruised and swollen. When she cried out in pain, Robert suddenly wished he had been the one to pull the trigger. "I'm so sorry," he whispered as he gently enfolded her in his arms.

"How is she? Will she be all right?" Devin asked. While

Robert had been freeing Miranda from her bindings, his captain had knelt at Winter's side.

Still holding her protectively, Robert said, "I think so." Leaning back a little so he could see her face, he asked, "Miranda, did he hurt you anywhere else?"

"No. I'm a little bruised, but beyond my wrists, I'm unharmed." Releasing a ragged sigh she said, "I honestly think he was trying to get up the nerve to kill me."

"Thank the Lord he couldn't summon the will to do that," Devin replied.

"No, thank the good Lord that you both found me in time." Treating them both to a watery smile, she said, "I was willing to do whatever it took to survive, but I was frightened half to death."

When she shuddered again, Robert enfolded her back in his arms and held her close. "You okay?" he asked Devin.

"Me? Yeah." Looking toward Winter, he added grimly, "It gave me no pleasure to end his life, but I am grateful he didn't harm either of you."

"Not as grateful as I am," Robert replied. "I owe you."

Looking grim, he shook his head. "You owe me nothing, Robert. I've lost enough people I care about. I'm in no hurry to lose one more. Keeping you and Miranda alive was a selfish move on my part."

Robert was about to say he understood when they heard the pounding of footsteps on the stairs. Turning, his body went on alert again as he loosened his hold on Miranda.

But instead of moving away from him, Miranda clung. "Who do you think that could be?" she asked.

He didn't bother to reply as he continued to stare at the doorway. There was no telling who was coming to join them, but the chance that it was yet another person out for trouble was high.

"Get down," he ordered as he freed his gun. To his relief, she didn't question him, but simply did as he asked.

Devin had already pulled out his Colt again. His face impassive, he slowly lifted his right arm and watched the empty doorway.

The pounding on the wood floor grew louder.

When it was obvious the intruders were men and they were heading their way, Robert exhaled and cocked his gun.

The moment two men appeared with guns drawn, Robert uttered, "Right," just as he placed his finger on the trigger.

"Don't shoot!" Kern called out.

Robert had already pulled the trigger. He only had time to raise his arm so the bullet pierced the wall above them. Behind him, Miranda gasped.

"Easy, now," Kern said. He, as well as his deputy, looked visibly shaken.

Robert dropped his arm with a wince. He'd almost killed a lawman. Unable to help himself, he swore under his breath. When he felt Miranda's reassuring hand, he glanced her way. "You okay?"

Her blue eyes were tinged with worry, but she gifted him with a tremulous smile. "Yes."

Now that he was reassured, he laced his fingers with hers, then turned his attention back to the other men.

Beside him, Devin was complaining. "You almost got yourself killed, Sheriff."

"I kind of noticed that."

"I kind of noticed that you were nowhere to be found when we got here. Where have you been?"

"Trying to track down the four of you," Kern said. "I think we went to every single run-down and abandoned building except for this one."

"I've seen more rats today than I care to admit," his deputy complained.

"We saw our fair share of rats ourselves," Devin said.

Kern's eyes narrowed. "Is that right?" Looking from Miranda, who was clinging to Robert's arm, to Robert himself, to Devin, he started to speak, then stilled as it became obvious that he had finally located Kyle Winter.

He was lying facedown on the floor behind them in a pool of blood.

Kern walked over to the body, crouched down, and pulled on Winter's shoulder, rolling him over. Winter's gun was lying next to his hand. "Looks like he was armed."

"He was seconds away from shooting Miranda," Devin said. "Then when he pointed his gun at Robert . . . I had no choice. I shot to kill."

The deputy whistled low.

Robert curved an arm around Miranda, who was now trembling again. Holding her closer, he whispered in her ear. "Don't look."

While Miranda kept her face hidden, Robert eyed both Winter's body and Kern's reaction.

After a moment, Kern lumbered to his feet. "Looks like you two men took care of things for me." He raised his eyebrows. "Can't wait to hear what happened."

"I'll be glad to fill you in, Kern," Robert said. "But after I get Miranda home safely and tend to her hands and wrists."

"That works with me. I'll walk back with y'all. I'm going to need to ask Mrs. Markham some questions. I'd prefer to get those out of the way so I don't have to bother her again."

The last thing she needed at the moment was to be pestered. "Sheriff, I think tomorrow will be soon enough."

"No, tonight will be fine," Miranda interrupted. "I'm not made of spun glass, Robert," she said into his ear. "And besides, I have a feeling our sheriff is going to want to check on someone else at my home."

"Point taken." Looking at Kern, Robert nodded. "Yeah, come on with us."

Kern turned to his deputy and pointed to Winter's body. "Take care of this," he said before gesturing for Miranda, Robert, and Devin to lead the way out of the loft.

Just before they started down the stairs, Kern said, "The more I learned about Kyle Winter, the more I started to worry about y'all. That man was a loose cannon. Though I would have liked to have put him on trial, I'm not disappointed to be spared that undertaking." Looking their way again, he said, "I really am glad you all survived this ordeal relatively unscathed."

Devin Monroe smiled. "Truax and I made a promise to each other long ago. We take care of our own."

Kern smiled in return. "It seems your loyalty knows no bounds."

29

Almost two hours later, Miranda was sitting on the sofa in her parlor beside Robert. The moment they'd returned home, all four servants had rushed to her side.

Upon seeing her condition, Belle—who had just returned from Major Kelly's bedside—ushered Miranda to her room. Once there, Belle had helped her change into a fresh gown.

Cook arrived mere moments after that with a pitcher of warm water and some rags. While sitting at her dressing table, the two women had gently bathed Miranda's wrists and wrapped them in the clean cotton.

"I don't think you will scar, ma'am," Cook said with a frown at her wrapped wrists. "Though your left looks pretty bad, I'm afraid."

Miranda had to agree. Both of her wrists were swollen, bruised, and cut. However, her left one looked the worst. "It's a small price to pay for surviving that experience," she said with a shudder. "I was so afraid. I felt certain Mr. Winter was going to kill me today."

"Those men are true heroes, they are," Cook said.

"I owe them my life," Miranda agreed. She'd given Cook and Belle a brief account of her ordeal while they'd cleaned her wounds.

"They did save you, but I think you saved yourself, too, Mrs. Markham," Belle said. "You didn't give up."

Another time, Miranda probably would have pushed aside any praise. But at this moment, she was feeling glad that she had been as brave as she possibly could. "I'm so glad I didn't give up. And now I just need to give my statement to Sheriff Kern."

"Would you like me to stay with you, ma'am?" Belle asked.

"I would appreciate that very much. Thank you," Miranda replied, exchanging a knowing look with Cook. It was beginning to become pretty apparent that she wasn't the only person to have been recently granted a chance for love.

When she got back downstairs, Robert immediately walked to her side. "How are you feeling? Do you want me to tell Kern to go away? It's near midnight. I'm sure you can tell him your story tomorrow."

"I'd rather get it over with. When I finally go to sleep tonight, I want to know I can put this all behind me, not dread going over it yet again."

"I can understand that." He looked at Belle.

"I'm going to stay with her, too, sir. Just in case she needs anything. I can help serve refreshments as well. Cook went to go prepare something."

Robert nodded as he escorted Miranda to the sofa. "Let's get this over with, then."

He sounded so weary, so disgruntled, she couldn't help but smile. "I promise, I don't mind speaking to Sheriff Kern now. I'm grateful to be alive."

His expression softened. "Well said, Miranda. Indeed, we have much to be grateful for. More than I ever imagined."

An hour later, Belle walked Sheriff Kern to the door. Though it was apparent Mrs. Markham, Mr. Truax, and Captain Monroe were surprised—and perhaps amused?—at her bold offer to see Sheriff Kern out, Belle didn't care.

The day had been so stressful, so incredibly nerve-racking, it had made her want to finally take some chances. She would always regret it if she didn't at least make a bit of an effort.

When they reached the impressive carved oak door, Sheriff Kern bowed gallantly. "Thank you for seeing me out, Belle. Given the time of night, it is very kind."

The right thing to do would be to say it was no trouble, open the door, and wave him on.

But if she did that, she might never have another chance like this.

"Do you have to go right this minute?" Belle blurted.

"No." He looked at her curiously. "Is there something you need?"

"Only a moment of your time. If you aren't in too big a hurry, can we stand outside for a moment?"

His dark eyes flickered. "I'm never in too big of a hurry for you, Belle. But it's chilly. Do you have a cloak or something to put on?"

She grabbed a blanket that she'd folded on one of the chairs by the door. "This will do."

After the front door closed and they were alone under the dim gas lantern by the door, Sheriff Kern looked at her with concern. "Now, what is on your mind? Is anything wrong?"

Because she was so nervous, her voice was sharper than she intended. "Do you mean beyond my employer getting kidnapped and almost killed?"

He looked down at his feet. Sighed. Then raised his chin to meet her gaze. "I'm sorry. Of course you are right. There has been more than enough 'wrong' today." Still eyeing her carefully, he added, "It's just that, well, you seem . . . well, you seem distraught. I was afraid something else happened tonight that you didn't feel you could share in front of everyone else."

"Something did."

"What happened?"

"I was worried about you."

"Me?"

"I was so worried that you would come to harm. The moment I heard you were out looking for Mrs. Markham, I worried."

"You did?" Then he looked embarrassed. "I didn't hardly do anything."

"Of course you did! Why, you were out searching in the warehouse district all evening for Mrs. Markham!"

"This is true, but Truax and Monroe were the ones who found her. Not me."

"That hardly matters."

"Winter pulled a pistol on Mrs. Markham. Monroe's quick reflexes prevented a terrible tragedy from taking place. So I would say what he did does matter. It matters a lot."

Now she was the one who was feeling foolish. Backing up, she said, "I'm sorry. It's just that I didn't want you to go home without me saying anything. I am very glad you are all right . . . sir."

"To be honest, even though you said that day at the docks that you would give me a chance, I didn't think you cared about me," Sheriff Kern admitted.

She was stunned. "Why would you say that?"

Looking increasingly uncomfortable, he looked down at his linked hands. "Well, I heard you spent much of the evening with Major Kelly." Raising his chin, he shrugged. "I don't blame you, though."

"What?"

"After all, I'm just a man, Belle. I fought in the war and have settled here in Galveston. I now try to keep the peace in this melting pot of Northerners, Southerners, refugees, and foreigners from all parts of the world. Never have I gained a reputation like Ethan Kelly's."

She realized then that, even though she thought of him as powerful, he was just as confused about his self-worth as the rest of them. And for some reason, that made her feel more at ease around him than ever before.

Choosing her words with care, she said, "To be honest, yes, I was glad to sit with Major Kelly. He's helped Mrs. Markham and Mr. Truax, and because of that I would sit with him as long as anyone needed me to."

His expression was still guarded. "He is wealthy and handsome."

"Indeed. And yes, I think he is dashing."

"I am far from that."

She couldn't help but smile. Did he really not know how handsome he was?

"Well, he is not the kind of man for me." Based on some of his mostly unintelligible ramblings at Dr. Kronke's, she also was pretty sure Ethan Kelly was hiding some secrets of his own. She had no desire to discover them.

"He's not?"

She shook her head. "First of all, I don't think someone like him would ever care for me. We are too different."

"Ah." He stared at her for a long moment. What was he thinking? Had she been too bold?

She turned to leave. "Sheriff Kern, I do beg your pardon. I shouldn't have run out here."

"Wait. I'm glad you did."

"Truly?"

He nodded. "There's something about you that I can't get over, Belle. Maybe it's the way you look so fragile, but you never give in. Or maybe it's the way you always put other people's needs before your own." His voice lowered. "Whatever the reason, I can't always seem to think coherently when I'm around you."

"How do you think we might solve this problem?" She smiled as she felt his gaze float over her.

"I think we need to see each other more often," he said, his voice strong and sure.

"I've heard that practice does make certain tasks easier," she teased.

He nodded. "When is your next afternoon off?"

"In two days."

"May I take you out then? We could go to that new tavern in the Tremont and have some supper."

He was asking her out. Just like a real lady. "Yes, Sheriff Kern, I would like that."

"I only eat meals with people who call me Jess. Will you finally call me by my given name?"

"I'll let you know . . . in two days' time," she said with a smile.

"I'll look forward to discovering your answer then, miss." He tipped his hat and nodded, then started down the stairs.

And when Belle opened the door, the lantern by the door illuminating her way, she was delighted to hear his chuckle float toward her.

Sweetening her dreams.

30

Two weeks later

THEY HAD DONE IT.

Miranda would no longer be receiving threatening letters. Phillip's honor and reputation were restored—some folks were even saying his name should be added to the monument on Recognition Square.

People were talking to her again, though she suspected it would take some time for Mercy to be willing to face her. She even had more reservations for guests than she had room for.

Mr. Winter was dead and Major Kelly was recovering well from his wound. Captain Monroe had left that morning.

She was going to be just fine now. Better than fine, actually. She felt like smiling all the time. At last, all the darkness that had permeated her life had lifted and she felt optimistic and grateful again. She was feeling blessed.

So yes, Miranda knew she had every reason to celebrate each day's new dawn. And she would . . . even though she was going to miss Robert terribly.

Last night after supper, he'd told her he felt it was time for him to go. Though everything inside her had wanted to beg him to stay, she couldn't think of a single reason that would convince him. After all, he'd certainly accomplished everything he'd set out to do.

Therefore, instead of crying or attempting to cajole him to stay even one day longer, Miranda had simply nodded her head and attempted to look happy for him. This act had been important. After all, she was stronger now. She didn't want his last memory of her to be of her crying yet again.

When he came down the stairs, duffle in his hand and a determined expression on his face, Miranda prepared herself to see him off with as much grace as possible.

She needed to do this. She wanted to do it. Robert Truax had fulfilled his mission and she was grateful for his service. To expect anything more from him was selfish. And while she had a great many faults, selfishness had never been one of them.

As he set his bag on the floor near the door, she walked to his side. She was wearing a crimson dress today. It was slightly daring, but the bold color had felt right. She was ready to conquer the world—or at least Galveston, Texas—thanks to him.

"I guess you are all set?" she asked.

"I believe so." His voice was quiet, his gaze reflective as it skimmed over her face and body. "You look beautiful today, Miranda. Fetching."

"Thank you." Like always, she felt every word he said all the way down to her toes. "Would you care for something to eat before you go? I know Cook would be delighted to make you something. Or even a small repast to take with you on your journey."

"I . . . I think not."

"Are you sure? I promise, it's no trouble. Cook, Winnie, Belle, and Emerson are almost as grateful to you as I am."

"I'm sure, Miranda." Shifting from one foot to the other,

he looked down at his spotlessly shined boots before staring at her again. "To be honest, taking my leave of you is going to be extremely hard. I don't know if I'm strong enough to drag it out."

Extremely hard? Strong enough? "What . . . what do you mean?" When something lit his eyes, she hurried to explain. "I mean . . . I thought you were eager to leave."

"I am eager to remove myself from temptation," he blurted. The moment the words were out, he inhaled sharply, just as a fierce blush lit his skin.

Miranda couldn't recall another time she'd seen him either blush or act so ill at ease.

"I beg your pardon, ma'am," he said, now standing tall and straight, and seeming to stare at a point directly above her head. "I didn't mean to place that burden on you."

Unable to help herself, she reached out and pressed her hand on his arm. "I'm confused, Robert, not burdened. What, exactly, are you saying? What are you tempted by?" She was beginning to have a very good idea, but she needed to hear the words.

He pressed his lips together, as if he had been waging a private war with himself, then blurted, "You, of course."

Her. He was tempted by her.

His words warmed her insides and caused her cheeks to flush. Happiness and hope sprang forth, and she yearned to clutch those two long-lost emotions tight to her chest.

But that didn't mean she understood what his temptation meant to him. "I'm sorry, but you said you wanted to leave." Though it was tempting to simply let him be the one to bare his heart, she realized she was stronger now. It turned out that she, too, could be completely honest. "I wish you wouldn't, though."

"Miranda, as much as I would hope otherwise, I fear you and I could never suit."

And right then and there, hope and happiness vanished. "Because you feel I am too fragile," she said, forcing herself to state the obvious. "Too weak."

He shook his head. "Never that." Stepping closer, he reached for the hand that was still on his arm and placed it in his own. "Miranda, I knew Phillip well. I know what kind of man he was. I know the kind of man you deserve. I am nothing like him."

He caught her off guard. "What are you talking about?"

He looked down at his feet. "I have no formal education. I have no pedigree." He rolled his eyes. "Sometimes I'm surprised I even have a name. I'm as far from a West Point graduate as one might get."

She was so taken aback, she almost laughed. "Robert, I never cared about where Phillip went to school. I only cared about him."

"Yes, well . . ." He swallowed. "There was much in Phillip Markham to care about."

"Just as there is in you, Robert." She squeezed his hand gently. "I know this, because I've grown to care about you too."

Longing filled his expression before he firmly tamped it down. "Miranda, when the relief you are feeling about being free from Winter's tyranny subsides, you will realize that you are a wonderful woman with a bright future. You are beautiful. Any man would want you. And you, my dear, will get to have your choice of whom to pick. You won't have to settle for someone like me."

"Settle for you?" she asked, incredulous. "Robert, you saved me. In more ways than one. Before you arrived, I wasn't only scared and afraid . . . I had run out of hope." Didn't he understand what a gift he'd given her? Didn't he understand what a difference he had made in her life?

Robert closed his eyes as if even the idea of her giving up hope was painful. "I helped you, but you saved yourself."

"Yes, but—"

"You didn't give up," he interrupted. "You learned to trust. You fought Winter and were determined to stay alive in that wretched warehouse."

"Actually—"

"Just as importantly, you helped me."

"How?"

"You gave me a reason to continue living. You let a man like me believe that goodness was still present on this earth. Even after a war. Even after so many very good men died." He lowered his voice. "Miranda, you let a man like me believe there really are people like you in this world. And for that, I will always be grateful."

It seemed there was only one thing left to say.

"Don't leave me, Robert."

He stepped closer, slipped one of his hands around her waist. "Miranda, I don't think you understand. The reason I'm leaving is that I cannot simply be your friend. You see, I've fallen in love with you."

"I've fallen for you too," she said through a smile. Hardly able to believe that she was the one who was taking the lead, she strengthened her voice. "Please, don't leave. Stay here with me. Help me."

He smiled then. "Do you want me to remain here as your husband or your boarder?"

She laughed then. "Robert Truax, are you proposing marriage or are you waiting for me to do so?"

He flushed, then before she quite knew what was happening, he pulled her into his arms and kissed her soundly. "I told you I don't have the words I need."

"I think you are finding them."

"I want you to be mine. Say you'll marry me."

"I will, Robert."

He smiled, then kissed her again and again, holding her close, being everything she ever needed.

It seemed that Robert Truax did a great many things well. He had been a fine soldier, an influential officer, and a brave protector. He was personable and confident. Chatty and romantic.

But a man of words he was not.

That was why, when he leaned down to kiss her again, Miranda realized that she was tired of talking.

Though words were always well and good, there were times—like the present—when they weren't even needed at all.

Discussion Questions

1. The five men at the Confederate Officer Prisoner of War camp are central characters for the entire book. What is your first impression of them?

2. Miranda Markham is without hope at the beginning of the novel. Is there any part of her character that you can relate to?

3. How do you feel about Robert Truax not telling Miranda the complete reason he is visiting? For that matter, what would you have done if you were Robert and were asked to check on Miranda? Would you have gone?

4. As the book progresses, it is evident that there are many people in Galveston who betrayed both Miranda and Phillip. Do you think Miranda should have left?

5. What is your impression of the inn's staff? What do you foresee happening with Belle?

6. The men at the camp have sworn their loyalty to Captain Monroe. Do you think he is worthy of their trust? Who in your life would you follow without question?

7. The novel focuses on the toll the war took on a handful of people in a southern Texas town. Do you think it was

realistic? How do you think some of these same themes might be played out in the world today?

8. In what ways was Miranda strengthened throughout the book? Do you think she is a worthy match for Robert?

9. The verse from Psalm 51, "Create in me a clean heart, O God. Renew a loyal spirit within me," is a favorite of mine. I thought it fit both Robert's and Miranda's faith journeys well. What does this scripture mean to you?

10. What former soldier are you most interested in reading about next?

ACKNOWLEDGMENTS

Dear Readers,

Thank you for reading this book! I hope you enjoyed this first book in the *Lone Star Heroes* series and getting to know Captain Devin Monroe and his friends and comrades as much I did.

I have to share that the inspiration for this series came from my kitchen table! One evening, my husband and I were cooking together, and I told him about a discovery I had made regarding Johnson's Island. Soon, we were talking about a series based on former POWs who made promises to look after each other for the rest of their lives. I scribbled notes on old pieces of notebook paper, stuck them in a folder, then pulled them out when my editor expressed an interest years later. That is how this book began.

With that in mind, I owe many thanks to the people who helped make this novel come together so well. First, I am grateful to my husband Tom, who not only helped me plot a whole series but also traveled with me to the C.S.A. Officer Cemetery on Johnson's Island and ventured down to Galveston one hot July weekend to do research. Tom is the best. Really.

I also owe many thanks to my friend Tiffany Crona and her mother Mary Wharton, who helped me discover more research materials about Galveston Island in the 1870s. I did take a few liberties with some of the information I discovered. Those inaccuracies are purely my own!

I'm also grateful to my agent Nicole Resciniti of The Seymour Agency. She helped make the dream of publishing this trilogy a reality. Thank you, Nicole!

I'm so appreciative of my editor for this project, Becky Philpott. Becky, thank you for chatting with me about Texas and soldiers and prisoner-of-war camps one sunny day in San Antonio. Thank you, also, for your belief in me and my writing. Every author dreams of having a champion like you.

Thank you, also, to incredible editor Jean Bloom for making this story actually follow a timeline that makes sense. You are amazing, Jean!

Finally, no note would be complete without praising God for His words, and my family, especially my brother and sister. We, like so many others, know how devastating both suicide and depression can be for loved ones. I'm so thankful for them!

With blessings and my thanks,
Shelley Shepard Gray

An
Uncommon
Protector

For my Thomas, Tom Sabga

I promise this very day that I will repay two
blessings for each of your troubles.

ZECHARIAH 9:12

It is well that war is so terrible, or we would grow too fond of it.

ROBERT E. LEE

PROLOGUE

Johnson's Island, Ohio
Confederate States of America Officers POW Camp
July 1865

It was hot. As hot as July. Wiping the sweat from his brow, Sergeant Thomas Baker gazed out at the waters of Lake Erie and watched the waves leisurely lap its banks. It was a peaceful sight since the lake was so calm. Its surface was smooth, reminding him of a sparkling pane of glass. For once, not a boat or craft was in sight or in hearing distance.

Indeed, it was peaceful. Tranquil.

So much so that Thomas could almost imagine he was out and about, taking a turn along the shore with a lady friend to enjoy a bit of warm weather. She'd have one delicate hand on his arm, and her hand would be bare, allowing him to admire her soft, pale skin. His goal would be to encourage her to smile at him. And because his intentions weren't all that good, his next goal would be to pull her closer. Close enough to smell her sweet scent. Close enough to brush his lips along the smooth nape of her neck. Just to see her shiver.

He stretched his right arm and imagined taking her on an

outing in a little rowboat, nothing fancy. Once he rowed them out a ways, he would lay down the oars and encourage her to lean against him. Then there she'd be, trailing her fingertips in the water as the current lazily moved them along. They wouldn't be hungry or cold. They wouldn't be afraid of death or pain or rats.

They would simply be at peace.

That moment would be perfect.

"Baker? What ails you?" a guard called out, his voice as coarse and biting as his accent.

Thomas didn't bother to reply. Instead, he knelt down into the mud. Pain shot through his knee as it hit the soggy ground. He ignored it, though. Just as he'd learned to ignore most aches and discomforts over the years.

He hadn't had an easy life. Losing his family at far too young an age had marked him. Fighting battle after battle in this never-ending war had been filled with its own fears and challenges.

But gardening while confined in a prisoner of war camp in the middle of Lake Erie certainly held its own brand of torture.

Especially for a man like him who wasn't finding much success while doing it.

In an effort to keep his men occupied, Captain Monroe had somehow managed to talk one of their guards into allowing them to plant the pouch of fruit and vegetable seeds one of the captain's admirers had sent him.

Not surprisingly—after all, their guards were a dim-witted, lazy lot—no one could think of a single reason not to let the officer prisoners plant a garden. Looking pleased as punch, the captain had allocated a good section of their yard for the effort.

As the guards stood by, the captain had a group of them hoeing hard dirt and clay, planting seeds, and carefully watering and tending the seedlings as though they were newborn babes. Now the plants had borne fruit, and every afternoon a couple of men knelt in the dirt or mud, fought off grasshoppers and mosquitoes, and weeded.

Thomas wasn't sure why he was continually on weeding detail, but since it was a far sight better than latrine digging, he went about the task without complaint.

He enjoyed being near the water, liked looking out into the expanse of it and letting his thoughts drift like one of the paddleboats he spied from time to time. It was a gift to look at something so serene while toiling in the soil.

Except on days like today, when the humidity rose from Lake Erie like a specter and he was sweating like a racehorse in August. Feeling as though his cotton shirt was suffocating him, he began unbuttoning it.

"Baker?" the guard called out again. "What are you doing?"

Mentally, Thomas rolled his eyes. The Lord had given Clyde Carson both a big mouth and a small brain.

"Taking off my shirt!" he said as his fingers worked the buttons. Again mentally, he added his pet name for the guard— *Taking off my shirt, Clay*—on account of the man being so slow.

But he had probably said too much, even without the name. Been too free with his tone. It really was no wonder the Yankees had festooned him off in the middle of the Great Lakes. He never had learned to control his mouth.

When the guard stared at him suspiciously, Thomas held up his arm. "It was getting soiled."

"Oh. All right. But be quick about it."

Like it even mattered whether he stripped quickly or slowly. They had nothing but time to kill on this island.

After he removed his oft-mended shirt, he knelt down again

and pulled at a clump of weeds. It was muggy enough that he had to wipe the sweat from his brow every five minutes.

He grunted. When they got out of here, he was going to high-tail it back to Texas, back to Fort Worth. He wasn't sure what he was going to do, but he sure wasn't ever going to weed again if he could help it.

The men around him—his fellow prisoners—grinned at him. One or two even laughed at his grimace. His total dislike of gardening was a constant source of amusement for the lot of them.

"You ever grow anything before, Baker?" Major Ethan Kelly asked from about two yards away.

Thomas glanced up from his row of string beans to meet the major's eye.

As usual, their elegant major was handling the chore with ease. He still had on his cotton shirt. It looked clean and fresh. Actually, the only indication of the major's physical exertions was two neatly rolled sleeves. "No, sir. You?"

The major chuckled as he walked over to the next row of plants, then crouched down. "Never. But I'm finding digging in the dirt rather restful." Fingering the small green clump of tomatoes on one of the vines, he said, "I have a feeling these are going to be the best tomatoes I've ever eaten."

"I bet they will be . . . if you get to eat them. Old Philly over there is looking like he's already planning his next meal."

Major Kelly sat back on his haunches. "You and your names," he scoffed. "One day the guards are going to overhear your made-up names for them and you'll pay for the disrespect."

"Probably," Thomas said, agreeing easily. But that was the thing, he supposed. His mouth always had gotten him into trouble. He reckoned it always would, until something happened that taught him to learn from his mistakes once and for all.

But that was no matter. He was already so used to hardship and scrambling for everything that he wasn't sure how to handle easy days with no hint of despair. Only in his dreams did he act like a gentleman.

Then, as he remembered the direction of the daydream he'd just had, he reckoned he wasn't much of a gentleman there either.

Eager to get back to the task at hand, he moved down his row, pulling weeds and swatting away mosquitoes.

When he stood up to wipe the back of his neck, Old Philly cackled. "What's wrong, Sergeant? That scar of yours paining you?"

He stilled. Though he knew he shouldn't, he traced a finger along the thick, raised line that ran down the back of his neck to a couple of inches above his shoulder blade. Even after all these years, the skin felt sensitive and burned.

Old Philly scoffed, "Looks like one of our boys got you good. With what? A bayonet?"

Comments like that made Thomas sure they were being guarded by the worst soldiers the Union army had to offer. Only a man who had never been up close and personal with a bayonet would think that type of blade would leave such a fine scar.

And only a man who had never had to fight for food and shelter would ever think a scar like the one on his neck could heal so quickly.

Resentment boiled in him. How was it that he'd constantly had to fight and scrape to survive while men like Old Philly simply coasted through?

Furious, he turned to the man. "My scar sure ain't from some blasted Yankee bayonet. If you had ever held one, you might even know that."

Philly's smirk vanished abruptly. "What did you just say to me?"

"Watch your mouth, Sergeant," Major Kelly muttered under his breath.

But the warning came too late. His mouth had gotten the best of him yet again. And because he was sweaty and mosquito bitten, and there was little to no chance he'd ever escort a fine lady around any body of water in his lifetime, he let his temper fly.

"You heard me," Thomas jeered. "I swear, every time you open your mouth, I have more respect for Yankees. No wonder they have you guarding a bunch of injured officers instead of fighting. You'd be worthless on the field. This scar is well on twelve years old."

Old Philly was now tromping toward him, passing the rest of the Confederate officers who had stopped working to watch his implosion with various degrees of regret and dismay. "What did you do to get sliced like that when you were a kid, then? Steal something?"

Now, how he got his scar was something he never talked about. Only a masochist would revisit the night his brother and parents were killed. And while Thomas Travis Baker was a lot of things, he sure wasn't the type to sit around and feel sorry for himself. "You need to stop talking."

Old Philly stiffened and his eyes bugged out. He looked so fired up, he was about to turn purple. "Did you just tell me to stop talking?"

"I did. But was that too difficult to understand?" he taunted. And while his brain was telling him to be quiet, his mouth—like always—couldn't seem to listen. "Can you not understand simple words either?"

Phillip Markham, Thomas's lieutenant, cursed under his breath.

Pulling out handcuffs, Old Philly restrained Thomas's hands.

Then, with a rough pull and a shove, he marched him to the stocks by the barracks. "Five lashes for insubordination!" he called out.

Thomas felt a shudder race up his spine. Yet again he'd gone too far.

Clay and one other guard stepped forward, grabbed his wrists, and carted him toward the whipping post. As they jerked him forward and tied him to the six-foot pole, they didn't seem to notice he wasn't putting up a bit of protest.

As other men gathered around and sweat poured off him, Thomas braced himself for the pain that was coming.

Tried to concentrate on the present.

Because even though it was a bad place to be, it was easier to bear than the dark, frantic thoughts filling his head. Easier than remembering the last thing his father told him before he pushed Thomas away and told him to hide.

For once in your life, do what you're told without argument, Thomas. Go to the secret crawl space under the kitchen. Go there now. Do it, son! Crawl in there, and don't come out. No matter what you hear, don't come out.

To his everlasting shame, Thomas had done just that. He'd torn open the tender skin on his neck when it met a protruding nail as he crawled under the cabinet. It had bled for what felt like hours as he remained folded into a small ball in a dark hole in the ground. It bled as he heard his mother scream and his older brother beg for mercy. It bled as he heard his father being stabbed repeatedly. It bled as he heard men rummage through their house, steal their horses, and at last run off.

By the time Thomas came out, the wound had clotted and the blood on his clothes had dried.

When he saw what his family had endured at the hands of the Comanche while he stayed hidden, Thomas had known one thing.

Never again would he follow instructions he didn't agree with.

As the first lash cut into his back, he welcomed the pain. Then he stared out at the water and imagined he was back in that rowboat with the sweet woman. Where everything was peaceful and lovely.

It likely would never happen, but he allowed himself to dream.

1

July 1867

EVERYONE SAID THEY WERE DANGEROUS. LAUREL ASSUMED it must be true.

But that didn't stop her from taking another peek out her open sitting room window at one specific prisoner. One of the men currently repairing the fence framing her yard, the one so close she could see more detail than ever before. Without the benefit of a hat, he was squinting as he bent over a split piece of rotted wood. Though he had an iron shackle on his right ankle, he seemed unperturbed by the weight of the heavy metal.

Instead, he concentrated on the task at hand, positioning a fresh piece of lumber in the ruined wood's place. The sharp lines of his face framed deeply tanned skin and brown hair that was already bleached by the sun.

The guard who stood by his side wasn't Ollie. He was the stranger. In contrast to the prisoner, his skin was flushed and damp with sweat under his Stetson. He seemed both bored and ill at ease.

The prisoner, however, continued to set the wood into its slot, then hammer it into place. He was now perched on one knee, his expression quietly intent on his job. As with his shackle, he didn't look uncomfortable or even that bothered by the oppressive heat.

Laurel craned her neck and looked at him even more closely. He had to be hot. Terribly hot, actually. His sleeves were rolled up to his elbows, revealing darkly tanned forearms lined with veins and more than a couple of scars.

He shifted, giving her a new view of his body. A line of perspiration trickled down his neck, right along a long scar that disappeared under the collar of his shirt. That perspiration made the thin fabric of his shirt stick to his skin, revealing just how muscular he was.

She knew she should look away. Her staring wasn't seemly. Then, too, there wasn't really anything to see that she hadn't viewed before. But for the life of her, Laurel couldn't seem to help herself. There was something about the man that had caught her regard and held on tight.

The ragtag team had been here for three days now. It was a charity mission, the idea of Sheriff Jackson. He'd served in the war with Laurel's father and was a distant cousin of her mother's. Laurel knew the sheriff felt sorry for her, essentially living on her own the way she was.

After all, she was attempting to run what was left of a pitiful cattle operation with barely twenty head, little money for alfalfa for them to graze on, and far too many squatters in the area. She was exhausted and beginning to think she was never going to be able to keep the ranch going. No matter how hard she tried, there were never enough hours in the day to do everything that needed to be done.

After she'd said as much to Will Jackson at church, he'd offered to send out a team of prisoners from the jail to repair her fence line.

Laurel was grateful her longtime friend was now the sheriff and could help her out. She was grateful for the prisoners' help too. Would have been even more glad of it if the team hadn't been overseen by Ollie Burnside—a man who hadn't been much of a worker when he was a teen and seemed to have grown lazier with each year.

He also, Laurel decided, wasn't very good at managing convicts.

Otherwise Ollie would have noticed those men were hot and thirsty. Parched. Even she knew men worked a lot better if they were given water breaks every now and then.

Unable to stop herself, her gaze fastened again on the man with the scars. He was working as industriously as ever, but his movements had slowed.

He was no doubt suffering from the heat. Her heart broke for him. All men—even criminals—deserved kindness. Giving one a sip of water in this heat was surely the least anyone could do.

And since the pair of guards seemed incapable of doing such a thing, Laurel knew that bit of kindness needed to come from her.

Yes. That was something her parents would have expected her to do.

But what would the prisoner with the scars do if she brought him a ladle of water? Would he snatch it from her, scare her half to death, and make her wish she'd never contemplated such a kindness?

Or would he take it gratefully?

Picturing the moment, she let her imagination fly. Perhaps he would take the ladle, meeting her gaze when their fingertips brushed. Smile knowingly when she shivered from the tingles of awareness sliding through her body as he brought the ladle to his lips.

Or would he look at the proffered water and speak? Maybe he would simply thank her. Maybe he would say something more.

And what would she do if he did speak? Would she reply? Dare to smile? Lost in her dreams, in her thoughts about the two of them meeting at last, she shivered.

"Laurel, step away from the window this minute!" Bess called, startling her.

Laurel jerked upright so abruptly that she knocked a book off the table next to her. It landed on the floor with a resounding *thud*.

Bess yelped.

Which no doubt startled the whole chain gang working in her yard. Laurel knew because more than one man had straightened and was now staring her way.

Oh! Had she ever been so mortified?

"Laurel, you really must present yourself in a more genteel manner," Bess chastised. "Why, those men out there are going to see you ogling them!"

Laurel was pretty sure they already had. But, unwilling to share that fact, she concentrated on saving what little bit of self-respect she had. "I wasn't gawking at them." After all, she was only ogling *one* man.

"Whatever you were doing, it wasn't seemly."

Laurel supposed Bess was right. She'd thought so herself just moments ago. But coming from Bess . . .

Here she was an orphan, barely hanging on to what little bit of property she had. Bess and Jerome, her stepsiblings who'd arrived a little more than six months ago, didn't help much. Actually, they didn't seem to be interested in Red Roan Ranch at all. Unless they were discussing how much it was worth, what could be gained by selling it. Frustrated with the whole situation, Laurel slapped her hand against the glass.

Which drew the men's attention back to her yet again.

Feeling her face catch on fire, Laurel turned away, but not before sensing her prisoner's scorching gaze.

Finally, after three days of watching him, she met his eyes.

He stared at her intently. As if he had all the time in the world to stare at her. As if he couldn't look away.

Her lips opened in wonder.

"Laurel!"

Resolutely, she shut her mouth before she caught flies, then turned to face her bossy stepsister. Bess was still glaring at her hard enough to sour buttermilk.

"Stop yelling at me, Bess. I'm not doing anything wrong."

"You're creating a spectacle of yourself, watching the prisoners like a loose woman. It's improper."

"I think not."

As Bess always did when Laurel didn't back down immediately, she harrumphed and then walked away, but not before flicking her dark-green taffeta skirts in disgust.

Once again alone in the sitting room, Laurel wondered how much longer she was going to be able to handle her stepsister's so-called help. At times like this, she feared she wouldn't make it another day.

Laurel's father had died in the war, and after a whole interminable year of mourning, her mother had remarried three years ago. Wayne Vance had been a good man, a kind man, and Laurel had been happy for her mother. He'd also had his own land, a sprawling estate two towns over. So he'd had no issue with her mother making sure Red Roan Ranch went directly to Laurel in the unlikely event of her death, especially since Laurel's brother, Anderson, had also died in the war.

But then, when both her mother and stepfather died in last

winter's influenza epidemic, everything Laurel had never wanted to happen had. She was the sole owner of a thousand acres of prime land just south of Fort Worth, near the small town of Sweetwater. It not only had a creek and several ponds, but it was also fertile farmland.

Bess and Jerome were supposed to have been happy with their father's land. But instead of holding on to it, they sold their inheritance the moment they could and, Laurel heard, for far less than it was worth. Then they'd gone down to New Orleans and Jackson, Mississippi, and spent every last dime.

Which was why they were now living with Laurel.

Almost daily someone came and offered to buy her land. Though her stepsiblings kept pressuring her to sell, she'd refused. Not only would selling make her homeless, but she'd have to figure out what else to do with her life.

She didn't have other goals. She liked her ranch. She wanted to keep it, wanted to live there. She wanted to increase her herd, send some to market. The land and cattle were her links to her identity. Her reminders that war and disease hadn't ruined everything in her life. Only most of it.

That was why, when Will mentioned that a crew of six men who were serving short jail terms for minor infractions needed work, and that he was thinking they maybe could do some work on her property, she said she'd be happy for their assistance.

Bess and Jerome had been up in arms when she told them.

But then she pointed out that no impropriety would be taking place since the men would be chained and guarded. She also took care to point out that the work needed to be done either by the men or by them.

They'd given in easily enough then.

She was starting to understand why her mother had never had

much respect for them. She'd said time and again that there were some folks who did and others who waited for things to be done for them.

For Red Roan Ranch to stay hers, it had to make a profit. Since she needed strong men like these prisoners who could work hard to help make that happen, she needed them hydrated at the very least.

Grateful to have come to a decision at last, she strode out to the kitchen that was slightly detached from the house, poured some cool water into a pail, added two chunks of precious ice, and took hold of a large ladle.

She was going to do it.

She was going to stop staring out windows, open up her front door, and walk outside. She was going to approach those men and offer them some water.

After smoothing her hair back off her face, she opened the door and walked toward the group of men. The walk was a short distance. But as each man stilled and watched her progress, Laurel felt as though she were walking two miles.

Now that she was outside and away from the shade of her house, trickles of perspiration slid along her spine.

The second guard, the stranger, the one who was most definitely not Ollie, strode to her side. He greeted her with an oily smile and the smallest of respectful nods. "Miss Tracey. What can I do for you?"

"Sir—"

"It's Foster Howell," he interjected. "Surely you remember? We met at the party on the square three years ago."

She didn't remember that party. Mr. Howell wasn't anyone she would have remembered speaking to if they had. He was rather coarse and crude. But since she couldn't very well admit such a thing, she played her part. "Yes, yes, of course, Mr. Howell. It's a pleasure to see you again."

"Indeed, miss."

Casting a glance at the line of men still staring at her, she held up her pail and ladle. "It's so warm. I thought I'd bring the men some water."

Looking eager, he reached for the pail's handle. "That is too kind of you. Thank you."

A sixth sense told her he wouldn't share the water with the convicts. Besides, she'd seen him and Ollie sip from flasks from time to time.

"Mr. Howell, I don't mind giving it to them myself."

The man looked appalled by the idea. "Certainly not, Miss Tracey. A lady like you needs to stay far away from these men. I believe Mr. Burnside told you they could be dangerous."

She glanced at the line of men again. "Sheriff Jackson said they weren't dangerous. That some were only convicted because of money owed."

"All men are dangerous. Especially around a woman like you."

A flicker of unease slid down her spine. Foster Howell could, indeed, be right. The war had taught them all that much could happen to the best of people under the worst of circumstances.

The right thing to do would be to hand him the pail and leave. To go back inside and busy herself with chores, then sit in silence and wait for the hours to pass. To try to converse with Bess about things that didn't matter. To hold her tongue when Jerome sat at her father's desk and attempted to look important.

But she couldn't do that for another day.

"My mother taught me to treat others as I would like to be treated, Mr. Howell. I'll take my chances now." Before he could caution her to stay away yet again, Laurel approached the line of men.

Now not one of them was even pretending to work on the fence. Suddenly, they seemed larger, more foreboding, and harder than she'd previously thought.

They were dirty and stained. They smelled of grime and sweat and disappointment. Upon closer inspection, she noticed their cheeks were hollow and their expressions as varied as their appearances. Some of them looked wary, others eager. All, however, looked terribly thirsty.

Telling herself she was merely doing a good deed, she walked to the man closest to her, the man who had consumed her thoughts and vision for the last three days. He straightened when she got close. When she stopped, he inclined his head respectfully.

"Miss."

His voice was deep and gravelly. Better than she had imagined. "Sir. I . . . I brought you men some water. Would you care for any?"

After a pause, he spoke again. "I would at that, miss," he replied in a slow drawl. "This is kind of you."

He was so mannerly. Even out in the heat fixing fences with an iron shackle cutting into his ankle. And his eyes . . . well, they were proving to be even more mesmerizing up close. He had blue eyes. Not gray blue. Not pale blue. Blue like bluebonnets. Blue like the summer sky in July.

Beautiful, piercing blue eyes framed by dark eyelashes. Fastened directly on her.

"Y'all are fixing my fence in the hot July sun. It's the least I could do."

Those blue eyes gleamed. "It ain't the least. It's more than we expected. And, I must admit, much appreciated."

She smiled at him before remembering she shouldn't do such

a thing. Hoping he didn't notice her hands were shaking, she held the pail toward him, allowing him to pick up the ladle and quench his thirst without her assistance.

He closed his eyes with the first sip, then sipped again.

One, two droplets of water remained on his bottom lip. The beads stayed there, taunting her.

When he swiped his lip with his tongue, she inhaled sharply.

While the other men snickered softly, her convict grinned, showing a truly fine set of teeth.

"Watch yourself, Baker," Mr. Howell called out. "You ain't out yet." Sounding gleeful, he added, "And there's no guarantee anyone is even going to want you tomorrow."

Ignoring the threat, the man—Baker—dipped the ladle into the pail again, then brought the water to his parched lips. Laurel watched each movement with bated breath.

After he released the ladle's handle, giving her leave to attend to the next prisoner, he said, "He's right, you know."

"About what?"

"You shouldn't be out here. A woman like you shouldn't be anywhere near a rough lot like us."

"You . . . you seem all right, Mr. Baker."

"I am all right." Looking amused, he smiled, triggering the startling appearance of twin dimples. "But that don't mean you should be anywhere near me."

Before she could respond to that, Ollie strode forward. "Quiet, Baker, or you'll feel the mark of my whip."

Like lightning, Baker turned on him. "Don't threaten me," he bit out, his voice hard and sharp. As far from the gentlemanly drawl as was possible.

To Laurel's surprise, Ollie stopped in his tracks.

Moving on to the next prisoner, she handed him the ladle.

As he drank his fill, she looked back at Baker. Pointedly ignoring Ollie's irritation, she said, "Mr. Baker, what did he mean about someone wanting you tomorrow?"

"Tomorrow is the first day I'm eligible to be released."

She smiled at him. "Why, that's wonderful."

He didn't smile in return. "It's only wonderful if I can get hired. That's the terms of it. Someone has to hire me tomorrow for me to be released."

Moving down the line, she smiled at the convict who greeted her with a head bob and a low "Miss" before passing on the ladle. While the man sipped gratefully, she continued her conversation with Baker. "And if no one does?"

"Then I might have the good fortune to be doing more chores for you in the future."

Feeling a bit speechless, she stared at him in wonder.

Just a bit too long.

"Bring it over here, miss," another convict called out. His voice suggestive and low, he added, "I'll take a sip of whatever you got."

Baker tensed. "Just give that pail to Watters there, miss," he said quietly. "We'll take care of ourselves now. One of the guards can set it outside your door when we leave. Go on in now."

"But—"

While the man she'd been giving water to held out his hands for the pail, her convict said, "What's your name, miss?"

"Laurel," she whispered. "Laurel Tracey."

"Miss Tracey, beg pardon, but you are a distraction. And I fear too much temptation for the likes of us. Go on in now."

"I'm not afraid."

"You should be. Now, go."

Her mind spinning, she did as he bid. She gave the pail to the prisoner and turned away. As she walked back to the house, she heard the low murmur of masculine voices, followed by the *clank* of the ladle against the pail. But she also sensed eyes watching her departure.

Tilting her chin down, she made sure to keep her pace steady. And tried not to think about how one man's attention could rattle her so much.

2

WITH A WINCE AND A CURSE UNDER HIS BREATH, THOMAS Baker stretched out on his bunk. He'd known Howell was going to enjoy doling out his punishment, but Thomas hadn't counted on the guard enjoying it quite so much.

Propped on his elbows, his cellmate, Bert Watters, watched from his own bunk with concern. "Yer back is bleeding. Blood's soaking through yer shirt."

"Figured as much." He left it at that. After all, what else was there to say?

"How many strikes did Howell get in?"

"I'm thinking at least eight."

Bert curled his lip. "I used to save all my hate for the Yankees, but I hate Howell too."

Thomas wasn't sure he hated the guard, but he reckoned if he didn't, he was mighty close to feeling that way. "He's definitely no good. Kind of a simpleton too."

Bert raised his thick, dark eyebrows. "You're a piece of work, Baker. That man took off a good portion of your skin for no reason and you only call him a simpleton." He shook his head. "Can't say I understand how yer mind works."

Thinking back to the more than eight months spent in the

Confederate Officers Camp on Johnson's Island, Thomas weighed his words. "I've had my fair share of cruel guards. Howell is bad, but he ain't one of the worst."

"I forgot you were up on Johnson's Island." After a moment, Bert continued. "You don't talk about it much."

"No reason to. It's over." Besides, the memories hurt too much.

"Makes sense."

Thomas hoped Bert did understand. But what he probably didn't understand was that it wasn't the pain or the boredom or the hunger that was so hard to remember. It was the realization that the friendships he'd made there were likely to be the best of his life. He'd had the dubious honor of being imprisoned with some of the finest men he'd ever met. Because of that, he'd found himself both hating and loving every minute of his imprisonment there.

No man should ever be so desperate.

"Lots of you die up there while you were shut away?" Bert asked, his voice sharp in the silence.

Thinking of Phillip Markham, his lieutenant who had suffered so much before his death, Thomas nodded. "Yep. But not all." Far more had died on the battlefield.

Leaning closer, Bert said, "I heard you served under Captain Monroe. Is that true?"

"It is."

"Really? What was he like? Were you with him on Johnson's Island?"

He respected Captain Monroe far too much to discuss him. "I was on the island with him, but I don't talk about the captain."

"Why not? War's over."

"The war's over, but my admiration for the captain hasn't dimmed."

Bert's mouth went slack before he collected himself. "So the rumors are true? He really was that good?"

"Yeah. He was." In fact, he was so good that if Thomas had contacted him about needing funds—or told him he had been imprisoned for his lack of funds—Captain Monroe would have paid his debts immediately. But Thomas wasn't going to take advantage of him like that. It was better to simply deal with his situation. Somehow, some way, his life was going to get better. He was going to make sure of it.

Bert sighed. He shifted, then flopped around on his thin, uncomfortable mattress like a fish flopping on dry land. In contrast, Thomas concentrated on attempting to stay perfectly still. If he didn't move, there was a halfway decent chance he wasn't going to start crying out in pain.

Minutes passed. Little by little his body relaxed. His back still burned, but at least he was now able to breathe in and out without agonizing pain.

"Hey, Thomas?"

"Hmm?"

"You remember that woman today? The one who gave us water?" As if Thomas had been in contact with any other woman in days.

"What about her?"

"She was something, wasn't she?"

"She was." She was more than that. She'd been the prettiest thing he'd had the pleasure of seeing in years. About his age, golden hair, light-brown eyes, full cheeks that made a man ache to see her smile. She had a figure that was as rich as it was alluring.

Perfect.

Though Thomas had cautioned himself to erase Miss Tracey from his mind, he couldn't help but dwell on her again. He just knew holding her in his arms would feel like heaven. He'd seen too many starving men and women during the war. The women who now tried to have minuscule waists and an air of angelic reed-thinness only made him feel ill.

"I keep thinking about her, and her name too. Laurel Tracey," Bert said around a sigh. "Pretty, ain't it?"

"Yeah." Pretty and feminine. Just like her.

"I think Howell aims to have her. It seems she owns some prime land out there."

"I can think of a lot of other reasons to pursue her."

Bert coughed. "It's that kind of talk that can get you into trouble, Thomas. You shouldn't be thinking about her like that. You really shouldn't have talked to her."

"I was only being polite. She spoke to me first."

Bert chuckled. "You did more than that. I saw how you looked at her."

"All of us watched her. She's a fetching thing. I couldn't help it. Besides, Howell was looking for an excuse to handle that whip."

"Maybe so, but I meant Howell wants her something awful," Bert continued in a low voice. "Two men were talking about it in the yard after supper. They said Howell intends to take more prisoners back to her place next week."

"Though that seems like an odd way to gain a female's favor, that doesn't surprise me. I can't imagine him spending much effort actually going courting."

"That's why he beat you good today. Howell doesn't want you anywhere near her." Bert snickered. "I guess he considers you a rival."

"I'm not much of anything at the moment." He certainly wasn't a rival. Howell was an idiot and liked to inflict pain on people who couldn't defend themselves. "But I can pretty much assure you Howell won't be choosing me to be within two miles of her ranch ever again."

"I don't think he'll be allowing you to get real close again either. No offense, but I sure hope the good Lord intends for me to be in Miss Tracey's vicinity again real soon."

Jealousy hit him hard, though it made no sense. But he did know that she was too pretty and too vulnerable to be the focus of a bunch of prisoners' minds.

With effort, he pushed those thoughts away. "You're from here. What do you know about her? Was she married? Is she a widow?"

"I am from here, but my kin never mixed with hers much. I know she never married, though."

"Surprising."

"Some say she had a sweetheart who went off to fight, but I don't know who."

"Most men married their sweethearts." He'd never done such a thing, of course, but he'd heard a hundred stories of men who married in haste before going off to battle.

"Well, no one married her. Don't know why."

She's young, beautiful, owns land, and seems to be in need of a man to help her manage that ranch. All of those things tugged on his heart. Thomas had never been one for compassion, but even he couldn't deny the appeal of a beautiful woman who was in need of a protector.

"I wonder what's wrong with all the men in this town," he murmured. If he'd been a different type of man—one who was actually worth something—he would have been pursuing her with everything he had. She was not only everything Bert had said, but she'd offered convicts water. Women like that were hard to find and even harder to claim.

"If they're all like Howell, it ain't no surprise she's still a miss," Bert said.

"I can't fault that reasoning. He would have fit in real well with the guards at Johnson's Island."

"If they had been working for the Yankees, us Rebs might have had a fighting chance."

A bark of laughter jolted through him, pulling on his skin, stretching the wounds on his back. Against his will, he cried out in pain.

Bert jumped to his feet. "You're sure in a bad way. You ain't still thinking about getting put up to bid in the morning, are you?"

The town had a tradition of giving prisoners who weren't violent the option of becoming a good citizen's indentured servant for a year. Sheriff Jackson had approached him about it that morning before the guards marched them out to Miss Tracey's ranch. He'd quietly told Thomas it might be the best thing for him.

Thomas had agreed.

Howell had overheard.

That, Thomas knew, was the main reason Howell had beaten him to within an inch of his life. There had been a chance that he was going to be out of this small-town jail in less than twenty-four hours. And if Thomas left, Howell would no longer have his whipping boy.

"I don't have a choice. I've got to get out of here."

"But you're in sorry shape. Real bad."

"No one's going to hire me for my looks." All he had to do was stand there on two feet until someone saw something of worth in him. Though he feared there might not be anything to find, not with injuries that could affect his ability to work, Thomas intended to pretend there was. "I'll be fine."

"They stick you in a cage, you know. You'll be standing in the hot sun like a caged bird. Your back's going to burn and blister something fierce."

He hadn't heard about the cage. Glad for the dim light of the cell, Thomas grimaced. "Probably so. But I still have to try."

After surviving too many battles and skirmishes to count, he'd survived his time on Johnson's Island too. There he'd learned to control his temper and tried to become the man his father had no doubt intended him to be.

But in the year or so after his release, he'd made mistake after mistake. He quit a good-paying ranch job in Oklahoma because they abused their horseflesh. In Abilene he'd been hired on as a guard for a group of men who were unscrupulous and no better than lying carpetbaggers.

Then he'd gone and gambled what little money he had in a card game with two well-known citizens of Fort Worth. Well, everyone knew who they were but him. When Thomas lost, he lost big . . . and ended up owing those men more money than he could ever repay.

And since one of them was Judge Orbison's kin, Thomas had ended up in Sweetwater's jail. Serving time for poker debts.

Thomas had had enough. Enough of making mistakes. Enough of trusting the wrong people and misjudging the right ones. Enough of simply trying to survive. Now he was willing to do whatever he could to never wake up to metal bars again.

All he had to do was hope that morning would come sooner than later and that he wouldn't be too much worse for wear when dawn did break.

It was faint, but Laurel could see it. The squatters in the north pasture had a campfire going again. Glancing at her timepiece, she saw it was close to midnight. At this hour, all she could do was hope and pray the wind didn't pick up and burn her fields and cattle.

Squatters were the bane of her and any good rancher's existence. They wreaked havoc on land that didn't belong to them. Over the years, she'd seen their destruction. Sometimes it was merely in the waste they left behind. Other times it was the damage they did to barbed-wire fencing. Or the thieving they did.

Now, here in the middle of summer, she lived in fear that one of their campfires was going to burn out of control and scorch her land. If that happened? No doubt they'd skulk off and she'd face the consequences alone.

During the war, she'd put up with some of the vagrants, mainly because she'd been too afraid to confront them. Deserters from both sides had run rampant. Having nothing to lose, they'd preyed on women trying to survive while living essentially alone. Sometimes literally alone.

But now something had to change. She needed to grow her herd, get some to market, and build on from there. Since Bess and Jerome weren't going to help her, she had to find someone who was strong enough to take on these squatters. She couldn't do it alone. She needed a man who was tough and hard and didn't frighten easily.

She was pretty sure Thomas Baker fit the bill.

Glad that she'd made her decision, she turned away from the window and climbed into bed. She needed to rest. Come morning, she was going to hitch up Velvet, drive herself into town, and bid on the prisoner.

Closing her eyes, she prayed Thomas Baker really was everything she hoped he was.

If he wasn't, she could be making her terrible situation even worse.

3

I fired Foster Howell an hour ago," Sheriff Jackson said to Thomas the next morning after he'd escorted Thomas into his office himself.

Thomas wasn't sure how he was supposed to reply. His back felt as if it were now home to dozens of sharp nails, each determined to make mincemeat out of the raw marks the whip had made on his skin. When he'd first opened his eyes, he'd yearned to cry out in pain.

He'd made do with allowing his cellmate to dip part of his shirt in some water and dab at his burning skin.

Soon after Bert helped him put on his shirt, Jackson had appeared at their cell's door. "Come on out, Baker," he'd said gruffly.

Then he'd led the way to his office, not even bothering to handcuff Thomas. Thomas had been surprised by that but hadn't complained. Once they were in the office, Jackson gestured for Thomas to sit as he took a fortifying sip of coffee.

But even though Jackson seemed like an upstanding man, Thomas was afraid to let down his guard. "Is Howell's firing supposed to mean something to me?"

"Maybe." As the sheriff continued to stare at Thomas over his mug, he looked increasingly disgruntled. "He whipped you like you were a blasted slave. Idiot."

Thomas agreed with him, of course, but he knew better than to disparage one of the guards. The sheriff might not think highly of Howell, but the man hadn't been a prisoner. Thomas certainly was.

"How bad are you, Baker? And don't tell me no tales. I want the truth."

"Not bad." It wasn't the truth, but it was going to take more than a few lash marks to stop him from doing everything he could to get out of jail as soon as possible.

Still looking at him skeptically, the sheriff said, "Do I need to send for Doc? I only found out what happened about two hours ago."

"You don't need to send for anyone." Especially not some doctor. He'd seen the worst of what those sawbones could do on the battlefield and wanted no part of them.

Sheriff Jackson didn't look so sure. "The back of your shirt don't look fine, but I won't push. Now, what do you want to do about today's proceedings? I gotta warn you that today might not be the best opportunity for you, son. Anyone who comes to bid wants an able worker—"

"I want to participate, sir." As long as there was the slightest chance to get hired on and out of jail, Thomas was willing to take it.

Jackson drained the last of his coffee, then set down the mug with a regretful look. "Yesterday morning I thought you might stand a chance of getting hired on, you're so able-bodied. But now?" He shook his head. "I just don't know. I should warn you there's not a lot of hope for freedom. So far, the only man who ever paid for prisoners was Kevin Oberlee, and he's gone now."

Thomas knew he wasn't much of a prize, but he had nothing to lose. "I'll take my chances."

"You sure? 'Cause the only thing you might get out of this is some food and a whole lotta cruel treatment tossed your way."

He was a man, not a child. He'd fought for the Confederacy and had been held prisoner on a forsaken island in the middle of Lake Erie. "I understand, sir."

"All right, let's do this, then." Pulling out a pair of metal handcuffs from his jacket pocket, he reached for Thomas's hands and securely cuffed them in front of his body. Then he gripped his elbow and led him out the front of the jail and into the town square.

Squinting in the sun, Thomas was surprised to see the area was fairly crowded with men, women, and children. Some looked at the cage in the middle of the square with doleful expressions. Others looked positively gleeful.

Thomas had thought nothing could ever surprise him, but it turned out he was wrong. It seemed for some people criminals garnered the same sort of lurid fascination that battlefields and human suffering did for others.

An almost carnival atmosphere prevailed. Folks were dressed in their Sunday best, chatting with each other. Laughing. One enterprising man was selling pickles from a makeshift cart. Above all of it was an air of expectation. The crowd was anticipating something out of the ordinary. Did they sense something the sheriff didn't?

Thomas stared at them, even going so far as to look several in the eye. Women tittered behind handkerchiefs and men blanched and gripped their children's hands. Through it all, Jackson kept his hand firmly on Thomas's elbow as they weaved their way through the crowd.

"It always this way, Sheriff?" Thomas asked.

"No. Maybe they heard about the whipping. Maybe they think you're something special to see. I have no idea." Jackson's voice was flat as he walked him up four steps to a pedestal of some sort. Sitting in the middle of it was a rectangular iron cage. It was tall enough for Thomas to stand upright, but barely.

It looked hot and uncomfortable and made him suddenly feel sorry for the animals carted around in the carnivals that toured the country from time to time.

Jackson sighed. "Here's what's gonna happen, Baker. I'm gonna lock you in this cage. You'll remain here for two hours or until someone makes an offer for your services."

"And until that time?"

"Until then, folks will mill around and get a good look at you. Judge Orbison will offer you up to the highest bidder."

"Until then, I wait."

"Yep. You wait. I'll be nearby, so no one should get too close. Burnside will be too. But prepare yourself, son. It ain't pleasant."

Thomas said nothing, but he was pretty sure the sheriff had just uttered a heck of an understatement. However, all he had to do was concentrate on the way his back burned and pained him—all he needed to remind himself was that some circumstances were definitely worse than others.

Since it didn't look as though anyone was about to whip him today for simply being alive, Thomas figured he could handle whatever was to come.

Jackson unlocked the cage, sent Thomas inside, then locked the barred door again.

The minute Sheriff Jackson stepped off the platform and moved to the side, the crowd inched closer from all sides. Thomas felt their disdain for him like a tangible thing. More than one person gasped at the blood that had seeped through his shirt.

Judge Orbison walked forward. Looking displeased to be out in the blazing sun in his three-piece black suit, he pulled out a spoon and clanged it against Thomas's bars.

The jarring sound, together with the vibrations the motion set off, made Thomas flinch.

At least the crowd immediately quieted.

"Citizens of Sweetwater, by now you probably know the drill. I've got a prisoner here, a Mr. . . . uh . . ." The judge turned to him. "Name, son?"

"Thomas Baker."

"Mr. Thomas Baker." As if he suddenly remembered something, the judge pulled out a sheet of paper from a vest pocket. "Ah. Here we go. This man here was once a sergeant in the CSA. He fought with honor and was captured and spent the last of the war in captivity up in Johnson's Island. By all accounts, he served bravely and was held in high esteem by one and all."

Thomas had no time to wonder where the judge had come across all that information before a thin farmer called out, "Then how come he's in jail?"

The judge glanced at his paper again. "Man couldn't pay his debts." Meeting Thomas's gaze, the judge raised an eyebrow. "That right?"

"Yes, sir." He decided to leave out the fact that the men he owed money to had been playing in a poker game.

To Thomas's dismay, the judge's account of his good character seemed a bit of a letdown for the assemblage. Perhaps they were hoping he'd done something far more dangerous or terrible.

"If he's only jailed 'cause he couldn't pay his debts, how come he was whipped?" another man asked.

"Foster Howell did that," Sheriff Jackson called out as he lit a cheroot. "He shouldn't have."

Judge Orbison motioned for Thomas to show him his back. After he took a good look at it, he frowned. "This ain't good, Jackson," he said to the sheriff, as if they were sitting in some gambling hall and talking about the weather. "Baker here might owe money, but I just received a telegram from a man about him this very morning. He's got some powerful friends. They aren't going to take it kindly when they discover how badly he's been treated while staying in our facilities."

Thomas stiffened. Who was the judge speaking of? He hadn't let anyone know he was here, especially not his friends from Johnson's Island. He looked over at the sheriff, waiting for him to ask the judge who it was. But Sheriff Jackson didn't look all that concerned.

Leaning toward him, Judge Orbison asked, "You need anything right now, son? Water maybe?"

There was no way he was going to sip water while half the town looked on. "I only need someone to offer me a job, sir."

"That would certainly fix things. We'll see what we can do." He inhaled, then turned back toward the crowd. "Alrighty. For those of you who might have forgotten, here's how our prisoner auctions work. This man here will be on display for two hours. If you have questions, deliver them to me or Sheriff Jackson." He cleared his throat. "If you are interested in hiring him on, come directly to me."

A hush fell over the crowd as more than one person approached, then turned away. After another twenty minutes passed, the square began to empty.

As the sun beat down on him, Thomas's optimism faltered. It had been a long shot, of course, but now it seemed he was doomed to spend many more nights in captivity. Even his "friends in high places"—or whoever had sent the telegram—couldn't gain him early freedom. Not merely with some good words. He wouldn't ask his friends for anything more anyway.

He passed time by staring out into the distance, much like he'd done on Johnson's Island. If he concentrated hard enough, he could imagine he was someplace else. Someplace better, more peaceful. Where his back didn't burn and he could sit down.

An hour went by.

He'd just pressed his chapped lips together and was considering asking for that sip of water when the lingering crowd parted and two rough-looking ranchers approached. Their faces were craggy from years spent out in the elements on horseback. Sharp eyes examined him as though he were livestock.

Thomas straightened and stared back. He wasn't afraid of hard work and he wasn't afraid of work-hardened men. But that didn't mean he was going to let them imagine they'd be getting a greenhorn if they freed him.

Time seemed to still. One of them nodded.

"I hope I'm not too late?" a sweet voice called out.

Immediately, everyone's focus changed. Thomas moved his head to the right and blinked.

Because there was Miss Laurel Tracey. She was moving gracefully through the crowd, dressed in a rather complicated-looking green calico and a straw bonnet with a bright-yellow ribbon threaded around its brim.

The bonnet set off her face and brown eyes. The dress was worn but in good repair. It had a bustle that emphasized her small waist.

She looked clean and fresh and perfect. Completely out of place.

Thomas tried not to stare, because, well, he was already standing in the hot sun in a cage with his back burning like the devil himself had set his pitchfork on it. The last thing he needed was to get punished for being disrespectful.

But Lord Almighty, she was a sight to see. Pretty and curvy and oh so innocent looking. She also had a little lift to her chin that said no one should make the mistake of thinking she didn't have a backbone.

Men and women moved to the side as she continued to walk toward him. Judge Orbison lifted his hat. Sheriff Jackson extinguished his cheroot and moved to her side.

"Miss Tracey," Judge Orbison said. "Afternoon."

"Sir." She smiled more brightly at the sheriff. "Will, hello."

"Miss Laurel. Good to see you," Sheriff Jackson greeted in a smooth tone, giving her a small bow. "What brings you here?" he asked, looking worried. "Are you having some kind of problem at the ranch?"

"I am, but it's nothing this man can't fix." Turning to Thomas, she smiled.

Sure he hadn't heard right, Thomas gripped two bars and leaned as close as his cage allowed.

Jackson pushed back the rim of his Stetson a couple of inches. "I understand he's been part of the crew that's been working on your fencing. Do you need them back?"

"Oh, I don't want that crew back. No offense, but I, well, I don't care for Mr. Howell's company much."

Judge Orbison stepped closer to her. "Did Foster Howell harm you, Miss Laurel?"

"Oh, no. It's just . . ." She opened her mouth and shut it with a firm shake of her head. "I don't think it matters anymore, does it? I mean, not if I'm here to hire Mr. Baker."

Thomas exhaled. Tried not to smile. Not because he wasn't pleased about what she was offering him. No, it was more like he wasn't sure if she *should* want him nearby. He was a war-worn man with next to no experience around ladies. Though he knew without a doubt that he'd never harm her, he wasn't sure if he'd always be able to hide his attraction to her.

And if he couldn't hide that, then chances were more than good she'd realize sooner or later that he wasn't necessarily the best man to have on her property.

Jackson narrowed his eyes. "Do your siblings know you're here?"

Instead of answering directly, she lifted her chin a tad bit higher. "Bess and Jerome are my stepsiblings, not my true brother and sister. Furthermore, they do know. And what they think is no concern of mine."

Jackson looked momentarily shamefaced. "Of course not. But I'm not sure you know what you're getting yourself into. This man might not be a felon, but he is no gentleman."

Miss Tracey darted another look his way. "Sir, I don't need a gentleman. I need a man willing to work hard and help me with my ranch. I also need him immediately."

It took Thomas everything he had to keep from laughing. She really did have a spark to her.

Judge Orbison seemed as though he was trying not to laugh as well. "I see," he said.

Laurel Tracey fastened her pretty eyes on the judge and said sweetly, "If I hire him, are there any stipulations?"

"You have to keep him on for one year."

She glanced Thomas's way. "And after one year, if he wants to leave or I no longer have a need for his assistance, we can end our contract?"

One of the two ranchers who had been staring at him grunted. "Hey, now," he said. "You can't just give him to her."

Jackson glared at the pair. "Judge Orbison can do whatever he likes."

After a pause Judge Orbison nodded in Miss Tracey's direction. "Yes, miss. That is how it goes."

"I see."

When she met Thomas's gaze again, he was pretty sure he flushed.

Leaving the judge and sheriff, she stepped up the first two steps of the platform. "Sir, do you remember meeting me yesterday?" she asked Thomas.

As if there was any chance that he'd forget. "Yes, miss," he replied, hating that his voice sounded a little hoarse, a little thick from nerves. "But there's no need to call me sir. Best just call me Baker, Miss Tracey. Or by my first."

"And what is that?"

"My full name is Thomas Travis Baker."

She looked about to comment on that when she seemed to notice his bloodstained shirt. She gasped as she walked around the cage to get a better look at his back. "My goodness! That's quite a scar on your neck. And, why, I do believe that is blood seeping through your shirt. What happened to you?"

"It ain't nothing to worry about, miss."

Walking back to the sheriff's side, she glared at him. "Did you do this?"

To Thomas's surprise, instead of telling her such things were none of her concern, the sheriff shook his head. "I did not, Miss Laurel."

"Then how did this happen?"

"There was some miscommunication last night in the jailhouse. It was taken care of."

Now staring at Thomas, she bit her lip.

As Thomas watched those perfect white teeth dig into the soft flesh of one plump bottom lip, he resigned himself to two things. One was that he could no more look away from her than he could get out of this cage on his own.

The second was that it was foolish to get his hopes up. After all, there was every possibility she was going to change her mind.

He didn't know her, but from what he could see, though she had a backbone, she was also a sweet, sheltered woman. She was gentle and she smelled good. She was everything he'd ever imagined a woman should be but hadn't really believed existed.

Time seemed to stand still again.

As she continued to look at him, she no doubt regretted her impulsiveness. He was dirty and smelled bad. He was standing in the middle of a cage and sweat was rolling off him like the tide at sunset.

Then, of course, there was the fact that he'd allowed himself to get whipped at all.

And even though she didn't know him from Adam, she had no reason to completely trust him. Even if she suspected he would never harm a hair on her head, that didn't mean his working at her family's ranch wouldn't have certain dangers all its own. She was liable to lose a good chunk of her reputation, and even he knew a woman could never afford to let that happen.

After staring at him so long that quite a few biddies in the crowd started whispering behind gloved hands, she seemed to come to a decision. "If I want Mr. Baker, can we take him out of there now, Judge Orbison?"

He was going to get hired on. A jolt rose up his spine as he realized his wish was about to come true.

When Miss Tracey met his gaze again, Thomas almost felt tears in his eyes.

She was the prettiest thing he'd ever laid eyes on. As far as he was concerned, heaven did exist, and it was right here in Sweetwater, Texas, in the form of one rather tall, buxom, blond-haired beauty with wide-set brown eyes.

4

As her question rang through the air, a collective sigh tore through the crowd.

Laurel wasn't sure if it was because everyone surrounding them agreed with her assessment or if they were eager to see her regret the consequences of her decision. Chances were good that either might be the case.

It didn't matter much to her either way. She'd ceased to care too much about everyone else's opinions. Verbal chatter didn't help a woman bury her relatives or take care of twenty head of cattle alone in the dead of winter.

As the seconds passed, she steadfastly did her best to look as if she were oblivious to the man in the cage who was staring at her in a bold way. Instead, she focused on the men standing on either side of her who could grant her wish.

Both of them looked a little surprised, but not completely dismayed.

"You sure about this, Miss Laurel?" Sheriff Jackson asked at last.

"I am. Now, it's hot, and I imagine the wounds on Mr. Baker's back are festering. I think it's time he got out of that cage. Don't you?"

Fingering the last of his cheroot, the sheriff said, "I'm talking about you hiring this man. Though he ain't known to be violent, he still isn't one for gentle company."

"I need a man to help me fight those squatters on my property. I need a man to work hard, Will. Not sip tea with me."

Judge Orbison's lips twitched. "Point taken."

Excitement bubbled up inside her. They were taking her seriously, and she was going to get the help she needed. "So may we release him now?"

"Yes. Well, maybe. We're supposed to wait another hour, in case someone else offers for him," the judge said doubtfully. "That's how we've always done things in the past."

It was obviously time to push a little harder. "I could be wrong. After all, I'm only a lone woman used to living on a ranch. But waiting a whole other hour seems kind of hard on everyone, don't you think? Surely you have many more pressing things to do than keep a caged man in the hot sun?"

As she'd hoped, the judge straightened his shoulders. "Indeed, I do."

"Then perhaps you could take care of things right now and move on with your day?"

After glancing over her head at the prisoner, Judge Orbison lowered his voice. "Miss Tracey, I know you need help. But . . . are you sure about this? Once this is done, it's done. Furthermore, I can't help but wonder if your parents would have supported this plan."

It was a legitimate question, one she should be pondering for hours, or at least a whole lot longer than a mere five or six minutes.

But something—something deep in her heart—was telling her to act now and to act quickly. It was as if she no longer had a choice.

Or maybe it was simply that she didn't have a decision to make. She wanted this man out of the cage. "While I agree that my parents wouldn't have necessarily wanted me to hire a prisoner, I don't believe they could have foreseen what my circumstances were going to be like. The truth is that I am sure, sir. In fact, I don't believe I've ever been more sure of anything in my life."

At last the judge inclined his head. "Well then, it looks like you've got a new ranch hand, Miss Tracey." Turning to the sheriff, he said, "Release him, Will. I need to get out of this blasted heat."

Laurel smiled at the judge as the sheriff pulled out a ring of keys. "Thank you, Judge Orbison."

"You're welcome. If it means anything, I'm plumb relieved he's getting out of here."

"I am as well." The moment the words left her mouth, she could practically feel the prisoner's hot gaze settle on her like a hovering bee. It was a tangible thing—so real, Laurel knew she wasn't imagining it.

She supposed she didn't blame Mr. Baker. She was talking about him as if he weren't right there, witnessing her transaction.

She hoped he wasn't scowling at her.

She didn't dare look at him. Not because she feared him. No, it was more that she feared what he'd see if he looked at her.

Inside his cage, Thomas swallowed hard. He wasn't real sure if he was eager to be a woman's ranch hand, even if that woman was Laurel Tracey. But he was definitely up to the task. He needed to get out of jail like he needed to breathe. Though he had few choices about what to do with his life next, most of them were a far sight worse than helping a woman in need for one full year.

His mother would've been proud of him for doing that. Well, he liked to think that such a thing was possible.

He was drawn out of his thoughts when the hefty judge turned and gently bent over Miss Tracey's hand.

"It's been real good working with you, Miss Laurel." Raising his voice, Judge Orbison said, "Jackson, bring him to my office. I'll prepare the paperwork and then he and Miss Tracey can get on their way."

"Yes, sir," the sheriff said.

Before the judge left, he turned to Thomas. Even though he was a good four inches shorter and was also standing four steps below the platform, the judge somehow managed to sound like he was talking down to Thomas.

"You've just been given the opportunity of a lifetime, Baker," he intoned. "Miss Tracey is a lady and gently bred. You'd best remember to give her the respect she deserves. If not, I don't even want to think about what could happen to you."

"Of course," Thomas said.

"Work hard and keep your head down." Hardening his voice, the judge whispered, "Squatters can be big trouble. Don't lower your guard."

"I won't, sir," he answered in the same tone of voice he used to answer Captain Monroe.

"Good. Hope it works out," the judge said before turning and walking away.

After Judge Orbison disappeared into his offices, Sheriff Jackson ascended the steps and placed his hand on the bars of the cage. Then he turned around and called out, "Alrighty, everyone. It's time to settle down and move on. The show's over. Our prisoner will now be working for Miss Tracey." Then he turned to his guard.

"Ollie, escort Miss Tracey to the judge's office. I'll bring the prisoner along presently."

"Yes, sir," Ollie said. Holding out an elbow, he smiled at her. "Let's go, Miss Tracey."

"Thank you," she whispered. "Please, just give me one moment."

Then, to Thomas's surprise, she walked up the steps to his cage.

Motionless, he stared at her. Her scent—lavender and magnolia and clean, fresh woman—caught hold of him and held him in its grip. It was a mesmerizing thing, and so beautiful he feared she could see its effect on his face.

"I'm glad this worked out, Mr. Baker," she said softly. "I promise that I'll do my best to be a good boss."

How did a man respond to that? Void of words, he nodded.

She smiled before walking back down the steps and taking Ollie's extended arm.

Not wanting to get caught looking after her backside, Thomas deliberately kept his expression empty and his eyes looking straight forward.

As his cage door opened and Sheriff Jackson grabbed his elbow, the sheriff muttered under his breath, "I don't know what you've ever done to be worthy of this opportunity, but you are currently the luckiest dog I know."

Since Thomas reckoned no reply was expected, he concentrated on negotiating the narrow steps with his still sore joints.

Most of the crowd had moved away, giving him and the sheriff a bit more room to walk back to the jailhouse than when they had approached the square.

When they were about halfway there, Sheriff Jackson spoke again. "Miss Laurel is about the sweetest girl I've ever met." Hardening his voice, he said, "Orbison wasn't lying. No one will go easy on you if she comes to any harm in your company."

"And they shouldn't." Afraid he wouldn't get another chance

to ask someone who might know, Thomas asked, "How come she never married?"

When the man inhaled, Thomas called himself ten times the fool. There went his mouth again. He was still in shackles but was asking personal questions about the lady who'd just purchased his freedom?

"Don't know," the sheriff said as he drew in another breath. "I like you, Baker. More than that, I respect the man who telegraphed the judge about your character. If Captain Monroe says you don't belong in a cell, you don't."

Thomas had no idea how Devin Monroe even knew he was in jail, but his reaching out didn't surprise him. "Thank you."

"That said, don't you ever forget something. You hurt one hair on Laurel Tracey's head, you'll get back in here so fast you won't know what hit you. And I'll make sure you don't see the light of day for months."

"Understood."

Thomas had no idea why a woman like her needed to hire on a man like him, why she didn't already have a man in her life. But he did know he'd do everything in his power to make sure she didn't regret her decision.

Besides his freedom from jail, she'd given him something he'd pretty much lost when he was captured and sent up to Johnson's Island prison—his self-worth. His new friends there had helped him see himself in new ways, but being thrown into Sweetwater jail, subjected to the whims of a man like Foster Howell, had set him back.

The return of his self-worth felt awkward and strange. But he was fairly sure it would, over time, fit him like a glove.

5

JUDGE ORBISON'S OFFICE WAS JUST ON THE OTHER SIDE OF the town square. But as Laurel and Ollie walked through the throng of people, it felt like one of the longest walks of her life. She felt weighed down by everyone's judgmental looks.

She also couldn't help but acknowledge that she'd just become part of the town's latest fodder for gossip. Chances were good that in mere hours, her formerly good reputation was going to become tarnished beyond repair.

"You're really going to go through with it, Miss Tracey?" Ollie asked after she'd barely taken four steps.

"I am."

"That man, he ain't what I'd call respectable. Like I told you before, might even be a bit dangerous."

Considering she'd just purchased Mr. Baker from a cage, Laurel figured Ollie's summation was a bit of an understatement. But instead of mentioning that, she kept her silence.

Looking down at his scuffed boots, the guard kicked at the red dirt underfoot. "I know we don't have much to say to each other," he mumbled, "but if you need something, or if you start to worry about your safety, come find me. I'll take care of him."

"I, uh . . . thank you, Ollie."

Just as he finally lifted his chin and smiled at her, another man moved to her other side. "I'll escort her the rest of the way, Burnside," he said.

Laurel inwardly sighed. The very last person she needed to talk to at the moment was Landon Marshall.

Ollie frowned up at him. "I can't let you speak with Miss Tracey right now, Mr. Marshall."

"Sure you can," Landon countered easily. "You know neither Judge Orbison nor Sheriff Jackson is going to have a problem with me escorting Miss Laurel."

"Maybe not. But still—"

"It's all right, Ollie," Laurel interjected quickly. Even though he had failed to recognize the needs of the men on the chain gang on a hot day, he was too kind to have to deal with the ego that was Landon Marshall.

My, how she wished he hadn't become so possessive.

"I'll walk the rest of the way with Mr. Marshall."

Though he didn't look happy about it, Ollie stepped away. "As you wish, Miss Tracey."

The moment Ollie turned away, Landon leaned close and gripped her elbow. "Laurel, tell me I didn't just see you purchase a convict."

"I didn't purchase anyone, Landon. I hired him to help me around the ranch."

"That's basically the same thing."

"Not exactly. Sergeant Baker is going to work for me for one year, then be on his way."

"Sergeant? He isn't a soldier any longer, Laurel. Now he's nothing. Don't forget, the war is over."

"I haven't forgotten." They were all still dealing with the war's effects, though, and likely would for some time. She was also fighting her own personal war to keep her land—and probably cattle too—safe from squatters and determined buyers.

Pulling her away from the judge's quarters, Landon hardened his expression. "I don't know what's gotten into you lately, but it is rather troubling. I'm beginning to worry for your emotional state."

She pulled her elbow out of his grip. "I beg your pardon?"

"You know what I'm talking about. You've been making a slew of poor decisions lately. Decisions that make no sense. This one is surely the worst of them all."

Before the war, she had wondered if she could love Landon one day. Their families were friendly neighbors and spent some time together. She knew some in town assumed they would marry when Landon returned from his service. But four months ago, after giving the possibility of a true relationship a fair chance, she'd told Landon she didn't welcome his suit and that she'd take it as a favor if he stopped calling on her. He hadn't taken her rejection well.

She supposed he had every reason to feel that way. His family was wealthy, and now that his father was deceased, he not only owned a great deal of land but was responsible for his mother and sister. He'd also fought in the war for a whole year. He'd been so brave that she'd heard he'd even been responsible for rescuing a group of unfortunate women from a burning building.

Most everyone said he fought with valor too.

In addition, he was handsome, blessed with golden-blond hair, bright-green eyes, and a strong jaw. He was everything most girls in Sweetwater—or Fort Worth, for that matter—would ever dream about having in a suitor or a husband.

Just not her.

Men like him had never appealed to her. Especially after he returned from the war, he was too confident, too full of himself, and too profuse with his compliments. He also had the unfortunate habit of sharing his viewpoints loudly and with force.

Only his parents' friendship with hers prevented her from severing their friendship.

"I don't believe I'm making a mistake, Landon," she said quietly.

"If you're wrong, you could be dead." Lowering his voice, he added in a dark tone, "That man . . . why, he could murder you in your sleep."

She shivered. "He's not a murderer." Aware that their heated conversation was beginning to garner attention, she said, "Now, I really must be going."

Landon paid her no mind. "Laurel, sweetheart, you are so naïve. Of course he's a murderer. I'm sure he killed during the war."

The fierce thread of disdain in his voice struck her as strange. Eyeing him curiously, she asked, "Didn't you? I thought all men did such things on the battlefield." Noticing he looked increasingly uncomfortable, she added, "I thought you were in several battles. Did you not fight the enemy then?"

"That was different."

"How so?"

"I'm not about to taint your ears with tales from the battlefield," he replied, his voice hard. "All you need to know is that I was a gentleman during the war. I fought with honor."

"But Mr. Baker didn't? How can that be?"

"Obviously this isn't a subject you are ready to discuss rationally. It isn't the right time or place either."

"You are right about that," she said before she could stop herself. Oh, it was certainly discomfiting how she'd started to become so used to speaking her mind. Discomfiting but exciting too. After spending most of her life holding her tongue and letting men tell her what to do, she was learning to be more like her mother had become during the war, to voice her opinion. Even make decisions on her own, like the one she'd made today. It made her feel stronger. She didn't want Landon's help. She didn't need to marry someone she didn't love to save her ranch.

"Now, I really must go, Landon. Judge Orbison is going to wonder where I am."

"I'll come check on you in a few days," he blurted. "That man needs to know you are not alone in the world."

"That is so kind of you," she said in a slightly exaggerated sweet tone before rushing away.

But just as she placed her hand on the judge's office doorknob, Geneva Forte pushed her way through the crowd.

"This is so exciting, Laurel. You buying a man is surely the most exciting thing that's happened in weeks, if not months."

Laurel couldn't help but agree even if Geneva, like Landon, had misunderstood what she'd done. However, unlike Landon's comments, Geneva's prattle was not mean-spirited. Just a tad vacuous. "It's taken me by surprise too."

"Are you nervous about having him on your property?"

She stopped to think about it. By all rights, Laurel knew she should be shaking in her shoes. But instead of feeling nervous, she felt completely at peace with her decision. She needed Mr. Baker's help, and for some reason she trusted him to give it. "No, I'm not nervous at all."

Looking eager, Geneva leaned closer. "Can I meet him one day soon? I promise I'll be everything proper."

"He's coming to work for me, Geneva. He needs to look after cattle and mend fences. You probably won't even see him."

Her blue eyes batted. "But can I?"

Laurel wasn't sure why, but everything in her body was rejecting Geneva's question. She didn't want the woman flirting with the sergeant or gazing at him too long, or even making him uncomfortable. Hadn't he already been through too much?

"I'm sorry, but I'd rather you not visit anytime soon."

"Sure?"

"Maybe you can in a few months." She smiled to ease the rejection. "Now, I need to go," Laurel said as she put her hand on the knob. "But, hey, Genie?"

"Yeah?"

"Help me with Landon, would you, please? Go smile at him or something. The last thing I want to tackle right now is him and his misplaced attempt to protect me."

As Laurel had hoped, her girlfriend looked excited about the task. With a bright smile, she turned toward Landon, who was still lurking nearby, watching Laurel with a cool expression.

When Landon's gaze skittered from Laurel to Geneva, her girlfriend started walking in his direction in a slow glide. It was her trademark move. Impossible for most women to accomplish anywhere but on a ballroom floor, Geneva had mastered effortlessly strolling across any surface by the time she was fourteen.

Finally opening the door, Laurel smiled to herself. Even Landon Marshall would be no match for that.

An hour later, standing beside the very tall Thomas Baker, Laurel wondered if she had overestimated her gumption.

He was a large man. Taller and more filled out than he'd looked when he was cooped up in a cage or lined up with other men against her fence. It seemed Mr. Baker also had an air about him that she couldn't quite put her finger on. It wasn't aggressive, but she sensed he would never be a passive kind of man either. Instead, he appeared to be tightly wound and watchful. Almost as if he had all kinds of thoughts and ideas floating just under the surface.

This new air about him might also have something to do with his appearance. He was no longer dirty, no longer wearing a bloodstained shirt and ill-fitting trousers.

Instead, he was outfitted in all new clothes, from his leather boots to his snug-fitting denims to his crisp white shirt and tan Stetson.

In short, he looked extremely dashing. So fine and handsome that every woman they passed was going to take a second and third look at him. So fine that Laurel was going to wonder how she'd ever felt sorry for him.

After they both signed the papers Judge Orbison prepared, they had walked silently through town, him carrying a small bag with, she supposed, all his earthly possessions. Eyes seemed to follow them from every window and doorway. She wondered if most everyone understood her reasons for hiring a convict or was simply shocked.

She imagined it was a little of both.

Now they were standing by her buggy and her horse, Velvet, and she wasn't sure what to do. Thomas was capable and powerful. Years ago, her father and brother had looked out for her. They'd taught her to expect all men to treat her with care. But the war had certainly changed things. She'd learned that not all men respected women. She'd also learned not to count on any help, not even from her stepbrother, Jerome. And she didn't want help from Landon.

But she was Thomas Baker's employer. And though he was

certainly dashing, he was no gentleman. Surely that meant she should drive the buggy?

She worried her bottom lip.

Was it even right for her to trust him? What if she gave him the reins, only to be thrown off the buggy so he could be on his way? He had broken the law, after all. She should never forget that.

After no doubt watching her internal debate for a few moments, Mr. Baker cleared his throat. "Miss Tracey?"

She popped up her chin. Looking into his eyes, she realized that was a mistake and shifted her gaze to stare just to the right of him instead. "Uh, yes?"

"I know we're standing on the street and everything, but it occurs to me this might be a good time to clear up a few things."

Forcing herself to look him directly in the eye, she said, "What would you like to clear up?"

Approval sure and solid slid into his expression before he appeared to collect himself. Clasping his hands behind his back, he took a deep breath and looked just to the right of her. "Well, first thing, what would you like me to call you? I heard the judge and sheriff call you Laurel. May I call you Miss Laurel? Or would you prefer Miss Tracey?"

His voice was low and soft. She knew he was speaking gently to her on purpose. "Miss . . ." She shook her head to clear it. Suddenly she didn't want even that barrier between them. "I mean, Laurel would be just fine."

His eyes settled on hers. "I don't think so, miss. Seeing as how I work for you, it wouldn't be right."

She realized he had a point, though she felt a bit disconcerted by the way he was leading the conversation. "Miss Laurel should do as well as anything. Now, should I call you Mr. Baker?"

To her shock, he chuckled. "Definitely not. I've never been

called that in my life and I don't aim to start now. In the army, I was a sergeant, Sergeant Baker. But since I'm not in the military any longer, I reckon either Baker or Thomas will do."

She had noticed something—a note of pride in his voice when he talked about the army. It wasn't the vague, prideful way Landon had talked about his year in the service.

No, Thomas Baker's military career had meant something to him. Meant a lot to him. For some reason, that made her feel good. Everyone needed to have some pride in their life. "I think, if you don't mind, I'll simply call you Sergeant."

Doubt clouded his eyes. "I don't know . . ."

"I do. You were a sergeant, right? I mean, that's not a lie?"

"No, miss. That is not a lie."

"Then Sergeant you will be, at least for now."

His lips twitched, as if he admired her spunk and was caught off guard by it all at the same time. "Yes, miss."

"Are we settled now, Sergeant?"

"Not exactly." Pulling back his shoulders even more, he continued. "I know you don't have any reason to trust a word I say, but I swear to you I will never harm you. Never. I'll even swear it on a stack of Bibles if you want."

She was shocked by his offer, but pleased. "There is no need for that. I believe you."

"You do?"

"I wouldn't have hired you today if I didn't trust you."

Slowly a smile—a rather cocky smile—appeared on his lips. "I'm glad we got that cleared up. Therefore, Miss Laurel, would you be so kind as to allow me to help you into your buggy? Then I will drive you home."

"I trust you actually do know how to handle a carriage?"

"Of course I do."

"Take care with Velvet too. She's a little skittish and requires a tender touch."

"You got me from prison, but I wasn't born there, Miss Laurel," he drawled. "I'll take care with your horse."

She felt herself flush. Realizing it was time to rectify the conversation, she nodded. "Thank you, Sergeant. Having you drive would be helpful."

"Yes, miss." Looking like he was attempting to conceal a smile, he held out a hand. "Miss Laurel?"

Gingerly, she placed her gloved hand in his hand, then started when he carefully placed his other hand on her waist to steady her ascent. But just as quickly, his hand pulled away. She decided to remain facing forward as he got in beside her, took hold of the reins, and flicked them lightly.

Velvet started forward.

After watching him for a bit and realizing he had spoken the truth, that he could control a horse and buggy easily, she exhaled.

He grinned. "Were you worried about my skills?"

"A little," she allowed.

"Only a little?"

"Maybe a bit more than that. I'm glad you didn't lie to me. It's easier to know the truth about things."

"I would have to agree with you about that. The truth always helps, I think." After a minute or so, he added, "I'm grateful you came out today. If it weren't for you, I'd be back behind bars or waiting for one of the men in the crowd to hire me on."

She shivered. "Most of the men who were gathering around you don't have the best of reputations."

One of his brows lifted. "Pointing out the obvious, I don't either."

Laurel knew she should agree, but something about this

man seemed different. She didn't think her intuition was that far off. "You seemed polite enough when you were on the prison workforce."

"Didn't have much choice."

"You might not have had a choice, but I would venture to say you didn't need much incentive to be respectful to me."

"No, miss, I did not," he said with a low drawl. "But I'd be lying now if I didn't point out that there wasn't a man there who didn't appreciate your offer of water."

"It was nothing."

"It was more than that. Prison—and war, for that matter—doesn't give a man much opportunity to feel such kindness. It was a reminder that we are still men and worthy of consideration."

His talk embarrassed her, especially since she had a terrible suspicion that her offer of water had somehow resulted in the lashes he received across his back.

"Sergeant?"

"Yes?"

She opened her mouth to ask about that whipping but chickened out. Instead, she asked a more obvious question. "How did you get your new clothes and boots? Is that customary?"

For the first time since they'd started their conversation, Thomas looked ill at ease. "No. They were a gift."

"From Judge Orbison?"

"Not exactly."

Though it wasn't technically her business, she prodded. "Then from whom?"

Still not looking her way, he said, "As I told you, I served in the Confederacy. I served under a captain and a major I thought the world of. I respected them. I also became friends with them and several others. We're scattered around the state now, but somehow the captain heard I was about to be eligible for release. He arranged for these items to be available. Since I didn't want to be around you looking like I did, I accepted his gift."

She had never heard of such a thing. "Those must be quite some friends."

The lines around his eyes relaxed. "They are."

"Why didn't one of them simply come get you? They could have lied and said you would work for them."

"First of all, I still don't know how the captain knew where I was. I didn't want any of them to know I was in jail. I got in trouble because I was gambling in a high-stakes poker game I couldn't afford. I'm not proud of that." He shrugged. "Then, too, there's the law. They couldn't have gotten me out no matter how hard they tried. And last, I would never allow any of them to pay for my release."

She thought about that. Thought about how hard it must have been for him to wait and have faith that somehow, some way, he would be freed. Visions of him sitting in a dark cell, hurting and alone, struck her hard.

"Sergeant, uh, how is your back?"

"I'll be fine."

"That scar on your neck—"

"That happened a good long time ago. It doesn't hurt."

She noticed he didn't say his back didn't hurt. "When we get to the ranch, I'll tend to your back. I made some ointment that works wonders for burns and cuts. I'll put some of that on it."

He stiffened. "That ain't necessary."

Laurel blinked at his harsh tone. "You might not know this, but we had our fair share of soldiers come through during the war. Some were grievously injured, and I tended quite a few. I promise there is little I have not seen."

"No offense, but I'm not the kind of man who would want his lady boss to be fussing over a couple of bumps and bruises on his bare skin."

She knew the wounds on his back were far worse than mere bumps or bruises. But he was sitting so stoically, she also knew it would be a mistake to push. "If your pain gets worse, will you let me know?"

"I'll let you know," he said shortly, but his voice was clipped. "You didn't bring me on to tend over me, miss. I'm going to work for you."

She nodded. He had a point. She needed to remember that and put the ranch first. Keeping it going was what counted. That was what she needed to care about. Not her loneliness. Not the way this man looked like he needed a friend as much as she did. All that mattered was the land.

Nothing else.

When they arrived at the ranch, Jerome and Bess darted out the door as though they'd been watching for her with bated breath.

Bess was dressed in a pale-pink dress and her hair was arranged in ringlets. She looked like she was about to go to a dance. Jerome was just as dressed up. Why they were outfitted the way they were, Laurel couldn't imagine.

"Laurel, it took you long enough," Jerome called out. "Bess and I have been extremely ill at ease and inconvenienced. In fact—"

Whatever he was about to add vanished as he suddenly realized she wasn't alone.

Bess placed a hand to her lips and coughed delicately. Laurel wasn't sure if she was doing that because she was stunned or intrigued.

Thomas stared at them curiously before pulling on Velvet's

reins and setting the brake in the buggy. Just as Laurel was about to dismount, he placed a hand on her arm. "Wait for me," he said.

She was surprised by his instruction—and rather amused by the way Bess's eyes had widened. She waited.

After Thomas walked around to her side, he held out a hand. Just as she was about to place her hand in his, he reached for her waist and swung her down from the seat.

Unable to help herself, she set her hands on his shoulders and felt a small cluster of butterflies fluttering in her stomach.

"Thank you," she whispered.

"It was my pleasure." His gaze was suspiciously warm.

Embarrassed for imagining something that wasn't there, she turned to Bess and Jerome, who were gaping at Mr. Baker and her as though they were part of a carnival show.

Seeking to quiet her nerves, Laurel gestured to their outfits. "You two look fetching. Where are you off to?"

Bess glared at the man beside Laurel. "We wanted to go into town. Now we're late."

"For what? I'm not aware of any parties going on today."

Jerome glared as well. "I had no idea you were going to be so long."

"It couldn't be helped." They were intently staring at her new employee. Seeing that they were hardly listening, and assuming they were only going to town to spend the bit of money she could spare for them each week, she said, "Bess and Jerome, this is Sergeant Thomas Baker. I just hired him on to work here. Sergeant, these are my stepsiblings, Bess and Jerome Vance."

Jerome stepped in front of his sister as if he was guarding her. "Where did he come from?"

Laurel was curious as to why he asked her. After all, she'd told Bess what she was going to do. Had she kept that information to herself? "Well, Sheriff Jackson sometimes allows men who have served time to be hired on."

Her stepbrother blinked. "Wait a minute. You were here yesterday, weren't you? On the prison detail."

Before Laurel could reply, Mr. Baker stepped forward, almost mirroring Jerome's stance. "I was. Miss Laurel has just hired me for one year."

Ignoring him, Jerome turned to Laurel. "And they told you he would be safe? I'm sure they would say anything to get him off their hands." He scanned her body as if she were a fallen woman. "Furthermore, I am shocked it seems you will do just about anything to ensure that you'll fall into this man's arms."

The sergeant stiffened. Thinking he was about to say something rash, Laurel stepped a little closer to his side. "I'm sure we'll all get along just fine," she declared. "We simply need to give it time."

Feeling panicked at their continuing stares, Laurel continued, "Listen, we need Sergeant Baker's help. He's strong, and smart too. He's not only going to help with the work, but he's going to help watch the squatters. Maybe he'll even be able to help us save the ranch."

"Save the ranch? We need to be done with it." Jerome frowned. "Laurel, you are overstepping yourself."

"You know I'm not."

"I just don't know what to think about this," Bess said. Her eyes looking like a wounded doe's, she lowered her voice in a dramatic way. "We'll be at his mercy."

Jerome nodded. "This is true. Why, this . . . this prisoner could attack Bess in her sleep."

She nodded. "I could be violated."

Laurel flushed in embarrassment. What must Mr. Baker think?

"I will not be attacking anyone, miss," Thomas murmured.

"You might," Bess said. "I've heard men can't always help themselves."

"I will."

"Let's believe him," Laurel said quickly. "It's the Christian thing to do."

"We cannot believe a thing he says. He's going to say whatever he needs to so he can stay here," Jerome sputtered. "While it may be true that you have nothing to worry about, Bess is another story. Everyone in the area knows how attractive Bess is."

Laurel felt like sinking into the dry Texas dirt right then and there.

But after glancing her way, Mr. Baker asked, "Why does she have nothing to worry about?"

"Because of her looks," Bess blurted. "She's . . . well, she's fat."

Then, to Laurel's dismay, the sergeant grinned. His smile lit up his face, and suddenly he didn't look so innocent. "Miss Laurel is a great many things, but fat ain't one of them. Truth is, I've yet to see a prettier female."

"Sergeant," she hissed under her breath. "Your words are not helping."

"Beg your pardon, miss. Though many a time I've said too much at all the wrong times, I don't believe this is one of them. I'm speaking the truth."

Bess gasped. Jerome glared.

And Laurel? Why, she had no idea what to say.

Her new worker seemed to have a true gift for stealing her breath and taking her by surprise.

6

AS THE SUN MARCHED HIGHER IN THE SUMMER SKY, TAYLOR
Orr shifted positions from his spot under the rock overhang.

Dang, but it was hot. He didn't know how these Texans could
take this summertime heat. He felt as if the sun were blazing a trail
across his face and hands. He surely had the sunburn to prove it.

Now, as he bided his time until dark, he fingered his view-
finder. It gave him a good sense of what was happening on the
Tracey property.

What he'd just witnessed was unusual and unwelcome.

Soon after he watched Laurel hire on that prisoner, he'd high-
tailed it back to his hideout. This rock overhang was a mere half
mile from an abandoned barn where he kept his horse.

Now that he'd seen the man escort her onto the property,
Taylor was coming to terms with the fact that the situation here
had changed. No longer was Laurel Tracey at his mercy or living
essentially alone on her property. She'd gone and hired herself a
man who looked like he was neither averse to fighting nor averse
to shooting anyone in his way.

Taylor would bet good money that the man had served
well during the war, too, and hadn't forgotten much in the way
of being brave and forthright. From the moment he had helped

Laurel alight from her buggy, he'd been looking around the area as though he was used to ferreting out any number of threats.

And when he wasn't doing that, he was gazing at Laurel. Even through his telescope Taylor could see the man had an interest in her.

If the look he'd seen the man give Laurel was any indication, he wasn't planning to just work his year and then leave the area.

No, Taylor had been in love once, and he remembered feeling that same sense of ownership that had shone in the convict's eyes. There was something between him and Laurel Tracey. This man wasn't going to give up her or her property without a fight.

And that, unfortunately, was a stinkin' shame. He was sick of being on this job. He'd been watching and waiting for weeks now. Waiting for his boss to say it was time to make a move. He was sick of sweating, and really sick of the fire ants that burned when they bit and the spiders that taunted him when they came out at night.

He needed to get back to Chicago. Chicago was cooler and more crowded. He knew how things worked there and didn't have to skulk around like a dang coyote.

The sooner he got this job done, the sooner he could go back and claim the life he'd lost because of his debts. He could go back to courting Dara. If she'd still have him after everything he'd put her through.

Well, she'd take him back if she never found out what he was doing here in the sticks outside of Fort Worth.

Thinking of the way she would no doubt look at him if she knew, Taylor felt a rush of bile scorch the back of his throat. What he was doing was a sin. He'd never been an especially faithful man, but he didn't think a man had to be God-fearing to be ashamed of the things he had done.

Looking at the kerosene he'd given the calf, Taylor shuddered. After the war, he'd never imagined he'd have a weak stomach for much. Killing good and healthy livestock didn't sit well with him.

It made him feel sick inside.

Poisoning cattle was nothing to be proud of. But it had been the only method he could think of that would do the trick. It was his job to do everything he possibly could to encourage Laurel Tracey to sell her land. The man who paid him to do anything and everything to get her to move hadn't been joking. Taylor knew, because he'd seen firsthand how the man dealt with anyone who got in his way.

If Taylor failed, no apology would be necessary. Instead, he'd pay for his mistakes with either a bullet in his head or a noose around his neck.

In his more desperate moments, he'd actually debated which way would be a better, less painful death.

But what was done was done.

As the first cool breeze of the day passed over him, Taylor slapped his hand on his thigh. His boss somehow knew Laurel Tracey planned to raise up her herd, make her ranch profitable. He had his own reasons for fighting that. But Taylor had no good reason to be even thinking about this woman or the people in her life in such a personal way. That would only create sleepless nights, and he already had those in spades. Besides, his boss didn't pay good money for bleeding hearts.

Getting to his feet, Taylor stepped out into the broad sunlight again.

Standing up straight and tall, he raised his face to the burning rays. As he felt them heat his skin, he figured remembering his boss's violent ways was all the encouragement he needed to continue to do what he had to do.

After he hid the kerosene container, he was going to get his horse and go back into town. He would continue to play his role—the not-too-smart greenhorn carpetbagger traveling through Sweetwater—for a couple more days. He'd play poker poorly and not hold his liquor well.

He'd also report to his boss and share what he'd done. And what he was going to do next.

God willing, then he'd hear Miss Tracey was getting desperate. He'd get paid and could go back to Chicago. He didn't need to be in Sweetwater and watch her sell her land to the man who was going to use her misfortune for his gain.

No, he would simply be back in Chicago and Dara's good graces. He could use his ill-gotten money toward paying off the ruthless men he'd borrowed from. And when those debts were resolved, he could return to Dara and she'd be proud of him.

Then he would do his best to be the man she believed him to be. He just hoped he remembered how to be that man. It had been a long time since he'd had much of an occasion to try to make himself into someone worthy.

Scurrying back to the horse, he pretended to think such a thing was even possible.

Pretended to believe a man really could sell his soul to the devil in exchange for mending a few broken dreams.

Pretended to imagine that the man who'd hired him was going to make good on his promises and pay him.

Pretended that he even had a future.

For a moment, a vision flashed in his head. He was sitting on a sofa, his feet propped up on a table, with a dog at his feet. Dara was sitting beside him, chattering about whatever women chattered on about. And his eyes were at half-mast as he pretended to listen.

It was a good dream. Real nice. He'd gotten really good at pretending too. Otherwise, the reality of his life was too harsh to contemplate.

Because no man lived long doing the things he'd done.

It simply wasn't possible.

7

STANDING THERE IN THE HOT SUN NEXT TO A HORSE AND buggy, facing Laurel Tracey's obnoxious stepsiblings, Thomas Baker realized he was a fool.

He was a headstrong idiot who still hadn't learned to keep his mouth shut. Not even when he should be doing nothing but giving thanks that he was standing in the hot sun instead of wasting away in a dark prison cell. One would think his time spent at Johnson's Island would have taught him that at the very least.

Truly, if his captain were standing in the vicinity, he would backhand him upside the head.

It would be no less than he deserved too. Men didn't go around saying such things to gently bred women. They most certainly did not speak of the female form and attributes in mixed company. He hadn't even needed the officers at the camp to teach him that lesson.

Of course, if he was being completely truthful, he didn't deserve all the blame. The problem was partly Miss Laurel's doing. The Lord had been generous with his gifts to her. Actually, she had a whole plethora of attributes that most of the male population would find difficult to ignore.

She was well shaped and soft looking. Beautiful, with golden hair and light-brown eyes that seemed to reveal every emotion.

She was also very sweet. And good. She was . . . Laurel.

All of it was pretty much impossible for a man like him not to notice.

And he would have been ashamed to call himself a man if he hadn't done anything to come to her defense. Why, the moment Thomas saw her flush in embarrassment, he knew he had to put her stepbrother in his place. Well, actually, he'd been tempted to slam Jerome against the door and keep his hand on the man's throat until he promised he would apologize to her.

So he'd been right to help her out. It was just that, well . . . he probably should not have done it quite so heatedly. He'd just made an awkward situation even worse.

As the silence pulled taut between the four of them, he heard Laurel's faint breathing. Glancing at her, he noticed her cheeks were rosy pink. He'd caused that. He'd embarrassed her something awful.

Thomas was about to apologize, to say whatever he could to convince his new boss he was not completely uncivilized when Jerome lifted his chin. "That little speech confirms my worries, Laurel. Obviously this man is not fit for decent company."

"I'm fit for anyone's company," Thomas bit out. Except, perhaps, the company of a good woman like Laurel.

Jerome's eyes flared again. "Laurel, if . . . if this *prisoner* stays, I'll have no choice but to take Bess out of harm's way. She's far too delicate to be near a man of his reputation."

Laurel gasped. "Surely you are overreacting."

"Not in the slightest." Folding his arms across his chest, Jerome continued, "If he stays, we're going."

Thomas forced himself to prepare to be shuttled back into that buggy. It was no less than he deserved. He'd been too bold and brash, and now he was going to be forced to deal with the consequences. No doubt Laurel was seconds away from sending him back to his corner cell in the town jail. Either she'd send her stepsiblings for Sheriff Jackson or she'd take him back there herself.

And he knew he would do whatever she wanted without a fight.

He deserved it. He'd soon have untold hours to contemplate the benefits of holding his tongue.

As the tension in the air heated like the noonday sun, Laurel sighed. "Sergeant Baker can't leave. I made my promise."

"Promises don't count when they're given to someone like him," Bess said. "He doesn't matter."

Thomas stiffened but kept his mouth shut. Bess wasn't completely wrong.

"Of course he matters," Laurel said, her voice full of righteousness. "He is a prisoner no more. He's my employee now. What's done is done."

"You are going to refuse me?" Jerome said.

"There is nothing to refuse. We need the help and Sergeant Baker is a good worker. I already signed a paper that said I'd pay him for the next year."

Bess sputtered, "You're going to spend our money on his wages?"

"Well, of course. He's not a slave."

As her relatives looked at her as though she'd slapped them hard in the face, a transformation came over his boss.

Stepping forward, she reached out to both of them. "Jerome, Bess," she began softly, "I know my bringing Sergeant Baker here isn't what you expected. But please don't do anything so hasty. I feel certain that once you get used to the idea, you'll be glad of the help. We're family, and we've already lost so much. I don't want to lose you too."

"Your parents never should have left you this ranch, and our father should have known better than to go along with it," Bess said. "You are in over your head. You need to sell it. That's plain to see."

"I agree. I am in over my head. Nothing in my life prepared me for this responsibility. But I'll get through it." She looked Thomas's way, and her voice turned hard. "I am not going to change my mind. And I'm not going to leave. And since this is technically my land, I still have that option. If you truly don't think you can abide by my choices, then I wish you both the best with your future travels."

After uttering a small cry, Bess turned around with a sniff and hurried inside. Jerome, on the other hand, continued to glare at his stepsister with something that looked dangerously close to malevolence. "Where am I supposed to live now?"

"I don't believe that's any concern of mine. You've made your choice."

Jerome's eyes narrowed. "Your weak-willed mother may have convinced my father to keep this place, but he did not intend for me to live here."

"Maybe not, but where he did intend for you and Bess to live is gone, and we need to help each other now. We need to try to find a way to live together as a family. You also need to start helping me more."

"I am not going to help you save a ranch that you shouldn't have in the first place."

"Again, it seems you've made your choice then, Jerome. I wish you well."

"You're going to regret this, Laurel. I'm going to make sure of it."

Just as Jerome reached out to grab her shoulder, Thomas

stepped in front of him. "Don't," he warned. "Don't talk to her that way, and don't ever attempt to touch her again."

"Or what?" Jerome scoffed.

"Or you'll regret it."

"How so? You being here is already ruining her reputation."

"It very well might be," Thomas returned. "But she will also be safe."

Looking as if Laurel's well-being only bored him, Jerome stepped to one side, visibly ignoring Thomas, and said, "Since you are casting us out, I'm going to need some money."

While Laurel closed her eyes in an obvious effort to gain patience, Thomas gaped at him.

Didn't that beat all? Her kin were living off of her. Thomas barely refrained from grunting in disdain. He wished he could send her inside and tell this fool what he could do with his proffered hand.

But of course, that wasn't his place. Instead, he stood silently next to her, hoping his very presence would remind her she wasn't alone. Not anymore.

She opened her eyes and, looking as dumbfounded as he assumed he did, stared at Jerome with those big brown eyes. Thomas would swear that a hundred retorts lay on her tongue, every one of them sharper than the next.

After almost a full minute, she spoke quietly. "I don't have any money to give you."

Jerome glared Thomas's way. "Because you spent it all on releasing him from a jail cell."

"No. It's because of everything." Turning to Thomas, she said, "Would you please go take care of Velvet and the buggy? You'll find everything you need in the barn."

This woman had more gumption than most soldiers he'd

witnessed on the field. Tipping his hat gallantly, he drawled, "Yes, miss."

Jerome cleared his throat. "No! Wait. I'm going to need the horse and buggy."

Thomas turned around, giving Jerome enough of a glare to make sure the man didn't consider reaching for her.

But Laurel was holding her own. "Of course you can't take Velvet or the buggy." Her voice full of hurt, she said, "Do you really think I would give them to you?"

"How am I supposed to leave?"

Thomas had had enough of the man's whining and verbal manipulations. "It's only eight miles to town. God gave you two feet. You'll do all right, I reckon."

"You'd cast out Bess and force her to walk?"

Laurel visibly steeled her spine. Then, after another fortifying breath, she said, "If that is the way you see it, then yes. I am casting you out and forcing you to walk to town."

Jerome narrowed his eyes.

Seeing the man's anger looming, Thomas stepped forward. He was prepared to do whatever it took to get the pair out of Laurel's hair, even if it meant using a little bit of force. Actually, he realized he wouldn't mind using his fists for a good reason. He'd even look forward to it.

Though Jerome stiffened, he pointedly ignored Thomas. Instead, he looked directly at Laurel and sent her a look that could only be described as deadly. "You have underestimated me, sister. I promise you will rue this moment."

Though her face remained carefully blank, Laurel's hands trembled before she fisted them.

And though he didn't know beans about being a gentleman, he knew a whole lot about defending someone who was in need.

He couldn't help himself. Stepping forward, he positioned his body so he stood slightly in front of her. "Miss Laurel, why don't you go on inside and rest a spell?" he said in a quiet tone. "I'll take care of your horse in a moment. But first, I think Jerome here and I need to have a talk."

He knew he had just overstepped his bounds by about a mile.

She stared at him, confusion lighting her eyes, before nodding. "All right, Sergeant."

The moment the door was closed, Jerome folded his arms across his chest. "I don't know who you think you are or what you're hoping to get away with, but I'm here to say you had better think again the next time you even consider interfering in my business."

"Is that right?" Thomas found he was almost enjoying this popinjay's dramatics.

"Absolutely. I don't know what kind of man you are, but I'm already counting the days until my sister figures out you are nothing more than a common criminal. Then she'll realize she's made a terrible mistake. There is no way she's going to kick me out and expect nothing to happen."

His temper unleashed, Thomas stepped closer and looked down. "I'll tell you who I am. I'm the man who grew up on the streets and learned to gain respect by the power of my fists. I've forced more people to bend to my will than you can ever imagine."

Jerome inhaled.

"I'm the man who fought on more battlefields than you've even heard of." Stepping even closer, Thomas glared. "I'm the man who held true heroes in my arms while they were dying, and made tougher decisions in a span of fifteen minutes than you've likely ever made in your lifetime."

Jerome's eyes widened. "Hey, now—"

"I'm the man who spent a winter in the middle of a northern lake in prison barracks and has just spent nine months languishing in a jail cell, the last two in the heat of a Texas summer." Thomas lowered his voice but took care to punctuate each syllable so there would be no mistaking what he was saying. "I've hurt and I've maimed. I've killed. I've done just about anything one can imagine to survive, and I'm willing to do it all again for Laurel Tracey."

"Because you are a reprobate."

"No, sir. Not that. It's because I am what I've always been. I'm a man without much to lose."

Jerome's face was pale and his hands were in useless fists at his sides. "I could send you back to jail."

"The only way you could do that is by forcibly taking me there yourself. Is that what you'd like to do? If so, I look forward to you doing your best."

Jerome's eyes nearly bugged out.

At last, feeling as though he was being listened to, Thomas continued. "However, it seems the Lord has decided it's time for a change. Somehow, some way, I did something to deserve getting hired on here. And I ain't leaving. So if I were you, I'd watch real close to any promises or threats you want to dish out to Miss Tracey. Because I'm not going to back down or give up. I'm going to fight you any way I can."

"You're nothing."

Thomas almost laughed. "You're absolutely right. I'm nothing. However, this man with nothing also has a place to sleep tonight, which is more than I believe you have at the moment. I suggest you get on your way and be quick about it. My determination to be here will far outlast any efforts on your part. I promise you that."

He turned then and led the horse and buggy to the barn, unhitched Velvet, and started rubbing her down.

She nudged him with her soft nose, flirting.

He rubbed her again, finding himself relaxing little by little. When she nudged him again, he murmured, "Look at you, pretty girl."

Velvet nodded her head as if she were in complete agreement, pawed the ground with a hoof, then nudged him once more, whickering softly.

Just like that, the memories came back. Of helping his father at the livery. Grooming horses while his dad fitted them with shoes.

It had been years since he'd allowed those sweet memories to take center stage in his head. Years since he'd let himself remember how good his life had been before the raids. Before everyone was gone.

He was so grateful that he leaned into the horse's chest and rested his forehead there. Just like he'd done when he was a boy. Velvet seemed to sense his need to hold her. She stilled and allowed him his moment. Then blew out a breath on his cheek.

As she'd no doubt hoped, he jerked back and wiped his face.

She whinnied, and before he knew it, he was smiling at the fool animal. Loving her affection. Loving the feel of being around a good horse again. It reminded him of serving under Major Ethan Kelly and Captain Monroe. Those men, as strong and stalwart as they were, had also been cavalry officers at heart.

Though he'd worked in a livery for a few years before enlisting, they were the ones who'd taught him to value a good mount, to trust a horse's good sense. The captain himself had taught him to truly care for his horse. His employer at the livery had done only what he could to get by with his customers, and Thomas had also forgotten much of his father's lessons as a way to survive. It had simply hurt too much to remember another life.

But under Captain Monroe's tutelage, Thomas had learned again. He'd first been struck by how individual each horse's personality seemed to be. And how much he'd come to enjoy the calming, solitary tasks of brushing and currying, the rubdowns and oiling of hooves. Other men took shortcuts. And if time was tight, Thomas would too.

But if possible, he would take as much time as he could. Because he'd had too little opportunity to coddle or fuss over anything or anyone. And horses . . . well, horses didn't ask why.

Just as he finished all the chores he could see needed to be done in the barn, the house's front door opened and shut and Laurel's two stepsiblings walked out. Each held a small bag of clothing. Their heads were lifted high and their steps were sure and brisk. Each looked to be wearing shoes far better suited to a cotillion than an eight-mile walk along dusty, rocky soil.

Thomas figured they'd be a sorry, sweaty mess before they'd gone two miles. He was glad Laurel hadn't asked him to take them into town. He'd rather see their backsides from here.

After washing off the worst of his sweat and grime, he turned toward the house.

Now that he could, he took a long look at it. It truly was a thing of beauty, with imposing white columns and a broad, long porch running the entire front. It was a little worn looking, a little tired. But though it had seen better days, it struck him as something special, though he couldn't say why. Hundreds of houses just like it dotted the state. Maybe the reason it looked so sweet was because he now knew he could count it as his home of sorts for the next year.

Counting his blessings again, he sat down on the front steps and waited for his new boss to appear. He didn't mind waiting. In fact, he kind of hoped she'd take her time.

After all, he had claim to the prettiest boss in the whole of the great state of Texas. If his buddies from Johnson's Island could see him now, they'd grin and remark that, against all that was logical, he had beaten the odds again.

Somehow, some way, Thomas Baker had landed back on his feet.

8

AS SHE STOOD AT A WINDOW AND WATCHED BESS AND Jerome walk slowly down the road toward town, each holding a small carpetbag that likely held less than a third of their belongings, Laurel attempted to maintain her composure.

Sitting down, she willed herself not to cry. They'd deserved what had happened to them. They really had. It occurred to her that she could have ordered Sergeant Baker to take them into town, but she was sure he and Jerome only would have provoked each other further.

Jerome and Bess had been twin albatrosses around her neck. They'd moved in just when she was at her weakest, and instead of offering help or support, they took advantage of her home, her savings, and what little bit of charity she had left to give. The whole time she'd kept waiting for them to help. Waiting for them to acknowledge how much she'd done for them.

But instead of doing any of that, they'd taken even more from her. They were part of the reason she'd grown so tired. They were part of the reason she'd been forced to hire a man to save the ranch.

Now, even when they knew their departure meant she'd be living alone on the ranch with a prisoner, they still left. Though she should have realized that nothing they did would likely surprise her anymore, their leaving this way had shocked her.

Even though she had so much to be upset about concerning their behavior, she had wanted to give them the benefit of the doubt. A small part of her had been sure Jerome was merely testing her. She'd naïvely hoped some part of him would feel responsible for her welfare.

But instead, he'd waged a war. Bating and badgering her. Tempting her with callous phrases, doing anything he could to get her to bend to his will.

She was done doing that.

If she had given in, he would take advantage and claim he was the head of the household. No doubt he would have then run the rest of the ranch into the ground—or worse, managed to somehow sell it right out from under her. Then she would be looking for a place to sleep at night.

But still . . . it was hard.

Of course, she wouldn't have gone back on her word no matter what happened. Not only had both Sheriff Jackson and Judge Orbison been relieved that a man they trusted was going to be free at last, but Laurel never could have done such a thing to Sergeant Baker. For some reason she felt warm inside just thinking about him.

Indeed, he was Sergeant Thomas Baker. *Thomas* in her private thoughts.

Thomas!

Realizing that she hadn't heard him come into the house, she felt her mouth go dry. Where was he?

Panic set in as she imagined the possibilities. She really hoped he hadn't turned her into a liar and taken off while she'd been sitting inside stewing and trying not to cry.

Getting to her feet, she wiped away the few tears she'd shed and hurried through the foyer to the front door. Perhaps he was sitting in the barn with Velvet, wondering what had happened to her. And he was also probably wondering about his living quarters and a meal. She rushed out the door.

Then, just as abruptly, she drew to a stop.

Thomas was standing on the covered porch facing her, leaning against one of the white columns her mother had begged her father to install years before war had infiltrated their lives.

He was also staring directly at her.

When she parted her lips, trying desperately to think of a reason she had practically flown out the door, something new appeared in those blue eyes of his. Pushing off from the column, he bowed slightly. "Miss."

That courtly gesture—so unexpected—made her flush. "I'm so sorry you've been waiting on me out here. Please forgive me."

He shook his head. "First off, I think we need to remember that you are in charge, Miss Laurel. You don't see to my needs. I see to yours. That means I can and will stand here all day long if that is what you need me to do."

His words might have been true, but it was his lazy drawl and slightly amused look that caught her insides and made her feel as if her world had just shifted to one side.

"I hope I will never treat you so harshly."

"Making me wait for you could never be called a harsh punishment."

There she went again. In spite of her best intentions, she found herself responding to something he said in a way that was completely inappropriate. Goodness! She needed to get back on a firmer, more professional foundation. She needed to get a grip on her emotions as well. Immediately!

"Did you put up Velvet all right?" she asked, hoping she sounded as if she was all business.

"I did. I watered her and gave her a good rubdown."

"You had time to do all that?"

"It wasn't all that much. Just so you know, I also fed her fresh hay and oats and mucked out her stall. And oiled the leathers. I did the same with the other horse too." He raised an eyebrow. "The pretty palomino."

"He's called Yellow."

"Yellow?" His lips twitched.

"I didn't name the gelding. He came with that name, such that it is."

"He is a yellow color. I suppose it makes sense."

"Actually, it kind of doesn't."

When he looked at her curiously, she filled him in. "The story goes that he was a sorry horse in battle. He shied away from the first gunshot."

"I can't say I blame him. The battlefield certainly ain't a pleasant place to be."

"I suppose not."

"For what it's worth, I'm thinking Yellow has the makings of a right fine horse."

"I thought so too. He's real gentle and doesn't seem to mind working long hours. We've been getting along just fine. No doubt he's had some eventful days, given the fact that I didn't know what I was doing when I first started herding cattle with him. But he's been patient with my struggles."

Instead of smiling at her little joke, he turned serious. "If he was being brave, you were too."

She liked the way that sounded. "Maybe so." Holding out her

hands, she said, "I've had my share of aches and pains and blisters. Some days I think it would have been easier to give up."

"But you didn't."

"Not yet," she joked, but it sounded rather pitiful, even to her ears.

But what else could she say? Ever since her father and brother left to fight in the war, and especially after her mother remarried and left to live with her new husband on the property Jerome and Bess later inherited, she'd been bearing the weight of running the ranch. When Jerome and Bess had shown up, their presence had only added more work for her.

She cleared her throat. "You know, I can't remember the last time anyone oiled the tack."

"It was nothing. A man in the cavalry learns real quick that his horse and tack make the difference between life and death."

The easy statement reminded her yet again of all he'd been through. Of what they'd both been through.

As if sensing her unease, he smiled softly. "What would you like me to do now?"

She didn't want to do this. Though she'd freed him from captivity to work, it was now going to be just the two of them on the ranch.

She was going to need to be his boss. A person he respected.

But she didn't want to start their relationship with her constantly giving him a list of chores.

Gesturing to the porch steps, she said, "Maybe we could sit down for a spell and visit?"

"Visit?" He looked a little confused, almost as if he wasn't sure of the term.

"Yes. I mean, if you don't mind. I could bring us some cold cider."

He looked completely taken aback, and she supposed she didn't blame him. "That . . . well, that would be real kind of you."

Feeling relieved, she opened the door again. "I'll be right back."

Laurel walked through the covered opening to the small kitchen, then pulled out two large, speckled stoneware mugs and poured cold cider from the cellar into them.

When she returned, Thomas jumped to his feet. Before she could figure out what to do, he took both mugs from her, set them on the floor of the wooden porch, then held out his hand to help her sit down on the top step. Just like they were in a parlor.

When she felt his touch, she trembled.

He felt it and froze. "Beg pardon, I didn't mean to act so familiar. Please don't be frightened. I would never hurt you."

"No, it wasn't that you scared me. It's just that it's been awhile since I was accustomed to such care." To her chagrin, she blushed again. Blast! She didn't know how to be coy and entertaining. She didn't even remember how to act friendly or relaxed. Obviously she had been keeping company with herself for far too long, though she'd been relieved to convince Landon to stay away.

After handing her one of the mugs, he sat down by her side and took a healthy sip. Pure pleasure lit his expression. "This tastes real good, Miss Laurel. By far the best drink I've partaken of in months. Thank you."

She took a small sip too. "You're welcome. I think it's just the right combination of tart and sweet. I bought it from a woman who was passing through town. She was . . . well, she was desperate for some income. Every time I take a sip, I think it's so much better than I anticipated. The quality of her offering was a welcome surprise."

"The best things are like that, I reckon."

"I've always thought so too." She took another sip of the cold drink, enjoying the way the liquid felt sliding down her throat. "Sergeant, there's a storage room at the back of the barn. There's a window in it, and it hasn't been used for much since the war. I think it might work out as a room for you."

"I'm sure it will suit me just fine."

Though he seemed perfectly at ease with her suggestion, she still felt bad. No matter how shady it was in the barn, it was still dusty and hot, and she had two empty bedrooms in the house now.

But how could she share a house with a man?

"There's no bedding in it yet. I was going to get Jerome to help me move a cot or one of the mattresses out there. But of course he's gone now. I'll help you with it."

"Don't worry about that none. I can sleep on anything you've got tonight, then I'll find a way to get a cot out there."

Looking doubtfully at his back, she said, "I can't imagine your back will thank you."

"Don't you worry about that. I promise it's been through worse."

That reminder made her feel even guiltier. Gathering her courage, she said, "Maybe it would be better for your back if you slept in one of the spare bedrooms upstairs? You would be cooler, and we wouldn't have to go to the trouble of moving a cot to the barn."

He stilled. "You want me to sleep in the house?"

"Yes. I mean, you could have Jerome's bedroom until you heal. It wouldn't be any trouble."

"I'm afraid it would, miss. It would mean a whole lot of trouble for the both of us."

Slumping her shoulders, she said, "I suppose you're right."

"I know I am. Don't spare me another thought. Like I said, I'll be fine out in the barn."

"I'll fetch you some blankets. And a pillow."

His gaze warmed. "That would be real good. Thank you, Miss Laurel."

Her invitation, along with his refusal of it, seemed to change the feeling of camaraderie between them. They sat in silence for a while, neither doing much but looking out at her land.

Laurel was mentally exhausted, thinking about how relieved she was to have hired Thomas, all while worrying about Jerome and Bess . . . and wondering if she was being hopelessly naïve to put so much trust in a man she knew next to nothing about.

After a good half hour had passed, she stood. "I'll, uh, go get your things together. I'll also make a meal." Still feeling frazzled, she brushed a stray strand of hair away from her face. "Is there anything you don't like?"

"A man like me hasn't had much opportunity to be picky. I'll like anything you prepare, miss."

Why did his statement leave her feeling a little breathless? "I have some chicken. And smoked ham."

"Don't put yourself to trouble on my account."

"It's no trouble. I mean, we need to eat, right, Sergeant? No matter what else happens, we need to eat."

"Of course, miss."

His thoughtful expression was a bit disconcerting.

So was his quiet demeanor while he ate every speck of the fried ham, creamed potatoes, and glazed carrots on his plate an hour later.

She'd tried not to let him see that she noticed the way his gaze lingered on her when he thought she wasn't looking. Or the way he insisted on washing both his plate and hers.

Or the way he thanked her for the meal before leaving for a long walk all around her property, and again after their light supper, before he once again went to the barn to care for her animals.

It was only when she climbed into bed and dimmed her lantern that she allowed herself to really think about his actions and words. About the way he seemed so grateful and tentative.

And she began to wonder what his life had been like. She knew he had fought in the war and been imprisoned, that he got into trouble with a gambling debt. But what other events had eventually led him to a jail cell in Sweetwater, Texas, and ultimately to sleeping in her barn?

Before sleep overtook her, she wondered if she really wanted to know.

9

Johnson's Island, Ohio
Confederate States of America Officers POW Camp
Winter 1865

His mouth had gotten him in trouble again.

As Thomas sat on his cot, shivering next to Robert Truax, he could practically feel the animosity rolling off the second lieutenant. Thomas didn't blame him in the slightest.

After all, he was twenty-two years old now. Far too old to be shooting off his mouth the way he had. He'd gotten mad at some new captain from Mississippi over an imagined slight. Before he knew what he was doing, Thomas had called him a few choice names. The captain had taken offense.

That had led, unfortunately, to Thomas punching him in the face with a powerful left hook.

The captain had fallen flat on his face. The man's fellow Mississippians hadn't taken that well and attacked Thomas—which had led, of course, to his own band of friends joining in the fray.

The guards watched the skirmish for a while, then broke up the fight. Soon after, they made sure Thomas's group felt the consequences. They removed their stove.

Since snow covered the ground and their quarters were

essentially hastily erected buildings constructed of green lumber, their usually cold conditions hovered at the freezing mark.

Now everyone was shivering on their cots, irritated with him and nursing various assorted injuries to boot.

Yep, this time the consequences of his inability to keep his mouth shut had been especially miserable. Hating himself, hating the anger that always seemed to be boiling on the surface of his tongue, Thomas swallowed hard and tried not to dissolve even deeper into self-pity. When a lump formed in his throat, he coughed, hoping he wasn't about to do something he was going to be even more ashamed about.

"You ain't about to start crying, are you?" Robert asked.

"Of course not," Thomas replied, his voice thick with emotion.

"Sure?" he asked, his tone now filled with distaste. "'Cause you sound like you're on the verge of tears."

Thomas bit the inside of his cheek and concentrated on that pinch. It was a welcome thing. Far better than coming off as weak. Everyone knew Robert had grown up on the streets of Fort Worth. Rumors abounded about who took care of him. Some said fallen women. Others said old war veterans from 1812.

All Thomas knew was that the man had had a harder life than even Thomas had and still didn't go around hitting captains or picking fights. "I'm, uh, just cold. The wind is blowing pretty bad tonight. It feels like we're sitting in the middle of the lake."

"I wonder why?" Major Kelly called out sarcastically. "Could it be because we have no heat? Thanks to you?"

"That's enough, Ethan," Phillip Markham said. "The boy has already apologized for his actions. Several times."

"Pardon me if I'm not feeling too kindly toward that apology. Words don't mean all that much right now. My feet feel like they might as well be submerged in Lake Erie."

"Just don't kick me with them," Captain Monroe bit out. "If you can help yourself, that is. I've never known a person to toss and turn as much as you do in your sleep."

"You aren't all that great to sleep with either, Devin."

"Yeah, but I'm still better than sleeping alone."

Thomas could practically hear Major Kelly grit his teeth before he exhaled with a bark of laughter. "You may have a point. The only thing worse than sleeping beside any of you would be to sleep alone. I'd have frostbite by morning."

Robert chuckled. "By the end of the night, I reckon all of us will be spooned up like dance hall girls."

"I don't believe spooning is what those girls do," Phillip said, joking.

"Oh, like you would even know," the major said. "You've only been around one woman." He sighed dramatically. "The fair Miranda."

"That is nothing to be ashamed of."

"Indeed it is not. It's a blessing the likes of us have never known," the captain countered. After a pause, he called out, "Do you not have anything to say now, Sergeant?"

Captain Monroe's voice held a definite edge. Feeling rather like a misbehaving child, Thomas cleared his throat. "No, sir."

"Ah, don't be so hard on yourself. If it wasn't you picking a fight with Creighten, something else would have set the lot of us off. We're a group of soldiers used to a lot of physical activity. Sitting around in the middle of a snow and ice storm didn't do us any favors."

"I still regret my actions."

"I regret them too," Major Kelly moaned.

"Oh, stop," Phillip said. "You know as well as I do that Creighten had it coming. That man is an idiot and a blowhard. And a braggart."

"This is true." Amusement entered Major Kelly's tone. "He's a fool. Only a fool would say he could outride the lot of us. Like it even matters at this point in time."

Captain Monroe started laughing. "The man grew up on a farm in southern Mississippi. He was not racing horses; he was planting alfalfa. He certainly never learned to ride like our Thomas Baker can."

For a moment, Thomas let himself luxuriate in the feeling of pride the captain's offhand comment gave him. He could indeed ride well. His father had made sure of that.

"Can you really ride so well, Baker?" Major Kelly called out.

Thomas considered lying, but since there was so little he felt proud of, he couldn't do it. "Well . . . yes, I can."

"How come? You have a natural gift?"

"No. I . . . well, I mean, my father was a blacksmith. He loved horses and made sure I loved them too. He had me riding practically before I could walk. I grew up in the saddle."

"Our sergeant is being too modest. He can ride like the wind. He and the horse move like one," Phillip said. "I've never seen anything like it."

"My brother was better," Thomas blurted.

"Is he gone?" Captain asked.

"Yes, sir."

"What battle?"

"No battle, sir. My brother, Jeremy, died long before the war began." Thomas hesitated, then decided to tell the whole truth. "My family all died when I was eight years old."

"Good Lord," Major Kelly uttered. "What happened? Did they get scarlet fever?"

He didn't want to answer. But he supposed he deserved the pain. "Indian raid. Everyone in my family fought them but me.

Said I was too young," he choked out. "My father made me go to a hiding place and told me not to come out, no matter what." Swallowing, he said, "So I hid while they were attacked and killed."

"And you heard the whole thing," Robert muttered.

"Yeah. I heard everything. Every bit of it."

The silence that met his statement made Thomas want to curl into a ball as a grown man and pretend to be anywhere else. Now they had a whole other reason to look down on him. Only a true coward would admit to hiding while his mother was being tortured by the Comanche, even if he had been a child at the time.

Yet again, his mouth had gotten him into this mess. If he'd held his tongue, they never would have known what he'd done.

At last Captain Monroe cleared his throat. "I'm real sorry that happened, Thomas."

"Yes, sir. Me too."

"What happened after?"

"After? I lived on the streets."

"You didn't go to any relatives' homes?"

"No, sir. I didn't have anywhere to go."

"So you've lived on your own since you were eight."

"I did until I got a job in a livery around the time I was eleven. I slept and worked there until I was seventeen. And then I enlisted."

"And now here you are, living with a bunch of broken men in the middle of a frozen great lake."

"Yes. I mean, no, sir."

"No?"

"I may be living in the middle of a frozen lake, but I'm surely not with a bunch of broken men. You all are some of the best men I've had the honor of knowing."

Major Kelly sighed. "You had to do it, didn't you, Sergeant?"

"Do what?"

"You had to go and prove me wrong. You have shamed me. Made me realize there's quite a bit of you to admire."

"I don't know about that, sir."

"Don't argue with a major, Thomas," Robert said. "Let him win this one."

Thomas smiled in the dark and kept smiling until his eyes got heavy and snoring reverberated around him.

Only then did he start to fall asleep, feeling like he'd finally found a home.

10

DOING THE RIGHT THING WAS DEFINITELY OVERRATED. If he hadn't been so chivalrous, Thomas could very well be sleeping in the comfort of one of Laurel's extra bedrooms.

Instead, he was lying on a pile of blankets in the dusty tack room in her barn. Though it wasn't the most unpleasant bed he'd ever lain upon, it was far from what could have been.

And that loss, the knowledge that for the first time in a very long while he'd had options and had chosen the worst one, was tough to swallow. Was that what doing the right thing felt like? Finding contentment in discomfort?

If so, Thomas realized it was going to take some time to get used to. He moved again on his makeshift bed and tried not to wince. The heat made the wounds on his back fester and itch and ache, which in turn kept him awake.

Realizing he was simply going to have to wait until his body became so exhausted that he fell asleep, Thomas bided his time by chewing on straw and listening to Yellow's and Velvet's breathing. The horses' easy slumber brought back those rare, peaceful memories of being a small boy in his father's blacksmith shop. He used to sit in the back of the shop, near where the horses were stabled, and listen to the familiar clang and sizzle of his father fashioning horseshoes. The horses had seemed to know that his father cared for them, because they always stood easily, eventually lightly dozing.

It was a good memory, one of the few he had. It was also far safer to dwell on than the other matter that occupied his mind— his new boss, Miss Laurel Tracey.

From the time she'd gazed at him with those slightly upturned eyes that seemed to change their hue with every mood, he had been lost.

Added to the mix were her golden tresses, kissable cheeks, and feminine figure. Though he truly felt respect for her, he was only a man. And he'd be lying if he didn't admit to himself that other thoughts had crossed his mind besides distant, cool respect.

Even her personality lured him like no other woman's ever had.

Without doing any one thing in particular, Laurel Tracey was everything he thought a woman should be. And if he was honest, he'd have to admit it was appealing that she needed a protector. Few people in his life had actually needed him, and he loved that she needed him to help with the ranch, to protect her, and to shield her from the cruel remarks of Bess and Jerome.

He still couldn't get over the way those two had belittled her attributes. He found her terribly attractive. He knew he wasn't the only man to notice her beauty either. The judge was certainly smitten with her, and the sheriff too.

From what he could tell, half the population of Sweetwater didn't seem inclined to do much besides covertly stare at Laurel. If he had been her man instead of her new hired hand, he would have stared them all down until they looked away in shame.

What they didn't seem to understand—as far as he could tell, anyway—was that Laurel Tracey's looks weren't what set her apart from most every other woman. No, there was something more about her. Something far less apparent but far more extraordinary.

She was kind and generous. Decent and honest. Tenderhearted and sweet. Almost as if she still believed in goodness in the world, even though she had survived a war, just like the rest of them had.

For the life of him, he couldn't figure her out. She didn't act like any woman he'd ever known. Not that he'd known all that many, of course. But still, she was far too trusting. For heaven's sake, he was a criminal! Surely she knew that meant he didn't always obey laws or do what was right. She should want to keep her distance from him, not invite him into her home.

But that was what she'd done.

He decided right then and there to do everything in his power to look out for her. He didn't know if he could actually help her save her ranch, but he could definitely make sure she came to no harm while he was there.

He was looking forward to it too.

His body relaxed as he imagined her looking at him with gratitude. As if, for a split second, she stared at him with appreciation, like he remembered those officers had in their barracks in prison all those years ago.

As if he was far more than she'd expected.

If that happened, he would count himself fortunate indeed.

He closed his eyes, thinking about her look of wonder. At last, exhausted, he felt himself drifting off to sleep, comforted by the gentle snores of two horses.

Taylor Orr was a desperate man. He was also running out of time.

That was the only reason he could give himself for sneaking

around Laurel Tracey's house after one in the morning with a dead calf in his arms.

Viewing the calf's suffering and eventual death had brought Taylor no joy. It had only cemented his determination to wrap up this loathsome job as quickly as possible so he could get away.

That was why he ended up carrying the calf on the back of his mount well beyond the house's perimeter, then carried it in his arms all the way to Laurel Tracey's doorstep. He had to be especially quiet with that prisoner sleeping in the barn, but this way there would be no mistake about what had happened. The last thing Taylor wanted was for its owner to mistakenly think the animal died of natural causes if it was found alone. Or worse, not even find it.

After he deposited the animal in front of her door, he quietly darted back into the shadows and headed to his horse. He had no desire to catch sight of the woman to whom he'd been ordered to cause so much pain.

He was going to go to his small room in the boardinghouse tonight and sleep until midmorning. By that time, he should hear word of Laurel Tracey contacting the sheriff in fright.

When that happened, Taylor could let his boss know he was making progress. Surely then he would get another payment.

Mounting his horse, he quietly urged it into a walk, then a canter. Thought about how getting paid so he could pay off his debts and provide for Dara was worth all this.

Some things were so worthwhile that they made even the most evil actions justifiable.

Maybe if he told himself that enough he might actually believe it one day.

11

LAUREL COULDN'T SEEM TO STOP CRYING.

She'd not only slept late, but realized she couldn't be sure Thomas would automatically care for all her animals. Especially the chickens, since she'd cared for them herself yesterday. Knowing Velvet and Yellow would be anxious for their food, and the hens would need their grain before they would willingly give up any eggs, and her dairy cow, Bonnet, would need to be milked, she'd thrown on her oldest worn calico dress and did little more than pull her hair into a makeshift braid before splashing water on her face.

Electing not to even put on shoes since the ground would no doubt be warm already, she scampered down the creaking stairs, threw open the front door, and almost tripped over the dead calf lying just on the other side of the entryway.

The sight of the sweet young thing, with its vacant brown eyes and stiff body, was so horrible, so unexpected, that she hadn't been able to stop herself from screaming. Not once, but twice.

Then, when she realized someone must have placed it on her doorstep in the middle of the night while she was sleeping just up the stairs, she began to sob.

Who could have done such a thing? Had it been Thomas? Was this stranger she'd invited to live by her side evil?

Almost in the next breath, she dismissed the idea. Her new

worker might be a little rough around the edges, but he wasn't the type of man to kill baby animals and leave them at her doorstep. That wasn't who he was.

Ashamed and alarmed at the train of her thoughts, she pressed her palms over her mouth. Anything to help her regain control. Because if Thomas hadn't done such a thing, it was someone else.

Maybe it had been one of those squatters she'd spied a couple of days ago. Everyone knew some of those men were desperate for land, desperate for something to hold on to. Maybe they'd assumed a lone woman, whom they somehow knew was low on assets and money, would be no match for the likes of them.

Maybe it was someone else, someone who knew her well and knew just what would frighten her the most.

Regardless of who had done this, the fact remained that someone had been on her land without permission, killed that calf, and stood right outside her door last night.

All while she'd been in her bed, sound asleep.

Why, she hadn't even locked her doors!

Thinking of how easy it would have been for the trespasser to have entered her home and attacked her, her trembling increased.

"Miss Laurel, what is it?"

Dropping her hands, Laurel turned to see Thomas stride toward her. His hair was sticking up this way and that, his denims hung low on his hips, and his chambray shirt was partly unbuttoned. He was barefoot too.

But what held her gaze the most was the concerned expression he wore. He looked sleepy and unsure and worried. She was no sleuth, but nothing about him indicated he had any inkling of what she'd discovered on her doorstep. It seemed that he, too, had been sleeping while a perpetrator had been lurking about on her land.

Shivering uncontrollably, Laurel curved her arms around herself in another weak effort to gain control of her emotions.

"Miss Laurel?" Thomas called out again.

Running toward the porch steps, he kept his gaze on her. "What's wrong? Did something happen to you?" His tone darkened with obvious worry. "Did you fall? Are you hurt?"

She shook her head. "No. I mean . . . I mean . . . look."

His next words froze as he looked down to where she pointed. Then he drew in a sharp breath. "This was here when you came out this morning?" he asked as he knelt down by its side.

"I almost tripped on it." Not even caring that sloppy tears were still sliding down her face, she continued, "Look at his size. He can't be more than a couple of days old. What do you think happened to him?"

He ran a finger along the calf's side. "God only knows. He feels cold. I reckon he's been dead for a while."

"Someone brought him here while we were sleeping and put him on my doorstep. Who would do such a thing?"

"I couldn't begin to imagine. I've seen a lot of things in my life, but this does beat all."

Staring at Thomas looking at the little calf, Laurel's head spun. She needed to take care of the poor animal. Or at least walk around it so she could talk to Thomas without staring at it. Or even go inside.

But unfortunately, she couldn't seem to make herself do anything but stand frozen.

Thomas took the decision away from her. Stepping around the calf, he wrapped one arm around her shoulders. "Let's get you inside. There's no reason for you to stand out here any longer."

Grateful that he was taking charge, she allowed him to usher her inside.

Once they were in the dim interior of the foyer, Thomas closed the door. The next thing she knew, he was pulling her into a warm hug.

Laurel knew she was not a small person. She was taller than most women. Her body was rather generous too. She usually felt too large, too ungainly when compared to other, more delicately formed women.

In Thomas's arms, however, she felt almost small. Releasing a ragged sigh, she leaned closer to him.

"You go ahead and cry," he murmured, hugging her tight as she laid her cheek over his heart and let the tears fall. He was warm, and to her surprise, his skin was smooth.

Placing both of her hands on his shoulders, she realized that she felt secure. She felt cared for.

Not alone.

How long had it been? Since her stepfather and mother died? Her father and brother? When was the last time anyone had held her while she fell apart? When was the last time she'd actually had someplace to fall?

Far too long ago.

The next thing she knew, she was crying for the loss of her loved ones. And crying because Thomas was there.

"It ain't okay, but I'll make it that way," he murmured, making some kind of sympathetic clicking noise with his tongue while one of his hands began to smooth back her hair. "I'm so sorry."

After giving in to her weakness for another half a minute or so, she straightened and pulled back.

As he stood tall and strong, looking down on her with an intense expression, Laurel knew she should be blushing like a schoolgirl. Her cheek, her face had been nestled against his bare skin. She'd pressed herself against his body.

Not only would her behavior have been inappropriate even if they were friends or sweethearts, but it was especially so because she was his employer! She'd released him from his prison less than twenty-four hours ago and now . . . now she was just wrapped in his arms.

What would he think?

It was going to be up to her to fix this. Two awkward steps backward carried her even farther away from him. "I seem to be forgetting myself. I'm sorry, Sergeant."

He reached out and curved two fingers under her chin. "Why do you feel the need to apologize?" he drawled, his voice rough. "Being upset that some son of a gun placed a dead newborn calf on your doorstep last night? A sight like that would have shaken up most anyone."

She shivered. "I can't believe this happened. It's awful. But I should have handled it better. I shouldn't have . . . leapt into your arms the way I did. It was inappropriate."

But instead of accepting her apology or making one of his own, her sergeant surprised her. "Stop it," he ordered. "We're not going to do this. Not anymore."

Caught off guard by his sudden change in demeanor, she looked at him in confusion.

"We're not going to start apologizing for being human," he said, his voice hard. Before she could question that comment, he added, "Miss Tracey, *Laurel*, you have nothing to be sorry for." When she froze, staring at him in wonder, he continued, his voice sounding more confident. "What you saw, what someone did?" He shook his head. "It's beyond comprehension."

His words, so sure and certain, were able to do something all the voices and doubts in her head hadn't been able to. Feeling far more calm, she breathed in deep. "What should we do now?"

He quirked an eyebrow. "Well, first off, *we* are not going to do anything."

"I don't understand."

Instead of explaining, he curved a hand around her elbow. "Miss Laurel, you need to sit down and rest. While you do that, I'll go take care of that animal. Then we can talk about whether we should ride into town to talk to Sheriff Jackson about it."

Though his words made sense, she dreaded the thought of being on display for the second time in two days. "I'm not sure what I want to do."

"Miss Laurel, I've never been a man with a lot of interest in bringing lawmen into my life, but this might be the exception, don't you think?" Gentling his voice, he said, "Like you said, that little thing didn't get here on its own. And I think we can be sure it came from your own herd."

"I know. It's just that I don't know what anyone else can do. And I'm afraid Sheriff Jackson might even want me to bring back Bess and Jerome so I'm not here alone." Just imagining how difficult it would be to interact with Thomas while her stepsiblings looked on, she shook her head. "I can't have them back here."

"Of course you can't, and I won't let that happen."

"You think he'll listen to you?"

"I know he will, just as I know you don't have to do one single thing you don't want to." Leading her to the sofa, he said, "Now, take a seat and try to relax."

Though she allowed him to guide her, she said, "I can't simply sit here and do nothing, Sergeant. The horses need to be fed and my cow needs to be milked."

"I'll take care of them."

"You will?" she asked in surprise. "The chickens too?"

Looking a little embarrassed, he said, "I never could abide chickens."

There was something about the way he looked when he said "chickens" that made her giggle in spite of the traumatic morning they'd shared. "Are you afraid of a few birds?"

"Yep. And I'm not ashamed of it neither."

"I'll go take care of the hens, then. And I'll make some breakfast too."

"All right. But please rest for a while first, give me time to do those other chores. Then come out to care for the chickens. You can tell me all about them."

"I will. I'm shaken up, but I'm not about to sit and do nothing all morning." Actually, she couldn't think of anything worse than to sit in the house alone and let her mind drift. It would be far better to keep busy.

"We've got a plan, then." Reaching out for her hand, he squeezed it gently. "Don't look out the window, though. I'll take care of the calf. You don't need to look at it again."

Grateful for that, she nodded.

After he closed the front door behind him, she pressed her fingers to her eyes once again. She needed to regain her composure. She needed to stop thinking about what used to be accepted and what was going to cause talk. None of that mattered. She needed to start thinking about herself and her needs.

What was more important than anything else was the future of the ranch. She needed to keep it, needed to get some cattle to market. That, not anything else, was what she needed to concentrate on.

If that was even possible, now that someone seemed to be going to great lengths to threaten everything she held dear. She just had no idea why. Or who.

12

Assured Laurel was resting in her sitting room as comfortably as she was able, Thomas wrapped the calf in a worn sheet he'd found at the bottom of her rag basket near the kitchen and carried it to the barn.

The calf was stiff in his arms and so very pitifully small. Probably only a day or two old. His death was such a shame.

When Thomas walked by the horses, both whinnied in alarm. He guessed it didn't take much for them to sense death.

After depositing the calf in an empty stall, he peeled back the sheet and examined it for cuts or any other signs of foul play. But beyond the blank stare and an odd set to the animal's jaw, he couldn't find anything amiss.

Now he was going to have to get other people involved. Definitely the sheriff, and maybe even the doctor if he was willing to take a peek at the animal. Thomas was as sure as the scars on his back that the animal had died of unnatural causes.

If the calf had merely died from a snakebite or from disease and someone had come across it, that person would have knocked on the door in the light of day.

No, someone had gone out of their way to intentionally scare

Laurel. The questions, of course, were who would do something like that, and why?

Though he'd only been around Jerome and Bess for a few minutes, they didn't strike him as the type to do such a thing. It was too much trouble, for one. They both had seemed rather squeamish too. Killing an animal and carting it to Laurel's doorstep in the middle of the night seemed like a lot for a pair like them to take on. Besides, he was sure he would have heard them. No, this was someone who knew how to keep even a former soldier from being aware he was there.

After covering the calf with the sheet again, he hurried to his room. There, he buttoned his shirt, wincing as he realized how exposed he had been in front of a lady, but remembering, too, the soft touch of her cheek on his chest. Shaking his thoughts away, he put on his boots and belt. Then, after caring for the animals, he washed his face and teeth. Feeling more fit for her company, he headed back toward the house to get Laurel.

Whether she saw him walking toward her through the window or the timing had worked out, she exited the door and hurriedly met him on the limestone walkway.

It seemed she, too, had used some of their time apart to put herself together. Her hair was braided more tightly and pinned into a neat bun at the nape of her neck. She had also slipped on stockings and boots, and carried a basket.

He had to admit he was a little disappointed by that. He had loved seeing her bare toes peeking out at him. He'd loved seeing her in a way no one else ever did.

"You put your boots on," he said when she got to his side.

As he'd hoped, her cheeks bloomed into a faint flush. "Oh, yes. I hadn't meant to go out barefoot in the first place."

"I didn't mind."

"I see you've put your boots on too."

He grinned. "A man learns to cover his feet when he's around farm animals."

"A woman learns to do that too."

Looking at her closely, he said, "Are you doing a little better?"

She shrugged. "I can't say that I am. Who do you think could have done such a thing?"

"I was just doing some thinking about that myself." Knowing they would no doubt need to talk about potential enemies soon, he said, "Let's not think about it now, though. Come on and show me how these hens greet you."

She looked at him in a bemused way, but Laurel acted agreeable enough. Leading the way to the henhouse, she said, "I have a dozen hens, ten of which are good layers."

"And the other two?"

She frowned. "They are destined for the stew pot," she whispered as she picked up a scoop of feed and scattered it along the ground.

With a flurry of white feathers, the majority of the hens trotted out and began pecking at the seeds. As they pranced importantly, Laurel went to their nests to gather eggs. She talked quietly to the hens, even going so far as to touch one of the chicken's heads.

Thomas watched with his arms resting on the fence, unexpectedly charmed. He liked that she treated those birds as though they had as much right to be there as she did.

Of course, that made him realize just how heavily that calf's death must be laying on her heart.

When she walked back out, he held out a hand for her basket. "I'll carry your eggs for you."

"I can handle carrying eight eggs."

"No doubt. But I'll feel better giving you a hand."

"Thank you."

He followed her into the house and back toward the kitchen. "Do you want me to wash them for you?"

"If you do that, I'll get right to work on breakfast."

While he primed the pump and washed eggs, she competently made biscuits, then put them in a cast iron pan and into the oven.

"Gravy?"

"Sounds good."

He watched as she sliced off a thick piece of ham, fried it, and then added milk and flour.

While she cooked, he said, "It's kind of surprising to see a lady like you so at home in the kitchen. Did the war teach you to cook?"

"I suppose so, though my mother taught me to cook by her side at a young age. This is a working ranch, you know. Neither of my parents had much patience for men or women who didn't want to pull their own weight."

"I'm guessing, then, that it was fairly hard to stand by and watch Bess and Jerome do next to nothing around here."

After checking on the biscuits, Laurel nodded, her expression pained. "I don't understand their ways, if you want to know the truth. Their father had always been a hard worker, and he always looked pleased about the work I did here."

Thomas was doing his best to keep their conversation general to try to keep her calm. It was a difficult endeavor, however, because all he really wanted to do was swear a blue streak and then go find whoever had done such a thing and make them pay for upsetting her so much.

He was supposed to be beyond all that, however. His moral fiber was stronger, his faith more pronounced. He hoped he'd always be that way. All that time in captivity had to have been good for something.

With all that in mind, he said, "Do you think they might have gotten so mad at you that they would be capable of doing something like what we found this morning?"

"Killing a calf?" She shook her head. "Not at all. To be honest, I don't know of anyone who would do such a thing. Not only would few people be so cruel as to hurt a young calf, but no one around these parts would knowingly put an end to something that could bring in money. Not even if this is one of the men who has been trying to persuade me to sell."

"I wondered about that too." He was tempted to brush a knuckle across her cheek, but he didn't. "How about we do some more thinking about this later?"

"I think that's a good idea, since breakfast is now ready."

He grinned. "Your timing is perfect. I'm starving."

After serving himself, he sat down across from her and stared in wonder at the plate of food in front of him. Just like the meals she'd made the day before, it was more than he'd had at one time in months and was certainly better than anything some jail cook had made. It all smelled wonderful.

He was truly thankful.

"May I lead us in prayer?" he asked.

She blinked, bringing a wave of appreciation into her gaze. "I'd enjoy that, Sergeant. Thank you."

"Dear heavenly Father, please bless this food and the hands that prepared it. Please also be with all creatures on your earth, great and small, and let us not forget to give thanks for even the smallest of blessings, for each day is a gift. Amen."

"Amen," she echoed. When she opened her eyes, she said, "That was a lovely prayer."

"You sound surprised."

"I guess I am. Well, a little bit. I didn't take you for being a praying man. You seem so hard." She blinked. "I meant that in the best way."

"I'll take it in that way. I am hard. But because of that, I've learned to reach out to our Lord. I'm a man who needs all the help he can get."

"I don't know if you're teasing me or not."

"I never joke about my faith," he replied before biting down on a biscuit and tasting heaven.

It was almost impossible to talk after that. Each bite was a revelation. She might have been surprised by his prayer, but he was just as amazed by her expertise in the kitchen.

Beside him, she ate as well, but in a far more desultory fashion.

Realizing he'd probably just inhaled his breakfast with the grace of a feed horse, he said, "I guess it's obvious I haven't had too many opportunities to eat in the company of ladies. Or with anyone who knows how to conduct himself in a proper way. Have my poor table manners taken away your appetite?"

"Not at all. I'm glad you're enjoying your food."

"I am indeed. You are a very fine cook, Miss Laurel."

"Thank you." She motioned to the stove. "I made lots, so go get some more if you're hungry."

Since he couldn't argue with that, he gave himself a second plateful, then took care to eat it far more slowly. When he was done at last, he pushed back from the table and stood up.

"How should we handle things? Do you want to go into town? Do you want me to go in your place? I can do that, you know."

"As much as I'd like you to talk to the sheriff without me, I think I had better go with you. After all, it is my ranch."

Glad that she stood her ground, he nodded.

"We need to do this today, don't we?" Dread filled her every syllable.

"Yes, I think we do." Picking up his plate, he said, "I'll work on the dishes while you get ready to go into town."

"You helped with the dishes last night."

He looked her way as he picked up a bowl. "And?"

"I should have stopped you. Washing dishes is women's work."

"I ate from my plate. I think I can wash it too." When she still hesitated, he smiled. "The faster you get ready, the faster we can get this errand over with."

"This is true. I'll be right back."

When she disappeared up the stairs, he got busy scrubbing pots and washing each dish and fork and spoon with care. He'd just dried the last piece when she appeared again, this time in a light-blue dress with rows of pin tucks across the chest.

On her head was a lovely wide-brimmed straw hat. It was flattering, highlighting her many attributes, and he hadn't thought she needed any help to improve her looks.

"You look real pretty, Miss Laurel."

Twin spots of color appeared in her cheeks. "Thank you, Sergeant. I . . . well, I thought maybe I'm going to need all the help I can get for this errand."

It was on the tip of his tongue to utter that, because she had him now, she wouldn't need to worry about facing the world on her own, at least not anytime soon.

Thank goodness he caught himself in time.

Laurel Tracey had enough to worry about without her new ranch hand making a pest of himself.

13

AFTER THEY FINISHED THEIR ERRAND IN TOWN, LAUREL couldn't wait to depart. Leading the way to the posts where Yellow and Velvet were tied up, she arranged the reins and looked for the block to help her get up into her sidesaddle.

But before she could do anything more than pull the mounting block closer, Thomas was at her side. "Allow me."

Well aware of the many eyes watching them, Laurel slipped her hand in his as he used his other to give her a boost into her saddle. He held her steady while she looped one knee around the horn and arranged her skirts.

Once she was settled, he swung into his own saddle as though he'd been born to it. Then, with barely a nudge, he guided Yellow onto the street.

She and Velvet reached his side, then together they guided their horses the short distance down Sweetwater's dry, dusty main street before heading in her ranch's direction.

After breakfast, Thomas had been prepared to hitch up the buggy again, but Laurel had asked if he'd be willing to ride instead. She liked to ride her horse, and she hated riding in the buggy in the middle of summer. It always felt too stifling and hot.

Thomas had readily agreed. Soon she learned why. Thomas

Baker on the back of a horse was truly a sight to see. He and the horse rode together as one. Whereas everyone else had seemed to need to fight Yellow over every command, Thomas controlled the gelding with ease.

Though she hadn't thought it would be possible, her ranch hand seemed stronger, more confident, and even handsomer in the saddle.

She'd been glad of the distraction the whole way to town, since he'd put the wrapped-up calf across his lap. Laurel's thoughts had alternated between wondering what the sheriff and doctor were going to say and worrying about running into Jerome and Bess.

However, her worries were for naught. After Thomas told the sheriff about discovering the dead calf on Laurel's doorstep, Sheriff Jackson said he'd take the calf to the doc and try to get some answers. As to who might have done this, he, too, had trouble identifying anyone both capable and willing to harm cattle to scare Laurel into selling her land, the most likely motive.

Not even squatters seemed to be likely suspects, though no one really knew how desperate any of them could be.

The sheriff encouraged Thomas and Laurel to head on back home. Doc Barnes was seeing to a mare and likely would not be back for hours. Jerome and Bess were nowhere to be seen.

Now as they rode home, Laurel felt contemplative. She was somewhat surprised to realize that after spending only twenty-four hours with Thomas, she felt as if they were a unit. A team.

"I know I said I didn't think Jerome would ever do such a thing, but do you think it could have been him who carried that calf to the doorstep?" she blurted.

"Like you, I wouldn't have thought so, but it is just under-handed enough to seem like he might have thought it was a good way to scare you into selling the ranch."

"I've started to think about that too. And whoever is doing this, I agree that has to be the reason, to get me to sell. But it's not as if this part of Texas has no other land available. Many a war widow has been forced to sell."

"I know it's hard, but we'll figure it out. You've got the sheriff on it too."

His words soothed her. So much so, it drew her up short. What was happening?

How could she have gone from feeling completely alone to feeling as though she had finally found someone to depend on? It made no sense, especially given the fact that the man she was depending on had just spent several months in jail.

When the house and barn came into view, they slowed their horses. There was a bit of shade now, thanks to a thicket of pecan trees that had been determined to grow and thrive for decades. Since Velvet and Yellow acted pleased to simply meander along in the shade, Laurel relaxed her grip on her horse's reins. All of them needed a few minutes to relax a bit.

She was just about to comment on the weather when Thomas turned to look at her, his blue eyes as striking as ever under the tan rim of his Stetson. "Miss Laurel, I think we should talk about something."

"Yes?"

"I don't like the idea of someone wandering around the ranch at night, especially with you alone in the house. It's not safe."

"I've thought about that a time or two as well," she said with a small smile. Actually, she didn't know how she was ever going to be able to sleep through the night again. Every creak and moan in the house was certain to draw a healthy amount of fear inside her.

Looking as if he'd just solved a difficult problem, he exhaled. "I'm glad to hear you feel the same way. Frankly, the idea of someone bothering you in the house while I'm sound asleep a hundred feet away in the barn scares the heck out of me."

"It scares me too," she admitted after debating for a moment. She didn't want to come across as any weaker than she was, but they were talking about someone killing animals and leaving them for her to find. Not just petty fears.

"Will you allow me to sleep in your house for a spell? I promise I'll sleep on the sofa in the sitting room if you don't want me in a bedroom upstairs. I need to be near in case something happens."

"You're right. But there's no reason for you to sleep on the sofa. I'd like you to take a room."

"If you're sure."

"I'm positive." She would also sleep better knowing he was just down the hall instead of downstairs near the front door.

The lines on the outside of his eyes crinkled in amusement. Then he seemed to gather himself together. "I don't want to worry you, having me so close and all. I promise I'll do my best to only come inside the main house to sleep."

"Sergeant, I don't know why, but I feel safe around you. I think it's also pretty obvious that if you had wanted to harm me, you could have done it by now. I'd rather trust you."

"Thank you, miss," he said as they stopped in front of the barn. Once again, he dismounted easily, then moved to assist her.

When she felt his warm grip on her waist, she didn't dare meet his gaze. She'd worn only a light corset and the minimum of petticoats. Though it was surely only her imagination, she suddenly felt as if she could feel his touch through the layers of her cotton gown.

The moment her feet touched the ground, he let go of her and cleared his throat. "Well, I'd best take care of Velvet now."

"And Yellow?"

"I'm going to let him give me a tour of the ranch. I think it's time I got the lay of the land."

"Would you like me to go with you?" She was tired, but she was willing to sit in a saddle for hours if it would help the ranch.

"Maybe tomorrow. Today I think it's best that I do a little bit of riding and familiarize myself with the area on my own, see what repairs and work need to be done. I think it will probably take me several hours."

Since she'd already told him the boundaries—the creek and the barbed wire to the north and east and the largest pond and wooden fence on the south and west—Laurel knew he wouldn't have any trouble staying on her property.

"Well then, I'll make some food for you to take along and then prepare your room. When you get back, come into the kitchen around six for supper."

"I'll be back on time." He paused. "Miss Laurel, do you have weapons? I had a rifle, but it was confiscated when I was arrested. I think it would be best if we were both armed. I don't want to go out there without protection, and I don't want to leave you here without it."

Agreeing, she took him into the house, where her father's and brother's rifles were safely locked away. After assuring him she knew how to handle a rifle and giving him her father's to load, he left the house to ready Yellow.

She noticed his gait seemed stiff and he seemed intent on keeping his back as ramrod straight as possible. With all the commotion of the calf on her doorstep, she'd forgotten about the lashes he'd received.

As she moved to the kitchen to pack some food, she promised herself to check on his wounds that evening.

14

HE'D BEEN AS GOOD AS HIS WORD.

Thomas had ridden out with Yellow as soon as she'd given him the food she prepared. When she saw him return close to five with a contemplative look on his face, she figured he'd had a good look at her property and now understood why she was willing to do almost anything to keep it.

When he entered the kitchen for supper, his hair was wet and he was wearing a fresh shirt, no doubt another gift from his captain.

She served him chicken stew and some more of the biscuits he'd liked so much. This time she said grace while he bowed his head in prayer.

Then they ate in relative silence.

After he cleared his plate and refused seconds, she finally asked him about his ride.

"Did you find your way around okay?"

"I did. At least, Yellow did." Smiling softly, he said, "That horse could have ridden me around the perimeter without me giving him a lick of guidance."

"Did you see anything?"

"I didn't get to where you say the cattle are today, if that's what you mean. But if you mean anything suspicious, nothing beyond a cleaned-up campground in the north pasture."

"That was from the squatters. Did you see them anywhere?"

"No." He seemed to contemplate the problem as he took a sip of water. Then he shrugged. "Could be they've moved on. That's what most do—stay until they feel they've outlived their welcome."

That explanation felt too pat, but Laurel supposed it had merit. "Maybe that is what happened."

"When we ride together, you can let me know if you spot anything out of the ordinary. Do you know your neighbors well?"

"I do. The Pipps are to the north, and Landon Marshall is on the south."

"Tell me about Landon Marshall. Is he a family man? Did he serve? Is he married?"

"He did serve, though I don't recall the name of his unit. He's about our age. He's unmarried and lives with his mother and sister, Eva. His father is deceased." She wondered whether she should share her recent conversation with Landon, then decided to go ahead and tell Thomas. "He wasn't real pleased to learn I was going to be having you on the ranch."

"Since he doesn't know me, I bet he was worried." He cocked an inquiring eyebrow. "Especially if the two of you are close. Are you?"

"Not exactly."

"That sounds intriguing."

"It's not."

Thomas examined her expression for a moment before nodding. "Perhaps he'll feel better about my presence here when we meet."

"Maybe so. But maybe we could keep the fact that you're going to be in the house at night just between the two of us for now."

The corners of his mouth turned up. "Yeah, I reckon that might not go over real well. Hopefully we'll be able to keep it our secret."

She hoped so too. However, that morning's discovery had served to remind her that there was far more for her to worry about than shocking her neighbors.

"I hope so as well. At this moment, however, I might be too tired to care."

For a moment he was quiet, contemplative.

"I meant what I said yesterday. I might have been in jail, but I certainly am not a man you ever need to fear."

Gathering her courage, she looked him directly in the eye. "I'm not going to start looking for ways to judge you."

"Point taken." After draining the last of his water, he set the glass back on the table, then lifted his chin. "Though I've already said this, it might be worth saying again. I need you to know that I would never hurt a hair on your head. I'd rather cut my own arm off than see you hurt or harmed."

It felt as if they were vowing to do so much more than set the foundation for a work relationship. She wasn't sure if that made her feel better or more nervous. His words, together with the heartfelt, sincere way he was speaking, touched her more than she cared to admit, even to herself.

"I trust you, Sergeant. And I would never send you back to jail any more than I would go there myself."

After staring at her for a moment, he blinked and smiled. "I guess we've made our vows then." Chuckling softly, he said, "I'm thinking what we just promised is more than how most marriages start out."

His statement was so disconcerting, she giggled. "Perhaps so, though I would like to think most marriages start with love."

His gaze softened. "Listen to you."

"What did I say? What is that look for?"

"Your talk of love."

"Goodness. Surely you believe in love."

"I believe it's nice there are still people who want to believe in it," he said lightly. "How about that?"

Feeling both happy to be talking about something as sweet as love and also strangely exposed, she said, "You don't ever think about love?"

He looked down at his empty plate. "Actually . . . no. Not often. What with the war and all, I haven't had much occasion to contemplate love and marriage, Miss Tracey."

She knew she should let the conversation go. Thomas Baker was a man who had fought in many battles and suffered in a Yankee prison. No doubt he had been filled with anger and pain in many moments of his life.

But she'd also spied something in his eyes that was soft and warm. He was not all cold and battle-worn. That tenderness came from somewhere.

"Were your parents in love?" she asked.

And just like that, the pleasant spark that had filled his eyes vanished like the sun in a dust storm. He seemed to be at a loss for words before he quickly regained his composure. "I . . . well, yes, they were."

Her instincts had been right. She never should have prodded. But now that she had brought up the subject, she didn't know how to retract it without making things worse.

"Mine were in love too." She stared at him. "Mine are gone, of course. Do you still have either of them?"

"No. I haven't had them in a very long time."

"That's so sad. Did they get the influenza? Or smallpox?"

"No." Sounding almost as if he were being strangled, he added, "They, uh . . . they were killed when I was a child."

She hadn't expected that. "I'm so sorry. That had to have been horrible."

He rubbed the back of his neck, almost like he was trying to think about that. "I suppose it was."

The cold bluntness of his words made her feel even worse. "I'm sorry for bringing it up."

"There's nothing to be sorry about. I want you to ask me anything you want. Though I am sorry it happened, growing up without parents probably saved my skin in the war."

"How so?"

"After they died, I had no one. Because of that, I could fight with honor. Nothing held me back on the battlefield."

"What did you do after they died?"

"I lived on the streets." Not meeting her gaze, he looked just beyond her. "I learned to fight and scavenge and do whatever it took to survive."

She gasped. "Oh, Thomas."

"It wasn't all bad. I got used to living with next to nothing. I even got used to being uncared for." His chin lifted. "Amazing how a good dose of neglect can serve a man well."

Tears pricked her eyes as she studied him. He was such a handsome man. With his dark hair, truly beautiful blue eyes, and exceptional smile, she imagined he had been a beautiful child. A beautiful child fending for himself. "I'm so sorry."

"Don't be." His voice gentled. "As you can see, I'm just fine."

His words said one thing, but his tone told a different story. As much as he protested, his lack of family did bother him. She took another sip of water and tried not to glance his way.

She wanted to point out the obvious. He had just come out of jail and had welts on his back that still obviously pained him. But if he was going to pretend, she supposed she could too.

She took another sip of water and tried to think of something else to say. But he beat her to it.

"I'm hoping your childhood was much different. You said your parents loved each other?"

She nodded. "They loved each other and were happy with each other too. I had an idyllic childhood. I spent most of it either following my older brother around the ranch or helping my parents. We were happy." She sighed. "You know the rest. The war started, and Anderson and my father rode off to fight."

"Leaving you and your mother to fend for yourselves."

"Yes, but it wasn't so bad, not at first. Like everyone else, my mother was sure the war would be over in a few weeks and then everything could go back to how it used to be. She kept my spirits up."

"I remember thinking that way too. But the war dragged on."

Feeling the dark memories return, she nodded. "First Anderson died, then less than a month later, we got word that my father had too. Mother and I were devastated."

"Of course you were."

Whenever Thomas said things like that, her estimation of him rose. Now that she knew how terrible his childhood had been, she wouldn't have been surprised if he had no compassion for her loss. But instead of making light of it, he looked nothing but compassionate.

After smiling at him softly, she said, "About a year later, Mother met Wayne Vance, who was a truly kind man."

"He was Jerome and Bess's father?"

She nodded. "Wayne had some money. After his wife died, he'd felt unable to care for them well. He sent Jerome and Bess off to a fancy boarding school. They spent most of their lives away from home, learning all sorts of things and being attended to. Neither of them was much touched by the war."

"I didn't know that was possible."

She shrugged. "I feel sorry for them, in some ways. They have little in common with most everyone. They weren't even that close to their father, on account of him sending them off for so long. His death didn't faze them too much."

"Didn't he leave them anything?"

"He did. But not a lot. He left most of his wealth to charity. Then, of course, his Confederate notes became worthless. And I think . . . well, I think his good intentions came back to haunt him. He didn't like how Jerome and Bess turned out. Though he left them property so they would have a place to live, he didn't leave them much for expenses. I believe he thought that would force them to work and become more humble."

"No offense, but I don't think that worked too good."

She chuckled. "It didn't. They sold the house and land he left them and spent their money like water in New Orleans and Mississippi. They arrived here with a whole lot of clothes but little of real worth. They seemed to assume I'd take care of them next."

"Did their father not leave you anything?"

"Not money, no. But he made sure this ranch would go to me. So in that sense he gave me everything."

He thought about the beautiful house, the barn, the land. "I think you might be right."

"If I can get this ranch back on its feet, I believe I will make my mother, father, and even my stepfather proud. I'd like to honor their legacy."

"I'll do my best to help you make that happen."

She smiled. "Thank you. If that does happen, I'll feel like I can breathe again. Maybe actually begin living."

"That's a good goal, then. A woman like you should be living as much as she can."

"A woman like me?"

"Are you fishing for compliments, Miss Laurel? If so, I'll be glad to hand them to you, though they probably won't sound all that good, seeing as they're coming from a criminal."

She laughed. There was no way she was going to focus on her looks again. Not after Jerome's hurtful comments.

Instead, she ached to tease him a bit. To remind him that he was about to do his fair share of living now too. After all, living on a ranch had to be much better than living in jail.

Especially when he was getting whipped there.

"Oh my goodness! I was going to help you with your back."

He stared at her, his expression alarmed. "There's no need for that."

"Oh, yes there is. I noticed you favoring it today. I think I need to check on your wounds."

He stood up, pushed in his chair, and then stood stiffly behind it, almost as if he was hoping the chair and table between them would keep her from him. "Checking my wounds means taking off my shirt."

Surely he didn't think she was that delicate? "I realize that, Sergeant."

His throat worked. "Since we're going to be doing our best to keep some distance from each other, I don't think me taking off my clothes would be the best idea."

She knew he was right. It was going to be scandalous enough with him sleeping in Jerome's room. She didn't need to make matters worse by looking at him when he was half-clothed or touching his bare back. She'd already experienced some of that after her scare with the dead calf.

But it would be even more shameful to leave his wounds untreated.

"Sergeant Baker, I'm not merely trying to be kind. If your wounds fester, you could get blood poisoning. You could die."

"And if I passed on, then you'd be out of both your money and one new worker."

She winced. "Please don't even joke about such things."

"Never, miss."

Yet again, that drawl of his sent a little shiver down her spine. Feeling rattled by the curious response she had to him, Laurel jumped to her feet. "Let's get this over with. Clear off the table and I'll heat up some water to clean your wounds."

He didn't move. "Miss Tracey, I'm still not sure about this."

"You don't have to be. I'm sure," she said as she put the kettle on. "I heated water for supper, so it shouldn't take long to heat up again."

"You know, after we ride out together tomorrow, I plan to start mending some of the fencing I saw today."

"I'll appreciate that. Clear the table, if you please."

He picked up his supper dish. "The reason I'm telling you this is so you understand that whatever good you do on my back might get undone tomorrow. That's a consideration, I think."

Scraping out the remainder of food from a bowl into a compost bin, she raised her eyebrows. "If you fear that you'll undo all my efforts, it's fortunate that we will both be here again tomorrow evening."

Grudgingly, he walked back to the table, retrieved a serving platter, and carried it over to her. "You aren't seeing the point."

"Oh, I see it," she said. "I know accepting a woman's assistance must pain you, but it can't be helped."

"It ain't that. I'm trying to think of what's best for you."

She didn't want to hear another word about what was right and what was wrong. "I know you don't want or need my help, but I think it would be best if you allowed me to assist you. Let's not waste another second on this conversation."

"Yes, miss."

But of course he sounded as skeptical as she did. Actually, he sounded as if he were on his way to another punishment.

As the kettle whistled and she began tearing a clean muslin dishcloth into strips, Laurel said a hasty prayer. Her hands were shaking, her stomach was in knots, and she wasn't at all sure she was going to be able to sound as calm and collected as she needed to be when she was examining his bare skin.

"Help me, Lord," she whispered to herself. "You've been here for me many, many times in my life. Although it might not seem like I need you now, I really and truly do. So help me do my best, would you please?"

It wasn't a good prayer. It was actually kind of frantic and self-ish sounding. But still she hoped for an answer.

Half holding her breath, she waited for a response. But no matter how hard she strained her ears, she heard no clatter of thunder or angelic voice.

But she did see Thomas Baker loosening the collar of his shirt. He was going to allow her to help him.

Perhaps that was enough of a sign for anyone.

15

THOMAS WOULD BE LYING IF HE SAID HE'D NEVER TAKEN his shirt off in front of a woman before. After his family's death, the years he spent on the streets of Fort Worth had taken away most of his innocence and all of his modesty.

But he'd also learned that a person's body was merely a shell that guarded far more important things, at least to him. He now placed far more importance on a person's heart and soul than on one's outward appearance.

Spending what seemed like an eternity in a unit of men only reinforced those feelings. Personal space and privacy became things of the past during the war. He'd gotten used to never being alone. He'd seen other men bleed and cry and hurt while standing or lying beside him. He'd grown to know those men almost as well as he knew himself. Actually, he'd probably learned far too much about the men in his company. They most likely felt the same about him.

His time in the prisoner of war camp had helped him remember that all that really mattered about a person's body was that it worked.

If a man wasn't dying, that was good enough.

Though he'd matured and learned a lot in the army under

Major Kelly's and Captain Monroe's guidance, he'd also spent time with the camp women.

He wasn't proud of that fact, but he didn't dwell on his faults or baser instincts either. The women had been there for a reason, and his upbringing on the streets hadn't exactly prepared him to reject anything offered freely.

He was a man who had never expected to live long. He'd also become selfish enough to yearn for instant gratification. Plans and goals usually meant little to him.

It was only during his months on Johnson's Island that he'd begun to learn the benefits of patience and perseverance. Those attributes paid off when a man yearned to grow into something more than he was.

He'd learned a long time ago to stop feeling guilty about the past and concentrate on looking forward. That was his chief survival skill.

But as he sat down again in Laurel's kitchen, Thomas experienced a new and fairly forgotten sensation. He felt self-conscious.

As he sat and watched her busy herself with heating water and gathering supplies, Thomas realized he'd rarely felt so exposed. For the first time in his twenty-two years, he was going to knowingly allow another person to see his failings. He hated that. He didn't want to ever appear anything other than strong and fit.

He wanted Laurel Tracey to think of him as her protector, as a man who would do whatever it took to guard and take care of her. He wanted her to view him as strong and stalwart. Not weak. Not as someone who needed tending to.

Maybe it was because he didn't have a whole lot of experience in this area, but he was fairly certain if she saw him like this, that memory would be forever burned in her head. Whenever she looked at him in the future, she'd be reminded of a time when he'd sat while she stood, when he rested while she worked.

How could a man of worth ever be all right with something like that?

However, he didn't have much choice. He worked for her. His back also needed help. It was sore and festering. Only because of those reasons did he resign himself to the inevitability of what was about to happen.

"What would you like me to do?" he asked.

She paused at the stove, looked at him carefully, then seemed to take care to hide her true feelings under a guise of steadfastness. "Take off your shirt and sit down. After this water is heated, I'll wash your back and put some ointment on your cuts."

Realizing that she'd see both these new welts as well as a whole mess of older scars, he tried to prepare her. "Miss, my back . . . well, it ain't pretty."

"I should hope not," she teased. "Grown men shouldn't aim for pretty backs."

He swallowed. Thinking of his worst wound, the jagged ridge along his neck, he said, "I meant that I have older scars."

"We've already gone through this. I am not attempting to judge you, only help." Sounding slightly exasperated, she said, "Honestly, Sergeant, I hadn't pegged you to be so timid or shy."

"I'm not shy."

Facing him, her expression one of gentle compassion, she sighed softly. "How about we stop asking questions and giving excuses and just get this over with?"

"Yes, miss." She was right. Turning so he didn't have to face her, he began unfastening the buttons. His hands working the small holes were a little unsteady. Sometimes it took him two and three times to manipulate a button through the fabric.

He told himself it was because, despite sleeping through their nighttime visitor's arrival, he hadn't slept all that much in three days.

But when he slipped the cotton fabric off his shoulders at last and felt the air kiss his back, he felt pure relief. The burst of fresh air felt wonderful. Cleansing. Like a gift.

Until he heard her gasp.

"Oh, Thomas."

Embarrassment made his voice hoarse. "If it's worse than you thought, too much for you, I'm sure I could find a way—"

"Your wounds are terrible. I have no idea how you got through the day without complaining," she interrupted. "I should have tended to you last night."

"I'll be okay."

After a small pause, she ran cool fingers along his neck. "You certainly do have scars."

He tried not to notice how welcoming her fingers felt against his skin. How gentle she was. Each brush was featherlight and made him almost wish she wouldn't stop. So much so, it was almost worth the pain and embarrassment he was feeling.

Seeking to think of more clinical things, he said, "I warned you it looked bad."

"Some look years old, like before the war."

They *had* happened years ago. Well before the war. "Those ain't nothing to be worried about."

As if she'd finally put together a puzzle, she cried out, "Thomas, someone whipped you when you were a boy."

He closed his eyes even though he couldn't see her reaction. "Yeah. A boy sometimes needs persuasion from his boss."

She paused, then said, "I'm sorry to say that cleaning these new wounds might cause you further pain."

Her voice sounded so aggrieved, so thin, he began to get a little worried.

After another endless moment, she gently touched his shoulder. "I'm going to get started. I'll try not to hurt you."

So far, both her voice and her touch had been sweet. He couldn't remember a time when he'd received so much care. "You won't hurt me."

"I might. If I'm too rough, let me know." She added, "It's just that, well, I think I'm going to need to clean them real good. Dirt and who knows what else are embedded in your skin."

Unfortunately, he knew exactly what else he'd been exposed to. The jail cots were infested with all sorts of vermin. "Do your worst, Miss Laurel. Just, well, whatever you do, please get started."

He heard her dip a cloth into the hot water she'd prepared, then felt a sharp sting as she placed it on one of his lash marks.

Unable to help himself, he flinched.

Her voice hardened. "Who did this to you?" She gasped. "Sheriff Jackson said there was some 'miscommunication' at the jailhouse, but who was it? Another prisoner? One of the guards?"

She sounded so incredulous. She was so naïve. Did she really have no idea what cruelties befell men in captivity? Swallowing back a curse as she rubbed hot, soapy water on another cut, he muttered, "You know there ain't no way I'm going to start telling you names."

"Why not?"

"Because it doesn't matter. It's all over with, thanks to you."

"I'm sorry it happened in the first place," she murmured as she washed his wounds with soap.

The abrasive soap stung. He welcomed the feeling. It cleared his head, helped him focus on the present and not the past. When she ventured to a particularly bad spot, he flinched again.

And she apologized.

"Come now, hasn't anyone ever told you regret is for fools? It happened and it's over with. Done."

He was right too. What had been done was done. Fretting and talking weren't going to change the facts. Especially since he aimed to live in relative peace and comfort for the next year.

Sounding resigned, she murmured, "Move sideways, please. You have a few welts I can't quite get to."

Feeling vaguely like a boy again, he moved to the side and then leaned forward. Closed his eyes as she continued her ministrations. Little by little, he realized the pain wasn't so bad if he concentrated on other things.

Like the smell of Laurel's skin, for example. Or the way her soft touch felt on his skin. Or the way he was in her kitchen and was going to be sleeping in a bed just down the hall from her. Not on a pallet in a barn or in a stinking jail cell.

As the minutes went by, Laurel also seemed to relax. She got up once to rinse out her bowl and get more hot water, then continued.

"Whatever man you are protecting never should have harmed you like this," she muttered. "I wish you'd tell me his name."

Still leaning over, he found himself smiling at the thought of her rushing to his aid. "I'm not exactly protecting anyone. Merely saving you from worrying about something you can't change."

She harrumphed. "Didn't he realize you aren't violent?"

She made him sound like a mule for sale. It almost made him smile. "I ain't violent, but I sure am no saint either. I fought in the war, you know."

"That was different. You had no choice. You fought for the Confederacy."

She made that sound like a good thing. If she were anyone else, he'd point out that their side lost. But if he did that, he was liable to hurt her feelings. He'd rather take another lash than do that.

Therefore, he continued to sit silently while she tended to his back. Again and again, he felt the heat of hot water and the sting of soap. Though he tried his best, he was unable to prevent a gasp and a flinch every now and then.

Her hands paused. After hovering over his shoulder, she at last laid a palm on his bare shoulder. "I really am sorry."

Knowing his suffering was almost as painful for her as it was for him, he attempted to think of something good. Something free and sweet. Anything not to focus on the movements of her hand or the sharp pain that surrounded each dab she made.

But the only thing he could seem to think about was her smiling at him when he was on the chain gang and mending her fence. Or the way she looked at him so sure and true when he was in that blasted cage and she told the judge she wanted him.

Or the way she'd said she trusted him.

But, of course, he shouldn't be thinking of such things. He shouldn't be giving in to his feelings toward Laurel Tracey.

He let his mind drift back to the family who had loved him and to the lifelong friendships he'd made in a prisoner of war camp. He had to depend on the good memories he already had when he needed them, not try to make more with a woman who would never be his.

16

THOMAS?" MISS LAUREL REPEATED, HER VOICE TURNING A bit panicked. "Are you all right?"

Blinking, Thomas realized he'd done it again. He'd taken refuge in memories. And in doing so, he'd scared his new employer just a little too much.

She was facing him now, her eyes filled with worry. Her hands were clenched together. The worn cloth she'd been cleansing his wounds with was lying abandoned on the tabletop, bloody and soiled.

He cleared his throat. "Forgive me. Sometime along the way I picked up a bad habit of indulging in daydreams."

Her eyes widened, almost as if she was surprised he would admit such a thing. Then she composed herself again. "Oh. Yes." She straightened, absently ran her hands over her gown. "I must admit to getting lost in thought a time or two myself."

Those brown eyes of hers flooded with concern and compassion, filling him with gratitude. Filling him with a want he didn't dare acknowledge. He tried to force himself to look away. Instead, he examined the rest of her face. Noticed that a tendril of her burnished hair had sprung free from its confines and rested on her temple. It teased him, practically taunting him to reach out and brush it back.

Before he could do such a thing, he turned away. Breathed deep.

And realized that Laurel Tracey was a veritable minefield of distractions he needed to stay away from. She smelled good. Like roses.

It drew him to her. It was the same scent he'd caught when she brought him water that day at the fence. That same scent they'd all caught.

The scent more than one man had talked about in lewd terms late that night in their cells.

He needed space. Distance.

He really needed to get his shirt back on.

Scrambling to his feet, he shoved one arm through a sleeve, then the other.

With a cry, Laurel attempted to halt his movements. Reaching out, she batted at his arm. "Thomas, no! I need to apply the ointment and bandage you."

He most certainly did not need her hands on him again. "Ointment and bandages aren't necessary." Jerking his shirt together, he fumbled with his buttons.

"What is wrong?" Distress filled her eyes. "Did I hurt you that badly?"

She had enough to worry about. The last thing she needed to be thinking about was hurting a convict's back. "I'm fine."

"Then what is wrong? Why are you being so stubborn?"

He exhaled. Thought about fibbing yet again. Then decided it might be best if he was a little more honest. Given the fact that they were going to be living in each other's pockets for the next year, if she had a better idea about his feelings, things might go easier between them in the future.

"Miss Laurel, forgive my bluntness, but the fact is, I'm only a man."

"Yes?"

He waved a hand at her. "I am a man and you . . . well, you are a beautiful woman."

She blinked. "I don't understand."

Of course she didn't. Gritting his teeth, he attempted to maintain his composure and conduct himself in a way that would do the officers who'd become his friends proud. "You see, the thing is . . . I've been in jail, miss."

"I know that."

Lord, have mercy. "At the risk of being blunt, I've got to admit that it's been a real long time since I've, uh, enjoyed any feminine companionship. So while I am sincerely grateful for your ministrations, I think from now on it would be best for both of us if I kept my shirt on around you." And if she didn't touch him again.

"Oh! Yes, well, of course. I see." Looking down, she began to gather the rest of the cloths she'd had out to clean his wounds.

"If you don't mind, I think it would be best for both of us if I went to my room now."

She turned, picked up the bowl and a towel, and walked to the basin. "Of course. It's the one with the folded blankets at the foot of the bed. If you need anything, please let me know. And if you get thirsty or anything, help yourself."

"Thank you. I'll do that."

Then, like the coward he was, he turned and walked up the stairs and started searching for his room.

The scent of beeswax and lemon oil captured his senses. Little by little, his head cleared and his muscles relaxed. Feeling more like himself, he walked down the empty hall. Heard his boots clatter on the wood floor that needed to be sanded and smoothed.

Then, to his misfortune, he looked into her bedroom. And stepped inside. Immediately he was besieged by everything that was Laurel, including that same scent. Saw her bed, covered with two quilts and a great many down pillows. On one side of the room stood a full-length mirror. And on a chair rested a discarded white chemise, the bodice threaded with a pale-blue ribbon.

Startled, he turned away, but it was too late.

The memory of seeing something he shouldn't have, of entering her bedroom, would now be burned brightly in his mind. He'd had no business there. He should have turned around the moment he'd realized this was her personal space, not staying for even a second.

Hardly aware of what he was doing again, he darted into one of the other bedrooms, saw the blankets she mentioned, and shut the door behind him.

He pulled off his boots and pulled off the shirt already sticking to his back. Then, clad only in his denims, he climbed onto the bed, curved his arms around a down pillow that smelled like sunshine, and stretched out on his stomach.

He'd just embarrassed himself, but he'd done worse things. Therefore, it didn't really matter.

What mattered was that he was in a room all by himself. He was holding a real pillow, and soft sheets and blankets and fresh, sweet-smelling air surrounded him. His wounds were clean.

More important, he wasn't running anymore. Not from his mistakes and not from his past. In short, he was in a better place than he'd been in a very long time.

With great care, he shifted, pulled over one of the light blankets Laurel had set out for him. As the soft fabric swooshed around his lower body, he enjoyed the clean scent that wafted upward and held him close.

It smelled like a faint memory, like a time before he'd learned to be afraid.

Feeling better and more content than he could remember being in years, Thomas gave thanks and counted his blessings. He had many. Even better than enjoying physical comforts, he knew where he was going to be sleeping tonight. He had a great many things to be thankful for indeed.

Only then did he allow his eyes to close and his mind to drift.

17

ONE FULL HOUR HAD PASSED SINCE THOMAS HAD PRACTI-
cally run from the kitchen. He'd cited exhaustion. Laurel had
been concerned that she'd done more harm than good to his back
and that he was suffering from her best efforts.

After going out to the barn to care for the animals, she
returned to the kitchen, poured a glass of cool cider, and worked
on mending. As she threaded her needle and repaired the torn
hem of a dress, she listened for Thomas to descend the stairs.

But as another hour passed, she realized he had retired for
the night.

She didn't blame him.

And she was used to being alone. She'd spent most of her days
and nights after her mother remarried alone. Even when Jerome
and Bess were living with her, they didn't spend time together.
She should have been used to her own company. She'd thought
she was.

But even after just a couple of days, Thomas Baker had
altered everything. She'd begun to look forward to his company,
even if so far it had been filled with more worry and stress than
anything else.

After putting away her mending, she sat on her sofa in the

sitting room and tried to come to terms with all that had transpired since she'd stood at the window to watch Thomas work
with the other convicts. She'd freed him, Jerome and Bess had
left, and a calf had died. Then they'd returned to town together.
She'd become part of a team. Half of a partnership that was
built out of necessity but seemed on the verge of turning into
something else too.

She didn't know how to stop the way she was starting to feel
about Thomas. Didn't know if she was capable of stopping.

And if she didn't?

Well, the consequences would alter her life, and that was
almost too much to take in. Maybe far too much to take in.

Laurel woke on the sofa with a start the next morning when she
heard Thomas open and shut the front door. Embarrassed that
he'd seen her asleep, she ran upstairs, changed her dress, and
washed her face. Next she went to the kitchen, made coffee and
flapjacks, and waited for Thomas to return to the house.

When he did, he was pleasant yet distant.

"I fed the animals and milked Bonnet," he said as he set her
egg basket next to her. "I even gathered these. Everything looks to
be in good order."

"Thank you." Pointing to the serving plate next to her range,
she said, "I made flapjacks."

"These look real good." He grabbed a plate and placed three
on it.

"Go ahead and eat. I'll fry you a couple of eggs too."

"Thank you."

She washed two eggs, then cracked them into a hot pan, all

while casting furtive looks his way. He was eating methodically, his attention solely focused on his flapjacks.

When she placed the eggs on his plate, he thanked her again but said nothing more.

Her stomach began to feel like it was in knots. "Would you like anything else to eat?"

"No, Miss Tracey. This is more than enough."

"Are you sure?"

"You always give me more food than I got in a day in jail, miss. It's plenty for me."

"Ah." Placing one flapjack on her plate, she sat down and nibbled a bit of it. It tasted like sawdust.

Pushing it away, she said, "Is your back hurting you this morning?"

"My back is mending," he said quickly. "You won't need to bathe it again."

Though she realized he was trying to ease her worries, she still felt a little hurt. "I didn't mind helping you."

Thomas set down his fork. "I'm here to work for you. Not be tended to."

Feeling like there was nothing she could say to erase the unease that was festering between them, she got up again and washed her dish.

A couple of minutes later, Thomas set his dish on the counter next to her. "Thank you for breakfast. I'm going to go back out to the barn now. I have something I'd like to do before we head out on our ride."

"All right, Sergeant."

When she heard the kitchen door close, she felt more alone than ever. Not for the first time, she wished she'd been blessed with sisters or cousins. An aunt. Some woman who was smarter than she was in the ways of the world, who would freely give advice and offer suggestions. Like what to do about Thomas.

But what would this mystery woman say or counsel her to do? Laurel was fairly sure there was no correct protocol to follow when it came to developing a relationship with a scarred and secretive former prisoner.

Tired of waiting and stewing, she picked up her broom, went out to the front porch, and pretended to sweep off some of the debris and dust that had gathered there overnight. It was a rather silly task, and a poor use of her time. She had far too many other things to do besides pretending to sweep while actually spying on her worker.

But she couldn't help herself.

Soon she realized Thomas was cleaning out the barn. Velvet was tethered to a hitching post and Bonnet was bawling mournfully in one of the holding pens her father had built a year or two before the war. Scattered in front of the structure were saddles and blankets, jars and buckets, and a hundred other tools and implements men had stored in its depths over the years.

She went out there and offered to help him, but he brushed off her offer like it was a painful thing.

Now she was back on the porch, reduced to spying on him again.

She was just thinking about taking him some water when she noticed two riders approaching.

Resting a hand on her forehead, she tried to see who it was, but all she could see was an appaloosa and a paint. Both horses were stepping lively. The faces of the men astride them were hidden by dark Stetsons.

Glad she was at least wearing a clean calico, she stood motionless and watched the riders come closer.

Seconds later, Thomas exited the barn and walked to her side. "Who's here?"

"I'm not sure."

He nodded, his expression intent as he watched the riders' progress. Minutes later, he sighed. "One of the men is Sheriff Jackson."

"Maybe he has some news about the calf."

"I hope so. I hope it's that and not the twenty-five other real good reasons he has to be here."

Realizing Thomas was referencing the amount of money she'd paid for him to be set free, Laurel looked at him dubiously. "The transaction has already taken place, and Will knows I'm happy with how things have turned out. Everyone should." Herself, for one.

Thomas snorted. "People don't care about feelings, Miss Laurel. They're going to revel in the fact that you made a mistake."

"But I didn't."

"Even if you think you didn't, they won't care. Their minds were made up about me the moment they saw me in prison rags."

"They might have been wary of you, but they'll change their minds."

"Not necessarily."

"They will. After all, lots of people saw how helpful you were yesterday when you helped me take the calf to town."

"For some people, what they saw will mean nothing. They'll only care about what I am."

She wasn't sure what more she could say to Thomas to ease his mind—or their relationship. Since it was doubtful that he was going to be of a mind to listen to anything she said, Laurel decided to focus on the approaching visitors. Now that they were fairly close, she recognized the man by Sheriff Jackson's side. "The other man is Landon Marshall."

"Your neighbor and friend, right?"

She nodded. Remembering the way Landon had spoken to her in town, and how vaguely she had described her relationship with him to Thomas, she said, "We've, uh, recently drifted apart."

Thomas studied her. "Usually a person is a friend or he isn't," he drawled.

"Our relationship isn't that easy to define." Kind of like another relationship she was in.

"Huh."

She thought that sentiment said it all. The man's appearance was certainly unexpected. After she'd refused his suit, he had stopped visiting her. Then, of course, there was what had happened in town. He hadn't liked her standing up to him at all.

When they were a mere hundred or so yards away, Sheriff Jackson raised a hand.

She raised a hand in return, taking note of their solemn expressions.

Thomas must have taken notice of their serious looks, too, because his expression turned less combative and far more protective. He stepped a bit in front of her, almost like he was attempting to shield her from whatever was about to take place.

Though she knew she probably shouldn't, she allowed herself to relax. Maybe the tension between them was about to ease.

When the men drew their horses to a stop and dismounted, Laurel moved around Thomas to greet them. "Hello, Sheriff Jackson, Landon."

"Good day, Laurel. Baker," Sheriff Jackson said.

"Miss Tracey," Landon said, tipping his hat as his gaze strayed toward Thomas, who was looming behind her. She didn't need to see him to know he was staring at Landon.

She turned awkwardly and tried to smile at each of them. "Landon, this is Sergeant Thomas Baker. My new hand."

"I've been concerned about you. I hope you are faring all right." Landon didn't so much as even glance in Thomas's direction.

Thomas stiffened by her side but didn't say anything.

Eager to get to the point of their visit and then send them on their way, Laurel said, "Did you discover what happened to the calf, Will?"

The sheriff shook his head. "I'm afraid not. Doc promised to look at the little thing, but he hasn't had a chance yet. It might have simply died of natural causes."

"And it decided to die while on her doorstep?" Thomas asked, doubt thick in his voice. "I find that hard to believe. Someone is attempting to frighten Miss Tracey."

"We don't know that for sure," Landon said. "After all, a good Samaritan could have brought it over."

Thomas blinked. "Really? Like who? You?"

"Of course it wasn't me. But that doesn't mean it wasn't another of Laurel's friends." Looking at him derisively, Landon added, "Here in Sweetwater, we look out for each other. We're a close-knit community made up of good people. You're probably not familiar with such relationships."

Thomas lifted his chin. "Even if a friend did leave the calf, I'm not real fond of the idea of someone dropping off dead animals on Miss Tracey's doorstep in the middle of the night, Marshall."

"You almost sound as if you *are* insinuating that I brought her the animal."

"I'm guessing you had as much opportunity as anyone."

"I wouldn't have done such a thing. I want the future of this ranch to be as profitable as anyone, and killing any of its cattle would hardly make sense." Crossing his arms over his chest, he added, "I'm also not fond of convicts living in such close proximity to my neighbor."

"Who would you rather see here? You?"

"Of course me. At least I would not be attempting to take advantage of her."

"And how would I be doing that?"

"Don't act so innocent," Landon drawled, disdain lacing his tone. "You probably don't know the first thing about being around decent women. But if you harm one hair on her head, you will definitely regret it."

Thomas stepped forward. "Are you threatening me?"

Before Landon could reply, Laurel raised her hands. "Gentlemen, please stop! I can speak for myself."

"You shouldn't have to, Laurel," Landon said. "You need a real man to speak for you."

Realizing that Thomas was barely holding on to his temper, Laurel ignored Landon and turned to the sheriff, who had been noticeably silent. "Thank you for coming out all this way to check on me. It was real kind of you to go to so much trouble."

Sheriff Jackson's expression turned pensive. "I hate to tell you this, but we didn't ride over here to check on you or talk about the dead calf." Rubbing the back of his neck, he said, "You see, something else has come up."

Before she even realized she was doing it, she stepped closer to Thomas. "What's happened now?" Thinking quickly, she asked, "Does it have to do with Sergeant Baker's freedom?"

"No. That's done, much to your stepsiblings' dismay, I should add." Smiling a bit wryly, he said, "They were in quite a state when old Alan Corntree picked them up in his wagon two days ago."

She almost grinned back at him. Mr. Corntree was a peddler who drove a donkey cart around the area in the summer. She doubted Bess or Jerome had ever deigned to give that man a second look, much less speak to him. And now they had been reduced to accepting a ride in his wagon. She had a feeling that set their high horses back a notch or two.

"Now that you've had time to think about it some more, Sheriff, do you think there's any chance one of them could have harmed that calf?" Thomas asked. "They've been after Laurel to sell. I'm not sure how they would have managed it, but maybe they resorted to trying to scare her into it."

Sheriff Jackson's expression hardened. "Their involvement is doubtful, but I haven't ruled it out yet. They have rooms at a boardinghouse, and I mean to keep my eye on them." He cleared his throat. "But we came to talk to you about something else that happened. Last night."

"Yes?" Laurel asked.

"One of my outlying storage buildings was ransacked," Landon said. "It was completely cleaned out."

Sheriff Jackson added, "Several items of note were taken. Some extra equipment, grain, and a trunk with some ammunition in it."

Thomas raised his eyebrows. "You stored ammunition in an outlying building?"

"I had my reasons for keeping it there," Landon said.

"Which were?" Thomas asked as he stepped closer to Landon.

Landon glared. "The point is that the ammunition is now gone."

"We suspect it might have been the squatters you've been worried about who've been coming onto your property from time to time," Sheriff Jackson interjected smoothly. "Any chance you saw them yesterday, Laurel?"

"No, Sheriff. I haven't seen anyone for days."

"I rode much of the ranch yesterday," Thomas said. "I found evidence of someone being in the north pasture, but nothing else."

"Interesting that this theft happened after you arrived," Landon said.

"What is your point?"

"I don't have a point. I'm merely making an observation."

Thomas looked at the sheriff. "Did you come out here to accuse me of raiding this man's shed?"

"Not at all," Sheriff Jackson said. "We just wanted to let you know what happened so you could keep your eyes open."

"I'll do that. If I see something amiss, I'll be sure to let you know."

Landon coughed. "I can't see how we can start relying on a man like you."

"Like me?"

"Don't pretend to act so surprised. You must have known your reputation would be in tatters after you went and got yourself arrested."

"I didn't go and get myself anything."

Sheriff Jackson sighed. "Gentlemen, this is beyond enough."

Landon stepped closer to Laurel. "This is exactly the kind of thing I was worried about when we talked in town. You are at far too many people's mercies, living alone like this. You need someone looking after you. You're just a woman, you know."

"Landon—"

He smiled as he cupped her cheek. "You know I'm right."

"I have help now."

"You wouldn't have needed to hire a convict if you'd simply let me help you in the first place," he murmured. "Let me help you, honey."

She felt the hard stare of Thomas's appraising eyes on them as she stepped back from Landon's touch.

"Watch yourself, Mr. Marshall," Thomas growled.

But Landon ignored Thomas's warning as if he weren't there. He ran his fingers down her arm. "Are you afraid of me? Don't be afraid. You know I don't want to do anything besides make you happy."

"I'm not afraid of you." However, though she wasn't afraid, she wasn't completely sure her happiness was the main thing on his mind. Stepping a little farther out of his reach, she eyed him carefully. "We've known each other for a good long while, Landon. Let's keep things the way they are."

"I'd love to do that. And since we're still such good friends, let me have you over one night soon. Eva will make us supper."

"Thank you for the invitation. Maybe I'll take you up on it one day soon."

"How about tomorrow?"

"Tomorrow?"

"I'll come fetch you, say, around five?"

Before she could accept, Thomas interrupted. "There's no need to pick her up. I'll drive her wherever she needs to go."

They all three looked at him in surprise.

"I don't want to burden you, Sergeant," she protested. Plus, though it made no sense, she felt a little apprehensive about involving him in her invitation.

He shook his head slowly as his gaze warmed. "Now, Miss Laurel, don't you be forgetting what we talked about," he drawled, his voice suddenly sounding a bit like honey. "I'm your hired hand. You're supposed to burden me."

"I don't believe driving me around is what either of us intended for you to be doing when I hired you."

"That don't matter. I'd be happy to drive you wherever you need to go. Always."

His offer was so sweetly worded, she couldn't resist smiling.

However, Landon didn't look all that enchanted by the idea. "There is no need for you to drive Laurel anywhere. I'll fetch her tomorrow evening."

Before Laurel could comment, Thomas spoke again. "No, sir. With squatters and so forth creating disturbances, I'd feel better if I was looking out for Miss Tracey as much as possible."

Before either Laurel or Landon could respond, Sheriff Jackson clapped his hands. "Well, that's settled. Turns out this little visit has been productive in more ways than one," he said brightly. "We got out our news and Mr. Marshall got his wish." He tipped his hat with a smirk. "We'll be on our way. We've got two more ranches to visit. And, Laurel, when I hear something about your calf, I'll let you know."

"Thank you, Will."

Landon didn't look nearly as pleased but tipped his hat as well. "Until tomorrow, then."

"Until then. Thank you both for coming out."

"I wanted to," Landon said, "even if I'd had no theft. You know how worried I've been, thinking about you living here like this."

Thomas stayed still and intent until they mounted their horses and took off. Only when their images were blurred in the distance did he speak again. "Does that happen often?"

"Does what happen? Does the sheriff come out often to pay me a house call? No."

Still staring off into the distance, he shook his head. "I'm talking about you getting asked out by your neighbor."

"No." She felt her cheeks heat even though she knew she had

no cause for embarrassment. "Mr. Marshall has asked me for a drive before, but never invited me to supper."

"I wonder why he's asking you now."

Laurel looked at him curiously. Thomas's posture hadn't eased. He was still standing alert in his shiny new boots and dark denims. The new, stiff cowboy clothes should have made him seem awkward. Maybe weak. Perhaps like a greenhorn. Instead, his clothing emphasized his toughness. She was starting to see that, unlike with most men, clothes did not affect him in the slightest. He looked just as dangerous and aloof dressed in a new chambray and denims as he had in his prison garb.

She swallowed. "To tell you the truth, I think he was always afraid to ask me to supper because of Bess and Jerome."

"He wasn't a big fan of theirs?"

"He was not. I think he was afraid they'd join me," she said. "They were truly insufferable." Before Thomas started asking more questions about Landon, she gestured toward the barn. "I know you've been doing some cleaning, but I think we should saddle up the horses now. I want us to check on the cattle. We can be back in time for our noon meal. I'll go put on a better bonnet and meet you in the barn."

Just as she was about to turn away, he called out, "Miss Tracey?"

"Yes?"

"Are you in the market for a man?"

She wasn't sure if she was or not. But because she was all too aware of the way Thomas was looking at her, as though she was something to be sought after, she stated uneasily, "I don't believe that's any of your business."

"I reckon it isn't. But it would be good to know."

His words made her feel flustered. Maybe a little warm. "That is something you won't have to worry about, Sergeant. I'm simply a woman trying to hang on to my family's ranch."

"Do you really believe that's all you are?"

"I believe I'd rather not discuss my personal life anymore," she said. She didn't like the idea of making choices about her future marital status that weren't based on love. She really didn't like the idea of thinking about making a future with a man who was nothing like the man she was walking beside.

"You might aim to pretend you're ordinary, but nothing could be further from the truth."

His words were soft. Kind. Still altogether too personal.

She ignored that familiar flutter of awareness as she ran inside and switched bonnets.

Later, when Thomas easily lifted her onto Velvet's saddle, she did her best to appear unaffected by his touch.

But instead of easing the tension between them, it seemed to increase it.

After assuring himself she was situated comfortably, he took hold of her father's rifle and mounted the gelding.

"Lead on, miss. Wherever you want to go, I'll follow."

Laurel motioned Velvet forward, trying all the while not to think about how his statement made her feel.

18

THOMAS HAD BEEN AN EXCELLENT HORSEMAN AND A PARticularly good soldier. He'd ridden across half of Tennessee and Kentucky during the war without complaint.

He'd charged into battles, sure the whole time he wouldn't survive. He'd also been sent on scouting missions, walking through swamps and woods and enemy lines to obtain information. Once he even pretended to be a Yankee lieutenant to procure vital coordinates for Major Kelly.

He'd ridden beside officers without a hint of uneasiness or self-consciousness. Even when he served under Captain Monroe, he felt fairly sure of his abilities. He attacked each task with the intention of doing his best and hoping it would be good enough. That said, he had many faults—that couldn't be denied.

He was impatient and could be emotional. He was barely literate and shamefully ungentlemanly. He was definitely not a good choice to be any woman's suitor.

But now, as he accompanied Laurel Tracey across her ranch, Thomas was starting to wonder if he knew himself at all. For the first time in forever, he felt like a weak-kneed greenhorn. He was antsy and uneasy. A sixth sense told him something was about to happen. He just didn't know what it could be.

Because of that, he kept gazing around their perimeter as though they were on a dangerous mission.

No, he felt as if he were a rattler, ready to spring at a moment's notice. Or a skittish colt, wary of everything in sight. It was disturbing, and more than a little unsettling . . . until he realized he wasn't worried about them being ambushed.

No, he was dwelling on the woman beside him. It was she who occupied his mind and kept him on his toes. The problem was, of course, that he was too conscious of Laurel Tracey.

He doubted she could brush a strand of hair away from her face without his notice.

Though his infatuation was his fault, he perversely wanted to put the blame firmly on her shoulders. It was Laurel's fault he was so smitten. She was too pretty, too kind, too delicate. Too everything.

He was running out of ideas about how to treat her too. When she'd purchased his release, he intended to push aside his attraction to her and simply treat her with the respect she deserved. Keep it as a business arrangement.

But last night everything had changed.

The feel of her hands on his back had ignited a need he'd forgotten he'd ever possessed. Her tenderness and care had washed over his heart the way the warm water had soothed his skin.

And those feelings had encouraged him to think about all the wishes and dreams he buried when his parents and brother died so long ago. Then, just when he had a handle on himself, he had gone and accidentally spied her bedroom. That hadn't helped matters one bit. He hadn't been able to get out of there fast enough.

A night of fitful sleep, as all along he assumed she was down the hall from him, had only sent the rest of his body on alert. He'd lain in bed on his stomach, wishing it had been his sore, aching back that occupied his mind. But instead of reviewing his injuries, Thomas spent hours remembering the conversations he and Laurel had shared.

By the time he got up with the sun, he'd almost convinced himself he had the two of them firmly back in place in his mind. She was the owner of the ranch. He was her hired hand. For one year he would do his best to help her keep the ranch afloat. In three hundred sixty-five days, he would leave and never see her again.

That was what was supposed to happen. Somehow, over time, he was sure he was going to accept that and be fine with it.

After finding her asleep on the sofa, he vowed to continue this plan. It almost felt as though it was possible.

But then Sheriff Jackson and Landon Marshall arrived, and he saw the way Marshall gazed at Laurel.

Then and there, Thomas had realized there was no way he was going to be able to sit by and watch another man court her. It had come on suddenly, but the possessiveness he'd felt had been so strong he didn't even attempt to tamp it down. Some emotions couldn't be hidden.

That was why, when Marshall asked Laurel to come to his home for supper tomorrow, his first instinct had been to step completely in front of her and refuse the man's proposal.

He'd had to make do with gritting his teeth while Marshall cajoled and Sheriff Jackson looked on like a doting father. The only bright spot was that he'd made sure he was the one who was going to take her back and forth. At least then she would be under his protection.

Watching Marshall put his hand on Laurel had been the last straw, but somehow he managed not to shove him away from her, letting her manage him herself.

Still, when the men left, Laurel hadn't been happy with him. He didn't care. He aimed to see her safe. Unfortunately for her, the only place he could be sure she was completely safe was by his side.

All the time.

Now, as they rode, Laurel pointed out various landmarks he might have missed on the ride he'd taken alone. Thomas pretended to be attentive, but all he really did was attempt to figure out a way for her to accept him as a suitor one day.

It was likely only another one of his daydreams, but he couldn't resist imagining such a thing actually happening.

"As you can see, the creek isn't wide, but it stays filled most of the year," Laurel called, bringing him back to the present.

"Most?" He raised his eyebrows. Now that she'd caught his attention, he wasn't real pleased with the news she was giving him.

"We have dry spells from time to time, but that's rare."

He glanced to his right and left but didn't see anything other than more of the same rolling hills. "Where do you run the cattle when that happens?"

"There's a good-sized pond on our southwest. The family that owns it is fair and doesn't object if other ranchers use it from time to time. My father and brother used to take the herd there when needed."

"That's generous of them."

"Indeed. They're good people, but older. They wouldn't be a lot of help if I had to lead my herd to their property. Thank the Lord, I haven't had to do that yet."

He hated the thought of her having to do so much on her own. To cover up his unease, he teased, "Are you thanking the Lord because you don't like the terrain or don't like moving cows?"

She grinned. "Both, I suppose. I have no problem with managing one or two or three cows at a time. When they are in a large group? I can't explain it, but they still intimidate me."

"That's not so surprising. Rounding up cattle can be arduous for the most experienced cowboy."

"Thank you for not saying it's difficult *for a woman*."

"I would be lying if I didn't admit to feeling concerned about a little thing like you taking on so much. You could get hurt."

Even in the broad sunlight, he could tell her cheeks flushed. "Only you would say I'm little."

Before he could reassure her, Laurel fanned her face. "Forgive me. I'm not usually so eager to fish for compliments."

"I never thought you were. And you weren't fishing. You were just being your usual modest self."

Smiling, she tucked her head. He let her take the lead again, happy to lazily scan the area while she told him more of the land's history.

About twenty minutes later, they rounded the top of a hill. "Here they are," she said as they looked down on the small herd of cattle, their brown-and-white hides standing out against the pale-green grass like Easter eggs.

"Good-looking cattle," he said.

"They're in good health. Some of them must be farther up the creek, but their numbers are increasing. Altogether we have twenty now." She blanched. "Would have been twenty-one."

"Don't think of that," he said quickly. "It does no good to dwell on the past."

She swallowed. "You're right. Well, tomorrow or the next day we'll need to guide all of them to another pasture." She turned to him. "I just realized herding cattle might be a new experience for you. I hope cattle don't intimidate you too."

"Not yet, miss. Those cows and I should get along just fine."

"You sound as if you've worked with your fair share of cattle."

"Some." Eyeing a mother heifer nudging her calf, he continued, "My father was a blacksmith. I was used to being around animals at a young age, and I worked in a livery before I went into the army, where I also worked with horses. And when I first got out, I did some odd jobs, one on a ranch."

"You've always been a hard worker, haven't you?"

"Learning quickly helped garner me extra nights on a cot. I've never been a fan of sleeping on the ground."

All traces of humor vanished from her expression. "I'm so sorry, Sergeant. You've had such a difficult time of it. Even after the war you were jailed."

"That was my fault. I was attempting to make some money in the wrong way and lost in a poker game to a pair of powerful men. I deserved what I got."

"You certainly didn't deserve to be beaten."

"Maybe not. However, it's all over now." He smiled her way. "Thanks to you."

"Don't thank me too much. You're going to be working hard for me over the next year."

"I'm planning on it. The hard work will do me good."

Their conversation turned easy as they continued on, riding along the filled creek bed. Eventually they slowed their pace to a walk. The sun was bright overhead and sent the temperatures skyrocketing. The shade from trees by the creek was a welcome relief.

Velvet whickered, showing her appreciation. Yellow, on the other hand, pranced a bit, illustrating his displeasure with the slower pace.

Thomas had been about to suggest they dismount and allow

the horses to drink, but he quickly discarded that idea. Until Yellow got over whatever was making him so skittish, he would likely be difficult to control.

Since Laurel didn't mention a need to stop, Thomas stayed quiet and concentrated on examining the area, looking for traces of squatters. He was so focused on tracking he only half listened as Laurel continued talking about the history of her family's land ownership.

"Oh!" she called out, interrupting herself.

"What?"

"Oh no!" she whispered as she motioned Velvet into a canter.

"Miss Laurel, what is it? Please slow down and—" He stopped talking as he caught sight of what had her in its grip.

At least six cows were lying on the ground in front of them. From the position of their bodies and the flies buzzing about them, it was obvious they were dead—and that they hadn't died of natural causes.

"Stay here," he barked as he dismounted, then hurriedly tied his reins to a nearby tree.

She ignored him.

More quickly than he had thought a woman could move in long skirts, Laurel leapt off Velvet and hurried to his side without bothering to tether her horse.

Thomas didn't know whether to order her to see to her mare or reach for her hand. Ultimately, he decided to do neither. He needed to focus on the poor cows and attempt to discern what had happened. As he approached, he noticed a pungent smell first. It wasn't death as such; it had more of a copper tint to it.

It was the scent of blood, the scent he would know anywhere, thanks to three years of standing in the middle of bloody battlefields.

Instinctively, he turned to the horses. If he'd been riding his old mount, Settler would have been dancing awkwardly and breathing hard. Thomas was having a difficult time not reacting to the scent of blood himself, even after all this time.

It was impossible to breathe in the scent and not be reminded of death and danger. However, neither mount looked ready to bolt. Their nostrils were flared and their ears were standing up, alert. But beyond that they seemed calm enough.

Stepping closer, he resolutely pushed the scent from his mind and scanned the ground for the evidence he was looking for. Eventually he did find blood, but it wasn't from either a bullet or a blade. Instead, it looked as if the steers were bleeding from their mouths.

It looked to him like they'd been poisoned.

The hairs on the back of his neck stood up. As Laurel said before, killing cattle made no sense. Especially in war-torn times like these, cattle were a valuable asset. No man he'd ever come into contact with, no matter what issues he might have with his enemies, would seek vengeance by killing five head. That was a waste of good money and a squandering of thousands of future dollars.

"This is terrible. No, it's worse than that. It's . . . it's a trag-edy," Laurel whispered. "I don't understand how someone could do something like this."

"I was thinking the same thing."

"What happened to them?" she whispered.

"My guess is they were poisoned."

She looked around. "Thomas, over there. What's that?"

A paper had been nailed to a tree next to the creek. Thomas opened it.

"It's a note. It says, 'Next time the kerosene will go in the creek.'"

Just as Laurel gasped, they heard a rustling in the distance, followed by a loud crack.

Unfortunately, Thomas was as familiar with that noise as he was with the scent of blood. Grabbing her arm, he forced her to the ground and covered her body with his own.

"Thomas!" she called out. "I can hardly breathe. I'm lying facedown in the dirt."

"Settle," he ordered as he braced his hands on either side of her, lifting his chest and shoulders so he could scan the distance.

But instead of serving to calm her, she fought him with a cry. Her efforts were futile. He was far bigger and heavier.

"Laurel, calm yourself. Someone fired a weapon," he said in a low voice.

To his surprise, she stopped thrashing. "Do you think someone is hunting?"

"Maybe." He shifted slightly, giving her a bit more space. "Could be one of those squatters you mentioned you saw."

She shivered.

Though he longed to hold her close and comfort her, military training kicked in. He concentrated on their surroundings, attempted to find a place where Laurel could remain safe and out of danger.

A minute passed. Another two.

Just when he was about to exhale, he heard another rustling, followed by another sharp crack. As Laurel's shoulders began to shake, he bit the inside of his cheek so he wouldn't let out a stream of the vilest curse words he could think of.

Whoever was out there was coming closer.

19

SOMEONE WAS SHOOTING AT THEM. RATHER THAN ANYONE hunting, it was likely whoever had poisoned six of her cows, and they had now set their sights on her and Thomas.

Well, Laurel thought so. It was hard to know for sure, seeing that she was currently pinned underneath her hired hand. He had his elbows propped up on the hard earth, his rifle clutched in his hands. From what she could tell—and she couldn't ascertain much from her position—his focus was on whoever was firing shots.

She, on the other hand, couldn't seem to concentrate on anything other than the fact that she was lying on the ground underneath a very large man.

She was sweating profusely. It was making her hair stick to her neck and her durable riding dress feel like it weighed two hundred pounds. A smattering of gravel and rocks was digging into her palms and cheek. What little bit of air she could inhale was infused with dust and grime.

She should be in pain. She should be terribly uncomfortable.

Instead, as each second passed, all Laurel could seem to think about was how Thomas's skin smelled of soap and leather. How he was holding his body firm and still, seemingly from sheer force of will.

She realized then that he'd probably participated in many such battles. His body was conditioned to respond to danger.

After several minutes passed in silence, she whispered, "Are they still out there?"

"I can't tell," he muttered under his breath as he shifted again, obviously attempting to cover her even more completely.

There was no way she was going to let Thomas get shot while trying to protect her. They both needed to move to safety. "Thomas, I need to get up."

"Stop squirming."

Feeling certain that she would rather face whatever was about to happen head-on than continue to lie underneath him, Laurel pushed against his torso with her shoulders.

He groaned. "Laurel—"

"No, this won't do," she protested. Though the way she was half squashed on the ground, there was no doubt her words came out garbled.

"I'm trying to keep you safe, woman."

"I understand that, but you are also stifling me. I'm finding it difficult to breathe."

He shifted, somehow managing to cover her body even more. "If you are alive, that's all I care about."

Though she appreciated his gallantry, she knew she wouldn't be able to live with herself if he died shielding her. Thinking of the only thing that might encourage him to ease up a bit, she hissed, "I'm not going to be alive if I suffocate. Please. Allow me some space to breathe."

At last he moved, but it was with obvious reluctance.

"There," he said when he shifted a few inches to his right. Now he was only covering a portion of her body. "Inhale."

The fresh, clean air felt like a gift to her lungs. She breathed in deep. "Can you see who's out there?"

"No. This old rifle is better than nothing, but it doesn't have the scope my old Winchester did." Ruefully, he said, "I'd give a whole lot to have it in my hand right about now."

She was wishing she'd brought her brother's rifle. She wasn't a sure shot, but she could certainly handle a weapon well enough to feel safer with one in her hand.

Glad that he hadn't yet pushed her back down, she kept herself close to the ground as she took several more fortifying breaths. She also scanned the horizon, silently hoping the people who'd already done so much harm had already left.

Beside her, Thomas was looking intently to the west, his eyes squinting in the sun. "Down," he commanded.

She pressed herself flat again, but not before she saw a sparkle of metal in reflection off the creek. Seconds after, she heard another crack of a gun.

"Whoever it is, he's closer," Thomas said. "We need to get you out of here."

"We both need to get out of here, Sergeant."

"I thought we'd moved to calling each other by our first names."

She didn't want to waste time verbally sparring. Instead, she stayed silent, hoping and praying she would be able to follow whatever instruction he was about to give her.

After another minute passed, he tilted his head toward Velvet and Yellow, who for some reason hadn't run off. "How well can you ride?"

"As well as you need me to."

"Good." After looking in the direction from where the shots

were fired, he said, "On my mark, we're going to rush to our horses, mount them quickly, and race to the house."

"I can do that."

"Laurel, when you're on that horse, you keep your body low and ride fast. As fast as you've ever ridden in your life," he continued, his voice rough with worry. "You understand?"

She was getting nervous now. Doubting her abilities. But she couldn't let him know that. "I understand."

He looked at her again. "If I fall behind for some reason, you continue without me. Don't wait."

No, that didn't sound good. "Thomas—"

"I'm real glad you're calling me by name now, darlin', but what I need to hear is your promise."

"I can't promise you that. If you're hurt—"

"You can. You must. Promise me." He paused, obviously waiting.

"What kind of woman would I be to leave you?"

His tone became more emphatic. "I'm trying to keep you alive, Laurel." Before she could protest again, he glared at her. "On three, move," he bit out. "Promise me you'll do it."

"I promise."

"Thank you." His blue eyes scanned her face, softening for the briefest of moments, then he spoke. "One."

She tensed, pressing her palms against the rough terrain. The corner of a sharp rock dug into her skin.

"Two."

Her mouth went dry as she moved to a crouch.

"Three."

Not daring to focus on anything but her promise, she sprang to her feet, turned with a stumble, then rushed toward Velvet.

As she ran over the rough earth, dust and gravel lifting into a cloud around her, she concentrated on making it to her mare.

She felt Thomas's presence behind her. Still shielding her. Still urging her forward.

The horse was skittish, looking at her with one wary eye, pawing the ground with one hoof.

"Velvet," she whispered.

As she reached out a hand for the reins, another crack filled the air. Closer to the horses than before. Velvet whinnied, then reared in fright. Laurel scrambled backward, ducking to avoid being inadvertently struck.

When Laurel straightened, reaching out a hand to try to calm the mare, the horse whinnied again, then tore off into the distance.

When Yellow cried out, then stumbled, Laurel cried out, too, as Thomas attempted to calm the spooked horse. But just as he got the reins loosened, the intruder fired again, this time even closer.

Kicking his hooves, Yellow let loose a sharp cry. Thomas jumped back, barely preventing himself from getting kicked.

"Thomas!" Laurel called out.

"I'm okay," he said around his panting as Yellow reared and snorted, then darted to their right. Seconds later, the horse raced away, a cloud of dust rising around his hooves.

Though Laurel ached to be tough, it was disheartening to see their mounts disappear like birds in flight.

They had nothing now.

Hooves pounded the ground, the vibration feeling like a train was approaching. Their attackers were much closer now. At least two riders by the sound of it.

Thomas reached for her, pulling her back to his side as they took shelter next to the creek's bank.

Fearing the worst, afraid as those who seemed to enjoy preying on them drew near, Laurel closed her eyes and silently cried out to the only One who could help them.

Why, God? she asked. *Why would you take away my parents, my brother, my future, my cattle, but then bring me a helper in Thomas . . . only to take even that away?*

What was she going to do? The situation felt so hopeless. She'd never felt so alone. Tears flooded her eyes and began to trickle down her cheeks.

"Don't, Laurel," Thomas said roughly.

Confused by his words, she turned, only to realize he was now crouched and pulling her against him as he guided her next to the deceptive safety of a pair of mesquite trees.

"Don't you start crying," he ordered.

"I'm trying not to."

"Good. I need you tough now. Don't you dare give up on me."

"I won't." After a few endless minutes passed, she realized she could no longer hear the riders.

"I think they're gone," he said, affirming her thoughts.

His voice was flat. She imagined that he, too, was realizing that not only could their attackers come back, but they were in the middle of her ranch in heat that had now risen to at least a hundred degrees.

"It'll be okay."

"You sound so certain."

"I've been in worse situations. I'm not worried."

His words were so welcome, so needed, that she allowed herself to lean against him, taking refuge in his solid form, even though her head reminded her there was little he could do to ensure their protection or propel them to safety.

"Breathe, Laurel."

Dutifully, she did as he bid. But even the intake of oxygen did no good. The air was so hot it felt like it was burning a path down her insides each time she inhaled.

After a few seconds, Thomas shifted and wrapped one strong arm around her shoulders. She felt the hard muscles of his arms and chest against her curves. His scent surrounded her once more. Leather and man.

Against her will, she found comfort in it. Even though it was all too much. Too intimate for two people who really didn't know each other all that well.

Nonetheless, she leaned into the comfort and took refuge in it. "I'm scared," she admitted. "I'm trying to be brave, but I fear I'm all out of bravery. I'm sorry."

"Don't be sorry." Rubbing her shoulder and arm, he said quietly, "Matter of fact, I'd be real concerned if you weren't scared."

Something in his voice caught her in its grip. Was it the thread of doubt? The thin wavering of his confidence? "Are you?"

"Scared? A little bit."

Laurel twisted to examine his expression. When she realized he was being completely serious, she blurted, "I'm scared we won't get home. Is—is that what you are afraid of too?"

"I'm afraid someone is going to try to hurt you again and I won't be able to prevent it. I'm afraid my best efforts won't be enough."

They heard another thundering of hooves, sending them both back to high alert. But to Laurel's surprise, the two riders were moving away from them. "They're not circling back toward us," she said after a moment.

"It seems so."

"Why would they do that? Now that we're here without horses, it would be so easy to finish the job."

"I couldn't say why they're leaving," he said after a pause. "Perhaps they only wanted to scare us, and then scare the horses as well to strand us."

"That makes sense." Poisoning cattle was bad enough. But horses, of course, were even more valuable than cattle. No one shot at horses, unless their intention was to run them off.

He tilted his head back so he could see her whole expression. "You doing all right now?"

"Yes. I think so."

"Good." Carefully, he removed his arm and stood up. "You're right about all this not making a lick of sense. It certainly doesn't. But I don't suppose it really matters. What is a concern is that we're currently at least three miles from your homestead in this heat."

Leaning down, he offered his hand to assist her to her feet. "We need to get you home as soon as possible. Or at the very least, out of the sun. That means we had better get started."

"Yes." She looked back at the dead cattle. "I also need to inform Sheriff Jackson about all that's happened."

"We both will. After we get back to safety."

"Walking will take us hours." She sighed. "Bess and Jerome aren't even on the ranch anymore to miss us. Too bad Landon didn't ask me to supper for tonight. He would no doubt come over when I didn't show up at his house. Maybe he'd even send out a search party," she added.

"Though it pains me to say it, I would hope he'd come quickly." He smiled then, showing his beautiful teeth. The effect was no doubt what he intended—blinding.

She barely refrained from rolling her eyes as they started walking. He truly was too much. "You have attitude in abundance, sir."

"I've been told that once or twice before."

"When you were a boy, did your mother despair of you?"

The muscles in his cheek twitched. "She did. She, uh, thought I was incorrigible. She said I would never be the scholar my brother was destined to be."

485

"And were you ever like him?" she teased.

"No."

She looked at him in surprise. "Why not? You didn't care to be?"

"I was too hotheaded, I'm afraid." He held out an arm as they climbed over a small thicket of large prickly bushes. "Careful. These thorns can hurt."

She held on to his hand as she maneuvered her way around the thicket. Once she was satisfied her calico wasn't stuck in the thorns, she smiled up at him. "What did you do that was so wrong?"

But he didn't smile back. If anything, he looked more pained. "Nothing I would care to talk about."

Realizing she'd struck a nerve, she refrained from pushing anymore. After all, she had just as many people in her life who were long gone and memories she didn't care to talk about.

After another twenty minutes, she wiped at the trickle of sweat dripping down her forehead. "Do you think we've gone a mile yet?"

"Maybe half. No farther."

She pulled at the collar of her dress. "You sound so sure."

"You're talking to a man who spent the majority of his days in the war marching across miles of fields and roads. My feet have a good idea of what walking a mile feels like."

Staring forward, she said, "Maybe Velvet will be waiting along the vista."

"I hope so."

"We should have taken a sip of water from the creek."

"It's good we did not, Miss Laurel," he said, his voice rough. "We can't be sure that note told the truth." He paused. "Though the cattle looked like they had been dead long enough for the other cattle to have been poisoned by the creek, too, if there was something in the water. After all, they were positioned downstream, but they looked fine when we saw them. I'll find out what happened. I promise."

Thomas looked so certain, his expression so determined, she began to fear what he was going to do when he did discover what happened. "And then . . . and then you'll tell the sheriff?"

"No. And then they'll pay."

His voice was so cold, his words so dark and filled with terrible promises, she stumbled again.

Automatically, he took hold of her elbow. "Careful now. You almost hurt yourself."

"I'm fine."

He didn't release her. "I see that. But still, slow down now. We've got time and it's hot."

That was where he was wrong. She needed to do something. She needed to do anything she could to make things better! Shaking her head, she said, "No, Sergeant. We need to hurry. We've got to inform the sheriff about what happened. And the men . . ."

Instead of moving away, he held her closer. "And the men are long gone," he finished, his voice gravelly in her ear. "That means we don't need to get overheated. We need to pace ourselves. Everything will happen when the time is right, Laurel. I promise, the Lord takes care of his children. Somehow, some way, he's gonna make sure we get back to your place okay."

"You . . . you really believe that, don't you?"

"I used to not believe. But now I know better. I still make mistakes, do things my own way too much. But I haven't forgotten what I learned from the men who became my friends on Johnson's Island. They knew that no matter what, God was in control. And they lived accordingly." Gradually, he released his hold on her. "Okay?"

As his words permeated at last, she realized everything he'd been saying made sense. They needed to trust in the Lord. They needed to bide their time and be cautious. Only then would they survive.

She drew in a ragged breath. "Okay."

He flashed her one of his perfect smiles. "Good girl."

She nodded. Thinking about his advice, about everything he'd done for her in the last twenty-four hours, she said, "Thomas, have I thanked you enough?"

He pulled back his hat so she could see his bright-blue eyes. "You shouldn't be thanking me for anything, Laurel."

"How can you say that?"

"Easily. You're in my care but walking miles in the heat after being shot at."

"You know what just happened was not your fault. There were only two of them, but they had the advantage. We were no match for them, especially with only one rifle." She frowned. "And since I cried out and hid, I don't think I even count."

"I should have been able to handle them. Two against one ain't much of an obstacle."

"Surely you don't mean that."

"I mean everything I'm saying. I know better. I know I didn't respond to any of what's happened like I should." His voice was harsh.

"Even though I hate to admit it, if you weren't here, I would be hopelessly lost."

"You're not giving yourself enough credit. I have no doubt that you'd find your way home without a problem." He winked. "You'd do your horse proud, for sure."

Her horse. Even after everything that happened, he could still manage to make her smile.

"That's quite a compliment, Thomas."

"You watch out, Miss Tracey. Before my year with you is over, I'm liable to say all kinds of sweet things to you. You might even become used to it."

"I'll try to prepare myself."

When he laughed, the sound echoed around them. Caught her heart and made her wonder what she was ever going to do when he left her.

The thought was almost enough to make her start crying all over again.

20

Johnson's Island, Ohio
Confederate States of America Officers POW Camp

THOMAS HAD JUST FINISHED EATING HIS SUPPER OF BEANS
and a couple of ripe tomatoes and cucumbers from their makeshift
garden when he noticed the other members of his group looking
at him funny.

He dropped his spoon with a clatter. "What?" he asked, feeling suddenly self-conscious. No matter how hard he tried, he
could never remember the "right" way to eat everything. It was a
constant source of amusement for the other men. It seemed half
of them had learned the right way to hold knives and forks by the
time they'd learned to walk.

When no one jumped at the chance to point out his mistake,
he began to get irritated. Why couldn't one of them just spit it
out so they could laugh at him, and then he could go back to
eating? It wasn't like they got many opportunities to eat fresh
vegetables.

Just as he was about to say something about how each of them
should mind their own business, he noticed their expressions
looked different than usual. Especially the major's. He looked
almost pleased about something.

"What is it now, Major?" Thomas finally blurted. "How did I hold my tomato wrong? *Whom* have I offended? I could have sworn I've been doing real good tamping down my temper."

Phillip Markham leaned back his head and laughed. "You know what? I think you have been calmer than usual. It's been impressive."

If his manners and behavior had been so much better, Thomas really didn't understand why Phillip was laughing. Or why the lot of them had been eyeing him in such a funny way.

Looking from Phillip to Robert Truax to Major Kelly to Captain Monroe, he searched for answers. "Is that it? You wanted to tell me I've been doing better?"

The captain sat down on the bench next to him. "Settle down, Sergeant. No one is trying to make you uncomfortable."

"Well, I am. You'd be uncomfortable, too, if four men were staring at you like your pants were unbuttoned."

Captain Monroe's blue eyes sparkled. "I didn't look, but I think your trousers are securely fastened, Thomas."

"Y'all are just staring at me for the heck of it, then?"

"No. It's that we just discovered something new about you."

This wasn't good news. Thomas had taken great care to try to keep his worst traits and the worst parts of his past concealed. "What did you find out?"

"Something of note," Major Kelly said with a grin. He was sitting across from him on the ground. His legs were stretched out before him and he was bearing the rest of his weight on his hands. "See, when Monroe and I went over to greet the newest arrivals, one of them happened to see you from a distance."

"So?"

Sharing a smile with the captain, Major Kelly continued. "The long and short of it is that the man was in awe."

The major had lost him. "In awe of what?"

"Of you, you idiot," Robert said.

"What are you talking about?" he asked.

Robert slapped him on the back. "Thomas, only you would take something good and turn it on its ear. The major and captain are talking about how you've been holding out on us."

Thomas stared at the captain and silently begged him to get to the point.

Thankfully, Captain Monroe did. "The gentleman we talked to happened to be a lieutenant colonel with a unit out of the Carolinas."

"Lieutenant Colonel Isaac?"

"Uh-huh." The captain's eyes brightened. "Ring a bell?"

"Yes, sir." Thomas nodded. "I met him down in Kentucky."

Lieutenant Markham folded his arms across his chest. "He told us how you fought off no less than five Yankees by yourself to save a young lady and her daughter."

"And that you were bleeding from numerous cuts and gashes but still spent the majority of one afternoon helping them get packed up, then took them to their nearest relative's house," Captain Monroe continued. "Five miles away."

"All while bleeding and sporting any number of cuts and bruises," the major added softly.

Thomas swallowed. He had been in a heap of pain that day, but his pain had paled compared to the things the woman had endured. "It was nothing more than any of you might have done. I can't believe Colonel Isaac remembered me."

"It's more than that, Thomas. He said he'd never forget you as long as he lived," Major Kelly said. "The colonel remembered you because that woman was his eldest son's wife. You saved her. You saved his granddaughter too."

The lady's name had been Helena. She'd been a sweet thing.

So scared, though. He vaguely recalled hoping she would be one of the few women who got to welcome her husband home. "Do you know what happened to her man? Is he still alive?"

Captain Monroe nodded, a big smile on his face. "He is, and after incurring a nasty wound, he got to go home. When he heard what you did, he swore he'd pray for you every night for the rest of his life."

Thomas reckoned no one besides himself had ever prayed for him before. It made him feel good, almost like he was worth more than he'd thought. "That's something."

"That's more than that, son," Phillip Markham said. "The old man said you've got quite the reputation among his men."

He was embarrassed now. "I sure hope not."

"Thomas, you're their hero," Captain Monroe said.

Thomas looked at each of the men, the men he respected more than most anyone in the world. They'd all put themselves in harm's way and had saved countless soldiers. "That happened almost a year ago. I'm not sure why you all care."

"Because you never told us, you nitwit," Robert said. "We had no idea you hide a heart of gold underneath all your cagey ways."

Putting his plate down at last, Thomas cleared his throat. "I appreciate you letting me know Helena and her daughter survived. Thank you for that."

Robert Truax blinked. "That's it?" he asked, dismay thick in his voice. "That's all you're going to say?"

Thomas got to his feet. "It was one afternoon. I'm pleased they're faring well, and will also admit to being gratified to know they remembered me. But I don't understand why you all think it's worth getting into such a fuss about."

Major Kelly shook his head. "You *don't* get it, do you?"

There it was again. Another reminder that he didn't catch on to things quick enough. "Don't get what?"

"I knew you were brave. I knew you were sent behind enemy lines, and I knew you could ride like the wind. I knew you had a bad temper, and I knew you had an excellent right fist. But this . . . well, this proves you have heart too." Looking him up and down, Major Kelly smirked. "The truth is, I'm kind of smitten."

"Smitten?"

"Indeed, soldier. If I were a girl, why, I'd likely be in love." While the other men chuckled, Major Kelly winked. "You are destined for great things, Thomas Baker."

"Because I was able to help a woman and her child?"

"No, Sergeant. It's not because you were able. It's because you did," he said before walking away.

As Thomas stared at the major, Captain Monroe gripped his arm. "We're right proud of you, son." He smiled then. "I'm tickled that man has been telling your tale to everyone for months. You deserve all the recognition. You are a good man. One of the best."

Thomas nodded as he felt his face flame.

Only when he was going to sleep that night did he dare allow himself to feel that euphoric bubble of worth lift inside him.

He wasn't smart. He had no money. He didn't have any family. But he had friends who valued him, and he also had done something worthwhile.

He realized then and there that even if he died in his sleep tonight, he had already become the kind of man he could be proud of. A faithful man. A Christian.

July 1867

TAYLOR HAD BEEN DREADING THE MEETING FROM THE MO-
ment a boy knocked on his door at the boardinghouse and delivered his boss's missive. But he had no choice but to send him word
about what had just been reported to him.

Nothing good happened when a man didn't follow through
on his directives. With weighted feet, he'd wandered to the edge
of Clearwater. Earlier, he'd threatened to tan their hides if they
weren't cleaned up and ready when he got there.

Luckily, they'd taken him seriously. They'd been a quiet trio
when they walked the half mile to meet their boss.

Now the four of them were standing in the middle of a field
full of overgrown prairie grass and littered with prairie dog holes.

"I knew y'all weren't smart, but I didn't take you for complete
idiots," Landon Marshall said once he'd gotten a good look at them
all. "What were you thinking, shooting at Laurel Tracey that way?"

Taylor looked at George Irwin and Foster Howell, the two
men he'd persuaded to work by his side. They, like him, had been
in dire need of some quick money. Unfortunately, they were more
unreliable than Taylor had ever imagined. He should have known
better. Not only had Irwin deserted his unit during the war, but
he'd since made his living cheating at cards. He was as lazy as all
get-out.

And Foster Howell? Well, he'd always had a bone to pick with
anyone in authority. But now he was eager to put both Thomas
Baker and Laurel Tracey in their place. For some reason, Howell
was sure the woman had been the force behind Jackson's firing
him. Not that that theory made any sense. Howell had been fired
before the woman showed up on the square that day and wouldn't
have known about Baker's beating before that.

Taylor was beginning to wonder why Sweetwater's sheriff had hired him in the first place. That man couldn't follow instructions if they were painted on rocks and placed in front of his feet.

"They weren't thinking," he muttered as he glared at the two men standing sullenly by his side. "I told them to poison more cattle, not shoot at people. But when they went to make sure the cattle were dead and saw the woman and her man, they got all riled up."

Howell spit a good amount of tobacco juice on the ground. "Seeing Laurel Tracey there was a surprise. I'll admit that we shouldn't have scared her so bad."

Marshall gritted his teeth. "You shouldn't have scared her at all."

Howell shrugged. "Yeah, all right. But I don't know why you care about what happened to Baker. A man like Thomas Baker is nothing but a waste of space." Waving a stained hand in the air, he said, "He was a prisoner. A prisoner in my jail."

Taylor rolled his eyes. "It wasn't your jail. You only worked there . . . until you got fired."

"Like I said, he's nothing. I still can't believe Sheriff Jackson got in such a tizzy. Why, if I had gotten my way, Baker would already be dead."

"However, he is not," Marshall said with a sneer. "Plus, didn't you say Baker has friends who matter?"

"Yeah." Howell looked away.

"Who are they?" Taylor asked.

"Some former captain of the Confederacy, the one who sent that telegram to the judge. Though he's of no consequence, on account of us losing the war and all."

Marshall tapped his foot. "The judge thought otherwise."

"Judge Orbison is easily impressed. Don't worry about any friends of Thomas Baker's."

Marshall seemed convinced. Looking a bit calmer, he eyed Taylor. "Let's pull back for a while. A third of her cattle are dead, and thanks to these two, she no doubt now fears for her own life. And I convinced the sheriff someone is also lurking about stealing supplies. Laurel doesn't know what's going on. But I'm going to pressure her to accept my suit one more time. I'm hoping she realizes she has no choice but to marry me. Then I'll get what I want."

"Are you sure you don't want me to scare her myself?" Taylor asked. "I can do some damage to her house in the middle of the night. Maybe even scare Baker away, if today's gunfire didn't do the trick."

"Like I said, hold off. I'll send word when I'm ready for more."

"All right." When he'd first seen his boss's irate expression, he'd been worried that the man was going to take out his frustration on him. Now he could spend the rest of the day in the saloon.

Just as Marshall turned away, Irwin whined, "What about my payment? You promised me ten dollars."

Marshall turned back around and said softly, "You want to be paid for almost killing my future bride?"

"Well, yeah." Irwin folded his arms over his thin, lanky frame and nodded toward Howell. "Orr hired me to ride with him. I did that. It weren't my fault he got all trigger happy."

"It wasn't your fault," Marshall repeated slowly.

Irwin raised his eyebrows. "You heard me. Now give me my money."

"Or?"

"Or else you're going to regret it."

Marshall lifted his Colt and shot Irwin between the eyes.

The man died instantly and fell, his expression forever looking surprised.

Taylor stared down at the man with a sinking heart. When he lifted his head, he saw that Marshall directed a chilling stare toward him and Howell.

Taylor swallowed and tried to stop his hands from shaking like leaves.

Marshall lifted his gun again. "Do you two reckon you need your payment right now too?"

"No, Mr. Marshall," Howell bit out.

"I can wait too, sir," Taylor said.

Looking pleased, Marshall lowered his gun. "I was hoping you would say that. Now, deal with this."

After Marshall left, Howell groaned. "What are we gonna do with Irwin? He weighs a ton."

This was why Taylor had been brought down from Chicago. Foster Howell was as dumb as a box of rocks. "All we have to do is put him in a shallow grave over there by the thicket of brush and the creek. I'm certainly not about to cart his body anywhere."

"Let's find something to start digging with then. At least Marshall got him in the face. Belly wounds make more of a mess. We have that to be thankful for."

This is what's wrong with Howell, Taylor thought as he looked around for a stick or something else to dig with. *A man is killed in cold blood by his side and he only thinks about how easily he can get rid of the body.*

As he lifted Irwin under his arms and began dragging him toward the thicket of bushes, Taylor realized he was hopelessly failing in his efforts to become a better man for Dara.

Actually, at this rate, it was unlikely she'd even recognize him when he returned. If he ever returned.

21

THEY'D MADE IT HOME. AT LONG LAST, HER HOUSE WAS IN sight. Laurel felt like both raising her arms in triumph and falling on the ground in thankful tears.

But instead of doing either, she settled for stating the obvious. "Thomas, we're almost there. We did it!"

When he smiled at her, the lines around his eyes crinkled. "Yes, ma'am. And I must admit that no building has ever looked more welcome to me than this one does right now."

His voice was raspy, no doubt because he was so parched. And hungry.

She was too. They were covered in sweat and grime, and the sun had burned so brightly her face was likely blistered, despite any shade from her bonnet. "The moment we get inside, I'm going to drink seven glasses of water."

"I hope you will," he said, his gaze turning soft. "You must be parched."

"You know I am. We both are." They had been walking so long. At least four hours, though she'd stopped guessing after they'd walked two or so. She'd soon learned that attempting to figure out how far they'd gone or how far they had to go did neither of them any good. All it had done was make each footstep heavier.

"I'll be drinking my fair share of water too," he said after they'd gone another fifty or so steps. "However, I'm looking even more forward to taking a cool bath. I feel like I'm wearing half of your ranch on my skin."

"I'm certain it's only half, because I know I'm wearing the other half on mine," she said. Fingering her dress's fabric, she grimaced. "I think my dress is a new shade of brown."

"I think I have a buffalo nickel somewhere. We can flip it to see who gets to bathe first." He smiled then, letting his perfect teeth flash.

Laurel smiled back at him because they both knew he was joking. Thomas had proven to be an especially attentive companion. There was no way he would ever bathe before she did. He wouldn't do anything before making sure she was taken care of first.

"I think I'll let you bathe first, Sergeant," she said. "Even more bothersome than the dirt and grime on my body is the condition of my feet."

He looked at her in confusion. "Are they paining you?"

"I'm afraid so. I have blisters on top of blisters."

He frowned. "But I haven't noticed you limping."

Somewhat proudly, she lifted her chin. "I've been taking care not to limp. I didn't want to worry you."

But instead of looking proud of her, he looked even more agitated. "You should have told me you were in pain."

"There was nothing you could do, Thomas." Realizing he was blaming himself all over again, she ordered softly, "Stop, now."

"Stop what?"

"You know what. Stop taking on my burdens. I wouldn't have mentioned it if I thought you would be upset."

"After we get cleaned up, I'll take a look at them." When she was about to protest, he gave her a hard look. "And don't go getting all delicate on me. I've seen bare feet before. Even yours."

"I remember." Could it have been just yesterday when he'd found her barefoot and screaming about the calf on the front porch? It felt like years ago.

"So you'll let me tend to you?"

She simply nodded.

"Thank you. Now let's get you to the house so you can have those glasses of water."

The house's proximity seemed to blur now. It teased her eyesight. Every time she was sure they'd reach it within a few minutes, it seemed to bounce farther backward. "These last few yards feel the longest, don't they?"

"They always seem to," he said.

She figured truer words had never been said.

They walked quietly side by side until they reached the bend and saw that both horses had returned and were standing near the front of the barn. Velvet was watching Laurel intently, almost as though she'd never seen her owner walking down the lane.

"Thomas, I can't believe Velvet and Yellow are here. I never imagined they would have both come home."

"They are smart horses, to be sure." When they got near the house, Yellow turned his head and whickered in their direction. Thomas grinned. "That horse is quite full of himself. I do believe he's looking at us in confusion. As if he's wondering what took us so long!"

Laurel found herself giggling. "I'm sure you're right." Now that they'd reached the front porch, she said, "Let's go get some water before you do anything with the horses."

"No. First, you wait out here a minute."

"Why?"

"I want to walk through the house to make sure it's safe."

She was exhausted. She was dirty. She also wanted to take a much-needed break from the stress and danger they'd been under in the last few hours.

But she had obviously been terribly naïve. She hadn't even imagined they could still be in danger. A shiver ran up her spine. "Surely you don't think those men are lying in wait for us."

"I hope not, but we can't know what they're capable of or predict what they'll do." His expression was cold and hard, illustrating just how upset he was about the day's events—and how serious he was about staying vigilant. "Stay here while I go inside, Laurel."

She hadn't been afraid, but now she didn't want to be alone. Suddenly every outbuilding and corner of the house looked like an ideal place for someone to be hiding. "I want to go inside with you."

"Honey, if there's trouble, I'd rather not worry about guarding you."

"If there could be trouble inside, it could be lurking around here as well. Thomas, I don't want to face it alone."

After studying her for a long moment, he held out a hand, his rifle in the other. "Come along, then."

Slipping her fingers into his clasp felt right.

When they walked in, she steeled herself to see overturned furniture or damage, or worse, bandits sitting on her settee and calmly waiting for them.

But everything looked exactly how they'd left it all those hours ago. As they walked down the hall and up the stairs, Laurel found herself peeking tentatively around corners and keeping a death grip on Thomas's calloused hand.

"Do you think they've been here?"

"It doesn't look like it." His voice sounded noncommittal as he guided her into Bess's old room, her mother's old sewing room, and then his bedroom.

She hadn't been inside since he'd taken it over. She was surrounded by his usual scent and a plethora of discarded items on one of the dressers. Otherwise, his bed was neatly made and his clothes were hanging on pegs on the far wall.

"Does everything seem like you left it?"

"I reckon so." He walked her down the hall to her bedroom. After pausing at her doorway, he let loose of her hand and walked around the room. "Was this your parents' room?"

"Yes. I moved into it when Bess and Jerome came. Otherwise they would have taken it over."

"It's a pretty room. I'm glad you're sleeping here."

"Thank you." She noticed he was examining every nook and cranny the same way she'd looked in his room. In a way that had little to do with looking for signs of trouble and everything to do with looking for signs of her.

She thought he was imagining her in it.

A new tension festered as she realized that such a thing wouldn't bother her.

Eager to dispel it, she cleared her throat and tried to focus on their safety, not the curious feelings sparking inside her. "Maybe they don't know where I live?"

"There's no telling what they know."

When he walked out of her bedroom, then headed down the stairs, she followed on his heels. She was starting to get the feeling that he knew far more than he was letting on. She hoped he'd share.

He stopped outside the bathing room at the back of the main house. "I think everything is as tight and secure as we can hope for."

"Thank you for checking on everything. It's very kind of you."

"Not kind, Miss Tracey. This is why you have me working here for you."

She felt a little deflated, though she knew what Thomas was doing. He was reminding both himself and her of their roles and relationship.

She realized he needed that line drawn once again as much as she probably did. Therefore, she didn't argue the point but merely nodded.

He looked relieved. "I think it's safe for you to take your bath now."

"Did you forget? I need to have my seven glasses of water first. And you need some too," she teased.

To her relief, he smiled. "I can hardly wait."

She was thankful he didn't protest. Instead, he followed her to the kitchen, stood by one of the rows of cabinets as she retrieved two heavy stoneware mugs, then accepted his mug gratefully after she poured some water she'd kept in the ice chest.

Oh, but that first sip felt and tasted like heaven! Laurel drained her mug in record time. Just as she was about to pick up the pitcher, Thomas took it from her hands and refilled their mugs. Again they quickly drained them.

After the third round, he set his mug on the counter. "Thank you. That helped a lot."

"Are you done already? You can have as much as you want."

His gaze settled on her before he turned with a jerk. "I'll get some water from the spigot in the barn. I need to see to the horses."

"But—"

"And you need to see to yourself," he said lightly, his blue eyes lingering on what had to be her sunburned face. "You need to take your bath and rest your feet."

"You'll come back inside after you see to the horses?"

His expression was almost tender when he replied, "Of course I will. Don't worry. I'll let you know when I've returned."

After she heard the kitchen door open and shut, she carefully pulled off her boots, then walked as best she could upstairs on her sore, blistered feet.

When she got to her room, she gathered some clean clothes, then hobbled back to the bathing room. She was looking forward to this bath like she hadn't looked forward to one in years. Almost like it was going to be a life-changing experience!

Or maybe it was? This bath was going to remove all the dirt and grime from their horrifying journey. And serve to remind her that she had survived it, and grown stronger too.

Returning to the kitchen, Laurel turned on the spigot, then set about heating water, all while drinking as much cold water as she could. When at last the tub was filled with enough warm water to be both practical and relaxing, she sighed, feeling as if she'd just accomplished a great feat.

Sitting on the side of the tub, she winced at the condition of her feet. She hadn't been wrong. She had some terrible, broken blisters on her toes, heels, and the pad of one of her feet. For some reason they began to sting more when the fresh air came in contact with them.

Gingerly, she stepped into her tub and allowed the warm water to soothe her sore feet for a couple of minutes. And then she went about the process of becoming as clean as she possibly could, focusing on dirt and sores instead of what they'd just overcome. If she dwelled on how close they'd come to dying or being seriously hurt, Laurel knew she wouldn't be able to think about anything else.

She'd just finished slipping on a fresh dress and combing out her hair when she heard Thomas calling.

"You decent?" he teased.

"Of course." Striding from the main house into the kitchen, she said, "I'll heat you up some water, Thomas. You start gathering a towel and your things."

After he had everything he needed, he closed the bathing room door behind him. Then, in the kitchen, though Laurel knew she needed to concentrate on making something for them to eat, she couldn't seem to do anything other than imagine him getting undressed, filling the tub with cool water, then adding the hot water little by little to make it more comfortable. He would test the temperature, running his hands through the water again and again.

Finally, at last, he would lean back against the metal side and wash his skin.

Her face and neck heated.

She pressed her hands to her cheeks, attempting to clear her head. There was no reason to dwell on his ablutions. After all, he was doing nothing that she hadn't just done herself.

It just seemed different somehow.

Because, she realized, she was different. And her feelings for him were different too. This realization was as much a surprise as anything else that had happened to them today.

Suddenly, she knew. She was falling in love with Thomas Baker.

22

THOMAS MIGHT HAVE BEEN TWENTY-TWO YEARS OLD, BUT he wasn't too old to appreciate the soothing comfort of a warm bath. From his time on the streets to the war to this very moment, he hadn't had all that many opportunities to luxuriate as much as he was in this private room while resting in a half-filled tub of water.

Picking up the bar of soap Laurel left him, he noticed that it smelled good, like lavender. It felt good on his skin too. It didn't burn or sting.

It was a woman's soap. Laurel's.

Closing his eyes, he allowed himself a moment to think about her, to think about how close he'd come to losing her. It had scared him half to death. It would have been a tragedy if he'd lost her. If the world lost someone so precious.

His heart pounded like a dozen horses' hooves every time he recalled hearing the gunshots and forcing her onto the ground. He'd always been a praying man. But in those precious few moments, he'd felt as if he couldn't pray enough or hard enough for the Lord to be with them at that moment.

He'd been willing to do anything to keep her safe.

His objectives hadn't changed after they began their long walk home. He'd kept a vigilant eye about them, ready to shoot whoever or whatever attempted to disrupt their journey.

After the first couple of hours, when his breathing had slowed and he no longer felt as though he were standing in the eye of a hurricane, he'd begun to watch her even more closely.

He was aware of each tentative step of hers, each pained expression. He noticed when she stumbled, when she swatted at a hornet, when her lips had turned chapped. He noticed it all.

The only thing he hadn't seemed to notice was that she'd injured her feet.

He was torn about what to do about his attraction to her. Part of him didn't exactly blame himself. He was a man who'd been given precious few sweet things in life.

Most of the time he'd been given only the leftovers, what no one else wanted. His only exception had been his relationships with the other men in Captain Monroe's unit.

Those were the best men he'd ever met, and he'd felt as if the Lord had given him those men's regard as a gift for all that he'd endured in his lifetime.

He'd certainly never had the opportunity to be around a woman like Laurel.

As he rested in his bath and imagined what she was doing in the kitchen, Thomas knew he didn't deserve a woman like her. But he didn't care.

The fact of the matter was that he needed Laurel. He needed her, and he wasn't ready to give her up. Not now.

Maybe not ever.

It might even be for her own good. If the rest of the men in Sweetwater were anything like that arrogant Landon Marshall, he doubted any of them could treat her as well or care for her as completely as he could. It might have been his pride showing, but he knew no other man around those parts was any better for her than he was.

It seemed God had given him a gift in Laurel. And though he was far from perfect, she needed him, just like he needed her. To turn his back on her at this moment, when she needed him the most, would be like turning his back on one of the best presents he'd ever received.

"Thomas?" she called out. "I mean, Sergeant?"

He smiled to himself. No matter how hard her heart told her otherwise, Laurel was still attempting to keep their relationship businesslike. When she remembered.

He decided to answer her in kind. "Miss?" he called right back, smiling as he rested naked as the day he was born, leaning against the back of the tub.

"Would you mind if we had eggs and spoon bread for supper? I know it's not much."

"It's everything. It's perfect."

"I'll get to work on it when you get done. But take your time," she said hurriedly.

"I will. Thank you."

When he heard her move away from the door, he smiled again. Then gave in to temptation and closed his eyes. Tried to come to grips with all that had happened to the two of them. He'd almost lost her today.

He had almost lost himself too.

And he wasn't convinced those men had intended only to scare off Yellow and Velvet either. Perhaps it was only thanks to the horses' good sense to run off as quickly as they did that the gunmen hadn't shot and killed Laurel's two fine mounts.

But why was anyone doing all this?

The squatters seemed to be gone, so who were these men?

Did they really want Laurel to die, and him along with her? Or did they just want her to give up the ranch, thinking she'd be too beaten down and frightened to stay if they killed her cattle and threatened her life? Either way, he imagined Bess and Jerome were the only ones who could benefit from her death, and he doubted Laurel would give them any proceeds from the sale of the place. But he still couldn't see them as the culprits.

Then there was Landon Marshall, someone Thomas was sure he couldn't trust. Was he trying to destroy Laurel's future on the ranch so she would marry him? But why not just bide his time? Or was he doing this because Thomas was now a threat to getting his way?

But Laurel had known him a long time, and she didn't seem afraid of the man, only annoyed. So maybe he would never turn to this kind of violence. Besides, he was rich. Why would he need Laurel's land anyway? And someone had stolen his supplies in that outbuilding, too, assuming that was the truth.

What if all the ranches in the area were under some kind of attack?

He was in over his head.

Sinking down into the soothing water, he took a deep breath, then let his neck and head submerge. Little by little, his muscles relaxed. He only lifted his head when he couldn't hold his breath any longer.

He figured that action was a fitting metaphor for all that had been happening to him. He was close to drowning, and it was only by sheer force of will that he hadn't yet drowned either himself or Laurel.

He needed to face facts. There was too much against him and what he had at stake. If he didn't open his eyes and reach out to others, he could put everything—Laurel, her ranch, her future, and maybe her life—in jeopardy.

He needed to do whatever it took and whatever he had to do to improve her situation.

And that meant he had to come to terms with the fact that he couldn't continue to try to handle all this on his own. Laurel had someone poisoning her livestock and shooting at her. Both were heinous crimes. Who knew what was next?

While he felt like he was keeping her safer by sleeping just down the hall, it wasn't much of a help. Maybe if he could sleep with her in his arms he might ensure her safety for the time being.

But obviously that was not a possibility. And if trouble came stealthily when he was asleep, it wouldn't matter where he laid his head. Yet he couldn't stay awake all the time.

It was also painfully apparent that he couldn't keep Laurel safe and watch her livestock at the same time. He certainly couldn't do either of those and hunt down the men who had dared to take aim at her.

Instinctively, he knew the men in town weren't the ones he needed to help him. While he might trust the sheriff, he didn't trust him enough to put Laurel's life in his hands.

Therefore, there was only one thing left to do. He would send a telegram to Captain Monroe and ask for help.

Just as he often called on the Lord to help him find the strength he needed, Thomas realized there was no shame in reaching out to the best men he knew to ask for the same thing.

Actually, it was comforting and made him feel as though he had finally matured enough to be the man a woman like Laurel needed him to be. It took a strong man to know it wasn't a sign of weakness to reach out to others.

Perhaps, at long last, he'd finally become the kind of man he'd always wanted to be. Yes, he'd regained some self-worth in the army, he'd become a man he could be proud of, but he'd never fully become everything he could be.

Feeling better about himself and his goals, Thomas pulled himself out of the tub, drained it, then hurriedly got dressed. He was eager to tell Laurel about his plans. He was also eager to put her fears to rights. He didn't want her to worry that he couldn't take care of her.

When he entered the kitchen, Laurel was sitting at the table with her feet propped on a chair. Her eyes were at half-mast.

"Laurel?" he whispered.

Hearing his voice, she sat up abruptly. "Sorry. I was just taking a rest."

"I'm glad you were." Reminded of how she'd complained about her feet, he took the chair next to where they were resting and studied them.

They were certainly in a bad way. Her toes looked red and swollen, and there were already scabs and some bleeding. Gently, he picked up one foot and set it on his thigh.

Her eyes widened as she attempted to free her foot. "There's no reason to do that, Thomas. My feet are fine."

"I beg to disagree." Lifting one slender foot in his hand, he noticed there was a sizable blister on her heel and another on the pad of her foot. "Laurel Tracey, what kind of boots were you wearing? Could they have fit you any worse?"

"They were old ones of Bess's."

"Why were you wearing them? Surely you have boots of your own."

"I do, but they're worn out." Blushing a bit, she said, "Hers were so pretty."

"You wanted to wear pretty boots?" He was beginning to wonder if he'd ever understand the complexities of the female mind.

"Yes."

"Laurel, you're smarter than that."

"In my defense, I hadn't imagined that I'd be walking several miles in them."

He chuckled. "You have a point there." Knowing she was still embarrassed, he said, "I'm a little surprised she left anything here of worth."

"Based on the condition of my feet, maybe she knew something about those boots I did not," she quipped.

"Indeed." After resting her foot more comfortably in his lap, he brought the other one up and inspected it.

"Thomas—"

"I'm not doing anything untoward. Merely looking at your toes." Carefully, he placed her feet back on the chair.

She sighed. "I hope Bess and Jerome are doing all right."

"If they didn't get shot at today, I'd say they're doing a far sight better than we are."

"This is true."

"Don't worry about them. They weren't helping you, only wearing you out."

"Jerome was the culprit, I think. Maybe I should have tried to speak to Bess alone."

Thomas didn't think Bess would have listened to anything Laurel would have said. "I can't help you there. I don't have much experience talking to women."

Luckily, instead of feeling awkward, Laurel seemed to find his statement amusing. "You didn't learn how to manage women when you were riding in the cavalry?"

"I did not. Our conversations revolved around guns and horses, I'm afraid."

"That's too bad. I could use some good advice."

"I have none to offer. Even though I learned a lot from the officers on Johnson's Island, we never covered that topic," he said lightly. He leaned back slightly, stretching his legs.

She opened an eye again. "I can't help but notice that you don't talk about your time in the prisoner of war camp as being especially horrible."

"It was bad at times. Sometimes worse than that." Remembering the cold and the boredom and the ever-present hunger, as well as the feeling of hopelessness, he said, "Don't get me wrong. The men who guarded us reveled in their power. They didn't make it easy on us, especially as the atrocities came out about Andersonville and such."

"But you choose not to think about it that way?"

"It ain't that." He swallowed. "It's more a case of me choosing to remember the friendships I made there. The men I was with were some of the best men I'd ever met." Meeting her gaze, he said, "Actually, I can't imagine that I'll ever meet another group of men I admire more. I felt privileged to be thought of as their friend."

"Based on what I know of you, I'm sure they felt the same way."

Thinking of the day they'd brought up his bravery, he murmured, "Sometimes I think they did."

"I'm sure it was more than sometimes, Thomas. I've never met a braver man."

Her sweet honesty was so kind. Far kinder than he deserved, given the fact that her life hadn't been any easier since he'd entered it, and in some ways it was much harder. "You see, the thing of it is, I wasn't supposed to be there in the first place. I was enlisted, and most times enlisted soldiers didn't mix with the officers."

"Not even in a prison?"

"No." When she shifted and moved her feet back to the floor, he shifted as well and stared across the room, once again reliving those moments as though they had just happened. "But I had done a lot of missions for Captain Monroe. Capturing him was quite a coup for the Yankees because he even had a good reputation among them. He demanded that everyone in his unit who'd been captured go with him to the POW camp."

"I'm surprised they listened to him."

"If you met the captain, you wouldn't be surprised. He's a formidable man." He sighed. "In any case, I'm glad they did listen to him and transfer me. You see, before we were imprisoned, I hadn't really known him. I merely did what I was told."

"You followed orders."

"I did." Smiling at himself, he added, "It might be hard to believe, but I was an excellent soldier. I followed my directives without question. It was only when I had spare time that my temper and my mouth got the best of me."

She smiled then. "Forgive me, Sergeant, but I do find that hard to believe. I would have liked to have seen you be biddable."

"You would have been impressed." He grinned back at her, thankful that he'd found a way to make her smile after such a horrific day.

"Speaking of being impressed, I think we should eat the meal I made," she said, getting to her feet and walking awkwardly to the stove. "I scrambled some eggs and baked them with some bread and cream and ham. I think it should be ready by now."

When she picked up a towel to get her pan out of the oven, he took it from her and did the honors himself. "You sit down. I'll do the serving today."

"Thomas, that isn't necessary."

"Your feet are hurt and I don't mind. Let me do this."

"All right. Thank you."

After filling two plates, he brought them to where she was

sitting and returned to her side. Then, as they were now in a habit of doing, they prayed together.

Thomas led the prayer. "Heavenly Father, we give you thanks for this meal. Thank you for providing for us with water to drink and enough food to allay our hunger. Thank you for the hands that made the meal and even for the chickens that provided it. Thank you for looking out for us today and for helping us arrive back here safely. Now please watch over us tonight so that we might both rest. Amen."

Her lips twitched. "I know you like to eat eggs, but you're giving thanks for the chickens? I'm impressed."

"You should be, given how much I don't care for poultry."

She giggled before taking her first bite. Thomas followed suit, enjoying the warm goodness of the simple fare after missing their noon meal, enjoying even more the company and the fact that somehow they'd been able to arrive home with nothing more than a couple of sore feet and some rattled nerves.

When he cleaned his plate, he decided he was going to have to tell Laurel about his decision right away. Tomorrow he was going to send the wire. Time was of the essence.

"Laurel, I'm glad we talked about the men of my unit tonight, because I think I need to contact Captain Monroe."

"You want to fill him in on what we've been going through?"

"No. I need his help," he said, correcting her. "We both need his and my other friends' help."

She wrinkled her nose. "They'll be strangers here. They won't know me or the land. Do you think they'll truly be of use?"

"They are smart men, and we vowed to be there for each other, always. I think we both know I can't protect you and your cattle while tracking the men who fired at us. It's an impossibility, even for a good soldier like me."

"If you think we need more hands, then you don't need to send a wire to Captain Monroe. All you have to do is contact Sheriff Jackson. He's a good man."

He might be a good man, but as far as Thomas was concerned, the sheriff hadn't been doing anything at all to help Laurel. "I think we need more help than what Jackson is able to provide. After all, he has a town to run. And it's possible the theft of Marshall's property was the work of squatters. He'll have to stay on that."

But instead of looking reassured, worry and disappointment clouded her eyes. "I'd rather you didn't ask your friends for help."

He was surprised, and not a little bit dismayed. "Why not? I promise they are better men than me. You wouldn't have to fear them or worry that they would behave inappropriately or that you would be in danger. They would even sleep in the barn if you wanted them to."

"While I appreciate that, and believe you, that isn't what gives me pause."

"Then what is it, Laurel? I don't understand."

Regret filled her pretty eyes. "Everything happening to me isn't your concern, Thomas," she said quietly. "And the men who shot at us are dangerous. Violent. I don't want you bringing your friends into a harmful situation. I don't want them to get hurt."

This girl was too much. She didn't seem to understand how much she meant to him.

Taking a deep breath, he said slowly, "Laurel, first of all, they didn't just shoot at you, they shot at me too. That has made it my problem as much as yours. No man is going to attempt to kill me without me taking it personally." Only all his years of practice enabled him to keep a handle on his temper. "I didn't survive a war only to die by a coward's bullet in the middle of your field."

She bit her lip. "Maybe it would be best if you just left."

"If I left what?"

"My employ."

"And return to Sweetwater's jail cell? Thank you, but no."

"I'm not speaking of going back to jail," she said, hesitant.

"What are you speaking of, then? Sheriff Jackson didn't leave me any other options that I recall."

"Actually," she said, "I wasn't thinking of following the sheriff's directives." Before Thomas could protest, she said, "You could leave in the middle of the night. I wouldn't tell anyone you were gone."

She was offering him the opportunity to slip off in the middle of the night. But not only was the thought of leaving her in the lurch repugnant, he also had nowhere else to go. "Miss Tracey," he said, "I would never do that to you."

"I promise I won't tell—"

"I am not that man. I am not the kind of man who abandons women when they are in need. And frankly, I'm a little offended you think I would."

Now she was the one who looked hurt. "I am not questioning your honor, Sergeant."

"I hope not. Because you need to understand something. You are stuck with me." When her eyes widened like saucers, he continued, "Let me be clear. When you offered me water, I became intrigued by you. When you freed me from that cage in the square, I became enraptured." He lowered his voice. "And when you took the time to see to my wounds, to attempt to heal me when I had done nothing to deserve it?" He inhaled. How did he bare his heart without becoming vulnerable?

"Yes?"

He met her gaze again. And realized that maybe being vulnerable wasn't necessarily a bad thing.

"Well, I began to care for you," he said at last.

Her eyes widened and she swallowed. "You care for me?"

He held up a hand to stop her from protesting. "I don't say any of this to scare you."

She swallowed. "I'm not scared."

"I don't even expect you to return my feelings. I don't expect you to ever feel obligated to me either. Even if you were to fall in love with someone else, I wouldn't begrudge that of you. Because I want the best for you."

Surprise filled her gaze before she tucked her chin and fiddled with a fold in her dress. "You want the best for me because you are under my employ for the next year."

"No, because, well . . . actually . . . I more than care for you, Laurel. The truth is that I have fallen in love with you."

"You've fallen in love. With me." She sounded rather stunned. And who could blame her?

Yet again, he was saying too much. Far too much. But since it was too late to take it back, he added in a lighter tone, "Now perhaps you will understand why I want you to be as happy and cared for as is possible for this year."

When she raised her head again, he saw that her eyes were clouded with worry. He wondered if it was a reaction to his profession of love or if it was because he set the deadline for one year. "I want you to be happy, too, Thomas."

"If you do, then you're going to have to accompany me tomorrow in the buggy so I can send off that wire."

"I could stay here alone."

"That isn't possible. Until I know for certain that you're safe, I never intend to let you be alone again."

"You mean for this year," she said, correcting him this time.

Blast it all. She sounded hurt and sad like he'd just kicked her in the shin. Why had he said so much?

More important, why, if he'd been so intent on telling her his feelings, did he not go ahead and be completely honest?

"I mean I'll be here with you for as long as you need me. Even if it is longer than a year."

Something new lit her eyes. Getting to her feet, she said, "In that case, I suggest we wash these dishes and get some rest. We have another full day tomorrow."

As he followed her, Thomas couldn't resist smiling. He felt like he'd just achieved a small victory.

No conquest had ever felt so sweet.

23

Sitting by Thomas's side, dressed in her Sunday finest, Laurel felt almost pretty. Maybe it was the way Thomas had stared at her when she walked out to join him in the barn. He'd been hitching up the buggy to Velvet but had stilled when he saw her approach. She'd felt his gaze pass over her. It lingered, as if he was almost reluctant to look away.

As she came closer, he straightened and his eyes filled with appreciation.

"Miss Laurel, you look very fine today."

Instead of reacting in a cool and composed way, she'd nervously fussed with her skirts and blushed. "Thank you."

"I'm almost ready," he said. "Velvet seemed to enjoy the ride out to Landon Marshall's property this morning, but she needed a bit of coaxing to get hitched to the buggy."

"She's not a great fan of leading my buggy, I'm afraid."

"I don't blame her. However, we all have to do things we'd rather not do."

She wasn't sure if he was making conversation or making a veiled comment about seeing Landon. When she'd asked if Landon had been upset that she'd changed her mind about having supper with him, Thomas had only said the conversation had gone well enough.

Because she'd been relieved the visit was no longer looming, she didn't ask him to explain. Now the silence seemed to suit them both. She simply stood to one side and watched him situate Velvet. When he was ready, she took Thomas's hand when he held it out to help her into the conveyance.

When they approached the town's square, she felt everyone's eyes on them. She didn't fault their curiosity. But instead of demurely averting her eyes, she took care to sit proud and tall by Thomas's side. No matter what everyone else thought, she knew he was a man of honor. He was honest and true. He was also brave. He'd not only saved her life yesterday; he'd saved her soul. She'd needed someone to believe in her, to believe in her future.

Thomas certainly did.

The goal they'd chosen was honorable too. It was time to fight whoever was intent on hurting her animals and threatening them.

After Thomas parked the buggy near the mercantile, he walked around, tied Velvet's tethers, then at last helped her down.

"Let's go to the bank first, Miss Tracey," he said, his formal manners out for show. "I can send a wire from there."

"Then we can get some supplies."

"Whatever you want," he said as he held out an arm.

She placed her hand on his arm and walked into the bank.

It might have been her imagination, but it felt like the room went silent as they walked to the line to wait their turn for the teller. Nervously, Laurel looked around.

A few women nodded her way, but most seemed intent on pretending they didn't know her. No doubt they assumed her relationship with Thomas was far more intimate than it was.

She tried not to let their cool reception bother her. After all, it wasn't as if anyone had come to offer her help over the last year. Though she might have had a better reputation, she had still been essentially alone.

When Mr. Cassidy called them over, he smiled at Laurel. "What can I do for you today, miss?"

"Our errand is actually for Sergeant Baker here."

Mr. Cassidy's smile faltered. "Oh? What may I do for you, sir?"

"I need to send a wire."

Mr. Cassidy pulled out a small sheet of paper. "I'll be glad to handle it, sir."

"It needs to be sent immediately." Thomas stared at the teller with some suspicion in his eyes. "You will do that?"

"Of course."

"Very well, then. Please send the following missive to Captain Devin Monroe of the Tremont Hotel, Galveston, Texas."

Mr. Cassidy scribbled his notes and then looked up expectantly. "Message?"

"Attempt on my life. STOP. Help needed. STOP. Red Roan Ranch. Sweetwater."

Mr. Cassidy's pen slowed. He began to write each word with extreme care. After he finished writing the last of it, he stared up at Thomas with a new respect in his eyes. "Is that all, sir?"

Thomas nodded. "After it's transmitted, I'll pay."

"I'll get to it momentarily."

"Please, Mr. Cassidy," Laurel said. "If you could do as we ask, it would be most appreciated."

Looking far more intent, he turned, walked a few steps to a long table with a wireless machine, put on some headphones, and began tapping out the message.

Laurel noticed that Thomas visibly relaxed once the teller began to send the wire.

"Things will be better for you now," he said, looking far more at ease.

She wanted to believe him, but how could one friend's arrival make such a difference? "How long do you think it will take for him to get here?"

Mr. Cassidy returned, and Thomas asked, "What is the time?"

"It is nine in the morning."

Ignoring the teller's curious expression, Thomas replied to her comment. "Someone will be here by nightfall."

"That soon? You're that sure?"

"Very sure. The captain will not let me down."

"That'll be three bits, sir."

Pulling out the correct amount, Thomas nodded his thanks before holding out his elbow again. Laurel had been prepared to pay for the wire, but Thomas said the captain sent a little money to go along with the new clothes.

Laurel waited until they exited the building before commenting. But once they were standing on the hot sidewalk, she stared at him in wonder.

"Inside, when you talked about how quickly help would come . . ."

"Yes?"

"Were you making a jest, or were you serious?"

"I'm always serious about Captain Monroe."

"But if he's in Galveston . . . plus he's got to ride all the way here. And make preparations."

"He will leave within the hour once he receives my message. He'll also take the time to contact the other three men in our unit. They'll come as well, and some of them are no doubt closer."

Thomas's expression was sure. His voice was sure. She saw

no doubt in his face. He actually believed these other men would rush to his side.

She couldn't imagine such a response.

Besides her parents, had anyone ever dropped everything to help her?

With a start, she realized someone already had. Thomas had placed his body over hers. He'd been willing to be hurt or killed to keep her safe. Now he'd even swallowed his pride and asked for help.

"I'm beginning to think this band of brothers of yours is an impressive group."

He laughed as they walked back toward the mercantile. "You will see for yourself when you meet them."

Opening the door to the mercantile, he said, "Get what you need to feed four or five men."

Laurel didn't question his request. She was beginning to think that whatever Thomas wanted to happen would.

As she mentally reviewed her own kitchen's supply of dry goods, she opted to purchase coffee, some dried black-eyed peas, and cornmeal. She had enough flour, beans, leavening, and sugar to make most anything else the men might need.

After telling the clerk what she wanted, she went to check on Thomas, who was looking at a box of ammunition and a very fine-looking Colt.

Just as she approached him, he looked over her shoulder and narrowed his eyes.

Quickly, she turned.

There was Foster Howell, one of the guards who had come to the ranch with the prisoners. He was eyeing Thomas with a look of suspicion and glanced at her with a small smile.

She felt uncomfortable but decided to brazen it out. "Hello, Mr. Howell."

"Miss Tracey. Good morning." His gaze swept over her, making her feel strangely exposed. Then he smiled. "I see you are out with your man."

She didn't like anything about his greeting. She didn't like how he was making her feel or how he was acting as if Thomas weren't worthy enough to be standing by her side.

Just as she was debating whether to tell Howell off, Thomas leaned closer. Placing a hand on the small of her back, he whispered into her ear, "Don't say a word. He ain't worth a bit of your time."

Unfortunately, the former guard heard his comment. "I'd watch who you're calling unworthy."

Thomas stared at Howell with a look that could only be described as loathing. "Did you need something? If so, you need to direct your questions to me."

"To you?"

Thomas seemed to let the man's scorn roll off his shoulders. Standing up straight and tall, at least a full three inches taller than his former guard, Thomas said, "There isn't a reason in the world for Miss Tracey to ever have to converse with you again."

Howell's gaze darted from Thomas to Laurel and back again. Laurel felt a trickle of perspiration slide down her spine. Was this how it was going to be for the next year? Everyone coming into her path and feeling free to judge her?

Howell rocked back on the heels of his boots. "I was only checking to see how Miss Tracey is doing, living in sin with the likes of you." He smirked. "How are you, miss? Is he treating you good?"

Thomas stepped closer to her when she flinched.

"Her welfare is no concern of yours," he said. "This is the last time I'll warn you. Don't speak to her again."

Howell backed up but didn't look completely cowed. "I can't wait to see you get your comeuppance, Baker. And you will, I promise."

"Do you know something I don't know?" Thomas asked.

"I know a lot you don't know. But I'm thinking most people do." Before Thomas could respond, he smirked again. "I'll be going on my way now." He stepped backward, then paused before turning around. "Miss Tracey, if this one lays a hand on you, you be sure and let me know. It would give me pleasure to get him back in line."

Though her brain was telling her to say something and stand up for herself, Laurel couldn't seem to make either her feet or her mouth comply. Therefore, she simply stood frozen and wished she was bolder.

Feeling the other customers' curious stares, she drew in a ragged sigh. "We're causing a scene. It's time we left."

But instead of dropping his hand and stepping away, Thomas bent his head a little so she could see his eyes. "We haven't done a single thing wrong," he said quietly. "We're simply shopping in the mercantile. There ain't a thing irregular about that."

"People think differently."

"It doesn't matter. Don't dwell on it."

"I hate that Howell looked at you the way he did, as if you are less than him."

"Honey, trust me when I say his scowl didn't bother me none. I've had far worse directed my way."

She smiled, though she knew her effort was likely more than a little wobbly. "I don't know how you managed to make me feel better, but you did."

Stepping to her side, he held out his arm. "That's because I'm a charmer, Miss Tracey."

His irreverent comment sparked one of her own. "You are incorrigible."

"Yes, I am." Pressing a hand to the middle of her back again, he murmured, "Come now, let's go inform Sheriff Jackson of the latest developments, then head back home."

Since she, too, was ready to end their visit to town, she followed him to the counter to buy her supplies.

Thomas seemed to be making a purchase as well.

24

By four in the afternoon, Thomas knew his nerves were shot. He couldn't count the number of times he'd gazed out toward the horizon, hoping to see a cloud of dust signifying that his friends were on the way.

He only hoped Laurel was handling the wait better than he was.

After they'd finished their shopping at the mercantile, Thomas loaded everything into the buggy, then got Laurel right home. Though he'd tried to pretend otherwise, the townspeople's curious, intrusive stares had bothered him. He also despised having to stand still and watch Howell leer at Laurel.

But what he hated even more was that he was the cause of all that. If Laurel hadn't taken a chance and gotten him out of that cage, he'd still be in jail. And though a better man might be thinking only about how such a kind woman felt, he had hated seeing the man who'd beat him so badly look at him with disdain.

After they returned, he took care of the buggy and Velvet, then saddled Yellow and rode around the house's perimeter. Laurel was still too shaken up for him to feel comfortable leaving her to check out the far areas of her property. To be honest, he didn't feel all that good about being out of sight either. Someone was watching her, watching them, and he wasn't going to stop until he got what he wanted.

Just as he directed Yellow to head back home, Thomas saw some hoofprints on the ground and what looked like a skid from either a foot or a knapsack.

Climbing off the saddle, he knelt down and inspected the area. Rocks were disturbed.

Someone had definitely been here recently, and they'd taken care to keep their appearance a secret. Had it been those squatters and they simply wanted a piece of Laurel's land? Picking up one of the rocks, he saw a dark stain. Or had his shot yesterday met its mark? He hoped so.

While he was debating whether to circle back around or go back and stay closer to Laurel, Yellow raised his head and pricked his ears forward.

"What is it, boy?" Thomas murmured as he got to his feet.

Yellow pawed the ground with a hoof. He looked uneasy but was waiting for Thomas to give direction.

As he ran a hand down the horse's flank, Thomas shook his head. Whoever named the horse hadn't known a thing about him. This gelding was exactly what every soldier needed—steady and responsive. A partner.

Grasping the reins, he listened harder.

And then he heard it. The faint rumbling of hooves. Had one of his comrades arrived? Or was it the men who'd shot at them yesterday?

Directing the horse around, Thomas felt behind him for the Winchester that had belonged to Laurel's father. He wasn't eager to start pointing a rifle at approaching riders on Laurel's property, but he was far from a greenhorn. There was no way he was going to allow himself to ever be at risk again. Clicking softly, he nudged Yellow forward with his knees.

Yellow seemed to sense his suspicion, because the horse slowly stepped out into the clearing, each hoof moving delicately and silently. It was as if he'd had as much experience dodging the enemy as Thomas had when he'd been asked to spy on enemy troops in the area.

Squinting against the hot glare of the sun, which had barely begun its descent in the west, Thomas found what he was looking for.

Two riders.

From force of habit more than a real awareness of what he was doing, Thomas grabbed the rifle and laid it across his lap.

Yellow continued to patiently step forward, each step slow and measured. They were in a clearing of sorts. It was obvious that he was as visible to the men riding forward as they were to him. And they weren't shooting.

Now, if he could only figure out who was approaching. Old memories of riding along with his friends slammed into his brain but dissipated with almost as much force. The problem, he knew, was those memories of the men on horseback had faded. Most of Thomas's memories of Major Kelly, Captain Monroe, and the other two men rested firmly on the soil of Johnson's Island. He could recognize their voices and even how they rolled a cheroot or held a tin cup better than the way they were seated on a horse.

Drawing Yellow to a stop, he watched the riders come closer. Unlike him, they were moving across the open field at an easy clip. Then one raised his hand, and Thomas saw a hint of a sparkle on the man's cuff.

Unable to hide his relief, he laughed. Enemies weren't approaching. His friends had arrived.

He reckoned there was only one man in the state of Texas who would ride into a potential battle zone with gold cuff links on his wrists, and that would be Major Ethan Kelly. The man came from money, and had never been particularly shy about it either.

He wasn't sure who the other fellow was, but it didn't matter. If Kelly was here, Thomas knew everything had just made a turn for the better.

Nudging Yellow forward to a brisk trot, he rode out to greet them, a smile on his face.

When he was about a hundred yards out, he called, "Welcome!"

Major Kelly pulled his dark-gray Stetson from the top of his head and held it out in greeting. "Baker, after the things we heard about you in town, the last thing I expected to see was you riding along on a fine-looking palomino like you were out for a Sunday stroll."

"There's a story there, I bet," the major's companion said, who Thomas now realized was Robert Truax.

When they drew to a stop in front of each other, Yellow's nostrils blowing air out impatiently as he tried to get a sense of the other horses, Thomas held out a hand. "Robert, Ethan, you two are a sight for sore eyes."

The major clasped his hand, his brown eyes lighting on him as though he was inspecting every new wrinkle and scar on his face. "I can't wait to hear what's been going on."

"From what Monroe said, it sounds like you should have called for us a whole lot sooner," Robert said, his voice lightly chiding. "Were you really locked up in this town's jail?"

"I was."

Robert frowned. "Someone told me you'd been whipped too. Was that a lie?"

"It was not."

Robert looked toward the sky, like he was asking the Almighty for patience. "It pains me to hear that. You really should have reached out to us earlier, Sergeant."

"I had my reasons for not contacting you."

"I would certainly like to hear them!"

"At a later date, perhaps."

"Well, why did you contact us?" Robert asked impatiently.

Thomas opened his mouth to try to describe Laurel's problems in a nutshell, but the words stuck in his throat. How could he attempt to convey Laurel's situation without the men guessing how much she meant to him?

Looking for help, he turned to face the house. Laurel was standing on the front porch watching them. Her hands were clasped in front of her. "I'll tell you more when we get to the house."

Both men turned to stare at the large home with its Southern grace and five majestic white columns. Major Kelly whistled low. "Ah, now I understand," he said. Smiling softly, he said, "Robert, I do believe I'm beginning to see what, exactly, is at stake."

"Indeed," Robert said, his voice thick with humor.

Noticing their looks of appreciation, Thomas hardened his voice. "No matter what you might think of me, you gentlemen need to be respectful. Miss Laurel Tracey is a lady through and through."

Major Kelly adjusted his Stetson, his gold cuff links glinting. Turning to Thomas, his expression filled with respect, he said, "Of course she is, Baker. Forgive me if I gave you the impression I thought otherwise. Now, lead on."

Just as he turned toward the house, Thomas asked the question that had been on his mind. "Is Captain Monroe coming too?"

"He is," Robert said. "I happened to be in Waco when he got your wire in Galveston. I fully expect him by nightfall. I believe he was going to take the train partway. He pulled some favors and got a compartment on the first one out."

"I am obliged."

"You call and we come," Ethan Kelly said as he encouraged his mount to a trot.

"Though I had expected as much, I have to admit that it's nice to realize that my hopes were not vanquished."

"Never fear. Some promises will never be forgotten."

The major had never said anything truer. He was exactly right. Some promises would always be fulfilled, no matter what the cost. Come hell or high water.

"Thank you, sir. Thanks to both of you."

"Don't mention it again," Robert said. "It's an honor to help a friend in need."

And with that, the three of them headed to the woman who was waiting for them.

To the place Thomas now considered home.

25

JOHNSON'S ISLAND HAD ONE THING THOMAS WAS FOND OF, and that was lightning bugs. From the moment they made their first appearances on the Lake Erie shore at the end of May, the bugs had become a source of fascination for Thomas. He spent a great many hours watching their flickering lights dance across the camp and light up over the calm waters as though they were stars falling from the sky.

Their dancing and darting had become a source of hope for him. Thomas liked to think their appearance in his life was a sign from God, a reminder that good could be found anywhere and at any time. One just needed to have his eyes open and be watchful.

"Looking at the fireflies again?" Major Kelly asked as he sat down on the ground beside him.

Though he was a bit self-conscious about it, Thomas nodded. "Yeah." Thinking he needed to share some kind of explanation for his infatuation, he added, "I ain't never seen them before here."

Kelly smiled softly as he watched the insects flicker and flutter across the field next to him. "I hadn't seen them before I signed up. Don't know why they aren't in Texas, but I guess we can't have everything."

"Just fire ants and hornets."

"And roaches the size of men's hands." Grimacing dramatically, he said, "I'd be happy to trade the roaches of San Antonio for these little things."

Thomas grinned, liking the easy conversation. In many ways, he was closest to the major, though they sure didn't have much in common. Major Kelly was from a well-to-do family outside of San Antonio. He'd gone to the military academy and was book smart. He had money and was rather eloquent. Rumor had it that he was also the son of a well-respected man who was serving with Lee himself. The major never spoke of his father, though.

In short, he was rich, educated, and well connected. Thomas Baker was none of those things.

However, something about Ethan Kelly was a little flawed, which made him—by Thomas's estimation, at least—far easier to relate to than Captain Monroe. Their captain was the best man he'd ever met. Thomas looked up to him like none other. But the major, though he was higher in rank, hadn't garnered quite so sterling a reputation. He had to be told things, often hesitated when he needed to charge forward, and was sometimes a bit indolent.

If the world was fair, then Captain Monroe should have outranked Major Kelly. Actually, the captain should have been a colonel or a general, someone really important.

But the world wasn't fair, and neither was the military.

However, the reason no one begrudged the major his rank or his authority was that he was just so darn likable. He often blurted out loud what the enlisted men were thinking but were too afraid of facing discipline to say.

Major Kelly also had a habit of doubting rumors, questioning orders, and overthinking strategies. It drove Lieutenant Markham crazy. However, when Kelly made his decision, he charged ahead, fighting with great valor and tenacity.

Thomas admired the man for that.

Kelly could also, as he was doing at the moment, sit in silence for long periods at a time. Bracing his elbows on his knees, he said, "Mail came today."

"I saw." Thomas never got any mail. Thinking that maybe the major wanted to talk about something in particular, he said, "Did you receive anything good, sir?"

"A letter from each of my sisters and one from an aunt, who seems to have a strange fascination with some of the bawdy girls in a saloon down the way from her house."

Thomas grinned. "Shame, that."

Kelly chuckled. "Indeed. I need to find a way to tell her to guard her reputation." After a pause, he added, "I also received a letter from Faye."

"Four letters from four women," Thomas teased. "An impressive mail call, I'd say."

"Not hardly. All this correspondence can become rather taxing." Looking him over, he said, "I ought to tell them to start taking pity on a certain sergeant. Then you can write to them every week."

Thomas could barely read and write. No matter how many times Ethan or some of the other men had tried to work with him, Thomas couldn't seem to grasp it. For some reason, every time he tried to read the words, letters got all jumbled up and turned around.

He didn't know why God decided he needed to be so stupid, but he must have had his reasons. "I don't think they'd be wanting to hear from a lowly sergeant, sir. Women like the officers' uniforms."

Major Kelly's teeth flashed in the dim light. "You are right, Thomas. Some women like my uniform very much."

Searching his brain for something of worth, Thomas said, "Your Faye certainly does, I believe."

"That she does. Well, she used to."

"Used to?"

"Yes. She ... well, she wrote to tell me that she no longer favors my uniform."

Thomas sat up. "Sir?"

"Faye has regretfully ended our relationship. It seems she has been making friends with a certain lieutenant who was severely injured and is recuperating in the hospital."

"He must be quite the man for her to turn you over for a lieutenant." Realizing how that sounded, Thomas blurted, "No offense, sir."

To his relief, Major Kelly laughed. "None taken. It seems that a lieutenant with a broken and beat-up leg bests a healthy major locked in a prisoner of war camp."

"She's a fool, then. Injured lieutenants are as plentiful as ... well, as fireflies on Johnson's Island. You are one of the best men I've ever met."

Major Kelly stilled as he turned to stare at him. "You mean that, don't you?"

"Yes. I mean, you are a good man, sir. And you have everything. Money and family. Education. She should be waiting for you. Not letting you go while you're here."

Slowly Major Kelly smiled. "Thank you for saying that. To be honest, I've been too embarrassed to tell Devin or any of the other officers that I've been discarded. I was afraid they'd act like they knew something about me that Faye did as well. Or simply look at me with pity."

"Oh, I'll look at you with pity, sir. What she did ain't right. She never should have broken things off while you're behind prison bars."

"I did find that rather heartless."

"If it's any consolation, I don't imagine too many women are like Lieutenant Markham's Miranda."

Major Kelly chuckled low. "I think you're right about that. Miranda Markham is the epitome of womanhood."

Thomas wasn't exactly sure what that meant. "She's real pretty too."

"Yes, she is. Phillip is blessed to have found a woman sweet in both appearance and heart." After a pause, he asked, "Have you ever had a sweetheart, Thomas?"

"No."

"Probably just as well. If you did, you would be doing what I was doing, trying to keep a relationship going through letters. That doesn't warm a woman's heart or body."

"I don't think I'll ever be the kind of man ladies write to, sir."

"Why not?"

Thomas saw no need to hedge. "I'm too rough. Too big. I'm not smart, and I get in fights all the time too. None of those things are what women want."

"You may be right, you may not. But I will tell you something every man in our unit knew, Sergeant. If there was something that needed to be done, we all knew who should take care of it. You."

Those words sounded so good Thomas was tempted to ask him to repeat it. But of course he didn't dare. Instead, he simply pointed to the woods. "It looks like someone lit a hundred candles out there, don't it?"

"It does. Those fireflies aren't much in the daytime. But at night, they sure do shine."

"Yes, sir," Thomas murmured, realizing that most things were like that. When one was by himself in the clear light of day, he didn't look all that special. But then, at just the right moment, his light could certainly shine.

26

Two of Thomas's friends had arrived.

As Laurel watched the men ride closer, each one sitting so tall and straight in the saddle, she felt her stomach twist into knots as her memories from the war slid into place. She'd stood on the porch countless times, watching groups of soldiers approach, never knowing how they were going to treat her.

Though she didn't think she had anything to fear, she could tell even from a distance that they were a formidable band of three. Each man looked almost as large as Thomas, which was quite a feat in itself. In addition, they rode with a confident air, the way only someone who had spent a great amount of time on a horse could.

She noticed that even after such a long time apart, they weren't talking a lot. Instead, their eyes were constantly searching. Each also had a rifle resting across his lap as if he was prepared to take on any sort of trouble at a moment's notice.

What kind of men were they? What kind of men dropped everything and rode miles and miles on the basis of one telegram?

Men unlike any she'd ever known.

Continuing to watch them, Laurel decided that, together, they looked like an unmovable force. Now she was able to see their facial expressions. Like Thomas, their faces looked tanned and their mouths were set in thin lines. They looked hard.

Another flicker of unease coursed through her. What would the men be like? Thomas had said he knew them from the war, from being in the prisoner of war camp. But what did that even mean? Were they good men who had been at the mercy of an enemy? Had they just happened to have been captured and were victims?

Or was there something else about them that had set them apart from other soldiers on the battlefield?

Did they, too, have dark pasts that had marked them like Thomas's did? Or were they everything she'd grown up to believe gentlemen and officers of the Confederacy should be?

Everything she'd been brought up to believe was so blurred in her mind now.

To her surprise, Thomas didn't bring them right to the hitching posts at the front of the house near where she was standing. Instead, the three of them rode toward the barn. At first, she was a little hurt and confused. Wasn't he eager to introduce them to her?

Then it all began to make sense. Of course. The horses would need to be watered and taken care of. The men had likely ridden for hours in the hot Texas sun. No doubt the animals were exhausted.

No doubt the men were too. Should she go right in and prepare for them or wait until Thomas gave her some direction?

After debating a moment about the right course of action, she walked to the barn to greet them. She would say hello, then let them take care of their mounts while she prepared a simple meal. That seemed to be the most polite way to act.

All three of the men stopped what they were doing when she approached. She hesitantly smiled back at them.

Then, to her bemusement, Thomas walked out to meet her halfway. When he reached her side, he presented his elbow for her to take.

She clasped it as he led her to the other men, liking how she now had Thomas to hold on to.

"Miss Tracey, may I present Major Ethan Kelly and Second Lieutenant Robert Truax?" He took a breath, then continued in a firmer, more authoritative tone. "Ethan, Robert, may I present Miss Laurel Tracey, owner of the Red Roan Ranch?"

Both of the newcomers bowed slightly at the waist.

"Miss," Robert murmured.

"Miss Tracey, it's an honor to make your acquaintance," Ethan said with a kind-looking smile.

Though it had been awhile since she'd done so, Laurel moved her right foot back and executed a curtsy. "Gentlemen, welcome. Thank you for coming to our aid."

"The pleasure is ours, I assure you," the major said with another smile. "Plus, it gave us a reason to see each other, which is always a blessing."

"A blessing," she murmured.

Thomas groaned a little bit under his breath. "Don't mind Major Kelly, Miss Tracey. He can't seem to help but be charming. It's a character flaw."

In spite of the gravity of the situation, Laurel felt her pulse race a bit. The major really was extraordinarily handsome. Blessed with an impressive height, wide shoulders, slim hips, and chestnut-colored hair, he no doubt had set many a woman's heart aflutter. Especially when dressed in his officer's uniform of gray and gold.

Beside him, Robert Truax appeared far less refined. He had piercing dark eyes, almost black hair, and pronounced cheekbones.

He looked as if he could take anyone on in a back alley and come up the winner.

Realizing she'd been staring, she turned to Thomas. "Sergeant, please do bring your friends into the house after you get your horses settled. Their rooms are ready, and I'll set out a light meal."

A pair of lines formed between Robert's brows. "There's no need for you to go to any trouble on our account, miss. We can bed down here in the barn and help ourselves in the kitchen."

"Of course you'll do no such thing! Just come in the house when you're ready." Turning to Thomas, she said, "I'm counting on you to make sure they listen to me."

"Yes, Miss Tracey," Thomas said with a hint of a smile.

Major Kelly chuckled. "Thomas, you've just answered the question every officer has ever asked after they met you."

"And what was that?"

"If it was ever going to be possible for you to settle into your skin."

"And what was your answer?"

"Get you a woman to order you around, obviously!" Robert finished with a laugh. "Miss Tracey, I would have paid good money to have you at my side when I gave Thomas orders during the war. Your presence would have saved us from many hours watching him pace and fidget."

As the major's grin broadened, Thomas scowled. "Don't you pay them any mind. I wasn't ever that bad."

Enjoying the light bantering, Laurel couldn't resist joining in. "Somehow I can't help but think they might not be exaggerating too much."

"We are not," Ethan Kelly said. "He was as difficult to supervise as he was a skilled tracker and horseman."

"It sounds as if you are a man of many talents, Sergeant."

Cheeks red, Thomas said, "My former officers enjoy bringing up my flaws a bit too much. I'm sorry for their clumsy conversation. They are usually as polite as preachers on a Sunday morning."

"I think I'd rather have them like this. Take your time, gentlemen. I'll see you inside."

Laurel couldn't help but smile when she turned her back. Something told her she was just about to learn a whole lot more about Thomas, thanks to these friends of his.

Though she regretted the reason for their visit, she was certainly looking forward to getting to know more about Thomas. From the moment she'd first seen him, he'd intrigued her more than any man she'd ever met.

It was almost a full hour later when the men entered the house. She'd expected them some time earlier and had even heated up water so they could bathe before supper.

But a quick glance told her that wasn't going to be necessary. Each of their faces looked freshly scrubbed. The edges of their hair were damp too.

"Please tell me y'all did not bathe outside. I've been heating up some water for you to bathe in the bathing room," she blurted before realizing it was rather unseemly to talk about such things.

"That's right kind of you, but my mother would've had my hide if I'd come inside your home smelling of dirt and sweat."

"Well, my mother would have been ashamed of my poor manners, allowing you to bathe in the barn."

"I'm not sure what my mother would have said," Robert said. "But I do think she would have cautioned me not to worry about such things when one was among friends."

Thomas, who was standing to one side with his hands clasped behind his back, looked a bit aggrieved by his friends' gentle flirting. "Miss Laurel, would you care to serve supper now, or wait a bit longer?"

"Everything is ready and warm in the oven. If you would follow me?"

She led them to the dining room, then brought in bowls of bean salad, fried chicken, and mashed potatoes. She also set out some pickled cucumbers and peppers she'd been saving for the right occasion. This had seemed as good as any.

The men stared at the table as if in wonder.

Robert cleared his throat. "Thomas led me to believe you didn't have any help in the kitchen."

"I don't. I made it all myself."

"Just now?"

She shrugged. "It's never too much trouble to fry up chicken and boil potatoes."

"It looks wonderful," Robert said. "I'm obliged."

Thomas led her to her seat and held her chair for her. She smiled up at him, feeling as if the situation was becoming more awkward by the second. Sure that the newcomers wouldn't enjoy a blessing, she said, "Gentlemen, I hope you will enjoy your meal."

"I'll lead us in prayer," Thomas said easily.

After they bent their heads, Thomas spoke. "Dear heavenly Father, thank you for this food we are about to receive. Bless the hands that made it. Be with our captain as he makes his way here. Let him feel your protecting arms as he makes his way across the state to come to the aid of friends. Amen."

"Amen," Robert and Ethan murmured. Laurel followed suit.

Moments later, after all the serving dishes had been passed around and the first tentative bites of her meal had been taken,

Robert sighed in appreciation. "Only you would be taken prisoner, be beaten, then land in a spot as fine as this, Thomas. You really do always land on your feet."

"One could say the same of you." Looking pointedly at the man's gold ring on his finger, he said, "I didn't know you had gotten hitched."

"It's a recent development. It only just happened. Two weeks ago."

"There's a story there too," Major Kelly said with a ghost of a smile. "He married Markham's widow."

Thomas set down his fork. "You married Miranda?"

"The one and only," Robert said.

"I can't wait to hear how that came about."

"It's quite a story, I'll tell you that."

"Major, were you there to witness the nuptials?"

"I was there when Robert sent word that he needed help. Monroe and I did what we could."

Thomas looked hurt. "I didn't receive such a missive."

"It all happened just weeks ago. The captain told us you were unable to join us, but I know now how you were otherwise occupied. In, uh, your jail cell."

"Indeed, I was." Looking back at Laurel, he said, "I'd still be there if Miss Tracey hadn't seen fit to release me."

"I'm glad I did, though I fear the sergeant has probably spent more than one evening wishing I'd left him where he was," Laurel said.

Thomas grinned before turning solemn. "I wish I could tell you this"—he gestured toward the table—"is all I've been doing since I arrived, but that certainly hasn't been the case. Miss Tracey has had to endure one loss and fight one problem after another since the war began. However, her troubles have escalated as of late."

"Care to tell us about it now?" the major asked.

Not hungry, Laurel spoke. "I'll do it. The first morning after the sergeant arrived here, just two days ago, I discovered someone had left a dead calf at my doorstep."

"Strange calling card."

Thomas nodded. "Feeling sure that it hadn't died of natural causes, I took it into town to the sheriff and to get looked at by the doctor."

"What did he discover?"

"As far as I can tell, nothing yet. No one has been out here to tell us."

"Then, one day after that, yesterday, we were out riding. We not only discovered six more cattle dead, but someone shot at us."

Robert turned to face them. "Say again?"

"One moment we were reading a note left by whoever had poisoned the cattle, and the next I had pushed her to the ground and was trying to get in a shot," Thomas said.

"Do you know who did such a thing?" the major asked.

"I wish we could tell you, but we never saw them close enough to know," Laurel said. Unsuccessfully fighting a shiver, she added, "It was frightening."

Laurel noticed that all three men exchanged concerned looks.

"Forgive my sad manners," Robert said. "Thomas might have told you that I had to learn about comporting myself in social situations. Apparently I still have to learn. We'll discuss this at another time. Most especially when we are not enjoying your delicious meal."

"Indeed," Major Kelly said.

But Laurel wasn't about to let them decide her future without her input. She had come too far to pretend she didn't need to be completely involved.

Though she was nervous, she raised her chin and spoke with

complete sincerity and not a little bit of force. "Forgive my bluntness, gentlemen, but I think we are far beyond such social niceties. Lately I've been inundated with squatters taking advantage of my lone state, been approached by multiple men offering to purchase my beloved ranch, been browbeaten by my stepsiblings to sell, and now someone is killing cattle and attempting to kill me."

She sighed. "Please don't treat me as though I don't count."

"You count," Thomas said, his voice firm and sure. While she gazed at him, struck by the depth of emotion she saw in his blue eyes—and how his words made her feel—he softened his tone. "Of course you need to be part of this conversation, Miss Laurel. However, I would rather not start making suggestions or bantering about ideas until Captain Monroe arrives. When he arrives, we'll just have to go over everything again."

She didn't need to look around to realize the two other men at the table were listening to their exchange with interest. No doubt they were imagining something was going on between them too.

Laurel was sure her face was probably bright red. "Oh. Yes. Please just forget what I said."

"Never that." Getting to his feet, Thomas said, "Gentlemen, if you have had enough to eat, would you mind making yourself at home while I help Miss Laurel with the dishes?"

"I'll do one better," Lieutenant Truax said. "I'll help with them too."

Laurel was just about to assure him that was not necessary when someone knocked at the front door.

She stood up eagerly. "Sergeant, perhaps your captain has arrived?"

"Maybe so," Thomas murmured, though his expression didn't match his tone. "I'll go see if Captain Monroe has, indeed, arrived. But until I know for sure, you stay here."

She attempted to smile. "Not every person who comes here is a suspect."

"We'll see," he said as he turned for the foyer.

"Thom—" she began, but stopped herself just in time.

Because she noticed then that he was armed. He was holding a beautifully crafted new Colt in his right hand. He also looked ready to use it.

27

Uh-oh," Mabel muttered under her breath. "Look who's back."

Taylor turned to the entrance of the saloon and experienced the same empty feeling Mabel must have. Landon Marshall was back. This was not good news. He'd hoped for another day's break at the very least.

When Marshall's eyes lit on him and then he started sauntering forward, Taylor drummed up a lifetime of experience not to shy away from the man's glare.

Without saying a word, Marshall took the bar stool next to him and pressed a palm on the hammered copper surface. "Whiskey, neat."

"You got it."

When Mabel set the shot glass in front of him with a fake sultry smile, Marshall slapped two bits on the bar. "Thank you."

"Anytime, sugar." Turning toward Taylor, she arched a brow. "You want anything?"

Taylor was terribly thirsty but low on funds since Marshall had reneged on his last payment. "No thanks. I'll wait."

"Give him another anyway, darlin'," Marshall said. "I'm buying."

When Mabel took his glass to refill it, Taylor nodded. "Appreciate that."

"It's the least I can do. Given that you lost one of your partners yesterday."

Remembering how hard it had been to dig even an inch in the hard soil, Taylor pressed his lips together. It had been an ugly job, and Howell didn't seem to have much going for him in the way of upper-body strength. When Mabel set his shot glass in front of him, he drained half of it.

"You got something more for me to do?"

"Yeah. I'm still going to get her to marry me, and I've got something else up my sleeve too. But do something different this time, just as long as it's as threatening to the ranch as killing her cattle."

With effort, Taylor kept his expression impassive, almost glad for the request. The opportunity to change up his scare tactics made a difference when he had no choice but to do what this man wanted. Not only was he too far in to extricate himself, but he had no money and nowhere to go. "Yes, sir."

"Then be on alert. I'm told Baker and Laurel sent a wire to someone earlier today, and I'm thinking something is about to happen."

"Yes, sir. Do you need me to get any assistance?" He hoped Marshall didn't want him to hire Howell again. It was a whole lot easier to take care of everything himself.

"No." After slapping down another two bits on the bar, Marshall got up, sauntered toward a table, and motioned Mabel forward. "Come spend some time with me now, honey."

Mabel picked up the coin and slipped it into the bodice of her dress before visibly steeling herself.

Thinking of Dara, Taylor looked at Mabel with some concern. "You going to be okay with him?"

"Probably not. But why are you even asking?" she whispered, her expression filled with derision. "It ain't like you can do a thing about it."

He threw back the last of his shot and stood up. It was time to leave. He had no desire to witness Marshall mistreat her, because Mabel was exactly right. There wasn't a thing he could do about much anymore.

Even the soiled doves knew it.

Thomas respected Captain Monroe more than just about any other man on earth. And from the many years when he fought by his side, Thomas knew how his captain liked to do things. He was careful and methodical. He rarely did anything on impulse.

For these reasons, if Thomas were still a gambling man, he would say the chances were slim to none that the captain had decided to ride his horse onto the ranch, dismount, then walk up to Laurel's door and knock as if he didn't have a care in the world.

That wasn't how he did things.

Especially not after receiving a telegram like the one Thomas sent. Instead, his captain would ride to the barn, dismount, and simply wait until he saw Thomas or one of his other men. The captain had always been a man to be assured of his surroundings before making any move.

And that was why Thomas had his new pistol in his right hand at the ready when he opened the door.

"She's got you opening doors for her now?"

He'd been right. It definitely was not his former captain at the door.

"Marshall. To what do I owe this pleasure?"

"Don't play games with me, Baker. I need to see Laurel immediately."

Instead of backing away, he merely raised his eyebrows. "Care to explain why you have brought this pair with you?"

"We live here," Jerome said.

"Not anymore. Don't you recall that conversation? Because I do. I remember it clear as day."

"I recall that you kicked us out of our own home without reason," Jerome said. "I know you have insinuated yourself onto our land and into our lives with the ease of a poisonous snake in tall grass."

"While that's rather colorful, I don't find it to be fitting in this case."

Marshall glared. "Watch yourself, Baker. Laurel's siblings have every right to be here, and you had no right to influence her to drive them out. I've come to help Laurel see that. While you might think you're now someone high and mighty, it is an absolute certainty that you will eventually be nothing more than a dirt-poor criminal again."

Marshall's words stung. But instead of fighting them or pretending they hadn't met their mark, Thomas welcomed the hurt. After all, that was how he had felt most of his life until he'd lived side by side with his friends in the barracks on Johnson's Island. "You may be right," he replied without a bit of animosity in his voice. "Being here is most likely fleeting, and I am nothing more than a poor example of a man. However, the fact remains that I am currently here and you are not."

"Who arrived?" Robert asked as he joined them. His voice and demeanor seemed as if he were greeting Christmas carolers.

Thomas hid a smile. Robert was a master at hiding his true feelings. Thomas had once watched his lieutenant look much the same way when a blowhard major described his excuses for implementing asinine battle plans.

Somewhat eager to see what the man was going to do next, Thomas performed the necessary introductions. "Robert Truax, these are Laurel's stepsiblings, Jerome and Bess. Miss Laurel's already had to kick them out one time since I've been here."

Before their eyes, Robert's pleasant demeanor transformed into something far darker. Actually, he was eyeing them the way one might examine an unwelcome rat in a cupboard. "Interesting." Then he turned to the third visitor standing on the stoop. "And you are?"

Obviously running out of patience, Laurel's neighbor thrust out a hand. "I'm Landon Marshall. I own a sizable spread of land just to the west of here."

After a pause, Robert took Marshall's hand. "Robert Truax. I fought by this man's side during the altercation between the states. And while he might say otherwise, I can say with honesty that he is not some poor criminal. I would watch how you describe him in the future."

Marshall relaxed. "So you're an old friend."

"Of a sort."

Looking just beyond Robert, Marshall took on a wary expression.

The major held out his hand. "Ethan Kelly of San Antonio. I'm a friend too."

"Nice to meet you—" Recognition flew into Landon's eyes. "Any chance you're a relation to the Michael Kellys?"

Ethan nodded. "Michael Kelly is my father."

"He owns one of the biggest ranches in the area."

"The Bar X is one of the biggest ranches in the state," Ethan said, clarifying Marshall's statement.

Thomas couldn't help but stare at Ethan in surprise. He'd known Ethan's family was wealthy and well connected, but he never dreamed they were that well-off.

Marshall's smile was so slick oil could have run off it. "I'd very much enjoy the opportunity to talk to you about your ranch. I have some questions about the train lines and managing a full crew."

"Excuse me," Jerome said. "We are still standing out here on the doorstep." He waved a hand at Thomas. "Step aside now and let us in. Bess and I need to get settled."

"You are not moving back in," Thomas said. "However, I will go ask Miss Tracey if she desires company."

Bess harrumphed. "I fail to see how it is up to her to decide anything. After all, this was our father's house before it became hers."

"Your father ensured this ranch would come to me when he and my mother died," Laurel said quietly from her position next to the staircase.

Thomas gripped the door. "As entertaining as this reunion is turning out to be, I don't believe there's anything more to be said."

"Hold on, Sergeant," Laurel said. "We should let them say their piece."

"Sure?"

Before she could answer, Landon Marshall pushed his way in. "Laurel, I became even more worried when your help relayed that you would not be coming to my home for supper tonight. Please tell me you've reconsidered your decision to manage this ranch and all your troubles on your own. Your siblings and I want to help you."

Sharing a look with Robert and Ethan, Thomas stepped to one side as Bess and Jerome wandered inside too. After looking outside for any sign of Captain Monroe but seeing nothing, he shut the door, then walked to Laurel's side. "You don't need to do or say anything," he said.

Her gaze softened. "While I appreciate your efforts to shield me, I think I should hear what they have to say."

"At last you have regained your senses in that regard," Jerome said. "Let's sit down and discuss why you men are here."

Bess was already walking toward the sitting room. "I'll have some tea, Laurel. With cream and sugar."

"Of course. Please make yourselves comfortable," Laurel said as she walked toward the kitchen.

"What is going on?" Robert said under his breath to Thomas.

"I'm not exactly sure, but I aim to find out. Lead our visitors into the sitting room, would you? I'll go get some answers."

"My pleasure."

Satisfied that Robert and Ethan would keep Laurel's stepsiblings and wannabe suitor in line, Thomas followed her to the kitchen.

Laurel had just set the kettle on to boil.

"Why are you serving them tea?" he asked. "You don't need to lift one finger for them."

"I know. But I can't avoid them forever. Jerome and Bess have a way of twisting information and situations to get what they want."

"Yes, I noticed they don't take rejection well."

"They don't take much of anything well. I'm afraid I'm not above using you and your friends to help me get my point across."

"And Landon Marshall?"

"I started wondering if he might be able to give us any helpful information about the problems occurring around here. But I don't want to face him alone either."

"Fair enough. But I'm putting a time limit on this visit," he warned. "They are not staying longer than half an hour."

Setting cups and saucers on a cart, Laurel nodded. "That suits me just fine." After she set out a plate of shortbread cookies, a small pitcher with cream, and a sugar pot, she poured the now boiling water into a fine-looking blue teapot. "You may push the cart, Thomas," she said lightly.

"My pleasure. You know, I do believe this is the first tea service I've ever pushed."

"So far you are doing an exemplary job."

Thomas found himself smiling as they entered the sitting room. As he saw that Bess and Jerome were sharing the sofa, Landon Marshall was ensconced in the largest chair, and Robert and Ethan were standing in front of the fireplace, he raised his eyebrows.

Laurel's grace, on the other hand, seemed to have no limits. Standing at the cart, she politely served everyone tea. Only after they had all been taken care of did she perch on the edge of the remaining chair.

Unable to help himself, Thomas walked to her side.

After casting him a look of gratitude, she said, "Now that everyone has met, I must ask why you have come, Landon. Were you simply escorting Jerome and Bess here?"

"Not at all. There has been talk in town of some problems taking place on your ranch. I heard rumors about more dead cattle and gunshots being fired at you. Is this true?"

"It is," Thomas replied.

"Why would anyone want to harm you?"

"I don't know," Laurel said. "I can only guess that someone who wants me to sell my land is hoping violence might sway me. That is, unless he actually wants me dead."

Thomas noticed Jerome and Bess exchange a look with Marshall. He jumped on that. "Miss Tracey has told me that each of you has been attempting to persuade her to sell."

Bess gasped. "What are you insinuating?"

"It seems fairly obvious to me," Robert said.

Jerome got to his feet. "While it is true that I have been unsuccessfully encouraging my sister to sell, I would never resort to killing animals."

"Or shooting at her?" Robert asked. "If you killed Miss Tracey, your problems would be solved."

"Think what you will, but I am not a murderer."

Thomas agreed. Jerome still didn't look like he had ever held a pistol. And from what Laurel had said, he also didn't have any money to pay someone to do his bidding.

Landon Marshall was a different story.

"What about you, Marshall?" he drawled. "I know you also have been hoping to persuade Miss Tracey to sell."

"That is true."

"Would you resort to violence to get your way?"

"While it is true that I fought in the war, I am still a gentleman." The look he gave Thomas showed he definitely did not consider Thomas to be the same type of man.

Thomas was not affronted. After all, he was no gentleman.

"Where did you serve?" Major Kelly asked.

"I was with the Texas militia unit."

"Oh? Did you fight alongside the Tennessee Army?"

Marshall looked uncomfortable. "No. I was stationed near Dallas. I'm afraid I didn't see much action."

"Ah."

Landon turned to stare at Laurel. "I am becoming concerned about you, Laurel. You shouldn't be here alone, and especially not alone in the company of these soldiers. You need to consider not only your stepsiblings' needs but your own. I would still like to marry you."

Laurel clasped her hands together. "I have told you several

times now that I would like you to stop pursuing me. I also told you the other day that I didn't need you looking out for me."

"But something is going to happen to you."

"Is that a threat?" Thomas asked.

"I am stating a fact. As I told you the other day when Jackson and I stopped by, I have had nothing to do with the attacks on the Red Roan Ranch. Also, don't forget that one of my barns was broken into as well. I am also a victim."

Just then Thomas felt a prickling on the back of his neck. Turning around, he saw Captain Monroe standing in the doorway that led out to the kitchen. "Sir."

Immediately, all the other occupants of the room turned to stare at the newcomer. Everyone wore various shades of surprise.

"Good evening," Captain Monroe said. "I decided to come on in when I saw the doorway was cracked and heard such an intriguing conversation." Looking as if he was harboring a secret, he said directly to Laurel, "I hope you don't mind that I barged right in, miss. I couldn't seem to stay away."

28

IT TOOK EVERYTHING LAUREL HAD NOT TO PRESS A HAND to her chest as her latest guest stepped into her sitting room. She'd been so focused on the conversation that she hadn't even realized another person had joined them.

Even more disconcerting was the rush of adrenaline she felt when Captain Monroe turned her way. He had blond hair cut close to his scalp, a ruddy complexion that testified he'd spent most of his life out in the elements, and clear, light-blue eyes that seemed to burn into her very soul.

No part of his face was exceptional. However, the sum of its parts made one want to take a second, more lingering look.

Luckily, he seemed oblivious to her stare.

"Miss Tracey, I presume. Please forgive my rude entrance." Executing a small bow, he said in a deep, almost scratchy voice, "My name is Devin Monroe. At one time I was Thomas's captain."

She stood and curtsied deeply. "Sir, your appearance is most welcome. I hope your journey wasn't too strenuous?"

"I am happy to say that it would take a far more taxing trip to make it a strenuous one."

"May I bring you something to drink or eat?"

He looked at Bess, Jerome, and Landon. "Thank you, but not at the moment."

Major Kelly stepped forward and held out his hand. "Glad you could join us, Devin. As you might have surmised, we were just discussing a few things that have been occurring recently on Miss Tracey's property."

Turning to Landon, Captain Monroe surveyed him from top to bottom. "I overheard much of what was discussed," he said, his voice cold. "Trust me when I say that it would be in your best interests, sir, to conclude your visit at this time."

Landon narrowed his eyes. "What are you insinuating?"

"That while thousands of men were in the Confederacy, few earned the reputation you did."

Landon blanched. "I don't know what you think you heard, but I assure you I served with honor."

"I'm sure you served many women extremely well," Captain Monroe said sarcastically. While Landon sputtered, the captain turned to Thomas. "Thomas, I'd like an update as soon as possible."

"Yes, sir. I will do that presently."

"What a minute," Jerome called out. "Our business is not done."

Before Laurel could step in, Thomas said, "I beg to disagree. I believe it's time to bid you good evening."

"Laurel, are you simply going to stand there and let these men push us out the door?" Bess asked.

Laurel thought Bess looked crestfallen. So much so, she was tempted to ask her, at least, to stay. Though Bess hadn't treated her well, Laurel wasn't proud that she'd sent Bess away. It wasn't a Christian way to behave, especially toward a woman who was essentially on her own in the middle of Texas. Bess was also family. Even though she had neither been grateful for Laurel's sacrifices on her behalf nor lifted a finger to help her, she could change.

Maybe she already had changed?

While the men in the room waited on her reply, Laurel pursed her lips. Maybe she should ask the men to move back out to the barn and strive to make it work with Bess and Jerome? Her step-father had been so very good to her. Surely he would be pleased if Laurel took them back.

Her mother would be proud of her too. After all, hadn't she taught Laurel time and again to do good deeds without expecting anything in return? Surely this was in that category.

Having made her decision, Laurel cleared her throat. "Bess, as a matter of fact—"

"Good," Bess said, interrupting. "I'm glad you're coming to your senses. For a moment I was worried you were actually thinking of continuing this façade."

Laurel blinked. "I'm sorry, I don't understand."

Bess waved a hand impatiently. "Look at you, primping among all these gentlemen."

"Primping?" Laurel looked down at herself. She was wearing a faded and worn calico. No doubt her hair resembled a rat's nest after being pushed off her face for the last ten hours.

When she raised her head, she saw Bess looking her up and down, disdain heavy in her eyes. "You know what I'm talking about. Don't pretend you don't. It's unseemly. And if I may be blunt, embarrassing for you." Raising her chin, she said, "We both know you would never catch the eye of men like these. Why, they were officers."

Mortified that Thomas and his friends were hearing such accusations, she sputtered, "I have not been attempting to catch anyone's eye."

"You need to accept Landon's suit. He is your only chance for matrimony. And he has promised that Jerome and I can live in this house too."

Landon got to his feet. "My offer of marriage still stands, Laurel. I can protect both you and Red Roan Ranch. And if you feel guilty about how you've treated Miss Vance and her brother, I can buy the ranch and you can give them the proceeds."

Oh, but this was awful! Her cheeks burned as Thomas, his captain, Robert, and the major all looked on with varying degrees of distaste. What did they think of her now? She could only imagine.

And though she hated to continue to air her dirty laundry, it didn't seem as if she had much choice. She ignored Landon and turned to her stepsiblings.

"I need to keep the Red Roan Ranch. It's all I have left of my parents. It's all I have left of your father too. Surely that means something to you. He loved this ranch."

"If he loved this place, his affection was misplaced," Jerome interjected in a bored tone. "Besides, if he had truly loved this land, he would have asked Bess and me to come here years ago. He never did."

"Why would he ask you to live here? He and my mother lived on the property he left you. And besides, you two were still in boarding school when he married my mother."

"Yes, I believe you were studying math and whatever while the rest of us were fighting," Thomas murmured.

Jerome folded his arms across his chest. "I was studying business and law while you all, I have learned, were languishing on an island during the end of the war. There's a difference, I think," he said.

Robert Truax's whole posture changed and his fists clenched. Looking at his expression, Laurel realized he was holding on to his temper with care.

Luckily, she was also coming to the conclusion that nothing

was ever going to change her stepsiblings. No matter what she did or said to Bess and Jerome, they were never going to respect her. They also were never going to appreciate the ranch the way she did. To them, it was simply a piece of land that, one way or another, would allow them to continue their rather aimless lives.

It would never be their legacy.

It would never be their home.

That realization bolstered Laurel's resolve. She had to keep the ranch. If she lost this land, she would feel like a failure. She would also feel as if she had lost an important part of herself. She couldn't allow that, not when she'd already lost so much.

Turning to Landon, she said, "I do think you have had my best interests at heart, and I understand you think marrying me will be of help. But I can't marry only for the ranch's future, and I will not sell this land."

"You will regret this," Landon warned.

"I don't think so." As he glared at her, she turned to face Bess and Jerome. "Time and again I have tried to give you both the benefit of the doubt. I have waited for y'all to help me work the ranch. To help me keep your father's legacy alive and well. But you never did. Now it is very apparent that you never will. I have had enough, I'm afraid. Please leave."

That seemed to be all Thomas needed. He turned toward the foyer. "You heard the lady. It's time to go."

Jerome glared at the assembled men, his expression holding nothing but disdain for the war heroes in the room.

Then he turned to Laurel. "From now on, I will cease to know you. You are no better than a soiled dove working the alleys, living the way you are with multiple men. It's shameful and unseemly."

Just as she was about to sputter a reply, Thomas threw out a punch and hit Jerome square in the face.

Uttering a startled cry, Jerome's head jolted back from the force, though he did remain on his feet. After a few seconds, he blinked his one good eye, his other hidden behind one palm. Blood began to pour from his nose. "You will regret this."

"You are full of threats, aren't you?" Lieutenant Truax asked as he grabbed Jerome's elbow. "I've rarely seen or heard the like."

"Are all of you going to allow him to get away with this? He struck me."

"If he hadn't hit you, I would have done the deed myself," the lieutenant said. "There is no way I would stand quietly while you disparaged Miss Tracey. Though I may not have Thomas Baker's size, I can pack a good wallop."

Holding a handkerchief to his face, Jerome merely walked out of the room without a word.

"It is evident that this situation has disintegrated," Landon said. "I'll see myself out."

Bess said nothing, just followed Jerome and Landon and scurried to the front entrance.

After Robert closed the door, he grinned. "Good riddance to them."

Thomas stepped close to her. "Are you all right, Laurel?"

"Yes, of course. Thank you for coming to my defense. Thank you, too, Lieutenant Truax."

"It was my pleasure," he said. "I must say, I always thought having siblings would make my life better and more complete. But after meeting those two, I'm kind of glad I missed out. They couldn't have been harder to bear."

"I'm afraid I've often felt that way myself," Laurel replied. Wanting to get everything out in the open, she looked curiously at Captain Monroe. "Sir, what did you mean about Landon Marshall? I thought he'd served with honor."

"No, he didn't do that. Not exactly. But I'm afraid the things I know are not suitable for feminine ears."

Thomas rested a hand on the middle of her back. "He's right, Miss Laurel. Let it go, at least for now."

Realizing he was right, that there were far more important things to dwell on besides Landon's past, she drew a deep breath. "Gentlemen, would you care for some fresh coffee?"

"That would be much appreciated, miss," the major said. "Thank you."

Just as she left the room, she saw Captain Monroe hug Thomas like a fond old friend. She imagined Thomas was asking how he knew he was in jail and thanking him for his gifts. Thanking him for coming now to his aid.

When all the men started chuckling, then began to talk as though they'd never been apart for more than a day or two, she knew it was a welcome reunion. A needed one.

It was a blessing in the middle of a terrible situation. And because those moments were hard to come by and should be treasured, she decided to take her time with both the coffee and the captain's supper. Some things were far more important.

29

Johnson's Island, Ohio
Confederate States of America Officers POW Camp

MAIL HAD ARRIVED AGAIN.

Thomas knew the routine, and in his more maudlin moments, he resented the men who looked forward to each mail day like the arrival of a long-awaited lover.

Whenever rumors circulated that a boat had arrived with a pack of letters, a new tension would flurry around the camp. The men would rest on their bunks, gazing at the door of the barracks. And while they waited, they would mope and whine and talk about how the hours passed so slowly.

Then their eyes would light up when one of the guards wandered in with a handful of precious correspondence.

It happened again and again, with Thomas never receiving a thing.

Usually he dealt with his disappointment by muttering caustic remarks to whoever was nearby. But this day found him in a more reflective mood. Instead of glaring at the guards or mercilessly teasing the recipients, he sat on his cot and watched.

As usual, Phillip Markham had a handful of letters. Each

one was addressed with care. Each letter of his name was carefully formed, as if his beloved Miranda cared so much about her husband that she needed to make even the letters of his name perfect.

Phillip received so many letters from his wife that he wasn't stingy when he read them. While most men retreated to corners in the barracks or empty spaces on the grounds to read mail, weep, and mourn, Phillip simply sat down on his cot, placed his letters in chronological order as best he could, and read them one right after the other.

Thomas, sitting on his cot next to him, would sometimes sneak a glance and attempt to read some of Miranda's words and phrases. It was hard for him to do. He didn't want to be rude and intrusive.

But he had a whole other more embarrassing reason. It was plain and simple too. He couldn't read well. Not hardly at all.

He liked to tell himself it was most fortunate that he didn't have a sweetheart to write him. If she did write, he'd have to ask another man to read her words. And then he'd have to ask him to write for him too. A man's pride could take only so much.

Therefore, he lay on his back on his cot and made do with feeling the happiness that drifted off the lieutenant.

"Hey, Thomas," Phillip said after almost a quarter hour had passed.

Thomas turned his head to face him. "Yeah?"

"Want to hear part of Miranda's letter?"

He did. He ached to hear the words, to pocket them away so he could one day pretend they had been written for him. But such eagerness would be misunderstood.

So he propped himself up on his elbows. "If you want. What is she pattering on about today? Her daffodils?"

Phillip laughed, the sound lighthearted and sweet. "Not this time. It's . . . it's about our house."

"Don't keep me in suspense," he teased. "Read on."

Phillip cleared his throat. "'I hope you don't mind, but I decided to redecorate some of the downstairs rooms. They seemed so dusty and drab. You know they do, Phillip, dear. Why, your office alone feels like a dark tunnel with those plum-colored velvet curtains and heavy carpets. And the smell! We've had so many fires in that fireplace I fear everything will forever smell like a chimney sweep.'"

Thomas closed his eyes and imagined such a place. Thick curtains, heavy carpets, roaring fireplaces, and a woman living in the center of it all who actually cared what it looked and smelled like.

Phillip inhaled. "Don't fret, Thomas. It gets better. Listen to this: 'With your comfort in mind, dear husband, Winifred and Emerson and even Cook and Belle and I pulled out the rugs and beat them on the front lawn. Then Belle and I—Belle is the new girl from New Orleans, remember?—set to work taking down those drapes. It was difficult. They were so heavy, and they were fastened with those awful brass rings your mother is so fond of.

"'Anyway, just as we were halfway done, a mouse scurried out of the hem of the drape Belle was holding! A mouse had been living there! That was how long it had been living in your office unattended, Phillip. Which, as an aside, means those drapes were in desperate need to be removed.'"

Phillip chuckled as he flipped over the sheet of velum. "Isn't this something, Thomas?"

Thomas's throat was so tight with jealousy he could only nod.

Clearing his throat, the lieutenant continued. "'Well, you must surely imagine what happened next! That rodent scurried toward me! I cried out and jumped on a chair. Belle was stranded, so I pulled her up on the same seat as me! Us in our skirts . . . why, there was hardly an extra inch to breathe.

"'Then, when Belle saw another mouse, we squealed again, so loudly that we startled Mr. and Mrs. Clark, who were out for their usual Friday evening stroll. They came running up the lawn and burst into the foyer without even knocking first.'"

Phillip looked at Thomas. "I never cared for Mr. or Mrs. Clark. They don't have much of a sense of humor, I'm afraid."

"Pity," Thomas muttered, eager to hear the rest of the tale.

"'And . . . oh, Phillip, it was just awful. There they were, standing in the doorway, watching Belle and me clasp each other on top of a chair. When—and I am sorry about this, Phillip, I really am—the chair broke—'"

Thomas leaned forward. "Broke, you say?"

Phillip's face lit up as he continued. "'We fell to the ground, startling the mouse, who went running toward Mr. and Mrs. Clark! Mrs. Clark ran out of the house while Mr. Clark attempted to bash the poor thing with his umbrella. He missed, thankfully.'"

Unable to help himself, Thomas interrupted. "Thankfully?"

Phillip chuckled. "That is one thing you're going to learn when you get yourself a wife, Thomas. Women are fretful creatures. They change their minds on a moment's notice and feel sorry for small furry creatures." He sighed. "I don't know what we men would do without them."

Thomas laughed. "You mean you don't know what you'd do without your Miranda, sir. You, I'm afraid, are well and truly smitten."

Staring down at the letter, Phillip grinned. "I can't deny it. I'm afraid I am."

"What are you going to write to her about all that, sir? Are you upset about the chair?"

"The chair? Of course not. I don't care about the mouse either.

All that matters to me is that she's there at home, waiting for me to return."

"You are a blessed man, sir."

"I know I am. But don't worry, Thomas. When you get back to Texas, I'm sure some gal will claim your attentions too." He laughed again. "I am only going to be sorry that I won't be there to hear the stories about all she puts you through."

"I won't be marrying anyone, sir."

"Don't be so certain. Love and marriage happen to the best of us."

"Not to men like me, I'm afraid."

Carefully folding Miranda's letter into its envelope, Phillip glanced at him again. "That's where you're wrong, Sergeant. It happens especially to men like you."

Not wanting to argue that point, Thomas lay back down. He rested his head on his folded arms and closed his eyes, and finally gave in to the temptation of imagining what it might be like to be Phillip Markham. To have a pretty woman waiting for him in a comfortable house.

But no matter how hard he tried, he couldn't picture it. It seemed such a thing was beyond him.

30

THOMAS WOKE UP BEFORE DAWN. EVERY NERVE IN HIS BODY felt raw, every sense on alert. Startled, he realized he'd felt the exact same way before going into battle. His stomach was in knots and his head felt clearer than it had in months. Even a faint metallic taste was in his mouth.

He was both bemused and relieved to realize that his body hadn't forgotten how to prepare for war. Maybe a small part of him had missed fighting after all.

After hurriedly dressing, he carefully walked downstairs and stepped out to the kitchen. He hoped he hadn't awakened Laurel. She'd sat with him and the men late into the night, listening while they made plans and answering questions about various parts of the Red Roan Ranch.

He'd been proud of the way she answered each man's questions. She had been both thoughtful and observant, and hadn't acted either rattled or nervous when the men listened to her answers intently. He'd seen many men handle Captain Monroe's questioning less well.

Much later, well after midnight, Thomas had heard Laurel's light footsteps going down the stairs. He'd sat up in bed, waiting to hear her ascend again. It had been a lengthy wait, almost an hour.

While he'd waited, he let his mind drift again, imagining how pleased he would have been to have the honor of taking care of her. If she hadn't been able to sleep, he would have held her in his arms into the night, soothing her worries by reminding her that he and his friends weren't just former soldiers with battlefield experiences. No, they had years of practice tracking men in all sorts of terrain. They each had also fought several battles in hand-to-hand combat. She wasn't going to have to worry about getting hurt.

Unable to stop himself, he'd let his mind wander to places it shouldn't. He thought about pressing his lips to her temple and brow, softly kissing her lips. Imagined whispering things only a lover would. That she was important to him. So important that he would be extra careful when he was out, because he now had someone to come home to.

The bright light of morning reminded him he was a fool. He would never be her sweetheart, her husband, or her lover.

No, he was destined to be only her hired hand, a prisoner in her eyes. A poor man without relatives to vouch for him or money to improve his situation. He was simply a man she would know for only a small amount of time. He was expendable.

That was all right, though. Even if he did get nicked by a stray bullet, he wouldn't mind dying to help her live a better life.

After shaking off his doldrums, he entered Laurel's kitchen. By now he knew his way around it well enough to make a pot of coffee. As he boiled some beans and reviewed their plans for the day, he heard footsteps. Turning, he saw the captain was already up.

"Good morning, Thomas," the captain said as he joined him, his blond hair damp and his cheeks freshly shaved. "I was hoping to find you here."

"Just making coffee."

Monroe looked around and smiled. "I never thought I'd say this, but domesticity looks good on you."

"I like to help Miss Laurel when I can. She didn't sleep well." Of course, the moment he said that, he wished he could take back the words. He didn't want any of the men to think he wasn't treating Laurel with anything other than respect.

But if the captain had thought his comment was odd, he didn't dwell on it. "That's understandable. Today is a big day."

"Yes, sir." Pointing to the pot on the stove, he said, "I'll pour you some coffee momentarily. It's almost done."

Leaning against the counter, Captain Monroe shrugged. "No hurry. Have you seen Miss Tracey yet this morning?"

"No, sir. I'm hoping she's still resting."

The captain seemed to relax. "Good. Poor thing. I thought I'd seen everything, but those siblings of hers were rather insufferable."

Thomas grinned. "That they were." Satisfied that the coffee had been boiling long enough, he poured them each a cup. "Here you are, sir."

"Thank you." Smiling at the dark, rich brew, he murmured, "No matter how many years pass, I find I can never take a decent cup of coffee for granted."

"This is certainly better than some of the drinks we ground up and sipped around campfires."

Monroe groaned. "Remember when we tried to make coffee out of ground black walnuts? To this day I haven't tasted a more vile concoction."

"We were thankful for it at the time. I do remember that."

"We were thankful for a great many things. One had to believe that God had our backs, otherwise our reality was too hard to bear." After draining half his cup, the captain looked at him. "How bad is your back, Thomas?"

"From the whipping?"

"Of course."

Hating that Monroe had brought it up, Thomas shrugged. "It's nothing to be concerned about. It's healing."

"Are you sure? Are you in a great deal of pain?"

He certainly wasn't eager to discuss his back with his former captain. "No, sir. Miss Tracey cleaned my wounds. That helped."

"Did she now?" he murmured. Staring at Thomas intently, the captain said, "She's a good woman. Kind."

"She is." After looking toward the door to make sure she wasn't within earshot, Thomas shared what was hard to admit even to himself. "I guess it's pretty obvious that I'm fond of her."

"I did take notice of that." As he filled his mug to the brim again, the captain said, "If the way you stayed close to her side didn't clue me in, the facer you gave her stepbrother demonstrated how you felt."

Now that his own mug was empty, Thomas set it on the counter and folded his arms across his chest. "I don't understand the way those two are constantly putting her down. Laurel is just about the prettiest thing I've ever laid eyes on."

"She is fetching, that is true."

Thomas was rather surprised that the captain's statement didn't sound more emphatic. After all, she was so much more than that. "She's more than fetching, sir. She's beautiful. It's not just me who thinks that either," he rushed on. "Why, when I accompanied her in town, I saw men watching her. I tried not to get too riled up. After all, how could they help themselves?"

"Indeed."

"It's all I can do not to keep my hand constantly on her arm or back," he continued, since it seemed he was unable to stop himself. "People need to know she is not someone to be trifled with."

"I reckon she's grateful to have such a devoted servant," the captain said lightly. "Have you told her how you feel?"

"That I admire her? I have. Not that it really matters."

"Why doesn't it?"

"It's pretty obvious even to me that she deserves someone other than a worn-out ex-prisoner."

"I fear we are all ex-prisoners, Sergeant."

"You know what I mean. She paid money to release me from a cage. She deserves someone a whole lot better than the likes of me."

Captain Monroe walked to the pot, picked up a rag to hold the hot handle, and poured himself more coffee. "Forgive me, but it sounds as though you're having confidence issues."

It was on the tip of his tongue to deny it, but he couldn't do so without flat-out lying. "Maybe I am." He didn't like the thought of that. Men needed to be confident and strong, not full of self-doubt and impulsive. "I'll work on that."

Just as the captain smiled, Robert Truax poked his head into the kitchen. "Good. You're both here."

"I'm surprised you found us," Thomas said.

"I followed the scent of coffee."

"I'll pour you some," Thomas said. "Let me just find another mug."

"That can wait," Robert said with a grim look. "I need y'all to see something," he said, then turned before Thomas or the captain could ask any more questions.

Suddenly realizing that Robert smelled faintly of smoke, and feeling no small amount of dread, Thomas followed Robert into the main house, through the front rooms, and into the foyer. There he saw Ethan Kelly standing by the door, looking grim. His clothes were uncharacteristically rumpled.

"What happened?" Thomas asked.

Kelly opened the door farther so they could see outside without any barriers.

Half expecting another dead animal, what he saw instead made his breath catch.

A sizable plume of smoke was rising from the north pasture. "Fire?"

"Only a small one," Kelly said. "Someone took a barrel, lit a fire on the inside of it, and took off. If Robert and I hadn't seen it when we were shaving, the barrel could have blown, and with the direction of the wind this morning, this house and the barn might have been destroyed, along with all the horses."

"So they've upped their game," Thomas said.

"It seems like they have, but their methods are still confusing. They kill cattle, but only a few. Now they start a fire, but intentionally limit it to threaten these buildings," Robert said.

"They want Laurel afraid, or homeless, but the ranch intact."

"There's one thing more," Ethan said as he handed Robert a sheet of paper. "This was nailed to a nearby mesquite tree."

Thankful that Laurel wasn't there to read this one, Thomas said, "Major, have you read it yet?"

"I did. It says, 'This isn't over.'" Looking intently at Thomas's face, Kelly said, "Does that mean anything to you?"

"Only what it probably means to you. Escalation."

Looking at the other men surrounding them, Ethan Kelly's expression seemed almost lethal. "I don't know how y'all feel, but I sure as heck didn't survive the war and prison camp just to deal with some idiot setting fires while I sleep." His voice rose. "I don't take kindly to someone setting out notes for me to find like it's a bloody game."

Just then, Captain Monroe walked out the front door and

joined them on the porch. "My patience has reached its end," he said. "We need to ride out immediately. Track who did this."

"I'll be ready in ten," Robert said. "Just give me a minute to drink some coffee."

"I'll fish out something for us to eat on the ride while you're doing that," Thomas said. "I think Laurel has some biscuits left over from yesterday."

Kelly shook his head. "Appreciate you getting us some food, but we need to stick to the plan we devised last night. You need to stay here to protect her."

"I can't stand down while the rest of you take care of this business. I'll tell Laurel to stay inside with the doors locked. She has a rifle, and so far no one's tried to come into the house."

"We don't know they won't now, not after this fire. This could be a trap." Major Kelly shook his head. "You don't know what kind of men they are. Not for certain."

Kelly was right. But Thomas couldn't see another way to fight the men. "We need every man on horseback to track and fight. Plus, I know the terrain. You all need me."

"We'll make do," Captain Monroe said. "That lady is going to be scared to death when she discovers what happened. We can't leave her to sit and worry by herself."

"But—"

"You know I'm right." Lowering his voice, he said, "Think about what you just told me in the kitchen."

"That is precisely why I need to go. I can't stay behind while the three of you solve my problems."

Robert placed his hand on Thomas's shoulder. "If it's any consolation, I just went through something like this with my wife." He paused as he looked at Thomas more closely. "Do you really want what's yours left unguarded?"

Thomas exhaled. He didn't dare meet the major's or captain's eyes. No doubt they were amused by his newfound love for such an innocent, sweet girl.

But he couldn't deny his friends' words made sense. If he rode out, he might feel better about what he was doing, but he would also be putting Laurel at risk. She would always be on his mind. And he would never forgive himself if something happened to her while they were all away. "You have a point," he said around an exhale. "I'll go find some food for y'all. And thank you for what you're doing."

"I'm just glad you contacted us," Captain Monroe said. "Whoever is doing this needs to stop."

Thomas turned to walk back inside . . .

And was brought up short by the sight of Laurel standing right inside the open door. Her face was pale, and a question was in her eyes. "Thomas, what happened?" she asked, her voice tremulous.

"There was a fire, but it's out now."

"Where?"

"North pasture. Someone started a fire in a barrel." No reason to tell her what could have happened if the barrel had exploded, nor about the note.

"What are we going to do?" she asked as Robert and the captain joined them.

"You and I are going to stay here while Robert, the captain, and Kelly attempt to track whoever set the fire in your pasture."

She shook her head. "I can't do that."

"You can't do what, darlin'?" Robert asked. When he caught Thomas's glare, he rolled his eyes.

"I can't stay here. I'm sorry, but I can't do it."

Thankful that his friends had coached him, he reached out and rubbed both of her arms. She was frightened to death. Why had he ever thought it would be okay for him to leave her to worry and fend for herself? "You aren't going to be alone, Laurel. I'm going to stay with you. I promise, no one is going to hurt you while I'm nearby."

But instead of looking reassured, she shook her head. "No, I want to go too."

"Miss Tracey, forgive me, but you don't understand," Robert said. "We all rode together for months, if not for years. There's a trust there and a familiarity. If you came along, you would only get in the way."

"I can ride well too. I grew up on a horse." She straightened her backbone. "Plus, I know this land better than any of you could ever hope to. You need me."

While Thomas considered the best way to cut off her argument, she stepped away from him and raised her chin. "I am not going to be scared, and I am not going to slow you down."

"And if someone is shooting at us again?"

"Then I'll do my best to shoot back," she said. Staring at him, she said, "Look at me, Thomas. Really look at me. I am not a spoiled hothouse flower. I, too, survived the war. I am also the same woman who walked through a crowd and bought myself a convict."

Feeling the other men's approval, Thomas exhaled. It seemed there was only one thing to do. "Can you be ready within the hour, Miss Laurel?"

She smiled. "Since I'm nearly ready now, I believe my answer is yes." Turning toward the kitchen, she called out, "I'll gather some food to take with us and meet you in the barn."

"Before you start gathering, may I beg a favor?" Robert said, moving to her side. When she stared at him warily, he offered a sheepish smile. "I'm parched and half asleep. May I have a cup of coffee, Miss Laurel? Preferably right this minute?"

"Of course," she said around a relieved exhale. "I'll be happy to get you anything you need."

When they disappeared down the hall, Thomas met Captain Monroe's eyes. "I'm sorry, sir," he bit out. He hated to disappoint Devin Monroe. "I know you were right, but it seems I am hopeless against her. I couldn't think of another way to encourage her to stay."

But to Thomas's surprise, the captain chuckled. "Don't apologize, Sergeant. She was extremely persuasive. She also happens to be right."

"I never thought I'd hear you say that."

"At one time, I wouldn't have either. However, times have changed. During the war, our women had to take care of themselves without our help. Some even thrived. Now I'm afraid we can't expect them to always be content to sit and wait while we do our best."

"We sure couldn't have expected Miss Tracey to do that. She was determined."

"She made some good points too. I couldn't have said no to her if I'd tried. Buying herself a prisoner, indeed. You got lucky the day she decided to free you."

Trotting up the stairs to get his weapons, Thomas smiled to himself. No matter what happened next, he knew one thing for certain. Laurel Tracey was a woman like no other.

31

HER SKIN FELT TINGLY. EVERY ONE OF HER SENSES FELT AS though it was on alert. Actually, Laurel had never felt more alive, not even when she'd made the decision to walk through a crowded square and claim Thomas Baker as her own.

The reason could be the company surrounding her. The four soldiers were gruff and confident and seemed to be solely focused on implementing the plans they'd made. She'd taken a leap of faith when she made the decision to join Thomas and his friends on their mission, though she'd been fairly certain Thomas was going to refuse her request to join them.

A part of her wouldn't have blamed him. Although the war and the following years had changed her, she was still her parents' daughter. They'd taught her both to mind authority and to know her place. But she'd also witnessed her mother making decisions about their home or about her and her brother that her father hadn't necessarily agreed with.

But time and again he'd bowed to his wife's decisions.

But this felt different. She didn't have people to lean on. She had only herself. And while she might have Thomas for the year, and he claimed he would stay as long as she needed him, the day would come when she would be safe and he would be ready to move on. That day would no doubt come sooner than she was ready for.

Because she had that knowledge, she knew she had to do everything she could to help herself, and to learn too.

After she'd made some bacon sandwiches and served Robert a cup of coffee, she decided to put on her most comfortable riding boots, a brimmed hat, and her sturdiest gloves. She also took her brother's rifle from its resting place.

Then she gathered up the sandwiches and hurried out to the barn. The last thing she wanted to happen was for the men to be waiting for her to make an appearance.

She was pleased to see that only Thomas and Captain Monroe were in the barn when she arrived. They were inspecting their own rifles and storing ammunition.

It was a stark reminder that this ride would likely be dangerous. The men were determined to hunt down the trespassers, and they undoubtedly expected trouble.

"You ready to ride with a bunch of worn-out soldiers, Miss Tracey?" Captain Monroe asked when he spied her lurking at the barn door's entrance.

She rolled her eyes. "I doubt there's a person in Texas who would describe any of you men in that fashion. But to answer your question, yes, sir, I am ready."

"I admire your gumption, but don't forget that gumption and fortitude can get one only so far. Be sure to stay close to Thomas's side."

The captain's blue eyes were solemn. Looking in Thomas's direction, she noticed that he, too, was looking at her in complete seriousness. "I'll do my best to keep up with you, Sergeant."

But instead of smiling at her, he shook his head. "That ain't good enough. You need to promise you will."

She didn't believe in promising what she couldn't be sure she could do, but Laurel understood his point. She needed to set her mind on success, not just hopes and dreams. "I promise to keep up with you. I will."

"Good. I need to know you're going to be there, no matter what. The other men would no doubt rather have us stay here while they fan out and look for your intruder. We have both allowed our vanities to go against our better judgment."

Laurel felt a chill run down her spine. She believed in herself and knew she wanted to do everything in her power to help save her ranch. That included joining these men and helping out however she could.

Just as important, she needed to prove to herself and her parents' memories that they'd been right in leaving the ranch to her. She loved the land as much as they had. She was willing to make sacrifices for it too.

However, she also didn't want to risk putting other people in harm's way to feel good about herself. "Gentlemen," she asked hesitantly, "am I being foolish?"

"You are not," Captain Monroe said. "All of us need to put ourselves in harm's way at one time or another for something we believe in. If a person wants to be a person of worth, that's part of the territory."

His words reinforced her resolve. "Thank you for understanding," she murmured.

"Oh, I certainly do understand," he said with a kind smile. "However, I beg you to be honest with us. If you are having second thoughts, say so. There's no shame in letting a group of men do what they are trained to do."

"I'm not having second thoughts," she answered, though she was certainly a bit more nervous about what was going to happen next.

Thomas's reassuring hand on her arm drew her eyes to him. "It will be all right," he said. "I'll look after you. Plus, chances are better than good that we'll ride out and see nothing."

Relieved, she gave him a tremulous smile.

"Uh-oh, looks like our sergeant has brought out his game face," Major Kelly called with a touch of humor in his eyes as he and Lieutenant Truax walked into the barn. "Don't let that scare you, Miss Tracey."

She giggled. "I'm afraid I don't know what 'game face' means."

Lieutenant Truax answered that one. "Thomas here was known to put on a fierce persona before each battle or skirmish. He'd march up and down the line and spur our poor privates on, leaving them shaking in their boots."

Thomas grunted. "Hardly that." Holding up a canteen, he appeared eager to drop the subject. "We all have water. Let's ride out."

Immediately, Lieutenant Truax and the major became serious. "We following last night's plans, Devin?"

Captain Monroe nodded. "Thomas and I talked some more just now. Robert and Ethan, you head south and west. Thomas, Miss Tracey, and I will ride north and east. If you spy trouble or need assistance, shoot three bullets into the air. Otherwise, we'll convene back here in five hours."

"What if we don't see anything in five hours?" Laurel asked as she handed Major Kelly one of her food pouches.

"We probably won't. But that's long enough to keep the horses out in this heat. Plus, we'll need to check with each other and report findings."

Major Kelly swung onto the saddle of his fine-looking Tennessee Walker. "Gentlemen, miss, I suggest we get on our way."

"We'll see you at noon. God be with you," Captain Monroe said as he led his own horse out of the barn.

After helping Laurel onto her saddle, where she secured the other food pouch and her rifle, Thomas mounted Yellow, then directed the horse to follow Captain Monroe. Taking one last look at Laurel, he said, "You ready?"

She inhaled. Exhaled. Then finally answered, "I am."

"Then let's go." He smiled before motioning Yellow into a good clip.

Doing the same with Velvet, Laurel gripped her reins with one hand and her hat with the other.

They were off.

They'd been riding for three hours. With the exception of a few broken branches and a vague feeling in his gut that they were close to trouble, Thomas had nothing to report. Though he had known their hunt wasn't going to be easy, he felt disappointed for Laurel's sake.

It didn't help that as the sun rose higher, the faint wisps of clouds that usually formed in the sky vanished. The sky was now a vivid shade of bluebonnet blue, coloring the sky and making it possible to see for miles across the horizon. Because of that, Thomas was very aware that any movements they made could be observed by whomever they were after.

He also couldn't seem to stop worrying about Laurel. Though she was an excellent rider, he found himself concerned with the sun burning her nose, the heat burdening her, whether she was thirsty or becoming too tired.

Every thirty minutes or so, Thomas would slow his horse and make sure she was all right.

Captain Monroe no doubt noticed his inattention to his

surroundings, but he didn't say anything. Instead, he constantly moved from the front of their group to the back, circling his horse expertly. Taking up Thomas's slack.

When they came to the area by the creek where he and Laurel had come under gunfire, Thomas showed the spot to the captain. "They came from that bluff," he said, pointing. "Laurel and I ended up crouching next to the creek bed."

"Looks as good a place as any to make a quick stop, I think," Monroe said. "Let's stretch for a minute and let the horses get some water."

After Thomas dismounted, he walked to Laurel's side. "Here, honey, let me help you," he drawled, no longer caring that he was uttering a number of endearments. He was glad she didn't refuse his aid. Instead, she merely murmured her thanks and rested her hands on his shoulders as he swung her out of the saddle.

"You feeling all right?" he asked quietly as she held on to him a little longer than was necessary. He wondered if she was trying to get her bearings or was simply tired.

"I'm fine." Looking nervously around, she said, "This spot brings back bad memories, doesn't it? It feels a bit vulnerable."

"It does, but we're well prepared now," he replied, hoping he spoke the truth. "Before, we never would have imagined that someone would fire at us. Now we know better."

Laurel looked warily at Captain Monroe, who had also dismounted but was gazing around them with an alert expression, his rifle at the ready. "I hope the other men are faring better than we are."

"If something happens, we'll hear three shots. If not, it will be no more than we expect." Leaning closer, Thomas said, "Now I'm going to see to the horses. You take a rest or move your legs a bit. They'll thank you for it."

Laurel looked at Thomas gratefully as he walked Yellow, Velvet, and the captain's dark quarter horse to the creek. The captain's horse seemed able to follow the smallest command with high-stepping elegance. Velvet and Yellow looked ill trained by comparison.

However, she couldn't deny they had conducted themselves with honor so far that day. As had she, she reflected as she moved a bit to the side and stretched her arms over her head. When they'd first set out, she had been a nervous wreck. She'd been just as afraid of proving the men right by not controlling Velvet well or getting in their way as she was of encountering their attackers again.

But as they'd split up and quietly continued on, focusing on any faint shadows they spied on the horizon or noises heard in the distance, her body had relaxed. While she might not have been able to lead the search party, she had certainly been able to keep up.

"I must say you're doing a fine job, Miss Tracey," Captain Monroe said as he approached. "I have never been on a mission with a woman before, and I have to admit I was a little worried about how you'd do. But you are proving to me that you can handle just about anything."

"Hardly that," she said. "This has been hard, but even though we're out in the open, I feel safer with you and Thomas out here than I would at home, even if one of you had stayed with me."

"I'm glad you aren't there too."

After realizing Thomas was now taking watch, she smiled her thanks at the captain. "I was just coming to the conclusion that I was glad I had accompanied you," she admitted. "Now I'm torn between hoping we see those men and praying we do not."

He smiled in return. "I would be lying if I said I haven't experienced those same thoughts more than once this morning."

"Really?"

"Absolutely. It's the danger of the unknown that reminds a man he's only human. After all, only the Lord knows our future."

"Indeed." As she drew in a breath, ready to ask the captain about some of his past missions, Thomas cocked his gun.

Both Laurel and Captain Monroe froze.

"Report," Captain Monroe called out.

"Three o'clock," Thomas replied.

She had no idea what that meant. "What—"

Immediately, the captain pulled out his pistol. "Go to the creek, Laurel," he ordered. "Go there and crouch low. Now."

She didn't waste time arguing. She ran as fast as she could to do as he bid. And had just fallen to her knees on the soft, cool ground when a gunshot rang out.

She covered her head and prayed as Captain Monroe fired into the air three times.

It seemed their prey had become their predators.

32

THOMAS HAD ALWAYS CLUNG TO HIS FAITH. HE'D CLUNG TO it when he'd been hiding during the Indian raid that had killed his parents and brother, and during the hard, lonely years when he'd suffered so much on the streets of Fort Worth.

He'd trusted in the Lord to get him through each battle and mission he'd fought during the war and had prayed for strength and grace when he'd been imprisoned on Johnson's Island. In short, he'd always hoped and believed he was never completely alone.

But he'd never feared being forgotten by the Lord as he did at that very moment.

Standing by the captain's side, he watched two men scramble forward, their pistols drawn. One was a stranger. A wiry fellow with a desperate, almost scared expression on his face.

The other man was Laurel's neighbor, Landon Marshall.

Marshall looked grim and determined. Deadly determined.

While the captain raised his Colt, Thomas attempted to talk some sense into the man. He absolutely did not want Laurel to have to witness him killing Marshall. "That's far enough!" he called out. "Lower your guns. We can talk this through."

"I'm done talking!" Marshall yelled right back. And though his steps slowed, he continued forward.

He could sense Monroe closing one eye beside him. "Right or left, Baker?" he murmured, already choosing a target.

"Left," Thomas replied instantly. "But give me a minute."

"You got thirty seconds."

Only because he knew Laurel was witnessing their actions, Thomas attempted to get Marshall to talk. "What is this all about, anyway?" he asked. "We should be able to talk. There's no reason for you to be firing at us."

Marshall sneered as he stepped forward. "Of course there is. Haven't you learned anything in your sorry life? Some matters simply can't be settled without a show of force."

"I agree, but this ain't one of them," the captain said. He'd lowered his gun slightly. In fact, the pistol looked as if it were hanging limp in his right hand. "Now, what exactly do you want?"

"This land. I tried courting Laurel for it. I've even tried to scare her. Killing her cattle, staging property theft, that fire this morning . . . all so she'd sell it to me, if not marry me so I could control it. But nothing has worked. And now she's got you hunting us down."

"It's only one thousand acres," Thomas reasoned. "I was told you have over double that amount."

Landon nodded as he continued to approach, one slow step at a time. "I do. But this property here has two water supplies. Around here, water is more valuable than gold."

"You threatened to poison the creek."

"If I had, the water would have run clear after a matter of days. I need it."

Landon Marshall still wasn't making sense. "Why?"

"Rumor has it that the railroad has plans to come through this way. Anyone who can cater to the railroad is destined not only to survive but to prosper."

Monroe narrowed his eyes. "I was a Ranger before I was a captain. You and I both know a man can't go around staking his claim through poison, bullets, and fires."

Marshall ignored that statement. Glaring at the horses, he said, "There are two of you and three horses. Where's your other rider? Who else is with you?"

"No one you need to be aware of," Thomas said. There was no way he was going to give up Laurel's position if he could help it.

Marshall raised his pistol again. "How about you try answering me again?"

"Lower your weapon," the captain ordered. "There's no need for you to start murdering more people."

"More?" Marshall asked.

"Yeah. You already took down one of my men," Monroe said, lying easily. "You or your partner there shot him."

Marshall's pistol wavered. "Show him to me, Baker."

"If you want to see him, you'll have to dismount and check him out on your own. No way am I leaving my friend alone with you."

Marshall turned to his partner. "Orr, go down to the creek and take a look."

Without a word, the man started heading down the sloping hill toward the creek. Toward Laurel.

Thomas's heart was beating so hard he felt as though the other men could probably see it pounding in his chest. Not daring to even look in that direction, he prayed that Laurel had followed the captain's command and hidden herself well.

The air felt thick and cloying as the three of them watched the man disappear into the brush around the creek. Soon all they could hear was the snap of twigs as he searched.

While Monroe looked a bit bored, Thomas stared at Marshall and attempted to think of reasons not to simply fire a shot into his heart right that minute.

"You're looking a little tense, Baker," Marshall jeered. "What's wrong? Is freedom not suiting you? Or is it that you are coming to realize that Laurel Tracey ain't worth the effort?"

"If I'm tense, it's because I'm trying to convince myself not to kill you for the trauma you've put her through."

"I wouldn't have put her through anything if she'd agreed to marry me in the first place."

"She can't marry you. She deserves better."

"Why?" His voice was filled with thick sarcasm. "She's nothing. She's nothing more than a plain, quiet woman with too much land and too high an opinion of herself."

The captain shifted one foot forward, resurrecting an old move that he'd perfected during the war. Inconspicuously following the direction of his boot, Thomas could see Robert and Kelly approaching from the south. They were on foot and walking stealthily enough not to attract Marshall's attention.

Thomas knew he needed to keep Marshall talking until the other men got close enough to help take him down.

With that in mind, he lowered his gun. "Laurel might have a high opinion of herself, but that don't mean her cattle deserved to be slaughtered."

Landon stepped closer. "Slaughtered? All Orr did was poison them. Half a dozen cows and one calf are hardly worth thinking about."

"Most men value livestock a bit better," Monroe drawled.

"Most men are too afraid," Marshall scoffed. "Most men aren't willing to do whatever it takes to get what they need."

Thomas saw that Kelly and Robert were less than fifty yards

away now. They had separated and were approaching Marshall from either side. With luck one of them would be able to take him by surprise before he could fire.

Knowing he needed to goad him a bit, Thomas smirked. "Unfortunately, your plan didn't go so well. You were no closer to obtaining Laurel's land than before. I'm starting to understand why you didn't see much action during the war."

"I saw enough."

"Of the cathouses," the captain scoffed. "That's where you rescued those women, isn't it? Because you were with the harlots instead of with your regiment."

"I was doing what I needed to do."

Monroe's gaze was filled with pure loathing. "No. You were doing what you—"

"Marshall," his partner called out. "I found something, but it sure ain't a dead man."

Thomas's heart sank as he turned to the thicket of brush and saw Orr holding Laurel's elbow in a death grip. She looked shaken and frightened . . . and mad.

"Laurel!" he called out. When she turned her head his way, he pleaded with his eyes not to give up. He also sent a quick prayer to the Lord for his help. He needed to caution Laurel to keep quiet and meek-looking. Thomas needed her to do whatever it took to stay unharmed.

"You've been standing there lying to me?" Marshall yelled. "What do you think I am? Some pitiful, gullible, weak-kneed opponent?" He raised his pistol, but it hung limply in his hand. "Just because I didn't—"

The rest of his speech was cut off when, without a word, Robert knocked the gun from Marshall's hand from behind, pulled him to the ground, and subdued his protests with a solid blow to his jaw. Seconds later, he had him facedown on the ground and was calf-roping him. Marshall writhed in pain.

Meanwhile, Monroe had turned to Orr. "Let loose of the woman and you'll live."

The man looked wild-eyed, but he didn't let go. "This weren't my fight. I was only doing this for the money. I owed him money. And . . . and he killed a man. George Irwin, after Irwin poisoned the cattle by the creek and shot at her. So did Foster Howell."

"I'd venture to say you don't owe him anything no more," the captain said, his voice smooth and reassuring. "Landon Marshall isn't going to be harming anyone anytime soon, and neither is this Howell. Let go of Miss Tracey."

Orr's eyes widened as he turned to Laurel. He gulped as he stared at her, almost as if he couldn't figure out how he'd met her in the first place.

"Please," Laurel begged.

At last he lifted his hand.

The moment she was free, she started running toward Thomas. He walked down to meet her halfway and pulled her into his arms. "It's okay now," he soothed. "You're safe."

Kelly strode over, and as he tied Orr's hands behind his back, Laurel closed her eyes and burrowed her face into Thomas's chest. "I was so afraid."

"I know. I was too," he admitted as he stared at the other men. Robert now had Marshall sitting against a rock and Kelly was maneuvering Orr to a spot against an old pine tree.

The captain was facing Thomas and Laurel with a pleased look on his face. "It's over."

Relief flooded Thomas. He felt like he was on the verge of tears. "I'm beholden to you," he said to his best friends in the world. "I couldn't have done this on my own."

"You never should have thought you had to, Sergeant," Monroe replied. "We wanted to help."

Still tucked safely in Thomas's arms, Laurel looked up at all of them with shining eyes. "I'm so grateful. Gentlemen, I hardly know how to convey my thanks."

"No thanks are needed," Robert said. "We're only glad you're all right."

His expression now all business, the captain moved toward his horse. "I'm going to ride into town and tell the sheriff what transpired and get some assistance. Robert and Ethan are going to stay here with these men. Thomas, I think it might be best if you took Miss Tracey home."

Thomas couldn't agree more. Running a hand down the curls of her hair, free of its bonnet, he murmured, "How does that sound, angel? Do you feel like you can handle riding Velvet home?"

She nodded. "I can, but I don't want to leave here. Not yet."

Thomas wasn't eager for her to hear Marshall say any more harsh words against her. But he knew it was just as important that he let her see this through. She'd been dealing with this man's destructive behavior since before he'd met her, and she'd be dealing with the consequences of his actions long after he was put in jail.

Looking at both men tied up and silent, he sighed. "If you'd like to stay a bit longer, we will. But now is not the time to talk to Landon Marshall, you understand?"

She nodded. "I don't want to talk to him ever again."

"I think that can be arranged. You won't have to talk to Howell again either."

"I'll be back when I can," Monroe said, then set off toward town.

After helping Laurel get situated in a cleared spot near the creek, Thomas walked over to Kelly and Robert to see if they needed anything.

Each man shook his head before Thomas could open his mouth. "We're fine, Thomas. You know we are," Ethan said.

But that was their way, he knew. They would stay where they were needed for hours or until their captain or whoever was in charge said otherwise. Until that time, they would remain vigilant and silent.

Feeling satisfied that there was nothing else to do for the time being, Thomas returned to Laurel and sat down beside her. Then he took her hand, carefully pulled off her glove, and cradled her hand in between his. She didn't offer a single word of protest.

They sat and waited. No words were said.

That was just as well. Not a single word could be said that would make a bit of difference.

33

No matter how hard Laurel tried to get her body to comply, she couldn't seem to make it stop shaking. Fortunately for her, Thomas didn't notice. Or perhaps he had.

While the other men stayed a respectful distance away, allowing them to have a small semblance of privacy, Thomas had moved from holding her hand to holding her close in his arms, then pressed his lips to her temple and brow.

"Easy now," he murmured for what must have been either the sixth or the sixteenth time. "It's over. I promise, it's all over."

She'd kept her hand resting along the expanse of his chest. Her palm was flat against the soft cotton. Underneath the fabric, she could feel the line of his muscles, and underneath those hard planes, she could feel the beat of his heart.

It beat steadily, centering her. As the minutes passed, she was able to draw strength from its constant beat. She was alive, and Thomas was too.

Little by little, she once more became aware of the oppressive heat of the sun, the faint scent of soap, the gentle whickering of the horses in the meadow. She began to feel more secure, calmed by Thomas's heartbeat, his warm embrace, his soft assurances.

But even all that couldn't alter the fact that her world had just been shaken up. Yet again.

"I can't believe Landon was the man behind everything," she said at last. "I don't understand it."

Thomas sighed. "I know you don't, sugar. But that's okay."

"How can it be all right?"

"If you did understand such things, you wouldn't be the woman you are."

That statement felt as cryptic as any she'd ever heard. Lifting her head at last, she studied him carefully. "What about you? Do you understand it?"

His blue eyes, usually so bright, were cloudy with regret. "To an extent I do." Looking a little sad, he continued, "Marshall wanted everything to stay the same. He thought if he possessed this land and you, it could be."

"But marrying me would have changed everything."

"For you, it would have. For him? He would have gained the water he was fixated on. He would have had better access to the rail line people are talking about coming in the future. He would have even gotten your family's home and any money you had in the bank."

"He was willing to kill to get it all."

"Men kill for such things all the time."

She scoffed. "Thomas."

"It's true. People kill and hurt and maim for security and money. Sometimes even for a woman's love." Lifting one finger under her chin, he tilted it up so she would look into his eyes. "Those things are what dreams are made of. I know I sure dreamed of having such blessings many a time."

"I suppose. But Landon already had so much."

"Landon Marshall's problem was that he couldn't see beyond what was lacking in his life to realize what he already had."

Thomas sounded so sure. "Did you ever do that? Feel like

you needed to put other people in jeopardy to get what you needed?"

"Maybe I did. There have been a lot of times when I would rather eat than starve or sleep instead of suffer. Or kill, rather than be killed."

"That was different, though, wasn't it? Because it was during the war."

Gazing at her, one corner of his lips turned up, he nodded. "Yes, Laurel," he said as he smoothed a lock of her hair away from her face. "It was different. It was a matter of life or death, and I don't mean that in a dramatic, over-the-top way. I mean it was because I had no choice."

"Thomas, I remember the night before my brother and father left for the war. Landon and his father were over, and we were all in our sitting room watching the blaze in the fireplace." She remembered feeling as if she'd known exactly how her life was going to play out. She'd felt safe too.

She hadn't felt that secure or safe again until Thomas appeared in her life. "Landon promised my father he'd look out for me."

"Did he ever do that?"

"For a time. But then he left. When he came back, his personality was different. Altered."

A shadow filled his gaze. "War can change people, I'm afraid."

"I guess that's what happened." Thinking of the many men and women she knew and had known, she sighed. "I guess everyone is destined to change in one way or another. Do you think so?"

He shrugged. "Maybe. I know I have."

"Landon did. And when he did, the things he used to think were important—family, honor—didn't seem to matter anymore. I can't help but think about his poor mother and sister. This will devastate them."

Thomas changed positions and kicked his legs out. "Laurel, it does us no good to try to understand why a man like him did something like he did. You are right. War changed everything. Our land, our homes. People too. However, most of us clung to our values and our hearts. We stayed true to those."

Laurel nodded. Realizing she was no longer shaking and holding off tears, she dropped her hands and exhaled. "You're right. It is over. And it was foolish of me to wonder why he valued different things than he used to. After all, no one really keeps their promises anymore, do they?"

"What? Of course they do."

He sounded so indignant, she almost smiled. "I meant, besides you."

"Look at the captain and the major and Robert. They came here because of a promise we once made."

"They came here because you are a man worth helping."

"I'd like to think I am, but I also know they're honoring something we shared one night in the prison camp."

Lifting his chin, he let his gaze drift over the horizon. "We had just buried Rory MacDonald. He'd been younger than all of us. So fresh and young. So full of promise. We were all feeling the pinch of our confinement."

"I'm so sorry, Thomas."

"While we were all standing there, worrying over what was going to happen next and wishing our circumstances would somehow get better eventually, Captain Monroe had us all make a promise to each other. We promised to look out for each other the rest of our lives."

"That's why they came when you sent word you needed them."

"Yes, that's why. The only reason why. It wasn't because I

deserved it or I had earned their efforts. It was because they'd made a promise. A vow."

"They are truly good men."

"They are."

"You are worth it, you know," she said softly. "Even if you had to ask for help for yourself, not me, it would have been the right thing to do. You're worth it too."

"I'm beginning to think I am at that," he said lightly as he got to his feet.

Bending down, he reached for her hands. "Now, don't you think it's time I got you home? The major and Robert can wait for Sheriff Jackson here. If he needs to speak with you, he'll find you. Let's go home."

She loved how he referred to her house as his home. It was going to be a difficult day indeed when he left, when his year was up and she was the only one who lived in her house again. Thomas didn't seem like someone who would ever settle down if he didn't have to, and she felt sure he was the kind of man who probably never would, no matter how he felt now.

As Laurel placed her hands in his, she made a vow to herself to show her love for him as well as he showed his to her, for the time she would be allowed to do so.

No matter what happened in the future or how much she yearned for him to always stay by her side, she, too, could honor a promise. She could let him go.

Secretly, she knew her reasoning had nothing to do with honor and glory. It was simply because she loved him.

She loved him enough to one day encourage him to leave.

34

THOMAS WATCHED IN DISMAY AS HIS THREE BEST FRIENDS in the world packed their duffel bags in their rooms. After Marshall and Orr were safely jailed in town, along with Foster Howell, they had brought the sheriff and Judge Orbison to the house. And because the two officials wanted to meet with everyone involved individually as well as in a group, the three men divided their time between eating a light meal of cold pork and fried potatoes and bathing off the sweat and grime of the day.

Thomas had also checked on Laurel frequently. As far as he could tell, she was handling all that had happened as well as anyone could have expected. However, he had known many a green recruit in battle who had broken down from the shock of it all hours after seeing such violence and bloodshed. Thomas feared that such a thing would happen to Laurel as well.

He'd been hoping the other men could help him find the words to comfort her. He knew they'd all had more experience soothing tattered nerves than he did.

But less than an hour after Orbison and Jackson left, Thomas discovered the three of them preparing to leave.

"Surely y'all aren't planning to leave right now?" he asked.

Captain Monroe nodded. "I need to get to Fort Worth before it gets too late."

"I had hoped y'all would stay at least until morning. We could catch up."

Major Kelly flashed a smile. "As much as I would enjoy that, I'm afraid that's not possible, for me at least. I need to get back to San Antonio. I need to see to an issue at the Menger Hotel."

Ethan's voice held a note of desperation in it. "Are you in trouble?" Thomas asked.

He shook his head. "Of course not. My, uh, concerns have more to do with a woman than anything else."

Robert chuckled low. "Concerns, hmm? Perhaps I'm not the only one to be falling in love."

"I didn't mention love, Lieutenant," Ethan retorted sharply. "What Lizbeth and I have is just"—his voice lowered—"friendship. At least I think it could be categorized as that."

"Lizbeth sounds like a name to remember," Robert mused.

Feeling a little desperate, Thomas turned to Robert. "I didn't even get to hear the whole story about you and Miranda."

"There were some problems and threats . . . well, it all worked out for the best," Robert said easily. "Once we let our guards down, Miranda and I discovered we had room in our hearts for something more."

For the life of him, Thomas couldn't imagine how Robert and Miranda had fallen in love, but now it seemed he wasn't likely to learn the ins and outs of it anytime in the near future. "I see."

Robert laughed. "I know you don't see at all. But I'm thinking you will see what I'm talking about very soon."

"I suppose you need to leave tonight as well?"

"I do. Miranda doesn't do well without me nearby." Looking a little self-conscious, he added, "I don't do too well away from her either."

Thomas finally brought himself to look at Captain Monroe.

The captain was staring right back at him. However, unlike Ethan and Robert, he wasn't smiling. Instead, he was wearing a solemn expression that spoke volumes. "I have other pressing concerns as well. I am sorry."

"I feel like things are at loose ends." No longer caring that he sounded like a sulky child, Thomas added, "Captain, I haven't even thanked you properly."

Devin Monroe brushed off his words. "Like Robert said out on the range, no thanks are needed. They are never needed. We made a promise, remember?"

"Yes, sir." But still, Thomas knew this was a case where a mere thank-you wasn't good enough. He was going to need to do something more to convey his thoughts and gratitude, even if it was in the form of a letter. "Are you going back to Galveston? Is that where you'll be?"

"No." Looking a bit uncomfortable, Monroe said, "There's a small town out west, almost to the New Mexico territory. I've had my eye on it for some time. I thought I'd head out that way and maybe make a home."

"What are you talking about?" Kelly asked. "Big Spring?"

"None other."

Realizing that the other men were as much at sea as he was, Thomas dropped the subject. "I'll leave you to finish your preparations, then."

"Don't worry, we'll tell Miss Tracey good-bye before we depart," Captain Monroe said.

After going downstairs and ascertaining that the main house was quiet, Thomas looked for Laurel in the kitchen. He wanted to check on her again and let her know about the men's plans. As he walked, he was mentally trying out ways to let her know the men who had helped her so much were about to take their leave.

But she was nowhere in sight.

"Laurel?" he called.

Not hearing a reply, he glanced outside the kitchen door, hoping she was taking a break on the back porch, as she sometimes did. However, there was no sign of her there either.

After checking the bathing room and finding it also empty, he strode up the stairs and tapped lightly on her bedroom door, then turned the doorknob.

If she was sleeping, he would close the door again and tell the men he would convey their good-byes.

Peeking in, he saw that she was, indeed, lying down. But instead of seeing her resting peacefully, he saw her staring back at him.

He was so startled that he gripped the door for a moment to gain a few seconds. "I'm sorry to disturb you, but I couldn't find you downstairs. I thought you might be asleep."

"I probably should be." Moving into a sitting position, she shrugged. "I just thought I'd take a few minutes to gather myself." Her gaze warmed. "Someone keeps telling me I try to do too much and I should rest more."

"Sounds like a very smart man with good advice."

"I think so."

Her light response made him flush. "The men will be leaving soon. They'll be coming down to tell you good-bye. I thought you might want to see them off."

She sat up abruptly. "They're leaving right now? I was hoping they'd stay for a while. I wish they would."

"I asked for the same thing. Unfortunately, they couldn't be persuaded."

Pressing her palms to her cheeks, she said, "I'll freshen up and be down presently."

"I'll let them know. Thank you," he said as he edged out of the room and closed the door behind him.

As he walked back down the stairs, he realized things were about to change between him and Laurel. Now that she was no longer in danger, he needed to go back to his rightful role on the ranch. He needed to put some distance between them and move back to his room in the barn.

Funny, but he had a feeling that, in some ways, he was about to tell her good-bye too.

35

TELLING THE MEN GOOD-BYE HAD BEEN EASIER THAN
Laurel thought it would be. No doubt it was because they looked
so eager to be on their way. After another light but hasty meal,
they each bowed over her hand and wished her well. Then they
each shook Thomas's hand, gave him a hug, said a few words, and
went to fetch their horses from the barn.

Thomas seemed to handle their departure in a stoic manner.
He stood beside her on the front porch as they turned their animals and rode out.

Watching their forms change to faint silhouettes to eventual faint clouds of dust, Laurel felt Thomas's dismay. Though
of course he didn't say anything, she knew he was no doubt disappointed that he'd be bound to her for another eleven months.
That he couldn't be off on his own adventures, live his own life.

"They are good men," she said when there was nothing left of
them to see. "I'll always be grateful for their help."

"I know I've said it before, but they are the best."

Now that they were alone again, she felt a little awkward.
After all, what did you say to a man who had saved your world?
"Would you care for something more to eat?"

"No, Miss Laurel." He pursed his lips. "Actually, I was thinking I would go get settled back in the barn."

"Why?"

"You know as well as I do that it ain't seemly for me to be living in the house with you. People will talk."

"Surely we don't have to worry about what other people say anymore." Her reputation had undoubtedly been ripped to tatters the moment she'd walked through the crowd and paid good money to make him her servant.

Still staring straight ahead, he said, "Eventually Marshall's betrayal will fade and you will get lonely. When a man comes courting, he's not going to be real pleased to discover me sleeping down the hall."

"You moved into the house for my safety," she pointed out. "You were down the hall to protect me."

"I was there for that reason, but you're safe now. You don't have any need for me to be so close to you at all times."

She supposed he was right. Oh, not about her entertaining suitors, but about the other thing. She was safer now. At least, her head knew that.

But her heart and nerves did not. She did need him. She wanted him nearby. She wanted him as close as possible.

"Can you please wait a couple of nights, Thomas?"

"Miss Tracey . . ."

She hated that he was speaking to her in such a formal way again. Hated that he was putting up a wall between them that she wished didn't exist. "Please don't do this," she pleaded. "Don't push me away. Don't pretend we're nothing more than employer and employee. We've come too far for that."

"I agree." He looked pained. "But it's because we are more to each other that I feel we should return some of that distance between us."

"I disagree."

"Miss Tracey, please. Allow me this. I'm trying to do the right thing by you. I'm as far from a gentleman as a man can get, but I know at least this much."

"All right."

"Good."

"But not yet," she said quickly. "Stay down the hall two more nights. Please, Thomas? I already know I won't be able to sleep much tonight. Don't make it worse."

He stared at her for a length of time. Lifted his hand as though he wanted to curve it around her cheek, then let it drop to his side. "All right," he said around a sigh. "I'll stay in there for two more nights. But no longer."

"Thank you, Thomas."

"Don't thank me for this, Miss Laurel," he said in a low tone. "I'm doing this because I can't bear to say no to you. But that don't mean I'm doing either of us any favors."

"I understand."

"Good. Now, I'm going to go check the barn and see what kind of mess the men left for me."

"You think they left you a mess?"

"They're good men, not perfect," he replied with a dry smile before walking away.

Watching him walk away, she realized what she needed to do.

When she came back from town the following afternoon, tears were in her eyes. She could only hope Thomas wouldn't notice.

"I have something for you," Laurel said the moment she found him working in her garden, his sleeves rolled up and a disgruntled expression on his face.

Sitting back on his haunches, he looked at the paper curiously. "What do you have there? I thought you were going for more supplies. Did you get mail too?"

"Stand up and I'll show you."

After stretching his arms, he slowly got to his feet. "You came in the nick of time," he teased. "I was about to tackle these bean plants. Now you can help me with them."

Noticing the stage of growth the beans were in, she said, "What were you going to do? None of them are ready to be picked."

"They aren't? Huh. Well, in that case, it seems your arrival saved them from certain death."

In spite of the lump in her throat, she giggled. But that was always how it was with him. He brought light into her world even when she knew there shouldn't be anything but clouds or darkness. What was she going to do without him?

Almost immediately, she pushed that question away. It didn't matter what she was going to do or how she was going to feel. All that mattered was him. Thomas Baker needed to start living for himself.

"Now I know two things about you. You don't like chickens and you don't know anything about gardening."

Pulling the paper out of her hand, he flashed her another one of his brilliant smiles. "Well, I definitely do not like chickens, but I did learn something about gardening in that prisoner of war camp," he countered. "Just maybe not enough. I'd better be careful or you aren't going to think I'm worth keeping around."

That was as good an opening as any. She leapt on it. "I might have already come to that conclusion."

"Hmm?" he asked as he unfolded the paper and scanned through the writing. His right hand gripped the paper, wrinkling it slightly as he scanned the words again. "Laurel, what did you do?"

"I got you your freedom," she said, hoping she looked more triumphant about what she'd done than she felt.

"What? How?"

"I did pick up a few supplies, but this is the main reason I went into town. I talked to Judge Orbison and Sheriff Jackson about you and what you did for me. For Sweetwater, actually."

"For Sweetwater," he echoed.

"Yes. I reminded them that you helped prevent what could have been a horrible situation. If Marshall and his men hadn't been stopped, who knows what else they would have done to my cattle and my ranch, not to mention people could have lost their lives." Lifting her chin slightly, she added, "I was fully prepared to do whatever it took to convince them I was right, but it turned out I didn't need to do much convincing at all."

"No?" He still held the paper in one hand, looking for all the world as though he hardly cared what was written on it.

"Not at all. Actually, they agreed that such a service needed to be rewarded."

"So you got me my freedom."

She smiled. "Yes. A man like you never should have been an indentured servant in the first place. You're free, Thomas. You can leave me whenever you want."

His face turned expressionless, but then his lips curved up slightly. "Free to leave you, hmm?"

She wasn't sure she liked how that sounded, or the glint in his eyes that looked suspiciously like pain. "That was a slip of the tongue. What I meant to say is that you are free to leave the Red Roan Ranch."

"If I leave, how will you manage? This is a big ranch, Laurel. It would be a lot for a man to handle on his own, let alone a woman by herself."

She knew he was right. But some things were more important than even a family legacy or a home to live in. She was willing to sell the ranch if she had to. Nothing was more important than ensuring Thomas's freedom. "I'll make do."

"How?" he scoffed. "Are you planning to hire someone else?"

"Maybe. I'm not sure." Stuttering a bit, she added, "I don't know what I'll do." She was feeling defeated. How could she feel so optimistic one moment and so deflated the next?

"If you do try to hire someone else, what will you pay them with? I know you put the majority of your cash on me. Even convicts cost money."

"I know." Not liking the harsh way he was looking at her, she took a step backward.

"Laurel, did the judge give you your money back?"

"Of course not," she sputtered.

His gaze was cool. Cold. "So you have almost nothing."

That was where he was wrong. "I have a lot. I have my pride. I have my safety. I'm no longer afraid for my future." She was only sad that her future was going to be a lonely one.

He stared at her for a long moment, then seemed to come to a silent decision.

Dropping the paper onto the dark soil, he reached for her. "You're right," he drawled, his lips brushing her ear. "Those are all real good things. But still . . . what you have won't be enough."

His hands were covered with a light dusting of soil. He was hot and sweaty and was holding her so close she could practically feel frustration pour off him.

Yet she also sensed the way he made her feel so secure. The warmth of his breath against her skin. The faint smell of soap mixed with leather and earth and everything that was Thomas. And because of all that, he still felt right. So right.

Which was why she knew she had to do the right thing too. Firmly, she pushed away from him so she could look into his eyes. "You need to let me give you your freedom. I want you to be able to get away from here."

"No."

"What? Thomas, if you read that letter again, you'll see it says—"

"I can't read all that well. But that hardly matters to me at the moment. I know everything I need to know right here, right now."

"What is that?" she asked, dreading his answer. Her heart felt as though it had stopped beating.

"That I belong with you. I need to be with you, Laurel Tracey. And not as your worker. Not even as your protector. I want to be your husband." Lowering his voice, he said softly, "I want to be yours."

Her pulse jumped as she got warm all over. Was he truly saying what she thought he was? "You sound so sure."

The corners of his mouth lifted as he reached again for her hands. "Oh, I am. I don't know a lot of things. I've actually spent most of my life wishing I knew far more than I do. But one thing I know without a bit of doubt is that I want you forever."

He swallowed. "Laurel, I love you. If I promise to give you the best of myself, if I promise to work hard and care for you and work your land and do my best to protect you from the bad things life can bring . . . will you have me?"

"I will . . . if you can promise me one more thing," she said, now feeling as though her heart was pounding so hard in her chest that he could surely hear it.

"Anything. Name it."

"Will . . . will you promise to still love me tomorrow?"

"I promise, honey. And the next day. And the day after that," he said before his lips crashed down over hers.

He kissed her with no finesse, little gentleness, and complete fervor. His arms held her tightly, his body strong and solid next to hers. This, she realized, was Thomas.

Passionate and strong. Impulsive and sure. Everything that had been lacking in her life until he'd come. And everything that had happened since he'd stepped into her life.

She held on to his strength and reveled in his love.

Suddenly, they had a future.

Suddenly, they had each other.

And when they had all that, nothing else was needed.

They had enough.

Discussion Questions

1. What do you hope to discover when you read historical fiction?

2. This novel centers on various interpretations of protecting. Protecting land, values, other people, one's heart. Which kind of "protecting" are you most familiar with? Which theme in the novel resonated with you?

3. What do you think of Thomas Baker? Is he truly a hero? Why or why not?

4. What about Laurel? Was she actually in need of protection?

5. It might be obvious that my favorite parts of these novels are the scenes back in the prisoner of war camp on Johnson's Island. Did you care for them? Why or why not? What hero are you most intrigued by?

6. All of the characters in the novel have been marked by tragedy in some way. Each is attempting to come to terms with that and move forward. What has helped you recover from difficult situations in your life?

7. I loved the scripture quote from Zechariah: "I promise

this very day that I will repay two blessings for each of your troubles." I thought it described the storylines of the main characters in the novel very well. When have you received two blessings for each of your troubles?

8. Which Lone Star Hero are you most interested in reading about in the last book of the series?

Acknowledgments

Though my name is on the book's cover, there are so many people who worked very hard to guide this novel to publication! First and foremost is the amazing team at HarperCollins Christian Publishing. Not one but two editors helped me fine-tune this novel! Thank you to Becky Philpott and Karli Jackson! Huge thanks also go out to the amazing Jean Bloom, who somehow manages to locate every discrepancy! Jean's honesty and humor make working on this book for the fifth, sixth, and seventh time almost enjoyable.

I also owe a debt of gratitude to Lynne, my first reader, as well as my assistant Laurie Smith and my wonderful street team, the Buggy Bunch. Since writing is a very solitary job I'm so grateful for these ladies' (and men's) support!

I also owe so much to my own Thomas, my husband Tom. He spent a weekend with me on the shores of Lake Erie and stood by my side as I plotted and chatted with historians about Johnson's Island. He also very patiently explored the Confederate Officer Cemetery with me, taking pictures of almost every tombstone! Tom also spent many hours with me plotting each hero's journey. He knew how important they became to me, which says a lot, given that his ancestors fought for the Union while mine fought for the Confederacy.

ACKNOWLEDGMENTS

Finally, I am eternally grateful to God for being with me while I write. He has answered many a prayer while I fussed and worried over these characters. I'm so grateful that even in my basement office, I'm never completely alone.

Love Held Captive

To anyone who loves old westerns as much as I do

The apostles said to the Lord, "Increase our faith!" The Lord replied, "If you had faith the size of a mustard seed, you could say to this mulberry tree, 'Be uprooted and planted in the sea,' and it would obey you."

—LUKE 17:5–6

The past is dead; let it bury its dead, its hopes, and its aspirations. Before you lies the future, a future full of golden promise.

—JEFFERSON DAVIS

PROLOGUE

Johnson's Island, Ohio
Confederate States of America Officers' POW Camp
January 1865

There was almost nothing there. Almost.

Examining his surroundings, knowing he was mere minutes from ordering his men to take whatever this place still had, Captain Ethan Kelly forced himself to focus on his orders. General McCoy himself had given him this specific assignment, and failure was not an option.

Ethan was to make sure he and his men scoured the area and procured as much food and provisions as possible. By whatever means possible. Their efforts would make the difference between life and death for the men in their camp. The soldiers were hungry, cold, and about to be sent into battle. The Confederacy needed them to be strong of mind and able-bodied. No matter how hard it was to prey upon the South's women and children, Ethan could not allow any feelings of weakness to distract him from his goal.

His men weren't going to starve and freeze to death. They needed whatever supplies they could scrounge up.

Practically feeling his men's expectant stares on the back of his neck, Ethan steeled himself. Then he turned around to face them and began barking orders. "All right. You know what we came for. Wood. Ammunition. Food. Blankets. Fan out and be quick about it."

But instead of rushing to do his bidding, the small band of five eyed their surroundings warily.

"What about the woman, Cap?" Baker asked before Ethan could berate their slow reaction.

Caught off guard, Ethan turned to look where Sergeant Baker was pointing.

That's when he saw her. She'd come out to stand on the porch of the run-down ranch house. She was dark-haired and wore a dress that hung loosely on a form obviously too thin. A brown threadbare shawl was wrapped around her shoulders, the edges of it fluttering in the cold wind. But what struck him the most—and most likely, struck Thomas Baker too—was the way she was staring at them. As though she was mentally preparing herself for harm.

Ethan reckoned this woman looked a lot like the rest of the South. Ravaged and in pain.

Then he noticed she bore a scar. Even from his distance, he could tell it was recent. Its jagged red line tore across her temple and into her hairline. An accident?

Ethan forced himself to look away. He turned to his sergeant. Ethan could count on Baker to follow his orders, even when he didn't agree with them.

The man stared right back, bold as day. As he'd hoped, Baker's expression was carefully blank. Without distaste. Without interest. Really, without any emotion at all.

Ethan swallowed the rush of sympathy that had threatened to overtake him. And because he was afraid he might give in and decide they didn't need to search this house and barn, he turned to Baker. "Go explain to her what we're doing. Tell her we mean no harm."

"Yessir."

"But, Baker, make sure she understands we aren't going to leave until we get what we came for. The needs of our soldiers must come first."

After nodding, Baker started barking to the others. "You heard Captain Kelly. Go!"

The four other men scattered like fleas in a barnyard while Baker walked over to speak to the woman.

Ethan watched two of his men enter her storm cellar and breathed an inward sigh of relief. There had to be something down there. Maybe even some meat curing. They could take it to their unit, and for once those boys could have something to eat besides mealy hardtack.

He was warmed by that thought as he watched Baker move into the house, and his unease about the woman dissipated.

Until he noticed she was now holding one of the posts of her front porch in a death grip. She looked terrified.

He should have done the talking. Announced their intention to gather supplies for the soldiers of the Confederacy by order of President Jefferson Davis himself rather than asking Baker to do it.

Feeling far older than his twenty-nine years, he moved closer and studied her when she turned to look at him. He was sure she couldn't quite see his face in the shadows, but he could see tears forming in her eyes. She said nothing, but let go of the post and wrapped her arms and the ugly shawl around her chest and waist more securely. Almost as if she could shield her body from his men. Or perhaps he was the one she feared. He wasn't a small man, and he was also the one giving orders. His soldiers would do whatever he told them to do.

Looking at her more closely, he realized her hair was darker than he'd earlier thought. Almost black, really. It hung in thick, riotous curls down her shoulders, and when she had turned, he could see it went down her back. Almost to her waist. Her loose dress was a faded pink calico with frayed cuffs. Her feet were in worn boots that looked too big. Obviously she'd done a little bit of requisitioning herself.

But what caught his attention most was the way she continued to stare at him. Her eyes were dark. Maybe blue? Maybe green? Did it even matter? Never had someone looked at him with such stark terror.

It drew him up short. He'd supervised dozens of these raids across the South. Most of the inhabitants were resentful. Some had been downright cordial and sympathetic, sharing stories about their own boys in uniform.

As the men brought up jars from the cellar and carried a comforter from the house, her vivid eyes turned from his and tracked every move. Another tear ran down her face when Baker carried out a sack of flour in one hand and a quilt in the other. Two privates behind him came out empty-handed.

"Where's the rest, Baker?" he called out.

"Ain't nothing more, sir."

It wasn't a surprise—it was obvious other bands of men had done their share of looting.

Knowing many homeowners hid their best belongings, even from their own troops, he hardened his voice.

"Look harder," he called out.

The men paused, but after a nod from Baker, they rushed to obey.

The woman pressed a fist to her mouth as her eyes filled with more tears.

He hated seeing her cry. It went against everything he'd been raised to be. His father and mother had taken great pains to teach him to be a gentleman, as befitting their station in Houston society. But though he felt sorry for her, a far different emotion overrode his concern.

Resentment. He resented how her weeping made him feel—as though he were stealing from her for no good reason.

Now he had no choice but to speak to her. He stepped closer, out of the shadows. Close enough for her to see captain's bars on his uniform. Probably not close enough for her to see much of his face under the brim of his hat.

"You'd best dry your tears, miss," he called out. "Our soldiers need supplies. They are fighting for our cause. Everyone must make sacrifices. Everyone. Where have you hidden everything else?"

After a brief moment her fist left her mouth, but she didn't reply. She simply continued to stare at him in silence. What was wrong with her? Had this conflict already taken its toll on her? Some women were far too delicate for the ravages of war. Imagining his mother or his sister in such circumstances, he inwardly winced.

Who had he become? A man reduced to ordering soldiers not just to fight the enemy but to raid innocents and the afflicted? His father would hang his head in shame.

"Can you speak?" he finally asked, his voice sounding unfamiliar and harsh even to his own ears.

She nodded.

"Well then, an answer please, if you will. Where are the rest of your food and provisions?" He knew his tone was severe. Impatient. But he couldn't help it. This whole situation was hellish. He didn't want to spend his day frightening young women.

After visibly attempting to regain her composure, she spoke. "There isn't anything else, sir."

Her voice was husky. Deeper than expected. It was also soft, almost melodic.

In spite of himself, Ethan climbed the steps. As much as he wanted to remain detached and hard, a part of him needed to hear a feminine voice, if only for a minute. Needed a reminder that while many hurting soldiers depended on his successful objectives, many of them were fighting for their sisters, mothers, wives, and daughters.

Well aware of his men watching and listening, he kept his voice low. "I know there is more. There always is."

"There isn't. Other men have already been here. And when they came, they took everything of worth." The pain in her voice encouraged him to search her face. Once again, he eyed the scar running along her hairline on the left side. Jagged and thick, it curved from her forehead and temple, ending at the top of her ear. It was very red. It appeared to be fresh.

Deep emotion he'd tried so hard to forget existed slid into his heart and soul. Jolted him with a shock of pain as her silence and fear all made sense. Other soldiers had looted her house before. And she'd been attacked. Cut.

And now she was expecting that same of him and his men.

He turned on his heel. "Baker!" he called out. "Collect the men. We're leaving."

"But, Cap, we haven't finished searching the barn." His voice was filled with confusion.

"Silence, Sergeant," Ethan ordered in a hard voice—one he was certain Baker knew better than to argue with. When the only sound was the bitter wind blowing across the plains, Ethan made a great show of staring at the map he'd just unfurled.

Ten minutes later, they were marching back down the lane, their wagon pulled by his horse. Though the woman hadn't lied—she really hadn't had much left—they'd still managed to take what was there. But it was hardly enough to make a difference to a camp of soldiers.

Still, it would no doubt make a big difference to one woman living alone in a run-down house. Desolation coursed through Ethan as he realized what that meant. They were no better than anyone else. And maybe a whole lot worse—even if they hadn't physically harmed her.

Gasping for air, he tried not to care that he'd become everything he'd feared. He'd become everything—

"Wake up, Major!" a man said while giving Ethan a harsh shove. "You're dreaming again. Wake up!"

Inhaling, Ethan sat up. Realized he wasn't freezing. He wasn't back in Texas in the middle of winter. He was on his cot in his barracks on Johnson's Island. He was a prisoner of war, stuck in the Confederate Officers' POW camp under the desultory guardianship of Yankee soldiers. He was reduced to waiting out the remainder of the war in boredom and misery.

He was also safe and dry.

And far away from a damaged woman living on a desolate ranch.

"You okay?" Thomas Baker asked. "You were gasping in your sleep. Sounded like you were choking."

"I wasn't. I was just dreaming. I'm fine, Sergeant," he said, reverting to the man's rank. Hating that his shirt was soaked in sweat.

"Want some water? I got a canteen-full last night."

"Thanks, but I'm all right. Like I said, I was, uh, dreaming."

"I'd ask if the dream was a bad one, but of course it was. I mean, they all are, right?" Thomas asked with a wry look.

He was right about that.

"You okay, Ethan?" Devin Monroe murmured from his cot.

"I'm fine. Sorry I woke you." Realizing he had most likely awoken half the men in the barracks, he spoke again, this time a little more loudly. "Sorry, everyone."

But instead of grumbling, the rest of the men in the room remained silent.

Pure shame engulfed him. He had lost control. Struggling with how to accept that, Ethan held out a hand. "You know what, Thomas? I'll take that water after all."

When Thomas turned to retrieve the canteen, Ethan shook his head and tried to get his bearings. Then did what he always did after he dreamed about that house—prayed that woman was okay.

That he hadn't done any lasting harm.

But, of course, he knew he was only fooling himself. He *had* hurt her. Of course he had. He knew he was going to cause her pain and heartache the moment they stopped in front of her house.

She'd had so little, and he'd ordered his men to take what they could anyway. It hardly mattered that other men had done far worse. Pain was pain. It all hurt.

1

The Menger Hotel
San Antonio, Texas
Thursday, October 31, 1867

SHE NEVER SHOULD HAVE HAD HER BACK TO THE DOOR.
When it shut behind her with a sharp *crack*, Lizbeth Barclay
knew she was in trouble. But though everything inside her was
screaming to run, she froze while pulling on the heavy brocade
bedspread in the hotel's guestroom.

And just like that, she was transported back in time. Back
to another place where she should have felt safe but had been her
most vulnerable.

As she heard the faint brush of clothing, a muted jangle of
change in a pocket, the rustle of leather behind her back, her hands
held the spread in a death grip. Frustration filled her. She so wanted
to be braver. Tougher. Better.

But she wasn't. Not yet.

"You ever going to turn around?" the intruder drawled.

Her breath hitched. It made no sense, but she could have
sworn she recognized the voice. It was unmistakably deep and
thick and sounded much like the voice from her nightmares after

that day back in Castroville. Back in the middle of the war, when she was alone in her house. Alone and scared and completely sure there was no one in the vicinity to come to her aid if she screamed.

She'd been right, of course. No one had come before.

A thick bolt of dread coursed through her as she forced herself to turn. Pretending she wasn't as scarred and scared as she felt, she raised her chin and turned.

And stared directly into a pair of familiar dark-brown eyes. Confusion warred with dismay as she realized she hadn't been mistaken. She did know this man.

Intimately.

He haunted her dreams. Starred in her nightmares. She'd thought he was merely a memory. She was wrong.

"You," she whispered.

This time he wasn't wearing a uniform. He was dressed in a finely constructed black suit and highly polished black boots. But his hard jaw, the steady gaze, the way his arms hung loosely at his side . . . She would recognize him anywhere. Even now, as he stood with his back against the door. Barring it with his body.

He frowned before his expression cleared. Then, as she watched him, he turned his attention to her body. As if he had all the time in the world, his gaze slid over her. It paused on her face, lingered on her curves, then settled on her hips, covered by a neatly starched white apron.

The whole perusal made her feel dirty. Maybe he'd intended it to.

Or maybe she'd felt that way for so long she didn't remember how to ever feel clean again. By the time the war ended, Lizbeth had come to realize one never felt completely clean when one's soul—one's very being—was bruised and tarnished by pain.

Out of habit, she shrank into herself, gripping the voluminous fabric of her gray uniform. His eyes tracked her hands, following the movement of her fingertips with the interest of a predator. Perspiration dampened the fabric on her back. It fastened onto her skin, confining her movements even further.

It was becoming difficult to breathe.

"Do I know you?" he asked, his voice haughty yet curious.

Taking care to avoid his gaze, Lizbeth focused instead on his tailored suit. His cream-colored shirt. The silver pin puncturing the silk cravat at his neck. When she dared to meet his eyes again, she realized his showed no recognition.

He didn't remember her.

Realizing her cap was covering the worst of her scar, relief flowed through her. "Of course not, sir," she replied around a rush of air. "I'm just a maid here. I'm sorry I was still in the room when you arrived. I'll leave now."

"No need to do that, miss . . ." He grinned, encouraging small lines to form around his eyes. "What is your name?"

She didn't want to tell him.

"I'm going to leave now." Though she was barely able to move her limbs, she looked around for her feather duster and the little wooden crate that held her rags, the beeswax, the vinegar, and newsprint. She needed to escape.

She picked up the crate, ready to go. But still he blocked the door. Those highly polished black boots shining against the door's dark stain.

He wasn't a handsome man. Most likely he never had been, though it was hard to tell. His eyes were bloodshot and his skin was sallow. Much of the flesh on his cheeks was scarred from the pox. Everything about him screamed of dissolute behavior. But even in the midst of such disrepair, an intensity emanated from him.

He knew she was uncomfortable, and that pleased him.

It took everything she had to move forward. "Please step aside."

"I'd rather not. I'd be a fool to let an opportunity like this pass me by." His lips curved into a smile that didn't meet his eyes. "Why don't you stay awhile longer? The afternoon is still young. We can get to know each other."

She had to get out. On the other side of the door lay freedom. Relief. Air.

She had to do it. She had to find a way to get him to move aside, to allow her to turn that knob.

It was time to run. Fast.

She fought to keep her voice light and detached. "I have other rooms to clean. I need to go."

At last he moved away from the door. Clicking his tongue softly, he approached. "My bed isn't made. You haven't finished your job, have you?"

Her tongue felt thick. "I . . . I will come back. We're not supposed to bother the guests."

"Stay. You can work around me."

"I cannot, sir."

Just as she folded her palm around the door's knob, he reached for her forearm. "Reconsider."

His voice was hard. Demanding. It hurt almost as much as the memories. Images of all she'd tried so hard to forget flashed forward, making her feel weak and dizzy. She needed to get away before she passed out and made things worse.

Her lungs felt so tight, she had trouble catching her breath. She was beginning to pant. To hyperventilate. Hoping to regain her bearings, she grasped the crate's handle with one hand and pressed a palm to her face.

"There's no need to hide yourself from me. If you think I'm bothered by your looks, I'm not," he said with an almost-tender smile. "Don't be shy. Why, we're all marked from the war in one way or another. You'd probably be shocked to discover some of the things I've done." His tone had turned almost nostalgic, just as his gaze sharpened on her forehead.

Feeling sick, Lizbeth realized what he was seeing. She must have inadvertently slid her cap back when she'd pressed her palm to her face.

Memories threatened to overpower her. Teasing her with snippets of scattered, split images she worked so very hard to ignore during the day. But just like the four-inch scar that ran along her brow and hairline, the memories would never completely fade.

Bile rose in the back of her throat, making her gag. Her stomach churned, her vision turning spotty. If she didn't escape soon, chances were very good she was going to vomit. Right there in the hotel room.

She needed air. She needed freedom and comfort and relief. Without daring to glance his way again, she threw open the heavy door and tore out of the room.

If he complained about his service, she'd be in trouble. Though her second cousin and her husband managed this hotel, Aileen and Dallas weren't understanding. And she would never tell them who the man was.

Lizbeth looked both ways down the narrow hallway. She needed a moment to get her wits together before coming up with a decent excuse to explain herself. Quickly choosing to go left, because that end was far less occupied by guests, Lizbeth turned and hurried as fast as she could.

When she came to another junction, she glanced right and left again. Seeing both sides of that hall empty, she breathed a sigh of relief. So far, so good. If Aileen or one of her favorites caught her running like she was, they'd want to know what had happened. And they'd make her return to that room no matter what.

Lizbeth suspected Aileen would never believe what happened to her during the war. As with everyone else, she'd let her cousin believe her scar was the result of an accident. Or maybe she would believe the truth, but not care.

Aileen's parents were living in Galveston now, but she had been with them right up until she married Dallas Howard. Lizbeth's parents hadn't been the most giving or kind people. They'd thought of Aileen's branch of the family as far beneath their merit and had done little to help Aileen when she made her debut. While Lizbeth had been dressed in silks and had worn skirts filled with so many petticoats and hoops she could hardly fit through doorways, Aileen had been standing to the side. Largely forgotten.

Lizbeth had been embarrassed by that, and even offered to share her gowns. But her mother refused to let her. Aileen was just pretty enough to be competition. It was far better for their daughter to be the only one to shine brightly. Social status had counted for everything to them.

Right up until they died of an illness that had somehow spared her life.

No, she wouldn't tell Aileen this was the man who had ruined her.

She thought she heard heavy boots on the carpeting behind her, coming closer. Lizbeth's heart started beating even faster. Why had she stopped?

Desperate, she started scanning room numbers. She needed an empty room to dart into, and she needed it fast.

Just as she was about to scurry down the stairs, she realized suite 28 was just ahead. Only Major Ethan Kelly ever stayed there, and everyone at the Menger knew he wasn't currently in residence.

His suite would be perfect. It had its own bathing and sitting rooms. She could lock herself inside, splash some water on her face, and regain her bearings. Then, after a bit, she could go back to her duties. With luck, no one would be the wiser.

Rushing ahead, she set her crate of cleaning supplies against the wall and started sorting through her keys, their jingling echoing down the hallway. Hands shaking, she located the right key after two attempts and inserted it into the lock. Finally, the knob turned.

She swung open the door in relief. Feeling triumphant, Lizbeth went inside and slammed it shut behind her with more force than was necessary. Turning to face it, she laid her hands on the smooth, cool wood. She was safe.

2

After she caught her breath and turned around, the first thing Lizbeth noticed was that the major was in residence again. He must have come in late the night before. Clothes were strewn across the bed. Polished boots were lined up against the wall. Papers littered the desk, and personal belongings lay on top of the dresser.

Lizbeth was still rattled, but she found herself smiling. Major Kelly was such a mess!

Walking across the room to his bed, she ran a finger along his navy silk vest. Stopped to carefully fold his handkerchief back into a perfect square. She'd done such things more than once during the last couple of months. Unlike some other former soldiers, the major didn't seem to have retained any sense of order from his military life. Or maybe he'd had people to pick up after him during the war.

Whatever the reason, he always left his belongings scattered around. Some maids—Callie in particular—dreaded being assigned to clean his suite. It always took double the time to put it to rights. Lizbeth had never minded, though. It rather amused her to think the major, who looked every inch the dandy when he was out in public, was something of a mess in private.

Unable to help herself, she moved to the dresser. In the center was a beautiful gold pocket watch. Lying next to it was a pair of gold cufflinks. They were substantial and showy. She knew the major only by sight and reputation, but even she knew he wore them constantly.

Picking up one, she turned it this way and that. It was a carved gold knot. Beautiful, really. And far heavier than she would have imagined. For all her tidying, she couldn't remember him ever leaving the cufflinks out in the open. Picking up the other, she held them both in the palm of her right hand.

She really should put them in a safe place. Though she hoped none of the other maids would be tempted to steal them, she didn't want to test their honesty. Perhaps she should set them in a drawer. She could write him a note. Yes! That would be the best thing—

"May I help you?"

She jumped at the sound of the voice.

With a feeling of dread, she slowly turned around. And felt as though her heart had just dropped to her feet.

Major Ethan Kelly was standing in front of her. At first staring at her face, and then eyeing his cufflinks in her hand. All while standing in a pair of trousers.

In only a pair of trousers.

Though she shouldn't, Lizbeth let her gaze drift. Like a miserly banker, she catalogued each one of his scars and battle wounds. Allowed herself to notice the way his muscles flexed when he moved his arm. The way his olive skin was smooth except for a faint line of dark hair that ran down the center of his abdomen. She noticed the line of muscles across his chest. Along his arms, his shoulders.

Last, she raised her chin and met his stare. Felt her skin flush, knew he'd just watched her look him over like a trollop in a back alley. So very like the way that other man had looked at her.

She realized now that he'd been in his bathing room. His clothes weren't on the bed because he'd changed in a hurry but because he was about to get dressed.

"It looks like you've found something you like," he finally drawled.

With a start, she realized he thought she was stealing his cufflinks. Stealing from him! Her hands went limp, and the cufflinks fell to the floor.

Clattering against the floorboards like tiny symbols of her foolishness. Or maybe just symbols of how mixed-up and confusing her life had become. Despite her best intentions, everything she did only served to make her situation worse.

After the space of three beats—or maybe after she'd finally controlled her breathing and was able to concentrate again—Major Kelly raised his eyebrows.

Lizbeth scrambled to the floor, picked up the cufflinks, and set them back on the dresser's surface. As she stepped aside, she tried to decide how to explain herself.

She was stuck. Trapped between two men—this man, too filled with charm, and the other, the reason she had never become the person she'd always hoped she'd be. It was almost too much to take in.

She watched as his brown eyes drifted over her. Then did it again, pausing for the briefest second on her scar. To her surprise, he didn't look angry. He seemed to be assessing her, like an officer examining one of his men. Compassion might have entered his eyes. Or it might not have. She couldn't tell.

Still he said nothing. Still she waited.

When he raised one arm to absently scratch his other, he seemed to realize he was mostly unclothed. Without a word, he strode to the dresser, opened a drawer, pulled out a folded white shirt, and slipped it on. Then he proceeded to neatly button the shirt, as if what was happening wasn't completely irregular.

She needed to get out of there. She needed to simply turn and leave. Maybe, with God's help, they could eventually both pretend this moment had never happened. But just as she shifted, preparing to explain why she'd been holding his cufflinks, he spoke.

"I've seen you in the halls. What is your name?" He sounded bored as he continued to carefully slip each well-crafted button through its appropriate hole.

"I'm Lizbeth, sir. I mean, well, my full name is Elizabeth Barclay." Not that he cared. And, oh, did her voice just . . . squeak? This was only getting worse.

As he turned his attention to fastening his cuffs with the gold links, he murmured, "Would you, if you please, explain why you are in my room?"

"It wasn't to take your cufflinks, sir."

"No?"

She trembled.

Suddenly realizing he was still staring at her intently, awaiting a response, she walked toward the door. "I'm so sorry, sir. I thought this room was unoccupied. Then, when I saw your cufflinks, I thought I should put them away. For safekeeping."

"And your palm seemed like the best place?"

"Oh, no. I was going to put them in the top drawer and then write you a note," she murmured as she continued to edge to the door. "I didn't want anyone to steal them." Hearing her words, she felt even more foolish. Surely no other explanation could sound more unbelievable.

"So you came in here to do . . . what? A good deed?"

Glad that she could finally form a coherent thought, she grasped the ornate, heavily faceted knob behind her. The glass handle was cool underneath her touch and its chill soothed her. "I'm so sorry about this. If you could forget that I ever came inside, I would be so grateful." She turned the knob a quarter of an inch. "And, um . . . I'll just leave you in peace."

"Stay."

She dropped her hand. "I beg your pardon?"

He fastened a starched collar around his neck. "I said stay. Your face is flushed. Were you running? And if so, what were you running from?" His eyes narrowed. "And don't you start telling me some nonsense. I heard you darting in here like the devil himself was on your heels."

Funny, she'd felt as if that had indeed been the case. But what could she say?

"Well then?"

His voice was commanding. Authoritative. She didn't know how to not answer. "I had a small issue, but I'm sure it is better by now."

He'd tucked his shirt in his trousers and was now fastening the navy silk vest. His fingers stilled. "An issue. And what kind would that be? And please, do start talking."

Clutching her hands together, she tried to fashion a reply. But her mind went blank as he plucked a suit jacket from the back of a chair.

After slipping it on, he smoothed the fabric along his chest. If anything, he stood even taller. Right there on the expensive Aubusson rug, under a gilded chandelier and surrounded by dark ruby-colored curtains and wallpaper. He was a man used to being in charge. A man used to making decisions and commanding an audience.

For the first time since she'd arrived, his voice adopted a thread of impatience. "I am waiting for a response, miss."

Tell him, she cautioned herself. It isn't as if you have anything to gain by keeping your silence. There's no way you're going to have an ounce of pride left after this experience anyway. "I was, well, cleaning a guest's room when he returned unexpectedly."

"What happened then?"

How could she tell him she'd been so afraid? How could she when she was standing right here in the same room with the man? What was the difference between what was happening at that very moment and what had happened moments earlier? Was it because the other man was from her past?

Or was it because she didn't fear Major Kelly?

Beyond flustered now, she hedged. "It became difficult. He didn't want me to leave."

"Difficult? What is that supposed to mean?"

"I was afraid."

"Forgive me for being obtuse, miss. But am I to understand he made an untoward advance against you?"

Caught between a nod and a shrug, she kind of twitched. "Yes, sir. But it's all right, because I—"

"It's not all right. Nothing about that was all right."

No, it wasn't. But what could she say? "If you will excuse me, I'll be on my way."

"Not yet, if you please," he murmured as he turned to his dresser. Methodically, he slipped that very fine gold watch into his vest pocket. Then, just as calm as you please, he sat down on the dark-gray winged chair and slipped on his fine-looking black leather boots.

All while she stood and continued to watch him.

After rubbing his thumb along a scuff in the leather, he stood. "In what room did this occur?"

She'd already said too much. "I don't recall."

"Come now. Let us not start lying to each other."

Was it possible for one's skin to become any more flushed? "All right. The truth is that I would rather you not be involved."

"I'm already involved, though, aren't I?"

Was he? "Yes, but—"

"So what you really mean is you do not wish me to be any further involved."

"Yes, sir. That is what I mean." Just to make sure she was clear, she added, "I'd rather you not become any further involved in my business, Major Kelly."

A new, amused glint shone in his eyes. "I'm afraid it's too late to wish for that."

"It's not."

"I have to disagree." His voice lowered into a slow, languid drawl. "Don't forget, you've seen me practically naked."

She couldn't deny that. However, she could free herself from this travesty of a situation. She needed to leave. Just leave. Forget about asking for permission. Forget about how tarnished her reputation was going to be.

Yes. She needed to leave. Immediately.

She could go to her room and begin to make plans to start over somewhere else. New Braunfels, perhaps? Just as she reached for the glass doorknob again, a light knock sounded from the other side.

"Major Kelly, sir?" a high, shrill female voice called out. The woman followed with another series of sharp knocks.

As Lizbeth realized who was now standing on the other side of the door, she bit back a moan. She hadn't thought her predicament could get worse. But, as with rain, heat, and war, it seemed it certainly could.

3

A<small>FTER THE KNOCKS CAME A TENTATIVE VOICE</small> L<small>IZBETH</small>
knew all too well.

"Major Kelly? Sir, I hate to disturb you, but if I might have a
moment of your time?"

Lizbeth stared at the door in dismay. Aileen was on the other
side. Her employer. What choice did she have but to respond?

She looked at the major, and he narrowed his eyes just as she
started to turn the door's handle. "Wait," he said, his voice once
again low.

Lizbeth cleared her throat and lowered her voice as well.
"Major Kelly, I do believe my cousin is knocking at your door."

"Cousin, is it?" A new light, one a lot like amusement, she was
afraid, entered his eyes. "Is that right?"

"That is Aileen Howard. She and her husband, Dallas, manage this establishment."

"Yes, but that still doesn't help me understand why she is
knocking so urgently."

Lizbeth realized she did understand her cousin's persistence.
No doubt the other man had complained about her. But how did
Aileen know where Lizbeth was? "I think it would be better for all
of us if I went out to speak to her, sir."

He stepped forward, bringing with him the faint scent of bay rum and soap. "Will you trust me? I can help you, if you'll give me your trust."

Trust him? She didn't trust any man. Not any longer. Having no words, she shook her head.

His eyes darted to the scar on her face. A flash of concern she didn't understand entered his eyes before he spoke more forcefully. Did he feel sorry for her? "I won't harm you. I promise."

But he didn't realize promises meant nothing to her. "Beyond the fact that I know you frequently leave your clothing scattered around your room, I don't know you, Major," she said stiffly. "Furthermore, we both know I am none of your concern."

"Reconsider."

One word. The same word Bushnell had said to her minutes earlier. And just as forcibly said. Both men were used to giving commands. Even more used to being listened to.

The major wasn't Bushnell, but she wasn't one of his soldiers either. She was nothing to him, and he . . . well, though he was mannerly and polite, he still symbolized everything that had ruined her life. "I would like to leave, sir."

"All right, then." Motioning with his hands, he said, "Open it up, if you will, Miss Barclay. Let us see what your cousin desires."

Desires. His choice of words took her by surprise. She pulled open the door.

Aileen was, indeed, standing on the other side. As always, she was dressed becomingly. In one hand was Lizbeth's crate of cleaning supplies.

Lizbeth called herself three kinds the fool. In her haste, she'd put the crate on the hallway floor when she was fumbling with her keys. All the while she'd been attempting to hide, her supplies were right outside the major's door. They had been stationed there like a beacon, practically begging for her to be found.

She glanced at the major. He had clasped his arms behind him. He looked exactly like he was—a military man standing at rest.

For a split second, all three of them remained mute. Each staring at the other two. Lizbeth could only hope what was about to happen would do so quickly.

Ethan Kelly had liked to think that after four years of war, nine months in captivity, and six months of gambling in various disreputable saloons and on riverboats, nothing could surprise him.

He had been wrong.

He was now standing with two women. One whose voice was so brittle and high it grated on his last nerve. The other? Well, she was the star of his nightmares and the cause of his shame. He was torn between wanting to shield her from the rest of the world and turning his back to her in a feeble effort to retain what remained of his soul.

Impatient with the situation, he glared at the woman who was standing in his doorway. She was dressed in a becoming cranberry-colored day dress, stockings, and some fine black kid shoes. When she turned her head to look at Lizbeth, he could see her dark-blonde hair was styled in a low chignon.

"May I help you?" he asked with obvious sarcasm.

"I'm sorry, sir. I was looking for this maid."

Before Ethan could say a word, Miss Barclay stepped forward. "Obviously you have found me."

"Excuse us, sir," Mrs. Howard said to Ethan before directing her maid into the hall. Miss Barclay went out, never looking back in his direction.

Ethan knew the right thing to do would be to close his door. He needed to come to terms with the fact that he had just seen the woman whose home he'd raided in the war. Maybe have a drink. Maybe then he could pretend it had been a strange coincidence that their paths had crossed again but no harm had been done. She had obviously survived, just as he had.

But despite his best intentions, he found himself unable to pull his attention away. The two women were close enough for him to still hear every hushed word.

"Why were you inside Major Kelly's room?"

"It was a mistake. I was only trying to find a quiet place to collect my bearings."

Aileen's voice rose. "In a guest's room?"

"I didn't know anyone was inside."

"It is never okay to be in a guest's room unless you were called in to clean it. You know this."

"I know. But—"

"I can only assume you were in there for another reason." She folded her hands across her chest. "Perhaps you were in search of money?"

"I wasn't stealing anything!"

Ethan couldn't deny he had thought the very same thing. Now, though, he wasn't even sure if he cared. Who was he to deny something to a woman who had already lost so much?

With an exaggerated sigh, Mrs. Howard said, "Lizbeth, why were you trying to get your bearings?"

"I had to get away from a man who walked into his room when I was cleaning. He . . . Well, it was obvious Mr. Bushnell intended to take advantage of me."

Her voice started shaking, as though she hated even uttering his name out loud.

"Surely you were mistaken. Mr. Daniel Bushnell is a gentleman."

Daniel Bushnell?

Ethan jerked his head around the doorframe, but the women didn't seem to notice.

Lizbeth shook her head. He thought he could see tears glistening in her eyes. "I know what his intentions were."

Mrs. Howard pursed her lips. "That doesn't change the fact that you ran into another man's room while it was occupied. This is a problem, Lizbeth. My husband . . . I can't allow it. You know what a hard time Dallas and I have making sure we have decent, reputable maids of unquestionable character. If the other women found out I let you stay after this, they would think they could do the same thing."

Lizbeth slumped. "I understand."

"Do you? I hate to do this, Lizbeth, but you are dismissed. You can stay the night, but leave in the morning."

After nodding, Lizbeth turned and walked down the hall. Her cousin stood motionless, watching her for a moment before visibly gathering herself.

Ethan fought the torrent of emotions that boiled up inside of him. Dismay that the woman could dismiss Miss Barclay so easily. Guilt that he had somehow played a part in her dismissal. But even more powerful than that was the biting feeling of anger that flowed through him.

Daniel Bushnell, his former colonel, his enemy, was here in the same hotel. Just as Mrs. Howard started following Lizbeth down the hall, he strode after her. "Give me his room number," he ordered in a fierce whisper.

Aileen startled and then shook her head. "I cannot give that to you, Major."

"Of course you can, and don't you start telling me about privacy or reputations. I'm not some helpless girl in need of a job."

She flushed at his jab but lifted her chin. "I don't know what you overheard, but I really do value our customers' privacy. We wouldn't have any guests if I gave out room numbers."

"You *won't* have any guests if you don't give it to me." He hardened his voice, speaking to her in a way he hadn't spoken to anyone since he was ordering troops to retreat on bloody battlefields. "I will make sure your business suffers, and don't think I don't have that amount of influence. I assure you I do."

Mrs. Howard's expression tightened. For a split second, Ethan was sure she was going to refuse, but then she exhaled. "He is in room 240," she said before turning and retreating down the hall.

Back in his room, Ethan reached for his money clip on the dresser. He stopped with his arm in midair, staring at one of his gold cufflinks.

They were a gift from his father, given to him thirteen years earlier on his eighteenth birthday. That had been years before the war. Years before he'd realized he might have grown older but had never truly grown up. It had taken his first battle to do that.

Though he and his parents had had their share of rocky moments, he continued to wear the cufflinks out of respect for his father. To Ethan, they were a symbol of what his father had imagined he could one day be—someone of worth.

He grabbed his money clip, walked out of the room, locked the door behind him, and headed down the hall. What he was about to do might not seem like a sign of maturity to some. Perhaps others might even consider it shameful. Revenge was an ugly emotion. But at that moment, Ethan knew he had never been more sure about anything in his life. As far as he was concerned, the Lord had brought him, Miss Barclay, and Bushnell together for one reason and one reason only: for Ethan Kelly to make sure Daniel Bushnell firmly and completely regretted his actions.

For the first time in a long time, Ethan felt as though he was finally going to do something of worth. Few opportunities had ever felt as sweet.

4

HELLO, MAJOR KELLY," MRS. SANDLER CALLED OUT WITH a cheery smile as she approached on her husband's arm.

It was difficult, but Ethan forced himself to stop and exchange pleasantries with the esteemed couple. "Good afternoon, ma'am," he said as he offered a small bow. "You are looking as pretty as a picture." He didn't lie. Mrs. Sandler had hair the color of mink, violet eyes, and a truly beautiful smile. She also had a penchant for wearing rose-colored gowns that flattered both her skin tone and figure.

Her smile brightened. "Thank you. I hope you are doing well on this fine day."

"Better, now that I have seen you," he said with a wink.

Obviously amused by his flirtation, she turned to her husband. "Warren, you didn't tell me the major was going to be here this week."

Warren patted her gloved hand. "That's because I didn't know. Is there a tournament this week I don't know about, Kelly?"

Warren Sandler was in his early forties and an avid poker player. Ethan had spent many hours sitting at Warren's side, back when he'd spent most of his evenings in the gambling establishments around town. "No, sir. I just happened to be in the area for other reasons." He didn't see the need to mention he'd returned to San Antonio only to spend a few days at the Menger before heading to his family's ranch.

"If you plan to dine at the hotel this evening, please do join us," Warren said. "You can tell us how your family is faring."

Mrs. Sadler inclined her head. "Yes, please do join us if you are able, Major Kelly."

"It would be my pleasure." He bowed again as they parted ways.

After taking a few steps down the hall, he forced himself to stop again. Seeing the Sandlers had diffused the worst of the anger that had been threatening to consume him. He'd needed to see them, he realized. They were a gentle reminder of who he was. Yes, he was a former soldier. But he was also a gentleman. Not the kind of man to race down the hall of a hotel intending to brutally harm another person in cold blood.

Not even if that person deserved it.

Feeling more himself, he exhaled and reevaluated his mission. He needed to help Lizbeth, but even if he went so far as to kill Daniel Bushnell, would it really change her life for the better? He didn't think so. But he had to do something.

Thinking again about their meeting, Ethan realized it had taken everything he had not to simply stare at her in befuddlement. After all, she was someone out of his dreams.

Even from the back, before he had any idea who she was, he could tell she was a fetching thing. Dark, curly hair. Small waist. Not too slight. Not too petite. An armful.

But then she turned around. Her eyes? Luminous and dark green. And she had that scar on her temple.

He'd been jolted by the sight.

He'd seen that scar before. It had haunted his dreams. No, she had haunted them.

When she lifted her chin, obviously waiting for him to say something more, he was without words. Not because she invaded his room. Not because of her obvious beauty. No, it had been because of that scar.

What were the chances of another woman having such a mark along her hairline? Since he dealt in odds in his current occupation, he knew there were none. She'd been the woman whose ranch they'd raided. She was the woman who had barely said two words to them. Who had shaken like a leaf whenever any of them got too close to her. Even when he'd promised, as an officer and a gentleman, that all they wanted was food and supplies.

She was starving, scared. Completely alone. He'd still ordered his men to take everything that was of use.

And they had.

And just like that, he was lost in the past. Lost, back at a small house not too far from San Antonio.

Back in the war, when he was hungry and cold.

And so desperate to help his men that he'd done many things he was ashamed of. A great many things.

Most, he'd made peace with. The war had been difficult and far more painful than any of them had anticipated. Every man he knew had been forced to take horrible steps to survive. The ones who hadn't had died.

But even though he'd done a great many things he regretted, few came as close as his trip to this woman's home with his men.

And all he could think to do to hide his dismay was to accuse her of trying to steal from him.

Now that he'd learned she was still so alone in the world, and that very afternoon had been on the run from Daniel Bushnell—a man with whom he had a long history and thoroughly despised—Ethan realized it was time to pay his debt to her.

Miss Barclay might never realize he remembered her from the war. He hoped she didn't. It would ease his conscience. He hoped she would think of him only as someone willing to help her shoulder some of her burdens. Willing to protect her. To take care of anyone who threatened her again.

Now that he realized Bushnell was the reason for her flight. And that she was going to lose her job because of his preying on her? Well, he could only believe it was a matter of divine intervention that had brought him and Bushnell once again to the same place at the same time.

It was wrong to be feeling what he did, he knew. Wrong to be looking forward to extracting vengeance.

Why, God? he asked as he started back down the narrow passageway wallpapered with busy designs and adorned with rather uninteresting charcoal drawings of plants and animals. Why have you decided to bring us all together again?

Ethan hadn't thought of Colonel Daniel Bushnell in years. Ethan had been one of the many men who'd served under him. Frankly, if Ethan had spared him a thought, he would have assumed Bushnell had gone back to his mistress and his wife and continued to manipulate and use as many people as possible for his own selfish gains. After all, that was what he'd been so very good at.

But maybe he had been just as human as the rest of them. A lot of men had problems adjusting to life after the war and months in a prison camp. That was one of the reasons he, Captain Monroe, Lieutenant Truax, and Baker had vowed to look out for each other. A new lawlessness existed in men's hearts after the war. It was as if they were unable to give up their worst influences.

Many couldn't. After returning home and finding either their plantations or homes ruined or in pieces of rubble, they'd been at a loss for what to do. Then had come the punishment the union waged during Reconstruction. It ate upon their souls.

But now that he realized a man he loathed had accosted Miss Barclay here in the hotel, Ethan knew he owed it to her to warn him to stay away from her in the future. He hadn't been able to do anything except hurt her when he and his men had shown up at her house that day. Now, at last, he could make amends. He was determined to be her hero, even though it made no sense. He wanted retribution, and he was eager to get it. At any cost.

Situations like this—such that it was—were why he missed the army so much. In the army, there was a distinct order. His rank mattered. His disapproval mattered. Furthermore, dozens—if not scores—of men had been all too willing to do what he desired.

But this? Trying to help a gentlewoman like Miss Lizbeth Barclay? Well, that was dangerous.

Women like her made him yearn for things he'd already come to terms with never having. Like goodness and a home. Those were what he'd dreamed of and planned to have with Faye, his longtime sweetheart. But she'd grown lonely during the war and found someone else while he was in that prison camp. It seemed even majors lost some of their shine when they were reduced to mere prisoners.

That was yet another reason he yearned to do some kind of physical harm to an intangible object.

Glad he'd made Aileen Howard tell him the room number, he strode down the hall and rapped twice on Bushnell's door. He felt a pleased appreciation when it swung open immediately.

It took only seconds, but that was long enough for Bushnell to erase the shock that appeared on his face when he recognized him. "Kelly."

Ethan was thrust back in time. Back to his captivity on

Johnson's Island. To Bushnell's arrival after Ethan had already been living on the premises for two months. To the man interfering with most everything Captain Monroe had put into place.

Time had not been kind to the other man. The small pox scars on his cheeks had turned red and become more pronounced. The skin on his face and neck seemed loose, whether from hard living or some kind of sickness. He also seemed to have shrunk in size. Ethan wondered if that was indeed true, or if he'd merely shrunk in importance to him.

It was obvious that Ethan's appearance caught him off guard, but he recovered quickly. "Is it really you?"

"It was Major Kelly last time we saw each other."

"The war is over. Like in the camp, appellations don't matter much now." He raised one eyebrow. "Or do they?"

"They mattered at one time. Maybe more than I realized."

Bushnell shook his head. "It was men like me who saved the high and mighty generals from getting their hands dirty. Even your friend General McCoy."

"I never heard wind of you after we were released."

"I did what you did, I reckon. I attempted to put my life back together. I went back to Boerne."

"Ah. Yes. You had a ladybird there." Bushnell had often bragged of her beauty.

"Julianne? I did have her for a time, even after the war ended." He grunted. "But then I got rid of her, of course. I couldn't chance my wife's family discovering her, you know. After I paid her off, I went home to Fredericksburg."

"Where your wife and children live."

"Well, they did." He frowned. "My wife and son have since died, and my daughter married a blasted Yankee and moved up to Philadelphia."

"That's a pity."

"Indeed, it is." He cleared his throat. "Is there a reason we are standing here in the Menger Hotel reviewing my life? As you must surmise, I am finding it rather tiresome."

And just like that, all the patience Ethan had hoped to adopt after meeting the Sandlers dissipated like a morning fog. He loathed this man, loathed everything about him—including the fact he had preyed on a woman who had already been through far too much.

"There is a reason," he said softly. "But I wanted to know what had become of you before I say my piece."

"I doubt I will care to hear anything you have to say."

"While that is probably true, what you want matters little to me."

"You sound so sanctimonious. Don't tell me you're going to start casting stones. You might act like you are a self-made man, but we both know you built yourself around the comfort of your circumstances. Few men can boast of such privilege."

Bushnell's words were harsh, but they were also true. Ethan was from a wealthy, old, well-connected family. Their influence was far-reaching, and their holdings were substantial. He'd never been ashamed of that. But at the beginning of the war, his relationships with his family had been strained. His father had wanted him to dodge the war. To stay back and let other men put their lives on the line for their homes and convictions. His brother, Phillip, had agreed, convinced some of the young men were needed at home to protect the women and help manage family holdings. But Ethan had refused. On the night before he left, both he and his father had said a great many things they later regretted.

But as the war wore on, as he witnessed far too many good

men suffer painful deaths, Ethan was privately glad both his father and his brother were safe at home. And in their letters, both his parents shared how proud they were of him. Their letters, so full of hope and home, had helped him survive his life on Johnson's Island.

Bushnell cleared his throat, bringing Ethan back to the present. "So, say your piece, Kelly. Do it quickly now, before I slam my door in your face."

"All right, then. It has come to my attention that you accosted a woman just minutes ago."

"Is that right?" He looked amused. Leaving Ethan still standing in the hallway, he walked to a pack on his desk, pulled out a cigar, and lazily lit it with a match. As he puffed, smoke plumed from his mouth, spiraling toward the high ceiling in a lazy motion.

With another man, Ethan might have been irritated. But this small action showed that Bushnell, for all his bluster, was thrown. During the war, the man had always lit his tobacco whenever he was worried or uneasy.

Leaning against the doorframe, Ethan said, "We aren't going to play this game, are we? You know what I'm talking about."

"Do I?" Bushnell said around a smoke-filled exhale. "At the moment I don't know which woman you are referring to."

Only with the greatest effort did Ethan resist pummeling the man's face. "I am speaking of the maid you were dallying with. The maid with the dark curly hair."

He chuckled. "Ah, yes. I remember now. What of her? She is only a maid. No one of importance. Certainly no one to concern yourself about."

Bushnell's haughty manner was almost believable. Almost. His eyes gave his real thoughts away, however. They were lit with a new light that said volumes about his character. He enjoyed the game. He enjoyed both toying with helpless women like Miss Barclay and matching wits with men like him.

"Don't push me."

"Don't accuse me of things I didn't do."

Stepping into the room uninvited and striding across it, Ethan finally did what he'd been itching to do from the moment Bushnell opened the door. He grabbed him by the collar. "You attempted to violate her."

"She might have believed that. However, I did not."

"Don't lie, Daniel," he said, tightening his hold on the man's collar, nearly choking him.

To Ethan's dismay, Bushnell started laughing. "Now I understand. You aren't upset that I was dabbling with a maid, are you? You are concerned because you have feelings for her! For a maid! What is your family going to say, Kelly? Surely even they don't believe you've fallen this far from society."

"Leave my family out of this."

"You want to pretend you're suddenly just like the rest of us, bowing and scraping to get what we want and need? Well, so be it. If you want to lower yourself to fawn over a chambermaid, it ain't no business of mine." He smirked. "Just let me know when you tire of her. She might be scarred, but that won't hardly matter in the dark."

Finally, the moment he had been hoping for. He slammed his fist into the man's jaw and felt a glimmer of satisfaction rip through him as Bushnell fell to the ground with a *thump*.

Standing over him, Ethan stared at the man's face. When his eyes opened, Ethan bent slightly forward. "She is now under my protection. Do you understand?"

Bushnell's eyes narrowed and a look of extreme distaste passed through his expression before he spoke. "I understand perfectly."

Ethan was still shaking with fury when he slammed the door behind him and stood rooted in the hall.

He'd just made more of an enemy out of Bushnell. If he knew anything, it was that Bushnell wasn't going to take Ethan's assault and threat lightly. He would retaliate.

And though Ethan would have been happy never to see that man again, he now knew that wasn't an option. He would take out his retaliation on Miss Barclay because he knew hurting her would hurt Ethan too.

He needed to protect her. He also needed to discover everything Bushnell had done since the war and ascertain what his plans were for the future. He could use that to his advantage and hold it over the man. Only then would he be able to keep Lizbeth safe.

He had some choices. He could investigate him alone. He could also reach out to his brother and father. They would help him if he asked.

Or he could rely on his band of brothers, the men he knew best and knew would always have his back, no matter what the cost.

In the end, it wasn't really much of a decision. He needed to be available to Lizbeth, so he couldn't leave her alone for long periods of time. His family, while influential and powerful, would expect him to finally move back home and help run the family ranch and assorted holdings. He'd been planning to visit them in a few days to face that reality, but he wasn't going to return for good.

He'd been putting off the inevitable since he'd returned from Johnson's Island. He hadn't been in any shape to be around people in polite society. Instead, he'd been hovering on the fringes of that society. The easy laughter and high-stakes gambling he'd found in numerous establishments around the state had been far easier to deal with. All anyone had wanted there was his money.

But he'd also been able to help the friends with whom he'd been imprisoned when they called, and now he was the one who needed help.

He decided to ride out to visit Captain Devin Monroe as soon as he could. Devin was a man of honor, thoughtful and clear-headed. He also would understand Ethan's feelings about owing such a debt.

Looking around him in the empty hallway of the second floor of the Menger Hotel, Ethan realized his own head felt clearer than it had in months.

Maybe even years.

At last, justice would be served.

5

He was too old for this.

Standing outside Julianne Van Fleet's plain but neat and well-tended home, Devin Monroe felt as though his shirt was too tight, his feet were too big, and his bearing was too hard. Nothing about him was kind or relaxed. Nothing about him was comfortable or easy.

This was a problem.

He didn't know the first thing about courting a gentlewoman like Miss Van Fleet. Actually, he didn't know much about courting women at all. He'd spent the majority of his life in the company of rough soldiers. During most of the war, he'd been a captain, and that rank had fit him like a glove.

He knew how to take orders, and he knew how to manage enlisted men. He knew what to say to push men onward and what to do when he needed them to come to heel. He had been comfortable in the army. He'd instinctively known when to speak and when to stay silent. He'd been respected. Confident. Content.

But he knew next to nothing about talking with women, and even less when it came to knocking on the door of a lady's home. Chances were better than good that he would offend Miss Van Fleet within ten minutes of stepping foot in her parlor.

Turning away from her front door, he studied the other ten or so houses on her street. Each was one story, constructed of limestone and wood, and boasted wide front porches. The yards were carefully tended, and the gravel drives were neatly edged. It was a pretty place. Quiet. Perfect for a lady like her, but confusing for a man who was still getting used to a life out of the military.

Unease crept along his spine. He shouldn't have come. Why had he, anyway?

He knew the answer as sure as if he'd been leading a regiment of soldiers across a war-torn battlefield and his lieutenant wasn't sure whether to surge forward or retreat.

He was on Julianne Van Fleet's front porch because she was the first woman in his memory whom he'd wanted to know. Even after growing up the prized oldest son of two very ordinary people and living next to another ranch where a young lady had made no secret of her desire to be his wife. Despite his mother introducing him to every one of her friends' daughters by the time he was seventeen.

Even after all the cotillions and dances and officers' balls he'd attended, where lines of lovely women in white dresses had looked at his chest of medals with stars in their eyes. He had appreciated their beauty, but not a one had made a lasting impression.

Neither had the women he'd spent time with after his release from Johnson's Island.

He'd begun to think love and romance weren't meant for men like him. He'd killed and hurt and bled too much to even know how to be suitable company for a gently bred woman.

Then one day Miss Van Fleet appeared in his life unexpectedly. He first spied her when he was traveling to San Antonio to visit his friend and former comrade Ethan Kelly. Devin had stopped to water his horse in Boerne, and then decided to take a stroll around the sleepy little town to grab something to eat and give his horse a rest.

The action had been nothing out of the ordinary. He'd done much the same thing more times than he could count. But on that day, in that moment, everything changed.

After hitching his gelding, he walked through the town square, intending to get a dish at the local boarding house, assessing the area, as was his habit. He'd seen the courthouse. The saloon. Mercantile. A couple of men about his age lounging against the side of the bank, smoking. A mother with her brood of children. And one lady walking by herself just across the way.

She was striking. Wearing a well-fitted navy-blue gown that accentuated a nipped-in waist and an hourglass figure. Her features revealed she was likely close to his age of thirty. She was at least five feet seven and had been blessed with auburn hair and a heart-shaped face. She wasn't merely pretty. She was beautiful.

But he'd seen many beautiful women before.

Then she looked up. And he? Well, he'd been caught in that gaze.

Later he would recall other details about her. She'd worn an attractive hat festooned with ribbons. She'd been walking a dog. A book was in her other hand, and a patterned shawl was draped around her slim shoulders.

She'd been so quiet and gentle-looking. Sweet. Peaceful.

He hadn't been able to look away. She was everything he ever envisioned when he laid in too-small cots during the war. There was something about her that he wanted to get to know, if only for a little while.

He'd realized it was time. Time to stop living alone, living only for others. For most of his life, he'd done that. From his days with the Texas Rangers to the years in battle and the months in prison camp, he'd survived by putting his needs last. After what God wanted him to do. After what the Confederacy ordered him to do. After what his men needed him to do. It was time to be selfish and concentrate on his own wants, needs, and hopes.

And even though he wasn't altogether sure what all those things were, he'd acted on his impulse.

In short order, he crossed the street and somehow managed to introduce himself and strike up a conversation with her outside the mercantile. They had talked about nothing, really. Her dog. The weather. She'd been a little shy, easing his own nervousness.

But every word she said had imprinted on his brain. And her voice, her sweetly melodic voice—it rang in his ears like church bells. She laughed at her dog's antics and looked directly at him when he spoke. She didn't simper or flirt or giggle.

He'd been charmed.

Knowing she most likely didn't want to stand talking to him outside the mercantile long, and because he still had obligations to attend to, he said good-bye to her and Boerne and went on his way. But from the moment he left her side he felt her loss. Before he was even halfway to San Antonio, he was making plans to see her again.

The second and third time he sought her out, she smiled. Once, he stood with her a full five minutes talking about Ginger, her spry little beagle. She laughed when Ginger ignored his command to sit.

Amazingly, he laughed too.

Those few encounters had brought him to this moment. To finally behave like a gentleman instead of a war-torn, washed-up soldier.

He just wished he didn't feel more nervous than he ever had in battle. Maybe it was because he'd never feared death, but he did fear her rejection.

When a couple walking down the street gazed at him curiously, the man going as far as to stop and size him up, Devin knew he no longer had a choice. He needed to knock on Miss Van Fleet's door or he'd cause talk, standing outside her door like he was. He couldn't do that. The clerk at the mercantile had already looked at him strangely when he asked for directions to this very house.

Spurred on by that thought, he rested his left arm across the middle of his lower back, stood at attention, and rapped twice on her door with his right hand.

It opened before a full minute passed.

"Captain Monroe," she said in that quiet, melodic voice of hers. "Hello!"

He bowed formally from his waist. "Miss Van Fleet. Good afternoon."

Her eyes widened. She belatedly gave a little curtsy. Pressed her hand to her sternum. "What a nice surprise."

He smiled. Then realized something important had just happened. She didn't step backward to allow him entrance. Instead, she was looking at him curiously.

She didn't understand he'd come calling. How could that be? His aunt had given him specific instructions about the correct time to call on a young lady when he wrote to her for advice. Had she been mistaken?

His palms grew damp.

"Miss Van Fleet, I was just in the area—" No, he wasn't going to lie. Looking at her directly in the eye so he could view every nuance that passed over her expression, he cleared his throat. "The truth is I wasn't just in the area. The truth is I've come calling . . ."

Her eyes widened again, and her lips formed a perfect O. Yet she still didn't move.

This visit was not going according to plan. He should have done some reconnaissance. He should have asked more questions about courting from the men he counted as friends, no matter how much he feared their ridicule. Perhaps his aunt's directives had been antiquated. The men, once they finished laughing at his ignorance, would have gladly advised him about the appropriate way to behave.

But since it was too late for that, he had to make do with standing on her doorstep, sweating as the November sun beat on his back, and fumbling for the right words to say.

Miss Van Fleet was staring at him closely. "Calling . . . ?" she prodded.

He realized then that he'd stopped speaking midsentence. "Yes. Calling." He cleared his throat. "For you."

All at once, amusement entered her expression. She smiled. Stepping back, she opened the door farther. "Captain Monroe, as I said before, this is such a nice surprise. Won't you please come in?"

Barely stopping himself from thanking her for allowing him entrance, Devin entered her home with a profound sense of accomplishment. While she took a moment to rearrange the skirts of her dark rose-colored gown, he took the liberty of closing the front door. As it clicked shut with a healthy *snap*, he looked around with interest.

The entryway was very small. Almost immediately upon them was a sitting room with two well-made chairs upholstered in light-blue velvet.

As Julianne guided him inside, he noticed a small desk, a matching sofa, and two other tables, each next to the padded chairs. A fine-looking lamp with a glass globe was near one of the chairs. As was a book . . . and spectacles.

She wore glasses.

"Would you like to sit with me?" she asked. "I had just come in here. I was reading." She sat down in one of the chairs.

"So I see." Holding his hat in his hands, he sat down in the space she gestured to, the chair across from hers. "You wear glasses."

She tensed before nodding. "I do. Well, I do to read. You have uncovered my secret, Captain." She smiled, but it was obvious she was embarrassed.

He wasn't sure why. Growing tired of his ignorance, he decided to take the topic on. "Forgive me. I know a lot about ordering men about, but far too little about polite conversation. Were those spectacles something I wasn't supposed to mention? I promise I don't think they are a detraction. Quite the opposite."

"My mother used to ask me never to mention such things, but that was a lifetime ago." Rubbing her temples, she shook her head. "To be honest, I'm not even sure if I'm supposed to hide my imperfection anymore or not. We all have far too many other worries about now, I fear."

"At the risk of sounding boorish, I have to admit I am rather relieved you wear glasses. I kind of like knowing you are not completely perfect."

Her eyes widened once more. "I am certainly not that."

Just so she wouldn't think he was full of himself, he winked. "Neither am I."

Something new flickered in her eyes before she firmly tamped it down, and she stood. "Forgive me my rag manners. May I offer you some refreshment? Bula, my day maid, is in the kitchen."

He was too afraid he would either spill tea on her furniture or ask for the wrong thing. "No, thank you."

"No? Well, all right." She sat back down. Folded her hands in her lap. Thirty seconds passed. Forty.

He started to wish he would have swallowed his pride and at least asked Ethan Kelly for advice. He was a man who always knew the right thing to say and do, at least in the company of women. Kelly's advice would have come in very handy right about then.

6

As Julianne sat composedly across from him, her pretty blue eyes patiently awaiting his next comment or question, Devin's uneasiness increased.

His mouth went dry as he attempted to think of something to say. Unfortunately, he couldn't think of a single thing of worth. He should have planned. He should have made notes. Made stratagems. Considered possible outcomes. Honestly, he never got out of bed without a detailed list of goals and possible outcomes. How could he have just taken a bath, put on clean clothes, and appeared on her porch without any more forethought?

She laughed.

He focused on her again. "Am I amusing you, miss?"

"Honestly? Yes."

All thought drained from his head as he stared at her. "Have I just committed another faux pas I wasn't aware of?"

She laughed harder. "No, Captain. I was just thinking that we are two peas in a pod, aren't we? I'm so unused to having gentlemen callers. I have no idea what to say or do . . . while you are obviously out of your element as well."

Though his cheeks and neck were no doubt turning bright red, he said, "I cannot deny my inexperience."

"A man of worth like you?"

"Like me?"

"Well, yes. After we first spoke at the mercantile, I did a little bit of checking on you. It seems you have quite the reputation, sir."

"I find that hard to believe."

"You shouldn't doubt it, sir. It seems just about everyone in these parts has heard of the illustrious Captain Monroe."

"I'm surprised."

"You shouldn't be, Captain," she said as her beagle meandered in and positioned herself under his right hand. "The stories shared describe a man of great bravery and honor."

He rubbed the soft fur in between Ginger's ears. "Such talk about a common captain seems excessive."

"I would agree, except the stories were impressive. Your reputation has preceded you, sir."

The last thing he wanted to talk about was himself. "I wouldn't believe everything you hear, miss. It's all in the past anyway."

Gazing at him with a warm look, she continued. "So even though exaggerated tales bursting about your greatness on the battlefield abound, you have not gone courting much?"

"That is true. During the war I fear I was always otherwise occupied with survival. But I must confess that I'm surprised about your lack of callers. I expected to be one of many gentlemen here today."

She shook her head. "That is not the case." Quietly she added, "You could probably tell in our earlier encounters, but I have the dubious honor of being both shy and bookish."

"It's my reward, then."

Her eyes lit up as she pursed her lips. "Captain, I'd love to know more about you. From where do you hail?"

"I grew up south of Dallas. When I got to my majority, I joined the Texas Rangers and served all over the state."

"What about your family?"

"My family?" He drew a blank.

"Yes. Were you close to your parents? Do you have siblings? Did you ever shirk your chores?"

"Shirk my chores?" He couldn't hide the incredulousness in his voice. When he spied the humor in her eyes, he laughed sheepishly. "Are you teasing me, Miss Van Fleet?"

"Only seeking to know you better."

"In that case I should tell you I had a happy childhood. My father was the foreman of a large operation. I grew up learning to mind my mother and guide my two younger brothers, and wanting to do whatever my father asked me to do at the Diamond P Ranch."

"You loved him very much."

"I did. My world was small. I loved my parents, thought every child feasted on warm buttermilk biscuits every morning, and was sure the most powerful man in the state was Mr. Pennington, the owner of the ranch." When her gaze softened even more, he felt himself relax against the cushions of the chair. "I don't remember the last time I thought about those days. About how idyllic my childhood was."

"You didn't want to return to Dallas? Boerne seems awfully far away, both in size and consequence."

"It is. But not only do I currently live near San Antonio, not here in Boerne, I have no reason to go back. My family . . ." He paused, surprised that after all this time, speaking of them still brought pain. "They are all gone."

"All?"

He nodded. "My father signed up to fight even before Texas followed Jefferson Davis. My brothers, Colin and Will, perished at Antietam."

"And your mother?"

"Yellow fever."

"And Mr. Pennington?"

"You know what? I haven't thought about him in years." He rubbed a hand along his jaw, wondering how he could have forgotten about the fine man who had done so right by his family. "I hope he did survive. That would be a blessing."

"I hope he survived for you too."

Devin wasn't sure how to respond to that. Her compassion was unfamiliar and stirred him in ways he hadn't expected. It also made him uncomfortable. "How about you?"

"Me? I have no exciting tales or experiences to regale you with."

"You might be surprised by what I find interesting."

She smiled, charming him. "Not all of us can be heroes, I'm afraid. I've lived all my life in Boerne," she said, running her hand against the smooth grain of the table next to her.

"So you grew up around here."

Her smile brightened. "I grew up in this very house."

"Is that right?" He surveyed the room, looking a little bit harder for signs of other inhabitants. "Who lives with you now?"

"No one."

He stilled. "No one. You lost everyone as well?" For some reason he didn't want to think of her suffering the same losses he had.

"Oh, no, Captain Monroe." Her pretty smile turned brittle. "My sister married, and then my mother moved in with her and her family. In Amarillo."

Obviously there was a story there. But what kind of story was it? He debated, curious as to why she had stayed while everyone else left.

It seemed odd and vaguely alarming. Women of good breeding

didn't live by themselves. It was also too expensive for them to do so. Especially in these lean days after the war.

Was she that wealthy?

The house, while not terribly large, was finely appointed and well cared for. Her gown, while not all that fancy, was of obvious quality. She looked fresh and well rested. Healthy.

But if she was that wealthy, why wasn't she living in one of the bigger cities? A beauty such as hers would always attract a following. She could have had her choice of suitors.

A new wariness entered her eyes. "It's good you were a soldier, Captain, and not a poker player."

"Is my expression that transparent?"

"I'm afraid so. I can practically see the wheels turning in your brain. You are wondering about my circumstances."

He didn't bother to deny it. "Yes. Even though it is none of my business, I must admit I am curious."

"You deserve an explanation. But, before I give it, I want to thank you for this."

"For what?"

She waved a hand in the air, somehow managing to encircle the entire room. "For being so attentive and gentlemanly. For calling on me. It has been flattering."

He wanted to smile, to say she was finding worth in something that shouldn't be out of the ordinary for her.

He certainly couldn't relay that he'd waited his whole life to come calling on her. He didn't know much about courting, but he knew enough to sense that such . . . well, enthusiastic devotion was unseemly.

He made do with reassuring her. That was something he knew how to do. Not all men who fought were gifted soldiers. The majority were clumsy in battle and unsure of themselves. Or lonely. Or afraid. He'd spent more hours than he could count reassuring men of their worth. "Miss Van Fleet, though I don't have a great deal of experience with women, I am no stranger to life. I can't imagine taking exception with anything you could tell me."

"I hope that is indeed the case, but I have my doubts."

Instead of responding, he leaned back against his chair and folded his hands on his lap. And waited.

Looking pained, she started speaking. "During the height of the war, around '63 or so, my circumstances were far different from what they are now. I was hungry, so very cold, and out of options."

He was stunned.

"Were you alone?"

"Almost. My grandmother lived with me."

"What of your parents?"

"My father had already died in the war. My sister married days before her husband left to fight. Weeks later, she discovered she was with child. It was a difficult pregnancy. That's when my mother went to live with her."

"Leaving you responsible for yourself, the house, and your grandmother."

"Yes." She swallowed. "It was very . . . challenging."

"I imagine so."

"My grandmother was ill. In fact, she was wasting away because we had so little food. I asked my mother for help, but for one reason or another she never had funds to spare. That was when I knew I had to do whatever I could." Looking more agitated, she averted her eyes. "One reason I was alone, I'm afraid, is that I hadn't quite grown into my looks. That, along with my shyness and bookish nature, made me something of an oddity on the marriage market. I didn't take."

"Men don't always see what is right in front of them."

Instead of smiling, she cleared her throat. "Eventually I did grow into my features, and I learned to keep my glasses hidden. That seemed to help." She took a breath. "Anyway, when some of the young women I knew confided they were going to travel to San Antonio to attend an officers' ball in the hopes of making a match, I thought maybe I would do that too."

"So you did?"

She nodded. "I . . . well, I couldn't think of any other option. A friend offered to stay with my grandmother. I put on my best dress, went with those girls, and made sure I outshone them all."

"And did it work?"

Eyes still shadowed, she nodded again. "At first my social graces weren't much different from what they'd always been. I fumbled through conversations and stumbled through dances. But then I met a man who seemed different. He didn't seem to care that I loved books or that I didn't know how to flirt or be especially charming. He didn't even seem to care that I wasn't wealthy. He wasn't very handsome, but I didn't mind. I was sure I had met the perfect man for me."

"Ah." She'd been married. He relaxed. That was her secret? He hadn't known she was a widow, but the mystery officer asking for her hand made perfect sense. She was exactly the type of woman he would have wanted to marry quickly, and many, many men had done the same thing.

"You shouldn't be embarrassed about that, Miss—or should I say Mrs. Van Fleet? Women need protectors and men need to protect. I'm sure your husband was thankful to have someone to think about when he was far away from home, and you needed someone. All I can say is he was a lucky man."

Chewing on her bottom lip, she shook her head. "No, I'm afraid it wasn't quite like that, Captain. This man called on me several times. He was everything proper and very wealthy. Each time he visited he brought gifts for both me and my grandmother. I was sure I was in love." Her hands clenched. She cleared her throat once more. "I thought he was going to propose, you see."

His mouth went dry. What was she about to tell him? "He did not?"

"Oh, no. He admitted he was already married."

Devin was shocked by what an officer had done to her. "What a scoundrel. I'm sure you were devastated."

"Yes, I was. I was ruined, you see . . ."

He shook his head. "Miss Van Fleet—"

"This is very hard. I need to finish, please." Gazing at a point just beyond him, she said quietly, "One evening he said he was joining his regiment the very next morning. Still thinking he was going to ask me to be his wife before his departure, I let him . . . spend the night. It wasn't until the next morning I learned he was married, and that he wasn't going to his regiment for a week. I was upset and desperate, and this man, this colonel . . . well, he knew it. He did make me an offer, but it wasn't to be his wife."

He knew he shouldn't ask. He knew he shouldn't make her say it. But he wanted to be clear about what she was saying. Just in case he had misunderstood. "Miss?" Was his voice as hoarse as he feared it sounded?

She raised her head and looked him directly in the eye. But whereas before there was light in her expression, nothing remained but flat resignation. "You didn't misinterpret what I said, sir. Daniel Bushnell asked me to become his mistress. And though I no longer had stars in my eyes where he was concerned, I knew I had little choice in the matter. I said yes."

His body protested each word she said. "You were Colonel Bushnell's mistress?" he said slowly. She'd belonged to Bushnell.

One of the slickest, most corrupt officers he'd ever had the misfortune to know.

Pain entered her eyes. "I was. I felt I had no choice. My financial situation was dire. My grandmother and I were literally starving. I had to do something."

"And that was all you could think of?" he asked, his voice harsh. Scathing.

She drew back. "I had no other options, sir."

"Really? Or did you not want to be patient? I imagine many a man would have come up to heel in a few months."

"That wasn't going to happen. No other man had shown any interest in me, and as I told you, we were already starving. And now I was ruined." She shrugged. "I don't suppose it really matters. I entered an agreement with him that morning."

"You agreed to continue to lie with him for money." He didn't bother to hide the disdain in his voice.

"Yes." Her face was a mask of control now. "He said he'd married young, and neither he nor his wife was happy. He was determined to find happiness elsewhere."

"And you believed him?"

She lifted her chin. "Do you want the truth, Captain? The truth is no, I didn't believe him. I thought he'd lied to me, taken advantage of me, ruined my innocence, and erased the dreams I'd had. But I had no choice."

"What about your grandmother? What about your mother? Your sister? Surely they advised you against it."

"My grandmother was happy to have food and firewood. I don't know if she even realized how it had all come to be. If she did? Well, she pretended she didn't understand. When he was here that night, she was already fading . . ."

Pain flickered in her eyes. It was obvious she was hurt that he was forcing her to talk more about this. "At first my mother said she understood. Eventually, though, my reputation became too much for her to bear. I don't know what she told my sister, but I stopped hearing from both of them. I only know they are well through a friend."

"Yet you continued that alliance."

"It was a great many things, sir, but an alliance it was not."

"Perhaps it was more of a *dalliance*, instead," he said before he thought better of it.

"Well, I lived here, kept this home afloat, and opened the doors to the colonel whenever he came." Her voice softened. "With that money, and because that money allowed me to engage Bula, I was able to care for my grandmother until she died, and pay for her funeral as well."

He knew he was being judgmental. He knew sharing this wasn't easy for her to do. She could have simply turned him away at her door or kept up a pretense. Yet she'd elected to tell him her true standing.

He should leave, but he couldn't seem to stop himself from prying even further. "Are you still Bushnell's kept woman?"

She looked surprised. "I am not."

"What happened?" he asked, hating that he even cared.

"Eventually the war ended. He, of course, went back to his wife." She looked out the window. "Or maybe he found someone new. A woman younger."

"So he was the one who ended it."

"I'm not sure if that is always the case, but yes, Captain, in my case, that is how my 'association' with this man ended. He gave me an envelope of money and told me he would not be back." She sighed and at last looked at him again. "I used part of it to buy sewing supplies and started making clothes for some women in the area to support myself and keep this house in good repair. Even if more women had been able to afford new clothes during the war, I couldn't sew when my time and energy were reserved for caring for my grandmother. The rest I put away for safekeeping." She sat back in her chair. "So that is how I came to be living here on my own."

"Does anyone even associate with you? Beyond your sewing customers?"

She paused, as if she was attempting to regain her composure. When she spoke, her voice was arched. "What do you think, Captain?"

It all made sense now. Why he'd only seen her walking alone, never with other women or companions. The reason she had no other callers and was surprised to see him at her door.

She was nothing like the gentle lady he had imagined. She was used. She had traded in both her respect and her reputation. She said her circumstances had been dire, that she'd only been trying to survive. But was that true? Had Miss Van Fleet simply wanted more comfort while the South was at war?

Suddenly realizing he was sitting in the chair Bushnell had no doubt occupied many times, Devin sprang to his feet.

She watched him with wide eyes.

"I knew Colonel Bushnell," he said coldly.

With great deliberation, she stood as well. "Then you know what Daniel was like."

"I know the type of man he was. I not only served under him during the height of the war, but we were interred in the officers' prison camp on Johnson's Island together."

Surprise flickered in her eyes. "He hated that camp so much."

"I'm sure he did. I certainly hated being stuck there with him." With far too many memories of the man fresh in his mind, he continued. "He was the worst sort of man. Entitled. Lazy. Mercurial."

He could have gone on and on. Described how he'd used people to his benefit. How he was sure the man would have sacrificed his own mother if it would have benefited him.

Julianne looked shaken, but she didn't dispute his words. "So you did know him," she said softly.

"You knew these things too? You knew these things and still allowed him . . ." He couldn't even finish his statement.

She reached out a hand and gripped the edge of the chair behind her. Only then did she sit back down. "I came to know more about Bushnell's ways than either of us would care to discuss. Good day, Captain Monroe," she said after she arranged her skirts. "I trust you can see yourself out."

Indeed, he could. He turned on his heel and strode out of the room. He was shutting her front door firmly behind him mere seconds later.

Heading toward his horse, sharp indignation flew through him. After waiting for most of his life to find a prospective bride, he'd centered on the most unsuitable woman.

What a fool he'd been!

He had devoted so much time to her. He'd dreamed about her. Imagined how pure and sweet she was. Had concocted a story in his head about how she'd been waiting for him too. How he hadn't been the only person to believe in fate and the value of patience.

He couldn't have been more wrong.

This is nothing you don't deserve, Devin, he told himself. You ignored scores of perfectly lovely women, sure that none of them was the right match. And because of that, you've lived alone, only taking comfort in dreams. You should have dreamed less and lived more.

Mounting his horse, Midge, he rode off her street, out of her town. Determined never to return.

He only hoped he could forget Julianne Van Fleet just as quickly.

But just like the worst moments on the battlefield, he had a feeling the moments in her company would be forever seared into his brain. A constant reminder of his faults and the danger in believing in dreams.

7

JULIANNE WAS ALONE IN HER HOUSE ONCE AGAIN. NOTHING she wasn't used to.

So why did she feel so lonely?

Her breath caught in her throat as she stared into the entryway, at the door that had just closed in her face. It wasn't a surprise, but it still felt like one.

It had been two years since she'd seen Daniel. Two years of blissful freedom.

Contrary to how Devin obviously viewed it, she most definitely had not entered into her arrangement with him lightly. It had been exactly as she'd told the captain—a decision born out of fear and hunger and a willingness to do whatever it took to survive.

Though it hadn't been what she wanted, she knew women who had suffered far greater pain and injury than she had, especially since she hadn't seen Daniel all that much.

After entering their agreement, he'd gone back to his regiment, returning to her only a few times. He spent most of the next two years in battle, and then in his confinement on Johnson's Island.

When he was gone, she didn't have to endure his abuse.

And she'd tried to make him out to be better than he was. She wanted to believe he was a brave man, responsible for hundreds, if not thousands of men. He'd been captured and then fought for survival while in the hands of the enemy. He deserved her loyalty, didn't he? Especially since all he asked of her during his absences was correspondence.

She wrote to him. Dutifully, twice a week. Tried to think of entertaining stories about her days, most of which were greatly exaggerated. When he wrote her back and asked if she missed him, if she longed for him, it was easy to lie and say she did. After all, it was because of his funds that she hadn't starved.

However, she learned something about survival. She learned there was a great variance between being respected and being shunned. As word of her arrangement became public knowledge in Boerne, people of good faith began to avoid her. Eventually decent women wouldn't even look her in the eye. She didn't blame them. After all, there had been a time when she would have treated someone like her the same way.

After her grandmother died and she could leave home more often, the minister still permitted her in church. But she felt his disapproval. Once, she was fairly sure she was the subject of his sermon.

It had been hard. At first she'd been bitter. But then, as the months passed, she decided she needed to do something besides sit by herself in her home. She took some of Bushnell's money, bought chickens and seeds, and planted a large garden. Worked on it painstakingly. Then shared as much of her bounty as she could with anyone else in need. She'd volunteered at the hospital, working with injured soldiers.

By the end of the war, she had no friends, exactly. But she wasn't nearly the pariah she'd been before. She could go to the mercantile for supplies easily enough. Even sit in the back of the church without others turning to stare.

She almost—*almost*—pretended she was respectable again. Then he came back.

She still felt sick when she remembered how awful he looked. He was so terribly thin. His skin sallow, two of his teeth rotten. And he wanted . . . well, what he came for.

She'd had no choice but to give him that. For one week.

He'd been rough—more than before. He'd hurt her. Scared her. At times he was cruel.

War had changed him, from bad to worse. And by the time he was finished with her, bruised and pale—desolate—she realized she'd been a fool to think accepting that arrangement had been right.

No, it had been everything wrong.

She'd prayed for his abuse to stop. Prayed for any kind of relief. Then, miraculously, her prayers were answered. He told her he had no use for her anymore. He gave her an envelope of money, said he was returning to his wife, and left. She was free.

She didn't know where he was now, and she didn't care. All she had known for some time was that she didn't need much to survive. Until today, when she'd been almost courted by Captain Devin Monroe. That was when she realized she couldn't have been more wrong. She needed peace and acceptance and happiness. But those things were going to once again be out of her precious grasp. There was nothing she could do about it either.

She never thought her future would be so cruel.

Late the next morning Julianne forced herself to get up and perform her usual preparations. She looked in the mirror and tried to care about the smudges under her eyes and the lines of strain around her lips.

After brushing her hair a hundred times like her mother had long ago taught her, she pinned it up, slipped on a warm dress made of blackberry-colored soft wool that she'd made two months earlier, and then put on her cloak. She needed to get out of her house. More importantly, she needed to banish Devin Monroe and the silly, girlish dreams he'd brought out in her from her mind. He wasn't going to come back, and he wasn't going to change his mind about her.

The longer she dwelled on what she couldn't change, the more depressed she'd be. Deciding that her walk was as much for her well-being as anything else, she left a note for Bula, who was out shopping. Then she set off toward Boerne's only diner for an early lunch. After all, she hadn't had any breakfast.

The temperature had dropped overnight, and the cold had made the dirt roads hard and the air crisp. It felt exhilarating, and it improved her mood and outlook. She hoped her brisk pace combined with the cool air brought some needed color to her cheeks.

As she walked the few short blocks to the town square, several people nodded in her direction. A few even stopped to exchange pleasantries. Oh, how things had changed from when she was known to everyone as only Bushnell's ladybird.

Now, though some sticklers made a great show of walking to the other side of the street when she approached, most folks in town seemed as determined to move on as she was. Time—and the fact that she now lived so visibly alone—had done miracles for her reputation. She might always be whispered about as a woman with a questionable past, but she was no longer treated with overt contempt and scorn. It was a welcome relief—and a welcome reminder after Devin's departure the day before.

Once she arrived in Bonnie's Café, she greeted the owner, then walked to her usual spot, the corner booth in the back of the room.

She would have some soup and a piece of their roasted chicken, then walk back home, maybe even taking the time to stroll around the town square.

When she was halfway through her bowl of vegetable beef soup, a young man and lady approached her. Well-dressed and extremely proper looking, they were a handsome pair. They also looked apprehensive about speaking to her, but determined too.

She looked up at them and smiled slightly. Perhaps they were lost or needed directions.

"Miss Van Fleet?" the woman said.

"Yes?"

After the man gave what could only be described as an encouraging nod, the woman spoke again. "My name is Abby Bernard. This is my brother, Carl. May we join you?"

"I'm sorry, but you have me at a disadvantage. Do we know each other?"

"We do. Well, we do, after a fashion," Carl said.

"I'm afraid I still don't follow."

"That's what we want to talk with you about," Abby said. Gesturing toward the two empty spaces across from Julianne, she said, "May we join you? I promise we won't take up too much of your time."

She was curious now. "All right."

As the pair got settled, she eyed them inquisitively. Upon closer inspection, Julianne realized their clothing wasn't quite as good quality as she first thought. Miss Bernard's gown was well fitted, but there were marks from frequent alterations. The ends of the blue ribbons on her bonnet were slightly frayed. Her brother had on a smart-looking brown suit, but it had turned-in sleeves and cuffs.

Her first impression had been that they were in their early

twenties, but now she determined their ages were closer to late teens, perhaps eighteen or nineteen. The boy's build was still lanky, all arms and legs, and the girl still had the full cheeks of youth. Both looked very much like the siblings they were, with fair skin and thick brown hair—only the girl's eyes were dark blue while the young man's eyes were a caramel color.

She thought of a number of ways she could begin the conversation, but none seemed right. Then, too, was the fact that she was still exhausted after Devin Monroe's visit. She decided to simply sit and wait.

After another moment of awkward silence, the boy spoke at last. "Miss, I'm afraid there's no delicate way to begin . . ."

The girl nodded, looking rather embarrassed.

As the time stretched out again, Julianne began to grow impatient. "Perhaps you could simply start at the beginning. That usually works for me."

"All right, then," Miss Bernard said. "As you might imagine, we were children during the war. Our parents lived over near New Braunfels."

New Braunfels was not far, but at least several hours by horseback. "Is that where you reside now?"

Carl shook his head. "When the war broke out, our pa went off to fight. When he left, our mother, well, she had a tough time of it."

"She was with child, you see," Abby interjected.

Julianne fought to keep her expression neutral. Though their history was mildly interesting, she could sense nothing that pertained to her. "Ah."

"She ended up dying in childbirth," she continued. "God rest her soul."

"I'm, uh, very sorry. And your father? How did he fare?"

"He didn't survive either. He died in the war."

"So you two have had your share of hardship." Again, she felt sympathy for their past, but nothing in their story was unfamiliar. One would be hard-pressed to find a single person in Texas who hadn't lost either a parent or sibling.

When they both nodded, she tried to think of another reason why they wanted to speak with her. She couldn't think of one. Feeling vaguely uncomfortable, she said, "While I certainly feel for your loss, I am not sure how it pertains to me."

Carl cleared his throat. "Of course not." He began to speak more quickly. "You see, after our mother passed, we were on our own. So we were sent to live with a relative here. Our aunt, Dora Feldman."

"Dora?"

Miss Bernard sighed. "Yes! You knew her quite well, I believe?"

"Indeed I did." Now that the connection had been made at last, Julianne felt immeasurably better. "You're kin to Dora? Well, that is something. She was a lovely lady."

"I don't know if you remember, but you took care of her, and therefore us, during the last years of the war."

She shook her head. "I think that is putting it a bit thick."

"You brought her food every week."

"Nothing much to speak of," Julianne pointed out. "Sometimes it was nothing more than eggs or greens."

"It was everything. Those items were how we survived."

A knot formed in her throat. "I didn't know that." Remembering what a dark time that had been, she whispered, "I don't remember much about those years except trying to survive." She coughed. "After the war? What did you do?"

"Aunt Dora took us over to Fredericksburg. She had a cousin who was willing to take all of us in."

"So you went there."

"We did, miss." They exchanged looks again. "After a few months, Aunt Dora passed away, but our cousins couldn't have been kinder to us. We . . . well, we both have a very nice life now."

"I'm glad to hear that." Their gratitude made her feel inadequate. She hadn't done much. Maybe she could have done more. "Thank you for letting me know you are doing well."

Miss Bernard leaned forward. "Thank you, but that isn't the purpose of our visit. You see, we have been meaning to come see you for some time now. But we weren't sure if we should . . ." She blushed as her voice drifted off.

They weren't sure about seeking her out because of her reputation. "I understand," she said quickly. She wasn't about to make them refer to her tainted past out loud. Or to have it presented to her face.

The girl looked at her quizzically. "Do you? I don't."

She looked sincere, but Julianne knew better than to believe anyone could be so naïve. She began to resent their intrusion almost as much as she resented the reminder about her past.

She folded her hands in her lap with care while she took a fortifying breath. "It is no secret that I was an officer's kept woman, Miss . . . Abby," she said, her voice like ice. "Most people don't want to associate with me because of that."

When Carl averted his eyes and Abby blushed again, she fought back the temptation to snap at them both. How dare they allude to her past, but then act as if it was too much to deal with!

Frustrated, she pressed her lips together and began to hope this unexpected visit would soon end.

As if Carl was sensing her dismay, he said, "What we're trying to say, Miss Van Fleet, is that your past doesn't matter to us. We were reluctant to come see you because we didn't want to bring up that time in your life. On account that it is no doubt painful to remember."

"I appreciate your visit. Thank you." Now she wished they'd leave.

"I haven't spoken to you to simply express my gratitude, Miss Van Fleet. I came in the hopes that I might one day be your friend," Abby said. "So I might seek permission to call on you at your home."

Her friend? "I beg your pardon?"

"I would like to visit you from time to time. That is, if you wouldn't mind my company." Softly she added, "You see, I recently became affianced to Preacher Timothy. I am very excited about the match."

"I wish you much good fortune," Julianne said haltingly. "However, I must stress that you mustn't feel obligated to visit. You don't owe me anything."

"That is where you are wrong, Miss Van Fleet. We owe you everything," Carl said. "Please don't say no."

"I won't say no." She did her best to ignore the tears that had just formed in her eyes.

Abby's smile was nearly blinding. Or perhaps it was simply beautiful. "I'm so glad. Thank you, Miss Van Fleet."

It was time to let down her guard. It was obvious that God had brought these two people to her for a specific reason. They'd come to remind her that faith, hope, and trust were not pretty, antiquated words that meant little or pertained only to other people. No, God had brought them into her life so she would believe in a future again. And maybe that was the essence of it too. It didn't matter that the future wasn't promised to be perfect or free from hurt. What mattered was that she was going to have one. Yes, it was time to stop subsisting in near isolation, bearing all the shame of her past, and start living again.

And since she was well aware that faith, hope, and trust did exist—though she'd given up imagining they existed for her—she held out a hand. "Please, if we are going to be friends, you might as well call me by my Christian name. Julianne."

Immediately, Abby slipped her hand into hers and clasped it tightly. "I would enjoy that. Thank you, Julianne."

"And I as well," Carl said.

Thirty minutes later, when she was alone again, Julianne wondered how the Lord had known she'd needed Abby and Carl. They'd come at the perfect time, just when her heart had been breaking over the loss of Devin Monroe.

Just when she'd been at her lowest point.

How had he known? Was it simply because he was God and all-knowing?

Staring at the road out the café's front window, she decided it didn't matter after all. For whatever reason, they had come, and their kindness had transformed her. She felt lighter of spirit, fuller of heart. Her cloying depression had lifted.

That was enough. More than enough.

8

It turned out Aileen really hadn't minded if Lizbeth stayed the night. And an hour after firing her, she came all the way up to Lizbeth's room to say her husband would compute her final payment in the morning. He'd been sidetracked by attempting to wrangle a group of disreputable gunmen in the hotel's bar.

She also told her Bushnell had made no complaint, but she and Dallas still thought it was necessary for Lizbeth to go because of her interaction with Major Kelly. She'd had a strange look in her eye when she said that, but Lizbeth didn't have the energy to ask why.

Aileen told her all this after she made Lizbeth promise she would stay in her room like a wayward child. Lizbeth felt so fragile, she would have agreed to anything as long as she didn't have to leave the hotel immediately. She'd lain down early in the evening and tried to sleep, but every time she closed her eyes, memories of being alone in her house on the ranch invaded her thoughts.

Just as she had been pulling out a sheet of paper to begin listing all the options for her future she could think of, Callie knocked on her door.

Lizbeth answered it with mixed emotions. Callie was her closest friend in the hotel, and talking to her usually brightened her day. But Lizbeth was afraid this conversation would only reinforce how hard it was going to be to completely change her life once again.

To her surprise, Callie didn't look full of questions. She was wearing a concerned expression. "Oh good. I was afraid you weren't going to answer the door."

"Is something wrong? What do you need?"

"I don't need anything," Callie said in her breezy way as she sauntered inside. As usual, she'd taken off her white maid's bonnet and stuffed it into a pocket. Therefore, her brown hair was on display. Today it was artfully arranged into an elaborate configuration of braids. It always struck Lizbeth that Callie's penchant for a fancy coiffure, in stark contrast to her rather plain features, was an effort to present herself as more than a maid in a fancy hotel.

But Callie knew that's all she was. Lizbeth, on the other hand, had recently remembered her previous life made her more than that. Inside, she was still a lady.

Taking note of Callie's expectant expression, Lizbeth arched an eyebrow. "You came up here to say hello?"

"Of course not. Downstairs, we all got to talking about what happened to you. I was elected to come up as the representative." She smiled, looking very pleased with herself.

"So you came up here to check on me?"

"No. I came up here to give you this." She held up a canvas tote bag. "See? We all got together and brought you something."

Stunned, Lizbeth took the tote from her. "Thank you."

"Go ahead," Callie said, gesturing with her hands. "Open it."

Lizbeth pulled open the heavy tote and nearly gasped. Inside were two wrapped sandwiches, a container of cookies, and a Mason jar of lemonade. "This all looks wonderful. Thank you."

Callie lowered her voice. "We heard how Mrs. Howard warned

you to keep out of sight. It's just her way to forget that you need to eat and drink, same as anyone else. You'd think she wasn't related to you."

Lizbeth didn't comment on that. She had a feeling Aileen had other concerns on her mind.

Callie waved her hand. "Keep digging. There's more."

After carefully setting the sandwiches on her bed, she pulled out a large envelope. Inside were several notes . . . and a large collection of coins. "What is all this?"

"Come now. You know what it is. It's some money for you."

"I don't know what to say." Tears were threatening to prick her eyes, which would be a mistake. Callie was never a fan of emotional women.

But to her surprise, Callie reached out and clasped her hand. "You don't need to say a thing. Though it ain't a big surprise that you're getting fired on account of some horrible gentleman guest, it's still terrible."

"Please thank everyone for me. This . . . this is so very kind."

"I'll pass on your thanks, though it's a real shame you aren't allowed to come downstairs and do it yourself."

"I'll be all right. No doubt I'll catch up on my sleep."

"That would be a treat, wouldn't it?" After squeezing her hand again, she said, "Do you have any idea what you're gonna do now?"

"No. The only plan I've been able to come up with so far is to get a room in one of the inns in the area for a while."

Callie's eyes widened. "Which one? Some of them have terrible reputations."

"I'll stay at whichever place has a room for me. I'm not going to try to find work yet. No one is going to hire me without a recommendation." Carefully putting the sandwiches back in the tote, she said, "I've saved some money. That, along with what y'all have so generously shared, should be enough to give me a few weeks' reprieve while I decide where to go next."

"So you're planning to leave San Antone."

"I don't have a choice." Lizbeth needed to get as far from Daniel Bushnell as she could.

She also needed to distance herself from Aileen and Dallas. She didn't know what to think about her cousin. They weren't close, but Lizbeth had thought she meant more to Aileen than she obviously did. After everything they'd both been through during the war, Aileen was still putting the needs of the hotel above her cousin's. But she also knew Aileen wasn't about to upset Dallas. A husband had been hard to come by during the war.

Callie nodded. "I understand. I'd want to leave too, if I were you." She sighed. "I'm sure gonna miss you, though."

Realizing she was going to end the battle with her tears, Lizbeth crossed the small room to her side. "I'm going to miss you too. You've been a good friend."

Callie hugged her quickly and then hurried to the door. "I best get back to work. You enjoy the sandwiches now. And don't leave town without saying good-bye to all of us, okay?"

"I won't." She smiled bravely until her door closed again. She figured it didn't matter anymore if she cried or not, and she at last gave in to tears.

It wasn't as though there was anyone around to see them fall.

Now this morning, Lizbeth shook off the memory of her talk with Callie the night before and left her room, her cloak around her shoulders and her bag in hand. Just as she was walking through the lobby, about to claim her last paycheck from Dallas in his office, Major Kelly appeared at her side.

She was relieved he wasn't Bushnell, but still, he made her flustered. Her cheeks were no doubt burning bright red, but she forced herself to greet him. "Good morning, sir."

"And good morning to you," he said as he curved a hand around her elbow. "I'm delighted I located you so easily."

"Sir?"

"Miss Barclay, may we talk?"

Yet again he was standing so tall, so well dressed, and so debonair. Though she wasn't wearing a maid's uniform, her dark-brown dress made her feel like a plain wren next to him. Then there was the fact that his easy smile and charm affected her too much. Being around him made her think of things she had no business thinking about. He was everything she shouldn't want in her life. Everything that was beyond her grasp, even if she did want a man like him.

No, it was much better to work on putting some distance between them, which meant she needed to do what she could to get him to turn away. Attempting to tug her elbow from his clasp, she said, "I think we've said everything there is to say, sir."

"I happen to disagree." Instead of loosening his grip, he tightened his hold on her. It wasn't painful, but it also didn't leave any room for her to refuse to walk by his side.

"Come along," he said easily as he guided her into a hall. He didn't look down at her. Instead, he kept his hand on her arm and escorted her into one of the private lounges some of the wealthiest guests reserved from time to time.

For a moment she considered simply leaving, but then she decided to listen to what he had to say. The truth was she didn't fear him. She also no longer had anything to lose.

After she perched on the edge of a plum-colored velvet chair, he sat down across from her. "Do you know what you are going to do now?" he asked, obviously not wanting to waste another second.

He knew she'd been fired? Aileen had probably told him. Or maybe it was obvious because of the bag she'd been carrying. Glad that she had a plan, she nodded. "I do. I have some money saved up. I'm going to stay in one of the local inns for a few weeks while I look for work."

He frowned. "You plan to stay at an inn by yourself?"

"Well, yes."

"I don't think that would be wise, Miss Barclay. A young woman, living alone? That isn't safe."

She almost laughed. "It's dangerous for a woman on her own everywhere. Even here."

But instead of looking chastised, he seemed pleased that she'd brought up that point. "That is why I wanted to speak to you. I'd like to help you."

She stared at him guardedly. He seemed sincere. But even if she completely trusted him—which she did not—she couldn't imagine there was any way he could help her.

"Help me? How? Find employment? If so, I should tell you I don't intend to stay in San Antonio."

"You mean to move? Where?"

"As far as I can." She shrugged. "Maybe Fort Worth. Or, I don't know . . . Maybe I'll head to Galveston."

"That's very far, Miss Barclay."

"That's the point. I need to start over someplace where no one knows me."

"Doing what? Cleaning guest rooms?" His voice was thick with contempt.

"Maybe." Embarrassed, she said, "Or perhaps I'll try to find employment as a nanny or governess."

"Those jobs are around children."

She laughed. "I realize that, Major. I happen to like children."

Looking at her intently, he said, "I have a better idea."

"And what is that?"

"Allow me to intervene."

"I beg your pardon?"

"Miss Barclay, let me find you a new job. With my connections, I'm sure I could find you something better."

She would have rolled her eyes at his heavy-handedness if she wasn't fairly sure he probably could find her a better job than she could on her own. But that didn't mean she had to accept his offer. "Sir—"

"Let me help you," he pressed. "If you don't want my help finding employment, at least let me help you find a suitable place to stay. You need to be someplace safe, where you won't be fending off men like Bushnell. I know he was the one who accosted you. I knew him in the war. He was no better then."

He must have eavesdropped on everything she and Aileen said in the hallway outside his suite, but she decided to let that go when she noticed he was staring at her scar again. And that's when she realized he really did pity her. He wanted to find her someplace where she could be safe and secluded. Alone. Where no one would ever stare too long at the scar on her face. Or say anything unkind.

"You know I can't let you do that, sir." If she accepted his help, she would owe him.

"You could if you wanted to." He stared at her, his eyes filled with so many turbulent emotions she thought she could read his mind if she were so inclined.

"But I don't." She smiled slightly, needing to take the sting out of her words, though she knew there was no real reason to do so. "I need my independence. It's important to me."

He looked tempted to object but shook his head. "I don't want to argue with you."

"We agree on something, then." She stood. "Now, thank you for your concern, but as you can see, I am fine."

"You are very far from fine, Miss Barclay."

Her cheeks heated again. "Even so, I am not downtrodden. Not yet. Now, if you'll excuse me—"

"Hold on." He got to his feet. "I have been wondering something."

"Yes?"

"Forgive me for asking, but does this sort of thing happen often? Do men accost you in rooms often?"

"No."

His eyes narrowed. "I'm starting to realize you are a gifted liar."

"I'm not a liar, sir."

"Then tell me the truth. Do men accost you often when you are working?"

Had it happened before? Of course it had. They were in Texas, barely two years after the end of a long and bloody war. Everyone's morals were in upheaval. Women no longer expected to be cosseted. And men? Well, most of them had become hardened. Some were now cruel, as if all the softness and compassion in their hearts had been emptied on the battlefields.

But how could she say anything about that without including the major in that group?

Maybe it didn't even matter. "'Often' is a relative term, sir," she said stiffly. "I have been accosted before, but never, um, in the way Colonel Bushnell did."

The muscles in his jaw tightened. "You need a protector."

"I need a new life, Major Kelly. But since that isn't forthcoming, I am going to settle for a new job."

"Will you at least allow me to escort you to Harrison House?"

Harrison House was a small inn just a few blocks on the other side of the Menger. Though she'd never been inside the establishment, she'd walked past it many times. It had the air of a comfortable relative's house. It also was known to have an exclusive clientele. "I can't afford to stay there. And even if I could, I wouldn't be welcomed." It went without saying that Mrs. Harrison would no doubt look down at a mere maid's attempt to stay there.

"I know Mrs. Harrison. As a matter of fact, I went over and talked to her about you early this morning. She has a room for you."

"Still, I can't afford to stay there."

"She offered to give you a room at half price."

Her eyes narrowed. No one did things like this without wanting something in return. "Major, why—"

"She feels for your situation, Miss Barclay." He leaned a little closer, bringing with him the fresh, clean scent of milled soap. "Bushnell seems to have left the hotel, but we can't be sure he won't return. Don't say no. It's all arranged."

She closed her eyes. Her pride wanted her to refuse, but the rest of her was so very grateful. Major Kelly was exactly right. Harrison House was safe and reputable. No one would bother her there. And she certainly did not want to see Bushnell again if she could help it. He might remember he'd been the one to . . . She shook the memory out of her mind. "Thank you."

"Let's be on our way, then."

"I would appreciate your escort."

His smile was blinding. "I'm delighted to hear you say that. Especially since it didn't include ten minutes of argument."

"I only argue when it's necessary."

"In an effort to keep the peace, I'll refrain from commenting on that."

"I need to claim my paycheck from Mr. Howard. He should be in his office."

All traces of that sunny smile vanished. "Indeed you do. Well, let's go take care of that."

Though she imagined a part of her should protest his coming with her, Lizbeth was relieved to have the major with her. Right before the lobby, she turned down another, narrow hallway. The hotel's private offices were there. Just beyond was a private section of the hotel. It allowed guests who didn't wish to be seen to come and go with a measure of privacy. She'd never actually seen anyone who was staying in the rooms, but she'd heard rumors that both Grant and Lee had slept in those beds.

After knocking on the door and announcing herself, Dallas beckoned her inside. He abruptly got to his feet when he realized the major had accompanied her. "Major Kelly?"

"I came with Miss Barclay to ensure she received her monies without issue."

"We're not swindlers, Major." He opened the top drawer of his desk and pulled out an envelope. "Here you are, Lizbeth."

"Thank you, Dallas." For a moment she wondered if she should say something else. But what else was there to say? She turned back to Major Kelly. "I'm ready now."

Ethan's eyes warmed. "Let's go, then."

The moment the major followed Lizbeth out of Dallas's office, he held out his arm for her to take.

She stared at it. Hesitated, because it felt as if he were offering her something more. It felt as though they had a relationship, or, at the very least, an agreement.

It felt too forward, too fresh.

But in the end, she decided it felt right as well. Realizing she'd already gone too far to back up now, she rested her hand along his forearm. She felt his muscles tighten from her touch, sending a spark of awareness traipsing up her arm and reminding her that no matter how much she protested, she wasn't immune to his charm.

Major Kelly looked pleased when he slipped on his Stetson. "Shall we proceed?"

Walking by his side through the back of the hotel and out one of the side doors, she felt as if she wasn't just stepping outside; she was stepping back in time.

Back before the start of the war, when she and her parents lived on the ranch, she'd gone walking with quite a number of gentleman callers whenever they went to town to visit friends. Her worries had centered around her appearance and whether she would make an advantageous marriage. How silly she'd been!

After they'd walked one block, Major Kelly spoke. "This is nice, Miss Barclay. I've been hoping for this day for some time."

"To escort me to Harrison House?"

He laughed. "No." Sounding far more serious, he continued. "I've been hoping to do something of worth for a while now. You are giving me the opportunity to do that."

Being his charity case didn't feel good, but she resolutely pushed the feeling away. She couldn't change her circumstances. At least one of them was finding something good in her situation.

It was rather cold. She had been meaning to buy a new dress for the winter but hadn't wanted to part with any of her precious funds. In light of the recent events, Lizbeth realized that had been a wise decision.

But it also meant she felt the bite of the cold more intently than she wished to. When a burst of wind blew across her cheeks, she shivered.

Major Kelly looked down at her in concern. "You are chilled."

"A little."

He stopped. "Here. Take my coat," he said as he began peeling off his suit jacket.

"Absolutely not."

"Because?"

"Because entering Mrs. Harrison's inn wearing your coat will not improve my reputation."

"Mindy won't care."

He was on a first-name basis with Mrs. Harrison. For some reason, that knowledge pinched. Maybe it was because it was yet another reminder of how different their circumstances were. "Of course she will care. I promise you, no innkeeper wants a boarder of questionable repute."

"That would never be you."

Lizbeth didn't bother to argue anymore. The fact was, she knew how society worked, both from a society lady's and a maid's perspective. Major Ethan Kelly—with his money, good looks, and heroic reputation—didn't have a clue.

He looked far more somber when he escorted her into Harrison House. After he stated their names, the maid who answered the door led them into a small parlor decorated in shades of rose and gray.

"Mrs. Harrison, Major Kelly and Miss Barclay have arrived," the maid said to an elegantly attired woman sitting on a chaise lounge, calmly knitting what looked to be a long and intricately designed shawl.

She looked up with a smile. "Major Kelly. You have arrived."

He bowed formally. "Mindy, may I present the young lady I told you about, Miss Elizabeth Barclay. Miss Barclay, please meet Mindy Harrison."

"Ma'am," Lizbeth said, dropping a curtsy. She'd seen Mrs. Harrison before, but they'd never had the opportunity to meet properly.

Laying her knitting aside, Mrs. Harrison stood and practically glided over to them. "I have so been looking forward to meeting you, Miss Barclay. I hope you will be happy during your stay here."

Lizbeth felt completely tongue-tied. Was this how Mrs. Harrison greeted all her guests, or was she being especially cordial since the major was held in such high esteem? Neither possibility seemed correct. "I'm not sure if you understand who I am," she began. "You see, I was a maid over at the Menger."

Mrs. Harrison waved a hand. "Oh, I know. Ethan told me all about what has happened to you. I know it will be hard, but I hope you will put that all out of your mind. After all, that part of your life is over now."

Major Kelly was standing tall and proud, and looking extremely pleased with himself too. After giving him a pointed look, she smiled again at Mrs. Harrison. "Thank you, ma'am."

"Of course." She turned back to where she'd been sitting and rang a small bell. "Miss Fletcher will take you up to your room now. Be sure to let her know if it will be suitable."

"I will. I mean, all right."

"Please send for me if you need anything, Miss Barclay," the major said. "And if you leave this establishment for any reason, please do be cautious. A certain man could very well still be about the city."

"Yes. I mean, all right." Oh, what did she mean?

"If you would follow me?" Miss Fletcher murmured from behind her.

Following the maid to the stairs, Lizbeth knew her life was indeed about to change again.

She sincerely hoped it was for the better.

9

NOW THAT LIZBETH WAS SAFELY SETTLED AT HARRISON House, Ethan felt he could take some time to visit Devin Monroe. Ethan knew he was still living in that small place on the outskirts of the city.

Since the war, Ethan trusted few people, and rarely dared to rely on anyone other than himself and his three remaining best friends from the prison camp. He knew, deep in his gut, that he needed advice. His emotions around both Lizbeth and Bushnell were too intense for him to see clearly. Every time he tried to make sense of his plan for them, he became distracted by either Lizbeth's pretty face or how much he loathed Bushnell.

Devin Monroe would help him see things much more clearly. He felt sure Bushnell would show up again, and he'd need a plan. Bushnell was not the type of man to take Ethan's attack lightly. He was also not the type to seek vengeance only on Ethan. Ethan feared Bushnell would choose to take out his revenge on someone who couldn't fight back—Lizbeth or some other innocent woman Ethan might be acquainted with.

But short of killing the man, Ethan had no idea how to permanently end this threat. He needed Devin's clear head and reasoning to put together a plan to keep Lizbeth safe and himself out of jail for cold-blooded murder.

At the Menger stables, he saddled up Gretel and headed west. He rode for two hours, enjoying the November air. Even after two years, he couldn't help but contrast Texas's relatively balmy climate with Johnson's Island's bitter temperatures and unrelenting wind. He doubted few other places would ever feel as cold or barren. He also doubted he'd ever again consider a Texas winter unbearable.

Perhaps it was because his incarceration had begun at the beginning of winter. He'd been captured and eventually taken to northern Ohio by train in November of 1863. When the guards motioned them along, much the same way one would herd cattle, Ethan had been bleary-eyed and exhausted. The wounds he'd sustained in his chest and shoulders had begun to heal, but he'd suffered nerve damage. He'd often felt as if his insides were burning hot trails of pain down his arms.

When they arrived, snow lay thick on the ground. It was icy and gray, a sign it had been there for some time. The guards forced them to walk on the ice of Sandusky Bay, and he'd been afraid it wouldn't bear their weight.

The drafty barracks, desolate landscape, and long, gray days threatened to drain their spirits. Later, they all came to grips with the new reality of their situation. Only prayer and other men's support made the conditions bearable.

As prisoners, they were kept in a constant state of discomfort and insecurity. When there was no snow, a cloying dampness still hung in the air. It sunk into a man's bones and teased him. Making every injury he'd ever incurred ache as though he had only recently received it. Sometimes the morning would be filled with a fog so thick he wondered if it was ever going to clear.

Hours passed far too slowly. Small enjoyments began to take on greater meaning. When his family was able to send him cigars, he would stand against the fence and watch the fog dissipate. For those few minutes, the scent of tobacco would fill the air and he'd be transported to another time and place, one where he was safe and comfortable.

Other days he would watch Thomas Baker stare off into the distance, lost in his daydreams. He'd been envious of the man's ability to lose himself in his own thoughts. He'd been able to transport himself to anywhere else on the planet anytime he chose.

Gretel neighed, bringing him back to the present.

And back to how empty his life had become.

Now he had all the comforts he could desire, but with his freedom he'd also lost his home.

How had he plunged into such a situation? After visiting his family briefly when he was released, he realized that, though they'd overcome their differences about his service in the war, he didn't have much in common with them anymore. How could he? He'd spent years putting both his life and the men who served under him on the line. He'd buried dozens of soldiers and mourned countless others. Then, of course, there were all those lonely months on Johnson's Island.

When he first returned home and was in a room by himself, he hadn't even been able to sleep. He felt too alone and had been plagued by flashbacks. He eventually told his family he needed to leave to work through his demons. At first his mother had cried, but then even she realized he wasn't the same man who had left their home in a resplendent gray uniform with visions of glory in his eyes.

When he left the ranch again, the feelings among them all were bittersweet. They loved him, of course. Just as he still loved them. But love hadn't been enough for him to feel as though he belonged.

In the end, he had taken a portion of his sizable inheritance, deposited it into the bank, and then gone about reinventing himself.

But, of course, he didn't know how to do anything but order men to kill enemy soldiers. That reality hadn't set well with him, and he'd spent much of his time gambling in smoky saloons and riverboats, all while waiting to be needed from time to time by the only people who felt real to him anymore—his three fellow former prisoners.

But lately he'd felt as if he had changed again. He was ready to make commitments. Ready to lean on others again. Ready to be himself.

Lizbeth's arrival in his room had been a turning point for him as well—and he hadn't even realized he'd needed one. She needed a hero in her life. And he? Well, he needed to make amends for his sins, and he knew she was someone he had wronged, even if she never realized he was one of the men who'd scavenged her home during the war.

Out of all the blood and gore of the battlefields, the stench of death and infection, the men he'd lost, the loneliness of being held prisoner for months, that was the moment that haunted him the most.

Before he knew it, he and Gretel had arrived. Just over the bend was his captain's temporary home. It wasn't much. Just a simple stone-and-clapboard house next to a thicket of abundant pecan trees. He remembered Devin saying once that he liked living next to a constant source of food that could be brewed into coffee in a pinch.

That was Devin Monroe, Ethan supposed. A man who leaned toward both the practical and the worst-case scenario.

But what did surprise Ethan was that the captain lived so far from other people. He'd been a sociable man both during the war and in the prison camp. He'd also had something of a tender heart, though he probably would have threatened to maim anyone who dared say it. Ethan had always assumed the day Devin Monroe returned to civilization he would find himself a lovely woman to bind himself to.

As if the captain had been looking for him, Devin was standing in front of his house by the time Ethan dismounted. He was dressed in his usual attire of faded denims, a pure white shirt, and black boots. It seemed he wasn't concerned about the Texas November chill either.

"Captain," Ethan said. He outranked Devin, but he used the title as a form of respect. Devin had earned every bit of his rank, while Ethan's family's money had paid for his.

Devin clasped his hand. "Ethan, this is a welcome surprise. It's good to see you."

"I'm relieved to hear that. Sorry to show up unannounced."

"You know we are beyond worrying about such niceties. Do you have any news?" he asked, his voice smooth yet betraying a touch of concern. "Is Baker all right?"

"Yes," he said before realizing he'd probably spoken too soon. "I mean, I haven't heard anything from him. I'm assuming he's enjoying wedded bliss."

Devin chuckled. "I hope so, though it's hard to imagine him staying out of trouble for too long. What do you think the chances are of him keeping his head down for a while?"

"Married to Laurel? I'd say real good."

"Me too."

Ethan smiled, thinking of their sergeant who could once only be described as a loose cannon on the best of days. Now he was far more circumspect and married to a beautiful woman with golden hair. And a fondness for cattle.

"What brings you out here? You in trouble?"

That caught Ethan off guard. He knew Devin would want to know how he was doing. But he'd hoped they might be able to ease into the point of his visit. "You still don't beat around the bush."

"No need to with you. Is there?"

"No." Realizing it would be futile to postpone the inevitable, he said, "I came to get some advice, if you have some time to listen."

"Always. Why don't you take care of your horse and then come join me?" Looking a little embarrassed, he said, "Even though the temperature is probably in the fifties, I've been feeling the cold today. I've been in the kitchen making chili. You can come in and chop."

Ethan hadn't touched a kitchen utensil since he'd been freed from captivity. "You still don't have a maid to do that?"

"No. I guess after living among men all my life, I don't know how to live with women. I get tongue-tied." A shadow filled his expression before he carefully wiped it away. "Matter of fact, I've recently come to the conclusion that I'm not real good around females at all."

This confession startled Ethan. Devin Monroe was one of the most confident men he'd ever met. "I find that hard to believe."

"You shouldn't. We all have our gifts. Mine do not lie in understanding how women's minds work . . . or in conversing with them."

After settling Gretel, Ethan followed Devin into the simple house. The captain had told him a friend was letting him use the house for as long as he wished, and as one might have expected for a bachelor, the interior was plain. Nothing decorated the walls, and there were no knickknacks or frames on any surface. It reminded Ethan of their quarters at the beginning of the war. Back then, they'd had relatively comfortable spaces but nothing that wasn't needed or necessary.

The kitchen was in the back. It was really nothing more than a small room where the captain obviously prepared his meals, but it had a black cook stove, a wooden table, two chairs, a line of beautifully made cabinets, and a large basin for washing.

The room's simplicity suited the captain well. It had enough to satisfy his needs, but nothing extra.

Devin walked directly to a cast-iron pot on the cook stove and started stirring. "Ethan, slice those peppers and onions on the table."

After washing his hands, Ethan rolled up his sleeves and got to work. Back before the war, he had only ever thought of a kitchen as someplace to sneak into when his servants weren't available to bring him food.

All that had changed during the war. At first they'd had various enlisted men take cooking rotations. Toward the end, their ranks were so ragtag and he'd spent so many nights by himself, he learned to cook just about anything. He received a greater education in culinary arts when they were incarcerated on Johnson's Island. They had nothing but time on their hands. And since food was so precious, each of them had taken to learning how to prepare it.

That said, he certainly hadn't missed kitchen duty.

"This reminds me of cooking at the camp," he said as he lopped off the top of a pepper. "I got pretty good at slicing carrots and potatoes."

"We ended up doing all right once we started our garden, didn't we?"

"All of us except for Baker. He couldn't grow a batch of thistles."

Devin laughed. "That he couldn't. He was worthless at anything domestic. 'Course, that might have changed now that he's found Laurel."

"Did that surprise you?" Ethan asked as he turned the pepper on its side and began slicing. "That he found love while working in a chain gang?"

"You know what I mean. Thomas Baker is as rough a man as I've ever known. His wife is his complete opposite in every way." Devin shrugged. "Perhaps on paper the alliance might not make much sense. But I'm not surprised he found a woman to love him. Underneath all Baker's bravado and insecurity is a good man."

"Which Laurel discovered, even though he was wearing a prisoner's uniform when they first met."

"You are right. She discovered Thomas's best qualities in spite of a prison uniform." Devin looked at him quizzically. "*You* sound surprised. Why is that? You knew Baker even before I did."

"I'm not disparaging Thomas," Ethan said quickly. "Of course I'm glad he's found love and happiness."

"Then what's bothering you?"

"I'm just, I don't know, thinking about how two such unlikely people became enamored with each other. It's curious, don't you think? I never understand how and when the Lord chooses to bring people together."

"That's why we have God. We trust in Him so we don't have to try to understand such things ourselves." Grabbing a handful of the peppers and onions Ethan had chopped so far, Devin tossed them into his pot. "Is that what this visit is really about? Have you found yourself a woman, Major?"

The question startled him. "What? No." Then, as an image of dark, curly hair and the sound of a soft, sweet voice came to mind, he amended his words. "Well, maybe. But, um, not in that way."

As he should have expected, Devin latched on to his last two words. "What other way is there?"

Suddenly tongue-tied, Ethan stared at him. How did one answer that? He had no earthly idea.

10

THOUGH HIS MIND WAS NO DOUBT RACING WITH A DOZEN questions, Devin allowed Ethan a few minutes to gather his thoughts. He continued working on his chili, his movements sure and easy. As if there was nothing unusual about either Ethan's unannounced visit or what they were discussing.

Lulled by Devin's matter-of-fact movements, Ethan finally relaxed. Then he told Devin about Lizbeth's sudden entrance to his room at the Menger and how her cousin had fired her rather than take her concerns seriously.

Devin's expression had turned dark at the mention of the colonel's name. "Bushnell. That man was always a scoundrel."

"I want to help Miss Barclay because of Bushnell's involvement. But I must confess I have other reasons as well."

Devin put down his spoon. "Which are?"

"I think . . . well, I know she's from my past."

Devin watched him carefully. "Which past? Your home or from the war?"

Ethan swallowed. "I met her—more or less—during the war. On a requisition raid."

Devin stared at him. "That is surprising, but not unheard of, I reckon. After all, we all met our share of women. Some during dances, others when we were marching through wherever we went."

Ethan knew what Devin meant. They'd marched or ridden their horses through several states. Arkansas. Tennessee. Kentucky. Texas. "Like I said, I met this woman on a requisitioning raid. At a place near here."

"Ah. You haven't said. Did she recognize you?"

"Apparently not. It would be different for her, though. She probably only remembers groups of men in gray and gold stealing her belongings."

"Or men in blue. We weren't the only ones searching for supplies, Major."

"Probably so."

"No, I know so."

Realizing Devin Monroe had never talked about raiding homesteads, Ethan searched his face. "Did you ever do that?"

"Requisition supplies for our troops? You know I did."

"Did you ever feel guilty about it?"

"Truth?"

"Of course."

"Not at the time." He shrugged. "Come to think of it, I still don't feel guilty about those runs. We didn't have a choice. Our men were dying. Starving and cold, wet and hungry. It was our duty to provide for them in any way we could. Our duty as officers."

"I know."

Grimacing, Devin continued. "Early on, we visited a horse farm in Kentucky, and I almost got poked with a pitchfork because I wanted a pair of champion breeders. That blasted man wanted all of us to bleed and die on the battlefields while he raised horses and waited for the war to be over. I've never forgotten that. What kind of man prefers for other men to defend his home?"

"I agree with you there. But this woman? Well, her circumstances were different."

After inspecting his chili again, Devin said, "How so?"

"Back when I was still a captain, Baker, five other men, and I were covering a block of land, trying to get some wood to burn and food. The men were starving. And freezing."

"I remember."

"Anyway, we came upon this ranch house. It had obviously been a pretty house before the war. It was run-down, but we were sure it was going to give us at least some of what we needed. The woman I now know as Miss Barclay met us at the front." Realizing his friend had turned and was listening intently, Ethan tried to form the right words without breaking down. "She was alone. And skittish."

"And scared."

Ethan sighed in relief. He was glad he didn't have to explain in too much detail about her state of mind. "Yes. She was petrified of me and my men." Raising his hand to his temple, he continued. "She was also scarred from her ear to her hairline. Men had come to her place before, you see."

"Ah." Devin turned to his stew pot. After a couple of additional stirs with a wooden spoon, he spoke again. "The story is sad but not surprising, Ethan. Those were dark times for everyone. Desperate. What did your men take?"

Ethan knew what Devin was asking. "We took everything we could, but it wasn't much. When we left her homestead, I knew she didn't have anything left." Shame choked his words, but he continued anyway. "It's my fault too. I ordered the men to scavenge."

"You can't judge the past by today's standards. Our circumstances were different back then. We would spend days fighting and killing before spending weeks burying the dead and tending to the wounded." Devin shuddered. "I thought I was never going to get the scent of blood out of my head."

"I hear you."

"Good. You must also remember that it wasn't only our war. We were all under orders. Even esteemed captains." Looking a bit amused, he added, "Even elusive majors."

Ethan would have saluted the sarcastic quip if he weren't so in need of guidance.

Impatiently, he said, "My point is that . . . this woman I'm concerned about? Well, I did help her with Bushnell."

"Ethan, before you tell me what you did, are you sure she's the same one? That raid took place a long time ago, right? It had to have been almost a year before we were imprisoned."

"I'm as sure as if I'd visited her home last week. I knew I'd never forget her. Plus, that scar that has haunted my memories is on her temple." Sighing, he said, "When I found her in my suite, she was in danger again. Running from Bushnell after he'd cornered her when she was cleaning his room."

Devin cursed under his breath. "Our world keeps getting smaller and smaller."

"You're right. He is one man I would have been happy never to cross paths with again."

"What did you do?"

"After I heard her cousin fire her—Lizbeth is her name—I made the woman give me his room number and I went there."

Devin stared at him intently. "What did you do?"

"I threatened him." And he might have bruised his face a bit.

"Ah. And later, how did Lizbeth react when you relayed how you remembered her?"

"When I saw her again, I didn't mention it. Or tell her anything about my encounter with Bushnell. Only that she needs protection and assistance and I am willing to give her that."

"You didn't see the need to tell her you raided her home?"

Though he was mentally cringing at the dismay in his friend's tone, Ethan attempted to excuse himself. "Lizbeth has no idea I was with that band of men. I don't want to tell her."

"Of course you don't. You would become less of a hero, wouldn't you?"

This time Ethan didn't bother to hide his discomfort. "Your contempt might be no less than I deserve. But if you were in my position, you might find yourself doing the very same thing."

"Maybe. Or maybe not."

"I am not ready to tell her everything, but I still feel the need to do something. She can't keep living on her own. She's going to get hurt." *Again*, he silently added.

"You're right. She very well might. But her problems aren't yours."

Hardly hearing him, Ethan revealed what he'd been turning around in his head. "I think they could be. I might not want to admit being at her house, but I still feel guilty about it."

"What does your guilt have to do with her?"

"Everything. If I make things right, I might be able to find absolution too."

Devin sighed. "Ethan. That isn't how it all works. God grants absolution. God will help you find solace."

Ethan knew Devin had a deep faith. But his didn't run that deep. "I can help her and help myself, too, if I take Bushnell on. She needs a protector. It might as well be me. Late last night I even contemplated marrying her."

Devin started laughing. It abruptly stopped when he noticed that Ethan didn't even crack a smile. "Wait a minute. Are you serious?"

"I am. It will solve a lot of her problems." All of them, as far as he could tell.

"It will also create a whole slew of them for you," Devin said with an uncharacteristic note of derision. After glancing at him again, he walked to a back cabinet, opened a door, and pulled out a crystal bottle of whiskey. After filling two shot glasses, he handed one to him. Before waiting, Devin tossed back a good portion of the contents.

Only then did he speak again. "Ethan Kelly, have you lost your mind?"

"Not yet." He took a sip of the whiskey. Realized how fine it was, then took another sip before setting it down.

"That might be a matter of opinion."

"Look, I know I'm not responsible for her problems, but I couldn't do anything about what happened to her during the war. I can help her now."

"You may think you are helping her. But if you encourage her to marry without love, where does that get her? Trapped in a love-less marriage, I tell you."

"She's alone. Bushnell could have raped her in that hotel room."

"But he did not."

Just as he was about to confess more of his worries, he noticed Devin looked extremely agitated. Something more was troubling him than just his idea about marriage. "What did I say?"

"Other than you are considering giving up your life for a maid in a hotel?"

"No, there's something more afoot. Is it the mention of Bushnell?"

Devin hesitated. "Partly."

"Why? What do you know about him that I don't?"

"I recently met the woman who was his ladybird during the war."

Surprised, Ethan picked up his whiskey and drained it. "I remember him speaking of her." Closing his eyes, he recalled Bushnell bragging.

"So do I," Devin said, looking pained. After taking another sip, he seemed to gain control of himself. "So you remember Bushnell speaking of her? Was it at Johnson's Island?"

"He did then too, but I'm thinking of another time. It was when we were traveling south and spent the night somewhere in the middle of Tennessee." Thinking back, Ethan remembered how appalled he'd been by Bushnell's tales. Deciding to tread carefully, he added, "He said she was beautiful. Deceptively beautiful, whatever that means."

"She is." A muscle in his jaw tightened. "Auburn hair and blue eyes. She's . . . well, she's striking."

"Ah. You know her well?"

"No. I only recently met her. She, um, she practically lives in isolation now. Her alliance with him ruined her reputation."

"That ain't surprising."

"It's not, but I've been thinking. She had good reason to do what she did," Devin said with more force. "She was desperate. Hungry. Had a grandmother to care for." His lips thinned as he stared off into the distance again. "Actually, I would go so far as to say her actions were justified."

Since Ethan had come for advice, he decided to bring the conversation back around to him. "Lizbeth has suffered too. She's all alone, except for a miserable excuse of a cousin."

"You look as if something else is weighing on you. What is it?

Is there something you aren't telling me?" Devin stepped forward. "Did you hurt her in some way but don't want to admit it?"

"Of course not." He hadn't, except when he'd taken all her provisions and left her starving and alone.

"Then her pain is not your problem."

Everything Devin said made sense. But Ethan was starting to realize sometimes a man had to do what didn't make sense.

"What should I do about Bushnell? I didn't just threaten him. I knocked him to the floor. He's checked out of the Menger, but I'm afraid he's going to come back to retaliate—by hurting Lizbeth. My friend Mindy Harrison agreed to let Lizbeth have a room at her inn, but will she really be safe from him even there?"

"That would be like him." Lips pursed, Devin stared at their pair of empty shot glasses. "I need to take care of some business, but then I'll come find you at the Menger. We'll hunt down Bushnell and confront him together. Maybe find out more about why he was even in San Antonio. He's from Fredericksburg, right?"

"Yes, but there's no need for you to do that. I didn't come here to ask you for help. Just advice."

"I need to be there, Ethan."

"Do you think the two of us talking to him will make any difference?"

"If it doesn't, we'll come up with a plan to make sure he takes our warnings seriously. In the meantime, don't do anything rash. Don't offer that woman marriage yet."

As they walked into Devin's cozy living room, Ethan said, "I'm glad I came here."

"Are you? I don't think I helped you much."

"You helped more than you know. You helped me remember I'm not alone."

Leaning back on the couch, Devin nodded, his cool blue eyes

looking almost empty. "You've done the same thing for me. You also made me realize I may have been a fool. Honestly, Ethan, I think you might have helped me more than I helped you."

As that statement lingered in the air, Ethan leaned back in his chair and exhaled. He'd come hoping to solve his problems. But if he wasn't mistaken, he'd just uncovered several more issues. Issues he was certain weren't going to be solved with a threat or a thrown punch.

11

Johnson's Island, Ohio
Confederate States of America Officers' POW Camp

THE HOUR WAS LATE. IT WAS LONG AFTER DARK, LONG AFTER the time most of the prisoners had returned to their barracks for the comfort of sleep.

Devin Monroe wasn't one of them.

He was leaning against one of the barracks' outside walls, unsuccessfully attempting to come to grips with what Colonel Daniel Bushnell was saying.

Correction. What Bushnell had been saying for the last ten minutes, ever since he, Bushnell, General McCoy, and Major Ethan Kelly had decided to have an impromptu meeting about yet another grave that needed to be dug. Well, their "meeting" was actually an argument between Bushnell and Kelly. Devin and the general had stuck around in case blood was shed.

Usually Devin didn't put too much emphasis on their military rank at the camp. No one did, for there was no need. From the time they'd been forced to march across the ice to their prison, each of the men had come to realize his life was no longer his own. They had no power. Definitely no control of their needs or their wants. No man's rank would ever change the fact that they were all at the mercy of their enemy.

Because of that, usually Devin would have no reason to stay outside and listen to an argument between two other men. He figured he'd broken up enough fights during the war for a lifetime.

But tonight? Well, Bushnell was being more of a pompous jerk than usual. And Ethan was taking greater offense to the man's words than he usually did.

"Once again, I will not allow it, Major," Bushnell blustered, his voice deep and foreboding. "That private shouldn't have even been on these grounds in the first place. I won't allow him to be buried in the officers' graveyard."

"Private Gluck was a good man. His being here was a clerical error. Nothing more, nothing less," Ethan retorted. "And it's not like it matters anyway. He's dead. Everyone he'll be buried next to is dead as well."

Bushnell turned to Devin. "Is that the truth, Captain?"

Since he was forced to be involved, Devin decided to have a bit of fun at the man's expense. "Are you speaking of Gluck's ranking? His being here in the first place? Or are you possibly dwelling on the very fact that he's dead and so it doesn't matter anymore?"

General McCoy chuckled. "I was wondering the same thing."

Bushnell visibly attempted to keep his temper in check. "You know what I am speaking of. Did you pull strings for Gluck to be here? Because I know you did for Baker."

At the mention of Baker's name, all traces of amusement left Devin. "Baker is not at issue. He is alive and well."

"He is also no officer. He should be in one of the other POW camps, one for noncommissioned personnel."

Devin raised a brow. "Because we shouldn't mix with the men who have been doing the majority of the fighting?"

A vein popped out on Bushnell's forehead. "That is not what I meant and you know it. Just answer the question. Did you sneak Gluck in here?"

"Gluck was placed here by accident. I had nothing to do with his assignment. And that is the truth."

"Perhaps."

"I wouldn't start questioning my integrity, Colonel. I am a loyal Southerner and a gentleman."

Bushnell grunted. "Don't act so surprised, Captain. You have been the champion of developing your own rules. Unlike your sergeant, for example. A sorrier soldier I've never had the displeasure of meeting."

"Baker rode behind enemy lines and put himself at great risk doing so," General McCoy said quietly. "The South is in his debt."

Bushnell's expression tightened, but he didn't argue with generals.

"Is this discussion done?" Ethan asked.

"No. We still have not resolved our dilemma."

Devin gritted his teeth. For a moment he wished Sergeant Baker was in the vicinity. Then he could have counted on Thomas to have uttered something disparaging. Thomas called everyone pet names. Most were derogatory, but right on point. Which was why Bushnell was often referred to as Blowhard behind his back.

As it was, Devin knew better than to be overtly disrespectful. Not only did he need to conduct himself in a way befitting his rank, but his men needed him to do that as well. That, however, didn't stop him from sneaking a look at General McCoy.

McCoy raised his eyebrows at Devin. Telling him everything he needed to know. The general was just as irritated by Blowhard's insistence about poor Gluck's burial as he was.

Very well, then. "You are right, sir," Devin said stiffly. "This matter of Gluck's final resting place has not been decided. The fact is I disagree with your directive, Colonel. We may have ranks, but they were earned on the battlefield and in the company encampments. Here on Johnson's Island, we are all Johnny Rebs in the eyes of the enemy. Because of that, we all sleep in the same barracks, eat the same food, and line up the same way. Consequently, we all are the same in death. Military ranking doesn't signify in death."

Bushnell tensed, then turned to Ethan. "Are you holding firm to your decision? Or do you agree that we should bury him on the other side of the barracks?"

The colonel wanted to bury Gluck near the latrines.

Devin held his tongue, but only barely.

Sitting on a boulder, Ethan crossed his legs. The major was so elegant, he somehow managed to look at ease anywhere he was. Only the look of distaste in his eyes hinted at what he thought. "It would be detrimental to our group's morale to bury Gluck without our usual fanfare. He deserves it. He was a good man and an honorable soldier."

"The men here need to be reminded who is in charge," Bushnell said. "If we start acting as though we are all equals, discord could erupt."

Ethan froze. "We are all equals in the eyes of God, and in this prison encampment, sir. The fact that I am a major means next to nothing here."

"That's been patently obvious. After all, I've seen you follow Monroe's directives without hesitation."

"I would be the first to admit that not every soldier's ranking comes from merit. For example, my commissions were purchased with a respectable amount of silver and gold."

Bushnell sniffed. "I should have known."

Ethan uncrossed his legs, seeming to pause to pick off a piece of lint from his trousers' cuff. "That reminds me of something I've never asked. How did you obtain your rank, Daniel? Was it through bars of silver and gold like me . . . or through other means?"

General McCoy coughed.

And Devin? He was exhausted. If they'd been back on the battlefield, he would have given in to temptation and jabbed Ethan in the ribs so he'd shut up. He settled for muttering his name under his breath. "Kelly."

But it was doubtful that his utterance was heard. Ethan was staring intently at Bushnell. Practically egging him on with its intensity.

And the colonel? Well, Bushnell looked mad enough to snap in two.

Not another second passed before he jerked to his feet. Glaring down at Kelly, he bit out, "You sound as if you feel no respect for either me or my rank."

"I'm saying I feel no respect for your ranking, sir." Ethan grinned suddenly. "Though, of course, I will honor it here as much as I am able." His voice turning cold, he said, "Unless we are discussing the dead bodies of good men."

Bushnell's hands clenched. "I take offense to your words."

"What do you want to do, sir? Fight me at dawn?"

"Ethan, control yourself," Devin said.

"And you? Sit back down and stop being such a popinjay," General McCoy said to Bushnell.

"Sir. You had to have heard him. We cannot allow—"

"I can and will do whatever I please. I'm languishing on an island in the middle of a lake! Have you forgotten?"

Bushnell sat down. "No, sir."

"I hope not. Now, calm yourself. This fight you have wanted to win is over and you lost. Take it like a man."

"Yes, sir."

"Good." With a groan, the general lumbered to his feet. Devin, Ethan, and Daniel Bushnell got to their feet as well. After rubbing his thigh and cursing under his breath about Yankees, stray bullets, and sawbones in battlefield tents, the general glared at the rest of them. "Gentlemen, tomorrow we will get into formation, walk to the officers' cemetery, and dig a grave for Gluck. There will be no further discussion. Understood?"

"Yes, sir," Devin said.

"Glad to hear it. Now, Captain, you have been on this island double the time I have. Do you foresee any problems with our guards?"

They would need to be bribed, but he knew how to take care of that. "No, sir."

"Good. Good night, then," the general said as he strode away, his gait uneven and painful to see.

With McCoy out of sight, all Devin wanted to do was seek the privacy of his cot. Well, and hope that Thomas didn't snore too loudly for once.

But before he could take his leave, Daniel sneered. "Look at you both, jumping to your feet even though you just explained how the lot of us are all one under the eyes of the Lord."

"Perhaps I simply respect him," Ethan drawled.

Bushnell laughed quietly. "Fool yourselves with your high and mighty words, but I know what's really taking place. You jump to his pleasure as quickly as my mistress does when I call for her. You owe him."

"I didn't realize you had a ladybird," Ethan murmured. "Do you keep her near your wife?"

Surprisingly, Daniel laughed. "Of course not. I've got her off in another town, just outside San Antone. She's perfect. Gorgeous, even, with blue eyes and auburn hair. Real grateful for my money too."

After he left, Ethan sat back down and stretched his legs. "There you go, Devin."

"What are you speaking about?"

"Well, I know you enjoy looking for everyone's weaknesses. Now, next time we're all sitting around, wishing we were somewhere else, we can think about how there's someone in this world who's got things a far sight tougher than we do."

"Bushnell's mistress?"

"Absolutely. Just think. Somewhere out there is a woman hidden in a little hovel, whose whole existence is dependent on the likes of Daniel Bushnell." He shook his head. "Can you imagine a worse way of spending one's day? Jumping to the wishes of a man like him?"

Though Devin could imagine far worse things, he conceded that Ethan did have a point. "I hope she gets paid well."

"Whatever she gets paid, Captain, I'm telling you right now, it ain't enough."

An hour later, lying in his cot next to Thomas, who was blissfully silent for once, Devin closed his eyes and said a prayer for that woman. Ethan had been right. War was hard. So was imprisonment. But to be imprisoned the way that woman was—dependent on a man like Bushnell for her very survival?

That was something he wouldn't wish on his worst enemy.

12

Her coffee had grown cold. Yet instead of getting up and refreshing her cup with warm liquid, Lizbeth simply sipped at the cold concoction. She would much rather stay in her comfortable chair and continue to appreciate her new situation and surroundings at Harrison House than get up to refresh a drink.

The moment was simply too sweet.

She figured she needed this time too. Though she'd been at Harrison House for two days, she'd spent the first doing little more than sleeping. It shouldn't have been a surprise, for she'd been both mentally and physically drained.

Being a maid had been exhausting. Working for her cousin and feeling constantly beholden to her and her husband added another type of strain. When she added Colonel Bushnell's scare and the subsequent interactions with Major Kelly and Aileen?

She'd been on the verge of collapse and she hadn't even realized it. Her body had craved rest, and she'd been more than happy to comply.

That morning, however, she'd awoken feeling rejuvenated. Now she was gazing around her surroundings as though she were a brand-new visitor to San Antonio. Indeed, everything in the area looked rather unfamiliar.

Sitting on a cozy wicker chair on a wide front veranda while wrapped in a lavender-scented soft afghan was to be savored.

Unable to help herself, she stretched her legs and leaned her head against the plush cushions behind her. Took time to count her blessings. And she did, indeed, feel blessed.

She was no longer working on her feet before dawn, racing against the clock to do Aileen and Dallas's bidding. No longer living in dread of being in the company of strange men. No longer afraid of being approached by people she didn't know.

For the first time in ages she was in charge of her day. She could do whatever she wanted. It wasn't a one-time thing either. She could very well live like a lady of leisure for quite some time. Well, at least until she ran out of funds.

It made her giddy.

That had been the first thing she'd thought of that morning when she awoke far later than she usually had on her days off. After lazing about under the comfortable down comforter and watching the last of the embers extinguish themselves in her room's fireplace, she gave in to the day and got dressed. Then she ventured downstairs to the kitchen at the back of the house and poured herself a large cup of coffee.

Next to the coffeepot on the stove had been a container of muffins and a note inviting guests to take as many as they would like. Feeling decadent, Lizbeth helped herself to two.

She didn't know if she would ever take such things for granted again. After living in her small room at the top of the Menger and having to follow Aileen's directives about what she could and couldn't do, being able to help herself to a steaming cup of coffee was a wonderful experience. Even the kitchen staff at the hotel hadn't been allowed a beverage except at designated times of the day.

Curling her feet onto the chair, Lizbeth continued to watch the world go by. A pair of mockingbirds squawked merrily as they signaled for their mates. A trio of squirrels played tag on the pine trees that lined the property. Their noisy chatter made her smile as they raced up and down the tree limbs. Below them was an orange tabby cat. She was lounging on the top of a wide stone fence, her tail lazily swinging like a metronome.

No doubt these things had happened all day everyday both here at Harrison House and right outside the Menger Hotel. Maybe they happened everywhere? All she knew for sure was that she'd been too preoccupied with work and worries to appreciate them. She silently promised herself not to let that happen again.

As the minutes passed, Lizbeth directed her sight toward the road just beyond her. Little by little, it filled with horse-drawn wagons and buggies. Men and women walked on its dusty sides. Some were striding intently, obviously hoping to finish a great many errands in a short amount of time. Others were simply strolling. They were speaking in cordial tones to each other, going about their routines. Other guests at Harrison House came up the steps and greeted her before going inside.

As she continued to watch all those people move about, Lizbeth realized she'd been concentrating on surviving for so long that she'd forgotten to remember one very important point. She *had* survived. Even though she'd endured many hardships, she was still surviving. She hadn't given up.

And while that was good, she also knew she hadn't been living either. Not really.

She knew if she stopped each one of the people out for their walks and asked about the war, they would share stories filled with as much heartbreak and longing as hers were. She had not been alone in her suffering. She was not the only woman to have experienced a great many hardships at the hands of others. She was certainly not the only person to have lost her home. Others also bore scars. Men lost limbs, eyes. Their very being.

Many women had also experienced pain at men's hands. She knew she was not the only one to have nightmares or to fear being alone in the dark.

So why was she still pining over the fact that her life was different than it had been before the war? Different from what she'd anticipated? Why had she not felt the need to stop often and give thanks?

She should have.

Nothing about that made her proud. Her grandparents would have expected more from her.

"Lord, please forgive me," she whispered. "I have been so blinded by my pain that I've neglected to realize I have so many things to be grateful for. Instead of remembering that, I took them for granted. I promise I'll do better."

Closing her eyes again, she concentrated on the warmth of the sun on her face . . . and a new sensation. It was a feeling of completeness. As if God himself was taking time out of his busy day to reach out to her. To let her know her words had been heard.

She was stunned. She'd thought her faith was true. Strong. But like her daily attempts of survival, she had only seen part of the whole picture.

Feeling stronger than she had in months, maybe years, she reached down to take another sip of her coffee. Then turned when the French doors that guarded the side entrance to the verandah swung open.

"Good morning, Miss Barclay," Mrs. Harrison said. "I trust you slept well last night?"

"I did. Thank you."

Just as she moved to stand, Mrs. Harrison waved off the motion with a hand. "Please, don't get up. I came to sit out here with you for a few minutes."

"All right." Lizbeth smiled, but her insides began to churn. Was something wrong? Had Mrs. Harrison changed her mind about allowing her to stay there?

She yearned to ask those questions, but she forced herself to continue to sit quietly. She swallowed the last of her cold coffee and watched her new landlady settle herself on the chair by her side. Her morning gown was especially attractive. It was a deep shade of plum and sported a wide ruffled hem that no doubt fluttered with each step.

After folding her hands neatly on her lap, Mrs. Harrison spoke. "I hardly saw you yesterday. I was worried you were ill."

"I thought at first I was. But then I realized I was simply tired. The excitement of the last few days caught up with me."

"I imagine so. As you know, Major Kelly shared your situation. I don't know if I found it more disturbing that you were accosted while making a bed or that your cousin blamed you for running into what you thought was an empty room to protect yourself."

"Both were rather difficult to deal with." Not wanting to be seen as only a victim, she said, "However, I am better now. I plan to buy a newspaper and start combing the ads from some of the surrounding areas. I aim to get a new job by the first of the year."

Instead of looking relieved, however, Mrs. Harrison merely looked contemplative. "I see. Well, I am relieved you will be waiting until after Christmas to leave us. It will be nice to have you here."

"Thank you." Still feeling awkward, she moved to stand. "I was just about to get another cup of coffee. Would you like one?"

"Thank you, but no." Looking a little embarrassed, she added, "Before you refill your cup, may we talk about something first?

I must confess there's another reason I came out here to speak with you."

"Oh?" Here it came.

"Yes. Major Kelly sent word to me early this morning that he'd like you to call on him at the Menger. At your convenience."

"He didn't want to call on me here?"

"It doesn't seem so." A wrinkle formed in her brow. "I feel rather awkward delivering his messages."

"Of course you do. I would feel the same way." But at the same time, she wondered why he hadn't sent word directly to her. Perhaps he suspected she would still be asleep.

"All right. As soon as I put on a bonnet and a proper cloak, I'll be ready to go."

"I'm sure you could have that cup of coffee first. I don't think it's that urgent."

"No, if the major is waiting for me, I don't want him to have to wait longer than necessary." Besides, she knew the relaxing moment had passed. She wasn't going to be able to rest until she discovered exactly why Major Kelly had summoned her.

After hurrying up to her room, Lizbeth put on her best felt bonnet and then put on real stockings and her best kid boots. After slipping on her cloak, she carefully locked her door and slipped the brass key into her bag before walking back down the stairs.

She spied Mrs. Harrison sitting at a writing table in the front parlor. "Thank you again for letting me know about my appointment, ma'am," she said politely.

"Would you like me to accompany you? The streets are awfully busy right now."

"I don't mind walking alone. Thank you for the offer, though."

After sharing another smile with Mrs. Harrison, Lizbeth ventured out onto the road. The lady had been right. Even more people were out walking and riding in carriages than when she'd been observing before.

Lizbeth felt very strange going back to the Menger, especially when she entered the hotel through the front lobby doors instead of the servants' entrance.

Several people looked her way, and, hoping she looked more composed than she felt, Lizbeth nodded at a few of the women. When she felt some of the staff stare at her in confusion, she pretended not to notice. Though she did feel awkward and on edge, she had nothing to be embarrassed about.

She really did need to remember that.

She started for the reception desk, relieved to still not see Bushnell anywhere around. But then she almost ran into Aileen.

"Good morning, Lizbeth," she said with a puzzled frown as she rushed to her side. "Do you need something?"

Lizbeth realized Aileen seemed concerned about her. She was beginning to wonder if fear of Dallas's disapproval had been what had pushed Aileen to dismiss her.

But though she was still hurt, Lizbeth realized she was also in a better place. She might not know what the future held for her, but she hadn't been happy being a maid at the Menger. "I am meeting Major Kelly here," she said. "He, uh, sent for me. Have you seen him, by any chance? I was just about to ask if he is in his room or—"

"He's in the parlor, standing in front of the fireplace." Looking at her curiously, Aileen added, "Is everything okay?"

"I don't know." Smiling tightly, she said, "I guess I'm about to find out."

Lizbeth shook off her doldrums and walked into the parlor, where the major stood with his back to her.

"Major Kelly, good morning."

After turning to her and smiling, he bowed. "Miss Barclay. Thank you for joining me here. I regret that I couldn't come to you, but my appearance at Mindy's establishment might have only caused talk."

She realized he was right. Though, from the interested stares around them, Lizbeth knew this meeting would be on the tongues of many people as well. "It was no trouble. I'm sorry for the delay. I'm afraid I was lazing about on Mrs. Harrison's verandah this morning."

"You have nothing to apologize for. We had nothing scheduled. After being gone most of Saturday and yesterday morning, I did quite a bit of lazing myself. Only inside where it is warmer." He smiled and gestured toward two chairs that faced each other. "Please sit down. May I order you something to drink? Hot tea, perhaps?"

Lizbeth didn't think she'd ever feel comfortable enough in the Menger Hotel to be waited on by the rest of the staff. "No, thank you."

After Major Kelly seated himself, he said, "How are you finding Harrison House?"

"Wonderful." Unable to help herself, she smiled. "I think I will enjoy living there for the next couple of months."

"Ah. Well, yes." He cleared his throat. "That is why I wanted to speak to you."

"About my living at Harrison House?"

If anything, he looked even more pensive. "That, and other things. I have been doing a lot of thinking, you see."

She didn't.

"Thinking? About what?"

"I feel bad about your circumstances."

"How so?" Before he could reply, she added, "Sir, you secured a safe place for me to live until I can find employment. Mrs. Harrison is very kind. Already she's made me feel like I'm an honored guest."

But instead of looking relieved, his jaw tightened. "Perhaps we could talk about your job search for a moment."

"Sir?"

He looked as though he had to struggle to formulate his words. "Are you still hoping to look for work somewhere else?" When she nodded, he leaned forward. "As what? A maid?"

"Well, yes." Lizbeth felt a little stung. He was acting as if that wasn't respectable work.

He frowned. "Don't you want something more than that?"

"I've learned what I want doesn't always matter."

"I think it does."

She almost laughed. Didn't he realize it wasn't just the men who had been changed by the war but the women too? "Times have changed, sir. I'm no longer the woman I used to be."

To her surprise, pain entered his eyes. "That may be true, but you don't have to give up all your dreams."

His comment, while sweet, was misinformed. She certainly did have to give up all her dreams. But more importantly, she'd realized that she was okay with that. "Major Kelly, something happened to me this morning."

Before he could say a word, she leaned forward, eager to share her epiphany. "You see, the strangest thing happened when I was sipping my coffee on the verandah. It occurred to me that I am not the only woman who suffered during the war."

When Ethan stared at her in confusion, she flushed. She needed to explain herself more fully. "I mean, of course I know thousands of men died or were grievously injured. The women in their lives grieved for them. I know that. But, well, I think a small part of me felt that no one had gone through quite what I had. I assumed that was why they were able to pick up the pieces of their lives and move on."

"When you weren't able to?"

She nodded, glad he understood. "Yes. I decided I've been a bit selfish, only focusing on myself and my own hurts. I need to start thinking about other people. And I am going to!"

But instead of looking pleased, Major Kelly only appeared more taken aback. "Don't make light of what you've gone through, Lizbeth—may I call you Lizbeth?"

She nodded, flattered he would want to.

"Others might have suffered," he went on, "but what happened to you was terrible."

"I know . . . but what I don't think I had completely appreciated was that I had been so used to being in pain and hurt I forgot to look at everything good in my life." Seeing the interest flicker in his eyes, she straightened with a smile. "I decided to start telling the Lord how grateful I am instead of asking him for things that cannot happen."

"Such as?"

His prodding was making her feel self-conscious. Stuttering a bit, she said, "W-well, things like marriage and children—and a home again."

And just like that, the tense set of his jaw eased. He shifted. "Lizbeth, it seems my timing is perfect, then. I asked you here to speak of those very same things."

"Do you know of a governess or a nanny position?"

"Uh, no."

Racking her brain, she tried to think of another job she might be suitable for that didn't involve either cleaning a house or caring for children. "As a companion?"

"No." He shifted. "You see, I don't like you working so hard, from sunup until sundown. It isn't right."

She may have given him permission to call her by her given name, but she was starting to feel as though he was completely overstepping his bounds. "Forgive me, but I must point out that what I do with my time really isn't your concern."

"But it is."

She was tired of his riddles. "Why?" she blurted.

"Because I've decided we should marry."

She almost started laughing. Almost. But then she looked into his eyes. He was very far from making a joke.

"Major Kelly, thank you for the honor, but I—"

He clasped her hand, startling her. "Miss Barclay, would you do me the very great honor of becoming my wife?"

His words were beautiful. His voice was fluid and strong. No hesitation. No doubt in his tone. No flicker of unease in his eyes.

It was more than she'd ever hoped for. It was more than she deserved. To say no would be giving up so much.

Tears filled her eyes. Wanting to treasure the moment, even if it was for just another second.

13

As she did each morning, Julianne wrote in her journal, taking special care to write down the date. Today it gave her pause.

Four days had passed since Captain Devin Monroe walked away after entertaining a brief but misguided infatuation with her. Three days since Abby and Carl Bernard had rushed into her life like twin tornadoes, already upsetting everything in her daily routine and turning it on its side.

Amazing how God presented her with so much joy and so much pain at the same time. Amazing how she'd been able to bear both almost easily.

Abby hadn't been speaking lightly when she said she wanted to begin a friendship with her. Abby had visited her home on both Saturday and Sunday. She first brought her fiancé, Timothy, along with Carl. Julianne had been so surprised by the preacher being in her home that she had been flustered. The whole time they were talking, she'd been on pins and needles. She had been sure that, just when she relaxed, the preacher would choose to lecture her about the choices she'd made.

Timothy couldn't have been more different, though. He'd been friendly and open. As open in his conversation as his fiancée had been in her heart.

The second time Abby came alone. Carl was making a Sunday-afternoon call on a young lady.

Julianne was delighted with Abby. She was so chatty and friendly, and brought back memories of another time in her life. Back when she had little to worry about beyond what to wear to parties she was invited to. When they'd taken a stroll together, she was surprised to see their friendship was already doing miraculous things to her standing in town. It seemed seeing her with a companion was all anyone had needed to take the final step in setting her past firmly behind her.

As they drank tea when they returned, Julianne commented to Abby that she'd never expected to be so well received.

Abby brushed off her surprise. "It isn't as though you have a man living in your upstairs rooms right now, Julianne. Actually, even my aunt Dora was hard-pressed to remember a time when you did anything to cause talk. She said you conducted yourself like a lady at all times."

Had she? All Julianne could remember was being both alone and lonely. Except for when Daniel visited her. Then she had been at his beck and call until the moment he left, telling Bula her services were not needed when he was there. And when she had been a slave to him? Well, she'd been an emotional wreck. Sometimes a physical one too—especially when he took out his wartime misery on her, hitting her for some imagined slight.

Those had been dark days. She'd been embarrassed by what she'd done and scorned by others. The money the man gave her always felt tainted. Only when she used it to help her grandmother—and to buy chickens and garden seeds to help others during the war—was she reminded that everything she'd done had been for a good reason.

"If I haven't told you before, I am grateful for your kindness.

It says a lot about your character to befriend a woman with my reputation. You are going to do Timothy proud, Abby."

"I hope so, though I want you to know I didn't befriend you for any reason beyond my explanation when Carl and I first introduced ourselves to you, Julianne."

"I am glad we are getting to know each other," Julianne said, feeling self-conscious.

Abby beamed. "Now that you've gotten that off your chest, let's talk about something far more interesting."

"Which is?"

"How we should go about finding a husband for you."

Julianne was thankful she hadn't been about to take a sip of tea. If she had, she would have probably choked on it! Instead, she laughed, determined to keep the moment light. "As much as you try to champion my honor, some realities cannot be overlooked. My past with the colonel is one of them. I simply am not marriage material."

"I heard a handsome man called on you the other day. Was that not the case?"

"Well, yes, a man did. A Captain Monroe. But that was a few days ago, the day before I met you and your brother. Nothing became of it, though."

"Maybe he'll call on you again. Men get busy, you know."

"He might be busy, but it doesn't signify. He won't be returning."

"Are you sure?" Abby must have noticed the expression in her eyes, because she softly added, "Did it not work out?"

That was one way to put it. "It didn't work out."

"But you liked him, though. Didn't you?"

Julianne was tempted to lie, but there was no reason to. "I did. I liked him very much."

"Maybe he'll change his mind and return."

"I'm afraid not. But that's all right, Abby. I've learned some things can never be changed. The past is one of them."

Abby nodded. "I'm starting to realize the most disappointed people in the world are the ones who cannot come to terms with that reality."

Since she knew disappointment well, Julianne decided truer words had never been said.

When she was alone again, buoyed by Abby's words of wisdom, Julianne decided to call on a woman she had talked to at church several times. She had always been kind and friendly, but Julianne had been the one to keep a small measure of distance between them. She realized now that she'd been unconsciously distancing herself from a potential friend.

She'd told herself it was so she wouldn't taint anyone with her reputation. But after Abby's talk, Julianne realized she had been the one putting up barriers. While honorable men like Devin Monroe might find her to be a less than suitable bride, it seemed others were not as judgmental in whom they befriended.

Miss Blake was gracious and welcoming when she tentatively knocked on her door. She invited Julianne into her parlor and served her tea and cake. In turn, Julianne did her best to be a friendly and entertaining guest. She shared stories about her gardening mishaps and the war she'd been having with some wily squirrels.

After visiting a half hour, she started for home. Between Abby's visit and her own call, Julianne couldn't recall having a more social, conversational day. The idea that it might be the first of many days made her smile.

As she entered her street, she drew up short. Just beyond her house was a proud-looking man on a black stallion. His back was to her, but she knew both his bearing and the horse as well as she knew the contents of her linen closet. It was Daniel Bushnell.

Her first reaction was to stop in her tracks. Heart racing, she scanned the area, looking to her left and then right. She ached to dart off to the shadows and hide. There weren't many options. A thicket of evergreens. The Conners' shed. But she was willing to take a chance on anything. Anywhere would be better than being out in the open. If he turned around, he'd spot her immediately. But just as she started walking, Daniel and his horse sped up and disappeared out of sight.

After waiting another moment, Julianne hurried to her house. As she approached the front door, she scanned the yard, examining the area. For what, she wasn't sure. Maybe she couldn't imagine Daniel leaving her house without leaving his mark as well? When all seemed quiet, she unlocked her door and started to step inside.

Then she saw it. A small bouquet of flowers. No doubt the cost had been dear. Flowers in November would be. Daniel had been forced to lay them on the doorstep. He was going to be so angry that she hadn't been there to receive them!

She picked up the bouquet. Fingered the rose petals absently. She was going to have to take them inside. Display them for anyone to see. Her heart started pounding as she wondered how she was going to explain their appearance to Bula. Or to Abby and Carl.

Then, with a start, she realized she didn't have to accept the flowers. She could leave them on the doorstep or even toss them in the trash. She wasn't Daniel's mistress anymore.

But instead of feeling better, she was confused. Because while she wasn't his anymore, her insides didn't seem to realize the difference.

Even now, after all this time, a part of her was still under his control.

14

IT WAS COLD. DRESSED IN HIS OVERCOAT, BOOTS, AND FELT Stetson, Devin still felt the bite of the cool wind on his skin as he leaned against the side of his house. He should probably go inside. He had a good steak he'd bought from a nearby rancher. He should cook it up with a couple of eggs. Maybe even open the book he'd purchased on a whim the last time he visited the mercantile. It was a rag highlighting the escapades of the notorious outlaw Scout Proffitt. Perhaps it would be entertaining enough for him to forget about Julianne Van Fleet for a couple of hours.

Yeah, right.

When Ethan was here two days ago, he'd promised to ride to San Antonio as soon as his other business was done—not just to find and confront Bushnell for the honor of Lizbeth but also for the honor of Julianne, even if he'd never see her again.

But he doubted he'd ever forget the look she gave him when he coldly told her he was leaving. She'd been crushed, yet also unsurprised.

And that was what had stayed with him. She hadn't expected to be treated better by him. She'd grouped him in the same category as a blackguard like Bushnell. That had hurt. Worse, he feared she might have been right on the mark.

Because the fact was he had behaved abominably. When had he decided he was fit to judge others?

For that matter, when had he become so cold? Hadn't she told him Bushnell had deceived her? That she and her grandmother had been suffering? Hadn't she told him she'd practically been forced to accept his offer because she'd been ruined and they'd been cold and hungry?

What did it really matter if she had done what she had to do to survive? Was that very different from some of the things he'd done during the war?

Julianne was lovely. When she was desperate, she used what the Lord had given her, just as he used his gifts to lead men into battle.

He'd left her feeling ashamed, but he knew that, in actuality, he had shamed himself. Tainted much of what he was.

No, turning his back on a woman wasn't who he was. Especially when he was already half in love with her.

He had to go back.

Once he'd made the decision, it was suddenly so easy. Not only would he see Julianne, but he'd also follow through on his promise to join Ethan in San Antonio and hunt for Bushnell. Although Ethan could have already resolved his dilemma with Bushnell. Or perhaps the scoundrel had even left the area after Ethan threatened him. But he'd made a vow never to let his friends down when they needed help, and he wasn't going to start now.

Within fifteen minutes, he had walked to the barn, saddled Midge, and started toward Boerne. Pleased that he had a goal to accomplish, he felt better than he had in days.

Once in Boerne, he rode directly to Julianne's, even though the late-afternoon light was waning. He wasn't sure how he would be received, but he was willing to chance her displeasure for the opportunity to apologize.

When he got to her door, he knocked before he could talk himself out of it.

Almost immediately, he saw the curtains in a front window move. She had seen him.

Minutes passed. Then several more. He knocked again.

At last the door opened and Julianne stepped out onto the porch.

She was dressed far differently from the last time he saw her. She was wearing her glasses, her rich auburn hair was confined in a loose knot on the top of her head, and she was wearing a brown dress that was so shapeless it not only washed out her complexion but made her appear a bit like a baked potato.

Behind the glasses, he could see shadows under her eyes. There was a new wariness about her. Almost as if all her joy had been suctioned out of her.

"Yes, Captain?"

"Miss Van Fleet," he began after he bowed slightly. "May we talk?"

"I don't believe we have anything more to discuss, sir." Her hand was curved around the edge of the door. He knew he had mere seconds before she closed it in his face and turned around. With that same certainty, he knew he would not get another chance. If he could not smooth things out between them at once, she would never acknowledge him again.

"Miss Van Fleet, please reconsider. I won't take up much of your time," he continued in a rush. "Perhaps we could even talk out here." Even though it was getting colder outside.

She sighed. "Captain, I don't know what you want from me."

"Just your time."

"I gave you that, and it ended badly." Before he could apologize, she continued. "You seem to forget I never sought you out. I was also honest about my past."

"You are exactly right. I sought you out. You are beautiful, that is true. But there was something more that struck my fancy. I wanted to get to know you better."

"And you did." Wrinkling her nose, she murmured, "You don't have to feel any kind of misplaced guilt, sir. I didn't expect you to understand my circumstances."

"But that is why I am having such a difficult time. I know I disappointed you. But I disappointed myself as well." He straightened, holding himself so stiffly he might as well have been standing at attention. "I expect better of myself, you see."

"So this is about you."

"No."

"Are you sure about that?"

He felt his cheeks heat. Oh, but he was handling this badly. "It was wrong of me to leave the way I did. Please forgive me."

Her expression softened. "You are sincere, aren't you?"

"Very much so."

"I . . . I appreciate your words. But I feel I must remind you that nothing has changed. I can't change my past, Captain."

"I can't change mine either. Please don't give up on me yet."

She wavered, then opened the door farther. "Obviously I'm not dressed for callers."

"You look fine."

Placing her glasses in a pocket, she almost smiled. "Not so fine. If you would like, you may come inside. It's too cold for me out here."

"I would like to come inside. Thank you."

She smiled then. "I just made a pot of hot chocolate. Would you like some?"

He would consume anything she offered if it meant he could stay near. "Of course. Thank you."

"Entertaining again, Julianne?" a caustic voice called out behind him.

Julianne stiffened, and Devin turned.

Before he even realized what he was doing, Devin stepped in front of Julianne and faced the one man he'd hoped he'd never see again—even though he was planning to go to San Antonio to help Ethan find him.

Bushnell looked to be taken aback by his presence, but only for a moment.

"Sniffing after my castoffs, Devin?" he asked as he sauntered closer, finally stopping a few feet away.

Behind him, Julianne gasped.

And for the first time in memory, Devin acted without fore-thought. He punched the man hard in the jaw.

Bushnell flew back on impact. Then, surprisingly, he righted himself quickly and fisted his palms.

When he heard Julianne's cry behind him, Devin struggled for control. He could not lose his temper again, not if he ever wanted a chance with her. If Bushnell wanted to fight, he would fight him, but someplace far from Julianne. "You deserved my fist for what you just said about Miss Van Fleet," he said. "But if you think we're going to continue this discussion here, think again."

Daniel smirked. "What? So I'm supposed to just take that and walk away?"

"That is your choice. If you want to fight, I'll gladly do that. But I don't intend to beat you to a bloody pulp in front of Julianne."

"Like she matters?"

Comments like that were why Devin was so eager to pummel him into submission. "I'm warning you. I won't take kindly to you disrespecting her."

"Disrespecting her?" Bushnell spit on the ground. "She was my mistress, Devin. Nothing more than that. She lay on her back for my money."

Seeing red, Devin stepped forward. It seemed it was inevitable. He was going to have to beat this man on Julianne's front porch and pay the consequences later.

Just then Julianne placed a hand on his shoulder. "No, Devin. Please, don't trouble yourself."

"See? She knows what she is." Bushnell smirked.

Devin suddenly wished they were back in the army. At least then the strict code of conduct would have forced Bushnell to watch his mouth—or Devin to curb his temper.

Instead, he looked at the other man coldly. "I am advising you now to stop any and all interest in Miss Van Fleet. She is no longer your concern."

"Or else?"

He should have known that was coming. "Or else I'll make sure everyone knows about the secrets you sold during the war."

"What secrets? I was no traitor."

Devin knew he wasn't. But he also knew—thanks to what had happened to Phillip Markham in Galveston—how easily information could be twisted and misconstrued. "Good luck convincing everyone of that. One word from me and there won't be a man in the state who will give you the time of day."

Bushnell glared. "You have made a serious mistake, Monroe. I won't forget this."

"Neither will I. I can promise you that." Devin stood motionless, never taking his eyes off the man until Bushnell walked away, mounted his horse, and left. His only regret was that he'd not determined where he and Ethan could find him next.

Devin could hear Julianne breathing hard a few steps behind him. He moved to stand in the doorway until Daniel Bushnell was out of sight. Only then did he step inside, close the door, and face her.

As he suspected, she was in tears and pale. Staring up at him, her blue eyes looked murky with worry and dismay.

And, it seemed, fear.

That hit him hard. "Don't be afraid of me," he said, stepping forward. "I would never hurt you."

"What have you done?"

He drew up short. "I kept you safe." He'd also been marking his territory, establishing his regard, and setting ground rules. Now if Bushnell ever contemplated approaching Julianne again, he would think twice. And maybe he'd done enough to keep him from Ethan's Lizbeth as well. When the man calmed down, he was bound to realize he and Ethan were still friends, still in touch. Maybe the thought of the two of them coming after him would be a deterrent—at least for the time being.

Julianne shook her head. "He is very powerful, Captain Monroe."

"Not so much."

"He has powerful friends. And a lot of money. I have no way to fight what he wants or anything he tries to coerce me with."

"Yes, you do."

When she stared at him in confusion, he murmured, "You are not alone anymore, Julianne. Please. Calm yourself and don't worry."

"Don't worry. You make that sound possible."

"It is. He is not going to bother you again. I know he is not."

"You don't know that. Besides, what am I going to do when you leave and he comes back?" Her bottom lip trembled. "Now he's going to think we are more to each other than we are."

Her bitter tone. The way her arms were curved around her middle, as though she was attempting to comfort herself. Those words. That lack of belief in him . . . It all came together. Made something snap.

And so he did what he shouldn't do, what she was no doubt afraid of, what was undoubtedly a very bad idea.

He took the last four steps to her side, grasped her upper arms, and pulled her into his embrace.

She stumbled forward and braced her hands on his chest.

He almost smiled. That was exactly where she needed to be. Exactly where he wanted her.

"Captain—"

"I'm not your captain," he said, his voice rough. "My name is Devin. Call me by my name." Then, before she could protest again, he bent his head and claimed her lips.

She gasped. He took advantage and deepened the kiss. Then did what he had been dreaming about since the first moment he'd spied her across the town square. He pulled her closer and kissed her again. More thoroughly. And when she melted against him, he felt such a thrill that he groaned and continued.

Her hands reached up, curved around his neck. Her touch was so sweet. So precious. So exactly what he'd been imagining that he lifted his head to smile.

When he looked down into her face, what he saw there made all the pain and suffering in his life worthwhile.

Because Julianne Van Fleet was gazing at him in wonder. Her lips were slightly parted, and her blue eyes were bright with passion.

She'd desired him too. He felt triumphant.

Until she slapped him. Hard.

Hard enough that he flinched in response. Rubbing his hand along his jaw, he studied her curiously. "What was that for?"

"Need you ask?" Fire, mixed liberally with condemnation, burned deep in her eyes.

She was upset with him. Blamed him. Had he hurt her?

Horrified, he drew back. Dropped his hands from where they'd curved so perfectly around her waist. "I thought you wanted that kiss as much as I did. Julianne, I swear I didn't think I forced you." He knew he hadn't. He was enough of a man to know when a woman welcomed his touch.

Enough of a man to know when she didn't.

She was trembling now. "Please leave."

"Leave?"

Breathing heavily, she nodded. "And do not come back."

After that kiss? After he'd confronted Bushnell about her honor?

Then, finally, he noticed she didn't look frightened of him. No, it was more as if she was frightened of the things she was feeling. Maybe she was just unsure of his intentions, or what she meant to him.

"Julianne, I know you enjoyed that kiss as much as I did."

She inhaled. "I . . ."

He almost smiled as he continued. "Don't deny it." Lowering his voice, he murmured, "Maybe, like me, you are hoping I will hold you in my arms again soon."

She paled as disappointment flowed from her. "Is that why you came here today, Devin Monroe?" she asked quietly. "Did you come to claim my charms? Have you decided to become my new keeper?"

"Of course not."

"I have no desire to be another man's mistress."

He would have laughed if he hadn't been so disappointed that she thought he would ask her to do such a thing. "I did not come here to ask you that. I don't want a mistress."

"Oh? Is that simply how you greet all women you know?"

"Of course not." Becoming frustrated, he said, "Don't twist my actions into something dishonorable, Julianne."

She blinked. Her posture eased. "Maybe you could explain yourself."

She didn't sound as mortified now. How could he begin to explain the mixture of emotions he felt toward her? It was likely impossible.

But still he tried. "I came here for the very reason I told you when I first arrived on your doorstep. I wanted to apologize. I was wrong. I hold you in high regard. But then, that blasted Bushnell came and you were crying . . . and—"

"And you decided to kiss me without my permission?"

For the second time in ten minutes, his temper snapped. "Julianne, as much as I respect you and have worthy intentions, let's not start pretending you are an innocent miss."

She gasped. "Sir—"

"Let me finish. Listen to what I have to say. I don't want an innocent miss. And for the record, that wasn't my first kiss either." He edged closer. Close enough to smell the faint scent of roses in her hair. "But no kiss I've ever experienced was like that. It was perfect."

Her eyes were stormy as she gaped at him.

"Do you disagree?"

For a second, he was sure she wasn't going to reply. But then she shook her head. Almost imperceptibly.

Making him feel triumphant again.

Glad his emotions were coming in check, he said, "I wasn't going to tell you this because I didn't want to scare you, but I aim to marry you one day soon."

"Marry? Captain—"

"Devin."

"Devin, you don't know what you're saying. I cannot . . ." Obviously flummoxed, her voice drifted off.

"Finish that thought, Julianne. I want to hear what you have to say."

She pressed her fingertips to her lips. "But . . ."

He decided to make it easy on her. "I think it's time for a bit of space. I am coming back in one week. Please plan for me to take you out to dinner."

"We can't discuss marriage. We hardly know each other."

"That's exactly why I'm coming back. And if Bushnell returns, don't answer the door."

"I hardly know what to think."

He laughed. "Good. Now you know how I've felt from the moment I first saw you. I don't know what to think. I don't know how to act. All I know is that I want to know you better. I want you in my life."

"Devin . . ."

"If I'm going too fast, well, I'll slow down. I'll wait until you are ready. But I'm not going to change my mind about us."

"You sound so sure."

"I haven't been this sure about anything in quite a long time. Trust me, Julianne. Believe me when I say I am coming back and that my intentions are honorable." Staring at her hard, he said, "Okay?"

Tears pricked her eyes as she gave a purely feminine, adorable shrug. "Well . . . um, okay."

Pleased that he'd gotten his way, his tone gentled. "Good. Now, don't forget about Bushnell. Stay away from him."

She nodded. "I will."

"Good."

"You don't have to leave this minute. Would you like to come sit down?"

She was too tempting. So tempting, he knew he needed advice. He needed to go see Ethan. "I cannot. I need to go to San Antonio. I've got an old friend there, a fellow former prisoner with whom I need to confer about some personal business." Such as how to ruin Daniel Bushnell. "Major Kelly is a bit of a gambler now, but I know of no finer man. He's staying at the Menger Hotel there."

"Will you promise to be careful? Daniel was so angry . . ."

"Always." Reaching out, he cupped her cheek with one rough palm. "See you in one week."

Before she could ask any more questions or think of another argument, he bowed and then strode out her front door.

If all went well, he would be in San Antonio by nightfall and seeing Ethan Kelly shortly after. Hopefully, he could already shed some light on Bushnell's present occupation and usual whereabouts. Then, together, they could decide what else needed to be done to get him out of their lives—and out of their women's lives too.

It was time.

15

DEVIN TOOK CARE TO FOLLOW THE CURVE OF THE RIVER AS he rode east toward San Antonio. Though there was a bite to the air, it felt exhilarating. Fresh.

He knew, of course, the elements outside weren't what made it so. No, his response to the weather had everything to do with his state of mind.

At long last, he was hopeful about the future. His time with Julianne had been transformational. Not only had they mended their rift, but he had new goals in mind. He intended to one day marry Julianne Van Fleet and find a way to remove Daniel Bushnell from her life.

Both missions were daunting. Neither was sure to be a success. But it was because of those plans that he felt uplifted.

While keeping a careful watch for other riders in the distance, Devin allowed his mind to drift back to when he'd been a cavalry officer.

Oh, not to the bad times. Not back when all of them were bloody and hurting and exhausted. Or when everyone had been injured, suffering from stomach ailments, or hungry. But back at the beginning of the war. When he'd first enlisted and been so cocky and full of himself. Back when there was so much hope and excitement in the air it was almost impossible to think of anything else.

Because of his father's influence and his natural ability to lead, handle a rifle, and ride, he'd been able to gain commissions as a second lieutenant. Over the first year, he'd easily slid up the ranks. He'd been so gratified when he'd made captain. So comfortable with that rank that he'd stayed there.

Scanning the horizon again, he relaxed slightly as he saw a collection of lights in the distance. He would be in the Menger Hotel soon. Once there, he was going to spend a good hour at the bar. Indulge in a shot of whiskey. Maybe two. Talk to the other the men sitting around the bar who were usually amiable, often ready to trade stories about nothing that mattered. That was something he was looking forward to.

And get down to business with Ethan. He needed to tell him what happened with Bushnell at Julianne's.

"Not long now, girl," he murmured to his mare.

Midge whickered softly. Then, as if she'd understood his words, increased her pace.

Soon they were trotting across the cold surface of ground that had already settled in for a long winter. The wind brushed his cheeks, curled tight around the skin on his neck like a kerchief. His tan duster—stained, worn, and frayed at the edges—felt like a warm companion. Enveloping him with warmth without asking for much.

He realized he was happy. At last, he had been pulled from his inertia. Julianne was going to allow him to court her. One day he'd bend down on one knee and ask her to honor him by being his wife. And when she said yes, he knew he would push her to the altar as quickly as he could. No doubt, she'd protest. Maybe even remind him she was no innocent, blushing bride.

But she was perfect for him.

He'd have to remind her that he'd seen too much, done too much bad to be the right fit for someone too sheltered.

He smiled, imagining the conversation. No doubt, she'd shake her head. Say—

Crack.

The force of the bullet hit his shoulder with enough emphasis to make him gasp. His mind blanked. Only the memories that lay deep in his muscles allowed him to keep his seat in the saddle. Only the horse's knowledge of war and battle enabled her to continue forward without getting spooked.

When he heard another gunshot, he hugged his mare's neck and spurred her on, allowing her to run hell for leather. Though he figured the Lord had gifted him with more years than most soldiers ever deserved, he wasn't ready to die. Not yet.

He turned to look behind him. Needing to see how much distance he'd gained. Needing to see who had been so yellow as to shoot him from behind.

The rider loomed in the distance. He was wearing a pale Stetson, a black duster, and was keeping his pace. His familiar gray appaloosa was a fine piece of horseflesh. He was galloping steady, solid.

After another few seconds passed, Devin glanced behind him again. That's when the rider's head lifted. When Devin caught sight of who had shot him. He'd been right.

Bushnell.

Cold calculation settled in Devin's soul. As Midge continued to zig and zag and direct him to safety, as Devin's blood no doubt stained his tan duster more, he fostered that anger.

To keep his bearings, he planned his revenge on Bushnell.

And though it didn't make him proud, he knew he was not going to regret giving the man his due. No man was going to live long enough to attempt to kill him twice.

Not if he could help it.

16

Sitting on one of the bronze velvet chairs in the main parlor at the Menger, his marriage proposal looming awkwardly between them like an unfamiliar relative, Ethan had stared into Lizbeth's eyes.

What he saw hadn't been reassuring. Pain and worry distorted their green color. Made them look a little murky. Darker than they were.

Or maybe that had been his imagination.

It didn't really matter all that much. All that mattered was that she was about to say no. But without a word, she had risen to her feet and walked out to the lobby. He didn't have to follow her to know she was returning to Harrison House.

Ethan had expected a refusal. Lizbeth Barclay had more integrity in her fingertips than he did in his whole body. No doubt, she probably had more integrity than most of the men he'd served with and fought beside during the war.

She was certainly more upright than most of people he'd been spending time with of late. She would never marry him just to help herself. She especially wouldn't agree to a match between them if she thought he might later regret it. He was beginning to think she wouldn't promise to love and honor someone if she didn't—certainly not in a house of God. Maybe not even to herself.

The only people he'd held in such high esteem were his band of brothers. Monroe, Truax, and Baker were his best friends in the world. Their bond had been forged on scarred battlefields, in desperate fights, and during forced captivity.

And now, after he'd spent all day trying to determine where Bushnell had gone, trying to convince himself it would be wrong to pursue Lizbeth further, she had returned. When it was almost dark. They were sitting on a brown velvet settee in the lobby this time. But she wasn't saying anything. And neither was he.

As the silence stretched between them, he wondered how that could be. How could he feel so close to a woman he just met when it had taken years of pain and suffering to feel as close to other people?

Under his regard, she began to look uneasy.

And why wouldn't she? He was staring at her intently. So far, he'd done nothing in her company that was worthy of her.

But he wanted to. He wanted to change. To become better. He thought he might have a chance if he had her by his side.

And that was the heart of why he wanted her. It wasn't just that he felt he owed her for his part in her trials. It wasn't just that he ached to do something of worth again. Something that he could go to sleep at night feeling pleased about.

More than that, he yearned for someone good in his life again. Someone pure. No, not innocent. He didn't need innocence. He needed a pure heart and kindness far more.

It was selfish. He knew that. But he had long ago come to terms with the fact that he wasn't nearly as good as some thought. He was a study in missed opportunities and multiple faults.

That made him realize he was going to have to do something

harder than just about anything he'd done in a very long time. He was going to have to show his real self to her. Not the slick gambler who bent rules. Who used his looks and charm to get what he wanted. He needed to show her the man he was underneath the layers of gold cufflinks and silk vests. The man he'd been for the Confederacy, when having honor and integrity had mattered so much.

He was going to have to allow her to see a man of whom she could be proud. A cold chill swept through him, one that had nothing to do with the lobby door opening and allowing the frosty air to worm its way inside. He had to start talking.

"Don't say no," he blurted, defying all his good intentions.

Her expression turned even more pained. "Major—"

"It's Ethan. Call me Ethan."

"Yes. All right. Ah . . . Ethan," she began. "Your proposal shocked me this morning. You and I met only days ago, but that was no excuse to leave as I did. I simply had to . . . think. I did not want to offend you, because I do appreciate the sacrifice you are willing to make for my safety."

"It's not a sacrifice."

She kept talking. "What's more, you honor me, but I cannot accept. *Of course* I cannot accept."

Tears were now in her eyes. She was rattled. He'd upset her that morning, and she was still upset. "Please, let us discuss this," he said quietly. "Please know I don't propose lightly. I do not intend to make a mockery of these vows. I will honor them."

Glancing around the lobby, she stiffened. No doubt she was as aware as he that they were being observed. They were causing a scene. "Sir, how could I think otherwise? We don't know each other. And . . . and, Ethan, I'm just a maid."

"You are more than that and we both know it."

"But—"

"And I know enough." He'd told himself he wouldn't, but he persisted, using all the skills he'd learned to press his suit. "Don't forget that marriage is for a lifetime. We'll have years to get to know each other."

"But that isn't how it's supposed to happen. Is it?" She stood.

"Does it even matter?" Getting to his feet, he held out a hand. "Please. Sit down again so we can talk about this." When it looked as though she was going to refuse, he murmured, "Don't I at least deserve your time?"

She sat back down, but her back was tense. "Of course you do, but I don't see what can change." Taking a deep breath, she said, "As I thought about your proposal all afternoon, I was reminded that marriage is the culmination of a romance. It's the crowning glory, the opportunity to make promises and say vows honored by God. It is not the beginning."

Her words were pretty. But he also thought they were far too fanciful for the violent, desperate times they were living in. "Lizbeth, for others, perhaps that is how marriage comes about. But we both know that isn't what always happens. Sometimes a couple marries because it makes the most sense. Think of all the unions that formed before men went off to war."

"Ethan, perhaps I should have spoken more clearly. While others might venture into such a union, I will not."

"Lizbeth, if you consider it for a moment, you will see you need a protector."

"I need a great many things, Major. A marriage of convenience is not one of them."

"Not even for protection?"

"Not even for that."

He couldn't help it. He smiled. She had so much fire. She

was so earnest. Intent. "You could be wrong. Have you considered that?"

"Even if I am, it doesn't matter. I won't repay kindness by shackling a man like you with a woman like me."

"Don't speak as if we are worlds apart. You have much that I desire."

Her cheeks were now flushed. "You are embarrassing me. People are listening."

Feeling brash, feeling desperate, he shrugged. "Let them listen. I don't care. Aren't you going to allow me to explain my reasons? That's hardly fair."

"Do you have reasons?"

"Of course."

She still looked skeptical. "Real ones?"

"First, to be completely honest, you need me, and I need to do this. Lizbeth, Miss Barclay, there is more to me than you are aware. There is more to me than I've allowed you to see."

"Why is that?"

Because he'd been afraid. Afraid to revisit the memories. Afraid to admit he had changed. Afraid to share he had as many scars in his soul as he did on his body. He was marked, and sometimes, in the middle of the night when the things he'd done haunted him, he was very weak. "Maybe, like you, I need time. And I need to be able to trust."

A new light of vulnerability shown in her eyes. "You too?"

"Especially me."

"If you need to marry, a great many willing and desperate women are available. I suggest you set your sights elsewhere."

"For reasons I cannot explain, the bride needs to be you. Please consider it. I promise you will not be disappointed."

She was weakening. He could feel it. Felt it as sure as if he were sitting at a poker table and knew the man across from him was holding a straight flush in his hands.

Just as sure as if his enemy had a flaw, a gap he could identify.

He was going to get his way. It was all he could do to not smile.

Then the door swung open. In walked a man with blond hair in a tan duster. Hair cut short by necessity and bleached by wind and sun and years. A man with eyes so light in color that one might imagine they were gray or silver. But they were light blue.

They also looked filled with pain.

Concerned, Ethan surged to his feet. "Monroe!" he called out to get his attention. "Are you all right?"

Captain Devin Monroe turned to him, started forward, then stopped again, as if the step was too painful. "No."

By now Ethan was at his side. He reached out, intending to support him, but instead he ended up enfolding Devin in his arms. Realizing the other man had passed out, he eased him to the lobby floor.

"Ethan?" Lizbeth cried. "What happened? Who is that?"

"Get a doctor. Fast," he barked as he started pulling at Devin's duster. Blood stained his hands, sunk into the crevice of his fingertips.

It had been years since he'd seen a wound like this. Devin had been shot with a high-caliber shotgun. And, if he wasn't mistaken, he was staring at an exit wound. Devin Monroe had been shot in the back, just below his shoulder.

"Someone's already gone for help," Lizbeth said as she knelt next to him. "Use this."

Grabbing the soft fabric, Ethan realized she'd given him one of her petticoats.

Folding it tightly in his hands, he pressed it against Devin's wound. The fabric turned red in seconds. So much blood.

When Devin groaned, Ethan leaned closer. "I'm here," he whispered. "You are not alone."

"I'm . . . I'm okay."

Glad that Devin had spoken again, though weakly, Ethan felt a burst of anger surge through him. It was unimaginable that this friend, their captain, could survive so much only to be felled now. "Who did this?" He knew Devin would understand. If he didn't survive, someone would need to avenge him.

Even if it took the rest of his life, Ethan knew right then and there that it needed to be him.

"Bushnell," he whispered.

17

Bushnell?" Ethan repeated, leaning closer to Devin, ignoring the blood seeping through the linen cloth against his friend's wound and staining his hand. Surely he had misunderstood.

"Colonel Bushnell did this?" Lizbeth asked faintly. "How . . . how could that be?"

It didn't make any sense to him either. But he didn't doubt that Devin had spoken the right name.

He was aware that Lizbeth was upset and standing directly behind him, but Ethan forced himself to ignore her needs. He ignored the questions forming in his mind too. Only one thing mattered at that moment—ensuring Devin' survival.

"What is going on? Oh!" a feminine voice exclaimed behind him. Ethan glanced over his shoulder and saw it was Aileen Howard.

"This gentleman has been shot, Aileen," Lizbeth said quietly. "A doctor has been sent for. At least, I hope so. We need a room to place him in."

"Yes, well . . ."

"Immediately, ma'am," Ethan bit out. "And get someone outside to see to his horse."

"I'll take care of this, Aileen," her husband said as he joined them. "Go see if the physician has indeed been sent for." After a pause, he knelt on one knee by Ethan's side.

Though he resented the intrusion, the tone of Dallas's quiet voice reassured Ethan something was about to get done. "I need to get him off the floor this minute."

"I have just the place. Lizbeth?"

She stepped closer. "Yes, Dallas?"

"We're going to put this man in the Mockingbird Suite. Take my keys and open it, if you please."

As Lizbeth took the keys without a word, Ethan's admiration for her grew. Here she had just discovered the man who threatened her had tried to kill his friend. Furthermore, she was having to interact with her cousin and her husband, both of whom had treated her shamefully.

But instead of asking dozens of questions or breaking down into tears, she was calmly assisting them as if she were used to such things happening all the time.

"I'll help you carry him to the room, Major," Dallas said. "It's a private suite just down the hall here."

Ethan was hesitant to move Devin, but he figured it was the lesser of two evils. At least six or seven men were standing nearby, looking on. No doubt far more men and women were observing from more distant spots. This was no way to treat a war hero. "All right," he said at last. "I'll take his shoulders if you can take his middle."

"I'll help you carry him," another man said as he came forward.

Ethan eyed him closely and then nodded when he realized he recognized him from some of the better local gambling halls. The man was a former soldier and had always seemed competent enough. "Thank you."

The three of them bent down, surrounding Devin. As Ethan slipped his hands around Devin's upper torso, he gave a silent prayer of thanks that he was again unconscious.

"On my count of three," he barked, slipping into the tone he'd used in the army. It was forceful and allowed no discussion. "One. Two." He inhaled. Prayed they were doing the right thing. "Three," he said around an exhale.

And together, the three of them lifted Devin's form in unison. Devin wasn't a small man. Easily six feet and solid muscle. Ethan was glad the third man had offered to lend them assistance.

"We'll take him about ten feet, then turn down that hallway," Dallas said.

Ethan started walking backward. He was vaguely aware of another man motioning everyone who was gawking to get out of the way.

They turned and continued their slow pace. Blood from Devin's wound soaked Ethan's hand and dripped on the carpet. Each drop made him worry all the more. His friend was losing a great amount of blood. This was also too close to some of the worst battles he'd been involved in. He began to feel a little dizzy and lightheaded as the metallic, coppery scent of blood invaded his space and brought him suddenly too near memories he always tried very hard to forget.

"Not much farther, Major," Dallas said.

Ethan nodded. Hating the sudden weakness he felt, he forced himself to focus on the present and gazed down at Devin. His eyes were still closed, his mouth slack. His face deathly pale.

What was he going to do if they lost him?

"Here's the room," Dallas announced. "Lizbeth, is everything ready?"

"I believe so. I found Callie in the corridor. She's bringing hot water and clean linens to treat the wound."

"Good. That's good," Dallas said easily as he guided them toward the bed.

Just as they were about to set Devin's body down, Ethan noticed Lizbeth had placed an extra blanket over the coverlet.

Though it was awkward, the three men managed to lay Devin on the mattress with a minimum of jostling. Only when he was lying still but looking no worse did Ethan feel as though he could take a cleansing breath at last.

"Thank you," he told the gambler. "I'm sorry. I don't recall your name . . ."

"Harold Neidig," he said. "Formerly a sergeant out of Virginia."

The description, said with a small amount of pride, spurred a smile from Ethan. "I'm indebted to you, Mr. Neidig."

"Is that Captain Monroe, by any chance?"

"It is."

Mr. Neidig studied him closely. "I heard stories about him, but I never thought we'd meet."

"God willing, you will soon."

"I'll pray for his recovery," Mr. Neidig said, executing a small bow before exiting.

Right then a small maid carrying a wooden bucket of steaming water and a pile of linen against her chest entered the room. Lizbeth rushed to her side. Together, they emptied the water into a basin.

After the maid left, Dallas walked to the door. "I'll go see where the doctor is," he said. He closed the door again, giving them privacy.

Ethan found he was incapable of moving. "I'm afraid he's about to die," he said at last.

"I know you are, but we mustn't give up hope," Lizbeth said as she walked to the foot of the bed. "Let's take off his boots and make him comfortable."

Glad for something to do, he worked with Lizbeth to move Devin's leg enough to allow them to pull off the snug-fitting boots.

Devin groaned under his breath.

Amazingly, Lizbeth smiled. "See? We haven't lost him yet."

Her irreverent comment brought back his hope. Lizbeth was right. They hadn't lost him, and what's more, Ethan was going to do everything he could to make sure they didn't.

Determined to do something, anything, instead of allowing his fears and the memories of war to overtake him again, he pulled out a knife and carefully cut along the seam of Devin's tan duster, then his jacket.

When only a linen shirt covered Devin's skin, Ethan felt dizzy again. The fabric was soaked with blood. Some of it even looked like it was stuck to his flesh. He stared at the linen, unsure whether it was better to leave the fabric in place or clean the wound as quickly as possible. "We need that doctor," he said to Lizbeth. "Could you see what his status is?"

"Of course." But just as she was about to leave, Aileen peeked inside.

"Major Kelly, Dr. Palermo is on his way. He should be here very soon."

"Palermo, you say?"

Still hovering at the door, Aileen nodded. "Yes. He's Italian. Very knowledgeable."

"Thank you for coming to tell me yourself."

After Aileen exchanged a look with Lizbeth, she closed the door again.

Lizbeth walked to his side. "Major Kelly, all we can do is pray and wait."

Her words made sense, but he needed to do more than that. Devin's face was deathly pale. After feeling for his pulse again, he made the decision. He was going to pull off the last of the fabric and care for Devin until more help arrived. It's what he had done on the battlefield, and it was what he needed to do now.

After taking off his jacket, Ethan removed his gold cufflinks and rolled up his sleeves. "I need to bathe his wound. Get me some more warm water, soap, and more cloths."

"Of course." She turned and walked out the door without another word.

Glad to be alone with his thoughts, he took the cloth Lizbeth had placed by the basin and dampened it. Then he carefully removed what was left of Devin's shirt. As he had known it would, the wound started bleeding again.

Steeling himself, he pressed cloths to the wound, hoping his efforts would staunch the flow of blood. As he did, he also inspected the rest of Devin's torso, looking for any further damage he had inadvertently overlooked.

Devin's skin was as marked as his own. A product of the Rangers, then the cavalry, Devin looked as though he had survived as many close calls as any other veteran of the war. Funny how Ethan had never taken the time to think about Devin being a survivor like the rest of them. For some reason Ethan had always regarded Devin Monroe as impervious to cuts, bruises, bullet holes.

Stunned, he sat on the side of the bed. He'd seen Devin sleep, of course, but the captain never looked completely relaxed. His body had always had a certain tenseness about it, as though he were only moments from springing into action and taking charge of most anything.

Now he only looked vulnerable.

Ethan realized his hands were shaking. Not from fear for himself. No, it was from fear of failure. Fear that he wasn't going to be able to help Devin. That Devin could die in this room.

When the door swung open again, Lizbeth entered, along with another maid. He heard Lizbeth call the young woman Cassie. They were carrying a pitcher, a floral basin of steaming water, and several cloths. After the other maid set the basin on the dresser and left, Lizbeth spoke.

"I know you don't want or need my help, but could I stay in here with you?"

He was about to refuse, but he did need help. "I'm, uh, attempting to bathe him. But I can't seem to do that with this wound in such bad shape. I need to keep pressure on it."

"I can bathe him."

"Thank you, Lizbeth."

Without another word, she dampened another cloth, picked up one of Devin's arms, and carefully began cleaning his hand. His fingers were stained with blood. It was obvious he'd been applying pressure to his wound himself.

But instead of looking shaken by the blood and grime she was removing, Lizbeth seemed calm. He recalled that she hadn't flinched or launched into hysterics like the other women in the lobby had when Devin appeared. She'd been surprised and upset, of course, but seemed more intent on helping him than giving in to vapors.

"This wound doesn't seem to faze you," he said quietly. "Is it because you've seen bad wounds before?"

"I have."

"From the war?"

"Yes. But while growing up too." She moved to her left so she could clean the last of the blood from Devin's skin. "Growing up on a ranch, well, all sorts of accidents occur."

He was intrigued by the thought of Lizbeth working a ranch. Hoping to concentrate on anything other than the chance of failure, he murmured, "Any happen to you?"

"Yes. Once I knocked into the blade of a scythe that had been recently sharpened. Before I knew it, I had a sizable cut on my calf. My grandmother stitched me up."

"I bet your wound was painful."

She smiled faintly as she smoothed a fresh rag across Devin's brow. "Being stitched up hurt worse, I can tell you that. My grand-mother wasn't an especially gentle nurse."

"And your forehead? Did you get stitches then?"

"No." Her voice was tight and distrusting. He realized she was upset that he'd even brought it up.

He probably shouldn't have. She was helping him. The very least he owed her was to respect her privacy. But he couldn't bring himself to apologize. He needed to know about her, and what secrets she had.

"Do you remember how you got that scar?"

Her hand stilled. "Of course I do."

He waited, hoping she would expound upon it. When she didn't, he prodded again. "Was it, by chance, a ranch accident?"

"It was not."

Her voice, usually rather tentative, was as hard as the red dirt in the middle of summer. "What happened?"

"This scar isn't something I speak about."

He should have said he understood. After all, he didn't like talking about anything that happened in the war. Instead, he kept pushing. "Have you ever talked about it with anyone?"

"No."

"Perhaps it would help."

She turned to rinse out her cloth. "Help what? The scar has healed."

He swallowed, half feeling as if he was talking as much to

himself as he was to her. "I've heard that talking about painful topics makes them easier to bear." He wasn't lying. He had heard about that. But all the same, he felt like the worst sort of charlatan. He could barely handle the smell of blood now.

"Talking about this won't help."

He should leave it alone. Devin was bleeding, they were waiting on a doctor, her whole life had just been turned on its side, and they hardly knew each other.

But her voice had sounded so tight, so filled with pain, Ethan knew he had to say something. If nothing else, he owed it to her. After all, he'd seen that scar when it was fresh and he'd hurt her anyway. "I am used to hearing confidences," he said. "I wouldn't betray your trust."

"Sir—"

He talked right over her. "Holding something like that inside can be harmful to you." He drew in a breath. Stared at her pretty green eyes. Tried to make his words softer, more meaningful. "Take it from me."

"Whom did you speak to about your scars and injuries, Major?" she whispered softly. "And how did it help you heal?"

"I am surprised by your sarcasm."

"And I am surprised you think I am so naïve as to imagine that speaking to anyone about something that can't be changed would change anything for me."

He knew she was right. But she was wrong too. "I shared my pain and worries with my comrades at Johnson's Island. I complained about my wounds and injuries to the men I fought beside on the battlefields. I talked about my fears with the men on the cots next to me in the hospital tents."

"You aren't lying, are you?"

"I'm not lying."

Her voice lowered. "And when you shared your hurts with them, what happened?"

He knew this question was important. That it meant everything. Therefore, he struggled with how best to answer. Finally, he simply spoke from his heart. "I was free. Even there, in a prison barracks, behind enemy lines. Their acceptance freed me and made me almost whole."

She blinked. A hint of wonder lit her eyes before she firmly pushed it away.

But he had seen it.

And he knew then that she believed too.

18

HAD A MORNING EVER BEEN SO GLOOMY? JULIANNE STARED out on the horizon and searched for a glimpse of blue sky. But only dark clouds hung there. They seemed weighted by precipitation yet too stubborn to give up their precious water.

She could understand that. Part of her felt more than a passing kinship with those clouds. From the moment Devin had left the day before, she'd felt a heavy ache in her chest, convinced he would not return as promised. Experience had taught her a good cry could ease her pain and alleviate the pressure there. But she was so tired of crying. It didn't help, anyway. All her tears ever seemed to do was make her eyes red and her mouth parched. She was done crying over whatever she wished were different.

Instead, she realized bitterly, she seemed happy enough to stand out in the cold and look out into the distance. Wishing a certain man with light-blue eyes and blond hair would appear, already back from his visit to San Antonio and eager to see her again.

Folding her arms over her middle, she rested her head against one of the posts holding the porch railing. Sighed. And finally cautioned herself to stop making a spectacle of herself.

Just as she was ready to turn around, she caught sight of

a carriage. Holding a hand over her eyes, she peered into the distance. Her pulse began to race. Maybe Devin *had* come back early. Maybe he was bringing a carriage to take her on an outing today.

Then she realized it was Carl and Abby Bernard. Today's appearance was a blessing. She'd grown tired of her mournful thoughts. Their company would be a welcome change of pace. At the very least, she wouldn't be looking out into the horizon for hours on end.

When Carl parked their carriage, Julianne opened the front door and let her beagle, Ginger, outside. Ginger looked delighted by their visitors and scampered ahead, her soft ears flapping in the wind.

The moment Carl alighted, Julianne raised her hand. "Good day, Carl."

After a second's pause, he smiled broadly. "Indeed it is, Julianne. I trust you are well?"

The proper response would be to say she was, indeed, very well. But she was as tired of pretending as she was of her doldrums. "I've been better, if you want to know the truth."

He looked at her closely, then seemed to be waging a war with himself as he extended a hand to help his sister down from their carriage.

Julianne fought back a smile as Abby accepted her brother's gesture, but then practically jumped out of the conveyance as though she were on a newfangled pogo stick. Her brown hair was artfully arranged in a high chignon. It flattered her features. That, and her sparkling eyes, made her appear almost fairy-like. Julianne reflected once again that Abby's pastor fiancé had no doubt been charmed from the moment he spied her.

"Hello, Julianne! And Ginger too!"

Ginger barked while Julianne laughed. "Hello, Abby. Would you care for some tea or coffee? It's rather dreary out here."

"I would, indeed. I dressed in layers, but I still find myself chilled to the bone." She trotted up the steps and gave Julianne a hug.

Startled, Julianne wrapped her arms around the girl and tried not to think about how long it had been since she'd been the recipient of such a warm gesture. After Carl joined them, she led the way inside.

The fire was still burning in the parlor. "Please, do make yourselves comfortable. Bula is away today, but I'll return with tea—"

"Please, allow me to help you," Abby said, interrupting. "After all, we're more than mere guests by now."

Carl scratched his chin. "Well, now, I don't know if that is how one should behave . . ."

When Abby's cheeks flashed bright red, Julianne decided to save the conversation. "Of course you both are more than mere guests now. Abby is right. You are friends."

As they followed her to the kitchen, Carl said, "Is that why you were honest enough to share that something has been upsetting you?"

"Perhaps," she allowed. "Or I might have come to the conclusion that no good would come with me pretending otherwise."

"What happened?" Abby asked as they entered the small but well-appointed kitchen.

Though it was on the tip of her tongue to make up something inconsequential, Julianne decided to err on the side of honesty. "Captain Monroe came to visit me again. Yesterday, late in the afternoon."

"But that is good, yes?"

"It would have been, except it was rather, um, tumultuous."

She supposed that was one way to describe Daniel's visit and Devin's reaction.

"I'm sure you'll make things right again," Abby said. "I've had difficulties with Timothy before. But we've worked it out."

"This is a little different, I'm afraid. He, uh, was confronted with the consequences of my past. It wasn't pretty." She turned her back and fussed with the water pump, taking far more interest in priming it than necessary. Then there was his kiss and the way she'd responded to him.

"I am sorry to hear that," Carl said.

"Thank you. I am sorry about it too." After she filled the teakettle, she turned back to the siblings. "He did say he would return to take me out to dinner in a week, but I've been wondering if he really will. Thank you for listening. Speaking of it actually made me feel a bit lighter in spirit."

Abby nodded. "Speaking about problems does help." She pulled out one of the kitchen chairs and sat down. "Julianne, I guess you have two choices, then."

"And what are they?"

"You can wait and have faith he will return. Or you can go after him right now. Do you know where he's gone?"

Julianne laughed, sure Abby was making a joke. When she realized the girl wasn't, she felt more than a little tongue-tied. "Run after him in San Antonio? Just like that? That would be one way to finally dissolve the rest of my reputation."

"What does that matter if it means you will be happy?"

Abby was serious. "Well, I, um, I don't know. But that's beside the point."

"Why?"

"Well, I don't know if I can."

"Why couldn't you?" Carl asked. "The stage can take you there."

Was it their youthful enthusiasm that made them act as though anything was possible? Or was it more the fact that they had never been on the receiving end of rejection? When Ginger padded in, Julianne leaned down and petted the beagle. Then she got her a fresh bowl of water.

Anything to give herself some time.

"I'm afraid it isn't that easy. Besides, he told me he needed to visit a friend on personal business. Someone he knew in the war. I would never wish to interfere."

Both her visitors stared at her expectantly. It was obvious they wanted to hear more about what had transpired between her and Devin. But no matter how kind Carl and Abby were, Julianne wasn't about to share everything that happened. Instead, she kind of sighed, hoping they'd let the matter drop.

And they did. With a small smile, Abby walked over to the stove. "How about I help you with the tea tray?" Before Julianne could refuse the offer, the girl poured the hot water from the kettle into a teapot. After she added tea to steep, she opened a likely drawer and pulled out three teaspoons.

Julianne poured cream into a pitcher and set a few cookies she'd made yesterday on a china plate.

Moments later Carl carried the tray to the parlor. After she poured and they all sat down, he grinned. "We are quite the team now, aren't we?"

"I should say so." After she took a fortifying sip of hot tea, Julianne smiled too. "Why is it that something made by someone else always tastes better?"

"I couldn't say, but I will agree that it is true."

When she set down her cup, Abby clasped her hands primly on her lap. "Now that we've determined that for now, at least, you cannot follow the captain, we need to work on your belief in him."

"I'm afraid it isn't as simple as that."

"Of course it is," she said earnestly. "It's like faith, don't you see?"

"No, I don't."

"Remember the parable about Jesus and the mustard seed?" she said quietly. "How Jesus chastised his followers, saying one only needed the smallest amount of faith to believe?"

Feeling a little helpless, as though they were talking about two different things at the same time, Julianne sputtered, "Of course. But—"

"You need to have faith, Julianne."

"I do have faith in God."

"No, not just in God. You need to have faith in the captain too. Because they aren't two different things. The Lord wants you to have faith in him, and in how he is guiding your life. And I feel if you keep that faith, and you let Captain Monroe know how much you believe in him, in the two of you, well . . . everything will work out like it is supposed to."

Julianne frowned. This young girl, with her sprite-like mannerisms and perpetual optimism, made it sound so easy.

But it wasn't. Was it?

Or . . . maybe it was? Maybe that's what it took to understand how things worked, she realized. Life was hard. But love and faith? Perhaps they didn't need to be.

"I am beginning to believe your fiancé has found himself a perfect partner."

Eyes sparkling, Abby raised her chin. "Of course he did," she replied with a cheeky grin. "He asked for my hand in marriage, didn't he?"

Her brother grunted. "As you can see, the Lord has much to work on with my little sister. On her humility, for example. That's obvious."

"Not at all," Abby retorted. "I am well aware I have many flaws."

"And a lack of humility is a big one."

Julianne giggled. "I'm glad you two came over. You've done wonders for my mood."

Carl leaned forward, about to reply, when a noise outside caught his attention. Getting to his feet, he looked out the window. "Are you expecting more company?"

"No." Walking across the room, she looked out the window. Then felt her stomach drop. He'd come back. "Oh no," she whispered.

Abby joined them. "Do you know this gentleman?"

It took everything she had to keep from saying her visitor was most definitely not a gentleman. Instead, she merely nodded. "I know him."

"What is his purpose? Why is he simply standing on your walkway?"

"He knows he's not welcome inside."

Carl's expression hardened. "Has he been giving you trouble? Would you like me to ask him to leave?"

The very last thing she wanted was for these young people—so fresh, so innocent—to be tainted by Daniel Bushman. "I think it would be best if you stayed inside with Abby while I go outside to speak with him."

"Of course you cannot do that."

"He is rather unsavory." A knot filled her throat as she struggled with how to continue. How could she tell them this was the man for whom she'd been a mistress? And Devin had told her not to open the door to him, but she was afraid he'd create a scene—threaten Abby and Carl.

Looking out the window again, she felt Daniel's gaze right

into her heart. He was standing there, taunting her. And there was a new expression on his face. He looked triumphant.

But why?

What had he done?

Feeling as though she were about to enter a deep, dark hole, she rushed to the door.

"Julianne!" Abby called out. "What is wrong?"

Suddenly, she felt even more unkempt than she had before the pair arrived. Brushing back a strand of hair that had fallen onto her face, she realized she was going to have to confess all. "That man is Daniel Bushnell. I was his mistress during the war. He . . . he is everything you don't want to know, Abby."

"But I thought you were done with him," Abby protested.

"I thought I was too." She opened the door, stepped outside, and closed the door. All she could do was hope and pray neither of her guests decided to follow. She would really like to shield them. "Daniel," she said. "What do you want?"

A slow, knowing smile lit his face. "It seems pigs do fly. At last, you are speaking to me again."

"What are you doing here?"

He folded his hands across his chest. "I wanted to see your face when I told you your new protector will no longer come to your aid."

All the trepidation that had engulfed her fell away. And though everything inside her ached to simply turn her back on him and go back inside, she couldn't ignore his words. "Why not?"

All traces of amusement faded from his gaze as he stared at her. Hard. "Because I went after him, Julianne."

"After Devin?" She could hardly get the words out.

"Of course, Devin. I followed him out of town yesterday. Then I shot him."

She gasped.

"For what? For *calling* on me?"

"He threatened me with that false story about me giving away secrets during the war. But mostly because you are mine, Julianne. I wanted you when no one else did. I took care of you when no one else would. Did you really think I was going to stand aside and let a man like Devin Monroe have you? Touch you?"

She could barely hear his words. Could barely understand them. "Is he dead?"

"I shot him in the back. I doubt he made it another hundred yards before falling from his horse."

"So you don't know for sure? He could be suffering on the ground somewhere, all alone?"

Daniel narrowed his eyes. "That is extremely doubtful. You forget that I shot my fair share of men during the war. I know how to shoot to kill." While she gaped at him, he continued on, his voice gaining confidence with each word. "I don't know why you are concerned about him, anyway. He is of no consequence."

"If you killed Devin, you will rue the day."

"I'm sure I shall." He raised his eyebrows. "But perhaps the two of us will rue the days together, no? Because one day soon I'll be back. And since you'll have no one else . . . Well, I'm sure I'll have you again. It will be just like old times."

"Never," she countered as he turned and walked away.

"Of course I will. You're my property, after all," he said over his shoulder. "I bought and paid for you long ago." Then he mounted his horse and rode out.

Julianne felt frozen. She wrapped her arms around her middle again, trying in a futile attempt to keep herself together when all she really wanted to do was fall in a heap on the ground.

"You don't know he's dead. He could have made it to San

Antonio. You've got to find him," Abby said from behind her. "You need to get packed and let Carl help you get on the next stage."

Feeling as if she was still in a daze, Julianne turned. Abby was standing next to her brother. Close enough to have heard every ugly word Daniel had just uttered. The way they were both staring at her in concern confirmed that guess.

She hated that she'd tainted their innocence this way. "I am sorry you had—"

"Forgive me, but I think we're done with apologies, don't you?" Carl said crisply. "Now, please, stop arguing and do what we say. Listen to Abby. If this man you care for made it to his friend in San Antonio, he's going to need you as soon as possible. I mean, you aren't simply going to step inside and assume Captain Monroe didn't survive, are you? Or hope some old major was able to adequately help him?"

Eyes swimming with tears, Julianne bit her lip. Carl was right. So was Abby. She needed to stop waiting. Stop degrading herself. Stop worrying about her past. Stop being afraid Devin could have changed his mind about her.

"You're right, Carl." And with that, she walked through the front door, pulled a carpetbag from a hall closet, and walked to her bedroom. "I'll be out presently."

Abby called after her. "I'll stay here with Ginger until Bula returns and explain she'll need to take care of everything here. Carl can come back for me once you're on the stage. And I'll clean up the tea service too."

Julianne almost laughed. She'd completely forgotten about the tea.

All she did know was that Carl and Abby were right. She needed faith in the Lord and faith in Devin.

She also needed to embrace her reality. She cared for Devin Monroe, and she needed to get on the next stage to San Antonio.

There would be plenty of time to think about her future when she was sitting at Devin's side.

If she made it in time.

19

Johnson's Island, Ohio
Confederate States of America Officers' POW Camp

ETHAN COULD PRACTICALLY FEEL THOMAS BAKER'S INTENSE gaze. Stretching his legs out on his cot, Ethan tried to ignore the younger man's fixation on the letter he held in his hand. After all, this wasn't anything new. Thomas was alone in the world and had yet to receive a letter from a loved one. Consequently, he ate up everyone else's news from home like a starving man being given a Virginia ham.

But that didn't mean Ethan was always in favor of sharing his mail with him. Some news was meant to be private. Such as letters like this. Letters from Faye.

Wanting to draw out the anticipation of it, he ran a finger along Faye's perfect handwriting. One day she was going to be Mrs. Ethan Kelly. One day he wouldn't have to wait months and months to talk to her. He'd simply be able to roll over and pull her into his arms.

Thomas groaned. "You've been staring at that envelope for fifteen minutes, Ethan. When are you ever going to open it?"

Tearing his gaze from the letter, he glared over his shoulder at Thomas. "Whenever I feel like it. No offense, but it has my name on the envelope. Not yours."

A flash of pain appeared in Thomas's eyes before he spoke. "Yeah, all right. But at least answer me this. What are you waiting for?"

"I don't know."

"Oh."

Two cots over, Phillip Markham chuckled softly. "Guess he's in a selfish mood today, Baker. Want me to read you part of my letter from Miranda? They had a fierce storm in Galveston last month. She described it in detail."

"Thanks, but I'll pass, Lieutenant. While I'm sure Mrs. Markham's account is real exciting, we had our own storm here yesterday."

Phillip laughed. "You have a point there."

"I'll read you part of my letter, Baker," Devin said. "My cousin has a new baby."

"Thanks, Cap."

Behind him, Ethan could hear Thomas walk over to Devin's side. Seconds later, Devin was reading him a passage of his letter. It was obvious most of the men were listening too.

And that gave him the small amount of privacy he craved so badly.

Smoothing the envelope again, Ethan forced himself to wait another two minutes. Faye didn't write all that often. It was likely he wouldn't receive another letter from her for several weeks. He hated to rush it.

Which privately embarrassed him. Never would he have thought he'd be the type of man who put so much emphasis on a single letter.

Though it wasn't especially constructive, sometimes he couldn't help but reflect on where he'd been. He'd grown up a gentleman of privilege. His family had gained thousands of acres of land back when Texas was still a republic. His ancestors had nurtured their investment and tripled their wealth.

Consequently, before Texas entered the War of Northern Aggression, he'd lived a rather narrow and spoiled life. He'd had more servants than he could count to see to his every need. He'd been surrounded by beauty and comfort and had eaten well. His family, both his parents and his two siblings, had been affectionate and agreeable. Even his time at West Point had been successful. He'd distinguished himself by having an affinity for strategy. He'd also been able to get along with most everyone and been popular with both the instructors and his fellow plebes. For the most part, he'd lived a charmed life.

Then he entered the war. He'd fought with honor. He'd fought with valor. He discovered he was capable of not only guiding troops but devising strategies for battle. Truly, he'd felt at home being an officer.

But then, while on a scouting mission, he, Monroe, Truax, and Markham had been taken prisoner and put on a train north. Now he was living in circumstances that were unfamiliar and difficult. He was doing menial tasks, and growing hungry, and seeing good men die all around him.

All of this was hard.

But the worst was that he was no longer ever alone. Ever. He was sure it was a fact that man needed time and space. It was a necessity.

Feeling he'd waited long enough, he carefully opened the letter's seal and pulled out Faye's letter. He frowned when he realized it was only one page in length.

And only written on one side of the paper.

Dread filled his insides as he smoothed the fine stationery and began to read.

Dear Ethan,

As much as it pains me to tell you this, I fear I can no longer put it off. You see, I got married two weeks ago.

Ethan blinked, sure he had read Faye's words wrong. Hands now shaking, he turned the paper over and opened up the envelope, looking for another sheet of paper. Maybe he'd missed something?

There was nothing.

He turned back to the letter.

I am sure you understand how hard life have been for me here, what with you being taken prisoner and all. People have told me stories about the atrocities that happen in those camps. Thinking about you in such a situation has been hard for me.

He didn't. He didn't understand at all.

But maybe the opposite was true?

Maybe he understood too much. Faye was certain he was either being tortured or starved—if he was not already dead. She had decided he wasn't worth her loyalty or love. He'd become a burden she didn't want to shoulder.

It took every ounce of willpower to read the remainder of the letter.

I recently met a very nice lieutenant who was discharged because of an injured leg. Luckily, he healed well and won't even carry a limp. I didn't expect him to ask for my hand so quickly, but he claimed he could not wait to make me his.

If you do get this letter, I hope you will understand my decision. Please know, too, that I'll keep you in my prayers, just like I pray for all our brave men.

Mrs. James Chubb

She'd married another. A Lieutenant James Chubb, who was whole and present while he was not. Who was eager to place her in his marriage bed and willing to ensure Faye would not be shackled to an imprisoned soldier with an uncertain future.

Well, he guessed he now knew what Faye had wanted. He blinked, realizing tears had filled his eyes. It seemed rejection was as painful for him as anyone else.

Unable to stare at her words any longer, Ethan crumpled the thin sheet of paper in his hand, then tossed it on the floor beside his cot.

His movements didn't go unnoticed.

"Major, are you all right?" Thomas asked. He'd come to stand by his side. "Is something wrong at home? Was that from your mother?"

His mother wrote long, involved letters about nothing. Nothing besides her shopping, her gardening, and what minor inconveniences she'd been forced to endure because of the war. For some reason, Thomas found her letters to be his favorites.

"No. It was from Faye."

Gesturing at the wad of paper, Thomas cleared his throat. "I'm guessing she didn't send you any good news."

"She did not."

"Do . . . do you want to talk about it?"

"Baker, you would try the patience of a saint."

Thomas stepped away. "Sorry, Major."

"Don't be so hard on him, Ethan," Markham called out. "You know Thomas meant no harm. He was just asking what the rest of us were wondering. Besides, we've been stuck inside these bare walls for three days now. You can't blame a man for being curious about the contents of a letter you just crumpled in a ball and tossed on the floor. What did she say?"

He wanted to ignore them all. To tell Thomas his pain wasn't any of his business. To tell Phillip Markham Faye's letter was too personal to share. But Markham received regular missives from his beauty of a wife and read aloud much of what she'd said . . . all except the really private parts, where she supposedly professed her love in nauseatingly glowing ways.

Feeling as though he had no choice, he bent down, smoothed out the paper, and read aloud Faye's letter from start to finish.

Feeling helpless, he glanced at the other men.

As a whole they were motionless. Some of the men were staring at him. Others had their heads bent down, as though they were afraid to meet his eye. The barracks were completely silent. Only the sound of sleet hitting the walls and roof and sliding through the chinks in the mud cement could be heard.

The silence was so desperate, so out of sorts, that Ethan realized he had not misunderstood anything. Faye had found someone else and didn't even sound terribly regretful about breaking his heart.

He tossed the letter on the floor again. "So that is what was inside, gentlemen. A not-too-gentle dismissal of my love and my future, all wrapped in a dozen sentences."

"It's good you're rid of her," Thomas said. "I've known a lot of women and men who take what they can and when they can. They're a smarmy lot. She would have made you miserable in the long run."

"Would she? I'm not so sure about that."

As Thomas retreated to his cot, Ethan hung his head. He hated these barracks. Hated this situation. Why had the Lord placed him here? Why could he not even have a few minutes of privacy when his heart was breaking?

Needing to get out of the room before he broke down or broke something, he stood up. "I can't sit in here any longer. I'm going to take a walk."

"You think that's wise in this sleet?" Phillip asked.

"Does it really matter? I've already been assumed dead or worthless. I've already been tossed over for a Lieutenant Chubb. He's whole, you see. And hasn't had to live through the vulgarity of a prison camp." After throwing on his tattered jacket, he grabbed a blanket, threw it over his shoulders, and headed out into the elements.

When the freezing sleet brushed against his face, stinging his skin, he welcomed the pain. And when he got back inside, no one would realize he'd been crying.

Then, to his surprise, the door to the barracks opened again. Out came four of his friends, wrapped in blankets like he was.

"Couldn't let you have all the fun," Devin Monroe said. "Besides, after everything we've been through? Well, we figured a little bit of sleet and ice wasn't going to hurt us none."

"We're made of tougher skin than that," Markham added.

When Thomas started whistling and walking ahead, Ethan, Truax, and the other two men followed. And that was when he knew Markham hadn't been exaggerating. They were war hardened and mentally and physically tough. A little bit of bad weather wasn't going to faze them. It seemed only letters like Faye's could.

Receiving a letter like that? It cut like a knife.

20

SHE'D LIVED WITHIN A THREE HOURS' RIDE TO SAN Antonio all her life, yet Julianne had never ventured close to it except that one time when she'd met Bushnell at the officers' ball.

When she was younger, there had been no reason. Like children so often do, she'd been comfortable in her surroundings. She'd mistakenly assumed everything she saw and experienced was all there was in the world.

Then as a young woman, she realized there was far more to see than what was in Boerne, Texas. But she had been afraid to leave the security of home. She'd become aware that she'd been blessed with good looks but little money and no prestige.

And that, she'd come to realize, was a dire recipe for a successful match. She'd been afraid to go to any of the large assemblies in her town, fearful that her grand dreams of fitting in and being courted would be easily put to shame.

Then, when the war had come? Well, she'd ventured all the way to San Antonio—and circumstances had conspired against her.

When Devin Monroe approached her at the mercantile, Julianne dared to wonder if he was the answer to years of hopes and prayers. During the war she'd seen her world grow dim, and what she'd thought to be true had been turned on its ear. She'd lost hope in both herself and that anything could be different.

But from that first conversation, Devin had brought a good amount of light into her world. And by the time he told her he wanted to marry her someday? Well, her life had changed again. He'd restored her belief in humanity and the future.

But that didn't mean she had been willing to do anything but wait for him to make the next move, to come back as he promised. As hard as it was, she'd been willing herself to sit home and dream and wait. To hope.

The truth was, until Abby and Carl had encouraged her that morning, a part of her had been resigned to being alone for the rest of her life. It was too hard to believe a man like Devin Monroe would want to risk everything by taking her for his wife one day.

Until Daniel told her what he'd done.

Then everything in her world changed again. The moment she learned Devin had been shot, and wanted to believe he was still alive, she knew it was time to do whatever was necessary to be by his side. She owed it to them both to be stronger than she was. That was what love was, she guessed.

With Carl's help, she'd purchased a ticket for the stage to San Antonio. And now it had deposited her at the entrance to the Menger. She'd hardly had time to gaze at the sprawling brick building before she was greeted by two bellmen. In no time at all, they'd taken her small carpetbag in hand and were escorting her inside.

They were treating her with respect. Like a lady. As though she were a woman of means. Like she used to dream she would one day be treated. But that wasn't important to her now. Learning of Devin's fate was.

"Did you have a good trip, miss?" the youngest bellman asked, his expression filled with appreciation as he helped her walk up a small flight of stairs.

She forced herself to smile as she hurried. "Yes, I did. It was uneventful, which is always good, I think."

He smiled. "My ma says the same thing." Blushing slightly, he tipped his hat and nodded toward the reception desk. "Well, here you go. Mr. Howard, the manager, will get you set up in your room."

"Thank you for your help." Despite her urgent quest, she remembered she should give him something for his efforts. She pulled out a bit and pressed it into his palm. He blushed again before turning away.

"May I help you?" Mr. Howard was a rather haughty-looking man.

"Yes. I believe Captain Devin Monroe is here. I just learned he was injured while on his way here. I believe he would have come to one of your guests—a Major Kelly."

"And you are . . . ?"

"I am Miss Julianne Van Fleet, a friend. Please answer my question. I must know."

Howard looked reluctant, but he answered. "You are correct. Captain Monroe is here, with Major Kelly in charge of his care."

She lowered her head for a moment in relief before gathering herself again. "Thank you, sir." She was eager to go straight to Devin's side, but she knew she needed to wash off the worst of her travel dust. "Now, may I please have a room."

He lifted his chin and looked just beyond her, as if he was looking for someone important. When he directed his stare back at her, his voice was even cooler. "Do you have an escort?"

"Pardon me?"

"A chaperone?" he added with obvious impatience. "We only accept ladies here."

"I arrived on my own."

"If you are traveling by yourself, it would be best if you moved to a different hotel. This is the Menger, you see. We have a reputation to uphold."

They had a reputation to uphold? Well, so did she! And she wasn't leaving Devin.

Staring at the supercilious man, Julianne realized she'd had enough. She had had enough of men telling her what to do and where to go. She'd just survived several hours in a cramped and hot stagecoach next to a pair of men who had obviously not bathed in weeks and a pair of elderly women who insisted on talking about nothing the entire journey. Her head hurt, her body ached, and she was afraid for Devin Monroe.

She needed to see him, and as soon as possible.

She drew herself up to her full height and dared to look at the manager in the eye. "It would suit me best if you gave me a guest room, helped me with my baggage, and then directed me to where Captain Monroe is recuperating."

When the man gaped at her, she raised her voice. "Perhaps I need to speak more clearly. I demand that I be taken care of immediately."

His eyes darted behind her, glancing around the lobby warily. She, too, was aware their discussion was being overheard, and no doubt gossiped about.

Though she wished it wasn't the case, she had no choice in the matter. She had lived for years with a tainted reputation. She wished the same thing wasn't happening here, but Julianne knew she could handle it.

Keeping her voice firm, she held out a hand. "Mr. Howard? My room key, if you please?"

Looking resigned, he drew out his guest book, spoke to the gentleman behind the counter, and pulled out a key. "Here is your key, miss."

"Thank you. And now may I please have Captain Monroe's room number?"

"We don't announce guests' room numbers. When you are ready, Jim here will escort you," he said with pure ice in his tone. "He will assist you with your bag as well."

She was so relieved—not only because the man had acquiesced but at the confirmation that Devin was alive—she felt like crying. Holding on to the last of her composure, she turned to Jim, who was of African descent, and was also standing as tall and strong as a redwood. "Thank you, Jim. If you could accompany me now, I would be appreciative."

He nodded. "Miss," his deep voice lumbered.

Aware of the many curious glances, she followed Jim, taking care not to look either left or right.

"Your room is on the second floor, miss."

She climbed the stairs, her feet feeling like lead as she maneuvered her skirts. Then they walked silently down a long hallway. Both the hallway and the doors were painted a cream color. Brass gas fixtures cast a faint glow on the carpet and walls, making the hallway seem warmer and more inviting than her greeting in the hotel's lobby.

When they stopped at her door, Jim unlocked it for her, opened it wide, and then stood to the side. "I'll wait here for you, miss."

Eager to see Devin, she nodded. "I'll be back out in no time, Jim."

He shrugged. "Don't make no difference to me, miss. Take your time."

Smiling softly, she said, "All the same, I won't be long."

When she closed the door, she exhaled. She had done it. She had poked and prodded her way into San Antonio, and into the

Menger Hotel. Now all she had to do was hope and pray Devin would be pleased that she had come.

If he wasn't? Well, it wouldn't be the worst thing that had ever happened to her. Not by a longshot. She was a survivor, and no matter what happened, she would survive again.

Julianne felt all her bravado fade twenty minutes later when she was following Jim again. It didn't seem to matter that she'd donned a rust-colored taffeta gown with jet buttons and an attractive curve to the bodice and sleeves.

She might look her best, but she knew even when armed with a whalebone corset and a well-fitting garment, nerves could get the best of her.

Without a word, Jim escorted her back down the stairs, down yet another glowing hallway, then eventually to a large, ornately carved oak door.

"Where are we?"

"This here is where we put guests who don't want to be found, miss."

"And that is where Captain Monroe is?"

Jim shrugged again. "Seems that way."

"Is he a frequent visitor here, then?"

He looked down at her, his expression carefully blank. "Don't believe so, miss. To my knowledge, this is his first visit—at least as a guest."

"I'm told Major Kelly is with him. Is that correct?"

Jim didn't look as though he wanted to answer. After a small pause, he nodded. "Yes'm. I heard the major was watching out for him right now."

Realizing just how little she knew about Devin, she swallowed. "It's good to know he has a friend here."

Jim looked as though he was tempted to say something about that, but merely nodded. "Yes, miss."

He guided Julianne into a far dimmer hallway, then stopped at a closed door just off to their right. "This is it," he said, then turned before she could thank him for his assistance.

Seconds later, she was alone in the hallway and staring at the door. She hesitated, listening for voices on the other side. She heard nothing. But it was time. Drumming up her courage, she twice rapped her knuckles on the plain, nondescript door.

It swung open abruptly.

To her surprise, a tall, lean man filled the threshold instead of the older man she'd been expecting. Leaving her to face an attractive man about Devin's age with brown eyes, light-brown hair, and a forceful presence. "Yes?" He spoke in a low voice, and she followed suit.

"Are you Major Kelly?"

"I am Ethan Kelly, yes."

Feeling more assured, Julianne looked him in the eye. "My name is Julianne Van Fleet. I have come to see Devin Monroe. I believe he is in here?"

The man's expression hardened. "How did you know he was here in this room?"

"From Mr. Howard."

His eyes narrowed. "Howard simply came out and told you?"

"Well, I had to do a bit of persuading. And to be fair, he never did tell me the location or the room number. Instead, he had Jim escort me here."

"Jim."

"Yes. He's, um, he's a servant here, I believe. He walked me to my room, then here. He was very nice."

"Miss, perhaps I should rephrase my question. How did you know Captain Monroe was in residence at the Menger?"

"Someone told me he'd been hurt, and I knew he'd been on his way to see you." Feeling his intense gaze practically sear her insides, she swallowed.

"Who told you?"

Though she knew he deserved an answer because he was only trying to help Devin, Julianne didn't want to admit to learning about Devin's injury from the man who'd shot him.

Remembering that speaking forcefully had gotten her a room key, she adopted the same tone again. "Sir, may I please enter now? I've traveled some distance to get here, you see."

But still, he didn't budge. "Beg your pardon, but your needs do not interest me in the slightest."

His words were a shock. On the outside, he looked just as gallant as Devin appeared to be capable and forthright. At first glance, one might even assume they were polar opposites. But now she saw the similarities. They were both hard on the inside.

This man, this Major Kelly, seemed just as solid and steady in his views and viewpoints as Captain Monroe was. He did not waver. Ironically, instead of causing her worry, it made Julianne feel more secure in his company. She could handle anyone who was honest. It was the liars and the charlatans that gave her pause.

"Perhaps I should have given you more information when I introduced myself," she said slowly. "I know Captain Monroe is here because he told me he was coming to you. And I know he suffered a bullet wound on his way. And I know this because I also know the man who shot him."

"And how do you know that man?"

"Because I used to be Daniel Bushnell's mistress. When I scorned his latest attempts at my home yesterday, Devin was there. He threatened him, and he shot Devin in retaliation."

Something flickered in the major's expression. Because of the dim lighting, Julianne wasn't exactly sure what it was. Disapproval? Shock? A vague sense of humor about how small and insular their world had become?

Whatever the reason, he seemed to have at last come to a decision. And with that, he opened the door wider, stepped backward, and bowed. "After you, Miss Van Fleet."

Putting her extensive experience of looking composed to good use yet again, she walked through the doorway.

Then she saw Devin Monroe lying in bed, his chest and shoulder bandaged, his skin a deathly white.

She was going to lose him. Before she'd ever had Devin, she was going to lose him.

And the knowledge was so dark, so tinged with despair, Julianne burst into tears.

Uncaring of her lovely dress, uncaring of her audience, she went to the bed and sank to the floor by his side. Clasping Devin's hand, she pressed his knuckles to her lips and cried.

21

EVEN IF THE OPEN DOORWAY HADN'T BROUGHT A CHILL
into the room, Lizbeth was certain Ethan's frosty demeanor
would have. From her position, where she sat on a small wooden
chair next to Captain Monroe, it seemed as if Ethan had brought
in a cold wave of anger.

That was surprising. What was more surprising, however,
was the anger and irritation that had emanated from him as
he let one of the most beautiful women she'd ever seen into the
suite.

Concern mixed with a thick dose of jealousy hit her hard as
she watched him close the door behind the woman. Where had
she come from? And why had he let her into this sanctuary?

But although she had many unanswered questions about
Ethan, she couldn't help but stare at the woman. After all, how
could she not? It was dark in the room. Lizbeth thought for a
moment that it should have made the woman's hair look faded or
even dark. Instead, the rich auburn color fairly burned brightly.
As did her blue eyes. Her striking looks, combined with the rustle
of her well-made gown, made Lizbeth feel much like the country
mouse in the big, bright city.

Lizbeth wondered if the woman even realized she was in the

room. Because the moment she walked near the bed, she stilled. Her hand lifted. Pressed against her mouth.

And then, without warning, she sank to the floor and burst into tears.

Stunned, Lizbeth jumped to her feet and crossed the room. Eager to help, she glanced at Ethan to see if he wanted to give her direction.

He appeared just as taken aback as she was. Actually, he looked rather frozen in place, as if he had no idea how to deal with this. Then something clicked and he stepped closer. Bending at the waist, he reached for the woman's arm. "Miss, allow me to help you to a chair."

But the woman didn't acknowledge him.

Lizbeth didn't think she heard Ethan. After a small sigh, she pressed her lips to the captain's hand again. "I'm so sorry, Devin. So very sorry."

Her devastation and obvious love for Ethan's friend was both beautiful and heartbreaking. Lizbeth felt herself choke up.

After several more minutes, the woman whispered something in his ear. Then, with softly murmured thanks, she accepted Ethan's help and rose to her feet, looking bereft and alone, staring down at Captain Monroe with such longing in her eyes that Lizbeth felt like an intruder.

Ethan must have felt the same way, because he stood motionless as well. When he darted a look in her direction, Lizbeth knew she had to ease the situation. It seemed all her experience with tears was going to come in handy.

"Miss?" she asked.

Obviously startled, the woman turned to her. "Oh! Hello. I do beg your pardon," she said in a voice as smooth as fine cream. "I'm afraid I didn't realize you were here."

Lizbeth certainly didn't care about that. "Miss . . . uh, would you care for anything?"

"It's Van Fleet," the woman supplied.

She smiled at her. "Miss Van Fleet? Please, do sit down."

"Thank you." With a wan smile, she took the chair Ethan had provided for her. "Please forgive my behavior. It's just that it is difficult to see him in this state. Every other time I've seen him, I felt as if he was invincible." Her gloved hand shook. "I know it makes little sense, of course. I mean, I know he suffered injuries. I just . . . well . . ."

"Seeing the reality can be far more difficult."

"Yes." Looking frustrated with herself, Miss Van Fleet carefully unfastened the small buttons at the base of one glove, then pulled it off. After looking about her person in confusion, she simply swiped at her tears with two slim fingers.

"Miss Van Fleet, allow me," Ethan said as he handed her a white handkerchief.

"Thank you." Though she still kept her eyes on the captain, she murmured to Lizbeth, "My name is Julianne. Miss, are you another friend of his?"

Lizbeth caught the curious tone, laced with, perhaps, a touch of jealousy. "No, I'm afraid not. I've never met him. I used to be a maid here."

"This is Miss Elizabeth Barclay. She is a friend of mine," Ethan said, directing a warm look her way.

His warm reassurance made her heart lift. Maybe she and the major actually were on the road to a real relationship. "Please, call me Lizbeth."

"I am pleased to make your acquaintance. Lizbeth, Major Kelly, what is the prognosis?"

Ethan answered. "Devin was shot in his upper back, almost

at his shoulder. Miraculously, the bullet didn't hit his lungs or heart, but he did lose quite a bit of blood. The physician cleaned his wound and sewed it up as best he could. Now we can only sit and wait, I'm afraid."

Miss Van Fleet's bottom lip trembled. "Does he have a fever?"

Lizbeth shook her head. "Not yet. He's been either unconscious or asleep almost the whole time since he arrived."

"I see. Well, I came to help. How may I assist you?"

Lizbeth looked at the beautiful gown. Her polished demeanor. "Perhaps you could simply sit here with him?"

Miss Van Fleet looked at the cloths and the pitchers of water. And maybe she noticed how rumpled Lizbeth looked as well. "I put on my best gown, Lizbeth, but that doesn't mean I am a stranger to hard work. I am happy to attend to Devin as best I can."

The woman's matter-of-fact tone was a welcome relief. Maybe she could help her and Ethan after all. "Perhaps we could help each other how each one sees fit?"

"Thank you," she said hesitantly. "I'd like that."

To her surprise, Ethan came to her side and curved his hand possessively around her elbow. "Lizbeth, now that we have some help, why don't you take a break and rest?"

"I got some sleep last night."

"You slept on the chair. Go back to Mrs. Harrison's for a while. Get something to eat. I'll stay here with Devin and Miss Van Fleet."

The twinge of jealousy she'd been fighting grew. Lizbeth hated that she was thinking about herself when she should be thinking only about the captain's health, but she wasn't sure how to push it aside. "I really don't mind staying. Besides, Miss Van Fleet only just arrived."

"I rode in on the stage today to help Devin," she said. "I don't want to be anywhere else."

It seemed she had no choice. "All right, then." When she started toward the door, Ethan stopped her.

"Not so fast," he murmured, cupping his hands around her shoulders. "Promise me you'll get some rest. And that you'll think about my offer some more."

His offer? To her surprise, she'd forgotten all about his proposal of marriage! Feeling far lighter of spirit, she felt much of her jealousy drift away. In its place was something new and warm and comforting. "I'll do some thinking, but I don't believe my answer will change."

He leaned closer. "Then I guess I'll have to find a way to change your mind, won't I?"

She gasped. His words, his touch, the feel of his breath on her neck, it was suddenly all too much to take in. After clumsily saying her good-byes, she darted out of the room.

Ethan's words rang in her ears as Lizbeth walked to the lobby. Looking around the space, she scanned the few coat hooks near the main entrance. She'd somehow lost her cloak in all the commotion surrounding Captain Monroe's arrival.

Not immediately spying it, Lizbeth decided to walk the perimeter. Her cloak had to be somewhere out in the open. She didn't mind the search. It gave her a few precious moments to reflect on what had just happened . . . and the way Ethan had spoken to her. For the first time in her life, she wished she had more experience with men.

She didn't understand his repartee or his statements laced with hidden meanings. He made her feel uneasy and at a disadvantage. That conversation, together with the captain's injury and

Miss Van Fleet's arrival, had been a lot to take in. Aching for the quiet of her room, she increased her pace. With luck, she could be back at Mrs. Harrison's house in fifteen minutes. Then she'd be able to review everything that had occurred in her mind, pray for guidance, and try to make some sense of it all.

Finally, in a darker corner of the lobby, Lizbeth found her cloak tossed over the arm of a rather uncomfortable horsehair chair. Relieved to have located it at last, she quickly fastened it, then headed toward the front door. Lost in thought, she almost walked right past her cousin. But because she didn't, Lizbeth forced herself to stop and say hello.

Aileen looked just as surprised to see her. "You're still here?"

"I never left. I've been in the back rooms with Major Kelly and . . . his injured friend." She thought Ethan would rather she not mention his name, although she had a feeling Aileen knew it anyway.

"Oh. Well, where are you living now?"

"I'm at Mrs. Harrison's down the street."

"She allowed you to live there?"

"Why are you surprised, Aileen? Did you want me to be homeless?"

"No. Of course not." Her expression turned pained. "May I talk with you?"

"Are you sure your reputation will survive?"

She flushed. "I know I deserved that. I promise, this won't take long."

Lizbeth nodded. Talking with Aileen about her reputation was the last thing she wanted to do. But Lizbeth also had a feeling her cousin was being sincere.

"Thank you. We can walk outside. Let me go tell Dallas where I'm going and I'll get my cloak."

Lizbeth nodded and then tried not to feel conspicuous as she waited by the entrance for her cousin to return. Several workers looked at her curiously, but didn't say a word. It was obvious they were being observed by Dallas Howard.

Luckily, Aileen appeared mere minutes later. "Thank you for waiting," she said, glancing at her husband before they went out the door.

"What did you want to say?" Lizbeth asked once they were outside.

"That . . . well, that I am sorry about how things have been going between us."

As far as apologies went, Lizbeth figured this was one of the worst. "You are sorry for the way things have been going?" she sputtered. "You sided with that . . . *that man* instead of me. You said my reputation interfered with the hotel's and you asked me to leave. Dallas barely gave me my full payment. That is how things have been going between us."

"All of that is true. I really am sorry."

"You know, what I don't understand is how you could treat a member of your family like that."

"I guess a part of me always resented you." She closed her eyes. "It wasn't until you left last week that I realized just how badly I've behaved."

Lizbeth couldn't let her off that easily. "You have tried your hardest to make me pay for things that were never my fault, Aileen. I never wanted my mother to treat you badly. I never wanted the two of us to be in competition with each other."

"I realize that now."

"I wish you would have realized that before. You know it was hard to ask you for a job, but I did. And you know what I went through too—alone in that house during the war."

"Again, everything you have said is true. I don't have an excuse, other than I was so eager to start over. I was eager to push away everything from my past . . ." Her voice drifted off. "I guess that doesn't make sense, but in time, maybe you will one day be able to forgive me."

Aileen's statement struck a chord. Lizbeth actually did know how it felt to want to start over. To push away the past and pretend it never occurred. "You don't need to wait for one day, Aileen," she said quietly. "I forgive you now."

"I appreciate that. Thank you. What are you going to do now? I mean . . . do you want me to talk to Dallas about getting your job back?"

If there was a silver lining in all that had happened, it was that Aileen's harsh treatment had pushed Lizbeth out of her self-inflicted prison. No matter what God had in her future, she was certain she couldn't go back to the way things had been. "I don't know what my future holds," she said lightly. "I was thinking maybe I would move."

"Really? What about the major? You two seem close."

Lizbeth almost smiled. They had seemed to be getting close. So close he'd even proposed to her the day before! "We are becoming friends," she said.

"Maybe there will be something there, then."

"I don't know what will happen. Only God does." Suddenly feeling exhausted, she stifled a yawn. "Aileen, I'm sorry, but I must go. I fear I must get some rest."

"Yes. Of course. Take care of yourself, cousin. I mean that sincerely."

"And you too, Aileen," she said, surprising herself.

When she finally got to her room at Harrison House and lay down on her bed, Lizbeth's mind spun. She wasn't sure what was going on, but it had been an exceptionally tumultuous couple of days.

She could only hope the rest of this day was far quieter. She rather doubted that would be the case, however. After all, it was only a little after two.

22

Feel free to get some rest, Major," Miss Van Fleet said after the two of them had been sitting in silence for the last half hour. "If you would let me know how to send word to you, I promise to notify you the moment Devin's condition changes."

With a start, Ethan realized he'd been standing against the wall, lost in thought. He'd also been staring at her. That had been rather rude. Abruptly, he sat down in the chair next to the small writing desk. "Thank you, but I will stay here as well."

"There's really no need for you to do that."

"Actually, I think there's every need."

She turned to face him. "Are you staying because you don't trust me? I promise I won't leave his side."

It was true, he didn't trust her. But it was more than that. "Devin Monroe is one of my closest friends on this earth. I have no wish to be anywhere else."

Her expression softened. "I understand." Then, with a rustle of taffeta, she turned back to Devin.

He watched as she leaned closer to him. Pressed her hand to his cheek and forehead, obviously checking for fever. He hadn't thought to do that. Feeling awkward, he got to his feet again. "How does he seem? Is he running a fever?"

"There's no change. Not that I can discern, at least." She sighed. "He does seem to be sleeping peacefully. That's something, at least."

"I agree. Rest is what he needs." He started to bring up his experience when recovering from a gunshot wound, but stopped himself in time. Stories about war wounds were not acceptable conversational topics. The timing couldn't be worse either. After all, what could he say? That he'd felt blessed not to have died like the other men in the surgical tent had?

Her attention still focused on Devin, Miss Van Fleet nodded. He wondered if she had even heard what he said.

Though he knew he should probably sit back down again, he resumed his position against the wall. He watched her watch Devin.

Each minute passed more slowly than the next.

Miss Van Fleet was right. There was no reason for them both to keep vigil. But he could no more leave than heal Devin. Only God and time could heal his friend.

Bored, and feeling a bit at loose ends, he studied Miss Van Fleet. *Julianne.* Maybe it was her auburn hair, maybe it was the curve of her jaw and neck, but he found himself gazing at her in appreciation—much like one might stare at a painting or a particularly beautiful flower.

She was striking. He could see how she would have caught Devin's attention.

"You are very beautiful," he murmured.

Obviously startled, she turned her head, capturing him with her blue eyes. They looked wary, as if she didn't know how to respond.

He didn't blame her; his comment had been too blunt. Maybe too honest.

"Thank you," she said after another moment. After his nod, she turned away and went back to holding Devin's hand.

Ethan folded his arms across his chest and continued his bold perusal. In all the time he'd known Devin, the man had never displayed more than a passing interest in any female. How had this one come to mean so much to his friend so quickly?

"Is that what caught Devin's attention?" he blurted. "Your beauty?"

"I couldn't say. You'll have to ask him when he wakes up."

Her modest answer was everything proper. He appreciated that. But he couldn't help but wonder if his old friend—who was so capable and forthright among men but inexperienced with women—might have been taken advantage of by this beautiful woman. He'd watched his sister and mother use their looks to their advantage any number of times. "I guess you are accustomed to using your looks to get what you want."

She turned to face him again. "Not necessarily," she said, her voice noticeably cooler.

And why wouldn't it be? He was jabbing and prodding at her like a child might bother a stray animal. Practically goading her to retaliate.

This wasn't like him. Far from it! But part of him was glad he was goading her. If she broke her composure and admitted to manipulating Devin, he could have a reason to make her leave.

Then he would finally be able to do something of worth. To take care of something, even if it was to get this woman who was so unsuitable for his friend out of his life.

Returning his attention to her reply, he pushed some more. "No? Not many women can say they survived the war as well as you did."

"I imagine that is true." Her chin lifted.

That chin lift told him much. He wondered, if the room hadn't been so dark, would he have been able to see more of a reaction than she was showing now? Would he have spied pain in her eyes? Regret?

"Is that how Bushnell acquired you?"

She visibly flinched. It brought him the reaction he'd been searching for . . . and made him feel ashamed. "I beg your pardon, Miss Van Fleet. That was beyond the pale." His mother would have been ashamed too. Oh, who was he kidding? Lizbeth would be upset with him too.

To his surprise, she stood up and walked toward him. "Oh, no, Major Kelly. Let us not start begging each other's forgiveness, especially since we both know you don't regret your words."

Her words stung . . . and brought his worst thoughts back. "All right, then, perhaps you could tell me how you became the paramour of such a miserable man."

She cocked her head, stepping closer. The faint scent of rose, laced with an undertone of spice, wafted toward him. He hated that he noticed it.

"I don't owe you an explanation, sir. But if it will help you understand that I am not about to hurt Devin, I'll attempt to explain myself." She sighed. "By the time the war had been going on eight months, my grandmother and I were starving."

His mouth went dry. "Starving."

"Although my father maintained a nice enough home for us in Boerne, my family was by no means well off before the war began. Then, as you might imagine, after Texas joined the Confederacy and the fighting continued for months and months, our situation grew worse." After a pause, she continued, her voice thick with emotion. "My father had been killed, my mother left to live with my sister elsewhere—and sent no funds to help us—and my grandmother was ailing. I didn't know what to do. When I heard about an officer's cotillion in San Antonio, I decided to go. Women talked about how some men were eager to leave a wife behind when they were off fighting. Some were so eager, they weren't too particular about who said yes. So I put on my best gown and decided to find myself a husband."

"You went to make a match."

She laughed softly. "Yes. But I soon realized that was a fool's quest. Gentlemen officers like you were not so desperate as to marry a woman who was not only awkward and shy but also had no money to speak of. Then, out of the blue, one man did show interest in me."

"Bushnell."

"Yes. He said things, things to make me believe he cared for me. He called on me at my home, acted as though he was about to make me an offer of marriage." She swallowed, clearly in no hurry to share more of her story with him. "Suffice to say I misinterpreted his regard and soon had no options left but the one he did offer."

"So you sold yourself."

"I did what I had to do. Daniel Bushnell was, in many ways, the answer to a prayer."

He scoffed. "I find it something of a stretch to categorize Bushnell in those terms. He's as far from angelic as a man can get. Truly, he is a scoundrel of the worst sort."

"It was because he is a scoundrel that I was able to take care of my grandmother."

"And yourself," he pointed out.

"Yes, sir. And myself." She stared at him intently. "I'm curious as to why you are judging me so harshly, Major Kelly. You fought on battlefields. Instead of dying, you lived. I know from Devin that you also survived a lengthy imprisonment in enemy territory.

I would think you would have seen far worse than a desperate woman choosing to survive."

"You risked your reputation."

"I did. And I lost it as well. It was a gamble I had to take." She tilted her head to one side. "I must confess your disdain for my actions surprises me. Aren't you a gambler now?"

Her point, because it was valid, stung. And he wondered just how much Devin had told her about his friends. "My current occupation has nothing to do with this discussion."

"I beg to differ. We're discussing weighing probabilities of life and death."

"We are not. We are discussing your less-than-illustrious past."

"I'm not going to apologize to you for the choices I've made."

He shifted. She was right—to an extent. But she was also very wrong. Maybe she'd been alone so long that she'd forgotten what it meant to have close friends who looked out for each other.

Or maybe she'd been so self-serving that she forgot the rest of the world would judge Devin Monroe for courting a woman of her reputation. Devin had not let on that his acquaintance with her had come to that when he'd seen him days ago, but an understanding between him and this woman seemed obvious now.

"Bushnell used to talk about you," he blurted. "He talked about his ladybird." He'd used far coarser words, actually.

To his surprise, instead of being shocked, a faint glimmer of amusement entered her eyes. "I imagine Daniel did talk about me. He saw me as ornamental, you see. Having me made him feel important."

In contrast to the gleam in her eyes, her voice sounded empty. Almost hollow. "And you didn't find that distasteful?"

"Not enough to give up eating or having a roof over my head. Not enough to sacrifice my grandmother for misplaced honor."

"Is she still alive?"

"No. She died not long after my arrangement with Bushnell began."

"So you could have ended it."

"Not easily. The colonel and I had a business agreement. As you've just pointed out, it was very far from a love affair."

"Did you even try to break things off?"

"What, exactly, are you doing, Major Kelly? Are you attempting to understand why I did what I did? Or hoping to devise a way to make sure Devin distances himself from me as far as possible when he awakens?"

Her questions hit the mark.

She was smart. Smart and quick and proud. It was obvious why Bushnell had been so proud to call her his. She was beautiful, strong, and had gumption.

But she was also very far from the type of woman Devin deserved. He needed someone sweet. Innocent. A woman worthy of his honor and reputation. "Maybe I'm doing both," he admitted.

"Why? Do you imagine that I would have kept my past from Devin?"

Devin had told him what she was. And why. Still . . .

"Devin Monroe is a great many things, but wise to the ways of women is not one of them. How much did you admit to him about what you did?"

"*What I did?*" she scoffed. "Do you desire details, Major?" she asked, her voice thick with sarcasm. "Do you want to know what Daniel made me do when he visited my house when he was on leave? Is that the kind of thing you enjoy hearing?"

Her implication was shocking. So much so, he didn't even try to read the sarcasm in her expression or attempt to match her tone. "No," he bit out. "Of course not."

Her voice turned even more brittle. "Then what do you want from me?"

He knew in his heart that she was playing a role. She had put on a shield, acting in a way she must have perfected when so many people looked down on her.

But he, however, was not acting. His only concern was Devin, and Lizbeth. He didn't want this woman near either of them. Lizbeth was too fragile and Devin was too weak. "I want you to leave," he said, not feeling a trace of remorse. "I want you to walk away from Devin and give him space. Allow him to find a woman who is more worthy to stand by his side."

Even in the dim light, he could tell his barb had met its mark. He'd wounded her.

Though he knew she wouldn't believe it, he was sorry. He wasn't cruel by nature. But like a parent disciplining a child out of love, he felt he had no choice. "Miss Van Fleet, I'm sorry to speak so severely, but you mustn't be surprised. I've gone to hell and back with Devin, and I'd do it again to keep him safe from harm."

He was so focused on her face, on her tense expression, that the words he heard caught him off guard.

"Ethan Kelly, if I didn't have a hole in my back, I would beat you bloody," Devin rasped. "Apologize right now."

Julianne gasped and rushed to his side. "Devin!" she exclaimed as she fell to her knees next to him. "Look at you! You're awake. Oh, thank the Lord!"

Ethan didn't seem able to move. He stood frozen while Julianne knelt next to Devin, her hands reaching for his, tears already running down her face.

Slowly, the captain's fingers curled around hers. Gently.

But he was still staring at Ethan as if he were an enemy.

His spine prickled in unease. "You know I was only trying to help you."

"Let us not play games. I am not an innocent woman susceptible to your verbal innuendos."

Julianne ran a hand along Devin's jaw. "Devin, I'm fine. Please, don't worry yourself."

"What I heard was not fine," he said softly before staring at Ethan again. "You were being deliberately cruel. Disrespectful. After she's come all this way. You were taking advantage of the fact that I was lying here, unaware."

Each word was harshly stated. Each word was punctuated by scorn. Seen from Devin's perspective, maybe Ethan deserved his friend's contempt. But surely he wasn't so naïve as to think people who cared about him wouldn't hesitate to protect him. "If I overstepped my bounds, please accept my apology."

"That is not good enough," Devin rasped, his tone still cold. "You are apologizing to the wrong person."

Taking a deep breath, he continued. "Miss Van Fleet, I am sorry for the way I spoke to you. It . . . it was uncalled for and undeserved. Please accept my apology."

His mouth was dry. He wasn't surprised. He felt as if each word had been pulled from his insides. But Julianne didn't even turn to look at him. She didn't do anything but bend her face over Devin's hand. "I've been so worried, Devin," she murmured. "I prayed so much, I doubt there's an angel in heaven who didn't hear my prayers."

Ethan listened, dumbstruck. It was as if he didn't exist for her. It seemed only Devin did.

Devin whispered something to her before glancing at Ethan once again. No emotion flickered in his gaze. It was as if they were strangers. Definitely not friends.

Ethan felt that loss. His fists loosened as he racked his brain, wondering how to fix what was beginning to seem unfixable. "Devin, if I may—"

"Leave us."

He stepped forward. Ready to argue. To press his point. "But—"

Devin cut him off again. "Allow me to make myself perfectly clear," he rasped, his light-blue eyes glinting like shards of ice. "Get out, Major Kelly."

His voice was sharp. Hard. And his glare? Well, Ethan never would have imagined it would be directed at him. Not only because of Ethan's rank, but because of all they'd been through together.

Appalled at the situation, Ethan turned and strode from the room. Neither Devin nor Julianne acknowledged his departure.

When he was out in the hall, Ethan rested his head against the wall and closed his eyes. He felt sick. Obviously, he had gone too far.

"Sir?" a young maid asked as she walked down the hallway. She was the one who had helped Lizbeth with supplies when they first brought Devin to this suite. He was surprised to remember her name. It was Cassie. "Sir, are you all right? Do you need something?"

He laughed grimly. "There's nothing you can do for me, miss. Not a single thing in the world."

When she scurried away, he straightened and walked down the hall. Lizbeth had refused him; Devin had almost died. And he'd just gone out of his way to offend a perfectly decent woman.

It was time to pray and make plans . . . before the day got any worse.

23

DEVIN FOUND IT HARD TO BELIEVE JULIANNE WAS KNEEL-
ing by his side. When he'd awoken in the strange room, at first all
he could surmise was that his shoulder burned as though it were
on fire, but he was alive.

Then, little by little, he'd come to the realization he wasn't
back on the battlefield. He wasn't recuperating in a field hospital
on a make-shift cot with a score of men surrounding him in worst
straits than he was. Instead, he slowly became aware of the tangy
scent of lemon oil in the air and a soothing warmth emitting from
the fireplace across the room.

Then, as if he'd conjured it, he'd inhaled a familiar rose scent.
It was one he knew he would always associate with Julianne Van
Fleet. He'd been stunned, especially since he was in San Antonio,
not Boerne. She would have traveled to get to his side.

And then the fogginess in his brain subsided and he compre-
hended what Ethan was saying.

That was when he'd felt an anger the likes of which he'd never
experienced surge through him. It was as unexpected as it was
explosive and hot. If he could have stood on his own two feet,
Devin was fairly sure he would have slugged Ethan.

Thank goodness he'd only had the strength to demand he leave.

Now he was alone with Julianne and at a loss for how to soothe the pain she must feel after Ethan's words.

"I'm so sorry," Devin said when he felt he could speak in a coherent manner. "I don't know what got into Ethan. He usually is everything kind and gracious."

As Julianne rose to sit beside him in a chair, she raised one shoulder in a gesture that said so much. She was hurt but hadn't expected much else. "He cares about you."

"That was no excuse. His accusations were uncalled for." Glad her hand was still in his, he ran a finger along the delicate skin on the back, feeling the faint outline of the bones and veins underneath. "I don't agree with anything he said. I hope you know that."

"He wasn't exactly wrong, Devin. You are a celebrated officer. Everyone who admires you would no doubt hope to see you with a woman who is your equal."

"Of course you are that."

She looked down at her lap. "Let's just say a woman of better reputation."

"I don't want to discuss our pasts or reputations anymore. They don't matter. Times have changed."

Lifting her head, she cast him a doubtful look. "Not that much. People are more accepting, but not of a woman's reputation."

"It doesn't matter to me."

"But it will to other people," she said haltingly. "We can't live in a cave, Devin."

"No, we can't. But we can't live filled with apologies and regrets either. What matters is that I've found you." He slid his hand over hers, linking their fingers together. Maybe his grip was too tight, but he was willing to risk it. She needed to know he wanted never to let her go.

She blinked before gifting him with a tremulous smile. "I didn't know you were such a romantic, Captain."

"I'm not. I guess you're bringing that out in me." Realizing he was a new recruit to relationships, he added, "Is it too much?"

Julianne chuckled. "No. I seem to like it."

"Good."

"I never thought I was especially romantic either. But it seems we've been waiting for the right time, haven't we?"

He smiled. "I'd ask you to lean down and kiss me, but I don't think my heart could take it." He no doubt smelled to high heaven too.

"I guess I'll just wait in anticipation, then." Lines around her eyes formed as she smiled again. "Now, though, we need to see if we can make you better." Getting to her feet, she leaned over him, gently curving her hands around his uninjured shoulder and under his opposite side. "Sit up, sir, and I'll straighten your bedding and get you some water."

It hurt, but he bit back his moan of pain and let her move him about. Her hands were soft and cool, and her touch was gentle. So different from the way he'd been treated the last time he'd sustained a bullet wound.

"Are you all right? Am I being too rough?"

"Not at all. I was just thinking about the last time I was injured."

"During the war?"

"Yes. I was in a hospital tent, being treated by a medic and a volunteer nurse who was burlier than me."

As he'd hoped, she laughed. "I bet you were afraid of her."

"I was afraid to cross her." Remembering the woman, he said, "We were all a little afraid of her. I was as obedient toward her as I've been to anyone. Probably even more so than toward Lee himself!"

"She sounds impressive. And frightening."

"She was indeed. She probably saved more lives than anyone realizes."

After she helped him take a few sips of water, she looked at him in a worried way. "I could use another nurse at the moment. I want to give you some beef broth, but I don't want to leave you alone."

"Don't worry. Ethan will come back eventually."

"I'm not so sure about that. You told him to leave."

"I did. But he knows I need him."

"Another woman was here when I arrived. Maybe she'll return."

Devin didn't care about broth. "Tell me how you got here. What happened, Julianne?"

"Daniel returned to my house. He told me he shot you. Bold as brass, he was."

"I can't believe he had the nerve to do that." The ire that had settled after Ethan left slowly burned hot again. Hating that he was lying in bed so helplessly, he looked her over. "Are you all right? Did he hurt you?"

"I'm all right. I was actually talking to two . . . well, friends of mine. A young man and his sister have adopted me, of sorts."

"Is that right?"

"There's a story there, of course. But what matters is that the three of us were having tea when Daniel arrived. He was full of bluster, saying he took care of you."

"Thankfully, not yet."

"He said he'd be back."

"And?"

She bit her lip before continuing. "I think he wants what you might expect, Devin," she said softly. "He wants me to welcome him back into my life with open arms. He said he owns me."

"Over my dead body." When she flinched, he cursed his choice of words. "I do beg your pardon."

Her expression softened. "No worries. I knew what you meant. But it doesn't matter anyway. I sent him on his way."

Staring at her, watching the array of emotions run across her face, he was sure much more had happened than that. Knowing Bushnell as he did, knowing her as he was beginning to, he worried he had threatened or hurt her and that she was keeping it from him. "Julianne, don't shield me from the truth. I want to know what he did." So he could give those reasons to Bushnell when he beat him to a bloody pulp.

"Nothing you need to worry about, Devin. I handled things myself."

His eyes lit with admiration. "Good for you."

"To be honest, I don't know who was more shocked by my gumption!"

"I know I'm proud of you." He *was* proud of her and glad she'd stood up to the man. But that didn't mean he wasn't going to go after him the first chance he got. But for now? He was suddenly exhausted. "Julianne, if I lie still, could you rest next to me?"

"Certainly not."

"I'm under the covers. You could lie on top of them," he coaxed. "You could just stay for a few minutes."

"I don't want to hurt you."

"You won't. You'll make me feel better."

"Devin, now is not the time," she protested, but not very strongly. Her voice was warm. Her gaze was too.

"You can see my scars, Julianne. This is not the first time my body has been injured. I have spent my fair share of hours in hospital tents. When I close my eyes, those memories come back."

"I'll stay by you."

"They'll dissipate if you lie down next to me. And if you rest on my good side, I'm sure I'll hardly be aware of anything except your perfume." And the way she felt against him. And the way it felt not to be alone.

"Devin . . ."

Ah. She was wavering. "Come now. I know you must be tired too. No one is here, and they are unlikely to return anytime soon. Your reputation wouldn't suffer."

"If your friend discovers me there, it will discount everything I tried to prove to him."

"You have nothing to prove to him. But no worries anyway. He's not going to step in here for hours. After all, as you said, I was very firm with Ethan."

"I suppose that is true."

"Good." He patted the mattress. "Now, have pity on me, Julianne. I'm injured and exhausted. Come rest next to me. I'm not hungry now. Help me sleep."

"I'm beginning to think you survived by your wiliness instead of your expertise in the battlefield."

"I'd comment on that, but you'd realize I have no modesty."

She smiled. "I suppose I'm going to have to let you have your way. I don't seem to be able to resist you."

He might be lying in the bed, but her words made him feel as though he were a hero. He made sure not to look too pleased, though. "I think I should apologize in advance. I fear I won't be able to keep awake much longer."

Looking as if she were half afraid a bunch of scandalized women were about to step out from behind the curtains, Julianne crossed to the other side of the double bed and lay down beside him.

"You should take off your shoes."

"Certainly not."

"Whatever you wish, miss."

"Oh, hush, Devin."

He closed his eyes, smelled that faint rose scent, felt her soft-ness curve beside him. And even though he'd been shot by an arch enemy, he was angry with his best friend in the world, and his shoulder burned, he found himself smiling.

Few moments had ever felt so perfect.

24

WHEN LIZBETH RETURNED TO THE MENGER THE NEXT morning, she discovered Ethan lounging on one of the formal settees in the lobby of the hotel. Everyone who walked by was giving him a wide berth. Lizbeth wasn't surprised about that, given the way he was glaring at the closed door leading into the secret hall.

She was surprised by his appearance, however. His suit looked rumpled and his expression was haggard. He looked as though he hadn't slept at all. He looked the exact opposite of his usual, perfectly tailored self.

When he spied her, he got to his feet. "Lizbeth."

"Good morning, Ethan," she said simply.

He ran a careless hand through his hair. "Huh. I guess it is morning already."

"You look like you've been lounging here all night. Is everything all right?"

"I have. And no, it is not."

His voice had an unfamiliar rasp. He was upset. "What happened?" she asked as she sat down on one of the padded chairs nearby. "Is the captain worse?"

"I don't know," he said as he sat back down with a grateful sigh.

"I haven't been in his room since yesterday afternoon—although I made sure he let in the doctor when he came. And the maids in with some food and fresh water."

"But otherwise he's been alone?" She was shocked—and worried. The captain's wound had been angry, and he'd lost a lot of blood. He needed constant monitoring and was too weak to fend for himself.

"No. Miss Van Fleet stayed with him."

"Why didn't you join them?"

"Devin asked me to leave."

Her eyes widened as she tried not to let on how very shocked she was. But of course it was impossible to hide the fierce blush that was no doubt staining her cheeks.

Ethan did notice. "It wasn't like that, Lizbeth," he said, a touch of amusement lightening his tone. "I . . . well, I offended Miss Van Fleet. Devin heard and was furious."

Belatedly, she realized what that meant. "So Captain Monroe awoke when—"

"He did. Then ordered me from his room." He leaned back against the sofa's cushions and stretched out his arms along its length. When a lady tittered at his position, he glared at her.

Feeling sorrier for him by the second, she said, "That wasn't very kind of Captain Monroe. You went to so much trouble to care for him."

"It was no less than I deserved, I'm afraid." Staring at the closed door again, he shook his head. "What I said was cruel and crossed the boundaries of acceptable behavior. I do not fault Devin for sending me out. Only his injury kept him from hitting me. I would have."

"But you didn't want to leave, did you?"

He shook his head. "I decided to stand vigil out here, in case

Miss Van Fleet came out and needed something beyond what the doctor and maids provided. However, she has not."

"It's morning now. Maybe the captain's temper has cooled." Touching his arm stretched out closest to her, she added, "Let's go see him. Maybe we can take them both some coffee and pastries. That usually brightens any mood."

He got to his feet. "I think you're right."

"I'll go to the kitchens. One of the cooks is my friend. I'm sure she'll help me get a tray together." When he made a motion to accompany her, she shook her head. "You had better not wander around the servants' quarters, Ethan. You'd likely send the staff into a fit of vapors. Just wait for me here."

"Thank you. Once again, you've proven to me that while I hope to help you, you seem to be better at helping me."

His words settled in her heart as she walked to one of the servants' staircases and headed to the kitchens. She wasn't immune to his charm, it seemed. Even when he wasn't trying to be particularly charming.

When she opened the door, a blast of warm air and the low rumble of conversation greeted her. Though she didn't miss many things about working at the Menger, she did miss this place. The kitchens were made up of four large rooms, housing everything from china, glassware, cutlery, linens, and serving platters and trays to a walk-in pantry and an ice room, a washing station, and a huge stove.

Her appearance drew a couple of pointed stares, but then she spied Meg, who was rolling out pastry dough along a marble surface.

"Well, look who's here. It's Elizabeth Barclay!" she called out. "What brings you back to our world? Did Mrs. Howard hire you back on?"

Lizbeth had no desire to discuss her relationship with her cousin. "I'm actually on a mission for rolls and coffee."

Meg grinned. "I heard you're at Harrison House. You entertaining over there?"

"No, of course not. I offered to help Major Kelly. It's for him and a guest of his. Would you help me out?"

"I can. But does Mrs. Howard know you're asking?"

She shook her head. "Does it matter?"

Bertha, the dining room's head cook, strode forward. "Of course it doesn't, Lizzy. If the major wants something, he gets it immediately." She tossed Meg a chiding look. "Everyone here knows that."

Lizbeth hid a smile. It seemed her major had wrapped even their querulous cook around his little finger. "Thank you."

"Of course." Reaching out, she squeezed Lizbeth's shoulder. "But I should tell you that we'd do it for you too. We miss you around here."

"It's been far quieter ever since you left," Meg added. "No one else on staff is as well liked as you."

Lizbeth felt her cheeks heat. The women's kind words meant the world to her. She needed to remember she did have friends here at the Menger. "I'd best get these things together," she said. "The major is waiting."

"Did you say you wanted coffee and pastries?"

"Yes. For four, if you please," she said, figuring she might as well treat herself too.

Bertha pointed to one of the larger silver-plated containers. "Go grab one of those and a couple of cloths. The rest of us will set everything up."

"Thank you, Bertha."

"No thanks needed. You were one of ours. We'll keep claiming you too. As long as you'd like us to, anyway."

Ten minutes later, Lizbeth carried a silver tray toward Ethan. On it was a full coffee service, four china cups, four china plates, and a large silver container of pastries and muffins.

Ethan raised his eyebrows. "I was starting to wonder what was taking so long. Now I realize I should have been asking you to take care of my meals all along. That's quite a spread."

"I have connections in the kitchen," she teased. Thinking it was time for her to be the person who pushed things along, she said, "We should head right down to the captain's room, Ethan. The coffee is hot."

Steeling his nerve, he nodded and took the heavy tray. "It can't get any worse, right?"

She didn't dare comment on that. After all, she'd learned time and again that things could always get worse.

He hated this. Hated the feeling inside of him clamoring for acceptance and release. "I should probably let you know Devin might refuse us entrance."

"I understand."

With a sense of foreboding, he rapped on the door. "Devin, it is I and Lizbeth," he called out. "We brought you coffee and pastries."

They heard shuffling, then Julianne answered the door. She, too, was wearing the same clothes as the day before. He noticed she also looked rumpled. "Major Kelly, good morning."

"Miss. I trust you remember Miss Barclay?"

Her expression was somber as she nodded. "Indeed. Good morning, Lizbeth. Thank you for this."

"I'm happy to help," Lizbeth said with a smile.

Afraid she was going to shut the door in his face, Ethan managed to grip its side with one hand while balancing the tray with his other. "May we come in? Both of us?"

Julianne looked behind her, and then after she'd obviously gained permission she stepped backward.

Ethan placed the tray on the coffee table. Immediately, his gaze strayed to the bed, but it was empty. The covers had been straightened and the pillows fluffed. It looked as if a maid had already come and tended to the room.

Devin was sitting in one of the chairs next to the fireplace. Julianne had placed a blanket over his lap for warmth. "Ethan," he said by way of greeting.

Well, it wasn't much, but it was better than being refused admittance. "We've brought sustenance," he joked. "And Miss Barclay—Lizbeth—please meet Captain Devin Monroe."

She bobbed a curtsy. "Captain. I am glad to see you awake this morning."

"I'm told much of my recovery is because of your earlier assistance. Thank you."

"I didn't do too much. But you are welcome." Smiling at Ethan, she said, "I was told on good authority that you had a life worth saving."

Meeting Ethan's gaze, Devin said, "That's the benefit of a long friendship, I think. Even when things are not easy, they are appreciated."

It was an apology of a sort. Ethan hadn't expected to hear those words. Or to be let off so easily. Emotion gripped his throat. He knew what he needed to do. Turning to Julianne, he bowed again. "Miss Van Fleet, may I offer you something to eat or drink?"

She smiled as she sat down in the chair next to Devin. "If coffee is in that china pot, I will be forever grateful."

Ethan relaxed slightly. Things might not be good between them, but at least they'd gotten this far. That was something, he supposed. "Lizbeth, I fear I'm all thumbs when it comes to china pots. Would you please do the honors?"

"Of course." She competently poured a cup of coffee. "Miss Van Fleet, how do you take yours?"

"With both cream and sugar, if you please."

"I'll have mine black, miss," Devin said.

After preparing Julianne's cup, Lizbeth handed Devin his. "Here you are, sir."

"Thank you."

While Lizbeth continued the coffee service, Ethan handed out the pastries. Then he sat down by Lizbeth's side on the sitting area's settee.

After an awkward moment, they all began eating.

"Let us not waste any more time," Ethan said after swallowing his first bite. "Devin, you can give me details about your encounter with Bushnell at Julianne's home later, but I got the gist of what happened from her when she arrived. Now, assuming he gave you no clue about where we can find him, what do we need to do? He can't get away with this."

Devin looked at Lizbeth warily. "Perhaps we should wait to talk about this at a later time. I fear our plans might shock Miss Barclay here."

Before Ethan could say anything, Lizbeth spoke. "I am afraid I am not without my own concerns about Colonel Bushnell."

When Julianne suddenly looked up, Ethan knew he needed to explain what Devin already knew. "He attempted to force his attentions on her when she worked here," Ethan said quietly. "Just last week."

Lizbeth paled, and he reached out to her, glad he'd never told her about confronting Bushnell. He was still afraid Bushnell would retaliate by hurting her further, and he didn't want her to come to the same conclusion. "I know this makes you uneasy, but I promise, you are among friends. We can speak freely."

But instead of looking relieved, she seemed to become even more distressed. "I'm afraid I have more reasons to hate him than that, Ethan."

Forgetting they weren't alone, Ethan gripped her hand. "Has he accosted you here another time?"

"No. He, uh—" She stopped abruptly, cutting herself off as though she were slicing a knife through her thoughts. Ethan watched her closely, caught on her words. Bushnell had done what? A dozen scenarios crossed his mind, each more far-fetched and disturbing than the last.

As the silence pulled longer, and Lizbeth so obviously tried to gather her thoughts, he willed himself to wait impassively. During the war, he'd learned the value of patience, but never before had it been so difficult to put into practice.

He felt rather than witnessed Devin react the same way.

Looking apologetic, Lizbeth swallowed. "I'm sorry," she said. She smiled weakly, but at Julianne, not him. He realized it was easier for her to look at Julianne than at him.

A relative stranger.

At last, she lifted her chin and pushed a thick lock of her dark hair away from her face. His eyes traced the patch of skin that had been uncovered. Her skin looked pale and smooth. Her perfect cheekbones as finely sculpted as ever. And yes, even the red line of her scar looked as it always did. A faint mark emphasizing her other features' perfection.

"He is the one who gave me this scar," she said in a rush.

It took a moment for the words to register. With effort, he

pushed away the memory of what her scar had looked like when he first saw it. When he, Thomas, and the rest of the men had come on her property. The mark had still been bright red and thick on her forehead. Freshly healed.

Her hand shook as she loosened the stray curl she'd tucked behind her ear. As if it had been happy to be sprung, it curled back into place. Almost covering up the mark. "I got this during the war," she said. "I received it when Bushnell and his men raided my home."

He'd always known men had arrived before they had, and assumed one of them had harmed her. But Bushnell?

Ethan was vaguely aware of Julianne making a pained sound and of Devin cursing under his breath. Ethan felt chilled to the bone. How could such a coincidence exist? "What are you saying?"

"I'm saying Colonel Bushnell came to my house during the war."

It was too much to come to terms with. "Many men in uniform look the same at first glance . . ."

Lines of strain formed, settled in faint lines around her lips. She looked at him. "I wouldn't forget him, Ethan. He haunts my dreams almost every night."

"Of course. Forgive me for doubting you." Staring at her face intently, he said, "So Bushnell was the man who cut your face."

"Oh, he did far more than that," she said, her expression vacant. "He had his men take nearly everything of value—everything they could find. But then as they waited outside, he forced himself into my house, pressed a knife to my skin, and cut me." Her voice lowered, but her gaze did not. She kept her eyes directly on his own. "And then he raped me."

When a china cup crashed to the floor, Ethan wasn't sure if it was his own or someone else's.

He supposed it didn't really matter. He felt broken inside.

25

Johnson's Island, Ohio
Confederate States of America Officers' POW Camp

NEVER THOUGHT I'D BE PLAYING NURSEMAID TO YOU, CAP-
tain," Ethan Kelly said as he rinsed out the cloth he'd been using to
sop up the blood that didn't seem in any hurry to dissipate.

As Devin examined the jagged cut that ran most of the length
of his forearm, he tried to bluff the sting away. "I never thought I
was going to get my worst injury in the war from gardening. It's
embarrassing."

After folding the cloth into a thick rectangle, Ethan pressed
it on Devin's arm. The pressure hurt like the devil. "Easy, now."

Instantly, his pressure lightened. "Sorry. You hold it in place."
When Devin complied, Ethan sat down on the side of one of the
cots and started threading the needle in his hand. "It's not embarrassing. The blade on that hoe is sharp."

Indeed, it was. Razor sharp. "This is proof of that." Thinking
of how he'd gone and tripped on the pile of rubble Truax had left
out, Devin grimaced. "Still, it was a foolish mistake."

"The blame goes to Truax. Not you."

It was a childish maneuver to pass the blame. It wasn't like him not to accept responsibility for his actions either. However, he was in enough pain to make an exception. "I'll take that. Where is Robert, anyway?"

"I heard he's over at the cemetery," Thomas Baker said from where he was lounging two cots over.

Momentarily forgetting his injury, Devin turned to Baker. "Why? Did something happen?"

"No, sir. He, uh, well, he likes to pull the weeds around the markers."

"That sounds like Robert Truax," Ethan said as he lifted the cloth covering Devin's wound. "Still bleeding," he pronounced. As if Devin couldn't see that for himself.

Feeling a little lightheaded, Devin focused on the conversation, such as it was. "Hold on. Why does visiting the dead sound like Robert?"

"He has a soft spot for things like that," Ethan said. "I thought you knew."

Robert Truax was a lot of things. He was forthright, a good fighter, and extremely patient. He was also hard as stone. He had no family, born as he was on the streets. He looked after himself. That was it.

"No, I guess I didn't know that."

Baker got to his feet. "Do you need something, Cap? 'Cause I can go get him for ya."

"No."

"I need you, Baker," Ethan said. "Get over here and hold the captain's arm steady while I stitch."

"All right."

Baker was the biggest of all of them. The roughest too. No doubt his grip was going to be as painful as Ethan's stitching.

"No need for you, Baker. I'm not going to need anyone to hold me down."

"It might come as a bit of a surprise, but I have no experience stitching skin," Ethan said in that lofty way he adopted when his pride was stung. "I doubt I will have a tender touch. You're going to move. Baker will help you stay put."

Devin pulled his arm away and slapped the soiled cloth back on his arm. "Hold on. You've never given a man stitches before?"

"Of course not. Have you?"

"Once." Remembering what a mess he'd made of it, he frowned. His only saving grace had been that the soldier he'd been stitching passed out. He, on the other hand, was currently wide-awake. Eyeing the needle and thread in Ethan's hand, he said, "Where did you get the needle and thread? I thought it was in your kit."

"I got it from Thomas."

"You?"

Thomas shrugged. "I thought it might come in useful. And it did."

Devin noticed then that Thomas was eyeing Ethan with more than a little bit of wariness. "Baker, have you ever stitched a man?"

He nodded. "I have."

"More than once?"

"Yes, sir. Many a time." Darting a sidelong glance his way, Thomas continued. "There weren't a lot of physicians wandering around the slums sewing up nicks and scrapes. We took care of our own."

Ethan looked affronted. "It isn't my fault I grew up in different circumstances."

"Of course not, sir," Thomas said.

Devin made a sudden decision. "Baker, I want you to sew up my arm."

While the sergeant nodded, not looking the least bit intimidated by the length of the jagged cut, Ethan threw up his hands.

He was offended. "Do you not trust me?"

"In a word? No."

Devin shifted, holding his arm in a stiff way. "I'd be obliged if we could simply get this over with, Baker. We can discuss your experience at a later time."

"Yes, sir." Holding out a hand to Ethan, Baker said, "I'll take a thread. And light a candle for me, if you please."

"Why?" Ethan asked suspiciously.

"I need to put the needle through a flame first."

"Why?"

"Just do it, Kelly," Devin said through clenched teeth. His arm really was starting to burn. And the anticipation? He had never imagined himself to be nervous about anything involving an injury, but the men's bickering was beginning to take its toll.

As if Kelly had come to the same conclusion, he handed the needle and thread to Thomas, lit one of their precious candles, and held it steady while the sergeant held the needle over the flame.

A moment later, Baker sat down next to him, gestured for his arm, and lifted the bloody rag. The wound was still oozing, though the edges of the cut looked a little less fragile.

After examining the wound and the amount of thread on the needle, Thomas spoke. "I think I'm going to start in the center, sir. There's a sizable hole there, you see."

Devin was starting to feel he had no desire to discuss the wound another second. "No need to describe what I can already feel, Sergeant. Just begin, if you please."

"Yes, sir." And then, without another second's hesitation, Thomas pinched the aforementioned gaping section together and inserted the needle.

It stung. Stung like a mess of fire ants had descended on his arm. He clenched his teeth to prevent his body from flinching as the needle continued through his skin. There was no way he wanted Ethan to start holding down his arm.

"Huh," Kelly said. "You really do know what you're doing."

"Weren't no reason to lie," Baker said easily as he continued his work.

Devin held still as the door opened and more men entered. Seeing what was happening, they all walked over, peering at Devin's arm and admiring Baker's work.

"Looks like we can set you up your own dress shop when we get out of here," General McCoy said to Baker. "Those are some impressive stitches. I reckon that wound is going to heal real nicely. One day it will hardly have more than a fine line visible."

"Thank you, sir," Baker said as he did something painful. Devin turned his head to see Baker slice the thread with the tip of a knife someone held out for him.

"We done?" Devin said.

McCoy laughed. "You sound a little peaked, Captain. The sight of blood bothering you?"

Since they'd all seen more blood on the battlefield than any of them had ever thought possible, Devin grinned. "I guess so. Or maybe I've been sitting here worrying about my scar. I've got to get a wife one day, you know. Don't want to scare her off."

"Women like their men scarred and marred," Ethan joked. "Makes them think we are invincible."

"I'm sure all the women I court are going to be real impressed with my gardening accident," Devin joked. "Makes me sound like a real hero."

"Don't worry yourself," Bushnell interjected from the back

of the room. "Kelly is right. Men's scars don't matter. Only the women's do."

The statement was so outrageous, Devin looked over at the colonel, just to get a sense of how he looked. And there he was, standing tall and smug, full of blustery pride. "I'm afraid you've lost me, sir. What do you mean?"

"Nothing out of the ordinary, Captain," he replied, each word sounding like a lazy drawl. "Only that a man with a scar can still look attractive while a woman isn't so lucky. All she'll look is marked."

"Anyone who survives an injury is to be respected, no?" Ethan asked, his voice sounding frigid.

"Perhaps . . . unless the woman isn't the kind to be respected anyway."

A couple of the men surrounding him laughed nervously, but Devin stared up at Bushnell curiously. The comment was both in poor taste and rather odd.

Beside him, Baker pursed his lips as he ran the needle over the flame again. It was obvious that Thomas Baker knew what Bushnell was referring to and didn't approve.

"Colonel Bushnell, you sound knowledgeable on the subject. Do you know something in particular about women and scarring?" Kelly asked.

There was an edge to his voice. It also had a cadence to it Devin recognized as a warning. Whenever Kelly was particularly offended, his tone didn't just turn haughty. He started pulling out all his fancy vocabulary.

But Bushnell didn't look offended or caught off guard in the slightest. "Not especially. Only that their scars detract from their beauty."

"Because they had the misfortune to be cut?" General McCoy asked.

"I'm sorry if I've caused offense," Bushnell said. "I sometimes forget some of you are so fainthearted."

"That should do it, Captain," Baker said.

Looking down at his arm, Devin realized Thomas had, indeed, already finished. There on his arm were eighteen perfectly executed stitches. His flesh was neatly closed. He tested them, moving his arm this way and that. "You did a fine job, Thomas. Thank you."

"It was nothing, Cap." Looking bleak, he added, "As the colonel said, men seem to be able to handle cuts easier than women."

Of course, that wasn't exactly what the man had said.

But Devin had to agree with what Baker said. Men were tougher. They were built and conditioned to stand pain.

But of course, his father had taught him to protect women. Look after them. Not comment upon the state of their scars.

26

THE SOUND OF THE CUP CRASHING TO THE FLOOR SHOULD have spurred all of them to action, but Julianne couldn't seem to move a muscle. Devin, sitting next to her in an overstuffed chair, looked frozen.

That sweet little Lizbeth looked crushed, as if she regretted revealing a dark secret she had promised to take to her grave. Ethan Kelly looked even worse. Devastated.

Julianne understood how he felt. Even after enduring taunts and whispers for years, she'd never felt more unworthy or empty than she did at that very minute. After all, she'd allowed Daniel Bushnell to keep her in comfort even though she knew he was married. She'd allowed him into her bed even though she knew it was sinful. While she would never categorize those experiences as pleasant—he had certainly never raped her. He had beat her, but not this.

No, it seemed he had only done such things to innocent women when he raided their homes.

Feeling sick, bile rose in her throat. How long would it take before Ethan told Lizbeth about her being Bushnell's kept woman? And surely a gentleman like Devin Monroe would at last see the error of his ways and never associate with her again.

And Lizbeth? Well, that poor woman would probably go out of her way to avoid her at all costs. Julianne wouldn't blame her one bit.

"I beg your pardon for my clumsiness," Ethan said, breaking the strained silence. After reaching for a neatly folded cloth on the serving tray, he knelt on the floor and started picking up the shards. "I, uh . . . I fear I must be more tired than I thought."

Julianne knelt to help. Taking the cloth from his grip, she sopped up the coffee as he dropped the pieces of fine-bone china on a tray. Each one made a delicate *ping* as it landed on the silver, providing the only sound in the room.

After cleaning up as much of the coffee as she was able, Julianne reached for the tray. "I'll go see if I can get a maid to help me clean this up. I'll have her fetch you a fresh cup as well, Major."

"No, I can do that," Lizbeth said. "This . . . this was my fault, anyway."

"How can you say such a thing?" the major bit out.

"I shouldn't have shared what I did. Especially not right now. Captain Monroe is injured."

"You didn't offend me, miss."

But instead of looking reassured, Lizbeth appeared more agitated. "I'm sure I, uh, spoke out of turn. What happened is in the past. It's best forgotten."

"I, for one, am glad you spoke so freely," Devin said, his voice scratchy with suppressed emotion. "The truth is a far better ally than enemy."

Julianne had never heard that statement, but she supposed it was true—if one had nothing to hide. Not knowing where to look, she shifted uncomfortably.

Just as Lizbeth was making her way to the door, Devin's voice rang out. "Miss Barclay? I would be very grateful if you could fetch us another cup, and perhaps more coffee too. And, Julianne, if you wouldn't mind, please go with her."

"I don't mind at all." She knew what his request was. A thinly veiled plea for the two of them to vacate the room and give the men some privacy. She didn't care what the reasoning was behind it, however. She was grateful for the reprieve.

Lizbeth opened the door. "I'll inform the cook you'll need something with more sustenance as well, Captain," she said before departing.

When Julianne closed the heavy door behind them, she exhaled. "That was brave of you. Are you all right?"

Lizbeth lifted a shoulder. "I had never intended to tell anyone exactly how I got that scar. It just slipped out. My cousin knows a man cut me in the war, but nothing else."

"Maybe God decided it was time for your story to be told."

"Do you really think so? I wonder if that was the case. I saw Ethan's, I mean *Major Kelly's* expression. He looked angry."

"Of course he was. No one wants to think of you being hurt." She hoped she sounded more convincing than she felt. She felt as if she were balancing on a shaky tightrope. Any minute she was certain to fall and either injure herself or someone else.

Luckily, Lizbeth didn't seem to notice anything untoward. "I suppose not." Leading the way down the hall, she said, "As I told you, I worked here as a maid—until last week when I had my last encounter with Bushnell. My cousin and her husband are the managers."

"It's nice that you have family nearby."

"To be honest, of late I haven't been sure if it was a blessing or a curse."

"Are they difficult?"

"Not like you might be imagining. It's just that my cousin

knows how I used to be, you see. She can't seem to equate it with the person I am now."

Julianne smiled wryly. "Ah. Now I understand. But you shouldn't worry about that. What you are forgetting, I think, is that we all used to be different people. Time and experience change us. It can't be helped."

Opening a door partly hidden by a screen, Lizbeth said, "I'm going to try to keep that in mind right now. And keep you beside me, as well. Between the two of us, we should be able to persuade Cook to make the captain a real breakfast."

"That should be no problem. I've persuaded a great number of people to do a great number of things. I'm rather good at it."

"I'll watch and learn then, Miss Van Fleet. I could stand to have a few more things come my way."

The moment the door closed, Devin motioned Ethan to his side. "Help me sit up better, would you? I feel like an invalid, lounging in this chair in front of the women."

Ethan didn't bother disputing the notion that he wasn't an invalid. He placed his arms under Devin's arms and pulled him up. "Better?"

"Yeah." After taking a sip of coffee, he met Ethan's gaze. "Did you have any inkling about this?"

"Of course not. I would have shot him in his chamber if I had." With effort, Ethan tamped down the dozen swear words and threats rumbling around in his head. His anger wouldn't serve any purpose, especially since he imagined Devin was no doubt thinking of some kind of retribution that didn't involve bloodshed.

After relating the details of his encounter with Bushnell at Julianne's home, Devin said, "I want to kill him."

Huh. It seemed he had been mistaken.

Weighing his next words carefully, Ethan said, "Any special way you want to go about doing that?"

Devin grunted. "You mean besides picking up my Colt, tracking him down, and firing two shots into his chest? No."

"Ah." This conversation was becoming increasingly full of surprises.

"What? And don't look at me that way, as though you are attempting to figure me out. Of course you must feel the same way."

"I do. But I'm wise enough not to act on it."

"We need to. Justice hasn't been served."

"First we need to figure out where he is," Ethan said. "I couldn't locate him when I returned from your place a few days ago. No one seems to know where he's gone. When you feel better, we should start combing other inns and hotels in the area. I think he preys on women who are alone or have no one to fight for them. That was certainly the case with Lizbeth."

"We can't conduct such a search on our own."

Ethan knew that, but he didn't want Devin to get too agitated either. "Don't worry. I'll figure out something."

"Ethan, go to the telegraph office and send for Truax and Baker. We need their help."

"I know we need help searching, but let's wait. I can handle Bushnell." Plus, it was his right. Bushnell had scarred Lizbeth. Violated her. For that, the man would pay, and Ethan wanted to be sure he would be the one to make him.

"If it was a matter of you gunning down the man in cold blood, I would agree. But we need a plan to make sure no one discovers what we do."

An itch of foreboding flooded him. It was one thing to kill a man in battle. Or in self-defense. Maybe it was even understandable to seek vengeance when emotions were high and a man could be excused for letting his need to protect get the best of him. But to methodically seek vengeance in a cool and calculated way? Well, he didn't need to confer with a pastor to know that was a sin.

Devin was staring at him with those ice-blue eyes of his. "What's wrong?"

"I'm hesitant to get them involved."

"Why? Didn't we promise we'd help each other? Haven't we done that for them?"

"Yes. Of course. But Robert was fighting a nasty web of lies about Phillip Markham."

"He was also intent on making things right for Miranda."

"And Baker, well, he was fighting a gang of men threatening the woman who freed him from jail."

Ethan shook his head. "Make no mistake about his motives, Ethan. He wanted to help her not because she'd freed him. It was because he loved her."

Thinking about rough, jaded Thomas and how he'd gazed at Laurel with such tenderness, Ethan swallowed hard. Thomas Baker was easily the scrappiest of them all. He was rough around the edges and had a temper that could be ignited faster than a stick of dynamite. "Yes. That is true. However . . ."

"However what?"

"Is love involved now? I'm not sure."

"I am."

Devin was sure Ethan had fallen in love with Lizbeth?

"I don't know if I've fallen in love."

"Who said I was talking about you?"

Ethan wanted to ask if he was sure he understood what Devin

meant . . . until he got up to answer a knock at the door and saw who was there.

Things might eventually get better. But not yet. Certainly not anytime soon.

27

MISS VAN FLEET AND LIZBETH STOOD IN THE BACK OF THE
kitchens while Bertha, the cook, prepared a simple but substantial
breakfast.

Lizbeth had asked for food for the men, but, as she always did,
Bertha seemed to have a sixth sense about what was needed and
set her staff to creating breakfast for four. She'd been grateful for
the kindness, as well as the excuse to stand in the back of the noisy
kitchens and pull herself together.

Of course, she didn't try to fool herself into thinking she was
going to accomplish that goal anytime soon. She felt shattered
inside. Embarrassed too. For some reason, admitting her most
closely guarded secret had given her body permission to relive those
terrible hours all over again. Though a part of her felt it had been
bound to happen sooner or later, she would have given everything
she had to relive Bushnell's abuse in the far future, preferably when
she was alone.

It certainly would have helped the major, Captain Monroe,
and Miss Van Fleet. They'd looked shocked and disturbed.
Especially Julianne. Lizbeth couldn't blame her. She was soiled, at
least to most people of good breeding and class, of which Julianne
surely was.

It didn't matter that Lizbeth had been hurt by a soldier, that she was as much a victim of the war as the men littering the streets without limbs or disfigured from their injuries. Society had a different view of women who had been attacked and survived. They assumed they had allowed men liberties. That's why she'd never told anyone.

"Do you want to talk about it?" Miss Van Fleet whispered.

"I beg your pardon?"

Compassion warmed her gaze. "If you'd rather not talk about it, I understand, but I thought you might want to talk about it with another woman."

Talk about it? About how she'd been bleeding and hurt and alone for days . . . until yet another band of soldiers came through to take what few belongings she had left? About how they'd stared at the angry cut on her face and had known? *Surely they'd known.* But still they'd looted and grabbed until there hadn't been anything left.

A shiver ran through her. It seemed she was incapable of stopping her body from reacting to the memories. If she started talking about it now, in the middle of the kitchens? Chances were good she would collapse onto the floor.

"Thank you, but I don't think so."

Miss Van Fleet frowned at her stiff and formal tone. "Forgive me."

Her stomach sank. Somehow she'd managed to make things worse. "It's kind of you to still be speaking to me, Miss Van Fleet," she said. "Many women of your class would now be pretending I didn't exist."

"Please, call me Julianne. I certainly am not one to pass judgment." Staring at the women bustling around the kitchen in front of them, she exhaled. "Sometimes I wonder if men will ever really stop to think about what their sisters and girlfriends and mothers endured when they left to fight." She shivered.

"Being left behind to worry and make do on our own was difficult, wasn't it?" Hearing her words, she flushed. Calling those years difficult was like calling Texas in July simply hot. But if Julianne found an issue with her statement, she didn't let on. She merely nodded and continued to watch the staff making preparations.

Minutes later, Meg approached with a tray in her hands. "Here you go, Lizbeth. Cook wants to know who to charge for the payment. The major or the captain?"

"I'm not sure. Maybe the major?" She looked to Julianne for advice.

Julianne nodded. "That's a good start. If the men find fault with that, they can clear it up later on their own."

Meg smiled. "Good enough." Before she turned away, she said, "I guess you are truly keeping company with the major now, aren't you?"

"He's been a good friend."

"I just bet he has." After smirking at her fellow workers, she said, "Don't mind us none. We're just a little jealous, is all. The major is a man worth claiming."

Lizbeth felt her cheeks heat. Though she knew Meg hadn't meant to embarrass her, she still had. Hoping to transfer their focus to someone else, she looked around the kitchen. "Meg, have you seen Cassie? I just realized she usually comes down here to take her break right about now."

Looking pensive, Meg motioned them toward the door. "Lizbeth, no one's seen her today."

"Why not? Is she sick?"

Meg shook her head. "She's gone. All her things too." After looking over her shoulder, she lowered her voice. "Cook says Cassie probably took off with an admirer or something, but I don't know. That don't seem like her."

"That isn't like her at all!" Cassie was always full of good humor, but she wasn't flighty. Lizbeth knew she wouldn't have left without giving notice and careful planning. "Has anyone told Aileen? What did she say?"

"I guess Cook told her, but you know how Mrs. Howard is. If it don't concern paying guests, she don't pay too much attention."

Biting her bottom lip, Lizbeth nodded. "She can be that way, I suppose."

"No, she is that way," Meg corrected. Softening her voice, she said, "Look, don't worry about Cassie. I'm sure she's fine. I know you thought she was a good girl, but she had an eye on the gentlemen. Most likely she found her own Major Kelly and let herself get swept off her feet."

Lizbeth would have argued about that some more, but she was aware that Julianne was listening to every word and Meg was beginning to look uncomfortable. "Thanks for the tray and for letting me know about Cassie," she said at last. "I'll let you go before Cook gets upset."

As if on cue, Cook called out, "Meg, they don't pay you to stand around and do nothing."

Meg grinned. "I'll see you later. Work calls. Plus, you've got a tray to deliver."

After smiling at her again, Lizbeth led Julianne out of the warm kitchen. "I'm sorry about that."

"Think nothing of it. I'm sorry about your friend."

"I am too. Well, I'm surprised. No matter what Meg said, I can't see Cassie running after a man without careful thought."

"Maybe she had a reason you didn't know about."

Looking at Julianne, Lizbeth realized that could be the case.

Though she and Cassie had been friends, they'd been close work friends. Lizbeth had certainly never told Cassie about her past. It only stood to reason that Cassie hadn't felt compelled to share all her secrets. "Maybe she did at that," she said softly.

Julianne placed one elegant hand on her arm. "Are you all right? If not, I can carry the tray to Captain Monroe's room."

There was no way she would allow that to happen. "I'm fine. Though I am worried about Cassie, I'm not going to borrow trouble. I'm just going to have to assume she's moved on to some place better." She determined to ignore the fear that invaded her thoughts.

Looking relieved as they walked through the lobby, Julianne nodded. "Perhaps that's the best thing to do at the moment."

Lizbeth was just about to change the subject when Aileen called out her name. Unable to avoid her, they stopped again.

Her cousin was beaming. Beaming! She looked as though she were half floating with excitement. After quickly introducing her to Julianne and setting the tray down on a nearby table, she said, "Aileen, what has happened? You look so happy."

"Major Kelly's family just arrived."

Lizbeth was so surprised, she pushed all her worries about Cassie's whereabouts from her mind. Even she knew Ethan wasn't close to his family. She needed to warn him so they wouldn't catch him off guard. "Where are they?"

"Visiting him, of course. I escorted them to the captain's room myself."

"You did what?" Oh, he wasn't going to be happy.

"I had no choice, Lizbeth. That was Mr. Michael Kelly! He must own half of Texas."

"Did you warn the major first?"

"Of course not." She sighed and then spoke with even more

emphasis. "One more time, Lizbeth, Mr. Michael Kelly is here, with Mrs. Kelly and their other children. Of course I'm going to do whatever they ask. Besides, they're his parents."

Reluctantly, Lizbeth conceded that her cousin had a point. It wasn't a hotelier's job to screen guests' visitors—only to do what was asked quickly and efficiently.

Amusement lit Julianne's eyes. "Something tells me neither Major Kelly nor the captain is going to be excited to entertain guests."

"We better hurry."

Aileen trotted along as Lizbeth picked up the tray, and they headed down the secret hallway that wasn't much of a secret anymore. "Dallas is so excited. They requested three more suites too."

So they were staying. "Aileen, you had better prepare yourself to face the wrath of Major Kelly."

"What wrath? He's the most gentlemanly man who stays here."

Lizbeth felt like pointing out that his good manners didn't necessarily mean he was honorable at every occasion. After all, he was a gambler. He'd also fought in the war and survived a prisoner of war camp. A man didn't come out on the other side of those things without being tough.

Julianne paused a couple of feet before Devin's door. "Thank you for informing us, Mrs. Howard, but we will take it from here."

Aileen drew to a stop. "I was going to open the door for you."

"We'll simply knock."

"Lizbeth—"

She knew what Aileen wanted. She wanted Lizbeth to let her peek inside the room so she could report what was going on to her husband. But there was no way that was going to happen. Ignoring Aileen's look of longing, she walked down to the captain's door and knocked.

When it opened, six faces stared back at her. One of which was scowling.

"At last you have returned," Ethan said, his voice sounding as sharp as one of Bertha's butcher knives. "Do come in. You are just in time to meet my family."

28

TIME MIGHT AS WELL HAVE STOOD STILL FOR HIS FAMILY.
As Ethan stared at his brother, sister, and parents, each one decked out more elaborately than the last, he wondered if any other family in the state of Texas had been so blessed. The Kelly family had managed to survive the war without losing a member, losing their home, or, it seemed, their pride.

He'd only come to terms with the fact that despite his problems adjusting to civilian life, he had been just as blessed.

As he watched Lizbeth and Julianne enter the room, Lizbeth carrying a tray of food, he could sense their surprise and wariness. He hated it. Lizbeth's green eyes were clouded with worry. She was worried about him, about how he was feeling. After what she'd just revealed.

Before he could begin introductions, his mother stepped forward.

"I must say the service here couldn't be better. Set everything up along the back counter. Then you may go." Her voice lost a tad bit of warmth when Lizbeth and Julianne froze in confusion. "If you are waiting for a tip, you are going to have to do something more than stare back at me like deer lost in the glade."

Had his mother not noticed the women weren't wearing

maids' uniforms? Before Ethan could say a word, Lizbeth nodded and lifted the lid off the tray. Seeing her jump to his mother's bidding was more than he could take. Furious, he crossed the room and stopped her. "Don't," he said. When she flinched at his harsh tone, he gentled his voice and curved his hand around her own. "You are my guest now."

"I don't mind."

"But I do."

"Ethan, what is the problem?" his mother asked.

"Everyone, this is Lizbeth Barclay. She is a friend of mine. Also, may I present Miss Julianne Van Fleet of Boerne?" When they gaped at him, he continued the introductions. "Lizbeth, Julianne, please meet my parents, Michael and Genevieve Kelly. And these two are my siblings, Phillip and Margaret."

He noticed his brother and sister were studying both him and the women with interest. When Julianne curtsied, Margaret stepped forward and smiled. "It's a pleasure to meet you, Miss Van Fleet, and you too, Miss Barclay."

Julianne inclined her head. "Thank you."

Lizbeth curtsied but didn't say a word. It was obvious she was uncomfortable.

"I'm completely confused. Why are they bringing food in here if they don't work at the hotel?" his mother asked.

"I was an employee here until very recently," Lizbeth said.

Julianne moved to Devin's side and was now speaking to him softly. Before Ethan had allowed his family to enter, he'd assisted Devin back into bed. This was after he'd considered refusing to see them at all.

It was Devin who had insisted they come in. He said he had no modesty after the war and could not care less who saw him in bed—though he still wished Julianne and Lizbeth didn't have to. Because Ethan couldn't argue that point, he'd allowed his family to enter and explained how Devin was still recuperating after being shot. Of course, his family had looked somewhat alarmed, but they'd handled the news with grace. The Kelly family prided themselves on being able to adapt to any situation with ease.

Since then, Devin had been reclining in bed, just as if he usually received guests while lying down. Now, though, it was easy to see he wasn't pleased with Ethan's mother's assumptions about Julianne and Lizbeth. That was good, because Ethan was just as appalled. It was time to get his family out of the room and figure out why they'd suddenly decided to track him down.

"We need to allow Devin to rest," he said abruptly.

After studying Ethan's expression, his father nodded. "Yes. Of course, son." His father walked to Devin's side. "I will hope and pray you continue to heal, Captain. It was an honor to meet you."

Ethan could hardly believe his father's words. This was the first time in Ethan's memory his father wasn't acting as if he were the most important person in the room.

After his mother and siblings said their good-byes, his father opened the door and ushered the three of them out. Then he paused, obviously waiting for him as well. "Ethan?"

"I'll be right there. Close the door, please."

To his surprise, his father did as he asked. And his mother didn't even offer a word of protest! What in the world was going on? Feeling as though he were in the middle of a strange dream, Ethan turned to Devin. "Obviously I need to see to my family. After I ascertain why they have decided to pay me a visit, I'll send those telegrams posthaste."

Amusement lit Devin's eyes. "Thank you. Now, ladies, I think it would be best if you left as well."

"I am not leaving," Julianne said. "I came here to help you, and that is what I intend to do."

"I am better now, Julianne."

"All the same, I am staying."

"I'm going to go back to Mrs. Harrison's," Lizbeth said quietly. "I have a lot to do. Enjoy the time with your family, Major Kelly."

Knowing his family was lingering in the hall, waiting on him, Ethan nodded. "I'll call for you later. We have much to talk about." He was no longer concerned about gossip.

Lizbeth nodded before slipping out the door.

Ethan felt a loss—and the loss of everything he'd wanted to say deep in his heart. Lizbeth was embarrassed that Devin and Julianne knew about her past, having no idea Julianne had a past too. She'd acted as though his family should treat her like their servant too. It was all a mess. A complete and utter mess. He wanted to protect her more than ever. Be there for her. Reassure her that nothing she could say or do would distract him from convincing her to marry him.

But first he had to deal with his family. And, yes, go after Bushnell.

"I'll be back as soon as I can," he told Devin.

"I'd rather you take your time, Major. You have quite a list of people who need your attention."

Ethan felt like rolling his eyes. What Devin had said was a complete understatement.

Walking out into the hall, he studied his family. They were all standing rather leisurely, somehow managing to appear as though they loitered in hotel hallways on a regular basis. Knowing he had perfected that same way of behaving made his temper flare. Here again was another example of how he'd thought he was so different from his family, when in fact he was just like them. "Follow me," he said at last.

"Ethan, your men might be used to following your directives without question, but I assure you this family is not," his father pronounced. This was more like him. "Where are you taking us?"

"To my room. It's just on the second floor. We can confer there."

But still his father hesitated. "Ethan, I would rather not discuss our business while sitting on the edge of a bed."

"I have a sitting room. All of you will be completely comfortable." And he will have gained a few moments to accept the fact that his family had descended upon him without notice.

When his father looked as if he was tempted to question him further, Ethan started walking. He knew he was walking too fast for the women, for his mother most especially. But he couldn't bring himself to care. His mind was feeling too muddled. Why had they shown up? And what was he going to say about Lizbeth?

Seconds later, Phillip caught up with him. "So, who is that woman with the dark curly hair and green eyes? I am sure she is more than a mere maid."

What she was, was complicated. "Lizbeth is no one you need to worry about."

"If she matters to you, I will," Phillip said, surprising him. "Besides, you know Mother is going to have a dozen questions about her. You should prepare yourself."

In the face of everything they were going through, such worries struck him as laughable. "She can ask all the questions she wants. I'll be all right."

Phillip slowly smiled. "You are better. The shadows in your eyes have faded."

"I have recently realized that myself."

"I hope that means we'll be seeing more of you."

As much as Ethan wanted to make that promise, he couldn't

quite do that. He needed to know why his family had come to *him*—and see how they treated Lizbeth. If he couldn't be assured she would be treated with care, Ethan knew he would keep his distance as much as he could. Hoping to ease the tension between them, he changed the subject. "Phillip, how have you been?"

"You know. Doing the same. Working hard." Sounding aggrieved, he continued. "I've had to help Father find workers. We have to pay field hands now. Not much, of course, but that is a concern."

Ethan didn't dare touch that. His schooling at West Point had taught him a lot about how others viewed slavery. By the time he'd left the academy, he, too, had disdained the practice and privately promised himself he would do everything he could to help end it. He'd fought in the war to uphold the honor of the South, not to celebrate the inhuman practice of owning another man.

"How is Margaret?" he asked, eager to change the subject again.

Phillip shrugged. "About the same."

"Couldn't you share something more? Don't forget, I have not seen her in six months," he said as they walked up the stairs. He was aware of his father escorting their mother and sister at a far slower pace. "Is she well?"

His brother frowned. "She lost George. Remember?"

He had been in such a bad place when he'd been home, Ethan wasn't even sure if he'd been aware of how much she'd been grieving. "George McDonald, yes?"

Phillip nodded. "He was a fine fellow. He died two months before the nuptials were set to take place. Margaret already had her wedding gown and everything."

Ethan couldn't believe he hadn't known of all that, and since seeing Margaret, he had all but forgotten her loss. Forgotten his family *had* been touched by death. He didn't want to admit that. "How did he die again?"

"George had to report to camp for training. Then, right before he went out into the battlefield, he contracted some kind of stomach ailment. Margaret heard he'd died within two weeks of contracting it."

"It was most likely typhus." Far too many men had died from poor sanitary conditions.

"Whatever it was, he died. As you can imagine, she's still having a difficult time getting over his death."

"I'm sure she is," he said softly, realizing yet again that he wasn't the only person in the family who had suffered. He'd been so consumed with fighting his own demons that he hadn't spared a thought to theirs.

Which brought him back to his family's sudden appearance.

"Why did Father bring all of you here?" he asked, realizing he needed to prepare himself before all four of them were confronting him with something that would likely catch him off guard.

Phillip slowed his steps. "Not sure if I should be the one telling you."

Whether it was because he was still coping with Devin's injury, absorbing Julianne's arrival, or felt as if he still wasn't doing his best for Lizbeth, his temper snapped. "You are almost thirty years old. When are you going to be old enough to speak for yourself? Tell me."

They were walking down his hallway now. Every door was closed, no one else in sight. But the hall had never felt so long. Ethan was both eager to pull his brother into the privacy of his room yet also dreading the moment.

"Father wanted to be the one to tell you."

"What would it matter if he wasn't? Do you really think the world would end?"

Looking stung, Phillip stepped back. "Of course not."

"Then what has you so afraid?"

Phillip clenched his fists. "I am not afraid of anything."

If he wasn't, he was a fool. "What is the reason, then?"

Their parents and his sister would be joining them within a minute or two. Ethan pulled out his key, inserted it into the lock, and resigned himself to waiting.

"They want you to return home," Phillip said under his breath.

That was it? "I'll come home as soon as I'm able." He smiled encouragingly. "I promise."

"No, you don't understand, Ethan. Our father is dying. The doctors don't give him more than six months to live. We need you back. I . . . I can't do it all on my own."

An ache settled deep in his heart as shock overcame him. But though he knew he'd have to later come to terms with what he'd just heard, Ethan didn't dare give in to it now.

Therefore, he pushed back the pain just as he had done during the war over and over again. "Have you even tried?"

Phillip flinched. "I have, but it's never been good enough. I've never been good enough, at least not in Father's eyes."

He grunted. "I think we both know that is a lie. I've been the embarrassment to him."

"They have missed you, worried about you, and prayed for you," Phillip corrected, his voice thick with emotion. "But never, never did they feel embarrassed."

"I had nightmares. I couldn't adjust when I returned." Lowering his voice, he said, "I was weak."

"You were human, Ethan. You fought with honor. You are a much-lauded survivor of a prisoner of war camp. Everyone in

Houston speaks highly of you." He chuckled, the laugh sounding harsh and dark. "I promise, you are many things to our parents, but a disappointment is not one of them."

What if his brother's words were true? What if his father didn't regard him as a black sheep but as a prodigal son? "I don't know what to say," he said at last.

"No? Well, why don't you simply answer me instead? What is it going to take to bring you home, Ethan?" he asked between gritted teeth. "Would our father dying do it? Or does it need to be something more important to you? Maybe the idea of running your family's legacy?"

"That isn't more important than our father."

"Really? What about Mother begging? Would that encourage you to put us first?" Phillip stepped closer as he walked through the threshold into Ethan's suite. "Or do you make sacrifices only for strangers or your fellow comrades from prison?"

Ethan gripped the frame of the door as he struggled to answer. Quite simply, he didn't know.

29

ETHAN NEVER IMAGINED HE'D FEEL SORRY FOR HIS FATHER, but he was coming close to it at that moment. Standing in his suite next to his brother, and looking at his sister and parents standing together next to the windows, he felt a tension in the air that was almost claustrophobic.

When he'd entered his room, he'd been determined to merely stand and wait for his father to come to the point of his visit all on his own. Michael Kelly had always liked to be in charge, and Ethan had no desire to take that away from him.

But after watching him clumsily attempt to get to the point of his visit and fail, Ethan realized he couldn't do it. He couldn't act as though he weren't his father's son. He was. And that meant his father deserved his respect, even when he didn't feel comfortable giving it to him.

"Sir," he finally began. "I'm sure you are busy. Perhaps you could share why you have decided to visit me here."

"Yes, I'm sure it is difficult wondering why we have descended upon you without notice," his father said stiffly.

"I don't care about that," Ethan retorted, suddenly realizing he meant it. "You are my family. I might not have shown it of late, but I still love and care for you."

He could practically feel his siblings' approval beside him. Ethan didn't know if that mattered to him. But after getting to know Lizbeth, he realized he'd taken them for granted.

Only after talking to Lizbeth and realizing just how much she'd had to do on her own, how much she'd had to survive without any help or comfort . . . Well, it made him ashamed. Yes, he'd been hurt and imprisoned. But he'd also always known that, when push came to shove, he would never have to stand completely alone. Now he wanted to stand by her side and give her the support and love she needed.

And, perhaps, also reach out to the people in this room. It was time to stop focusing on their differences and pay attention to what they had in common. Because, at the end of the day, he was incredibly blessed to still have his family. They were imperfect, but so was he. Therefore, if there was even a chance to have a kind of new relationship with them, he had to try.

"We want you to come home, Ethan," his mother said, her cultured voice breaking the silence. "The war is over now. And . . . and we need you with us."

"Yes," his father said. "You have your life to reclaim. It's time you came home for good."

Home. The word brought up images of a wide front porch, the grove of pin oak trees, the stable full of fine horses. The deep burgundy rug that lay in the center of the house's formal drawing room. His great-grandmother had brought that rug over from England.

It all brought forth a wave of sentimental longing. He wanted to be a part of the family again. But was he ready to move home right away? He just wasn't sure. He also didn't want to say anything about his father's illness until he brought it up himself. Not trusting himself to speak, he remained silent.

"Ethan, what do you have to say?" his father prompted.

"I want to help, but I may need more time. I have a rather full life here."

"Doing what?" Father ran a finger along the top of the marble-topped dresser. "Gambling? Living in a hotel?"

Ethan couldn't help but smile. "I would hesitate to call my success at the tables a failure. Besides, I don't gamble as frequently as you might imagine. I've also come to the aid of my friends. Helping them in any way I can."

"But what about when your family needs you to come to their aid?" Phillip asked. "Do we not count?"

Margaret stood up and walked to his side. "Ethan, won't you reconsider? Just because there's been strain between us, it doesn't mean we can't make amends. Doesn't everyone deserve a second chance?"

Ethan swallowed. His sister's words were much like what he'd been meaning to tell Lizbeth. That she was worthy of a second chance. That just because her life had changed didn't mean it no longer had value. "Yes," he said at last.

When Margaret launched herself into his arms, he held her tight. In spite of himself, tears pricked his eyes. "There, now," he murmured, pressing his lips to the top of her head. "Everything will be okay."

But instead of nodding, she shook her head. "It won't. Father is dying."

Though Phillip had prepared him, he still flinched. He lifted his head and stared at his parents across the room. "Is she telling the truth?"

Their father nodded. "I . . . I have some kind of disease in my organs. The doctors say I won't last much longer."

"But, Margaret, we weren't going to tell him yet. Remember?"

"He needed to know, Mother."

Phillip looked at their parents with a pointed expression. "It's time for us all to be honest with each other, I think."

His parents exchanged looks. Then their father nodded. "Phillip is right. We came here to ask you to come home because we need you to run the ranch."

Looking at Phillip, Ethan said, "Are you sure you won't resent me being there?"

"I'll be grateful, Ethan."

"Faye's husband died, son," Mother said. "She is free now. Maybe that might make a difference?"

"Why would I want her back? She married another man while I was a prisoner of war. I didn't even know of it until after the fact."

"We can find you someone," his mother said. "So many women are available now."

"I already have found someone," he said. "I've already found Lizbeth."

"And who is that?"

"She's the girl we thought was a maid," Phillip supplied. "That woman with the dark curly hair."

"She's pretty," Margaret said. "She seems sweet."

"She is."

"Does this mean you're considering my request?" his father asked. "Would you return home?"

"Would you accept Lizbeth on my arm?"

The tension in the room grew taut as his parents exchanged glances again. Then his mother walked to his side and clasped both of her hands in his. "With open arms," she said.

Her expression was completely serious. In that moment, Ethan realized she was sincere as well. If he could convince Lizbeth to marry him, he could move them to the ranch and she would be secure. Settled.

Squeezing his mother's hands lightly, he said, "I'll come home soon. I need to take care of a few things first, but I'll come back. It's time."

When she pressed her lips to his knuckles, he could almost feel a collective sigh of relief fill the room.

Funny, but he might have felt a bit of relief too.

"Here you go, Devin. Are you ready for some nourishing soup?" Julianne asked as she carried a bowl to his side.

Devin yawned as he struggled to sit up. After everyone else left his room, he'd been so exhausted, he'd told Julianne he wanted to rest his eyes for a bit. To his dismay, he'd slept almost two hours.

During that time, Julianne had straightened the room, eaten some of the food she and Lizbeth had brought in, and then eventually had gone to get fresh water and some soup for him. She'd left him a short note, describing her errand.

He'd found it the moment he woke up. Then, while he was waiting for her return, he'd used the time to analyze his degree of pain . . . and make plans for retaliation. After so many years of war, he didn't take putting the law into his own hands lightly. But Bushnell had been more than a thorn in his side. He was a threat to all of them. He'd tried to kill him. He'd also treated Julianne disgracefully and, it turned out, violated Lizbeth. Surely there wasn't another man in his life who deserved retribution more.

However, focusing on such dark thoughts had drained him. He'd felt desolate and bitter. After taking a few sips of the broth, he set the bowl on the table by the bed.

Julianne's appearance was truly a ray of light. "I'm ready for your company," he said lightly.

She paused, not even hiding her surprise. Then she smiled. "I'm glad."

Oh, that smile. Just like that, life seemed better. Struck by a new sense of optimism, he inhaled deeply. She had such an effect on him.

Would he ever be able to look at Julianne without being completely struck by her beauty? It wasn't likely. Though he'd learned long ago that one's outward appearance didn't make or break a person, few people were blessed with a beauty like hers.

However, he had decided that was a good thing. He liked the idea of being a little tongue-tied around the woman he had chosen to love.

Yes, love. He'd come to terms with the depth of his feelings for her sometime around the moment he was bleeding and struggling up the front steps of the Menger Hotel. He'd had a momentary epiphany about the connection between bleeding to death and the pain in his heart. He'd decided if he was going to bleed out, he might as well die honestly. And that involved telling himself that he had loved his family. He'd loved his country. The men he'd fought beside and suffered next to in prison barracks.

And a beautiful woman who had suffered in her own way, but was still walking and breathing and looking her detractors in the eye.

Julianne picked up the bowl and carried it across the room. Then, with a rustle of taffeta, she returned to his side. "I'm so glad you slept. How are you feeling?"

There was no way he was going to share with her the ugly thoughts he'd been entertaining about Bushnell's fate. "Oh, you know," he murmured. "I feel like I've been shot."

She didn't smile at his quip. Instead, she leaned closer, bringing with her the faint scent of roses he now recognized was as much a part of her person as the striking auburn hair that framed her face.

"When did the doctor say he was going to return?" she asked.

"He didn't. Hopefully he won't be back."

"You dislike doctors that much?"

"I dislike being poked and prodded that much."

As he'd hoped, she perched next to him on the bed. Examining his bandage, she murmured, "I never took you to be squeamish, Devin."

"I'm not. I just don't necessarily trust sawbones. I saw too many drunken ones on the battlefield." Belatedly realizing the images in his mind weren't fit for feminine ears, he shifted restlessly. "Don't mind me. Everything seems to irritate me today."

"I'll watch myself, then."

"Everything except you." When her eyes warmed, he said, "I just don't like lying here like an infant." He didn't like being weak, and he really didn't like being weak in front of her. He was sure she was one of the strongest women he'd ever met.

After smiling softly at him again, she turned her attention back to his wound. Her fingers were light as she loosened the gauze strips and inspected his bare skin. "Everything seems to be doing all right."

He noticed she didn't look squeamish. "Do you have experience tending wounds, Julianne?"

She leaned back. "Some."

The very fact that she looked so uncomfortable talking about her skill made him curious. "How?"

"Like many women, I volunteered in the local hospital during the war."

"I didn't know." He really didn't know much about her, he realized. Suddenly, he wished she would tell him everything about herself. He wanted to know it all—her favorite foods, her favorite colors, how she'd gotten her beagle. What she dreamed about. He wanted to know it all.

She smiled slightly, though the warmth didn't reach her eyes. "Did you think I only waited for Daniel to visit me?"

"Of course not." Although his thoughts had been perilously close to that conclusion. "I guess hearing about your work at the hospital took me off guard because you look so delicate." He was not lying.

"If I ever was delicate, I learned to overcome it rather quickly." She walked across the room, gathered fresh gauze and scissors, then returned to his side. "At first Mrs. Mills acted as if my reputation was going to infect the injured men like a leper's disease might. But after some time passed, any help was welcome."

"I would have liked to see you tending to the men. I bet they thought you were an angel coming to them."

"Aren't you full of poetic words this afternoon?" She shrugged. "I don't know what they thought."

"Really? Most soldiers weren't shy about flirting with women." In fact, he would have been hard-pressed to imagine her not being inundated with all sorts of heartfelt sentiments of love and devotion.

She tensed as she seemed to take a moment to get her bearings. "I have neglected to tell you where I was," she said in a halting way. "You see, Captain, I tended to the men who were most grievously injured. Most of them died," she added, her voice thick with emotion.

He knew about those wards, of course. Doctors separated the worst of their patients so as not to hurt the morale of the healing.

On paper it made sense, but in practice Devin had always thought it bordered on cruelty for the men in those rooms.

He'd visited his men in those places more than once. He could still recall the dark feeling of doom and the smell of death lingering in the air. Never would he have imagined anyone putting a delicately raised woman in such a place.

"You were assigned there?" He didn't even try to temper the indignation in his voice.

"Mrs. Mills knew those men needed kindness too."

"Of course they did. But that was no place for a sheltered woman. I'm sorry, Julianne. I hate that you experienced that."

"I'm not. It was worthy work."

"Of course it was." He was making a mess of things. "How about this? I'm proud of you. Will that do?"

Her eyes lit up. "Yes, Devin, I think that will do just fine."

30

IT WAS ALMOST DARK BY THE TIME LIZBETH RETURNED TO the Menger Hotel. She'd considered staying away until morning, just so she wouldn't have to speak to either Dallas or Aileen again. Or see Ethan's face, now that he'd had more time to think about her ruin. Or the strain in Julianne's eyes. She didn't have the strength to fight another verbal battle, especially when she had no idea what she could say.

But while she did, indeed, have legitimate reasons to give the hotel a wide berth, she hadn't been able to do that. Not when Captain Monroe still needed help, knowing Julianne must be very tired by now.

And chances were good Major Kelly wasn't going to be able to do much for either of them for a while. He had his family here, and they looked both formidable and demanding. Lizbeth imagined they were going to require every bit of his time. She had decided to offer to sit with the captain so Julianne could get some rest. Spending the evening feeling useful would be the best thing for her state of mind.

To her surprise, the lobby of the hotel was bustling, a rare sight so late in the day. Several couples who looked well-to-do were sipping tea in the lounge areas while a great number of soldiers was standing near the entrance of the bar, their blue uniforms a stark reminder of who was in charge.

Lizbeth turned from them before one could catch her eye. She knew her habit of avoiding Yankee soldiers as much as possible was rather futile, but it couldn't be helped. Her brain and body would likely always tense up around any man in that blue wool uniform.

Her cousin was standing near the entrance, looking as if she would love nothing more than to exit the premises as soon as she possibly could. When she spied Lizbeth, she gestured for her to come closer.

"What's going on?" Lizbeth asked.

"It seems Major Kelly's parents have a great many friends in the area. When their appearance became public knowledge, scores of people descended on us. We are now filled to the seams. Every guest room has been taken."

"Dallas must be pleased."

Aileen shrugged. "I don't know if he is or not. By and large they are demanding in the extreme."

"It's a well-run hotel, Aileen. You and Dallas do a good job of managing it."

She looked just about to say more when Dallas approached. As usual, he was dressed in a three-piece suit. Unusually, however, he was sweating. She could see it on his brow.

Though she didn't owe him anything, she smiled. "Good evening, Dallas."

"Lizbeth. Hello."

"I hear you are filled to capacity."

His cursory nod stilled. Then he stared at her as though she were his new lifeline. "Are you here to work?" he asked.

"I am not."

"Any way I could persuade you? Since both you and Cassie left, we are extremely short-handed."

Ignoring the jab at her, she asked, "What happened with Cassie? Do you know where she went?"

"She left without a word," Aileen said. "I must admit to being surprised. It seemed out of character."

"Do you think something could have happened to her?" Lizbeth asked, feeling her anxiety rise again. "Maybe we should go to the sheriff."

With an impatient move of his hand, Dallas waved off her concern. "Cassie's departure is hardly noteworthy. Maids leave all the time without notice. What matters is that we are now extremely short-handed."

As much as he was heaping on the guilt, she wasn't going to feel a bit of it. "I hope you'll fill the jobs soon, Dallas."

He coughed, whether from embarrassment or irritation, Lizbeth didn't know. When he regained his composure, he said, "We have an important family staying here, you know." Looking around the crowded lobby, he added, "All their important friends too. Good service would cement the Menger's reputation as one of the top establishments in the state."

Lizbeth almost smiled. It was hard to imagine such things still meant so much to some people. "Since you're so busy, I had better let you both return to your duties. I only stopped to say hello to Aileen."

"You mean you came here to gloat. Now that you are connected with the major, I guess you're feeling high and mighty."

"Stop, Dallas," Aileen said, surprising Lizbeth. "As I told you earlier, we need to move forward. All of us do."

Dallas looked angry, but he held his tongue.

Knowing it wasn't the time to ease the tension between them, Lizbeth left for the captain's suite. When she arrived, she knocked on the door.

Almost immediately, Ethan opened it, then stepped into the hall. He closed the door quietly behind him. "I thought you would stay the night back at the Harrison."

"I thought I might be of some use here," she explained. "Since your family is in town, I assumed you would have other obligations to attend to."

"I already met with my family." Looking a little put upon—and a little bit resigned too—he smiled. "I believe they are currently holding court in the dining room. They have a great many friends here in San Antonio. Fortunately, one couple kept them occupied while I took care of some telegrams Devin asked me to send."

"I saw Aileen and Dallas on my way through the lobby. They said your family has created quite a stir."

He chuckled. "That's one way of putting it." Sobering, he continued. "I stopped here at Devin's room to check on him. I was planning to visit you next."

"Now you don't have to." Feeling conspicuous and a little embarrassed that she came when it was becoming obvious Ethan didn't want her to stay, she cleared her throat. "I will be seeing you, then. Julianne must be caring for Captain Monroe."

"She insists. But please allow me to walk you back. I want to speak to you about what happened earlier."

"There's no need."

"There's every need." He held up a hand. Almost reached out to touch her . . . then seemed to reconsider. "Please, stay here a second while I tell Devin and Julianne what I'm doing."

"All right."

"Don't you leave," he warned.

His expression was so hard, she almost smiled. "I promise. I won't go anywhere."

∞

True to his word, Ethan stepped back into the hall mere minutes later.

"How is he?" Lizbeth asked.

"He already seems much better. Julianne has put on a pair of spectacles and is reading to him."

Ethan sounded bemused. "Are you surprised they are doing something so mundane or that she wears glasses?" she asked as they walked through the hotel lobby.

"A little bit of both, I guess," he replied as he led her outside. "I'm ashamed to say I made far too many hasty decisions where she is concerned. At first I was sure she was nothing more than a pretty face."

Lizbeth might have felt jealous if the same thing hadn't crossed her mind. "They seem well suited. Perhaps they will have a long and happy future together. After all, people do say opposites attract."

"I don't know if we are opposites, but I hope you and I might find a future together one day as well," he said as they continued to walk down the street.

"Oh?" She couldn't be sure he was still talking about marriage.

"Yes. You see, it's a long story, but I think I finally mended things with my family." He took a breath. "Actually, I told them I will eventually return home for good."

"That's wonderful." She meant that sincerely. "Family should stick together." She was happy for him, but feared his new bond might ultimately force him to move on to a woman who was more of his social equal.

"They would like me to take over the running of the ranch and our holdings."

"Ah." He would be leaving soon. No doubt when they were apart he would wonder why he'd ever felt so attached to a maid. It was a struggle to keep her composure.

He looked down at her. "You don't seem to be sharing my enthusiasm."

"No, I am happy for you."

"Lizbeth, when I return, I want you by my side. I told my brother and parents that."

Shocked, she almost stumbled. "Ethan, I don't know—"

"Shh. You don't need to say anything yet. Just know that I haven't given up on us. I am looking forward to my future, Lizbeth. Just as importantly, I want you to want to be there with me."

It was on the tip of her tongue to say she wanted to be by his side as well. But those painful years during the war and experiencing so much loss made her wary.

"Say you'll think about it," he said.

"I'll think about it." Then, because she didn't want him to imagine she wasn't touched by his words, she curved her hand around his elbow and smiled up at him. No matter what, she wanted him to know she was proud to be walking by his side.

After a moment, the muscles in his arm relaxed and he smiled too.

It was so lovely, a new warmth filled her insides. Right at this moment, they were together. Her hand was on his arm. That was enough for now.

31

Johnson's Island, Ohio
Confederate States of America Officers' POW Camp

THEY'D BECOME A GREETING PARTY OF SORTS. WHENEVER one of them heard word of additional soldiers arriving, five of them would stand at the entrance of their barracks and welcome the newly imprisoned.

As the dozen or so men walked toward them, their expressions as ravaged as their bodies, Devin figured he'd done nothing harder in his life. He had nothing to offer them except acceptance. Sometimes that was received gratefully.

Other times? The men lashed out at them in anger. Resentful of their circumstances. Scared they wouldn't survive. Worse, that they would while their comrades who hadn't been picked up would die while fighting. It was a difficult transition to make, leaving the ranks of the brave for the company of the survivors. Devin knew. He'd experienced every range of emotion during his long months of incarceration.

Officer Crosby stopped at the entrance and looked at Devin with a practiced eye. "You ready for them, Monroe?"

Devin nodded. He wouldn't go so far as to say Crosby and he were close, but they had definitely come to an agreement over the last two months of Devin's captivity. They treated each other with respect, sometimes even bordering toward the friendly.

Devin thought the man was a lot like him. Unlike some of the other guards, Crosby had fought with valor during much of the war. He seemed to find the lack of exercise as difficult to bear as the whole feeling of helplessness that pervaded their surroundings.

Sometimes, too, Devin would catch Crosby eyeing the other guards with something close to impatience and disdain. And no small wonder. Devin realized some of these men wouldn't have lasted an hour on the battlefield. They were as unruly as they were lazy.

Crosby pulled out a heavy brass key ring and unlocked the doorway. "Listen up, you Johnny Rebs. You are under our jurisdiction now. Best mind yourselves and watch your backs. Save yourself some pain and worry and listen to Monroe here. He'll make sure you get on all right."

All at once, the dozen new prisoners turned to Devin and stared. Their expressions ranged from cautious hope to pure disdain.

Devin was used to that too. Some of the incoming prisoners were sure any man who survived imprisonment must be a traitor. Sometimes, after the guards left, the new prisoners would take out their anger and pent-up fears on him. He'd learned the hard way never to face a new band of men alone.

When Crosby left, locking the gate securely behind him, Devin spoke. "I'm not going to tell you welcome, because we all know this is no place where any of us would choose to be. Instead, I'll just introduce myself. I'm Devin Monroe, Captain, C.S.A. Behind me is Major Ethan Kelly, Lieutenant Robert Truax, Lieutenant Phillip Markham, and Sergeant Thomas Baker."

A man wearing captain's bars eyed him suspiciously. "How come you're greeting us? You work for the Yanks or something?"

Before Devin could answer, Markham stepped forward. "We have the dubious honor of being some of the longest residents of this place. We got sick and tired of watching each man new to our ranks enter here looking like they were weeks away from dying."

The captain eyed Phillip, then nodded. "Name is Underman. Randolph. I'm out of Kentucky."

Markham nodded. "Captain Underman, I'll do my best to help you and your comrades survive here."

"Is it possible?" another man asked, this one a colonel. His expression was slightly incredulous. "We heard no one survives here long."

"We do our best to beat the odds," Devin said. "Now, come along and we'll make sure you have cots to sleep on."

"Do you observe rank here?"

Devin barely refrained from rolling his eyes. In almost every group of new prisoners, someone always made sure Devin knew he didn't intend to follow the directives or advice of a lowly captain. "We try to honor each man's worth, Colonel."

"What does that mean?"

"It means we've learned that the men's ranks usually stem from honor and bravery on the battlefield, not while sitting in a prisoner of war camp."

"Rank and file means everything, Captain."

"Not here, it doesn't," Ethan Kelly blurted.

The colonel swung around to face him. "I know you. You were at West Point."

"I was. Markham was as well. I don't recall you being there, however."

His expression tightened. "I did not have that benefit."

"Seems like you've still done all right for yourself."

The colonel lifted his chin. "One learns quickly to prevail no matter what happens. All that matters in life is who comes out on top."

Phillip Markham, the man who'd always been their voice of honor, eyed him coldly. "No, sir. All that matters is who survives."

"That's the same thing."

Phillip shook his head slowly. "I beg your pardon, but I must disagree. That's not the same at all. It's not even close."

32

THE FOLLOWING EVENING DEVIN WAS FEELING EVEN MORE like himself again, and with Julianne at last getting some sleep in her own room, he and Ethan were spending a few late-night hours in the Menger bar. Though it was connected to the hotel, it was everything the lofty Menger was not. With its wide plank floors, polished copper bar, scuffed tables and chairs, and dim lighting, it was a man's retreat. Devin imagined scores of men over the years had found solace here, especially the men who had been to war.

Returning to civilized society was a challenge. Sometimes men needed to be around masculine comforts and away from elegant wallpaper, etched drawings, genteel voices, and feminine sensibilities. Devin had found it to be something of an oasis in the midst of so much fussiness. He was now used to soldiers' plain speaking. And many men like him were in San Antonio. Former officers, former Confederate soldiers—they were a rough-and-tumble lot. After spending years in only the company of men, they were uneasy at spending too long a time in feminine company.

Oh, some men were the exception. Devin figured Ethan was one. He was a true gentleman, and no matter how hard he protested that he didn't fit the title, it remained true.

But that didn't mean he didn't enjoy holding court with Devin in one of the bar's back tables. Smoking cheroots, sipping whiskey, and trading stories with other men who had survived.

Devin had just accepted a second round of drinks from the barkeep, paid for by a cavalry officer from Louisiana, when Mrs. Howard opened the bar's ornate door.

Right away, the atmosphere in the room changed. It was obvious her presence wasn't welcome.

Women weren't wanted here, that was true. But it was more than that. Ethan had told him there was something condescending about her, and Devin could tell many of the men in the room didn't care for that. As for Devin, he only needed one reason to stay as far away from her as possible: she'd sided with Bushnell instead of Lizbeth.

Leaning back, he watched Mrs. Howard make her way through the maze of tables. She ignored the men who stood up when she approached or nodded in her direction. Beside him, Ethan fidgeted.

"Looks like we've got company," he muttered.

Devin didn't reply, only picked up his cheroot and inhaled. When she stopped in front of their table, obviously ill at ease, he barely got to his feet. Then, after exhaling his smoke in a way that would make his mother cuff his ears, he raised his eyebrows. "Mrs. Howard. To what do we owe this honor?"

Ethan, who had stood up politely, tossed him a look as he gestured to the chair that had just been vacated by the Louisianan. "Evening, Mrs. Howard. Care to join us?"

She looked taken aback. "Uh, no, thank you, Major Kelly." After clearing her throat, she spoke again. "I am sorry to disturb y'all, but you have visitors."

She hadn't tried to contain the sarcasm in her voice, and Devin didn't attempt to hide his lack of respect for her. "Who is it?"

"A pair of, uh, men."

She had purposely not said gentlemen. Well, so be it. At the moment, he wasn't feeling like much of a gentleman either. "Well, where are they?"

"I wasn't sure where you were. Or if you wanted to see them . . ."

"Mrs. Howard, if you could show me where you left them cooling their heels, I'd be obliged," Ethan interjected as he stood up once again and circled the table.

Looking relieved to no longer be dealing with Devin, she smiled hesitantly at Ethan. "Yes, of course, Major. If you will follow me. I asked them to wait in the lobby."

After giving Devin a pointed stare that said to settle down, Ethan followed Mrs. Howard back through the smoky bar and out the door.

When the door firmly closed behind him, two men at the bar clinked glasses. That gesture returned the festive air back to the room.

And with it, the tension Devin hadn't even been aware he'd been carrying dissipated. He smoked his cheroot and sipped his whiskey while he waited. One or two men paused near his table, obviously eager for him to extend an invitation for them to join him.

He didn't.

After exchanging the minimum of small talk, he used the time to think about Julianne. She'd looked very fetching that afternoon when, over her objection about his readiness, he'd taken her for a short stroll on the street in front of the Menger.

She'd worn a dark-gray dress that should have looked drab on her. Instead, it only served to accentuate her auburn hair and blue eyes. She had held his arm and smiled at him as though he were the only person in the state. Under her spell, he'd told her a story or two about growing up with his brothers and how he'd gotten into far too much mischief. Despite her concern for his health, she'd laughed and teased him, coaxing him to chuckle too.

Their interaction didn't go unnoticed. Men eyed him enviously. She didn't seem to notice. He had, though. He hadn't needed their approval, but he'd understood their envy. He'd been amazed he had the honor of her company.

Before they returned to the hotel, Julianne mentioned she needed to go home, at the same time trying to extract from him a promise to fully heal before coming to Boerne to see her. He convinced her to let him pay for her room at the Menger a few nights more. He couldn't bear the thought of her returning to her house before he had Bushnell taken care of. He'd managed to scare her enough to stay.

He wasn't especially proud of that, but he was glad it had served its purpose. He wasn't going to play the fool again. No matter what, he would make sure she was safe.

And as soon as he did that, he was going to continue to court her. He still wanted to marry her. More than once in the last two days, he'd offered to marry her immediately. Of course she'd refused, but she looked at him in a way that told him a part of her had wanted to say yes. It had made him gratified.

When the saloon door flew open again, Devin put down his glass. Tension snaked up his spine as he watched closely for the newcomers.

When he saw who it was, he grinned. Ethan had entered with Robert Truax and Thomas Baker.

Tossing his cheroot in the brass spittoon nearby, he stood and strode over to meet them. "You are a sight for sore eyes, gentlemen," he exclaimed as he held out his hand.

Robert shook his hand first. "I would hug you, but I hear you're filled with holes," he joked.

"Only two—the bullet went in my shoulder and then out. However, they are sizable."

Baker grinned. "I'm sure they are impressive wounds, Cap. I'm just glad that bullet didn't kill you." And with that, he wrapped his arms around Devin and lightly hugged him.

Devin might have been embarrassed by the affection they were showing if these men weren't his closest friends in the world. In addition, he knew he owed them more than he could ever repay. These men had put their lives on the line for him multiple times and had suffered next to him on Johnson's Island. Never would he shy away from their friendship. "It's good to see you both. A nice surprise too. I didn't expect to see y'all for at least another day."

"I told them the same thing," Ethan said.

"You know the story. When one of us calls, the others come running," Thomas said. "No exceptions."

"I rode out yesterday after receiving your telegram, Ethan," Robert said. "And somehow Thomas and I arrived at the same time."

"Come on, let's sit down before somebody decides to take our spot," Ethan said as he beckoned them back to their table. Devin appreciated that. For the conversation to come, they'd need that corner out of hearing of other patrons.

The men didn't need any further encouragement. After calling an order for two additional whiskeys, they settled themselves, each covertly taking stock of the others.

"No offense, Cap, but you look like death warmed over," Baker said.

"I look better than that," Devin protested.

"Not by much. Shouldn't you still be in bed recuperating?"

"I should not. I got a bullet hole, not an amputation."

"Doc say you're gonna be all right?" Truax asked.

"He did. So stop staring at me like I'm gonna pass out."

Ethan laughed. "The problem is neither of us looks as fit and hardy as these two. Once we get hitched and set up a home, I'm sure we'll look like we're in glowing good health too."

Thomas smiled. "The major doesn't lie. Laurel changed my life."

Robert smiled. "Indeed. It's amazing what marriage and a home can do to you."

"And how is the lovely Miranda?" Devin asked. They all knew of Miranda because she was once their good friend Phillip Markham's wife. Phillip had died on Johnson's Island, and Miranda had mourned extensively. When they'd heard men and women were ruining Phillip's reputation and making Miranda's life unbearable, Robert traveled to Galveston to try to help her. While doing so, the two of them had fallen in love and soon after they married.

Robert smiled. "With child."

That news made every jest and ribald comment evaporate from his head. "Many felicitations," Devin said sincerely. "I hope she is feeling all right."

"Mrs. Truax is having to adjust to being a pampered lady of leisure. Between me and the rest of the staff, she's only allowed to take her daily walks and take care of herself."

Ethan chuckled. "How is she handling that?"

"To my surprise, she simply bats her eyelashes, smiles at me, and says, 'Yes, Robert.' Then she does what she wants. Within reason, of course."

Devin grinned. "Sounds like the South needed her in the army. She could have taught us all a thing or two about dealing with superior officers."

"She could at that," Robert said softly. When their drinks arrived, he took a sip of his whiskey, then looked at both him and Ethan. "Speaking of officers . . . What is going on with Bushnell?"

"He's the one who shot me," Devin said.

Thomas Baker gaped. "I knew he was an idiot and a blowhard, but this doesn't even make sense."

"It caught me off guard too, especially seeing as he shot me in the back."

"And he's still alive?" Truax murmured.

"If he was here in San Antonio, he wouldn't be. But he isn't," Ethan said. "That's why we called for your help. We need to go after him and see that justice is served."

"I'll be glad to hand out justice," Baker said with a satisfied look. "No one is going to get away with shooting you in the back, Captain."

"This isn't just for me, Baker," Devin said. "It's for a Miss Van Fleet and Miss Barclay too."

Robert looked at them both. "What does Bushnell have to do with them?"

"Unfortunately, far too much," Ethan said. Succinctly, he told them about Lizbeth—the fact that Bushnell had both marked and violated her, and then most recently had nearly forced his way with her in a hotel room.

Then Devin shared how he met Julianne, how she had come to his aid when he was shot, and that she'd been Bushnell's mistress during the war. He also explained why she'd allowed such a man into her life.

Both Thomas and Robert gaped.

"I don't know what to respond to first," Baker said. "This Lizbeth, is she all right now?"

"She is. I've got her resting and relaxing at a small inn nearby. She was fired for entering my room uninvited, despite her reasons."

Robert's eyebrows rose. "What kind of an establishment is this? I would string up any blackguard who tried to take advantage of Miranda or any of the staff at our inn."

"The couple who runs the place are relatives of Lizbeth's," Ethan said tightly.

"And that's supposed to help me understand?"

"Suffice to say she's under my care now."

"And Julianne? Where is she?"

"She is staying here at the hotel." Devin hesitated, then decided he might as well come clean about everything. "She's come to mean a lot to me. I . . . well, I intend to marry her one day."

Silence met his pronouncement. As each of the men digested his news, Devin felt his pulse slow and his body tighten. He knew what was going on—his body was preparing to fight. He had felt much the same way before every battle during the war.

And that made him realize he was making the right decision. He had fallen in love with Julianne Van Fleet and wanted her to be his wife. He didn't care what her past was. He didn't care what she'd had to do to survive. All he cared about was that she *had* survived.

Even if these men who meant so much to him didn't agree, he knew he wasn't going to change his mind about Julianne.

But then, to his surprise, Ethan raised his glass. "Here's to the lovely Julianne, men. May she be loyal, strong, and true."

Baker and Truax raised their glasses too. "Yes, here's to love and marriage and finding women to put up with us," Robert Truax added, finishing off the toast. "We aren't easy to live with . . ."

"But I reckon one day we'll be worth the trouble," Thomas said with a wink.

Devin raised his glass as well. "And if we aren't, may they never tell us to our faces," he said with a laugh.

"To Julianne!" they called out as they clinked their glasses together.

Few moments had ever felt so right.

33

THEY HAD BEEN DISCUSSING DEVIN'S DEPARTURE FOR A solid hour. Julianne knew Devin wasn't pleased with the way she was reacting, but she couldn't help herself. As far as she was concerned, if Daniel Bushnell was out of sight, he should be out of mind as well. "I don't understand why you are doing this," she said at last. "I don't understand what purpose going after Daniel serves."

Devin abruptly stopped his pacing and stared at her incredulously. "Well, first, there is the matter of honor," he said slowly, as if he were speaking to a small child. "He tried to kill me, Julianne."

"But he did not succeed."

His eyebrows rose, he snapped his mouth shut, and then, with a mutter under his breath, he began pacing the length of his hotel room. *Pacing*, just as if he didn't have two stitched-up bullet holes in his shoulder.

"Devin, maybe you should sit down for a spell?"

"I am fine."

"Not exactly. Your wound is still healing."

He stopped again. Stared at her and smiled somewhat grimly. "Exactly. I am wounded."

Maybe they were finally getting somewhere? "That's why—"

"Julianne, I'm not the type of man to be shot in the back and turn the other cheek."

She knew he was strong. She knew he was a leader. She knew he'd probably killed or maimed more men during the war than he could count. But that was during war, when he was fighting for a cause. Now was different. "You should speak to the sheriff," she said reasonably. "Then he would take care of Daniel for you."

"He's not going to do anything."

"Of course he will. You are well respected—"

"Don't you see? That's one of the problems. It shouldn't matter who I am or how much influence I have. And that is what it will come down to. Even if the sheriff does bring Bushnell in, he's not going to bring him to trial."

"You don't know that."

"I know how things work, Julianne. And you do too." His lips pursed. "He's a complete reprobate. He took advantage of you. But he has money, and money is influence."

Though it made her skin crawl, she was strong enough to take responsibility for her actions. "I knew what he wanted, Devin. And, while, um, I can't say my experiences with him were pleasant, I'm not going to lie and tell you he raped me. He did not."

But instead of the lines in his expression easing, he looked even more disturbed. "You are not the only woman he took advantage of, Julianne."

"I realize that," she replied, knowing they were both speaking of Lizbeth. "But that was years ago and during the war."

"He should still pay."

He opened a drawer and pulled out his pistol. "Some deeds are too terrible to excuse, no matter what the situation. He violated Lizbeth and he used you unforgivably." When she started to protest again, he interrupted her. "I'm not the only one who feels this way, Julianne. The other men agree with me."

Watching him carefully inspect his Colt, Julianne suddenly

realized what he meant. "I told Ethan I was Bushnell's mistress myself, and it's right that he knows. But you told your other friends, didn't you?"

"I had no choice. They needed to know."

He had no choice? Realizing Devin still wasn't meeting her eyes, she swallowed hard.

"And did you tell Lizbeth Barclay too?"

"Of course not."

"Because it would upset her too much?"

"Because I may not be a gentleman, but I know better than to speak of such things to young women."

Because Lizbeth would be scandalized that Julianne had done such a thing, and would hate her because of who that man was. Julianne wouldn't blame her either.

Devin walked to face her. Placing both hands on her arms, he held her secure in front of him. "Julianne, I care about you. I don't care about your past, and I don't care who knows. You are still the loveliest, strongest woman I've ever met in my life. Never doubt that."

He sighed. "Now, what I brought you here to tell you is that Robert visited a number of the less-savory gambling establishments in San Antonio late last night, finding men there you would never want to know. Near dawn he discovered that Daniel's kidnapped one of the maids from the hotel. An hour ago, he also learned where he's no doubt taken her."

Remembering the conversation with Meg in the kitchen, Julianne gasped. "Is it Lizbeth's friend Cassie?"

He nodded slowly. "Ethan is about to tell her."

And just like that, all her arguments died inside her. "That poor girl."

"Robert believes Bushnell is holding Cassie in a house just to the east of here. He's no doubt terrorizing her. We have no choice. He must be stopped."

Devin was right. Daniel did need to be stopped.

Eying him carefully, Julianne realized this was the man she'd fallen in love with. Devin Monroe didn't sit idly by while women were abused. He didn't persuade others to put themselves in danger. He certainly didn't hope for problems to be taken care of by someone else.

And now that they knew it wasn't just a faceless woman in jeopardy, but one of Lizbeth's friends, well, there was no choice, was there? "I understand," she said at last.

Looking as if she'd taken a load off his shoulders, he released a ragged breath. "Thank you. Now, will you still be here when I return?"

"I'll be here."

What other choice did she have?

Ethan knew stranger things had happened, but mending the rift with his family had been unexpected and had caught him off guard.

If he weren't a believer, what had happened here at the hotel would have made a believer out of him. No other reason could explain the way his family had reached out to him, the way he'd been able to forgive them, or the way they'd all come to an understanding. While their relationships might not ever be the same, Ethan realized they didn't need to be. They simply needed to exist.

Wasn't that how he felt when he was liberated from Johnson's Island? All the men released had been thin, exhausted by war and prison conditions. They were scarred and weaker than they'd ever been. But in place of muscle and good health had come an awakening of their spirit and a new appreciation for small blessings and true friends. In his more introspective moments, Ethan realized he wouldn't be the man he was without surviving that imprisonment.

After gathering his gun, Bowie knife, and ammunition, he prayed. Prayed that the Lord would one day understand why he was joining his three blood brothers to ensure justice had been served to Daniel Bushnell.

Just as he was rising, he heard a faint knock at his door.

It was Lizbeth.

"I was just on my way to find you," he said.

"I hope that means you have a few minutes to talk."

"I do have a few minutes, but only that. Something has happened. Come in." As she entered the room, he took a moment to admire her. Lizbeth was wearing a light-blue dress. It was made of a fine wool and was immensely flattering. Her hair was arranged in a mass of curls, framing her face. He didn't know if he'd ever been more struck by her beauty than he was at that moment.

If he hadn't, he was certainly a fool. Her goodness shined through her, and that was what had drawn him to her. Only now he saw things so clearly. It wasn't that she needed him and he needed to do something good without expecting anything in return. It wasn't that she was merely pretty. No, it was the simple knowledge that she was better than him. Being around her could make him better. And, he suspected, he could do the same for her.

It was only a shame that he was coming to this realization just when he was about to leave her.

She noticed his weapons on the bed. "You look like you're preparing for a duel."

He turned to face her.

"Lizbeth, we've known from the beginning we would need to

deal with Bushnell. Devin and I called in two of our comrades from the war, Robert Truax and Thomas Baker, to help us. They arrived last evening, and then Robert discovered where Bushnell is no doubt hiding." He drew in a breath. "He has Cassie."

Immediately tears formed in her eyes. "I . . . I was afraid of this. From the moment Meg told me Cassie had gone so suddenly, something inside of me knew he had her. He must have forced her to take her belongings, to make everyone think she'd left on her own. How can anyone be so evil, Ethan?"

He reached for her hand and clasped it in between both of his. Tried to steady her and pass on his strength, though what he really wanted to do was hold her close and promise that everything was going to be all right. "We're going to find them."

Her hand trembled. "He could have other men with him," she warned when she looked back into his eyes. "You could get hurt."

"I know," he said softly.

She looked even more worried. "I don't want anything to happen to you."

"I don't want anything to happen to me either." Trying to smile, he said, "We have so much to look forward to, Lizbeth. But I have to do this. How can I not?"

"You're right. Cassie needs you. She needs someone to help her."

Ethan felt in his heart everything that she wasn't saying. That she'd needed someone, but no one had been there. That reminder made his insides ache. He realized then that he needed to bring up what had happened to her during the war.

Steeling himself for her reaction, he said, "I also want to avenge what he did to you." Though he hated to see the pain he was causing her, he continued. "Bushnell hurt you unbearably. He scarred you. In more ways than one."

As he'd learned she often did when she was nervous, Lizbeth pressed her other hand against the jagged scar. "He did. But I'm all right now."

"Lizbeth, he needs to pay for what he did to you. He used his uniform to his advantage. There . . . there are no words to describe how despicable his actions were."

"Ethan, I want you to go after him. I want you to rescue Cassie. But . . . well, let's not dwell on what happened to me anymore. It's over and what was done was done. Nothing is going to ever change it."

It wouldn't. But bringing the man to justice would make him feel better. "Lizbeth, I have something to confess to you. I've been trying to find a way to tell you . . ."

"What is it?"

"I . . . well, first, as I told you, I want a future together, and my family wants me to move back and run the ranch. I meant what I said. I'd like to do that with you by my side."

She stared at him, wide-eyed. "You said they would accept me. Isn't that still true?"

"Absolutely. They'll accept you because they know you have my heart."

She smiled tremulously. "Why the long face, then?"

"Because there's something else I must tell you, but I don't know how to say it."

"I think you should just tell me then."

Feeling as if he were standing up to be court-martialed, he forced himself to say the next few words. "Lizbeth, you need to know . . . Well, I led a raiding party to your house."

"What?" she whispered.

"Soon after Bushnell's. I know it was soon after his visit because the scar on your face was still fresh." Though she was staring at him as if she'd seen a ghost, he drew himself up, straight and tall. "I was the officer in charge, Lizbeth. I gave the order to search your property."

"The man who stood in the shadows . . . That was you?"

He nodded. "I had orders to get whatever I could. We were freezing. Starving. Men were depending on me."

Her hands fisted. "But I was cold too," she said in a small voice. "I was starving too. You took the last of everything I had."

"I've dreamed about it since. It's haunted me."

"When did you realize I was the same woman?"

He wished he could lie. But he couldn't. He owed her every bit of the ugly truth. "The moment I saw your scar."

Pure pain filled her eyes. "Why didn't you tell me this days ago?"

"I didn't want you to hate me. I didn't have the words to try to excuse myself. I'm afraid I still don't."

"That is why you are going, isn't it? Not just because that man ruined me, but because you feel like you did too."

"To some degree, yes."

"Did you tell the other men? Is that why they are going?"

"They would have come because of Devin's injury. But I did tell them about what Bushnell did to you. They feel you need to be avenged too."

"Really? They are willing to risk their lives for something that happened to me long ago?"

"It is because of you. And Devin. And to help the woman in Bushnell's clutches now." He paused, then continued, knowing that Lizbeth needed to know everything if she was ever going to trust him enough to one day be his wife. "There's one more thing you need to know, Lizbeth."

Her eyes widened. "What else could there be?"

"Julianne was Bushnell's mistress during the war. She was starving and so was her grandmother. He used her need to his advantage."

"Julianne was his lover?"

"To an extent, yes."

"And you've known about this as well?"

Her eyes were shimmering with unshed tears. It was almost too hard to bear. "I learned a few days ago."

She said nothing for a long moment. Then, folding her arms across her chest, she spoke. "I suppose I should thank you. All this time I have been comparing myself to you and have come up lacking. But now I realize you are just as flawed as I am."

Each word stung. Hurt. But she was hurting, he reasoned. In time, she would come around. "Lizbeth, when I return, I promise we can discuss this further."

"I don't think that will be necessary, Major Kelly."

"What does that mean?"

"It means I am done being lied to and coddled for my own good. I need to start new."

"I want to start new with you. Lizbeth, I have fallen in love with you."

She shook her head. "No, love isn't like this."

His relationship with Faye came to mind. He'd thought she'd been his perfect match, but now he knew the truth.

"I've never been in love before, not like this. But I think you are wrong. I think it is exactly like this. It's messy and hurtful. Awkward and confusing. It's not neat and perfect. But don't you see? All these flaws and cuts are going to mend and make us stronger."

"Like mine?"

"Like yours."

Lifting her hand, she traced her scar with one fingertip. "Ethan, don't you see? This hasn't made me stronger."

He approached her. He yearned to reach for her. To hold her close and tell her everything was going to be fine if she would just trust him again. "That isn't what I meant. You know it."

"Isn't it?" She wiped a tear from her eye. "You say you love me, but you are about to commit murder. You say you want to protect me, but you've kept secrets to protect yourself. You say you respect me, but you've shared my shame with men who are strangers to me. You say you want to be my friend, but you introduced me to a woman who willingly entered into a relationship with the man who haunts my dreams. You don't know how to love. Or if you do, your concept of it is so stretched and scarred . . . well, it's only a faint parody of love."

He was having a difficult time speaking. "Lizbeth, please try to understand."

"No, you try to understand. You try to see things from my viewpoint. Then maybe one day you won't look upon your secrets with anything but shame."

Ethan knew he wasn't going to have to wait years for that to happen. He was ashamed at that moment.

It threatened to suffocate him.

"When I return, I'll find you."

Her eyebrow arched. "And if I refuse to see you?"

"Then I'll come the day after. And the day after that."

He strode from his room then, wishing he could yell or scream or break windows or do something. Anything to make the pain more bearable.

But he had a feeling nothing was going to do that. Nothing short of going back in time.

34

THE FOUR OF THEM SET OFF JUST AFTER FOUR O'CLOCK. Late enough in the day for Bushnell to have been lulled into thinking no one was going to search for him while still giving them the ability to easily scan the perimeter and watch one another's backs. They'd all learned it was a good idea to be ready for anything, just in case their best-laid plans went awry.

Whether it was by one of their designs or because they'd unconsciously fallen back into habits they'd adopted during the war, they were riding two by two. A good fifty yards separated the pairs. If one of them was shot, enough space was between the groupings to allow the others a fighting chance.

Ethan was in the lead, Truax by his side. Ethan was there because he knew the area better than any of them. Truax, because he'd been the one who had talked to the old-timer who'd ratted out Bushnell.

Devin took the rear next to Thomas Baker.

As usual, Baker was riding his horse as if he'd been born on it. He looked supremely comfortable on the animal. Of course, anyone would, Devin reckoned. That horse was a fine-looking appaloosa gelding. White with gray-blue spots on its hindquarters.

Devin was riding Midge. She was his favorite mare. She'd

miraculously survived the remainder of the war while he'd been in prison. At the war's end, she'd been escorted to his cousin's house. She and her husband had taken special care of the mare, spoiling her with fresh grass and lots of lazy days.

Though he would have missed her, Devin would have left her there if she'd shown a preference for it. But it seemed she, like him, considered them a matched set. The pain in his shoulder was a clear reminder that he'd been a benefactor of her loyalty. She'd delivered him, bleeding, to the Menger just a few days ago.

She wasn't as spry as she used to be, but she was stronger and smarter. He trusted this horse as much as he trusted Ethan, Baker, or Truax. He felt she had just as much heart too. As if she sensed the importance of the day's mission, she was trotting at a good clip. Maybe Midge was like him; she needed to be out in the world every now and then, just to prove to herself that she still had what it took to survive.

"Feels like old times, doesn't it, Cap?" Baker said after they'd ridden a couple of miles. "Even our formation is how it used to be."

Devin nodded. "I was just thinking that myself. Actually, I was just thinking Midge seems a little eager to prove herself this afternoon. I guess she needed to get out of the stable for a while."

Thomas looked at Devin's horse with a fond expression. "She's still got it, don't you, girl?"

Midge perked up her ears, as if she knew Thomas was speaking to her. Devin scowled at Thomas. "I think she's flirting with you."

He grinned. "Nah. She knows I'm a married man now. She just recognized my voice. I cleaned her hooves and brushed her coat more times than I can name."

Devin had forgotten that Thomas had often done such tasks for him. Most of the officers he'd served with had servants with them to take care of their horseflesh. Others had just found a private to do his bidding. For some reason, Devin had always taken care of his belongings himself . . . and then Baker had.

"How come you always took care of Midge?" he asked curiously. "Was it because she was that good of a horse? Did she matter to you that much?"

"You mattered, sir," he said lightly. "That's why I did it."

"Ah." Now, what did one say to that? Even after all this time, Baker's honesty could still get him choked up.

"So . . . Miss Van Fleet must be quite a lady."

Devin looked at Thomas sharply, ready to scold him if he was being disrespectful, if he'd had a change of heart from the night before. But the look in Thomas's eyes said he was being completely sincere. Embarrassed that he had been rushing to her defense for the wrong reasons, he nodded. "She's very fine."

"And you're going to marry her?"

"Yes, I told you men that in the bar when you arrived. I just have to convince her sooner than later."

"Cap, you were on the Red Roan Ranch when I was so besotted with Laurel I could hardly see straight. You know I'm not going to judge."

"We have a different relationship than you and Mrs. Baker. Julianne and I . . . well, we've had a complicated beginning."

"Yeah, I can see how meeting Laurel while I was working on a prison chain gang was real simple and easy in comparison."

Devin grinned again. "Point taken." Last summer Thomas had gotten into some trouble and landed in a small-town jail because he owed some money. Instead of reaching out to the rest of them, he'd planned to serve out his time . . . until Laurel Tracy paid for him to be her indentured servant for the span of one year.

"Is marriage agreeing with you?"

"Very much so. But that isn't to say we don't have our own obstacles to overcome every now and then."

"As you know, Julianne has a history. Though I've told her I don't blame her for what she did—and I don't—sometimes I find I still care. I'd be lying if I said it didn't bother me at all."

"Ah. Yes. I can see how it would bother you."

"You do?" For some reason, he'd been hoping Thomas would be on Julianne's side.

"Well, sure," he said as he scanned the horizon again, his expression sharp. "I mean, I'm sure you've told her about all the things you did during the war to survive." He lowered his voice. "And the way we handled things on Johnson's Island."

Devin was shocked. "You don't share such things with women. Don't tell me you've told Laurel about the things we did."

"Of course I haven't," he retorted, giving Devin a look equally as shocked. "She'd have nightmares."

"Then why are you bringing them up?"

"Because your Julianne probably wishes you didn't know about what she did to survive."

"That was different." Because his actions didn't involve losing his good reputation, he admitted to himself in a burst of shame. "Anyway, uh, I upset her for another reason. I mean, it's related, but different." Lord, but he was no good as sharing secrets!

"What did you do?"

"She knows I told y'all she was Bushnell's mistress. She's embarrassed, of course."

"And feels you betrayed her."

"Because I did." Maybe it was being on Midge and riding next to Baker, or maybe it was because Devin knew it was time to admit some things to another person. Whatever the reason, he felt compelled to continue to spill his innermost thoughts. "She seemed to let it go before I left her just now, but I don't know if she'll ever completely trust me after this."

"I guess we'll see," Thomas replied, his voice suddenly quiet and still.

Wrestled from his musings, Devin looked up in surprise. There, about a half mile up the road, was the dilapidated two-story hacienda they'd needed to find. Finally, they could do something to right so many wrongs.

He and Thomas guided their mounts up to Ethan and Robert. The horses exhaled softly but stayed completely silent.

"Do you think Bushnell has spotted us yet?" Baker asked as he gazed intently at the house.

Robert shook his head. "I doubt he's looking out the windows. No doubt he'll be focused on the woman he kidnapped."

The tension among the four of them rose. Devin clenched his jaw as he imagined how Bushnell was abusing Cassie. And, yes, how he'd no doubt hurt Julianne. Although she'd never said he beat her, Devin suspected it. He remembered what she said that day before he stormed out of her parlor.

"*I came to know more about Bushnell's ways than either of us would care to discuss.*"

"I've loathed few men more," Ethan said, no doubt voicing what all four of them were thinking.

Thomas shared a look with Robert. Devin wondered if they were thinking about their wives and how they'd feel if Bushnell were taking advantage of them the way he was no doubt taking advantage of Lizbeth's friend.

It was time to end this. End the pain. End the worry Bushnell had perpetrated upon so many.

Taking care to keep his voice down, Devin said, "Major, we

planned to arrive two in the front, two from the back. Is that still how you would like us to proceed?"

"Yes. We need to capture him. If he realizes we're here, I wouldn't put it past him to leave Cassie and sneak out."

"All right, then. Let's proceed." Devin felt his horse's muscles tense in anticipation. It mimicked his own body's response. Years of riding into battle on horseback brought back muscle recognition.

"Gentlemen, thank you for your support and your friendship. I am grateful for it," Ethan said. Then, after he pulled out his pistol and cocked it, he spoke. "Forward!"

Holding the reins tightly in one hand and his Colt revolver in the other, still ignoring the pain in his shoulder, Devin kept to Ethan's side as Robert and Thomas veered toward the back.

Whatever was destined to happen couldn't be put off any longer. It was time.

35

I NEVER IMAGINED A FILLED HOTEL COULD FEEL SO EMPTY," Julianne murmured to Lizbeth as she stared out the window. "I hope the men are all right."

"And Cassie," Lizbeth added. "I hope she will be okay." Though they'd already cleaned Captain Monroe's room from top to bottom, Lizbeth still was moving restlessly around the space, wiping shelves that didn't need dusting and polishing furniture that already gleamed.

It was a testament both to her nervousness about the mission and to her respect for the men that she was cleaning the captain's suite in the first place. After all, Aileen employed a capable staff to do such things. A staff she was no longer a part of. However, doing something as simple as cleaning both Ethan's and the captain's suites had felt like the right thing to do.

When she'd mentioned her idea to Julianne, the other woman had been eager to help, and even went with her to collect cleaning supplies. Though there was quite a bit of tension, no doubt because of their past experiences with Colonel Bushnell. Not that Julianne knew Ethan had spoken of Lizbeth's relationship with him. Neither had made mention of the past. It seemed it was far easier to discuss dirt and cleaning solutions.

But now, hours after the men had left, it was apparent neither of them could think of anything other than the men and the mission they were on.

Lizbeth walked toward Julianne. "They are capable men, don't you think?" she asked hesitantly. "I'm assuming they know what they're doing." What if they did something reckless and made things worse for Cassie?

Julianne turned to face her, a faint smile on her lips. "You really don't know about these men, do you?"

"I know Ethan." Well, as much as he'd allowed her to know him. "And Captain Monroe a little bit. Their friends must be nice too," she added weakly. Even to her ears, her praise of them seemed rather distasteful.

Julianne's smile widened. "They are more than that, Lizbeth. After Captain Monroe first called on me at home, I asked some former soldiers about him. Oh, the stories they told!"

"He was that impressive?" Lizbeth tossed her dust rag on a side table. Though she knew war wasn't a glorious enterprise, she still couldn't help but let her imagination take flight. The captain in his uniform, leading men into battle, must have been a sight to see.

"He was extremely impressive! It seemed his bravery and honor had no bounds, and that transcended to his best friends too. Major Kelly, Lieutenant Truax, Sergeant Baker, and Captain Monroe were a band of brothers whom many believed could take care of most anything." She sighed. "Even all this time after the war, people still talk about their bravery. Isn't that something?"

Lizbeth nodded. "It is. I'm glad you shared that with me. Even if the soldiers exaggerated those tales, I feel better about the men's chances of surviving today."

After a pause, Julianne said, "I should probably tell you, I heard about Captain Monroe and the other men from Bushnell too. During the war, Daniel wrote me about their battles. He mentioned all of them with pride." She rolled her eyes. "Of course, he listed himself too. And he wasn't on too many battlefields—not at the beginning, anyway. He was too busy strutting around and making connections so he could raise his rank."

There it was. Julianne's past was now out in the open and as unavoidable as the bed in the middle of the room. Choosing her words with care, she said, "Ethan told me about your past relationship with Bushnell. I, uh, honestly don't know what to say."

All traces of light vanished from Julianne's expression. "You don't need to say anything. I don't expect you to feel anything for what I did but contempt."

That seemed harsh, even though Lizbeth had been feeling very close to that. "I wouldn't categorize my feelings that way," she said hesitantly. "But I will admit it's hard for me to imagine any woman entering into a relationship with that man willingly."

"I understand."

Lizbeth doubted it. "He ruined me."

"He did. And you are right. He hurt you in many ways. He should and will pay for his actions." Her voice softened. "But let me ask you this . . . Did he ruin you forever?"

"How can you ask that?" she blurted. "He raped me. He cut me. I wear this scar on my face. Isn't that enough?"

"Of course it is," Julianne said in a rush. "You have every right to hate him. I, for one, loathe him." She took a deep breath. "But what I am trying to say is that when I look at you, I don't see a broken woman deserving only of pity. I see someone who is strong and capable. A survivor. I wondered if you ever saw that too." She shrugged. "I just thought you should know."

Lizbeth was shocked. Could it be that she was more than a victim?

"Do you think it's ironic that of all the people in the state, the two of us met, and that we have developed relationships with men who were in a prison camp with Bushnell? It brings a new definition to a small world, I think."

Julianne's gaze warmed. "It's ironic and disturbing and a great many other things. But maybe God thought it was fitting too."

"How so?"

"Well, how could one attempt to describe such a man? With the four of us, there was no need. We all know exactly what he was like. And because of that, maybe in time we can all help each other move forward."

For the first time since Ethan told her how he'd come to her ranch after Bushnell was there, Lizbeth smiled. "This is true. At least there's that."

"I couldn't help but notice you seemed upset with Major Kelly today. Was it because of what he told you about me?"

"No." She bit her lip. "He'd been keeping a secret from me. He led a group of men to my ranch just two weeks after Bushnell came. He recognized me when we met again last week, from my scar. But I didn't recognize him."

"Did he hurt you too?"

"Oh, no. Nothing like that."

"Did his men?" she asked quietly.

"No. They weren't especially kind, but they weren't cruel," Lizbeth answered, remembering that time as if it had happened just days ago. "The men were on a requisitioning raid. They took what few belongings I still had and then left. My head knew they had no choice. But my heart? Well, it was breaking. But of course, I was already broken." She shivered. Truly, that time in her life was so bad, she had rarely allowed herself to think of it.

Julianne plopped down in one of the chairs they'd just fluffed.

"I bet you couldn't believe it when you realized he'd seen you before."

"I was certainly shocked. He said he remembered me because of my scar."

"What did he say?"

"He said he dreamed about that raid. That he's always regretted it."

"Was he sincere?"

Of that, she had no doubt. "Oh, yes. But I was so upset with him for not telling me he'd been there I didn't care if he felt bad." Feeling worse by the second, she mused, "Actually, I thought I was going to be upset with him for the rest of my life."

"Because he took your belongings?"

She shook her head. "No. And not because he kept his raiding my home a secret from me. Because he saw me at my worst. Because he saw me damaged and despondent and lonely. And instead of helping me, he only took more. But now? Now I don't know why I thought it mattered so much. If it wasn't him, it would have been someone else."

"Someone recently told me writers and poets make wars seem glorious but only fools think that way."

Lizbeth smiled awkwardly. "That's true, I suppose. Right when war broke out, my parents dressed me up to go to the officers' dances. The men in the uniforms looked so handsome and brave. I think I truly believed they would look the same in battle."

"I can only think there's a reason the Lord put us through so much. Maybe he needed us to meet each other. Or to be the right women for these men, Devin and Ethan."

"Do you think we are the right women?"

"I think we might be the right women for two men who also thought their lives were going to be quite different."

Lizbeth felt the tears come. "They could be injured right now. Or dead."

"Don't think that way. We have to keep our hope."

"But what if they are?"

"Then I guess we'll accept it. But they aren't, Lizbeth. They are fighting for their own reasons. Not just for us, or even to rescue poor Cassie. And I happen to think they are too good for the Lord to take them while fighting a man like him."

Lizbeth was awed by the passion in Julianne's voice. She was speaking from her heart, and it was obvious she believed every word she was saying. Clasping Julianne's hand, she said, "We need to keep praying. For our men, and for Robert and Thomas. And for Cassie to realize that even if the worst has happened, she can be a survivor too."

Julianne smiled. "I can't think of a better activity to do right at this minute. They need our prayers, and we need the Lord's comfort."

36

Standing on the outside of the hacienda with Devin, reeling with the knowledge that he was about to end another man's life, Ethan waited for the moment that usually came on the eve of a battle. There was always a time when all the chaos in his mind shut off, doubts faded away, and his body settled.

Right then and there, his body and mind would meld and all the hours of preparation would pay off. He would suddenly feel nothing but cool intent. Nothing would matter except for the job at hand. That was when he had been able to raise his rifle, to surge forward, to command other men to stay strong and risk their lives for the cause.

But now, as he stood at the door of the hacienda, his body tense and his mind churning with a dozen mixed emotions, Ethan realized this was a completely different situation. Nothing in his life had prepared him for what he was about to do.

Probably because everything about this mission was personal. He knew Daniel Bushnell. He knew him well. Not only had Ethan slept in the same tents and barracks as him, he'd also shared bread and hardtack and water. Ethan had sometimes laughed with him. He'd sometimes argued with him. He'd usually followed his orders.

And while it was true that he'd never cared for Bushnell, Ethan could admit that he'd never had an overwhelming urge to do him harm.

That had all changed when Devin was shot.

And when Lizbeth told them what he'd done to her.

Even when he'd come to terms with just how badly he'd used Julianne.

Since then, anger and the need for justice to be served had boiled inside of him. Daniel had used his rank and the integrity of everything they stood for and twisted it all to his advantage. As far as Ethan was concerned, Daniel Bushnell had dishonored everything he, as a Southern gentleman and a man of honor, had stood for.

Every time he allowed himself to think of Lizbeth being brutalized by him he could hardly contain his anger.

"Ethan, you okay?" Devin asked, his voice low.

"Yeah. I . . . well, I can't seem to settle."

"This is right," Devin said. "Justice needs to be served. Not just for Lizbeth and for Julianne, not just for Cassie, but for the countless women he's taken advantage of . . . and intends to continue to violate."

"Not to mention that he tried to kill you."

His own words and Devin's explanations rang in his ears. At last, he found the quiet sense of peace he had been looking for. He breathed in. Out.

Then, without another second's doubt, he kicked the front door. He half expected it to hold firm. But instead it cracked. One more forceful kick and it sprang open. "Bushnell!" he called out.

Behind him, he heard Devin cock his gun, ready to shoot. But when Bushnell didn't appear, they entered, immediately each intent on a different angle. In front of them, Ethan heard the faint shuffle of someone scurrying around.

"Don't make us hunt you down, Daniel," Devin called out. "We're all too old for that."

Pistol raised, Ethan tensed, again waiting for a reply. He scanned the area, carefully looking for places where someone might be hiding. But he saw nothing. Heard nothing more than his own harsh breathing.

All that remained was an eerie feeling in the air. By mutual agreement, they spanned out farther into the house. Robert and Thomas had joined them after entering through a back door.

Mexican red tiles made up the floor. They were hard under his feet. Each step echoed through the house. They might as well have brought in a score of soldiers. Seconds passed.

"We sure he's here?" Baker whispered.

"I am." Robert stepped forward. "His horse is outside. I'll go find him."

"Not alone," Devin murmured.

He paused, then nodded. "All right, Cap," he murmured. There was a new slight edge to his tone, though Ethan couldn't discern whether it came from Robert being amused that Devin felt he needed help or whether it came from appreciation of the other man's concern.

Maybe it was a combination. They needed to remind each other that they weren't as battle-ready as they'd once been. Reflexes were slower, their responses a bit sluggish.

Just as Ethan was about to join Robert on the stairs, an ear-splitting scream pierced the air.

"Cassie," he stated, though none of them had needed an explanation.

Thomas let out a string of curses as Robert rushed on ahead by himself, all of Devin's warnings either completely forgotten or destined to be completely ignored.

As one, Devin, Baker, and Ethan raced up the stairs and down the hall. Each of them had their pistols drawn. Ethan's arm felt like it was on fire, the muscles were so tense. Their pace slowed, each man keeping an eye out for Bushnell, the woman he held, and ready for the possibility of any other men they didn't know about ambushing them.

When they reached the end of the hall, Robert stood outside a door. It was obvious he was impatient to go inside.

"At least you waited here," Devin muttered sarcastically.

Before Robert had time to say a word, Ethan pounded on the door. "Open up, Bushnell. You're outnumbered and outgunned. We both know you never could hit a target without taking five minutes setting up the shot."

"My pistol's already pointed at the door," Daniel replied. "The moment you open it, I'll shoot. Don't make me kill you."

When Cassie screamed again, Robert surged forward. Ethan had to put a hand out to stop him. They still didn't know what they were getting into.

But when she cried out once more, Robert tore forward. "Her death ain't going to be on my hands," he said as he pressed his shoulder into the wood. It didn't give.

"Step aside," Devin ordered as he raised his Colt and shot the lock. It swung open. "Bushnell, we're coming in!" he yelled. "Put your weapon down."

Ethan felt as if he were in a tunnel as he charged in after Devin and Robert.

Then he halted, stunned as he saw the sight in front of him. Daniel Bushnell was in his shirtsleeves and trousers only. His feet were bare. He held a knife in one hand and a pistol in the other. On the bed lay Cassie. Her torn dress was shoved up on her thighs, her lip was bleeding, and she was gazing at them in desperation.

It was so much like everything he'd envisioned happening to Lizbeth that Ethan felt himself sway.

Just as Bushnell raised his arm.

Finally, Ethan's heartbeat slowed and the doubts faded away. He raised his pistol and fired.

Bushnell jerked when the bullet hit its mark. Cassie screamed when he fell on the bed, obviously dead.

Only then did Ethan realize he hadn't been the only man to fire. The three men at his side had done the same. One of them—or maybe all of them—had ended Bushnell's life.

37

THE MOMENT JULIANNE SAW DEVIN ENTER THE LOBBY OF the Menger Hotel, she burst into tears.

Devin froze. "Julianne?" he rasped as he curved an arm around her shoulders and lowered her onto a nearby settee. He turned to briefly speak to Lizbeth and then helped her to her feet, guiding her to the hallway that led to his suite. "Sweetheart, what's wrong?"

Sweetheart? Had she ever been anyone's sweetheart? That, of course, made the tears fall even harder.

They continued until Devin unlocked his door and pulled her inside. Only when Devin stepped toward her with his palms up, as if he were attempting to still a skittish colt, did Julianne finally get control of herself.

"Don't mind me," she said, doing her best to dab at the tears on her cheeks. "I'm just so relieved you're okay."

His expression eased as warmth entered his eyes. "I'm okay," he affirmed. "I'm fine."

He wasn't hurt. "Oh, thank the good Lord!" Beyond caring about how she looked, or retaining any composure at all, she rushed toward him and launched herself into his arms.

After the slightest hesitation, he wrapped his arms around her tighter. "Julianne, careful now," he drawled, hesitation thick in his voice. "I've been on horseback for hours. No doubt I smell to high heaven."

She thought he smelled like man and leather and fresh snow. That wouldn't make a bit of difference to her, not in the slightest. "I couldn't care less," she murmured as she pressed her cheek to his chest. "I'm just so grateful you are here in one piece."

His arms tightened around her. "I am that."

She leaned back so she could see his face. "You really aren't hurt? You haven't opened your wounds?"

"I promise. I'm no worse for wear."

Now that worry had been put to rest, she dared to bring up the other concern. Because she knew him well enough to realize he wasn't going to easily give her any details, she kept her question simple. "Did you find Daniel?"

"We did, Julianne. You won't have to worry about him anymore."

Her body tightened. "What does that mean?" He might not want to tell her, but she needed to know the truth.

Sighing, he ran a hand down her hair. "You aren't going to let me cloak what happened in vague assurances, are you?"

She knew from his tone that he wasn't actually angry. "I cannot. Devin, tell me the truth. Is there a chance he could show up at my house again?"

"There's no chance at all. He's dead, honey."

Her breath hitched. Her mind spun as a mixture of emotions settled inside her. She was relieved, and maybe a little sad for the news too. Daniel Bushnell had done a great many terrible things. But no matter how others might perceive how he treated her, his money had saved her during the war. People could think what they would, but she would always be grateful she'd been able to survive.

"Did you do it?" she asked.

A muscle in his jaw jumped. It was obvious he was uncomfortable. Which made her feel terrible. Why did she even want to know? She *didn't* need to know. It wouldn't change her feelings for him. "Listen, forget I asked. It doesn't matter."

"I didn't kill him, Julianne. Rather, it wasn't only me."

That's when she knew she was a liar. Because she felt pure relief. Not because she would feel differently about Devin, but because she didn't want him to have to carry that burden. And she could tell by the set of his shoulders, the way his eyes looked tired, that he would have held that burden close to his heart. Maybe he would even eventually resent her for it.

Reaching up, she rubbed her hand against the scruff on his cheek, trying to console him in a way only a touch could do.

He closed his eyes for a brief moment as though he was drinking in her touch. "What happened was inevitable. When we got there, it was obvious he wasn't going to come out of that house alive.'"

Remembering there was another victim, she braced herself to hear the rest of the news. "What about Cassie? Was she really there? What happened to her? Will she be all right?"

For the first time since he walked into the room, his expression eased. "Cassie was there, but I think she is going to be okay. Right now Baker and Truax are escorting her to her family. She . . . well, Daniel had beaten her badly. She was bleeding. We got there just in time."

Julianne shivered. "The poor girl. I hope she'll recover eventually."

"I hope so too. Of course, we're living proof that a person can recover from some of the most adverse situations. We'll simply have to pray that Cassie will somehow find the strength and courage to do that."

Julianne liked how he'd phrased his statement. It was true, she realized. Not only did one's body have to recover from trauma, but the mind and heart did as well. Of course, faith played a big part in that recovery. "Lizbeth and I knelt and prayed for her and for you men for hours."

He ran his fingers through her hair again. "I'm grateful you did. I needed your prayers. Maybe God heard them and took pity on us all."

"God didn't need to take pity on you. You and Ethan were in the right. You saved that young woman."

His expression softened as he looked down into her eyes. "I have to admit I was more than a little wary. I feared you wouldn't want to see me when I returned. Will you ever forgive me for sharing your past with Robert and Thomas?"

Julianne was surprised he had to ask. Couldn't he tell how much he meant to her from the way she greeted him? But then she remembered what kind of man he was. He was a man used to taking nothing for granted. "I have already forgiven you."

"That quickly?"

"The moment you rode off, I realized anything could happen to you. It made me so scared. That's when I started to realize keeping secrets about my past from your friends doesn't matter all that much. I can't change the past. It's a part of who I am, and most everyone knows about it. For better or worse, while I'm not proud of what I did, I have decided to stop cowering in shame. So many other people had to survive far worse things."

"I can promise you they have." He rubbed his hands over her arms. "Julianne, I'm so sorry I made you regret trusting me."

"Like I said, it's over now. I don't want to dwell on regrets."

"I don't either."

He was still holding her arms. They were still facing each

other, barely inches apart. Her face was tilted up to his. Devin was staring down at her, his blue eyes looking languid and almost dark.

And just like that, the tension between them dissipated. Gone was the stress and the worry and the sense that they could be pulled apart.

In its place was something new and strong. A pull that had nothing to do with lies or truths and everything to do with something far more basic and primal.

"Julianne," he rasped. His hands curved around her body again, pulling her so close she was sure she could feel his heartbeat.

Maybe it was because she wasn't inexperienced. Maybe she'd lived long enough to know what he wanted from her. But there was a difference for her that was unchartered. Because she felt something new. She desired him too. It had nothing to do with debts or promises or contracts or guilt.

It was all about what was in her heart. She'd fallen in love with him. Even though she would have told anyone before she met Devin that she didn't believe in love, she realized now that she couldn't have been more wrong.

She had simply not been ready.

Licking her lips, she suddenly felt shy. What should she say? How should she convince him that he didn't need to hesitate? That she would never confuse what was happening with them with what she'd done with Daniel?

She felt his gaze fasten on her mouth. And just when she decided to say something, anything . . .

It turned out she didn't need to say anything at all.

He pressed his lips to hers. Then, with a moan, shifted her, lifted a hand to curve around her jaw, then proceeded to kiss her in a way she hadn't known was possible.

If she didn't know better, she would say his kisses were drugging. Encompassing. All consuming.

But really, what they were like was Devin. Powerful and brave. Direct and to the point.

Perfect.

Much, much later, he lifted his head. Searched her face. "Too much?"

Since she felt as though she could barely stand on her own feet, she sighed. "Oh, no, Devin. I think it was just right."

He smiled before he leaned down and kissed her again.

38

DEVIN HAD RETURNED TO THE MENGER OVER AN HOUR ago. After he talked with Julianne, he told Lizbeth they had found Cassie, and that Robert and Thomas were taking her home to her family. He also said Ethan was fine and only a few minutes behind him. Before Lizbeth could pepper him with questions, he'd turned back to Julianne and they'd retreated to his suite.

She didn't even know what had exactly happened with Bushnell. But she assumed by Devin's demeanor that their mission had been accomplished.

Then, a bundle of nerves, she settled on a chair in the corner of the lobby and watched the front door. Each time the door opened, she leaned forward, anxiously hoping to see Ethan stride through. Looking strong and proud and so heroic.

But as the minutes passed, and the hour grew late, she realized he wasn't going to come. Worrying her bottom lip, she wondered if he was in a saloon.

Just as quickly, she disregarded that idea. That wasn't who he was any longer. Determined to find him, she decided to begin at the first place he would have gone—the stable.

When she walked into the barn, the warm, musty air kissed her skin. It felt warm and inviting inside. Welcoming. Feeling optimistic, she walked down the center aisle. Each stall was filled. When the horses saw her, they shifted restlessly. A few whickered a greeting.

A palomino pushed his nose out between the slats of his stall, begging for a pet. Unable to help herself, Lizbeth slid a hand through and rubbed his soft nose. When he stepped closer, gently nudging her hand, she laughed. Just as she moved away from the horse, she heard a board behind her groan.

She turned, expecting to see one of the four grooms the hotel employed.

Instead, she found Ethan. He was leaning against one of the back stalls, half hidden in the dim light. He was standing quietly. Completely silent.

Everything about him seemed to be the exact opposite of the man she'd first talked to in his room. Gone was his proud and sardonic bearing. Gone, too, was his aura of confidence.

In its place was a man who looked exhausted by life.

She approached him carefully. She didn't want to intrude, but she didn't want him to be alone either.

He stood motionless, watching her approach. When she stopped in front of him, he finally spoke. "Lizbeth, why are you here?"

How could she not be? Keeping her voice purposefully light, she said, "I was looking for you, of course."

"Why? Do you need something?"

His voice sounded brittle. She decided to temper it with a bit of levity. "As a matter of fact, I do. I need you."

He straightened. A hand that had been shoved into one of his pockets fell to his side. "I beg your pardon?"

"I've been waiting for you in the lobby, Ethan. I've been waiting for over an hour. I thought you would walk inside directly after

Devin, but you didn't arrive. That's why I ventured out here. I started to worry about you."

"I didn't know how to face you. And, well, I'm not fit for company right now."

"Only horses?" she asked lightly.

"I don't know if I'm even fit for them. Gretel doesn't seem real fond of me at the moment either."

She couldn't let another moment pass before she said what was really on her mind. "I'm really glad you are all right. Are you hurt at all?"

"No. I'm just fine. We got Cassie. She's with Baker and Truax."

"Yes, I heard that." Staring at him closely, she noticed Ethan didn't seem happy about their mission. "What's wrong? Did Bushnell escape?"

"No, we found him. He was where we thought he'd be." He ran a hand along his brow. "He drew his gun, so I raised my gun as well. Actually, all of us did. He didn't stand a chance."

She released a ragged sigh. "So he's gone?"

"He's dead. It happened fast. So fast. After all that worrying and planning, it felt almost too easy." He grimaced. "I'm sorry. Like I said, I'm not fit for company right now."

He turned from her, but he didn't walk away. Lizbeth knew there would come a time when the harsh reality of what he was telling her would no doubt hit her hard. Maybe she would scream and cry. Maybe she'd dissolve into tears. But all she could think about at the moment was Ethan.

Carefully, she ran a hand down his back. "You're worrying me."

"Don't. I'm fine."

"What's going to happen next? Are you going to get into trouble?"

"No. After we, uh, left that house, we took Cassie to a doctor and I went for the sheriff. Between the four of us and Cassie's recounting of all she went through and what happened when we arrived, the sheriff seemed more relieved than anything."

"So he won't be taking you in for questioning or anything?"

"I don't think so." Ethan turned and tried to smile, but he couldn't seem to manage it. "Lizbeth, honey, I'm real glad you came out here. I'm sorry you had to go looking for me, but I think it might be best if you went on back inside."

"And do what? Wait for you some more?" she lightly teased.

He rubbed a hand over his face. "No. Of course not. I'll come find you at Harrison House tomorrow before I leave."

She gaped at him. "You're leaving?"

"Yeah. Like I told you earlier, my parents want me home. They left this morning. I was going to linger here a bit, but I think it's best if I go on my way."

She noticed he was avoiding her eyes. He thought she was still upset with him.

Impulsively, she reached for his hand and then pulled him down until they were both sitting on the ground, side by side. "Ethan, I know you want me to leave you in peace. And I will. But first, will you give me a couple of minutes? I'd like to tell you a story."

He shifted, stretching his legs out in front of him. "What's it about?"

Everything in his tone said he could not care less about any tales she might be telling. But maybe he'd think differently when she was done.

That is, if she could put everything she wanted to say in the right words.

"It's about a girl," she said.

"Okay . . ."

"Just hush and listen." She waited a beat to make sure he

kept his silence, then stopped worrying about the right words and aimed for the right thing to say. "When she was a teenager, she had bright dreams for herself. She was going to find herself a handsome man. He was going to be perfect too. He was going to be wealthy and kind and polite and even kind of fun. But most importantly, he was going to think she was something special."

He cleared his throat. "Ah. Did she find him?"

"Not exactly." She took a breath, hoping to settle the emotion rushing through her. "See, the war came. Her parents died. Other family members went off to fight and didn't come back, and no handsome man appeared in sight. Then, well, things got worse."

"Lizbeth—"

His voice was strained. She ignored it.

"She ended up alone. In a small house on a small ranch. On the outskirts of San Antonio, in a place called Castroville. Every day she just tried to survive. And then . . . when men did show up? Well, they didn't come to make her life better. They just made everything worse." She swallowed hard. And though it felt as if she were choking on her words, she continued. "And so she tried a little harder to survive."

"And then?" Ethan asked softly.

"And then the war ended. So she had to work in a big hotel and forget about her dreams." She smiled softly. "She was very good at that. As the months passed, she forgot she'd ever cared about love and marriage. Actually, she forgot she'd ever had any dreams at all."

She turned slightly. Took one of his hands. "And then she met him."

He blinked. "Who?"

"The man she'd always dreamed of. And he was just as handsome and kind as she'd dreamed he'd be. But he wasn't perfect."

Laughing softly, she continued. "Not by a long shot. But that was okay, because she wasn't perfect either."

Ethan stared at her. Tightened his grip on her hand. "What happened next?"

"He realized that was okay too." Staring down at their linked hands, she whispered, "Ethan, I don't care what you had to do today. I don't care why you kept secrets or why you did what you needed to do in your past. I don't even need you to be different or better."

His eyes turned glassy. "What do you need, then?"

"You, Ethan Kelly. I only need you." Smiling softly, she said, "Do you think you can one day need me too?"

Instead of offering her words, he reached for her and pulled her close. Bent his head so it rested in the nape of her neck and held her tight.

Then, just when she was about to relax against him, offering him comfort, Lizbeth felt his lips brush her skin. She pulled back slightly, intending to flash him a smile, but that idea evaporated as he whispered her name and then kissed her neck again.

She trembled, then gasped as Ethan traced a slow, lingering path along her throat. His mouth was warm. Each place it touched felt like a brand, making her aware of little besides how close she felt to him, how treasured. How very wanted.

When she shivered again, he lifted his head. "You okay, Lizbeth?" he drawled. His voice sounded deep, almost languid.

Wonderful.

As his question registered, she knew only one way to answer. And that was to circle his neck with her arms and raise her lips to his.

With a sigh, he pressed her close and kissed her at last. It was lovely. Perfect. No, it was even better than that. It was worth waiting for.

39

SOMETHING IS GOING ON," ROBERT TRUAX WHISPERED when he joined the ten or so men gathered around the wood-burning stove in the middle of their barracks. Though it was June, the air was still chilly. "None of the guards are around."

Intrigued, Ethan put down the figure he'd begun trying to whittle. It had been a hopeless task. He wasn't an artist and had no vision for how an ordinary stick could be made into a thing of beauty. But like Thomas and his constant attempts to better himself, he'd decided to at least attempt to push himself to learn something new.

That said, he was thankful to be concentrating on something else. Looking at the other men, they seemed to be having the same reaction he did. Some men were curious about Truax's information; others simply looked happy to have something new to talk about.

"I saw seven of them leave today on a skiff," Thomas said.

"They were probably going out to scout," someone said.

Thomas shook his head. "Nah, that weren't it. The guards wouldn't ask seven men to do the job of two."

"You forget who we're talking about," General McCoy said with a grin. "Our guards need double the time and double the manpower to do most anything."

"Yessir," Baker agreed. "But they had knapsacks. I've never seen them leave the island like that before. I don't think they're coming back."

Ethan's mind began to race. It was summer of 1865 now. The war had been going on a long time. Far longer than anyone had anticipated. And, if he was being completely honest, the South had hung in there longer than he ever would have imagined.

Turning to one of the newest members of their group, he said, "Where were you taken captive?"

"In Georgia, sir."

"Tell me the truth. What was Lee saying about our chances? What did you hear?"

His gaze darting around the assembled lot of them, the man sputtered. When he met General McCoy's eyes, he paled. "I couldn't say, sir."

"Come on. I've been here over a year. You were out there until just six weeks ago. What was happening?"

Again the man looked like he might throw up.

Baker shook his head. "He ain't going to tell you a thing, Major. Speaking against the cause is a treasonous offense."

Of course, Baker's voice was laced heavy with sarcasm. Baker was known for saying too much about half the time. He would never let a probable consequence interfere with spouting his thoughts. But he was the exception, not the rule.

"We were losing," another newcomer said. "Our men were sick and starving and had more problems than a mammy could shake a stick at."

"Watch your mouth, Lieutenant," Bushnell barked.

"Leave him alone, Daniel," General McCoy said. "Kelly asked for the truth and he received it."

"What are you thinking, Kelly?" Devin asked.

Ethan was afraid to give voice to his hope. But he couldn't very well expect other men to speak their minds if he was afraid to do the same. "I'm wondering if something significant happened," he said.

What he was too afraid to share, however, was that he couldn't help but think about what was going to happen to all of them if the South had lost and the war was over. Rules of engagement stated they should be escorted out, but few things happened during the war that followed any such rules.

Devin was staring at him intently, no doubt wishing Ethan would finally say what all of them were thinking. Then the door to the barracks burst open and they all turned in surprise.

There was Dunlap, the guard who had been there the longest and was far and above the men's favorite.

"Dunlap, you decide to join us for a spell?" Truax asked.

But instead of teasing Truax right back, Dunlap swallowed nervously. "Afraid I don't have time to be sitting around with you men today."

"I saw a half dozen of you Yanks leave on a skiff," Thomas said. "What's going on? Do they have to go fight again?"

Dunlap ignored Thomas's question. "I came for General McCoy."

"Only McCoy?" Bushnell asked.

"Uh, yes. He's the highest-ranking officer Reb, right?"

"That is correct," Bushnell said haughtily.

The general slowly got to his feet. "Where are you taking me?"

"The commander has requested your presence."

His expression tightened, but he walked to Dunlap's side. "Am I coming back?"

Dunlap's mouth pinched. "I believe so, sir."

"All right, then, let's see what he wants," he mumbled as they left the room.

After the door slammed behind them, conversation stumbled forward again, each person guessing why the commander needed General McCoy.

"This ever happen before, Kelly?" the Georgian asked.

Ethan shook his head. "Not that I can recall."

After another twenty minutes or so, conversation petered out and they all huddled together in silence. The tension in the room increased as each minute slowly ticked by.

After another thirty minutes passed, Ethan was so stressed out he picked up his stick and knife again.

Just as the door opened.

They turned as one to greet General McCoy, who quietly closed the door behind him. It was so silent, Ethan was sure he wasn't only hearing his own heartbeat, but the hearts of the men surrounding him too.

McCoy stood at attention.

One by one, each man in the room got to his feet and stood at attention too.

General McCoy's expression was carefully blank, though Ethan was fairly certain he had seen pain in his eyes before he hastily covered it up.

"Gentlemen, it is my duty, as the highest-ranking officer of the Confederate States of America here, to inform you that the War of Northern Aggression has ended. Last month, in the town of Appomattox, Generals Lee and Grant met and signed the treaty. Tomorrow morning Dunlap will take the lot of us on a boat to land, where we will be given tokens for a one-way train ride to Kentucky. After that, we are on our own."

"It's over," Robert Truax murmured.

"Almost over," Thomas said, never one to look at anything through an optimistic light.

General McCoy stared down the line of them. "I would be remiss if I didn't say it has been an honor and a privilege to serve with each of you. God bless and Godspeed on your travels home."

When he saluted again, every man assembled saluted him back, holding their hands and posture steady for several seconds.

After everyone relaxed, the general pulled cigars from beneath his cot. "My Mimi sent these to me months ago. I've been saving them for a special occasion. I can't think of a better time than now. You're all welcome to join me."

Most of the men followed suit, opening boxes and envelopes and pulling out cheroots and cigars, packages of tobacco, and, in some cases, pilfered containers of whiskey and moonshine.

Soon, only a few men remained in the barracks. Ethan was glad of that. He needed time to think and to come to terms with the wealth of emotions rushing through him. After all, was there anything more disturbing than despair mixed with joy? So many men had died for the cause. Just as many were maimed and disfigured. Now many would say they'd died for nothing.

Had they? Ethan didn't know. He supposed only history would tell that story.

He thought about all the hardships they'd endured. The things each of them had had to do, the women who had gone hungry and been at the mercy of the elements without their men at their sides.

The door opened, bringing in the crisp scent of fresh air.

"There's quite a party going on outside, Major," Devin Monroe said. "You coming?"

"I don't know."

"I think you should," he said, his voice light. "The stars are out and the air is clear. We have much to celebrate. After all, tomorrow is a new day."

"I don't feel like celebrating much right now."

Looking concerned, Devin eyed him carefully. "What's on your mind?"

To anyone else, Ethan would have smirked and said something meaningless. But he couldn't do that to Devin. Neither of them deserved that. "Everything. I've been thinking about how much we've all suffered."

"You speak the truth. We have suffered."

"We buried so many men here too. We'll never see them again."

"That's true. We'll only see them again in heaven."

Ethan was incredulous. "Do you still believe in heaven?"

"I never stopped." Devin breathed deep. "I might be wrong, but I like to think the Lord has something better for us than killing and sickness and captivity and pain. He's already sent Phillip Markham there. Too many others to count as well. One day, if it's his will, I'll join them. And maybe you'll be there too. And Baker. And Truax. And we'll all stand together and look down upon this island and nod our heads."

Devin wasn't making sense. "Why? Why would we nod our heads when we see this place?"

"Because when that day comes, we'll understand. We'll understand why this war happened, why we were brought here to Johnson's Island. Why we survived and lived for many years after." Striking a piece of flint, he lit his cigar. He puffed on the end, illuminating the air with a faint glow, surrounding them with the faint scent of sweet tobacco.

And then Captain Devin Monroe continued. "One day we're going to understand why he put us here." He lowered his voice. It turned thick with suppressed emotion. "And when we do?"

Ethan Kelly knew the answer then. "That will be enough."

DISCUSSION QUESTIONS

1. The scripture verse from Luke (Luke 17, 5-6) about the mustard seed guided me while writing this story. Were you familiar with this verse also? How might it apply to your life?

2. This novel features four characters who suffered and yet survived during the Civil War. With which character did you identify most? Why?

3. The themes of coincidence and God's will are explored throughout the book. How do you relate to these ideals? Have you ever experienced something that you considered to be particularly coincidental?

4. I really enjoyed writing about a band of brothers who vowed to be there for each other for the rest of their lives. Who might you consider to be part of your own band of brothers?

5. Did you find the flashbacks at the prison camp to be helpful or distracting to the story? Why or why not?

6. What do you think will happen to each of the four men now that they have found happiness?

7. Of the four couples in this series, Robert and Miranda, Thomas and Laurel, Ethan and Lizbeth, or Devin and Julianne, which would you be most interested in reading a novella about?

ACKNOWLEDGMENTS

ALTHOUGH MY NAME IS ON THE BOOK'S COVER, THERE ARE a great number of people who made this book possible. I owe a great deal of gratitude to everyone who worked so hard to make this novel as good as it could be.

First, I'm so very grateful for my husband Tom who helped me create Captain Monroe and his remarkable band of brothers one evening while we were making dinner. He and I both loved the idea of creating a hero who was larger than life. I owe Tom my thanks, too, for visiting Johnson's Island with me. I also want to thank my girlfriend Mendy who toured the Menger Hotel with me in San Antonio, and my first editor Becky Philpott who had tea with me at the Menger and encouraged me to set a novel there.

I owe a great deal to my editor Karli Jackson for her help in fine-tuning this book and Jean Bloom for helping me get the timeline and organize the many, many details in this story. Also important was my first reader Lynne Stroup, who spent a great many hours helping me turn in a very long book on time.

My heartfelt thanks also go out to Kristen Golden and Allison Carter. These ladies in publicity and marketing work wonders! I also want to extend my appreciation to all the bloggers and reviewers who have embraced this series and encouraged everyone to give it a try.

ACKNOWLEDGMENTS

Last but not least, I would like to give a little shout out to my father, who has been camped out up in heaven for over twenty years. It's because of my Dad's love of Louis L'amour, old westerns, and Palominos that I love them too. Thank you, Dad, for instilling in me a love of all things Texas. I think this series would have made you proud.

With blessings and my thanks,
Shelley

ABOUT THE AUTHOR

SHELLEY SHEPARD GRAY IS A *NEW YORK TIMES* AND *USA TODAY* bestselling author, a finalist for the American Christian Fiction Writers prestigious Carol Award, and a two-time HOLT Medallion winner. She lives in Loveland, Ohio, where she writes full time, bakes too much, and can often be found walking her dachshunds on her town's bike trail.

Visit her website at www.shelleyshepardgray.com
Facebook: ShelleyShepardGray
Twitter: @ShelleySGray

Enjoy Shelley Shepard Gray's

Chicago World's Fair Mystery Series

Available in print and e-book.